ALIEN WARRIOR MATES IV

GRACE KENSINGTON

THE ALIEN'S RETURN

1

———————

Eden could still feel Loralia shaking beside her as they stepped out of the lab and into the dim hallway. She couldn't imagine what the delicate, beautiful woman was feeling as she tried to process what she had just learned. All her life Loralia had believed that one man had been her father and that he had died along with the others of her kind during the mysterious plague that destroyed all but her in their underground realm. Only moments before, however, she had been confronted by another man who proclaimed himself to be her father. Though she had recently learned that she was not of pure Irisa blood and that she was, indeed, part Eteri, Eden could see in her eyes that she had not fully considered that that meant the man she had always considered her father, the man who she loved and who had taught her how to utilize the tremendous power that her Irisa heritage had given her, was not the man who had truly sired her.

"Loralia?"

The sound of the unfamiliar voice from behind them made Eden stop. She felt Loralia stiffen in her arms and saw the woman's lavender eyes close as if she were trying to block out the presence of the man by pretending that he wasn't there.

"Please," the voice said.

It was low and grainy in a strange, intangible way as if the man who was speaking hadn't used the voice in quite some time and was just now getting accustomed to forming words again.

"Loralia," Eden said softly. "Do you want to see him?"

Loralia stayed still and silent for a few seconds. Eden didn't rush her. She wanted to give her as much time as she needed to work through what was happening around her. A moment later, though, Loralia surprised her by turning suddenly and facing the man who was coming up behind her. Towering nearly as large as the Denynso warriors and bearing tattered wings that hung by his sides, the man was something that Eden had never seen. He was startling in an uncomfortable, out-of-balance way that was unlike anything that Eden had ever experienced. Even when she had first encountered the Denynso warriors, she had not felt this sense of discomfort. She didn't know if she could truly describe the feeling as fear, but it was something unnerving that put her on edge. As she met his eyes, however, she saw something deep within them that pled for calm and sought understanding.

"Who are you?" Loralia asked. "Who *are* you?"

"My name is Azrael," he said. "I'm your father."

"No," she said, shaking her head. "No. You're not my father."

Azrael nodded and took another step toward her. Loralia held her ground, straightening her shoulders and facing down the man in a way that somehow made him stop and look at her beseechingly.

"Please."

Eden felt a hand close around her arm and looked up to see Pyra standing beside her.

"We need to keep moving," he said. "We can't stop here. We have to get back to Penthos to the others."

Eden looked at Loralia and saw her eyes darken as she turned away from Azrael, stepped out of her grip, and moved quickly down the hallway. She watched as Bannack swept her into his arms for only a moment before she stepped away from him as well and continued their way down the hallway among the others. Eden followed the gentle tug of her mate's hand on her arm and they began to run down the dim hallway away from the lab where Ryan was imprisoned in the cage where he had held Aegeus for so many years. The thought made her shudder. The space had been so small, so cold, and the chains kept him brutally in place. It would have been nothing short of torture to be forced to remain in that place, unable to move more than a few inches, for years. Eden could see the pale, gruesome skin and skeletal frame that marked him as a Klimnu. Though he looked like one of the vicious creatures that had attacked her when she was first on Uoria and had caused such destruction and hardship among the entire Denynso clan for years, she knew that this man was nothing like those creatures. Yes, he was Klimnu, but Aegeus was far more. This was Maxim's father. The strong, powerful Mikana was still within him and with every breath he fought to maintain his connection to it. He refused to allow what Ryan had done to him pull him away from everything that he had ever believed and the goals that he had dedicated his life to achieve.

When she looked at Aegeus, Eden could see Maxim. The beauty was still there. The determination, gentleness, and intelligence that had made Ivy fall so deeply in love with Maxim was still evident in Aegeus's gaze and Eden felt an intense sympathy toward him. She had witnessed what happened to Maxim when he came into contact with the toxic flowers and began to change. He had fought against it with everything in him, struggling to stop the transformation and to keep himself as he was. No matter how hard he railed against the change, however, it was affecting more than just his skin. The anger, fear, and hatred that Pyra had wrongly directed at him had only fueled the transformation even further and brought the disintegration of who he was beyond his skin and into his heart. She had watched as he became angrier and more violent, and knew that if he had been left to his own devices he would have fully transformed into a Klimnu and been taken over by the vicious greed and violence that compelled those creatures. It was the love of Ivy and his determination not to justify Pyra's actions that had saved Maxim. These had kept him from disappearing completely and losing everything within him.

It was the same with Aegeus. She knew that he had clung to the love for his wife and his sons and his determination to protect his kind and everything that he had always fought for that had prevented him from giving in completely to the transformation that Ryan had tried to force on him. The corrupt scientist had tried to utilize the aggression, anger, and sadness of the Denynso to feed the change within him and send him further into the abyss of new existence as a Klimnu. The fact that Eden could still see the humanity and life in Aegeus's eyes only proved his incredible power and strength. She could see Maxim in him and could only hope that when they got him to Ciyrs, the healer would be able to restore him to his original Mikana state so that he could return to his sons and Ellora.

They reached the end of the hallway and Ciyrs and Elianna rushed toward them. Elianna swept Eden into her arms and Eden realized that she hadn't been communicating with any of them throughout the entire ordeal. She had maintained her connection with Pyra, but the stress and horror of what she was experiencing as she tried to save her son and mate from Ryan's grasp had closed off the unique connection that she had to the healer and his mate. This link had been created when she first came to be with the Denynso in the compound on Uoria. During her first encounter with the Klimnu, one of the creatures attacked her, nearly killing her. During Ciyrs's healing process he had created a close and inexplicable connection with her, somehow enabling her to communicate with him in the way that she could with Pyra. At the same time, it created the same connection with his mate, Elianna, enabling the three of them to communicate with each other freely. It was a strange ability, one that wasn't shared by any other members of the Denynso clan, and the moment marked when she changed from a human to a Denynso.

Eden stepped back from Elianna and turned to give Ciyrs a hug as well.

"Are you alright?" the healer asked, pushing her back by her upper arms and looking into her eyes. "Did he hurt you?"

Eden shook her head.

"I'm alright," she told him. "He tried, but he was more interested in Lysander and Pyra."

"Come on," Pyra said. "We need to keep going. I sincerely doubt that Ryan would only send the Valdicians to Uoria to capture Creia and not have anyone around here to guard him and his experiments. The longer we stay in place, the more vulnerable we are."

Ciyrs nodded.

"Pyra's right. We need to get back to the shuttle and get to Penthos as fast as we can." He turned toward Oro and the winged woman standing close beside him. "How did you find a shuttle to get you here so quickly?"

"We didn't take a shuttle," Oro explained.

"We took a hyper-speed vehicle," the man Ciyrs vaguely remembered as Jonah from the Nyx 23 settlement said.

"What is that?" Eden asked.

"We'll explain when we get there," Oro said.

They continued down the hallway, the group staying close together as they moved as swiftly as they could through the low light. Eden hated the shadows that filled the corners and made the doorways seem deeper. The controls were contained within an office at the front of the hallway, behind where they were traveling, so they would have to cope with the darkness until they got out of the lab and back to the university shuttle bay.

It felt strange for Eden to be running through the lab where she had once worked. Before she went to Uoria this lab had been her life. She'd spent more time in these halls and rooms than she had in her own home and felt like she could have navigated through it blindfolded. Now, though, those days of roaming the halls and dedicating all her time and energy to the research and experiments within the labs seemed like they had been lived by someone else. She could barely remember what it felt like to exist in those moments. The hallways felt strange and foreign to her and she found herself questioning each of the rooms that she passed. Though deep in the back of her mind she knew that she would be able to bring them through, it was as though she couldn't think any more than one step ahead. She couldn't see the layout of the lab in her mind or remember how to get out of it beyond taking that next step or that next turn.

Ahead of her she heard Lysander whimper and her attention focused in on him. Ty turned around and offered the infant to her. Eden gathered him into her arms and tucked him close to her chest so that she could wrap her arms around him as tightly as she could. The sound of her heartbeat and the gentle rhythm of her breaths seemed to calm him and her son fell asleep in her arms. Eden felt a surge of emotion and fought back the tears that formed in her eyes. Pyra's hand rested on her back and the weight of it comforted her and brought her focus back to getting through the corridors of the laboratory building as quickly as they could.

"What's the fastest way to get to the shuttle bay?" Gyyx asked from the front of the pack.

"Oro, you mentioned another vehicle," Pyra said. "Where is it?"

"It's right outside the shuttle bay," he said. "We were able to use tracking to get here, but the bay door was inaccessible. There's a blocking feature that prevents anyone without the proper knowledge of the machine to get to the doors. My only concern is that someone will see and destroy it."

"We'll get to it as quickly as we can," Pyra told him. "How many people can it accommodate?"

"As many as it needs to," Oro answered. "We'll figure it out when we get there."

They had reached the door at the end of the hallway that would lead them down toward the main floor of the building. Gyyx pulled on the handle, but the door didn't move.

"It's locked," he said. "It wasn't when we got here."

Eden pushed through the rest of the group to get to the

door and pressed her fingertips into the biometrics reader then input her personal code. The light on the reader should have flashed yellow then changed to green when it released the internal locking mechanism, but it didn't change from the glowing red.

"What's wrong?" Pyra asked as she tugged hard on the door with the hand that wasn't supporting Lysander.

"It won't open," she said.

George stepped up beside her and repeated the process that she had gone through. The light remained red and he glanced down at Eden questioningly before pressing his finger more insistently into the reader and imputing his personal code slowly as if to make sure that the machine was getting each of the numbers accurately.

"The lock isn't releasing," George said. "The authorized access system has been overridden."

"What does that mean?" Ty asked.

"It means that we can't open the door," Eden said.

"What?" Pyra asked, stepping forward and slamming his hand on the door. "You can't be serious."

Jonah stepped up beside Pyra and reached for the handle, shaking it briefly before pounding the keys on the number pad in random combinations.

"It wasn't locked when we got here," he said, repeating what Oro had said. "We were able to get right through."

"How did you find us?" Eden asked, a sudden sense of concern building in her mind.

"What do you mean?" Oro asked.

"How did you find us? How did you get here?"

"We told you," Jonah said. "The vehicle that we used has a built-in tracking system that allowed us to zero in on the shuttles that had traveled between the planets so that we were able to use the same path to get here."

"No," Eden said, her voice getting louder and more insistent. "Here. How did you get here? How did you find us in the laboratory? The vehicle brought you to the university, but none of you have ever been inside the laboratory buildings before. Once you were inside, how did you know where to find us?"

Oro and Jonah exchanged glances, and then looked over at Azrael and the lovely but silent winged woman who had been standing close to them since they appeared at the doorway of the lab. They all held expressions that looked as though none of them had really considered what she was asking. Oro looked back at her.

"The other doors were locked," he said.

Eden's heart started beating harder as she realized what was happening. She heard a low thud in the recesses of the building and some of the group turned toward it.

"The doors were locked?" Pyra asked.

"Yes," Oro said. "We came into the building and just started trying doors. Most of them were locked, but we found some that were open. We just kept going through the open doors."

There was another low thud, closer this time, and Eden felt prickly heat on the back of her neck.

"You didn't think that was strange?" she asked.

Jonah shook his head.

"We weren't thinking about it," he said.

"All we cared about was getting to all of you," Azrael said. "Like you said, none of us have ever been in this building. We didn't know anything about it. We thought that maybe the doors were always locked."

"They are," Eden said. There was another thud and Eden reached for Pyra's arm. "We need to go," she said. "Now."

She turned and started back down the hallway toward a short offshoot that she knew contained another access to the stairs that would lead them down to the main entrance of the building.

"What's going on, Eden?" Pyra demanded.

There was another thud, so close this time that she could nearly feel it shaking through her body.

"The doors are always locked," she said. "That's why I had to use my access code and fingerprint to get to the lab when we got there."

She tried the door to the stairwell and found it also locked.

"Then why were the others able to get through those doors?" Pyra asked.

"Ryan unlocked them," Eden said. "You said that there were only a few doors unlocked," she said, looking back at Oro. "Which ones were they?"

"The stairwells that led up," Jonah told her. "Every other floor we were able to get onto the floor and we would go down the hallway until we found another door that was open and follow that stairwell. We kept doing it until we heard your voices and then we just went toward them."

Eden handed Lysander to Pyra and pushed through the rest of the group so that she could run down the hallway toward another door.

"Why does it matter?" Gyyx asked.

"The laboratory was designed so that there are limited paths to each location within it. You can't just go from one place to another. You have to know which doors lead to which areas of the building. They created it that way to protect the labs and the research going on in them. The original building was much simpler, but scientists and their assistants were breaking into each other's labs and stealing research or sabotaging experiments. They redesigned the entire building and ensured that each person only has access to specific areas of the building."

Eden pulled on another door and it finally opened. Behind her she could hear another of the low thuds. She knew that it was the sound of the locking mechanisms within the doors somewhere in the building opening and that the only reason that that would be happening was that someone was coming through them.

2

———

Pyra followed Eden through the doorway and down the narrow stairs that led into near darkness beneath them. He could hear the fear in her voice when she was talking about the doors and the fact that she had handed him their son made him worry that there was something seriously wrong that she hadn't yet told them.

"But how were they open when Oro and the others got here, but they are locked now?" he asked.

Eden shook her head as she approached a door and pulled on it only to find that like the others it was locked.

"Ryan must have gained access to the master controls of the locks. He left the specific path of doors that would lead to his lab unlocked so that they would find us."

"But why?" George asked. "He already had Lysander and Zsilvia and me. You already knew how to get to the lab and would get there with your personal codes. He admitted that he wanted Lysander and to have us as a backup breeding couple. Wouldn't he want to prevent others from getting to us?"

"Not if he wanted to make sure that we were all vulnerable," Eden said.

"I don't understand," Pyra said. "We got out. We got him in the tank and we got away."

"We got away from the lab itself, yes," Eden said, pulling on another door until it opened. "But we haven't been able to get out of the building. Ryan said that the others are on Penthos and then Oro and the others came here and told us the same thing."

"He knew that they would come," Pyra said.

Eden stepped through the door and he followed her to the top of a stairwell leading further down into the building.

"At least he thought that they might. He knew that if there was going to be some way that they knew that we were here and in danger, however that was going to be, at least some of them would come for us. He made sure that those doors were left unlocked and that the rest weren't so that anyone who did come would be able to find us easily."

The next door that she tried opened out onto a hallway and she rushed down it. Some of the warriors followed behind while others went in the other direction, running down the opposite side of the darkened hallway pulling on the doors as they went to get them through the process more quickly. Gyyx called out to them from nearly the end of the hallway and they rushed toward him.

"Does anyone have a lightstick?" Pyra asked.

One of the warriors handed a lightstick to Pyra and he activated it. Holding it over his head to cast the light through the open doorway now in front of them, he saw that they were standing at the base of a staircase leading up.

"We just went down two flights," Gyyx said. "Why are we going up now?"

Eden shook her head and they started up the stairs.

"But we captured him," Ty pointed out. "I still don't understand the doors being unlocked and then then being locked again. And I thought that your personal code and fingerprint would unlock the doors that you were authorized to access. Why aren't they working now?"

"Ryan must have overridden the system," Eden told him. "Like I said, he planned for this. He planned for others to come. Remember that in the end what he really wants is Maxim and Kyven. The more people that he could get away from Penthos and then the more of us that he could eliminate before we had the opportunity to get back to the planet, the less of a chance there would be that we would be able to protect them from him. He might be completely deranged, but Ryan is not dumb. He knows that the Denynso are fiercely protective and that any allies that they build are going to be just as determined and driven. That is the primary reason he wanted to use them as the basis for his soldiers."

"He wants to offer up my sons to the slaughter," Aegeus said.

The sound of the Klimnu voice still made Pyra's skin crawl, but he fought to withhold the reaction. He knew that this man wasn't like the other creatures that he had encountered during the years of battle or that had nearly taken his mate from him so soon after he found her. Though his skin was grisly white and his body skeletal and misshapen, Aegeus was not the enemy that the Denynso had always perceived the Klimnu to be. In truth, he was as much a victim of the horror of the Klimnu as the Denynso. The creatures had threatened and attacked the Denynso kind, tearing their bodies and in some cases claiming their lives. At the end of the battles, though, they were able to return to their compound. They could walk away from the attacks and put them behind them, living the moments of their lives between the encounters with the creatures without the feeling of their breath on their skin or their eyes burning into theirs.

Aegeus didn't have that luxury. He was victimized in a way that Pyra couldn't even begin to imagine. The man, once a warrior so strong and powerful that even Creia respected his name, had been reduced to nothing more than a vessel. He could never escape the grotesque reality of the Klimnu. Their breath was the breath that filled his lungs and their gaze burned from his eyes. He could never walk away or put the clash with the Klimnu behind him. They had claimed his body and torn into his soul. Ryan had tried to claim his life in a way even more gruesome and horrifying than the deaths that some of the Denynso had faced. It was Aegeus, though, who had found victory over them. His body had changed, but his mind and heart had persevered.

Pyra saw Eden slow on the steps and look over her shoulder at Aegeus. Her eyes were filled with emotion as she nodded.

"Yes," she said. "If we can't make our way back to Penthos to help them and they can't get to the others on Uoria, that is exactly what is going to happen."

"But Ryan is in the tank," George said. "He's chained there."

Eden got to the top of the stairs and Pyra saw her rest her hand on the handle, hesitating for a moment as if she wasn't fully prepared to open the door and see what was waiting just beyond it. Finally, she opened it, revealing a small storage room. She rushed into it and he followed her through it back into the lab where they had faced Ryan. The warriors streamed inside and they immediately turned their attention to the tank where they had chained Ryan. It was empty.

"He's gone," Eden said, sounding desperate.

"He released the chains," Loralia said from behind Pyra, her voice weak. "I thought that they would hold him."

Pyra turned to see Bannack's arms wrapped around his mate, trying to comfort her.

"It's alright, Loralia," Eden said. "It's alright."

"He's gone!" Loralia shouted. "We don't know where he is."

The warriors suddenly erupted in shouts, and Pyra held out his hand to silence them.

"Be quiet!" he yelled. "You are doing exactly what he wants. He wants us to go against each other so that we are more vulnerable. We have to stay together and stay strong."

There was a sudden loud crash and Pyra looked up to see the door of the laboratory standing open. Four figures stepped in, each cloaked in the long black robes of the Valdicians. By their varying size and shape, however, Pyra guessed that these were not actually more of the creatures that had captured Creia on Uoria, but a few of the hybrids that Ryan had created. The lead warrior carefully handed his tiny son down to Eden and guided her back behind him without taking his eyes off the creatures that were slowly approaching them across the lab. Pyra could feel the other men around him tightening as they took hold of their weapons and prepared themselves for the conflict about to happen.

"Where do we go?" the winged woman who had come along with Oro and Jonah asked softly.

The group stepped in closer together as the Denynso warriors, Azrael, Aegeus, and Jonah moved up to the front to position the women behind them. Pyra glanced over his shoulder and saw Eden reach for one of the lab coats hanging beside her. She wrapped it tightly around her body, tying it so that it acted as a sling to hold Lysander against her and free her hands. When he turned back toward the creatures that were coming their way, he could see that each held a weapon in its hand. The hoods that they wore concealed their faces, but somehow that made them more infuriating to look at. There was no fear as he faced them down. Instead he felt only anger and the unquenchable drive to protect his family and his friends.

The clash was fierce and immediate. All at once all the men in the group surged forward and smashed into the wall created by the hybrid bodies. Pyra fought blindly. He barely knew what he was doing as his hands thrashed against them. He could feel his body coming into contact with theirs and the warmth of blood washing over his skin. The sound of screams and grunts filled the small lab around them. It was the intensity and horror of the battles that he had encountered countless times in his life condensed down into this small space and these few moments. Soon the bodies of the creatures lay battered and broken on the floor at their feet. Pyra could hear the labored breathing of the men around them and the strain in their voices told him that some were suffering injuries from the encounter.

"Pyra!"

He turned toward Eden's voice and Pyra saw worry in his mate's eyes.

"What is it?" he asked.

"You're hurt!"

Pyra glanced down and saw a narrow trickle of blood making its way down his skin, along the curve of the muscles of his forearm. He looked to Ciyrs, who was examining a deep gash in Ty's leg. The healer looked to his leader sternly.

"We need to get somewhere safe," he said. "I have to tend to these wounds."

Eden looked back at the door where they had come through from the stairwell and George started toward it.

"No," she said, reaching out to take hold of his arm. "We can't go back through there."

"Why?" Zsilvia asked.

The Denynso woman looked smaller and weaker than Pyra had ever seen her, as if the fear and strain of the day that they had just experienced had taken away all her energy. As soon as that thought went through his mind Pyra realized that he had completely lost track of time since they had been inside the laboratory building. He had no idea how long it had been since they had gotten there or how long they had fought the hybrids. It was a strange sensation and one that reminded him just how foreign Earth was to him and the rest of those who came from Uoria. When they were on their home planet they lived their lives based on the movement of the sun and the habits that they followed from day to day. Now that they were on Earth, though, he felt strangely bound by the arbitrary passage of time that they used to structure each of their daily activities. Kept away from the sun and stars inside massive, complex buildings, Pyra felt almost imprisoned by the unknown minutes and hours that passed them by.

"Ryan left those doors unlocked for a reason," she said. "He designed that path for us, knowing that eventually we would find our way back into this lab so that we could encounter those hybrids."

"But we defeated them," Pyra said.

"Those, yes," Eden said. "But I heard more than one

door open. I know that Ryan would not only send a few of his creatures to confront us. There are others and he has positioned them throughout the building to ensure that we encounter them as we are trying to get out. Remember how conniving and vicious he is. He even had a contingency plan for if the Denynso killed me when I first arrived on Uoria. He wouldn't automatically assume that he was going to be successful, or that his hybrids would be able to defeat us that easily." She shook her head and looked around at the hazy lab, the memories starting to become more obvious in her eyes. "No. He's ready. He planned for all of this. If we step back out into that stairwell, we are walking to our slaughter."

"So, what do we do?" Pyra asked. "Do we go back out the other door?"

"Yes," Eden said, nodding.

"And then what?" George asked.

She looked at him and Pyra could see an expression in her gaze that was guiding, forceful, almost as if she didn't want to say something but expected that it would occur to George if he thought about it.

"And then we go down."

3

Jem checked through his bag again and then glanced around to give one final look to the cave that had been his home. He didn't know how long it had been since he had left Uoria, but in the time that he had spent on this new planet he had become accustomed to it and to the lifestyle that it had afforded him. Especially since Angela had come to be with him, even before they had completed their bond and she had become his mate, he had become comfortable and settled into his existence in the peaceful and virtually uninhabited space. Though he was excited about the possibility of returning home to Uoria and seeing his clan again, Jem still felt a pang at the thought of not ever seeing this place again.

He walked away from the cave and found Angela and Jacob standing near the creek. They both turned to watch him approach, optimistic but cautious expressions on their faces.

"Are you ready?" Angela asked.

She reached forward to take Jem's hand in hers and as soon as he felt the soft comfort of her skin against his he knew that everything was going to be fine. As long as she was standing beside him, things were going to work out exactly as they were meant to be. Even if he got back to Uoria and found that his clan had turned their back on him and that he no longer had his place there, he knew that he would still have his mate and that they could return to the planet that they had shared and make their permanent home there. He squeezed her hand and offered the best smile that he could.

"Yes," he said. "I'm ready."

"Alright," Jacob said, stepping up to them. "Then let's go."

Despite the confidence and nonchalance in the words, Jem could hear the slight hesitation in the man's voice. This would be the first time in several years that either Angela or Jacob would be on Earth. Like he had, they too had disappeared from their planet. Unlike Jem, however, their families and friends had been given false explanations as to why they had gone to the excavation deep in the desert and simply not returned. Jem struggled to decide which would be more difficult, them returning to lives that had been manipulated and damaged by those who didn't want anyone to know that they had truly disappeared from the research site, or him returning to the life that his kind thought had ended the moment that he fell from the limb in the mirrored realm beneath the Denynso compound. Their family and friends thought that they had moved on into a new life and had simply been living without them. To them, Angela and Jacob had purposely left them and would be returning to the life that they abandoned. To the Denynso clan, however, Jem would be stepping out of death and back into a life that had likely already been put to rest.

Jem looked at each of them and Jacob and Angela

stepped up closer to him so that they were a tight cluster, their shoulders touching as they all focused on the necklace that Jem wore around his neck. He lifted the small metal cage and looked in at the piece of wall that it contained. This had once been a reminder of the first cave that he had settled into when he arrived on this planet and resigned himself to the reality that he would never be able to return to Uoria. Now he understood it as the method by which he would get back to the planet that he loved and the people he had thought of each day since inadvertently leaving them behind.

"Are you ready?" he asked them, repeating the question that they had asked him to ensure that all three were prepared for the brief but largely unknown journey that lay ahead of them.

Angela and Jacob both nodded and Jem returned the gesture before opening the metal cage so that they could access the piece of wall within. Ensuring that their bodies were touching, the three reached forward and touched their fingertips to the engravings in the stone that marked this small segment of stone the portal that would bring them directly back to Earth.

Jem closed his eyes as the tugging feeling began in his chest and traveled through his body until he felt as though everything inside of him was moving away from his body. A few moments later, he felt his body catch up with the pull from within him and the dizzy, near-blackness in his mind that told him that they would soon arrive in the museum. He struggled to maintain his connection with what was around him. In the times that he had used the portals to move from this planet to Earth and then to Vyker's stream and back he had learned that the transition could be extremely difficult on their bodies. He had seen the detrimental effects on Galadriel and worried that the same thing could happen to him if he wasn't vigilant about his mind and body and how they responded to the transition. Jem kept his mind moving as quickly as he could, forcing thoughts through it nearly indiscriminately in the few moments that it took for them to move through the portal.

Finally, he felt his body hit something solid and knew that they had made it to Earth. Jem lay still for a few seconds, giving himself a chance to recover from the transition and acclimate to being on the planet. When he felt his body relax, he opened his eyes and looked to the side to make sure that Angela and Jacob had both fared the journey well. Jacob was propped up on his elbow rubbing his forehead, but Angela was still lying on her back, her eyes closed. A sense of panic rushed through him as Jem remembered how Galadriel looked when they had traveled from the museum to Vyker's stream. She had looked very much like Angela did now, eyes closed and skin pale, only to be revived quite some time later after being brought to Vyker's home.

Jem knelt at Angela's side and rested his hand to the side of her face, then ran it across her forehead. Her eyes fluttered open and he felt relief flood through his body. Jem leaned down to rest a kiss to her lips as she smiled up at him.

"Let's keep moving," Jacob said in a hushed voice. "We probably don't want the guards to find us wandering through the museum when it's closed."

With that, Jem looked around and realized that the corridor where they had arrived was shadowy with only small lights along the ceiling glowing in the darkness. It had been like this when he came with Vyker and Galadriel, but he couldn't remember where they went or what they had done when they were there. It was an uncomfortable realization. As a Denynso warrior he had been trained to be aware of his surroundings and respond. Now that he was back in the museum he knew that he hadn't used this training when he was first in the museum, putting him in the unpleasant situation of not knowing where he was or what might happen as they made their way through the darkened building.

"Where should we go from here?" he asked.

"I think that it would be best to get out of the museum," Jacob said. "We can decide what to do from there. If the guards caught us in here, we would have a lot more trouble on our hands, especially considering that Angela and I are supposed to be in other parts of the world and you are from another planet and suspected dead. We get out first, then we figure out how to get to Uoria."

4

George could see the storm of emotion in Eden's eyes. He knew that she wasn't completely confident in what she was saying. The thought of stepping outside of the lab was frightening. He knew that the creatures that Ryan had talked about, more of what they had already encountered, were waiting for them throughout the building, and it likely didn't matter which direction that they went. The chances that they were going to be able to get out without finding more of them were slim. Eden, however, knew the way that Ryan thought better than anyone. If she believed that it would be more dangerous for them to leave through the staircase that they had used to get into the lab, they needed to listen to her.

"Down?" he asked. "Toward the main doors?"

Eden shook her head.

"Not yet," she answered. "They will be staking out every single entrance and exit to this building that they know about. If we go to the main doors, we'll have to go through the lobby, which means there will be nothing to protect us."

"That they know about?" Pyra asked.

Eden let out a breath and nodded. The blend of emotion in her eyes had seemed to fracture slightly, spreading out into more identifiable thoughts and feelings for a brief moment, and in them George could see fear simmering within them. It was a different type of fear than some might have expected to see in the eyes of a young mother facing such intense danger. It was guarded, as if the determination to defeat what had tormented her when she was on Earth and protect the home and family that she had built when she finally left the life behind had created a barrier around the fear and wasn't allowing it to control her.

"There are sections of the building that most people don't know about," she said. "Even I haven't been into them."

"Then how do you know that they are there?" George asked.

She looked at him with that same expression that told him that he should know what she was talking about.

"I don't know for sure," Eden said carefully, "but for now, it's really the only option that we have."

Without waiting for anyone to say anything to her, she crossed the room and rested her hand on the doorknob. She paused for only a moment, leaning toward the door as if listening for any movement that might be on the other side, and then opened the door. George could feel all the men around him brace themselves, preparing for the swarm of hybrids to come into the room, but none did. They left the room again and rushed out into the hallway. It felt strange to be following the same path that they already had, but there was no choice. Ryan had them like rats in a maze. At this moment, they were completely at the mercy of the building and of his whim; the only choice that they had was to follow the thoughts of Eden, who seemed even more driven now.

They followed the corridor until they reached an exit at the end in the opposite direction that they had originally gone. George noticed that there was no keypad beside it and realized that it might be a storage closet. There were doors similar to that on the floor of the building where he had his lab and offices, but they had long since been emptied and abandoned, or filled with crates of decades-old records being used in research projects. He knew that most of these closets throughout the building were rarely used and even when they were they didn't contain anything that was sensitive or confidential, which is why they didn't bother with keypads and personal access codes. This closet, though, seemed intriguing to Eden. She was staring at it in a way that told him she knew something about it that the others didn't.

"What is it, Eden?" Pyra asked, stepping up beside Eden as she rested her hand to the door.

"What if he knows?" she murmured to herself.

It was hard to tell if she was speaking to herself or the others, but Pyra brought his strong hand to her back and guided her up against himself comfortingly.

"What if he knows what?" he asked. "Ryan? Are you talking about Ryan?"

Eden nodded and looked over her shoulder at him. She seemed to be opening her mouth as if to saying something but then there was an extremely loud crashing sound in the direction of the stairwell and her eyes widened. Without another word of explanation, she pulled open the door and revealed that it was, in fact, a closet. There were a few crates sitting on the floor and pieces of outdated equipment shrouded in cloths tucked in the corner. Eden began to pull on one of the large pieces and Pyra guided her aside by her shoulders so that she was out of the closet. George saw her wrap her arms protectively around Lysander where he was tied to her chest and lean down to touch a kiss to the top of his head. It was difficult to see, a moment so tender and gentle, and yet so heavy with the emotion and energy of what was happening around them.

George stepped into the closet with Pyra and helped him move the objects inside out, handing them over to the other men in the group. Gyyx tossed one of the boxes behind them and the sound of its impact on the floor shuddered through the building.

"No, Gyyx!" Eden hissed. "We can't call attention to ourselves."

"I'm sorry," the massive warrior said.

He took another box from Ty and lowered it more carefully to the ground. They listened for a moment and heard another crash in the distance, sounding even closer this time than the one before. It seemed Eden had been right and the hybrids had been lurking in the staircase, waiting for them to come back in so that they could ambush them. Now that they hadn't, the creatures were making their way back up to the laboratory. The thought suddenly shot through George's mind that they still didn't know where Ryan had gone. He could be truly anywhere at this point. If he had actually figured out how to override the locking system of the building he had access to anywhere he wanted to go, which meant that he could move through the building at his whim, coming at them from any direction he pleased.

They moved more quickly getting the rest of the boxes and equipment out of the closet and stepped out of the way so that Eden could go inside again. She walked to the far end and ran her hand along the wall carefully as if feeling for something in the paint. Finally, she stopped and applied pressure to the wall. Nothing happened and she moved her hands to the side and pressed again.

"What are you doing?" George asked.

"Give me a minute," Eden snapped and moved her hands slightly again.

She pressed again and there was a slight cracking sound. Seeming motivated by the reaction, Eden lifted her hands and slammed them against the wall. Long, meandering cracks appeared in the paint and Eden repeated the gesture. Pyra stepped into the closet with her and reached up to dig his fingers into the cracks being formed by Eden's hands. His thick fingers pulled away at the paint and the wall material beneath it. As it fell away George realized that the pieces were nowhere near as thick as they should be. Pyra continued pulling at the wall and within a few moments they had revealed a large hole.

"Holy shit," he muttered. "What is that?"

There was a slight smile on Eden's face. It wasn't one of happiness, but rather relief, as if she had not fully believed what she had been thinking when she first stepped into the closet. She reached for the lightstick that Pyra had tucked into the waistband of his pants and climbed through the hole. The darkness engulfed her, but a moment later she held the light up above her head rather than in front of her and the glow illuminated an old, narrow staircase. A gasp rippled through the group and George felt a glimmer of excitement and hope in his belly.

"Let me go first," Pyra demanded, and Eden stepped out of his way.

The warrior started down the stairs, ducking down and turning slightly sideways to accommodate his tremendous size as he made his way along them. Eden fell into step behind him and George followed, reaching behind him for Zsilvia's hand. He knew that she would be there without even having to look. The connection that they had between them was far more powerful than anything that he had ever experienced. It was unexplainable how closely tied he felt to her and the way that they seemed to exist in the same moments, the same breaths. They seemed to orbit each other, always knowing where the other was and being able to move together without having to find each other. His hand wrapped around hers and he felt her body come up close behind him.

"Where does that lead?" she whispered.

George shook his head.

"I don't know," he admitted. "I've never seen it before. I don't know why it's there."

They stepped into the stairwell and followed the sound of Pyra's footsteps in the darkness ahead of them. He used the hand that wasn't holding Zsilvia's to guide himself along the handrail to one side. The metal pole felt cold, gritty, and sticky with cobwebs. It was evident that it had been many years since any other hand had used this rail as someone walked down the stairs. That was at once unnerving and comforting. Though it meant that they were moving into a section of the building that had been abandoned, meaning it might be unstable and filled with unknown dangers, it also meant that no one else had found that stairwell. This was reassuring, telling him that neither Ryan nor his hybrid creatures had used these stairs and they may be moving into an area that would keep them safe as they tried to escape the laboratory and get back to the ships to bring them to Penthos.

The group made their way down the stairs as quickly as they could. George followed them nearly blindly. Eden had moved far enough ahead of him that he couldn't see the light from the lightstick and he only had the sound of the footsteps and heavy breaths ahead of him to keep him going. He didn't know how far they would need to go. He simply let his feet follow them and waited for them to end. The stairs turned at points, following sharp bends that seemed to indicate that they were moving through the different floors of the building. There were not enough of them, however, to mimic the floors of the laboratory that they had already followed, indicating that wherever in the building they were, it was different form the section to which they were already accustomed.

Finally, ahead of him he heard the footsteps stop.

"There's another door, Pyra," Eden said. "Is it unlocked?"

"No," Pyra said. "It doesn't matter."

There was a tremendous crashing sound and George knew that the Denynso warrior had kicked down the door. If it was anything similar to the lightweight closet door that they had encountered before entering the hidden stairwell, this would not have been a challenge. Almost instantly George's lungs filled with thick, dusty air and he muffled a cough against his arm. The air smelled old, like it had been closed behind that door for quite some time without benefit of moving in and out of lungs or moving with an open window.

"We need more light," Eden called from ahead of him.

George relayed the message to the group behind him and soon there were several other pinpoints of light shining over his shoulder.

"Not all of them," Pyra said. "Those have traveled a far way without charging and we need to conserve the light."

A few of the lights turned off and George felt a tap on his shoulder. He turned and took the light that Ty was handing him so that he could pass it along to Pyra. A moment later they started moving again. Soon George stepped down off the final stair and felt himself surrounded by the stale air. The glow from another lightstick behind him revealed the outline of the broken door and he could see a large expanse of darkness beyond it. The shifting light that broke through the darkness told him that Pyra and Eden were standing slightly apart in the space and moving their lightsticks around to scan the room.

George gently pulled on Zsilvia's hand as he guided her further into the space and away from the door so that the others could join them. As soon as he was inside, he realized that the room that they were in was not as large as he thought that it was. Once the rest of the group was inside, he could feel their bodies close to him and could only walk a few steps to either side before encountering them.

"What now?" a voice came from the other side of the room.

"There has to be another door," Eden replied. "We find it and we keep going."

"What do we do about the door?" George asked. "Just leave it?"

"We can't," Gyyx said. "They'll find it. We need to cover our tracks as much as possible."

In the faint light from the lightstick beside him, George saw Azrael step back out of the broken door and heard his footsteps rushing up the stairs. Around him the others had gone to action exploring the room and soon he heard Ty and Ciyrs call to Pyra.

"There are some old shelves over here," Ciyrs called. "We can move them in front of the door. It might not stop them for long, but it will block it long enough to slow them down."

"We have to wait for Azrael," Oro said.

Only moments later George could hear the footsteps again and the winged man ducked back into the room.

"I closed the door to the closet and blocked it with some of the equipment so even if they do open it, they will have to move them out of the way to find the gap in the wall."

Eden nodded.

"Thank you, Azrael," she said. "We need to get these shelves in front of the door. Zsilvia, Elianna, help me find a door out of here."

Zsilvia's hand left George's as she moved toward Eden. He started toward the warriors and grabbed onto one of the tall sets of metal shelves that had been discarded in the corner of the room. Together they carried the shelves over to the door and positioned them so that four lay on their sides across the door with two more standing vertically in front of them. Gyyx lifted another set and slid it over the tops of the other shelves, following it with another so that those two wedged tightly into place between the other shelves and the ceiling. It would take strength and time to get past the barrier. This at once gave George a sense of security and reminded him that they were moving deeper into a space that was completely unfamiliar.

"Here's the door," Elianna called and the group rushed toward her.

George could see an extremely outdated version of the keypad beside the door, but it was clear that it was no longer connected. Eden took hold of the handle and the door immediately opened. They pushed through into another corridor and something seemed familiar to George. He pushed back out of the corridor into the room. He felt for the bag that he had grown accustomed to wearing at his hip since being on Uoria and realized that it wasn't there. He remembered that he hadn't carried it with him when he and Zsilvia came back to the lab before the wedding, and the lack of it made him feel angrier. Without the tools that he usually carried, he felt vulnerable and ineffective. Though he had never carried such items when he was at this laboratory before he went to Uoria, after his time on the planet he had developed a deep need to always feel prepared. Being there and engaging with the other species had brought a greater understanding of himself and awareness of his being in connection with others and with the world around him. Before he left Earth, his life had been controlled only by his mind and the research that defined him. After arriving on Uoria and meeting the Denynso, bonding with Zsilvia, and seeing the conflicts and clashes that had unfolded, however, he seemed to awaken to the presence and power of his body. No longer did he immediately go only to the logic and knowledge that he held as the only way that he would be able to help in any situation. Instead, conflict and challenges triggered a compulsion to protect, to work, and to fight. His mind and body had connected and he relied on the tools that he carried with him to allow him to react to whatever they encountered.

Now that he was without his bag and everything that he had carried inside it, he felt thrown back into the life that he had had before he left Earth. He hated the feeling of emptiness and this fueled his hatred toward Ryan even further.

"Can I use your lightstick?" he asked Ty.

The warrior handed him the light and George rushed back into the room. He held the light up over his head and turned so that it scanned across the walls around him. As he oriented himself to face the door where the rest of the group was streaming into the corridor, the light fell onto a boarded-up window. Another was several inches away; the crumbling remains of a counter sticking jaggedly out from beneath it. This was a medical wing.

5

E den moved along the corridor cautiously. The space was heavy with the feeling of abandonment, carrying that strange sense of memory that always seemed to linger in places like this. It was as if there had been such a concentration of life and energy there that it had saturated the walls, the floor, and the air itself, allowing the space to hold on to every moment that it had experienced so that even long after those moments ended, it didn't forget.

The floor beneath her feet was made of scuffed cream-colored polished cement and in the light of the stick in her hand she could see that the walls to either side were made of ceramic tiles. The tiles were crumbling in some places, further underscoring how long it had been since anyone had walked along this hall. There were closed doors every few feet on either side of her, some featuring small plaques with combinations of letters and numbers that she could only imagine were once a classification system to manage the rooms. Part of her wanted to try to open the doors, but another hesitated, unsure of what she would find if the doors were unlocked as the one leading from the small room had been. Finally, she knew that she couldn't keep hesitating. They didn't know where they were or what these rooms were, and they would need to find out if they were going to have any chance of making their way out of the building before Ryan or the hybrids caught up with them.

A set of large double doors loomed ahead of her. She wouldn't allow herself to hesitate. Pressing Lysander tightly to her with one hand, she pushed through the doors with the other, immediately thrusting the lightstick into the darkness ahead. The door opened out into an even wider hallway lined with more doors. Above her she could see old lights embedded in the ceiling and remnants of what looked like some kind of intercom or communication system positioned in the empty spaces between the rooms. It was an eerie feeling that made the tips of her fingers tingle and her mind intensely aware of each of her senses as if preparing her to respond to whatever the next step would trigger.

"Eden," George's voice called from behind her.

She turned and saw the man pushing through the rest of the group to her.

"Are you alright?" she asked as he approached.

"This is a medical ward," he told her.

"What?" she asked.

"A medical ward," George repeated. "That room that we found is an old registration room. I saw the windows in the wall."

"This laboratory building doesn't have a medical ward," Eden protested.

"Not anymore," Jonah said.

Eden turned to Jonah. The young man was walking toward her, an indecipherable expression on his face.

"What do you mean?" she asked.

"Before my crew left for our mission, we had our headquarters in the same complex as the old university. The buildings were actually connected by skywalks. One of the university buildings was a hospital."

"But the old university was demolished," George said. "It was torn down decades ago so that they could build the new university. All of the buildings in the complex came down."

"No," Jonah said, shaking his head. "They might have taken down some of the buildings, but for some reason they kept the hospital. This is the old medical ward. I remember coming into it a few times. When we first got here, I thought that it was the same area as the headquarters building and university, but none of the buildings looked familiar. Now that I'm here, though, I know exactly where I am. This laboratory is far bigger than the hospital was, but this," he gestured around him, "this is the hospital that was here when I was. It was old even then. They had tried to do some improvements. These keypads look similar to the technology that was implemented just when we left. A lot of the building was already totally outdated, though."

"So why did they keep it?" Pyra asked. "If it was already so old, why wouldn't they take it down when they took down the other buildings?"

Jonah looked around.

"I don't know. It doesn't make any sense. Why would they seal up an abandoned hospital and build a new laboratory off of it?"

"What's in these rooms?" Ciyrs asked, gesturing toward one of the doors.

The healer sounded intrigued by the idea of an Earth medical facility. On Uoria, Ciyrs performed his healing treatments in a small clinic attached to his home if they were in the compound. Otherwise, he used his inborn powers or the ointments and medicines that he crafted wherever he needed to, to heal and protect the warriors or whoever needed it. This was the first time that he had the opportunity to see where Earth doctors and surgeons used their skills, as outdated as it may be.

"These are examination rooms," Eden explained. "It's where the doctors would see their patients."

Ciyrs stepped up to one of the rooms and tried the handle. The door opened and Eden came to his side to hold her light up for him to see. The room beyond the door was filled with old chairs. They looked like they had been tossed into the room haphazardly, filling the space with leaning, precarious towers.

"Those were in the waiting room," Jonah said. "I remember what they looked like sitting out there."

His voice had become softer as if he were talking to her through the years that had passed since the last time he had stood in that building. They kept walking down the hallway, opening the doors to the examination rooms as they went. Some were completely empty while others held remnants of what the medical facility used to be, including stacked beds, file cabinets, and tangles of equipment. They paused in front of one of the doors and Jonah ran his fingers along the plaque. He gave a soft, mirthless laugh.

"This is the room where I got my final clearance exam before boarding for the Nyx 23 mission," he said. "Since it was a clandestine mission, we couldn't all go in together for our examinations like we usually did before a voyage. For the few weeks leading up to the launch a couple of us a day would come in and get examined, pretending it was just a regular department checkup. I was the last one."

He reached for the handle of the door and pushed, but it didn't move. He tried again and Eden could hear the clicking of the mechanisms inside the door that told her that the door was locked. She stepped aside and Pyra planted his boot just below the handle, forcing the lock out of place.

The door opened, revealing an intact examination room. Eden was startled by the appearance of the space. Of every room along the corridor, this was the only one that still looked like it would have when the hospital was still in operation. Jonah's eyes narrowed as he hesitantly stepped over the threshold into the room as if he was being drawn back into the last time he had gone into the room. Eden tried to reconcile the reality that when Jonah had attended that appointment before leaving for the mission, it was years before even her grandparents were born. When he stepped into that room, ready for the same type of examination he had undergone many times before in preparation for missions. He knew that there was a voyage ahead and that it would be unlike anything that he had experienced before as they ventured to an unknown planet. She wondered if he had been nervous, if there had been even the slightest indi-cation that this mission wouldn't go the way that the others had, that he wouldn't return until more than a century later.

Jonah crossed to the bed positioned in the center of the room and rested his hand on the mattress. The sheets and blanket had been pulled tightly and tucked in severe corners, the pillow rested at the head of the bed as if awaiting the next patient. Whoever had prepared the room for the hospital to close hadn't treated it like the room would never been used again. Instead, it had been put back together just as it would have been at the end of any other day, ready for the next morning.

"This is so strange," Jonah said. "Why this room? Of all the rooms on this floor, why did they keep this room like this?" He looked at the counter on one wall and Eden followed his gaze to the canisters and boxes of medical implements arranged neatly on the surface. A slim silver case sat in the center of the counter and even from the distance Eden could see the coating of dust over it. "Look at this," Jonah said, walking up to the counter. "They even left a patient file just sitting out on the counter."

"Wouldn't they bring something like that with them when they moved to the new facility?" Eden asked.

"I would think so," Jonah answered.

He picked the metal file up and brushed away the dust on the front. Eden saw his hand pause and his head lean slightly closer to the front of the file. He continued to brush away the dust with greater intensity and then Eden saw his hand begin to shake.

"Jonah?" she said. "Jonah, what is it?"

She stepped up to his side and held the lightstick up higher. The glow fell on the file in his hand. It was an old-fashioned version of a patient file, a design that hadn't been used in many years but might have still been in use when the old hospital had been closed many years before. She looked more closely at it and immediately saw what had caused Jonah to pause. There was a name engraved on the front of the file as it would have been on every permanent patient filed. *Jonah Kenyon.*

Eden remembered the first time that she had seen Jonah in the settlement on Uoria. Though she hadn't realized what it was at the time because they didn't yet know that these were not only humans but the members of a lost mission from a century before, he had been wearing a shirt that featured a remnant of his uniform stitched together with other pieces of fabric. On that scrap had been two letters. JK.

"What is it?" George asked from behind them.

Eden took the file from Jonah's hand and turned to show it to George.

"It's his patient folder," Eden said.

"What?" George asked.

"It's my patient folder," Jonah reiterated. "The doctor put it right there on the counter at the end of my examination before we left for Penthos."

"That can't be," Eden said, shaking her head. "The hospital was open for years after the Nyx 23 mission. At least a decade, maybe a little more."

"I remember when he put it there," Jonah said. "He input the information from my tests, scanned my fingerprints, and sent all of the information to the command leader, then closed the file and put it down right here."

"The command leader?" Eden asked. "The department head?"

Jonah shook his head.

"No. Nyx 23 was a clandestine mission even within the department itself. The department head and the governing bodies didn't want anything to do with Penthos or with the Valdicians. Nyx 23 was a small faction within the larger group and planned the mission."

Jonah opened the file and pressed the button that would have once started the file, but it remained dark.

"It's been more than 100 years," Eden said. "The energy cells would have worn out."

As if the words triggered him, Lysander began to cry. She patted him gently, but his wails only grew louder. The more he cried, the more aware she became of the exhaustion that was coursing through her own body. The voices around her started to sound muffled and the light faded as her eyes started to close.

"We need to get somewhere to rest," Pyra said.

"No," Eden said, her voice weak even as she tried to sound as insistent as she could. "We have to keep going. We have to get to the others."

"Eden," Pyra said over Lysander's cries. "Listen to your son. He needs to be changed and fed. He needs to sleep somewhere where he isn't being jostled around."

"We have to get out of here," she said. "Jonah has been here before, he can get us out."

"I've only been to this floor," Jonah said. "I know that the other floors have other rooms, but we don't know how much of the original structure was kept or what type of condition it's in. I wouldn't know how to navigate us out of here completely on my own."

"What do you think are the chances that anyone else knows about this?" Pyra asked, turning his attention to George.

Eden could see George glance around as if he himself was still shocked by the fact that they were inside the long-abandoned medical building.

"I don't know," George said. "I definitely didn't know about it and I've been working in this lab far longer than Ryan."

"Eden, how did you know about it?" Pyra asked.

Eden was starting to feel dizzy. It was as if the nearly two days that had passed since she had slept had all just pounded down into her and were making it so that she could barely stand. She shook her head slightly.

"I don't know," she said. "I don't remember. I heard about it somewhere. It was just a rumor, but I remember thinking that it seemed strange."

"What seemed strange?"

"The closets," she said. "Why so many closets?"

Lysander's cries seemed to pull away from her, disappearing into the distance as her consciousness pulled her away from the others like she was being pulled backward through a tunnel. She felt her body weaken and her legs give out. All she could do was scoop one arm around the baby as she collapsed toward the ground.

6

Jem pressed himself to the wall, trying to make himself as small as possible so that he could disappear into the shadows. He could hear the footsteps of the guard making his rounds through the gallery and he held his breath as they got closer. Behind him Angela and Jacob crouched in the recesses of an exhibit, their smaller forms making it far easier for them to be unassuming in the stillness of the closed museum. Finally, the guard passed by them and the sound of his shoes grew fainter in the distance as he made his way deeper into the galleries that wrapped around the center of the hall. Jem gestured for the others to follow and they rushed into the vulnerability of the open halls. Though he didn't think that there was more than that one guard patrolling this wing of the museum, Jem couldn't be sure, which meant that they had to stay cautious until they were safely out of the building.

"Which way do we go now?" he asked in as soft a whisper as he could manage while still making sure that the others heard him.

"There's a sign," Angela said, pointing several feet ahead of him and up on a wall.

Staying crouched low to the floor, Jem scurried toward the sign and looked up at it. Jacob came up beside him and pointed at the top word.

"Lobby," he said.

That wasn't a word used on Uoria, but Jem took Jacob's gesture and the way that Angela began to move in the direction of the arrow on the sign to mean that that was where they would find the exit. They moved as swiftly as they could and relief washed over him when he saw a wide, open area with a bank of doors ahead of them. He remembered this space. He and Galadriel had run across it during his first visit to the museum and escaped through those doors that stood just on the other side.

"Wait," Jacob said when Jem made a move to cross the atrium. "There's a guard at the front desk."

That guard hadn't been stationed there before and Jem could only imagine that his position had been added after Galadriel and he had simply unlocked the doors and run out amid the screaming of the alarm. Jem looked at the doors, narrowing his eyes to see them in as much detail as he could at the distance, and noticed that they were much the same as they had been the last time. Tall and wide, the doors were made up mostly of glass with the exception of black sections of metal across the center. It was on those metal sections where Galadriel had released the lock. Jem looked back at the guard. He knew that they weren't going to have the luxury of enough time to pause and unlock the door before getting out.

The desk with the guard was positioned at the far side of the lobby, tucked to the side of the bank of doors so that he would have full view of anyone going into or out of the building. This meant that he was several yards away from the far doors, which meant that he would have to move around the large, nearly full-circle desk and then across the room in order to get to them if they were to go for the doors at the furthest end.

"How do we get there?" he asked, pointing in the direction of another corridor that fed out into the lobby closer to the far doors.

Angela looked down the hall where they were crouched and then back toward the sign.

"It looks like the galleries wrap around," she said. "If we keep following this hall, eventually it will lead us through the exhibits and to that hallway. There will be other guards in those wings, though," she said. "Museums spread them out so that they can keep the entire building under surveillance."

Jem nodded.

"We're just going to have to be careful," he said. "We don't really have much of an option."

Angela and Jacob nodded at him and they started their way down the hallway again. Jem's heart pounded in his chest as they crept through the corridors and galleries. It was as though he could feel the pendant around his neck jump with each beat, reminding him heavily of the journey that he had already taken and the one that still lay before him. As they moved through the museum he found his mind reaching out to the displays that they passed as if trying to capture any little pieces of information that it could about the different times and places that they memorialized. Everything seemed so much larger now, so much more complex than he had ever considered before he left Uoria. Just as they made their way into the final corridor, he wondered if somewhere deep in the museum, in a section that they hadn't yet explored, there was an exhibit about the Denynso, and if there was, what it would say and how it would present his warrior kind.

When they finally reached the end of the hall, Jem, Angela, and Jacob huddled together behind a section of the wall that jutted out into the entrance to make a large, imposing arch. Angela looked around his arm at the doors and then up at Jem's face.

"What now?" she asked. "The guard is right there."

Jem looked at the guard and then back at the doors. They seemed further away from the corridor than they had when he first saw them, but this was their only chance. They had no other option for how to get out of the museum and every moment that they spent inside made it more likely that one of the other guards would discover them. The locking mechanism on the doors was more complex than it had been and it was even clearer now that they wouldn't have time to even attempt to unlock them. He took a breath and stood.

"Now," he said, "we run."

Jem shot out of the shadows without another moment of hesitation, hoping that the others would follow him. He squared his body toward the door, brought his arms up cover his face, and leapt. There was a brief moment of stillness before he encountered the glass. In the next instant, he felt the pane splintering around him and heard the familiar screaming of the alarm accented by the glass falling to the ground. He hit the ground, but got up instantly to turn and make sure that Angela and Jacob were making their way out.

Through the other doors Jem could see the guard running from his desk toward the door, a communicator held to his mouth. The door had broken in such a way that the metal bar across the middle was bent but still intact, but most of the glass was gone from both the top and bottom sections Jacob was climbing over the metal as Angela scrambled across the ground to get out through the bottom. They both got to their feet and came running toward him seconds before the guard reached the door. Jem latched on to Angela's wrist and he scooped her up into his arms as he took off running down the steps in front of the museum and down the sidewalk.

They ran until they reached a corner, then turned, starting a weaving path through the neighborhood surrounding the museum until he could hear Jacob's footfalls slow and then stop. Jem stopped and walked back to Jacob before lowering Angela to the ground.

"They won't find us," Jacob reassured them. "They'll look around the museum and in the immediate area, but until they watch the cameras, they don't even know who they're looking for."

"When they do, it will pretty hard to miss Jem," Angela said.

Jem felt a tinge of guilt, but then saw his mate smile. He reached down for her hands and turned them over to look at her palms.

"Are you alright?" he asked. "Did you cut yourself?"

"Only a little," Angela said. "I'll be alright."

"Let's get somewhere where I can bandage those for you," Jem said.

They started walking down the sidewalk and a few moments later noticed what looked like a small restaurant. A sign glowed in the window and the faint sound of music came toward them as they approached.

"Are they open?" Jacob asked.

"It looks like it," Angela replied.

Jem pulled the door open and the three stepped inside. He immediately noticed that they were the only people there with the exception of a grizzled man standing behind a long, narrow table that curved around the far end of the room. He lifted his eyes to the three of them as they walked in and his gaze focused directly on Jem. The warrior could feel the man evaluating him, scrutinizing him in much the same way that Angela and Jacob had when they first saw him. He anticipated a strong, possibly even violent, reaction, but there was none. The man simply gestured at the tables scattered around the room and then went back to cleaning the glass he held in one hand.

The three of them went to one of the tables and sat down, dropping their bags at their feet. Jem reached into his and drew out some of the bandages he had packed. He spread them across the table and then took out a cloth. Without warning the man appeared at the side of the table and place a large glass of water in front of Jem. He nodded toward Angela's hands.

"Everything alright?" he asked in a voice that was exactly what Jem anticipated would have come out of him.

"Yes," Jem replied. "She cut herself on some glass. I'm just going to bandage her up."

"Can I help you with anything?" the man asked.

His tone was long and slow, the words grumbling in his throat long after he said them, but there was something about them that sounded sincere and Jem shook his head.

"No," he said. "Thank you."

The man gave a single nod and walked away from the table. The interaction gave Jem a sense of comfort that he couldn't really explain, and he felt more secure and calm as he went to work rinsing Angela's hands with the water that the man had brought them.

"What do we do from here?" Jacob asked.

Jem started winding one of the bandages around Angela's hand and shook his head.

"I don't know," he admitted. "Now that we're here, I don't know any more how to get back to Uoria than I did when we were on our planet."

"I think the best way is going to be through the University," Angela said. "They have connections with Uoria and with your king. They might even have another group preparing to travel there for the exchange program, and if they don't they might be able to charter a special flight specifically for you considering the circumstances."

"Do you know how to get there from here?" Jem asked.

"We can't walk," Angela admitted. "We need a car."

"Maybe we should get in touch with Rilex," Jacob suggested. "Galadriel asked him to take care of her car and her apartment and everything when she and Ty decided to stay with Vyker. Maybe he would help us."

Jem wasn't sure how he felt about reaching out to Rilex. Convincing her that his name was Rick and that he was a researcher who shared her fascination with the wall that had eventually brought her to Vyker and then to Jem, Rilex eventually admitted that he was actually one of Vyker's species, the best friend of his father who had disappeared many years before. Though he had been extremely helpful to them in their efforts to restore the Star Wall and protect the universe from the StarKillers, Rilex had also been somewhat cool toward Jem, almost as though he were suspicious of the Denynso. He had chosen to return to Earth even after Ty and Galadriel agreed to stay with Vyker, which had struck Jem as strange, though now with the sense of attachment that he felt for the jungle planet where he had spent so much time since his own disappearance, he thought he might at least somewhat understand.

"How do we do that?" Angela asked.

Jacob reached into his bag and pulled out what looked like a small journal.

"This," he said with a hint of a smile on his lips. "Galadriel gave it to me before I left to visit you."

"What is it?" Jem asked.

Angela took the journal from Jacob's hands and opened it.

"This is Galadriel's journal," she said. "It has Rilex's contact information in it. Why would she give this to you?"

"She said that I should have it with me just in case I needed it. That I could give it back to her when she saw me again. It was almost like she knew that we were going to come here."

"How could she have known?" Jem asked. "Even I didn't know."

Angela's eyes dropped to the necklace that he still wore around his neck and then lifted back to his.

"Home is always home," she said.

The man from behind the bar appeared at the side of the table again and rested his hand to the table. When he moved it away there was a small black metal piece sitting on the surface. He made eye contact with Jem and then walked away again. Jem felt like the man had been listening to them, but even though it should have bothered him, he was also strangely grateful for his presence.

"What is that?" Jem asked as Angela reached for the object that the man had left behind.

"It's a phone," she said. "We can call Rilex."

Jem didn't fully understand what she meant, but then she picked up the device and input the combination of numbers that were on the page in the journal. A moment later he heard a buzzing sound coming from the phone and then a slight click followed by a familiar voice.

"Hello?" Rilex said with a slight tinge of confusion in his words. "This is Rick Abernathy."

He was using the human name he had chosen for himself when he arrived on Earth many years before after accidentally traveling through a portal, much as Jem had when he left Uoria during the battle with the Klimnu. That was the name that Jem had first used to refer to him, but it had never really fit him. Even though he looked fully human, there was something about him that had always struck him as different, as if because he, too, was a different species he was able to detect others. Soon, though, he found out that the man's name was actually Rilex and that had been lying about his identity to manipulate Galadriel's movements in an effort to complete the task that he had set out to do in a different time, in a different version of reality. Though the idea was difficult to wrap his head around when he first heard it, somehow it made everything fall into place. Suddenly his disappearance from Uoria and his arrival on the unknown jungle planet had begun to make sense.

"Rilex, this is Angela."

There was a brief pause before Rilex replied.

"Angela!" he said with excitement. "Where are you?"

"We're in a bar somewhere in the neighborhood with the museum. It's the only place we could find that's open."

"Perfect, stay where you are."

"What?" Angela said, but there was another slight click and she looked down at the phone with an expression that told Jem that the call had ended. "He hung up."

"Why does he want us to stay here?" Jacob asked.

Angela shook her head. Jem reached across the table to

hold her hand, finding comfort in the feeling of her skin. It was still so strange to think that she had only been his mate for such a short time. He felt like she had always been a piece of him and the thought of living only a second without her was unbearable. She looked back at him with the same intensity, the same reliance. It told him that even though she wasn't Denynso and hadn't been born with the same attachment that his kind developed for their mates, making it so that they could only ever truly love one person in their entire existence, she still felt the same level of passion and love for him.

For a third time the man appeared at the side of the table. This time he lowered a large plate to the surface between them and then slid the phone off the table back into his large hand. He walked away without acknowledging any of them and went back to his post behind the bar, wiping another glass with the cloth in his hand. Jem looked at the plate and saw it stacked with several types of food that he didn't recognize, but that Angela and Jacob grabbed up eagerly. Hunger burned in his belly and he wondered for the first time how long it had actually taken for them to transport to the museum and then escape. He picked up one of the pieces curiously and placed it in his mouth. The flavor was rich and strong, accented by something very much like the water that they drew from the purple sea on Uoria.

"Do you like it?" Angela asked with a laugh.

Jem guessed that his face expressed his surprise at the surprising flavor of the food and he nodded.

"It's different," he admitted.

They had only been eating for a few moments when the door to the bar opened and Rilex rushed in. Jem, Jacob, and

Angela jumped to their feet, surprised by his sudden appearance.

"Rilex," Jacob said. "What are you doing here?"

Jem noticed Rilex look up in the direction of the man standing behind the bar and give a slight nod. It was a gesture of acknowledgement, of familiarity. With that one gesture, the man stepped away from his post behind the bar and through a door that led deeper into the building.

"When I heard about the museum, I thought that it could be you."

"When you heard about the museum?" Angela asked.

"I have a police scanner," he said. "I like to be able to pay attention to what's going on in the area, especially with the wall here. I have to be vigilant. You never know what's going to happen – or who might show up."

There was darkness behind those words and none of them pushed him any further.

"What did you hear?" Jacob asked.

7

———

Rilex looked at the three faces that were staring back at him expectantly. He could barely believe that they were there. He had been trying to figure out how he was going to get in touch with them and bring them to Earth, and then the announcement came over the police scanner. It had been difficult to decipher at first. The code was complex and the voices overlapped until they were almost indivisible into words. Finally, though, he was able to figure out that it was alerting authorities to a break-in at the museum. Though they called it a break-in, the scanner specified that it was actually unauthorized people in the museum who seemed to break *out*, smashing through the front door and escaping the guard by a matter of seconds

"As soon as I heard that the people had broken through the door, I thought that it might be you," Rilex said. He gave a short laugh. "There's not many people I've ever encountered who could just smash through a door like that."

"But why did you come?" Angela asked.

"I'd been trying to find a way to get in touch with you," Rilex said. "With Jem, specifically."

Jem looked somewhat startled by the revelation.

"Me?" the warrior asked. "Why?"

Rilex felt what little amusement he had felt when thinking about Jem breaking through the glass drain away. He gestured toward the door.

"We should go."

"Go?" Angela asked. "Go where?"

"To the University. I'll explain on the way."

"The University?" Jacob asked. "That's where we were planning on going, we just didn't know how to get there. That's why we called you. We were hoping that you would be able to help us get there."

"That's where we're going," Rilex said. "I'll explain on the way."

"Wait," Angela said as they started toward the door. "The bartender. We didn't pay him for the food."

Rilex shook his head.

"It's alright," he said. "It's all settled."

He didn't go any further. That was an explanation for another time. Instead, he guided them toward the door and to where his car waited by the sidewalk. They piled in and he immediately set off toward the University. His heart was pounding in his chest as he tried to come up with the right words to say to Jem, to explain to him why he wanted to get in touch with him. Finally, he opened his mouth and simply let the words tumble out.

"I received a tip that an unauthorized shuttle appeared at the University and then another vehicle, technology that isn't recognizable, showed up as well. I have reason to believe that they are from Uoria."

"What do you mean 'unauthorized shuttle'?" Angela asked.

"The shuttle was marked for a different voyage and there

was no plan for it to return to the University at that time. The crew didn't report to the transportation department or give notice of their purpose for returning to Earth. They're currently missing."

"And the other vehicle?" Jacob asked.

"It's something that no one has ever seen. It doesn't look like any type of shuttle or ship that even the University has or is in the course of planning. It landed outside of the University laboratory building. I'm assuming it couldn't access the bay. The crew and passengers of that ship are missing as well."

"What is the University doing about them?" Angela asked. "Have they moved them?"

"No," Rilex said. "I went there before I heard the announcement over the police scanner. I wanted to see them for myself. The unknown vehicle has protective technology that prevents anyone from getting inside, but if the wrong people had access to it, I'm sure that it wouldn't last very long. I hid them to make sure that no one would be able to find them."

"How did you do that?" Jacob asked.

Rilex took a breath.

"I just did," he said. "But it's not infallible. They can't stay hidden forever, which means that we need to get there and figure out who brought them there and why before someone else does."

"Why do you think that the vehicles are from Uoria?" Jem asked.

It was the question that Rilex had known was going to come, but that he was at the most loss to answer. They were speeding toward the University and he knew that he had only limited time to explain what was happening and the urgency that he felt to get them there and figure out what was really going on.

"Since meeting you I've been devoting more of my research to Uoria and the Denynso. I wanted to understand your kind and what has been happening on the planet since first contact with the humans. I uncovered some information that might indicate that there are problems on Uoria."

"Problems?" Jem asked. "What's happening."

"I'm not absolutely sure," Rilex said. "But I feel that these vehicles have something to do with it."

"If you think that there's something wrong, why didn't you just call the University and let them know?" Angela asked. "Wouldn't they be the ones to help find the people who brought those vehicles to Earth and why?"

Rilex shook his head.

"I'm not exactly permitted to access the areas of the University that I have, and some of the research that I've been doing borders on unethical at best."

"And at worst?" Angela asked. "Illegal?"

"Deadly."

"So, you didn't call the University to protect yourself?" Jem asked, his voice angry and accusatory. "There could be countless lives at risk, but you are too afraid that you are going to get in trouble for your research that you didn't ask for help?"

"No," Rilex said. "That's not it. There are countless lives at stake *so* I didn't reach out to the University. You never know who you can trust. Sometimes the people who you think are the most on your side are actually the ones who are the most dangerous. I didn't want to risk that. I don't fully know what's happening, and I don't want to put anyone in more danger than they already are. The only one who can really help me is you."

"I don't understand why they would come without the authorization of the University," Jem said. His voice was softer now as if the anger had disappeared and given way to the fear and anxiety that he was starting to feel at the thought of his beloved home planet being in danger. "There is an alliance. There's a connection between the University and the Denynso. If my kind needed to come here for some reason, they would reach out to the representatives for the program at the University and get clearance to come."

"Maybe it doesn't have anything to do with the program," Rilex suggested.

"There's something wrong," Jem said. "The Denynso operate by duty and regulation. Laws and rules are binding. They wouldn't break the agreements made with the University lightly. Something very serious has to be happening for them to make that move."

Jem's words confirmed everything that Rilex had feared and made the urgency within him even more intense. He pushed the car faster, knowing that every single second mattered now and they needed to get to the University and to whoever was waiting there as fast as they possibly could.

Eden became aware of her heartbeat before she knew what was happening around her. Her eyelids resisted as she fought to open them, but eventually she dragged them open and was greeted by faint, hazy light. Pyra's face appeared above her and she saw a relieved smile come to his lips.

"Hey," he said. "Are you alright?"

Eden tried to sit up, but he pressed against her shoulders to ease her back down against the pile of blankets and pillows that had been propped behind her.

"Where's the baby?" she asked weakly.

"Don't try to sit up yet," Pyra said. "Ciyrs gave you something that he said would help you rest. It will probably make you a little dizzy for a while. Lysander is fine. He's with Zsilvia."

"I need to take care of him," Eden protested.

There were so many questions running through her head, but it seemed that they were so twisting and complex that she couldn't focus on them. All she could think about was Lysander and making sure that he was properly cared for.

"He's fine," Pyra said. "We changed him and I held him to you so that he could eat. Don't worry about him. You need to rest."

Eden settled back and let her body relax. She drew in and released several breaths until her heartbeat normalized and she felt the trembling from deep inside her ease.

"Where are we?" she asked.

"We're deeper in the hospital," Pyra said. "When you collapsed Ciyrs told us that we needed to get you somewhere to rest. We kept going until we found this room. Jonah says that it looks like one of the preparation chambers that used to be in hospital buildings. It seems to have served its purpose. There's bedding, clothes, emergency supplies, and even the rations are still safe after all these years. We decided to stop here for a while. We could all use something to eat and some sleep, even if it's just for a short time. We're a few floors down from the examination rooms."

Those words made a thought suddenly occur to Eden. Her eyes opened wider.

"Jonah," she said. "Where's Jonah?"

Pyra looked down at her and nodded.

"I'll get him."

A few moments later Jonah came to her side.

"Jonah," she said. "You said that the Nyx 23 mission was clandestine, and that's why each of you had to come in for your examinations separately."

The man nodded.

"Yes," he said. "Only part of the department was involved. The others didn't believe that the threat on the prison planet was enough to justify action."

"If it was a secret mission, why was there such a swift response by the Earth military?"

"What do you mean?"

"Everything I've read about the Nyx 23 mission points out that the response from the Earth military was swift and fierce. They went to the planet to try to find a trace of the crew, didn't find one, and wiped it out. That's when they named it Penthos in honor of you."

"Right," Jonah said, "but like Ryan said, that's not what really happened. The military didn't wipe out the Valdicians and free the prisoners. The general absorbed them and brought them back to Earth to use for the beginning of the breeding experiments."

"There's no memorial," she said quietly.

"What?" Jonah asked.

"No memorial," Eden repeated. "Don't you think that's strange?" They had talked about it before, but now that they were back on Earth it really sank in how out of character it was for there to be no memorial erected on Penthos for the lost team. "It is Earth's way to make memorials to honor people who have died and give others a place where they can go to pay their respects. So, an entire team goes out into the galaxy to try to fight against a rogue race that has created an illegal prison compound and goes missing, but when the military supposedly destroys the species that did it, they don't do anything?"

"What *specifically* did you learn about Nyx 23? What's in the textbooks?" Jonah asked.

"We learned that the team had identified a threat on a previously unnamed and unexplored planet. Under the belief that there was an illegal prison compound operated by a non-ally species, a small team set out on a mission with the goal of freeing the prisoners and pushing the enemies back. Mission control lost contact with the team and they didn't return as planned. A second team was then sent to the planet in an effort to find the team and understand what happened, but when they arrived they only found the prison and the enemies. There was no sign of the team. War units were deployed and the compound was destroyed. That's when they named the planet Penthos. The Nyx 23 team became martyrs, a symbol of devotion and the ultimate commitment to the quest for understanding, knowledge, justice, and protection."

"But there was never a memorial set up there? Nothing that our families could visit? Nothing even for the prisoners?"

"No," Eden said.

"Wait," Jonah said, his eyes widening slightly. "Ryan said that the general of the Earth military, his ancestor, teamed up with the Valdicians to start the breeding experiments. They were in on it."

"Yes," Eden said. "They shared the desire to breed the ultimate military force made up of hybrids, bred for their different powers and characteristics."

"So why did we end up on Uoria?" he asked.

"What do you mean?"

"Why did we end up on Uoria?" Jonah repeated. "The

Valdicians supposedly aligned with the Covra and sent us to Uoria after we raided the planet so that they could enslave us and use us in their plan to take over the Universe."

"Right," Eden said. "They had already sabotaged your ship and sent you to Uoria before the military units arrived on Penthos, though. They wouldn't have had any way of knowing that the war units would come and they would decide to go to Earth to participate in the breeding experiments."

"They wouldn't?" Jonah asked. "If they suddenly decided that they were going to go to Earth and start these complex experiments that they didn't want anyone to know about, don't you think that they would have mentioned to their new Earth allies that they had sent this mysteriously missing crew to another planet?"

"Why would they do that? Maybe they just figured that it didn't matter anymore and that they had a new venture."

"Three groups planning on taking over the Universe at the same time, specifically through the use of slaves curated from other planets and other species that have characteristics and abilities that the others don't. But they don't have anything to do with each other? Doesn't that strike you as a bit too coincidental?"

"The Covra," Eden said, her mind seeming to clear. "They wouldn't just let it go. If the Valdicians had made an agreement with them and then they reneged on it, they would retaliate."

"Exactly," Jonah said. "But they didn't. They waited. Then things went wrong and our ship crashed in the wrong place on the planet. Even then, the Covra didn't turn against the Valdicians. They waited for another generation to come so that they could continue the plan that had been put into place."

"It was designed that way," Eden said. "The entire thing. You were meant to go to the planet and confront the Valdicians. It wasn't a fluke. They didn't suddenly decide to send you to Uoria. It was all by design."

Jonah nodded.

"But whose?" he asked. "And why was my file still in that room?"

8

Oro stepped through the narrow doorway into the second preparation chamber and looked around. His eyes finally fell on the faint, almost imperceptible glow that was coming from one far corner and he moved toward it.

"Ariella?" he said gently.

The glow flickered slightly and he moved closer to his mate. She was crouched against the wall, her knees pulled up to her chest and her wings tucked in against her sides. The glittering light that emanated from her was weak, tremulous as if expressing the thoughts and emotions that she was going through. The warrior lowered himself to the floor beside her and rested his back against the wall. For a few moments, he simply sat with her, allowing his presence to give her strength and reassure her that she was safe. He knew that he would do absolutely anything to protect and take care of her. His own safety wasn't even on his mind. What mattered to him was guarding his mate and fulfilling his duty to his kind.

"How will we get out of here, Oro?" Ariella asked quietly.

"We will," Oro assured her.

Ariella looked at him, staring directly into his eyes.

"You really believe that," she said.

It wasn't a question. It was a statement, an acknowledgement of the emotions that she could feel coming from him. Oro nodded and brought his hand up to tenderly cup the side of Ariella's face. She was so beautiful. She was delicate and ethereal, softer than any woman he had ever seen. He had known from the moment that he saw her that she was crafted to be his mate. It was an honor to have been granted a mate so lovely, and he knew that he would spend his life devoted to giving her all the love, passion, and protection that she deserved.

The warrior leaned down and rested his lips to hers. It was a tender kiss at first, soft and reassuring. Soon, though, Oro felt Ariella's mouth press to his more insistently. Her lips parted and the tip of her tongue touched his, seeking hungrily. He responded in kind, giving over to the need that built within him every time that he was near her. The shimmering glow around Ariella strengthened the deeper that he kissed her, and Oro tucked an arm around her waist so that he could sweep her up and onto his lap. As soon as she settled onto his hips, Oro could feel his body respond to her powerfully. She rolled her hips subtly and the growing warmth of her core nestled against his already hardening erection.

Their bodies spoke to each other without their lips ever having to say a single word. They reached out to each other through the fear and uncertainty that surrounded them and urged them to find comfort and security in each other. Oro felt Ariella's soft, fragile hands come to the front of his shirt and dip into the gap at the neckline. Just the hint of their skin touching each other was enough to push him nearly to the edge of his control, but Oro didn't want to rush. He didn't want these moments to go past him too quickly. He wanted to savor every touch of her skin, taste of her mouth, and sound of her breath rushing through her plush lips.

Oro swept his hands lightly over her breasts and then ran them around her waist until they reached the tie of her dress just beneath her wings. Tucked defensively against her sides when he first saw her, they were now standing out from her back, their glow brighter and the shimmer more visible. Oro released the tie of her dress and eased the fabric down her ribs until it pooled at her hips. He groaned softly and lowered his mouth to one of the taut pink peaks of her breasts. Her skin felt cool and velvety against his tongue and he indulged himself by swirling the tip around her nipple until he felt it harden even further. His hand came up to cup around the other and knead into the flesh, the pad of his thumb nurturing her other nipple. Ariella's gentle whimpers made everything else around him disappear and Oro felt thirsty for more of the sound. He brought his hands down to her hips and gripped their full, feminine swells. Applying gentle pressure, he guided her up to her feet so that he could ease her dress the rest of the way off.

The angle granted him perfect access to her core and he could smell the warmth of her desire for him. Oro helped her step out of the dress and tossed it aside, then gripped the back of her thighs and led her slightly forward so that she stood straddling his stomach. He kissed her belly, running his tongue along her skin briefly before lifting his head and blowing a stream of cool air along the newly dampened path. Ariella's fingers buried themselves in his thick white hair and he felt them tenderly pulling as if guiding him down. Oro happily took the invitation and continue the path of his kisses down through the valley between her hipbones and toward the downy apex of her thighs.

When he reached his destination, Oro hungrily lapped his tongue through her folds. Ariella's grip on his hair tightened and she arched her back toward him. Oro drew his tongue through her again, then slid his hands up the backs of her thighs to the juncture between her legs and hips. This new positioning of his grip allowed him to use the pads of his thumbs to carefully part the wet petals of her core to reveal the tightened peak he had coaxed forward. Oro swept the broad portion of his tongue along the vulnerable pearl and then concentrated the very tip on it until he could feel Ariella's body trembling and shaking beneath his hands.

The sound of her whimpers told Oro that she was struggling to muffle the sound, trying not to allow the others to hear them. He continued to urge her forward, swirling and flicking his tongue masterfully. As she moaned deep in her chest, Oro moved one of his hands away from her hips to untie the cords at the front of his pants. He needed to release the surging erection that was pressing almost painfully against the fabric. His cock sprung out of his pants and Oro wrapped his hand around it. Slick fluid was already forming at the tip, but it wasn't enough for him. Closing his mouth over her clit to suck it between his lips, Oro dipped his fingers into her. Gathering the hot, silky fluid onto his fingers, he brought them back to his cock and rubbed it into his skin. He wrapped his hand back around his shaft and began to stroke, mimicking the movements of his mouth on her with his hand on himself.

Suddenly Ariella let out a cry and her knees buckled. Oro caught her and eased her gently down so that she rested on his legs again. The rosy flush across her chest and the brightness in her eyes made her even more beautiful and Oro felt an even greater need for her. Fortunately, it didn't seem that Ariella was close to wanting their interaction to end. The smile on her lips balanced somewhere between satisfaction and desire, and before her breath had even fully slowed again she was walking backwards on her knees so that she straddled his legs. She leaned forward to dip her fingers into the waistband of his pants and started to pull them down. Oro lifted his hips to help her and soon the garment joined her dress on the floor beside them. He stripped away his shirt, not wanting any fabric to separate their skin.

Ariella ran her fingertips reverently along the length of Oro's cock before dipped her head down to swirl her tongue around its crown in much the same way that he had worshipped her. The sensation was almost too much for him to handle. He closed his eyes and struggled to maintain his control. He didn't want to give himself over to the climax that was already rushing toward him. He needed more time. He needed to stay longer in the pure bliss that Ariella created.

Her hot, velvety mouth slipped around Oro's erection and Ariella sucked it tenderly, bringing the tip ever closer to her throat. Her hand cupped the base of his cock and her fingers massaged deeply into the hidden bundle of nerves there. Ariella seemed to know exactly what Oro was feeling at every moment and just as he was nearing the point when he wouldn't be able to control himself any longer, she removed her mouth from him and held his erection tightly to give him a few moments to cool and calm down. His body had just begun to relax and move back from the edge of oblivion when he felt her moving back up his legs. Oro opened his eyes and watched as Ariella lifted her hips up and positioned the tip of his cock at her still-wet opening.

Oro reached between them to take his shaft in his own hand, easing hers out of the way. Flattening his other hand on her lower back, Oro made tight circles with his sensitive head into the heat of her core. Ariella's breaths deepened and her hips started to move. Finally, he rested at her opening and allowed Ariella to sink down onto his lap, enveloping him completely in her tight, hot body. They both released groans of fulfillment as their bodies melded. It was a sense of completion like nothing else in Oro's life could create. He sat up from the wall and gathered Ariella into his arms. Her skin was smooth and slick with sweat and he could feel the quickening rhythm of her heartbeat reaching out toward his through his chest.

Ariella's hips rocked to move him within her body in deep, tight strokes and Oro lifted his hips to meet them. Powerful desire swept over Oro and he lifted himself up, taking Ariella with him as he repositioned himself onto his knees and then toppled her backwards. Ariella reached back and caught herself so that she reclined back with her knees up and her body open to him. Oro pushed forward over her so that he could capture her mouth with his again. Her legs parted further, sending him driving even deeper into her. He increased his pace so that each intense thrust seemed to correspond with his heartbeat. The sensations within him were spiraling out of control and he couldn't hold himself back any longer.

Each drive of his hips brought another deep grunt from Oro's chest. He heard Ariella's gasps getting higher and faster, telling him that she was quickly moving toward another climax. Just as she cried out, her body clenching down onto his in an intense, body-trembling spasm, Oro tore his mouth away from hers and let out a roar as his own body tightened and then released into her. Ariella frantically searched for his mouth and he gave himself into her kiss as each pulse of his cock met her delicious embrace.

Their bodies were starting to relax, cooling together and seeming to meld even closer, when Oro heard Pyra's voice bellowing from the other chamber.

"Everyone eat and get as much rest as you can. We'll move out soon. If you hear anything, let me know immediately."

Oro touched another kiss to Ariella's lips and rested his forehead to hers.

"We should get some sleep," he said. "It's been a long day and we don't know what tomorrow is going to bring."

Ariella nodded.

"I feel like I can sleep better now," she whispered.

Oro laughed softly and kissed her a final time before reluctantly withdrawing from her body. They dressed and walked hand-in-hand back toward the other chamber. Though he would have preferred to have curled up with her in the privacy of the other chamber and enjoy the warmth and bond that their bodies had created, he knew that the entire group was safer if they stayed together. They walked into the main chamber and saw the others spread out across the floor, some sleeping on the thick mats they had found rolled in one corner, others eating from the bags and canisters that held food crafted specifically to last nearly indefinitely in preparation for some unknown emergency. Pyra was sitting beside Eden, who cradled Lysander in her arms as she dozed with her head back against the wall.

"Close the door, Oro," the head Denynso warrior said. "All of us are here now and we'll be safer for the next few hours if we're closed in here."

"Not all of us," Gyyx said from the other corner of the room.

Oro looked toward him and saw the desolate look in the warrior's orange eyes.

"What do you mean, Gyyx?" Pyra asked. "Who's not here?"

"Leia," he said, naming his mate. "Zuri, Samira... except for Eden, Elianna and Ariella, the women went back to Zuri's house when we came here."

"They're safe there, Gyyx," Pyra tried to reassure the warrior.

"Are they?" he asked. "We don't know where Ryan or his soldiers are. If they could find the wedding, they can find them. We're hiding down here sleeping and eating, and they could be completely at his mercy."

Oro pulled Ariella closer against his body and touched a kiss to her hair, relieved that his mate was right beside him.

"We have to be strong to survive," Pyra said. "This isn't like any battle that we have ever fought, and not all of us are accustomed to what the Denynso go through. We eat, we sleep, and then we move on. It's the only way that we are going to be able to get out of here alive, and that is the first step before we can get to the women and then to the others."

Gyyx didn't seem fully satisfied by the response, but he fell silent and Oro could see him lean back onto the pillow behind him and close his eyes. He couldn't tell if he was truly sleeping or if he just wanted to be left alone until they moved on.

9

———

Kyven felt as though they had been walking for hours, but when he glanced back over his shoulder he could still see the dark outline of the quarry behind them. He could feel Maxim and Lynx on either side of him, supporting him as he struggled to make his way across the sand. When they first dragged him and Emerie from beneath the ground he hadn't thought that his injuries were so severe, but now that the adrenaline of their escape had eased away and they were traveling back toward the ship, he could feel the pain more intensely and the weakness caused by his blood loss seemed to be dragging him down harder with each step. He fought to keep himself on his feet and not to show on his face what he was going through. He needed to remain strong for Emerie and not allow his own suffering to frighten her.

His mate had been so brave in their time trapped in the cavern beneath the rocks of the quarry. The thought of the word brought the hint of a smile to Kyven's lips. It wasn't a term that the Mikana usually used, and the fact that his mind had immediately gone to it when he thought of

Emerie made him realize just how much his time with the Denynso had influenced him. It wasn't a negative feeling, but rather one of comfort and security, as if they were finally achieving the goals that their kinds had had for their alliances generations ago and truly coming together to defend themselves, their planet, and each other.

"Can you make it?" Maxim asked quietly.

Kyven looked to his brother and nodded.

"I'm going to be fine," he said.

"Yes, you are," Maxim replied. "We're going to get you back to the ship and fix you up. We have all of the supplies from Ciyrs there and we'll be able to heal these wounds before you know it."

It was one of the few times in his life that Kyven could remember his older brother actually sounding afraid. He had always been the stronger, more positive of the two. Even when their father had died and they were suddenly thrown into a life of confusion and loss, with just their mother, Maxim had been the one that ensure that they carried through. Though Kyven didn't have as many memories of Aegeus as Maxim did because he was far younger when he left, he still carried the love and respect for him that he always had, and treasured the thoughts of his father that he maintained. Often when he looked at Maxim he was able to see Aegeus in him. He could see him in his eyes and in the occasional expression that crossed his face. There was a presence there that kept Aegeus alive with every one of Maxim's heartbeats, and sometimes it was almost as though they had melded to the point that Maxim had taken Aegeus's place.

As soon as the thought crossed Kyven's mind, he felt a shock through his heart. He remembered that his father *was* alive. At least he had been when Ryan talked to them through the screen on the ship. The thought was as startling and disquieting as it was exciting. He couldn't imagine what Aegeus had been put through in the years since he had been gone and wondered what he would be like, if he was able to see him again. Would he be the same, or would the years of torture and captivity that he had suffered through have irrevocably changed him? Would he even remember his sons or his wife, and want to be a part of their family again?

He shook his head, trying to free himself of the bitterness that was beginning to creep into his thoughts. They would only weaken him further and slow him down, and they couldn't afford to be out in the desert for even a moment longer than they had to be. Night had fallen deeply now and he could almost feel the energy of the hybrids on the planet increasing.

"What's wrong?" Maxim asked. "Do you need to stop?"

Kyven shook his head again, forcing a smile this time in an effort to tell his brother that he could keep going.

"No," he said. "I was just thinking."

"About what?"

"Papa," he admitted.

Maxim nodded and lifted Kyven a little higher, as if the mention of their father had somehow given him greater strength and endurance to keep them moving across the desert planet back toward their ship.

"He's alive," he said. "It's a miracle."

"Another miracle," Emerie murmured from behind him.

"What does she mean?" Lynx asked.

Kyven didn't know if he should tell them about Mhavyrch. The man had stayed in the cavern with them only long enough to rescue them from the creature that lurked beneath and threatened to devour them when their light failed. He had only fought off the creature enough for them to get back in control and given them the light that they needed to keep the animal at bay before disappearing back out of the cavern and into the night. It was obvious that he had been a hybrid. His appearance showed characteristics of both Denynso and Mikana along with something else that he couldn't quite identify. It didn't make sense, though. If that man had been a hybrid, that meant that he had been sent to Penthos by Ryan. He was a member of the army bred and built specifically for the purpose of destruction, and put on the mission of eliminating Maxim and him. Why would he have climbed down into the cavern to rescue Kyven and Emerie rather than killing them, or just allowing the creature to tear them apart?

He suddenly remembered some of the few words that the man had said to them.

No one deserves to die alone in the dark.

"We're alive," Kyven said.

"It seems like that might be just barely," Zyyr said. "What was that thing that was underground with you?"

Meldor, he said to himself, remembering what Mhavyrch had called the creature. It was a word that he had never heard before and one that he would never forget.

"I don't know," Kyven said. "We couldn't see it."

"You couldn't see it?" Maxim asked.

"No," Emerie said. "It would only get near us when the light was gone. If we stayed in the light, it wouldn't get close to us. We never got a chance to see it."

"I know that it was huge," Kyven said. "We could hear it breathing and I could feel it's size when it attacked us. It had thick fur, sharp claws, and fangs. It was bigger than anything that I've ever encountered."

"Have you ever heard of anything like that, Maxim?" Lynx asked.

Maxim shook his head.

"No," Maxim said. "That doesn't sound like anything that lives near the Mikana."

"Emerie?" Lynx asked. "Is that something that might come from Earth?"

"I don't know," Emerie said. "It didn't seem like anything that I know. It was too big, and the fangs and claws were too sharp."

There were a few long seconds of silence as it seemed that each of them sank away into their own thoughts. Finally, Lynx spoke up, expressing something that had briefly crossed through Kyven's mind.

"Do you think that it could be one of the hybrids?" he asked.

Kyven hissed as a sharper pain shot through the wounds on his back and he felt his body crumple toward the ground. There was something more than just the cuts in his skin that was affecting him, but he didn't know what it could be.

"Put him down," Maxim said. "We need to check his wounds again."

"Not out here," Kyven said. He was desperate for the group to get back to the ship. "You can't all put yourself in danger because of me. Get me back to the ship and then check me over."

"No," Maxim said. "There's something wrong. If we don't figure out what it is, we might not have the chance to get you back to the ship."

Kyven felt the men lower him to the sand and begin to pull at his bandages to reveal his wounds.

"There's toxin in the wounds," Lynx said. "The creature must have it in its fangs."

"What will the toxin do?" Maxim asked. "Is he going to be able to recover from it?"

"I don't know what the creature is," Lynx said, "and I don't know any more about toxins than the little bit that I picked up from Ciyrs. He taught you more about his ointments than me."

The warrior's voice was tense, but it seemed to come more from helplessness than it did anger. Emerie came to kneel beside him and rested his head in her lap. He gazed up at her as the men moved his body around, trying not to focus on the pain that was tearing through him and the burning feeling in his blood. It was dizzying and with every moment he felt like he was being dragged further and further away from this moment. He knew that he had to fight to keep himself aware and awake while the other men continued to work on him.

"I don't think that it is one of the hybrids," he said, not really directing it to any of them in particular but needing to keep words coming out of him so that he didn't allow the black cloud that was creeping into the edges of his mind to take over. "I think that it was an animal that is native to Penthos."

"Why?" Emerie asked. "Why couldn't it be one of the hybrids?"

"None of us can think of any animals that could have been combined to make something like that," Kyven said.

"That doesn't necessarily mean that it couldn't be a hybrid," Lynx said. "We don't know what kind of creatures Ryan has access to."

"No," Maxim said. "That's not why. Ryan created the hybrids with the specific purpose of turning them into an army. He chose the species that he did because of their characteristics and their ability to fight. That creature wouldn't be able to fight."

"He's right," Kyven said, his eyes closed against the pain

now. "Ryan wants hybrids that can stand up against us. That creature wasn't able to go into the light, which means that he is only effective underground or at night. I don't think that Ryan would see any purpose in breeding something with such limited effect, especially since he would have to figure out how to keep it alive"

"I don't think that he cares if any of the hybrids live," Emerie said. "They're disposable to him. They're weapons, nothing more. He doesn't care what he created or if it is destroyed."

The tone of her voice was nearly as soft as the touch of her fingertips on his cheek and held meaning that Kyven didn't want to dwell on any longer, even though he could feel it beginning within him as well. Ryan didn't care about any type of life...but did the hybrids?

10

"I need to know what you've found out about Uoria," Jem said.

The warrior was trying to control the aggression that was building through him. It was a feeling that he hadn't experienced since he had been on Uoria. This was the feeling of impending battle, the fury and energy of a coming war. He knew that he had to keep it tampered or his warrior training would take over, making him incredibly dangerous to anyone he might encounter.

"I can't be sure about any of it," Rilex said. "These are just rumors, it is just hints that I've gotten that have led me down different paths in my research. I don't even know what it all means."

Despite the caution, Jem knew that if the information that Rilex had gathered didn't seem compelling, he wouldn't have acted as swiftly and insistently as he had. He had uncovered something that had made him feel concerned enough that he went to find Jem, and the warrior needed to know what that was. If his kind or his planet was in trouble, it was his responsibility, his duty to help them.

"What do you know about a woman named Eden?" Rilex asked.

Jem felt the nervousness inside him spike.

"I know her well," he said. "She came to Uoria as a researcher, but she ended up staying with us. She is the mate of the Denynso leader, Pyra. She was pregnant when I left."

"Pregnant?" Rilex asked.

"Yes. The first baby of the new generation of Denynso."

There was a pause and the tension in the car seemed to increase. Rilex seemed unnerved by his response, but wasn't offering anything more about it.

"Do you know about her boss, Ryan?"

"He was the man who she was working for when she came to Uoria. He's a scientist at the University."

"Yes," Rilex said. "But do you know why he specifically sent Eden to Uoria?" he asked.

Jem felt like the man was playing some sort of game and he didn't like it. He wanted him to just be straightforward and tell him what was happening. At the same moment, though, he felt that even Rilex himself wasn't entirely sure of what he knew and was using Jem's responses to try to confirm what he was thinking. He was piecing things together as he spoke and trying to ensure that he didn't incite Jem needlessly.

"She was the first of the people in the exchange program. She came to research the Denynso and to teach us about the ways of Earth. The goal of the program is to foster relationships between Earth and the Denynso and form lines of communication and alliance."

"He could have sent any of the people from the department. Why Eden?"

"She says that she was his assistant. She worked with him on all of his projects."

"And rumor has it that she rejected his thoughts of making their relationship more than just the professional one that they already had."

Jem felt himself bristle. He remembered Eden talking about the advances that Ryan had made toward her and how they had made her feel. It disgusted him that someone would treat her that way and it felt disrespectful toward her mate that he would acknowledge it.

"Yes," he said through gritted teeth.

"Did you know that she came to Uoria with more of a purpose than just learning about the Denynso?"

"I don't understand."

"Ryan sent her to steal some of Pyra's blood."

The revelation was horrifying. It wasn't something that Pyra or Eden had ever shared with him and the thought of her being sent into that mission made his head spin. To steal a Denynso's blood was to break the oldest and most revered of Denynso laws.

"If she had tried, she would have been killed."

"Exactly," Rilex said. "From what I understand, that was why Ryan chose her. If she could be successful, he would have the most powerful blood in the universe and be able to use it for his experiments. If she wasn't, she would suffer and he wouldn't have to deal with the embarrassment and frustration of her rejection anymore."

"He wanted to kill her just because she wouldn't go along with his advances?" Jem asked incredulously.

"Partially," Rilex admitted, "but I don't think that's it. I think that he wasn't forthright about the experiments that he was doing and that she was close to figuring it out. He wanted to eliminate the threat to his work."

"But she didn't die and she didn't bring him Pyra's blood. She joined the clan," Jem said.

"Exactly. What happened to the other women from the program?"

"They joined the clan as well," Jem said. "They bonded with other Denynso. I don't understand what any of this has to do with the problems that you said that you think are happening on Uoria."

"I think that Ryan's experiments are far more dangerous than anyone knew. Sending Eden to Uoria was just one piece of a plan that is in motion, and that's why people from Uoria are at the University. They were brought there for a reason."

"Why?" Jem asked.

"I'm not sure, but honestly I don't think that I want to know. We just need to get there as fast as we can."

The distance between the bar and the University seemed to stretch further and further with each moment, but finally Jem saw imposing buildings rising on the horizon in the distance. Lights positioned along their edges and along the perimeter of the complex made their silhouettes stand out starkly and Jem wondered which of them was the laboratory. Rilex pulled the car up to a massive gate and reached out to press a small piece of metal onto a screen positioned at the top of a pole at the edge of the road.

"Where did you get that?" Angela asked from beside Jem.

"What was it?" Jem asked.

"An access chip," Angela said. "Only people authorized to enter the University complex are supposed to have one."

"I stole it," Rilex said.

"What?" Angela asked, sounding shocked.

"I didn't have a choice," Rilex said. "When I came

through the portal, I didn't have anything and had no idea where I was. I had to create a life that was believable, and part of that meant that I had to steal parts of other people's lives. When this system was first implemented, I stole a chip so that I would be able to access the University if I thought that it might help me."

"If one of those chips is necessary to get into the gate to the complex, how did the unauthorized vehicle get in?" Jem asked.

"I don't know," Rilex said. "That's another reason that I have to believe that that vehicle didn't come from Earth. Either someone on it had an access chip or the vehicle is capable of utilizing the sky corridors like the shuttles, but didn't have access to the bay and was able to land on the grounds. Like I said, it's not technology that I've ever seen."

Rilex directed the vehicle along a road that circled around toward the back of the complex. They traveled past countless buildings and Jem found himself getting over-whelmed by the sheer volume of the space and the towering structures that seemed to bear down on him.

"How are we going to find them?" Jem said. "If that shuttle and vehicle are from Uoria, how are we going to find whoever was on them in all these buildings?"

"Ryan only works in the laboratory building," Rilex explained. "That's that tall building up ahead. All of the University's research and experimental laboratories are in that building. He doesn't have access to the other buildings except for the main administrative building, but there would be little benefit to him there. If he's doing experiments, no matter what kind they are, he would be doing them in the laboratory building."

"But wouldn't that mean that anyone in the building would find them?" Angela asked.

"Not necessarily," Rilex said. "Just like the access chips control movement in and out of the complex, there are controls in place in the building to keep people in the areas where they are authorized. That would put some level of protection for him. But I don't think that's it."

"What do you mean?" Jacob asked.

"Do you know how long this complex has been here?" Rilex asked.

"The buildings?" Jacob asked. "About a hundred years. It's the oldest standing University. There've been upgrades, but the structures themselves were built about a century ago."

"Not the buildings," Rilex said. "The complex."

"It was here for probably just as long before that. Maybe even longer," Angela said. "They closed the entire thing in phases, demolished it, and rebuilt."

"Right," Rilex said. "Only one portion took much longer to rebuild than the others."

"The laboratory building," Jem said.

Rilex stopped the car and reached into the glove compartment. He drew out a screen and input commands until what looked like a set of building plans appeared on it.

"These are the old buildings," he said. "You can see that they are laid out completely differently than the new University. Their laboratory building was on the complete opposite side of the complex. When they rebuilt the new laboratory, someone decided to move it, and then put it here."

He pointed to the screen and Jem looked at the word beside where his finger sat.

"Hospital?" he asked.

Rilex nodded.

"Look at these plans," he said, changing the screen to a

different set. These looked more basic, as if only showing the structure of each of the planned buildings. "What do you notice about the laboratory building?"

Jem looked at the plans, trying to understand what Rilex was trying to get him to see. Suddenly it struck him.

"It's smaller," he said.

"Exactly," Rilex said. "The original plans for the laboratory only had it as ten stories. Look at the current building."

Jem looked back up at the tall building ahead of them.

"Twelve," Angela said.

"And the hospital?" Rilex said, switching back to the other plans.

"Two," Jacob said.

"Right," Rilex said. "There was a floor of examination rooms and a floor of inpatient rooms. The surgical suites were underground."

"I've been in that building, though," Jacob said. "The first floor is all offices. The next two are student labs. There isn't a hospital."

"So, you've been to the third floor?" Rilex asked.

"Yes."

"Was it as deep as the first two?"

"What do you mean?"

"What was in the back of the building?"

"Staircases."

"Did they line up to the ones on the first two floors?"

"No," Jacob said. "It was built with extra space on the upper floors to give the researchers more room in their laboratories and offices."

"But the bottom floors are the same size from the outside," Angela said softly as if something was coming together in her mind.

"So, what's in that space?" Jem asked.

"There are no doors on either of the first two floors that lead into the surplus space. On the modified plans, the area is marked as being solid. The official explanation is that they wanted extra support for the laboratories and to make the building itself more stable."

"That doesn't make any sense," Angela said."

Rilex shook his head.

"No, it doesn't."

"That's where they are," Jem said.

"It's a start," Rilex agreed. "We just have to figure out how to get in."

11

———

"Are you sure that you want to come?" Samira asked, looking into the rearview mirror to where her mother sat in the backseat.

Valerie didn't hesitate before nodding.

"Absolutely," she said. "You and these people who you brought here rescued me. I'm not going to turn my back on them if I have the chance to do something for them."

Samira's heart swelled and she felt tears building in her eyes. Her mother had changed so much in just the brief time since she had walked away from Samira's stepfather. Valerie suddenly looked alive. Her eyes were bright and clear for the first time in as long as Samira could remember. She no longer held the expression of fear and exhaustion that always seemed etched on her face, and she was finally holding her shoulders straight rather than sagging down like she was trying to make herself as small and unnoticeable as she could be. It made Samira feel proud to see how much Valerie had improved, and gave her a sense of joy that it seemed her mother was finally coming out of the darkness that her husband had put her in and was going to take hold of her own life again. Samira would never be able to express enough gratitude to Ero for what he had done for her. In his first visit to Earth, when he had come for Zuri, he had gone to Valerie's home and confronted Samira's stepfather. It was that moment that had begun the change in Valerie's life.

"Have you been able to contact Gyyx, Leia?" Zuri asked.

Samira saw Leia shake her head. The small woman looked even more fragile than she usually did as she stared out of the car window into the darkness of the night beyond. She hadn't been able to reach out to her mate since they had escaped the wedding and she had become progressively weaker and quieter. Zuri drew in a breath.

"I haven't been able to get in touch with Ero, either," Zuri said.

"What do they mean?" Valerie asked.

"Usually the Denynso can communicate with their mates through their thoughts. It lets them speak to us without having to say something out loud, or communicate when we aren't together. None of us have been able to connect with our mates, though. They've blocked their minds," Samira said. "They're preventing communication with us."

"Why would they do that?" Valerie asked.

"There has to be a reason," Zuri said. "I know that there have been times when the warriors have blocked their communication during battles or other particularly stressful times. They don't want us to be able to sense what is going on with them."

"That's what I'm afraid of," Leia said softly. "I'm scared that they are in danger. They've been gone for too long. They should have come back by now. We should have gone to them sooner."

"They told us to stay at the house," Samira said. "They said it was too dangerous for us to go with them."

"Why did Elianna go?" Leia asked. "Eden's there. Zsilvia is there."

"Zsilvia was there before the Valdicians got to the wedding, which means that is it very likely she was captured. Eden went because it was her child that was taken. There's nothing that would keep a mother from her child in that situation and she too is a healer. And you know why Elianna is there," Samira said.

She didn't want to say it. She didn't want to put voice to the fear that was threatening to take over her thoughts and control her, distracting her from driving. Each of the women who had lived among the Denynso knew of the unique skill that Elianna had. Her arrival on Uoria had been extremely difficult and she nearly died after an attack, putting her in Ciyrs's clinic for days. The healer had put everything into healing her and though he was finally successful, she had not come out of the healing unchanged. During the course of the healing Ciyrs had transferred some of his healing capabilities to her, giving her the ability to heal injuries and illnesses, and imbuing her with much of his knowledge of the plants, ointments, and powders that could be used to further heal those who needed it. When Eden and the men had left for the lab to confront Ryan, Elianna went along in anticipation of violence. If any of their group was injured, having three healers would improve the chances that they would be able to get them out and back to safety.

"How much further?" Valerie asked.

Samira realized that her mother had never made it to the University to visit her in the entire time she had been studying there. Her stepfather had never permitted her much movement outside of the house and Valerie would never have gotten the opportunity to make the trip out just to see where Samira studied. Though she wished that it was under better circumstances, Samira was happy that Valerie was finally able to see the place that had been so important in her life up until this point. She knew in her heart that she wouldn't be returning here even after the conflict with Ryan was over. Her life was irrevocably changed by Ty and she would follow him back to Uoria.

"We're almost there," Samira told her. "Mom, please think about this. I don't know what's going on at the University or what is going to happen. I can't promise you that you are going to be safe once we get there."

"I haven't been safe since you were a little child, Samira," Valerie said. "I survived your stepfather. I'm not afraid."

The words stabbed deeply into Samira, though she knew that her mother hadn't intended them to. She knew that Valerie had suffered extensively under her stepfather's hands. She had gone through enough on her own. Now Valerie had finally gotten out from under him, but almost as soon as she had taken a breath of freedom, Samira was bringing her back into the face of unpredictable danger.

A few moments later the car pulled up to the gate at the University. She touched her access chip to the screen and the gates swung open, allowing her access. Looking around cautiously, she drove along the road toward the laboratory building. As they approached, she noticed that there was another car sitting in the small parking lot. Its appearance sent a shiver through her. She knew every vehicle of every person authorized to be inside the laboratory building, and she didn't recognize that car.

"Who is that?" Zuri asked.

"I don't know," Samira said. "Do you recognize it?"

"No," Zuri said.

They pulled up alongside the car and paused for a moment, each of them looking out of the windows to detect anyone who might still be in the area. Not seeing anyone, Samira climbed out of the car. The other women followed and Samira took her bag from Zuri, dropping it over her shoulder as she stared at the building ahead.

"Are you ready?" she asked, looking to the other women.

They all nodded at her and they started across the wide grassy expanse between the parking lot and the laboratory building. The feeling in the area was eerie. Everything was too still, too quiet. The air seemed to crackle with energy and it was getting harder to breathe with each step.

"How do we get inside?" Valerie asked in a tense whisper.

Samira looked to Zuri for guidance just as she had since she met her. Zuri scanned the area briefly.

"Let's go to the side entrance," she said. "It's less exposed than the front. There's less of a chance for anyone to see us going inside."

They picked up their speed as they moved toward the building, each one of them recognizing the urgency to get out of clear view. Samira strained for any sound to come to her over their footsteps, but there was nothing. They finally reached the building and Samira felt a strange sensation wash over her. She had taken this same path countless times before. Any other time she would have felt that she could navigate the grounds and even the building itself with her eyes closed, but now as she got closer to the entrance it felt less and less familiar. It was almost as though she didn't know where she was or where to go, as if she wasn't within her own body and was rather watching what she was doing from a distance. She struggled to get back in control of her emotions, to put herself back into the moment and focus on what she needed to do.

They turned the corner of the building and Samira stopped short. The other women stopped around her and she knew that they were seeing what she was. Ahead of them she could see movement in the shadows of the building. Samira stretched her arm out to block the other women from moving further. They crouched down closer to the ground, staying close to the wall. The movement in the distance divided into four distinct figures and Samira felt a sudden surge of anger. Her husband, her mate, was somewhere in this building and she needed to get to him. If these figures had anything to do with it, she wasn't going to back down.

Samira stood and stepped out of the shadow of the wall. Her focus narrowed on the figures and she started toward them. Suddenly she saw a flicker of something appear near the figures, then disappear. She took another step and it appeared again. This time it remained and she could see that it was a strange car parked close to the building. The figures stepped closer to it, moving further into the light, and she noticed that one of them looked extremely large, the size of a Denynso warrior, while the other three were smaller. They were walking around the car, examining it carefully. She wanted to call out to them, but at the same moment she didn't want to announce her presence yet.

Suddenly one of the smaller figures stepped fully into the light and Samira realized that it was a woman. As if she could feel Samira's eyes on her, the woman stopped and turned to look at her. She looked startled and stepped back against the car, reaching over the hood toward the massive figure still partially in the shadows. It stepped forward into the light and took her hand over the hood, then looked toward Samira. The impact of his gaze took Samira's breath from her chest. She felt like her legs were going to give out beneath her, but she had to keep standing to continue looking at him, to ensure that she was seeing what she thought she was. It had been so long, but she knew the curve of his face and the smile that came to his lips when he seemed to recognize her.

"Jem."

She thought that she had yelled out to him. She wanted to call out to him, but the name had come out only as a whisper. Zuri came up beside her and she felt the other woman's hand grip hers at her side. Jem came around the side of the vehicle and an instant later they were running toward each other. The warrior swept Samira into a hug and she immediately felt the intense heat coming from his skin. It wasn't as searing as it would have been if she didn't have a mate, but it was enough that she needed to step back from him. This was a protective feature embedded in the genes of the Denynso. Once one of the men found their mate, his skin became unbearably hot to the touch of any other woman. It often lessened the longer that he was bonded to his mate, which meant that Jem's bond was likely very new.

"You're alive!" she said as she stepped back from him and looked up into his smiling face. "How? How is this possible?"

"Samira, it is so good to see you. Zuri, Leia. I can't believe you're here. There's so much to tell you, and I'll explain it all, but right now we need to find the others. They need our help."

"The others?" Zuri asked. "You know that they're here?"

The three others who had been near the car with Jem came up behind him, looking at the women curiously. The younger of the two men looked slightly familiar to Samira, but she couldn't place him.

"This is Rilex," Jem said, gesturing toward the older of the men. "He told me that two unauthorized vehicles appeared here. One is a shuttle and this is the other one," he pointed toward the car. "He thinks that they're from Uoria."

"A shuttle?" Samira asked. "Another shuttle?"

"Another?" Jem asked. "What do you mean?"

"We arrived on a shuttle several days ago, but that was an authorized trip. If there is an unauthorized shuttle here, that means that others have come."

"The more of the Denynso who are here, the more danger there is," Rilex said.

"He's right," Samira said. "Ryan is luring us all here. This isn't just about Lysander."

"Lysander?" Jem asked.

Samira felt her stomach turn slightly. He hadn't been there when Pyra and Eden's baby was born. Lysander had become such an integral part of the clan as a whole that it was difficult to think of them without him, but she realized that in his mind that was the way things were. He didn't know of any of the changes that had happened on the planet or within the clan since that last battle, from the moment that he disappeared from them.

"Eden and Pyra's son," she said.

"Their son," he said with a soft smile.

Samira nodded.

"He was born a few months after you..." she paused, not knowing what to say. She was so accustomed to thinking of the moment when he threw himself into the sky in Loralia's realm as his death, but now he was standing before her and she had to change the way she thought. "After you left. Now Ryan has him."

She could see the panic rise in Jem's eyes.

"What?" he asked. "Why does Ryan have him?"

"We don't know. He sent creatures to my wedding and stole the baby."

"Your wedding."

It was another moment of painful reality.

"Ty and I got married," she told him.

"Congratulations," he said uncertainly. He reached behind him to take the hand of the woman she had first seen beside the car and guide her up to stand beside him. "This is Angela, my mate."

Samira nodded at Angela, but didn't greet her. They would have time to talk later. For now, they were letting precious moments slip away from them.

"Do you know where they are?" Samira asked. "You said Rilex knew the vehicles were here. Does he know where they've gone?"

"No," Jem said, "but he has an idea."

Samira listened as Rilex explained the plans of the building and pointed out a section that could be covering a building that had been abandoned many years before. It was something that she would never have considered, but she had no other idea. There was no other option.

"How do we get to that section of the building, though?" Samira asked.

"If it's sealed off so that none of us even knew that it existed, how would they have gotten to it?"

"I don't know," Rilex said. "We're just going to have to look."

"What about the locks?" Leia asked. "We'll only be able to access certain parts of the building using Zuri and Samira's codes."

"I'll take care of it," Rilex said. "Where are the master controls."

"They would have to be in the main administrative office," Zuri said. "But none of us have authorization to the controls."

"Just show me where to find them," he said. "I'll handle it from there."

From the moment that they stepped into the laboratory building, Samira felt the energy shift again. It was thicker here, more intense, and she felt like there were eyes on her from every direction. They were walking through the darkened main hallway when she heard a scuffling sound behind her. She turned and saw a shrouded figured come around the corner. Something glistened by its side and it started toward them aggressively. Jem turned and leapt at it, directing the impact of his shoulder directly into the creature's gut. There was a gasping sound as they hit the floor and Samira felt someone grab at her wrist.

"Come on," Zuri insisted. "Now!"

Jem was still thrashing on the ground with the creature but she let Zuri pull her so that they started running down the hall in the direction of the administrative office. Rilex pressed an access chip to the sensor at the side of the door and she was stunned to hear it click open. As they streamed into the office she could hear thudding footsteps behind her and when she glanced over her shoulder she was relieved to see Jem coming toward her. There was a streak of blood along his arm, but he didn't seem injured.

As if they could still feel the breath of the creature on their necks, they ran through each phase of the office until they reached a massive steel door that protected the main controls of the building. Rilex pressed his access chip to the sensor, but it didn't respond. Samira felt her stomach sink. Rilex took a breath.

"Step back," he said. "Turn your back and close your eyes."

"What are you going to do?" Samira asked.

"Please just do it," Rilex said sternly. "We don't have time for explanations."

Samira saw Jem take Angela by the hand and guide her to the other side of the room. The man who had come along with them followed and they turned their backs to Rilex without hesitation, as if they knew what he was planning on doing. Samira, Zuri, Leia, and Valeria followed and took their places beside the others. Samira felt herself drawing close to her mother, seeking out the same level of comfort that she would have when she was a small child. Valerie reached down and held her hand, squeezing it tightly. For the first time in so long, she was the strong one.

Samira closed her eyes and almost immediately heard a deafening blast from behind her accompanied by a searing light that brought her hands up to cover her closed eyes. It intensified until she thought it would burn through her and then finally darkened again. She felt breathless and it took a moment before the disorientation faded and she could move again. Turning back toward the steel door she saw that it was standing open, the sensor now melted and smoking. She ran past it into the room with the main controls and found Rilex standing over them, examining them.

"Do you know how to work them?" he asked.

Samira shook her head.

"No. Only authorized administration does."

"When I tell you to, I need you to leave the office as fast as you can. Go back out to the main hallway."

Samira nodded her agreement and Rilex returned the gesture. She watched as he reached beneath his shirt and pulled out a small pouch that was dangling from a cord around his neck. He reached into it and withdrew what looked like a tiny pebble. Rilex settled the pebble into a crevice in the main control panel, then leaned down and blew onto it.

"Go," he said.

Samira started out of the office and took only a second to glance back over her shoulder. She saw Rilex blowing on the pebble again, and where it was rested in the panel had begun to glow. The illumination began to intensify quickly and Rilex began to run toward her. They wove their way back through the office and out into the main hallway. They had just reached the body of the creature that attacked them when she heard another blast that made the building shudder and made her body feel almost liquid. Around her the air dissolved into the buzz of an alarm and a nearby panel in the wall flashed a red message.

Main Controls Deactivated. All Units Unlocked. Main Controls Deactivated. Please Utilize Alternative Security.

Whatever Rilex had done it had destroyed the main controls of the building, releasing all of the locks throughout it. They could now move through the building freely, but that still meant that they had to find their way to the abandoned section.

12

———

Dizziness swept over Ivy and she felt her body sway. Arms caught her and started guiding her away from the panic room and back into the main chamber of the shuttle. When she felt the soft cushion of the lounge chair beneath her she opened her eyes and saw Lila standing over her. Her cool hand brushed across Ivy's forehead and she gave a gentle, knowing smile.

"Rest," she whispered. "You have more to think about than the rest of us."

Ivy was surprised by the revelation, but she reminded herself that this woman was not only Mikana as they thought her to be when they met her in the kingdom. Instead she was a descendant of the Eteri, a beautiful and mysteriously skilled blend that allowed her to sense what was within those she came near. In that moment, she was utilizing her skill quite literally, sensing not just her, but the tiny child that she carried. She had told only Maxim, agreeing that they should wait to tell the others until after the conflict. Enough of her own thoughts and concentration were focused on her pregnancy. She knew that if she told any of the others about the baby that they, too, would worry about her and right then they needed each of them to be fully focused on the challenges that lay ahead.

"Please don't say anything," she said.

Lila shook her head.

"Of course not."

Ivy had just let out a relieved breath when Elise rushed into the chamber. Her cheeks were high with color and her fists were clenched by her side. She strode heavily across the chamber until she reached the windows and then turned back around, taking another few steps before stopping. She looked like she wanted to say something, but the fury she was feeling was preventing the words from forming. Rain quickly came in after her and rested a hand to her back.

"How could they do this?" Elise finally said. "How could they just hide?"

Ivy looked at the entrance to the kitchen but didn't see the three men who had been in the panic room.

"Where are they?" she asked. "You didn't put them back in there, did you?"

Rain shook her head.

"No. They went back to their quarters to take showers and change clothes. I don't think that they want to be seen in their uniforms right now."

"I don't blame them," Ivy said. "I will admit, though, that it disturbs me a little that there were three men onboard that we didn't even know were here. I mean, I knew that the ship had a crew when we got on it, but after we landed here, I just assumed..." her voice trailed off and she shook her head. "I don't know what I assumed. They were just gone and I didn't think about them again. Maybe part of me thought that the Valdicians had killed them."

"Like when Leia was headed to Uoria," Rain said.

Ivy nodded.

"Who's Leia?" Elise asked.

"The men in the panic room," Ivy said.

"Elon, Avery, and Michael?" Elise asked.

"Yes. One of them said that there had been a hijacking before and that's why they implemented all of the safety protocols."

"Yes," Elise said. "That was Avery, the pilot."

"Leia was on the ship that was hijacked," Ivy explained. "It was taken over by Klimnu when they were headed to Uoria. They killed the pilot and the crew and then took Leia captive. They held her in a prison on Uoria for months before Elianna discovered her and brought her back to the compound."

"So, they designed safety protocols that would protect the crew, but not the passengers?" Elise asked.

"Apparently," Rain said.

"I'm sorry." Ivy turned toward the voice and saw Avery step cautiously into the room. He was dressed in casual clothes now, but he still carried himself with the stiff formality of a pilot. "I shouldn't have gone into the panic room. The others were following my command, and I take full responsibility for it. I should have stayed out with the rest of you and faced whatever happened."

"You have no loyalty to us," Rain said. "There'd be no reason for you to do anything but exactly what you did: save yourself."

"It doesn't matter who I give my loyalty to," Avery contended. "I am the pilot of this ship and I should be the one that leads it no matter what happens."

"Maxim is our leader," Ivy said. "Even if you had stayed out, it wouldn't have changed that. You don't know what you're facing."

"You are the one who condemned us for hiding," he said, starting to sound angrier. "You pointed out that there were so many species out there right now unified and fighting, and that none of you ever hid."

"I know what I said," Ivy told him calmly, "and I know what I'm saying now. You did as you were told and that is probably the best choice to have made, even if it wasn't the courageous choice. You wouldn't have known what to do even if you had chosen to stay. You pilot pleasure cruises. This is war."

The man looked stung and he seemed to be getting ready to say something to her, but a loud knock on the door to the shuttle silenced him. His face went pale and he looked as though he wanted to run back into the panic room. Elise walked over to the door and stood close to it.

"Yes?" she called.

"Elise, it's us," Kyven's voice called from the other side of the thick metal. "Unlock the door."

Ivy turned to Rain, who nodded.

"It's them and it's safe. There isn't anyone with them."

"How does she know that?" Avery asked.

"My mate is out there with them," Rain answered. "He can communicate with me through his thoughts. No one else can hear them. If one of the hybrids had captured them and was trying to get inside with them so that they could overtake us and the ship, he would be able to tell me without them knowing and I would tell Elise to keep them doors locked. I guess you can call that *our* safety protocol."

Ivy watched as Elise input the codes to release the lock on the door and opened it. Maxim stepped in and moved out of the way to allow Zyyr inside. Kyven was draped across his shoulders and though his eyes were open, Ivy could see that the Mikana man was not well.

"What's wrong?" she asked, standing from the lounge and crossing to Maxim. "Was he hurt in the fall?"

The rest of the group came inside and Elise promptly closed the door, inputting the codes again to lock them inside.

"There was something in the quarry with them," Maxim explained. "Some kind of creature. It attacked him."

"There were toxins on its fangs or claws," Lynx said. "We tried the healing ointments that we brought with us, but it's still influencing him. It's getting stronger. We need to get the wounds completely clean and dress them again."

"Bring him to the infirmary," Avery said. "Elise, go to Elon's quarters and tell him he's needed there." Avery looked to Ivy and then at the others. "Elon is our medic. He might be of some help to you."

"We have our own methods of healing," Zyyr said protectively.

"I know," Avery said. "I respect that, and we wouldn't get in your way. But he might be of some service to you. What-ever you might need, he'll be there to help. Please. I know that we made the wrong decision when we first came here, but I'd like to show you that we want to be a part of this with you."

"You don't even know what's happening," Ivy protested.

"Ivy," Maxim said, quieting her. "He might not fully understand what's happening, but he's offering his service to us. Don't turn your back on help. Especially when we need it the most."

Ivy felt a hint of color splash across her cheeks. She knew that Maxim was right. She stepped back toward the lounge and rested onto it again, needing another moment to let the dizziness fade away again.

"I'm sorry," she said softly.

"Thank you," Maxim said, stepping toward Avery, his hand extended in the way that Ivy had taught him to greet humans.

"Avery," the pilot told him, taking his hand.

"My name is Maxim. Thank you, Avery."

Elise led Zyyr out of the room and Avery followed. Maxim watched until they were gone and then turned to Ivy. He came to the lounge chair and sat on the edge, leaning over so that he could rest his head on her chest. She cupped her hand around the back of his head and relaxed with the feeling of his breaths traveling across her skin.

"Where's Nylek?" Lila suddenly asked.

Ivy's eyes snapped open and she looked at Maxim, who had sat up sharply.

"Nylek didn't find you?" she asked.

"No," Maxim said. "He wasn't here when we left."

"He showed up just a little while later," Ivy said. "He insisted that he go to the quarry to help you. He figured that he would either get there while you were still there or he would meet you somewhere along the way. You didn't find him?"

"No," Maxim said, starting to sound nervous. "He's still out there somewhere. The hybrids might have found him by now. I have to go find him."

Maxim jumped up and Ivy reached for him, grabbing him by his wrist and trying to pull him back down to her. The thought of him going back out into the darkness was terrifying. She needed him there with her. She didn't want to be left alone in the shuttle again, pacing and waiting, helpless and ineffective.

"I can't leave him out there alone," Maxim said. "He left his mate and his home to come with us and help. We can't abandon him."

Ivy knew that he was right. Nylek was one of their number, a warrior who offered himself into service of his king even though he wasn't a part of the initial journey that had brought them there. If he was still out in the desert, he could be in serious danger, and they had to do whatever they could to return that courage. Maxim disappeared into the chambers deeper in the shuttle and came back wearing a thick cloak that he must have gotten from his pod.

"Lynx," he called. The warrior came out of the kitchen and Maxim tossed him another cloak. "Nylek is still out there. We need to go find him. Rain, could you please get Elise and ask her to unlock the door?"

"I can do it," Avery said, stepping back into the room. "Kyven is resting," he said. "He's in the infirmary and they were able to clean his wounds and apply ointments deeper in his skin. Elon put some sutures in, which should help them heal more quickly. He's resting now."

"Thank you, Avery," Maxim said.

He tightened the tie of the cloak around his neck and came back to Ivy. He stroked his fingertips along the curve of her jaw and looked into her eyes.

"I will be back as soon as I can," he said. "Go to bed. I need to know that you are safe and warm, and you need to sleep."

"Maxim," she started, but he leaned down and touched his lips to hers to quiet the words.

"I'll be back," he whispered. "Go to bed. I love you."

"I love you," Ivy whispered.

She watched as Avery went to the panel and input the code that unlocked the door. Maxim and Lynx stepped out and before they were even off the stairs, the former pilot closed the door again and locked it. He turned toward Ivy and she could see hope in his eyes. Despite Maxim's admonishment, she still couldn't bring herself to trust the man. Without saying a word to him, she stood and walked in the direction of the infirmary, hoping that she wouldn't encounter Elise along the way. She wanted to take a shower and change into fresh clothes so that she could slip into bed and drift away until Maxim was back with her.

Maxim dropped to his knees in the sand beside the form lying face down beneath a long black cloak. He tucked his hand beneath the form and flipped it over, revealing Nylek's face. Lynx knelt on his other side and lifted his head, feeling his neck for a pulse.

"He's alive," he said. "Check for injuries."

Maxim ran his hands down Nylek's arm and then along his chest and stomach. He felt something cold and wet against his hand and looked down to see blood shining on his hand in the moonlight. Even with his hand rested directly on the warrior's chest Maxim could barely feel his breaths, and he knew that they needed to get him back to the shuttle immediately if they were going to have any chance of saving him. Lynx scooped Nylek into his arms and they started back to the shuttle. As they went, Maxim's mind wandered to Ivy and the baby that she was carrying. Being a father was never something that he had considered before, but now that it was happening, it felt completely natural, as though it was something that was always there but he only now discovered it. Suddenly his entire world was focused in on two heartbeats and for now those hearts beat together, ensconced within the same protective body. Someday, though, they would be separate and all his love would have to exist in two places.

By the time that they got Nylek back to the shuttle, his breathing had stopped completely. Maxim pounded on the door, calling in to Avery or Elise to let them in. As soon as the door opened, Lynx rushed Nylek to the infirmary. Maxim watched as Elon left Kyven's side and came to the bed where Lynx had placed Nylek's limp and unresponsive body. He felt a shudder deep within him as Elon cut away Nylek's clothes and reached for pieces of equipment that were attached to the wall and ceiling. He attached them to Nylek's chest and the insides of his wrists, then pressed a button. The warrior's body arched, but fell limp again. Maxim tried not to think of what happened to him when he was out in the desert, to wonder what had caused the deep gash that he could now see meandering across his stomach and up to his chest, to feel the guilt crushing down on him that Nylek had left the safety of the shuttle to come to him and he had never found him. As hard as he tried, though, Maxim couldn't push away the thought in his mind, wondering if Nylek had called out to his mate as he collapsed to the ground and lay dying in the cold.

Suddenly there was a gurgling sound from the bed and Nylek's chest expanded as he filled it with a deep breath.

"Is he going to be alright?" Maxim asked.

"That's still left to be seen," Elon said. "For now, he's breathing and his heart's beating. If I can keep him stable for a while longer, I can attempt surgery on his wound. If he survives that, his next challenge will be getting through the night. After that, he has a good chance."

Maxim nodded and stepped over to Kyven's bed. He looked down at his brother, grateful for the look of peaceful sleep on his face. His lower body was covered with a sheet, but Maxim could see that nearly his entire upper body was wrapped in tight bandages. On the edges, some of the healing ointments had soaked through, giving the pristine fabric a green cast. He knew that beneath those bandages his brother's skin had been stitched back together, a concept that was both foreign and frightening to Maxim. He couldn't stand there any longer, listening to the strange sounds coming from the equipment attached to Nylek or looking at the bandages seeming to engulf his brother. They had been on Penthos for such a short time, and already two of their own lay tattered.

Maxim backed out of the infirmary and walked to the bank of showers in the room adjacent to it. He stood under the water until he felt all the twitching, adrenaline-fueled energy stream out of his muscles. Wrapped in a towel, he left the showers and returned to the chamber where his and Ivy's pods had been for the journey. The travel pods had been converted to sleeping accommodations and in the faint glow of emergency strips along the ceiling he could see Ivy resting quietly. She had left the space beside her open for him and it was one of the most welcome sights that he had ever seen. Maxim closed the door to the chamber and let the towel drop to the floor. Lifting the edge of the blanket, he slid into the bed and let his body sink into the mattress. Though he had been as careful as he could, the movement made Ivy stir and she gave a little sigh.

Maxim slid across the mattress to her and molded his body to her back. Through the gauzy white fabric of her nightgown he could feel the warm of her skin and it took away the deep chill that even the shower hadn't been able to remove. Ivy smelled sweet and clean and her skin felt soft as he ran his fingertips along her arm. Ivy sighed again at his touch and her back arched as she pressed her hips back against his. Maxim touched a kiss to her shoulder and returned the pressure of her hips. After a moment, Ivy rolled over onto her back and her eyes opened to look at him. She gave a sleepy smile and Maxim dipped his head to brush his mouth across it. Ivy caught his lips in hers and he felt her hands come to his back. The gentle pressure of her touch guided him over so that he lay on top of her and their kiss deepened. There was nothing urgent in the way that their mouths moved across each other. It was only calm, nurturing tenderness that reassured each that the other was there.

Ivy reached down and took hold of her nightgown, easing it up her thighs and over her hips. Maxim lifted his chest off her to allow her to remove it the rest of the way, and then settled back down onto her. The warmth of their skin touched from shoulder to their tangled feet and everything else fell away. Nothing else mattered but the rise and fall of her breasts against his chest and the fullness of her lips beneath his mouth as her hands ran languidly along his back. He craved her. Not in a way that was harsh or aggressive, but in the way that she filled him, satisfied him, and breathed life back into him when he felt that it was draining out of him.

One hand trailed along her side, feeling the ridges of her ribs and then the deep dip of her waist before the lush swell of her hip. He continued the touch down to her thigh and guided her leg up to his bend beside his hip. The movement opened her body to him and Maxim could feel the heat of her waiting core against his already hardened erection. Ivy moved her other leg out slightly to open further and Maxim felt his tip press into her opening. She sighed at the touch and Maxim lifted up slightly to sink the rest of the way into her. Her body molded around his perfectly and he paused deeply within her just to enjoy the way that it felt to have the embrace of her walls around him. He kissed along the side of her neck, creating a slow, gentle trail down to her collarbone where he let the tip of his tongue glide out against her skin.

When he finally began to move his hips, it was in long, unhurried strokes that ensured she could feel him touch every inch within her. The desperate need he had for her was nearly overwhelming. Watching Kyven and Nylek both nearly slip away had only solidified how precious she was to him and how vital to his life she truly was. Ivy was his breath and his blood, his reality and his dreams. Without her he knew that he could do nothing, and with her he was willing to endure anything.

There was nothing frantic or rushed in the way that his body delved into hers, but soon he could feel himself nearing climax. Pressure built throughout his body, fueling him to press slightly deeper and harder with each stroke until finally it broke and he felt everything within him pour out into her. Maxim rose up a few inches and ran his hand down her belly until he could press the pad of his thumb against her peak. He massaged it in tight, hard circles as he leaned down to draw one of her nipples in between his lips and suck it gently. It took only a few moments of this attention for her to let out a gasping cry as Maxim felt her body close tightly around him and draw him deeper with a series of intense spasms.

Maxim lowered himself carefully down onto Ivy and then rolled to the side, scooping her up against him so that he could cradle her body close to his. She tucked her head into the curve between his shoulder and neck and he felt her touch a kiss to his skin. After a few moments, Maxim pulled the blankets up higher over them, surrounding them in soothing warmth. Ivy was already falling asleep, but Maxim lay awake for several minutes longer. His hand trailed down her chest and settled on the swell of her belly. He ran his thumb along it, feeling a sense of awe come over him. When she hadn't yet told him about her pregnancy, he hadn't noticed anything different about her. Now that he knew, though, the difference was beautifully blatant. Though small, her belly was evident to him and it was as though he could sense the baby within it. It worried him that neither of them knew how this pregnancy was going to progress. Much like Eden and Pyra, this baby was unlike any that he had ever seen born. He didn't know if she would carry more like a human or more like a Mikana, which meant he couldn't predict when the baby might be born.

Cupping his hand on the side of her waist, Maxim eased Ivy's head off his shoulder and onto the pillow so that he could bring his lips to her belly. He kissed it tenderly and then turned to rest his ear against it. As he listened to the quiet sounds of her body, Maxim thought of his father. For so many years he had thought that Aegeus was dead and part of him had felt almost angered that he had allowed himself to be taken away from his sons. Now that he knew that his father was alive, however, it only confirmed what he was feeling toward the tiny child growing within his mate. He knew that there was nothing that would make him leave this child, and it would take everything to force him. He needed to see his father again and to be there when his own baby was born. He would survive whatever was to come, no matter what that took.

Maxim remembered what Elon had said about Nylek, and realized that it was the same for the rest of them. There were challenges ahead and they needed to prepare to fight, but first they needed to get through the night.

13

———

Sleep was brief and fitful for Pyra. He would allow himself to rest only for a few moments before he would suddenly wake so that he could check on Eden and their child tucked in her arms as she slept. Finally, some of the others around him began to shift and stir, and he knew that it was time to get moving. They had gotten a chance to refresh, but now they needed to forge ahead. As long as they were in the laboratory building, they were far more vulnerable to Ryan and his hybrids. Even though he knew that there were more waiting on Penthos for them, at least when they were there, they weren't trapped in a maze at the mercy of whatever was around the next corner. When they made it back to Penthos, they could fight.

The group was slowly pulling itself together and preparing to move on when the building around them shook and somewhere above them Pyra heard a tremendous blast. Eden sat up and scooped Lysander to her chest.

"What was that?" she asked frantically.

"I don't know, but we need to hurry," Pyra said. "Get

Lysander changed and gather anything that's here that you might be able to use. We need to move."

Pyra went around the room urging the group to prepare themselves. Soon they were gathered at the door to the emergency chamber looking to him for instructions.

"No hospital, not even one from a century ago, has only one stairwell," he said. "We followed the one on the same side of the building to get down here. Maybe if we find another one, we'll find a way out."

"Why don't we come back the way we came?" Ty asked.

"It's too dangerous," Pyra said. "We can't retrace our steps."

Pyra opened the door to the chamber cautiously, but the rest of the subterranean floor was still as silent as it had been when they found it. Several of the members of the group took out their lightsticks, while others used lanterns they had found in the emergency chamber to light their way. There seemed to be little on this floor of the hospital except for storage, and they soon made their way to the opposite side from the one where they had arrived. Here Pyra found a pale wooden door featuring a plaque with a jagged line etched onto it. He had come to recognize that symbol as representing stairs. Like the other stairwell doors that they had encountered, this one was unlocked and he stepped right through it, but paused when he noticed that there were stairs both leading up and down.

"What is it, Pyra?" Eden asked as she came into the stair-well with him.

"There are stairs leading down," he said.

"I thought that we were on the bottom floor," she said.

"I thought we were," Pyra said. "The stairs that we used to get down here didn't lead any further down."

"So, what's down there?" she asked.

"I don't know," Pyra said, "but I don't think going down is going to be the way that we get out. We should move back up into the new building and find the main exit."

They had moved up the first flight of stairs when Pyra heard a faint pounding on the wall. They all paused and Pyra listened more intently. The pounding came again and this time he thought he heard voices. Straining to hear them again, Pyra ran in the direction where he thought the pounding originated. He heard it again and this time the voices were stronger and more distinct. They were muffled by having to move through the walls of the contemporary building and the medical ward, but they were definitely voices.

Pyra!

Eden grabbed his arm.

"Did you hear that?" she asked.

Pyra nodded. One of the voices had called his name. They continued moving up the stairs and the pounding continued, seeming to grow louder the further they moved toward the main building. Pyra rushed up to the wall at the next landing and pounded his hands against it. He shouted, yelling anything to get the attention of whoever had called his name. For a brief moment he considered that it might be the hybrids taunting them and trying to lure them out, but he pushed the thought aside. Ryan hadn't bred them to be clever, he had bred them to destroy. It was far more likely that whoever was pounding on the wall was calling to him specifically, and if they were being that loud, they might not understand the danger that they were facing. He needed to get to them.

There was a beat of silence after he stopped yelling and then the pounding on the wall resumed. Pyra responded to it as he traveled up the next set of stairs trying to find it.

Suddenly it seemed that they had met. The voice cried out to him again and he heard it distinctly, the tone clear and firm. It sounded like Zuri.

"Gyyx, Ero, Ty," he called down the steps toward the men, "have you connected with your mates?"

"No," Gyyx responded as he approached. "I closed off communications with her right after we left. I didn't know what we were going to face here, and I didn't want her to sense any of it."

"Connect with her now," Pyra commanded. "All of you. Reach out to your mates. Find out where they are."

The three men each turned slightly away as they focused in on connecting their thoughts with their mates. If it was Zuri that he heard calling to him, Ero would be able to connect with her and confirm that the women were there. If it was a hybrid somehow mimicking her voice to get his attention, she would tell Ero that they were still at the house.

"It's me, Pyra," Zuri's voice shouted through the wall.

"It's her," Ero confirmed. "They're all here. They came to find us."

"They don't know about the hybrids," Pyra said. "They don't know that they're in danger."

"They must be in one of the closets," Eden said. "If they break through the wall, we'll all be able to get out."

"Tell them," Pyra said to the men. "Tell them to pick up the heaviest things that they can find and smash into the wall where they can hear my voice."

A few seconds later there was a dull crashing sound and then another. Soon the wall ahead of him looked like it was starting to crumble.

"Step back," Pyra shouted.

He waited a moment and then kicked at the weakened

section of the wall. It splintered beneath his foot and a large piece gave way. As it crumbled to the ground he could see through the resulting gap to the women and just beyond them, standing like a figment of his imagination in the shadows, was Jem.

The others standing with the women barely registered to Pyra as he scrambled through the broken wall toward the brother he thought he had lost. Jem laughed as they embraced and he held the younger warrior tightly to him. He pulled back and grasped Jem's face in his hands, holding his head still so that he could look at him. Some of the carefree softness that his face had once held was gone and he looked older, more weathered than when he had disappeared from that tree limb. As he stared at him longer, he realized that his eyes were now orange, the sign that he had found his mate.

"How are you here?" he asked. "Have you been here the whole time?"

"I'll explain everything," Jem said, "but not right now. Why are you here?"

The question broke Pyra out of the joy that he had felt at seeing Jem alive, and reminded him of the danger that they were all still in.

"Ryan captured Zsilvia and her mate George, then kidnapped Lysander. When we came here to free them he told us that he has been breeding hybrids to use as weapons."

"Hybrids?" Jem asked

"Yes," Pyra said. "He's been breeding and splicing together different species to try to create the ultimate military race so that he can take over the Universe, and he's starting with us. There are others on another planet, a planet called Penthos, and Ryan has sent some of his hybrid army there to eliminate them. The others are here, in the laboratory. We have to get past them or we won't survive."

"How many of you are here?" Jem asked.

Pyra stepped out of the way and allowed the rest of the group to stream out of the wall. He could see Jem's eyes widen as he saw Azrael and Ariella. Suddenly his expression grew dark and his hand moved to his hip the way that it had when they fought in battle.

"Get back," Jem commanded.

Pyra looked toward the wall and saw Aegeus climbing through. He held up an arm to block Jem from running toward him.

"No," Pyra said. "He's one of us. He's an ally."

"That is a Klimnu!" Jem growled.

"I know," Pyra said. "His name is Aegeus. He's been held captive by Ryan for years. He wasn't always this way. Ryan forced him to become Klimnu. He is our friend, Jem."

They heard a crash from behind Jem, followed by another, and then another. Pyra realized that all the doors along the hallway were opening and as they did, shrouded creatures stepped out of them. Pyra stiffened. Without looking away from the creatures, he tilted his head toward Eden.

"Go back down the stairwell," he said. "Get into the emergency chamber with the others and shut the door. Don't open it until you hear my voice." She hesitated and he pressed her backwards. "Go!"

14

Eden scrambled backwards through the broken wall into the stairwell again. She ran with Ariella, Elianna, and Zsilvia until they made it back to the emergency chamber. She turned and waited for Zuri, Samira, and Leia to come, and was surprised to see two other women along with them. One she recognized as Samira's mother, but the other she didn't know. They came into the room and Eden closed the door behind them.

She tried not to think of what was happening above them. She struggled to keep her mind away from the number of hybrids that could be swarming the building and whether the men would be able to fight them off. To distract herself, she turned to the unknown woman.

"Hello," she said. "I'm Eden."

The woman gave a tremulous smile.

"Jem has told me about you," she said. "I'm Angela."

"You're Jem's mate," Eden said.

Angela nodded. There were tears starting to build in her eyes and it was evident that she was overwhelmed by what was happening. Whatever she thought she was getting herself into when she came here with Jem, this was far more and she didn't know how to handle it. Suddenly Eden went from wanting to distract herself from the fear that she was feeling, to wanting to protect and surround this woman. She stepped up beside her and wrapped an arm around her shoulders.

"Come here," she said.

She guided Angela over to the side of the room where they had slept the night before and lowered her down to the makeshift bed. Zuri had found two more lanterns and hung them from the wall, providing enough light to help them see around them. Eden searched the nearby shelf of emergency rations and found coffee. She twisted the container to activate the automatic heating mechanism inside and handed it to Angela.

"Drink this," she said.

Angela held the container up to her nose and drew in a breath. Her shoulders relaxed as she filled her lungs with the rich aroma of the coffee. She took a sip and Eden heard the soft groan of someone who hadn't tasted coffee in quite some time.

"Where are you from, Angela?" Eden asked carefully.

She didn't want to push her overwrought emotions even further, but she couldn't deny her curiosity. She needed to understand what happened to Jem.

"Earth," Angela told her. She took another sip of the coffee and then shook her head. "Originally, anyway."

"Me, too," Eden said. "But you haven't been on Earth in a while, have you?"

Angela shook her head again.

"No," she said. "It's been five years since I've spent any time here."

"So, you didn't meet Jem on Earth?"

"No," Angela said.

She was starting to sound irritated and Eden settled down onto the floor beside her.

"I'm sorry," Eden said. "I don't mean to bombard you with questions. It's just...you've got to understand. We thought Jem was dead. We haven't heard anything from him since that day. He just..."

"I know," Angela said, cutting Eden off.

It wasn't a rude or aggressive gesture. Instead it felt like a desperate one, as if she couldn't bear the thought of hearing about Jem's disappearance. It was clear that she had heard the story before and it was painful to think of it again. Eden could understand. The story was only a reminder of how close Angela had come to never meeting Jem. Eden would never have wanted to think about it if Pyra had ever faced something like that.

"But where..." Zuri asked carefully, not finishing the thought as if she wanted to give Angela as much space as she could.

Angela took a final sip of coffee and rested the container on her lap. She took a breath and looked around at the women.

"Do any of you know about the HM-1313 wall?" she asked.

The women shook their heads. Angela looked down at the container in her lap and nodded. The expression on her face was pained.

"I've already been forgotten," she murmured.

"The excavation," Valerie said from behind them. She stepped up closer to the rest of the women and crouched down to look at Angela. "I remember watching about it on the news. It was a few years back. There was a research team that went into the desert across the country to do an excavation."

"Right," Angela said. "And a few of the researchers left from that project and joined other excavations around the world."

"I think I remember hearing about that," Eden said. "It seemed really strange to me that some of the team would get reassigned right in the field and wouldn't even get a chance to come back and debrief."

Angela nodded.

"That's because it is strange. Something like that would never happen, but because the investors and heads of the excavation presented a united front about it and had all the answers to all the questions, people just believed it. They went along with it rather than realizing how ridiculous that really was and demanding to find out the truth."

"What is the truth?" Valerie asked.

"We didn't go to another excavation. We went to another world."

"What do you mean?" Eden asked.

"Exactly what I said. We stepped into a cavern to explore it and in the next moment we were on a desolate, frozen planet."

"You went through a portal," Eden said in surprise.

"Yes," Angela said. "There were five of us when we went. Jacob and I are the only ones who stayed together. We haven't seen the others since just a short time after we arrived."

"Why didn't you come back?" Leia asked.

"We didn't know what had happened," Angela said. "We had no idea that we went through a portal or how to go back. It is not so simple as to just move through the same portal to go back and forth. The portal in the cavern brought us to another cavern on the frozen planet. That portal didn't connect directly back to Earth, though. The portals cross different locations and different times. When we finally found our way back to the frozen planet where we started, we stayed. It was difficult, but it was what we knew."

"How did you find Jem?" Eden asked.

"Others found us first. Galadriel and Vyker. They were traveling the streams and they found Jacob and me. They offered to bring us along with them, possibly even getting us back to Earth. We went with them, but we lost them along the way. They found another planet and Jem was there. He traveled back with them and discovered that he had a portal that brought them back to Earth. From there, they made it back to the original stream and to Vyker. That's when I met Jem. After that we figured out the path that connected Vyker and Galadriel's planet and the one where Jem had been living. His planet was so beautiful. Warm and untouched. I chose to go live there with him."

Angela was breathless when she finished and Eden felt the same way. It was a complex and overpowering story, difficult to even fathom, but she knew that Angela was telling her the truth. Jem's reappearance proved that there was so much that Eden didn't understand, so much that was still unknown about the world.

"We're very happy that you're here now," Eden said. "Both of you."

Angela tried to offer a smile, but the tears had built in her eyes again. She hung her head and ran one of her fingertips along the rim of the container of coffee in her lap.

"We were just trying to get back to Uoria," she said weakly. "Jem wanted to get home, even for a time. When we got here, we found Rilex and he told us that there were problems on Uoria."

Eden felt a heaviness in her chest. She nodded. She wished that she could explain everything to Angela, but there was just too much. For now, she was going to have to trust in them. As Jem's mate, she was bound to him for life. It would be her decision if she would follow that bond and stay with Jem or if she would turn her back on him. Knowing her own devotion to Pyra and the unbreakable tie that she felt to him, she knew how unlikely it would be that Angela would be able to walk away from her mate. She was one of them now, part of this, another piece of the resistance they were building against an enemy that was seeming larger and more oppressive with each passing moment.

"What's happening up there?" Angela asked.

Eden lifted her eyes to the ceiling of the emergency chamber.

"The hybrid army," Eden said. "The men are fighting them. We have to get through them before we can get out of the lab and back to our vehicles to travel to the others."

Angela's eyes suddenly went clear.

"Why are we sitting here?" she asked. "If they are up there fighting, why are we down here?"

"Pyra told us to stay here until he came for us."

"And we are all just supposed to listen to him?"

"He's Eden's mate and the leader of the Denynso warriors, which makes him the leader for the rest of us."

Angela set the container to the side and stood.

"He's neither to me," she said.

She stalked to a shelf along the wall and took up a long metal pole with a sharpened blade on the end. Eden watched her cross to the door.

"What are you doing?" Eden asked.

"I survived for five years with nothing. I came up against creatures that I had never seen and conditions that seemed completely insurmountable, but I survived. I didn't do that by hiding. I don't know what's up there, but I do know that I'm not going to let Jem face it alone. If there is someone who is trying to take over the Universe, I'm not just going to let it happen. He's going to have to get through my mate, and he's going to have to get through me."

Angela's words reawakened the fire that had burned within Eden. She had fought alongside the Denynso before. She had stood up and refused to give Ryan the satisfaction of knowing that he was still controlling her, that he was succeeding in the plan that he had manipulated her into being a part of long before she even left Earth for Uoria. Now she had been weakened and broken down, and instead of reaching within her to find the Denynso that dwelled there and letting it power her through as it had when she faced off against Ryan in the lab, she had hidden. Not anymore. She stood and nodded.

"She's right," Eden said. "What happened to us? Why are we here with our men? Because we fought to be here. We stood by their sides and fought to get here, and I'm not going to stop fighting. Ryan started this with me, and I'm going to be a part of ending it. I don't know where he is right now. For all I know he could be watching every move, delighting in us running through this place like mice and hiding from the creatures that he designed for this very purpose. He wants Pyra's blood. He wants to be able to take out the Denynso and turn all of us and all of our allies into slaves to help him conquer the Universe. I am not going to just let that happen."

"What about Lysander?" Valerie asked.

Eden leaned down and touched a kiss to her son's head.

"Lysander *is* Pyra's blood. He has the soul of a Denynso warrior. He was born for battle. When he's grown and has taken his father's place as the leader, he will know that he is the strongest and most powerful Denynso warrior that has ever been because he was conceived against adversity, carried through battle, born into conflict, and raised in war. He will never back down." She used a blanket to tighten the sling around the baby, crossing it over like armor. "And neither will I." '

A few minutes later the women marched up the stairs, each bearing a weapon they had scavenged from the emergency chambers. They could hear the grunts and crashes of the conflict going on above them and the sounds fueled them forward. The door to the closet concealing the sealed stairwell had been closed, but Eden forced it open. The corridor that stretched in front of her was strewn with bodies, the walls splattered with blood. The rest of the space was filled with figures tangled in combat and Eden scanned them to find Pyra. When she did, her heart steeled even further and she lifted the sharpened blade above her head.

The women streamed into the corridor and instantly Eden's mind was clouded by the compulsion for battle given to her by the Denynso DNA now in her cells. She clashed against the impending enemies with everything in her, using her incredible strength and the skills that she had learned from watching her mate. She fought nearly blindly, keeping her back to those that she fought against to protect Lysander from their weapons. Around her she could see the others engaged in their own battles against the tremendous array of hybrids that confronted them. Some fought independently against the smaller creatures, while others teamed up against the larger ones. Blood streaked against their skin and clothes hung in tatters, but they kept going.

The sound of the battle began to lessen as more of the hybrids lay dead or dying at their feet. Soon the intensity with which it had raged reduced to an ember. Eden had reached the end of the hallway and leaned against the wall in front of her, catching her breath. She turned slowly to survey the carnage scattered on the floor, praying that she would see all of their group standing. As she let her eyes travel across the shadowy hallway she saw some of their number crouched or lying across the marble. Jem was sitting leaned against the wall, his large hand clutched against his chest. His breathing was ragged and his eyes were closed.

Eden rushed to Jem's side and dropped down beside him.

"Jem," she said. "Jem, open your eyes. Ciyrs!" She shouted for the healer, then looked for Angela. Their eyes met and Angela ran over. "Jem, Angela's here."

Jem's eyes opened enough that he could see his mate kneeling beside him and then closed them again. Ciyrs came to him and touched his hand to Jem's chest above the warrior's hand.

"Jem, is this the only place you're injured?" the healer asked.

Jem nodded.

"Yes," he said. "Glass."

Eden looked up at the tremendous window that stretched across the front of the administrative offices and saw that it was shattered. One of the hybrids must have used Valdician powers to throw Jem into the glass, splintering it. Ciyrs took Jem's hand and carefully moved it aside. Eden could see a large shard of glass protruding from the wound in Jem's chest. Her hand flew to her mouth and she closed her eyes briefly.

"Alright, Jem," Ciyrs said. "We're going to get that out

and I'm going to fix you up. We already lost you once. We're not doing it again."

Jem managed a meager smile and weak laugh as he shook his head.

"I'm not going anywhere," he said. "Dying once was enough for me for now."

Ciyrs stood and called out to Pyra.

"We need to get Jem down to the medical ward," he said. "There isn't time to try to get him to the shuttle. I need to get that glass out of him and start the healing right now. I'll check the others here and bring down anyone else who will need healing. We're going to have to spend at least the night here."

The idea of spending another night in the laboratory sent a chill through Eden. She had spent enough time there when she was on Earth. She wanted to put it behind her and never think of its corridors and doorways again. If they were going to be strong enough when they made it to Penthos and the others, however, she knew that the warriors would need their injuries healed. For now, the hybrid forces had been pushed back and it didn't seem that more were on their way. They could spend some time recuperating and then escape to the shuttle bay and head to Penthos the next morning. As the group began to make their way back through the closet wall and down the stairs, Eden evaluated the bodies lying on the ground. If they did return, she was confident they'd be ready.

She waited as those who made it through the battle uninjured helped the wounded out of the corridor and down into the abandoned medical unit. It seemed Jem was the most grievously injured. When only Zuri, Ariella, and Jacob were left in the corridor, she headed toward the door. She was nearly at the closet when she felt a hand clasp around her ankle. Eden gasped and clutched Lysander closer to her chest as she tried to pull out of the hybrid's grip.

"Please."

The voice was weak and raspy, startling Eden enough to make her look down to whatever had her in its grip. The hood of the creature lying on the ground beneath her had fallen away, revealing a bloodied face and close-shorn black hair. Beneath the veil of oil-like blood along one side of its face she saw what looked like a tattoo etched into its skin.

"Please," the creature said again. "Downstairs. Help them. Please. Help them."

15

Maxim walked through the main chamber of the shuttle in the faint early morning light, trying to keep as quiet as he could as he made his way toward the infirmary. The others had only laid down to sleep a couple of hours before, but he had been unable to rest more than an hour after feeling Ivy fall tenderly to sleep in his arms. There was so much on his mind that it wouldn't let his body rest. He didn't want his movements to wake Ivy, so he climbed carefully out of bed, dressed, and started toward the infirmary to check on Kyven.

"Good morning, Maxim."

Elise's voice in the hazy corridor between the main chamber and the kitchen startled Maxim and he whipped around to see her standing in the kitchen stirring something in a tall cup. She was fully dressed and looked as polished as she did when they first entered the shuttle, telling him that she hadn't been able to sleep well, either.

"Good morning," he said. "Is everything alright?"

She let out a sigh and shook her head.

"I still haven't been able to communicate with Azra," she said. "I haven't heard from him since we first got redirected to Uoria. I'm really worried about him. What do you think they're doing? Why hasn't he communicated with me?"

"Have you tried to communicate with him?" Maxim asked.

Elise looked down into the cup that she was stirring as if whatever as inside was going to give her the answers to all her concerns.

"Yes," she said. "Many times. He just isn't responding. I didn't even know that I had the ability to communicate with him like this, but now that I can't I feel panicked all the time."

"I'm sure that there's a reason he isn't communicating with you," Maxim said. "He needs all of his concentration and focus right now. You heard Ryan just as well as I did. What we're going through here isn't the end of it. He drew the others to him there and has them at his mercy. The Denynso wouldn't just allow that to happen, though. They are fighting and they will continue to fight."

"What am I supposed to do?" Elise asked. "Am I supposed to just sit around here and wait for him to show up or to find out that he's dead? How do I even keep going? What am I supposed to do if he dies?"

"You can't think about that," Maxim said. "You can't worry about him. He is a Denynso warrior. This is what he is made for, Elise. It is his life. Now that you are his mate, it is your life, too. What you do now is honor him by being courageous and giving yourself to the same cause that he has given himself to."

"How do I do that? I can't fight. I've never seen anything like what's going on here. I've spent my whole life sheltered, and then when I started my career I thought that I was choosing something that would be adventurous. I wanted to see more and explore the galaxy and other planets. What I didn't know is that I was still completely sheltered. I wasn't seeing reality. I was seeing what these planets and travel companies constructed for their customers to see. Then I met Azra and everything changed. Suddenly it was like my world expanded. It had been watercolors and pastels and then it was vibrant and full. It wasn't until all of this happened, though, that I realized just how much everything had really changed. I'm never going to be able to go back. I've seen it. I've witnessed this and I know, at least partially, what's happening, and I can't pretend that it didn't happen or that it isn't out there. My life won't ever be the same."

"Of course it won't," Maxim said. "My life isn't the same since I met Ivy. The moment that I found her, everything was different, and I wouldn't change it for a single second. Even though we've struggled and had to face things that I never would have imagined, knowing what I do now, I would never go back to the life that I had before the Denynso came into the kingdom and brought us back to the Earth settlement. Even more, I know that I never would have been able to do any of this without Ivy. What you are going through is hard, and I promise you that it is only going to get harder. You're a part of this now, though. From the moment that you met Azra and realized that you were his mate, you became a part of something so much larger than you can imagine. Probably much larger than any of us can imagine, even those of us who have been in it since the beginning."

"Aren't you scared?" Elise asked.

"Yes," Maxim admitted. "But there are things worth being scared for. Even if I don't live through this, what I've done is worth it."

"Why?"

Her voice was quiet and strained, as if she was reaching out to him desperately, needing for him to tell her something that would make what she was facing make sense and reassure her. She looked smaller and more frightened than she had the day before. It was as if she had been filled with adrenaline and anger when she confronted the crew that had abandoned her, but now it had all drained away and only left the uncertainty. He took another step closer to her so that she could better see his eyes in the glow of the sun that was rising behind him.

"Because this moment and this world aren't yours alone. If you pretend that they are and keep your eyes covered to what's going on around you, you are just existing. To live is to honor the past, serve the present, and craft the future for yourself, for those who have already come, and for those yet to arrive. Even if I had to give up my life for it, it would be worth it, knowing that I didn't just sit by and allow Ryan to disrespect the past and try to steal the future."

"This is really happening, isn't it, Maxim?" she asked.

Maxim nodded.

"It is. There's nothing that you can do to stop it. All you can do is look inside yourself, find the strength, and hang on."

Elise held the tall cup out to Maxim.

"This is for Kyven," she said. "You can bring it to him."

"He's awake?" Maxim asked, feeling a boost of hope.

Elise nodded.

"I checked on him when I first woke up. It seems like the healing has really set in. You can go ahead and see him."

Maxim took the cup from her hand and rushed toward the infirmary. He stepped inside and saw Emerie sitting on the side of Kyven's bed, her hands pressed to his chest. Kyven looked over at her and a smile crossed his face.

"Kyven," Maxim said. "Are you alright?"

"I'm getting there," he said.

Emerie nodded and took her hands away.

"He is," Emerie said. "He should probably rest a little longer, but the healing ointments worked. The effects of the toxins have ended and his wounds are mending well. The sutures haven't been rejected and I don't see any signs of infection."

Maxim walked to the edge of the bed and offered Kyven the cup.

"Elise said that this is for you," he said.

"Drink all of it," Elise said, stepping into the room. "It will help keep infection at bay."

Kyven took a swing from the cup and Maxim saw his face clench and contort. He made a gagging sound and pulled the cup away from him as fast as he could, holding it out to Elise. She glanced down into it and shook her head.

"What?" he choked out.

"All of it," Elise said. Maxim saw Kyven clench his lips and shake his head. "*All* of it."

Maxim laughed as Kyven let out a groan like she was asking him to undergo torture and pulled the cup back so that he could swallow down the rest of the cup's contents. Kyven coughed as he pushed the cup insistently back toward Elise.

"What was that?" Maxim asked.

"Medicine," Elise said. "It's part of the supplies that Elon brought with us."

"That stuff might be worse than the toxin," Kyven said, his face still contorted. "I don't understand how you humans handle it."

Maxim laughed again. The happiness that he felt from seeing his brother back to himself was indescribable. He felt strengthened and revived, ready to face whatever the day was going to bring. Suddenly he remembered Nylek. He turned and looked at the bed across the room. Nylek was still lying still, his eyes closed. Elon was standing beside him evaluating the lines and symbols appearing on a screen above his head.

"How is he?" Maxim asked.

Elon looked up at him and the strained look in his eyes told Maxim that he hadn't slept much the night before, if at all. If he was anything like Ciyrs, Elon was too committed to watching over the patients that he was trying to help to think about himself. The thought was reassuring, but Maxim had to admit that the methods Elon was using were intimidating. The doctors in his own kingdom were far more like Ciyrs, though even the Denynso healer had more complex and advanced healing techniques than the Mikana. All of the machinery and medicines seemed to put a separation between Elon and the man he was trying to save, though Nylek did look stronger than he had the night before. The thought made Maxim wonder if he would ever really understand the humans and if Ivy ever felt the same way about him and the Mikana.

"He's showing improvement," Elon said. "Whatever got to him last night did some pretty serious internal damage and he was nearly frozen. I'm trying to stabilize his body temperature and regulate his vitals before I attempt surgery to repair the damage."

"Surgery?" Maxim demanded, standing up from Kyven's side and stalking across the Elon. "You didn't ask if you could perform internal surgery."

"I didn't know that I needed to," Elon said. "This is my

infirmary. You are passengers on my ship and when medical decisions need to be made, I will make them."

"We are not your passengers," Maxim said. "We're hostages. As we've already established with Avery, you have no power over us."

"Nylek is Denynso," Maxim said. "If he needs further healing, he should be given the healing that he is accustomed to. The healing of his kind. Ciyrs trained both Lynx and me to use the ointments and herbs that we packed to handle injuries."

"This man is severely injured," Elon argued. "I need to perform surgery to see the full extent of the damage and repair it effectively. I have access to advanced medical technology that will make it safer and easier, and give him a chance to survive."

"He doesn't need medical technology," Maxim said, offended by the man's words. "Ciyrs has been healing his kind since he was barely out of childhood. The herbs and ointments that he sent with us are powerful enough to handle virtually anything that we might encounter."

"There's a reason that humans once only used herbs to handle their medical needs and then progressed past it."

"That'll be enough, Elon," Avery said as he stepped into the infirmary. "I won't have you disrespecting them."

"It's not a matter of disrespect," Elon said. "It's facts. It's reality. Their healer isn't even here, but I've seen this man do what he passes as medical care. All the other Denynso did was clean his wounds and apply ointments."

"It worked, didn't it?" Avery pointed out. "Kyven is awake and regaining his strength by the minute."

"Because he's been taking strong doses of medication and I stitched his wounds. This is different. Nylek was seriously injured out there and we don't know how. Unless we know what is happening inside his body, doing anything else could cause him far more harm than good. I know that man feels that he knows best and that he taught the others how to do things well enough to handle these situations, but we both know that that's not the case."

"That man's name is Ciyrs," Maxim said, "and he is a Denynso healer. Humans developed tools and technology because the entirety of the understanding of herbs and plants for medical care doesn't even begin to compare to what only Ciyrs has. What he does is far more than just putting his hands on them. The powers and capabilities that this man has are unfathomable to you."

Maxim felt like his chest was going to burst with the anger that was causing his heart to pound heavily against his ribs. How dare this man question Ciyrs and his abilities? How dare he imply that because he had machines and complex medications, he was automatically better than the born healer who had been saving the lives of his entire clan for nearly his entire life?

"How do you know?" Elon asked. "You aren't even Denynso."

"No," Maxim said, shaking his head, "I'm not. You're right about that. But I was nearly Klimnu."

"What's that?" Elon asked.

"Something more horrible than I can begin to tell you. I would have suffered more than you can ever understand. The only reason that that didn't happen to me was because of Ciyrs. He kept me as I am. He has saved countless lives, including that of his own mate, who nearly died at the hands of their enemies but was brought back from the brink by his care. We weren't born to heal the way he was and the only tools that we have might be the herbs and ointments that he sent along with us, but I trust that that's enough.

Even if it isn't, you have no place questioning it just because we aren't human."

Elon looked stung and he stepped back slightly. It was clear he didn't know what to say. Avery stepped forward and reached a beseeching hand toward Maxim.

"I'm sorry, Maxim," he said. "I promised to help you and reassured you that my crew was here for you. I've already failed at that."

Maxim shook his head.

"You didn't fail," he said. "I still appreciate the assistance you've offered."

A groan from Nylek's bed broke the tension that had built among the men. Maxim looked down and saw the warrior's head moving slowly back and forth. He didn't open his eyes, but his lips parted and he let out a breath before speaking.

"Mhavyrch," he murmured.

Maxim heard Kyven gasp behind him and he turned to look at Kyven.

"What did he just say?" Kyven asked. "Did he just say Mhavyrch?"

Maxim nodded, confused by the word that had come from the apparently still unconscious warrior's lips.

"Yes," he said. "Mhavyrch. Miracle. How does he know an ancient Mikana word?"

Kyven shook his head.

"No," he said, sounding excited. "No, it's not a word. It's a name. It's a person."

"A person?" Maxim asked.

"Mhavyrch," Emerie whispered. "How does he know?"

"A person?" Maxim asked again. "How does he know what?"

Maxim hated the feeling of confusion that was rushing

over him. It felt like he was missing something, like there was a piece that he somehow overlooked so he wasn't able to keep up with the conversation that was unraveling around him.

"We weren't alone in the quarry," Kyven explained. "When we fell through the rocks into the cavern, it was just Emerie and me. Our lightstick was fading and we could hear the creature coming. The Meldor."

"Meldor?" Avery repeated.

Kyven nodded.

"The less light there was, the closer it got. When our light went out, I was sure that we were going to die. I did everything that I could to protect Emerie, but I couldn't see what was in that chamber with us, so I couldn't fight. It attacked me, but before it could kill me, there was suddenly light."

Kyven seemed out of breath and Maxim walked back to the side of his bed so that he could guide his brother back to lie down.

"You need to rest," he said. "Emerie, can you tell us what happened?"

She nodded as she reached for Kyven's hand.

"The light was blinding, but it was the most wonderful light that I had ever seen. A man had come down into the cavern with us and brought a ball of light that pushed the creature back. He told us that it was called a Meldor and that few who ever encounter it live. Before he left he told us that his name was Mhavyrch."

"Why didn't you tell us this?" Maxim asked.

"He was gone by the time that you got there to help us. I didn't know if I should tell you."

"Why?" Maxim asked. "He helped you. He saved your life."

"He was a hybrid."

The words struck Maxim silent. In the stillness that fell over the infirmary they heard footsteps rushing toward them. Lila appeared at the doorway with a look of fear in her eyes.

"What is it, Lila?" Elise asked.

The woman shook her head as if she couldn't speak and gestured for them to follow her. Maxim looked at his brother again, and then ran out of the room and down the hallway toward the main chamber. He was partway there when he heard the low rhythm of drums in the distance. It was a slow, steady beat, like one that would correspond with a controlled march. The sound seemed to hold more resonance than its volume justified and Maxim felt like it was pricking at his skin.

He got to the main chamber and saw that the sun had finally made its way all the way up. It glowed through the window on the far wall and splashed like gold across the floor and furniture throughout the room. It should have been soothing. It should have invigorating to finally see the sun again, as dark as the sun on Penthos might be, but it didn't represent the newness and possibility that a fresh day should. Instead, it was exposure, forcing them to see the planet where they had been dropped into Ryan's disturbing game and what was waiting for them there.

The sound of the drums continued, seeming to get louder. He rushed to the window and looked out, but he didn't see anything except the never-ending expanse of sand that stretched around the desert.

"What is it, Maxim?" Elise asked as she came into the room.

"I don't know," he said.

He ran through the pod chambers to the room that he

shared with Ivy. She was sitting up in the bed, looking around with wide, confused eyes.

"Do you hear that?" she asked. "What is it?"

Maxim shook his head. He pressed a button on the wall across from the bed and watched as the flat panels that covered the window slid open. He pressed his hands against it and looked out, trying to see if there was something more out there that wasn't visible from the window in the main chamber. Not seeing anything else but the shimmering sand did nothing to comfort him. If anything, it only made the fear that was beginning to prick the back of his neck more intense. He could feel the rhythm of the drums in his blood and the threat that they carried in a chill that rolled down his spine.

"Get dressed," he told Ivy. "I don't want you to leave the shuttle, but I want you to be ready."

"Ready for what?" she asked as she stood from the bed.

She was still undressed from him gently pulling away her nightgown the night before, and her beautiful bare body in the morning sunlight underscored the vulnerability that was setting in. Maxim stepped up to her and wrapped an arm around her waist so that he could sweep her up against his body and crush his mouth down on hers. He kissed her with all of the intensity that he was feeling, the desperation to keep her close, and the brutal, primal energy that was building within him with each beat of the drum outside. She sought him in that kiss, connecting with him and reassuring him with her sweetness and familiarity, but also with the promise of loyalty that she had given him when they were still on Uoria.

When their lips parted, Maxim crossed to the luggage pod on the opposite side of the chamber and lifted its lid. He withdrew the weapons that he had brought along with him and the supply bag that he had packed before leaving Uoria. Maxim loaded his body with the weapons, ensuring each was easily accessible so that he would be able to grab and use them however and whenever they were needed. He picked up his cloak and looked down at it in his hands. Now that the morning sun had come to burn away the chill from the night before he didn't know if he needed the cloak, but he still swung it around his shoulders and tightened it around his neck. He pulled the cloth around his body, concealing all of the weapons and providing a slight layer of additional protection.

Maxim walked back to the bed and leaned down to lift Ivy's nightgown off the floor. He took the pale blue silk ribbon around the neckline in his fingertips and eased it out of the gauzy fabric, using it to tie his hair at the back of his neck. Feeling fully prepared, he turned back to the window and closed the panels again to conceal the inside of the chamber again. He stepped up to Ivy and touched his hand to her cheek.

"Stay in the shuttle," he said again. "Stay with the other women and wait for me to come back."

"I'm not just going to sit around here, Maxim."

Maxim touched a kiss to the center of her forehead.

"I love you," he said.

He took a moment to touch his fingertips to her belly and then rushed out of the room. The sound of the drums was louder now. He could feel each beat shaking through the air around him. He knew what it was. He had heard of it before. When he made it back to the main chamber he saw Rain standing at the window, her arms wrapped around her body. The panels were only open a few inches but she was staring intently through them. She turned to him as Maxim stepped into the room with Zyyr and Lynx close behind him. Her eyes met his as if she could transfer the images that she had just gathered into him with only that look. There was a long, tense moment with only the sound of the heavy, pounding drums reverberating from the metal around them to accent each breath. Finally, she spoke.

"They're here."

UNTITLED

To be continued...

JACOB & PHAEDRA'S STORY

1

———

The silence that had settled in the hallway made Jacob's breaths sound heavy and ragged in his ears. He paused where he stood, his arm still holding his blade out to his side as if even the sight of all the fallen creatures strewn across the ground didn't convince his mind that it was over. Around him the silence began to crumble away, eroded by the sound of groaning as the wounded became aware of their injuries and poured their pain and desperation out into the shadowy space. The adrenaline that coursed through his veins was familiar. If he closed his eyes he could have felt the cold, biting wind of the frozen planet where he and Angela had struggled through the last years. They had been faced with danger there before. Many times when he stepped out of the cave that they had created into their shelter to find food or to gather fresh snow to melt down into water, he had come face-to-face with fearsome beings that he had to fight off to survive.

As he lowered his hand to his side and slowly steadied his breathing, he thought of all the times when he wondered why he fought so hard. Why was the compulsion to survive so hard that he would put himself through the struggle and threats that waited out in the snow? They had little hope and every moment that they spent huddling against the freezing temperatures was a reminder of what they had left behind when they tumbled inadvertently through the portal. He had had a life on Earth. Much of it had revolved around his career with the excavation team, but there was more. There were people he cared about, places he thought of when his eyes closed and he could pretend, if only for the few hours that he would sleep, that he was. There had been so much more than the daily struggle clawing just to stay alive. During those clashes, all his mind could focus on was the fight. He would use the weapons he and Angela constructed out of the meager plants and other materials that they could find and battle until he had either destroyed the creature or managed to escape. When he returned to the cave, he was thrown right back into yet another struggle to survive, trying to keep warm in the frigid temperatures and stinging snow, and scrambling to find enough food to keep them going.

Now as he stood in the hallway looking out over the aftermath of the battle that had come up so suddenly and yet had consumed his focus, he realized that it wasn't just the frozen planet that had driven him to fight to survive. There was something deep within him that went beyond just the basic desire for survival that had kept him alive when he thought that the life that was ahead of him in the endless snow was hopeless, and it continued to fuel him as he faced down an enemy that he didn't understand and that posed a threat not only to him but to all of those around him.

Jacob heard a groan and he looked around the space to try to find its source. His stomach sank as he saw Jem leaned against the wall, his hand clutched at a wound in his chest. Though he hadn't spent much time with him, the warrior had come to represent so much to Jacob. Not just the new mate to the only friend he had had throughout his time lost in the streams, Jem was also the most courageous and honorable man he had ever met. In even the brief time that they had spent together, Jacob had developed a great sense of loyalty and dedication to Jem. Seeing him stretched across the floor with blood spilling between his fingers was gut-wrenching. Eden ran to Jem's side and soon the others who weren't injured in the battle burst into action. They started gathering the wounded and bringing them toward the gap in the closet that led down the concealed set of stairs into the abandoned portion of the laboratory. They still hadn't gotten an explanation as to how the others ended up in the ancient hospital, but as unnerving as it had seemed when Rilex had first mentioned that as a possibility, now Jacob was relieved that there was a place where they could go to come back together and recuperate after the battle.

Tucking his weapon away, Jacob reached down and helped one of the women off the ground. She was clutching her shoulder, but otherwise seemed like she had weathered the fighting well. She nodded as she got to her feet.

"Thank you," she said. "I'm alright."

"Leia," one of the massive Denynso warriors said from behind her, "what happened?"

Jacob watched as the tiny woman turned toward the warrior. In an instant, he swept her into his arms and Jacob saw him rush her toward the stairs. He knew that that must be her mate by the ferocity in his orange eyes. It was one of the things that he had learned from Jem as he watched his relationship with Angela grow. Jacob looked around and watched as the others made their way down the hidden staircase. He grabbed under one arm of the large winged man who appeared injured and helped support him into the closet. They climbed through the broken portion of the wall and he helped guide the man through it and down the narrow stairs. The only light in the staircase was the glow from the lightsticks that had been placed on a few of the steps. It wasn't enough to fully illuminate the space, only to break through the thick blackness of the abandoned core of the building and allow him to see each of the steps.

Jacob felt like he couldn't remember being in the light. He knew that he had been under the shine of the bright sun that surrounded Jem's planet before they left, but he couldn't remember how it looked or felt. They had been ensconced in darkness since they arrived on Earth and though it had only been a short time, the intensity of everything that he had gone through after had made it so that darkness seemed to define him. He couldn't imagine ever seeing the light again. For now, they would live in shadow.

Jacob followed the others down the corridor to three adjoining chambers. One seemed to have just been opened and the group had divided so that those helping the injured brought them into this chamber while those who had gotten through the battle unharmed went into the other two. He saw Pyra and another Denynso helping Jem into the makeshift infirmary and followed them. He helped the winged man sit on a large cushion on the floor and then turned back to check on Jem. Pyra rushed to lay out mats and blankets and the other man carefully lowered Jem on top of them, propping a pillow beneath his head. Angela dropped to her knees beside him, but the second Denynso man touched a hand to her arm and gently pressed her back.

"I need to work on him," he said. "You need to give me space."

"I can't leave him," Angela protested, reaching for Jem's hand. "He's hurt. I need to be here with him. He needs to know that I'm here."

"He *is* hurt," the man said, "which is why I need to have as much space as I can get. I need to be able to work on him without interference."

"I'm not interfering!" Angela shouted.

Jacob crossed the room quickly.

"Angela," he said. "I know you're worried about Jem, but there's nothing that you can do for him right now. He knows that you're here. Please, let..."

He looked to the man now tearing away Jem's shirt uncertainly.

"Ciyrs," he said. "I'm the healer of the Denynso clan."

Jacob nodded.

"Please let Ciyrs do what he can. I'll stay with him. I can help."

Ciyrs looked at him questioningly.

"I had some first aid training before going to the excavation," he explained. "It's not much and I'm sure it's nothing compared to what you know, but I might be able to do something to help you with these injuries. Maybe that way you can move through them more quickly."

Ciyrs nodded.

"Human methods are nothing like the healing ways of the Denynso," Ciyrs said in a voice that was both warning and appreciative. "If there is something more that you can do for him than I can..."

"Together," Jacob said.

Ciyrs nodded again and Jacob saw him turn his attention back to Jem and the glass that was protruding from his chest. The healer rested his hand beside it and reached for one of the pieces of cloth that Pyra had put beside the bed. He wrapped the glass in cloth and looked down into Jem's face.

"Take a deep breath," he said.

The warrior drew in a breath and clenched his eyes closed, knowing the pain that was to come. Ciyrs gave a hard pull on the glass. Jem's body arched as the piece emerged from his body and blood began to spread further across his skin. He gritted his teeth, but he couldn't muffle the cry of agony and Jacob felt his heart clench, but he knew that they couldn't stop working on him. They had to stop the bleeding and ensure that there was no internal damage or Jem could die. Jacob reached for a small stack of the cloths and pressed them to the wound. The blood soaked through them almost instantly, and he reached for more.

"What are you going to do?" he asked Ciyrs.

The healer was searching through a bag that Pyra had also placed beside him. He pulled out a small vial and pulled the stopper out, tossing it aside. Lifting Jem's head with one hand, he placed the mouth of the vial to Jem's lips and tilted it so that the pale blue liquid inside slipped into his mouth and down his throat. Almost instantly the warrior's shaking stopped and the look of agony on his face relaxed. His body went limp and Ciyrs eased him carefully back down onto the pillow.

"That will help him rest and keep him still while we finish," he said. "I have to apply the herbs and then perform the healing, but the cloths can't be there when I do it. I have to work quickly to limit the blood loss."

Jacob nodded.

"Just tell me when you're ready."

Ciyrs stared at the bloody cloth on Jem's chest for

another few seconds, allowing it to do as much as it could for him, then nodded.

"Go ahead," he said.

Jacob peeled away the cloth and Ciyrs immediately poured the contents of another vial directly into the wound. He wiped away as much of the blood as he could and then coated the entire area in a thick paste.

"Is that it?" Jacob asked. "Should we add the bandages now?"

Ciyrs shook his head.

"No. I have to do the first healing and then we can put the bandages on."

"Is there anything that I can do to help?" Jacob asked.

"No," the healer said. "This is something that I have to do on my own. Please go check on the others, get a list of their injuries, and do what you can for them. When I'm finished here we can move on to the others."

Jacob climbed to his feet as Ciyrs rested his hands on Jem's chest, placing one over and one beneath the wound. He closed his eyes and drew in a breath. Jacob started over to the winged man he had helped into the room, but just before he reached him he heard heavy footsteps running toward him.

"Pyra!"

Jacob turned and saw Eden rush into the room, her eyes bright and frantic.

"I need your help."

2

Pyra crossed to Eden and took her hands.

"What is it?" he asked.

Jacob continued toward the winged man, but kept one ear turned toward Pyra and Eden, wanting to know what was upsetting her. He had seen her fighting in the corridor and she had shown no hint of fear. Now she looked nearly frantic and it made Jacob strangely nervous.

"We need to go downstairs," Eden said.

"What do you mean?" Pyra asked. "We're safe here."

Eden shook her head.

"No, it's not about us. When I was leaving the hall one of the hybrids that was on the floor grabbed me. It said I needed to save them."

"Save who?" Pyra asked.

"I don't know. It didn't say. It just pleaded with me to save them and said 'downstairs'. Those stairs that lead down, the ones that we noticed earlier, it must have been talking about those. We need to go down there."

"Eden, we can't do that."

"Why?"

"That hybrid was created as a weapon specifically for the purpose of fighting against us. Anything that they say to you is just as dangerous as them fighting against you."

"How do you know that?" Eden asked, sounding more desperate. "It was lying there dying. It was asking for help."

"Exactly, Eden," Pyra said. "It was dying. It was taking the last chance that it had to find a way to hurt you. It couldn't do it itself, but it could lead you downstairs where others might be waiting."

"If there were others waiting down there, why didn't they come up when we were spending the night here? Why didn't they hear the battle and come reinforce them?"

"I don't know the military techniques that Ryan has taught them. Just as the Denynso has methods and maneuvers, so do these hybrids. Those that were up in the hallway with us had the commands to go up there and fight us. Those downstairs might have been given orders to stay down there until we got there."

"These aren't the Denynso. They have no reason to fight against us except that they were told to. I don't think it was trying to manipulate me," Eden protested. "I really don't, Pyra. It was asking for help. It was desperate. I know that there is something that we need to see downstairs."

"We aren't going downstairs," Pyra said, his voice saying that he intended this to be the final say in the conversation.

The massive Denynso leader started to walk around his mate to go further into the room and check on the wounded, but she wouldn't let him. Though a fraction of his size, Eden stepped into his path and squared her shoulders at him, commanding his attention and refusing to allow him to simply walk away from her without hearing everything that she had to say to him.

"What if there really are people down there who need our help?" she asked.

"There is no help that we can offer them," Pyra insisted. "They are an enemy army, whether they are confronting us in battle or lying in wait for us. We are going to stay right here in these emergency chambers where we are safe and have the supplies that we need to get us through. You are going to stay here and take care of the baby."

Eden straightened even further, her hands seeming to clench slightly at her sides.

"The Klimnu were our enemy, but we helped them when they needed us. The Denynso have no alliance with the Eteri or the Irisa, but we have helped and connected with both."

"We helped Maxim," Pyra argued. "He is not Klimnu."

"There was a time not too long ago when you wouldn't have argued that," Eden said. "You were ready to kill him, but you changed your mind."

"I'm not going to change my mind this time, Eden."

Eden looked at her mate for a long, scrutinizing moment, and then started untying the sling that she had created for Lysander to hold him tightly to her chest.

"You don't have to," she said as she pulled the baby away from her body and started toward one of the other women. "I already have." She held Lysander out toward the Denynso woman. "Zsilvia, will you please take care of Lysander for me?"

Zsilvia looked slightly startled, but held out her hands to take the baby.

"Yes," she said.

"Thank you," Eden said and stalked out of the room.

For a moment, it looked as though Pyra was going to follow her, but then he let out an exasperated sound and whipped around. When he did, his gaze fell on Jacob and he strode toward him aggressively. Jacob stood and faced the warrior, unsure of the intention behind the approach.

"Who are you?" Pyra demanded.

"I'm Jacob," he answered.

"Who *are* you?" Pyra asked again, more forcefully this time. "You just showed up here with Jem without any explanation of who you are or where you came from or how you found him."

Rilex came to Jacob's side and looked up at Pyra's face.

"What's going on here?" Rilex asked protectively.

"You," Pyra said. "You, too. The two of you, and that woman, showed up here with no explanation."

"Who are you to ask who we are or our intentions?" Rilex asked.

"I am Pyra, the head of the Denynso, and the leader of this group," Pyra said angrily.

Jacob felt the muscles throughout his body tighten.

"You may lead the Denynso and even those who have joined you, but we came here on our own volition and without any expectation of loyalty or leadership," he said.

"Are you rejecting cooperation with us?" Pyra asked, a hint of threat in his voice.

"We are rejecting nothing," Rilex said. "We came here. We joined you and fought alongside you in a battle that was not our own. But this was not our intention when we came to Earth. It was never in our plan to encounter a battle or to join an army. We aren't rejecting cooperation with you, but we also don't owe you anything, particularly a promise of following you as our leader."

Jacob could hear the bitterness in Rilex's voice and fully understood its origin. This was a man who had spent years alone, away from everything that he knew and everyone who had meant anything to him. He had been committed to fulfilling the quest of his dearest friend, a man who had died far too young, and had found himself thrust into a world that he didn't understand when a portal on his planet sent him through time and space to a planet thousands of years ahead and in a different iteration of existence. There was no loyalty for Rilex outside of the loyalty that he still carried for the best friend whose family he had left behind and the mission that he knew was the only thing that would preserve all of reality. To be told that he had to give his allegiance to the leader of a species that he hadn't even known existed during his life on his own planet and that now he had never encountered went against everything that he believed and offended his very nature.

"Do you have a problem with my leadership?" Pyra asked.

He had taken a step closer to Rilex and squared his chest. His sheer height made it so that unless Rilex was looking directly up it was only the warrior's chest that he was able to see. This didn't seem to intimidate Rilex, who simply lifted his gaze further.

"I have no problem with you leading anyone who is willing for you to lead them, but I am not. I have no leader. Not anymore. That doesn't mean that I'm against you or that I will resist simply for the purpose of resisting, but if I agree not to stand in the way of your leadership for those who have pledged loyalty and allegiance to you, you must agree not to stand in the way of my not being led."

"If you refuse to be loyal to us and to allow my leadership, how can I know that I can trust you? How do I know that you won't betray us?"

"I fought alongside you," Rilex repeated. "Being loyal does not have to mean pledging yourself. To truly trust is to acknowledge that a person has no ties and yet knowing that they will still stand beside you. I am nothing but loyal to Jem, yet he is in no way my leader. I don't think it's too much to ask the same of you."

"Jem was dead," Pyra said.

There was a sudden wavering in the warrior's voice, a hint of vulnerability that broke through the strength and aggression that had been in his words. They were startling, uncomfortable words, ones that carried with them far more meaning than they would have if spoken by anyone else. This was not a statement, but a plea, a desperate need for him to understand what was happening. In that moment, Jacob felt like he was beginning to understand Pyra, at least so far as to no longer feel the threat that had been emanating off of him when he first approached. His demeanor had been accusatory, as if he believed that the two men had somehow been responsible for Jem's disappearance, or even for the war that had just been waged in the hallway. Now, though, Jacob realized that was not the true motivation behind Pyra's sternness and anger. Instead, the powerful, intense leader was protecting his kind. The thought that one of his warriors, something that he very obviously felt passionately about, had gone missing without explanation, apparently dead, was deeply upsetting and he was determined to understand what had happened to him and why.

Deep within himself Jacob knew that he wished there had been someone who had been as committed to finding out what had happened to him when he disappeared. It had been so much like Jem. One moment he was there, under the eyes of many others, and then in an instant he was gone. Unlike Jem, though, Jacob had disappeared along with four other people. It was obvious that the Denynso had been immediately worried about him and devastated by his loss. Even now, so long after it had happened, they were still deeply impacted by it and questioning what had happened in those first few moments after he was gone from their sight. Jacob wondered if there had even been a moment when the people he had left behind worried about him or wondered where he was. Though he had been out of a romantic relationship for a few years when he signed up for that expedition so he didn't have a partner at home waiting for him like Angela had in her fiancé, he did have friends, a roommate, and parents. They should have known that he wouldn't just decide to go off on another expedition without letting them know. No matter what the company had said to them or what type of measures they put into place to make it seem like he was still alive and well and just out of regular contact with them, they should have questioned it. He had always been fully devoted to his career and to the work that they were doing in the excavations, but he had never been one to just disconnect from the people he cared about. It wouldn't be like him to communicate with his family and friends only through letters. They should have known that. They should have questioned what they were being told and what was happening.

Jacob glanced over at Jem where he lay on the mat on the floor, now covered with a blanket as he slept. The people Jem had left behind never stopped thinking about him. He wondered what might have been different if those he had left behind had done the same for him. What might have changed if, even for a moment, they hadn't believed what the company had told them.

                                    3
                              ____

Jacob rested a hand on Rilex's back, wanting to both reassure him that he was there and to calm and comfort him. Though the two men were not as close as he and Jem were, Jacob could sense the tension continuing to build within the man and now that he had made a greater connection with Pyra he didn't want him to let that aggression control him any further. He started to explain the situation to Pyra, but before he was able to get further than opening his mouth to tell him how Galadriel and Vyker had made their way to the planet where they found Jem, Eden rushed back into the room.

"I need you to see something," she said to Pyra as she came to his side.

Pyra looked down at his mate with an indecipherable expression. There was something there that bordered on anger, but it wasn't forceful and violent like the anger that the warrior had expressed toward Rilex and Jacob. Instead it was the type of anger that someone experiences when they feel that they have not done what they needed to do to protect someone they love.

"I told you not to go down there," he said.

"Pyra, I need you to come with me," Eden said, ignoring his admonition. "I think that I found what the hybrid was telling me to find."

"I don't care, Eden," Pyra said. "I told you not to go down there. I told you that it was too dangerous for you to go down there."

"Please come with me," Eden said. "I need you to see this."

Jacob could see the desperation in her face and felt a pull that told him he needed to know what was happening.

"What did it say to you?" he asked, not wanting them to realize that he had been listening to them when she first came into the room.

Eden looked at him, her eyes narrowing slightly as if she hadn't fully processed that he was standing there.

"It asked for my help," she finally responded. "It told me to find them and help them."

"Who is 'them'?" Jacob asked.

Eden shook her head.

"I don't know. I can only guess that it's more of them, more of the hybrids."

"Can you show me?" Jacob asked. "Show me who asked you for help?"

He wanted to see the creature that had reached out to Eden. The concept of the hybrids was still something that he didn't fully understand. He felt like he had been thrown into this reality and that he was trying to learn it, to under-stand it as it unfolded around him. Eden nodded and started toward the door again. Pyra grabbed her around the wrist to stop her and she turned to look at him, unflinching as she stared up into his face. A moment later he released her and Eden continued out of the emergency chamber and back toward the stairs.

Jacob followed her, listening carefully as they climbed to try to detect any sounds in the hallway above. It was silent, but there was still an eerie, uncomfortable feeling permeating the space around them. He didn't feel calm or as though they were stepping back into a space that was free from the threat that had been there before. Instead, it felt like the final breaths that had been breathed there were still lingering in the hallway, poisoning the very air.

They made it to the top of the stairs and Eden climbed through the hole in the wall that led into the closet. She had picked up one of the lightsticks from the steps as they climbed and as she pushed open the door to the closet she held the stick ahead of her so that its glow illuminated the space. They stepped cautiously out of the closet and back into the hallway. At first Jacob thought that it looked just as it had when they left after the battle. As Eden stepped further into the hallway, staring at a section of the floor that was empty, he started to notice that there didn't seem to be as many of the bodies strewn throughout the space as there had been.

"Where did it go?" she muttered.

"What?" Jacob asked.

Eden rushed across the hallway and held the stick up higher to spread more of the light across the hallway floor. Jacob could see streaks of dark fluid in the light, creating a trail that led several feet and then disappeared.

"It was right here," she said, pointing at the ground. "It was right here. It was lying right there when I was leaving."

"Are you sure?" Jacob asked.

Eden looked around at the few other bodies that were still lying on the ground. She nodded.

"Yes," she insisted. "It wasn't any of these. It was here. Right here."

Jacob felt a chill run across his skin. She was standing among the dead, seeming unfazed at their presence. He wondered what she had seen, what she had gone through to make it so easy for her to simply overlook the bodies just at her feet.

"Where could it have gone?" Jacob asked. "None of us brought them downstairs. I was one of the last to go through there when I was carrying the winged man to the chamber. I know that I didn't see anyone picking them up or moving them."

"Are you sure?" Eden asked. "Are you sure that when you were carrying Azrael downstairs you didn't see anyone else still up here, or go back upstairs? No one could have moved them?"

"No," Jacob said. "No one."

'I don't understand," she said. "It was here. I know it was. It grabbed onto me. It asked me for help."

"I believe you," Jacob said. "We need to tell Pyra. Something is happening here and I think we need to figure out what it is."

Eden nodded and they rushed back through the hole in the wall toward the stairs. Jacob felt relief as he shut the closet door behind them and began down toward the others. When they ran back into the emergency chamber they found Pyra crouched down beside one of the injured warriors. Eden reached down and took his shoulder, pulling on him until he stood and followed them back across the room away from the others. Jacob could tell that she didn't want those who were injured or who were trying to help them to hear what they were saying.

"Pyra, please. I need you to listen to me. I know that you

don't want to, but you need to. We aren't on Uoria now. We are on Earth. We are in the laboratory where I spent my career. I know this place. That makes it my domain and I need you to listen to me."

Pyra looked at her for a few tense seconds and then nodded.

"Alright, Eden. What is it?"

"The hybrid that asked me for help is gone. Several of them aren't there anymore."

"Could it have escaped?" Pyra asked, finally looking as though he were invested in what she was saying.

"No," Eden said. "It was dying, Pyra. I could feel its hand on me. It was weak. It was barely able to speak. There's no way that it got up and walked out of that hallway, especially in the time that we've been down here. Someone got it. Someone got all of them."

"What did you want to tell me before you brought Jacob upstairs?" Pyra asked.

"There's a door," Eden said. "At the bottom of that set of stairs that we saw. It doesn't look like it fits with this part of the building. There's something about it that bothers me. I think that whatever is behind it is extremely important."

Pyra reached down and lightly stroked her cheek with his knuckles.

"Alright," he repeated. "Show me."

Eden started out of the chamber again and Pyra followed. Jacob was close behind. He was a part of this now. He felt drawn to it in an inexplicable way, pulled to whatever was happening and to what it meant for him. They made their way down the stairs, moving deeper into the building than Jacob would have imagined it went. In the back of his mind he remembered the time that he had spent in that building before they left for the excavation. He never would have thought that this crumbling section existed just beneath the polished, sparkling floors of the laboratory. The thought was unnerving and he felt vaguely sick to his stomach as he wondered what might have been happening here when he was in the laboratory.

When they reached the bottom of the stairs Jacob saw a massive door built into the aged wall. Jacob immediately understood what Eden had meant when she said that it didn't fit with the abandoned part of the building. It was far larger than any of the other doors in the building, but it was also of a completely different design. While the other doors were simple and lightly colored, this door was the color of darkened steel and featured long, narrow bands of metal down the length, thick, rounded bolts bordering each side. It was strangely primitive and yet was obviously several decades newer than the surrounding building, as if part of the wall had been torn away and this door built in its place. There was a lock pad positioned beside the door, much like the others in the newer portion of the building though less complicated.

Eden reached for the door handle and pulled, but the door didn't move. Jacob felt a strange prickle at the back of his neck. He stepped past Eden and took the handle, giving it a harder tug, but the door still didn't move. He touched the lock pad, checking it carefully.

"What is it, Jacob?" Eden asked.

"This lock," he said. "It shouldn't still be engaged. Rilex destroyed the master controls when we first arrived. All of the locks in the building were destroyed."

"That means that this lock wasn't on the master controls," Eden said. "It was put here independently. Whoever made it didn't intend on anyone else being able to access it."

"But if they didn't think that anyone else was going to know that it was here, why would they bother to lock it?" Pyra asked.

"Not they," Eden said.

"What do you mean?" Jacob asked.

"Not 'they'," Eden repeated. "He. This is Ryan's doing. He made this just like he made all of those hybrids." She touched the lock pad and then flattened her hand on the door. "Locks aren't always to keep something out," she said. "They can also be used to keep something in. Whoever we are supposed to help is here," she said. "We just need to find a way inside."

"Rilex," Jacob said. "He was able to destroy the master controls. Maybe it will work for this lock, too."

He turned and started back up the stairs, his heart beating heavily in his chest. When he had agreed to come to Earth with Jem and Angela it was because he had wanted to spend more time with the one friend he had had during his long and challenging time on the frozen planet. He had seen little of her since she had decided to leave Vyker's stream and join Jem on his planet, even before she had become Jem's mate. The thought that she would be going to Jem's planet with him was upsetting to Jacob, though he hadn't told her that when they discussed it. Angela had suggested that their time on Uoria would be brief, but Jacob doubted it. Even though Jem understood that he had moved through a portal to get to his planet from Uoria, he didn't know where the portal was or how to find it again. That meant that they would have to travel back to Earth and then follow the other portals, hoping that they would all still be open as they moved. The sheer risk and challenge that this presented would only make Jem's attachment to his planet more pressing and the chances were low that they would ever leave Uoria again.

If he had known what they would face when they got back to Earth, Jacob didn't know if he would have been so willing to go along. As he got to the top of the stairs and started for Rilex, though, he reconsidered the thought. The compulsion to be a part of what was happening burned in his gut and told him that he was meant to be here. This was more than just traveling to Earth to help Jem get to his planet. Jacob had a purpose here. It was only a matter of time before he discovered it.

4

———

Jacob found Rilex crouched down beside Jem. The warrior's eyes were open and Jacob felt a flood of relief. He regretted how he had felt toward Vyker and Galadriel when he first encountered them, and he had been committed to not allowing himself to be controlled by his distrust and the coldness that had set in during his time stranded. Though he was still having a difficult time in some ways with Rilex, he trusted Jem completely. Now he knew that he was going to have to put his trust into Rilex as well as he asked for his help, and the sight of him checking on Jem reassured him.

"How are you feeling?" Jacob asked as he came to Jem's side and crouched down beside Rilex.

"Tired," Jem admitted. "Ciyrs's healings are phenomenal, but they take a lot out of you."

"So, he's healed you before?" Rilex asked.

Jem nodded.

"This isn't the first time that I've been wounded in battle," he said. "It will likely not be the last." He gave a soft laugh. "And Ciyrs will be there again."

His eyes started to drift closed and Jacob patted him on the leg.

"You rest," he said. "When you are ready, I'm sure Angela will be beyond relieved to see you."

Jem nodded, seeming nearly asleep even as he spoke to him. Jacob turned to Rilex and gestured for him to follow him out of the room. When they got out of the chamber, Rilex looked harried and uninterested in what Jacob had to say to him.

"I need you to come with me," Jacob said. "Eden found a door downstairs and it's locked."

"It can't be locked," Rilex said. "I disengaged the master controls. There's nothing to control the locks."

"That's what I thought, too, but the lock is fully engaged. Eden says that the door must have been built independently and never integrated into the master controls. She thinks that Ryan built it."

As soon as he said it, Jacob suddenly remembered everything that Rilex had told them as they approached the University. The name Ryan jumped out at him, reminding that that was the man who had tried to send Eden to her death among the Denynso and had now thrust them at the mercy of his engineered army. They ran back down the stairs toward the door and found Pyra standing at the bottom of the stairwell trying to pull the door from its hinges.

"Step out of the way," Rilex said as he approached.

Pyra looked back at him, the disdain that he had carried in his eyes lessened now. He stepped away from the door and Jacob watched as Rilex examined the lock pad. He touched his access chip to it as if experimenting just to ensure that this was not the one lock of the building that had escaped the destruction of the master controls. When the lock didn't release, he gestured toward the corner of the stairs.

"Go up there," he told the three of them. "Go around the corner and stay there until I tell you that it's safe."

"What are you going to do?" Eden asked.

"I'll explain later," he said. "Just go."

It was the same thing that Rilex had commanded when he went into the administrative office to deactivate the master controls and Jacob knew that it was best that they do as he said. He moved up the stairs and turned his back to the corner. He closed his eyes and an instant later he heard a sound that wasn't as loud as the one that came from the office but that still shook through him. Then he heard Rilex's voice call up to them, telling them that it was safe to come back to the door. Jacob followed Pyra and Eden down the stairs and saw them staring at the now-destroyed lock pad on the wall. Pyra reached up and touched his fingertips to it, hissing and pulling them away almost instantly.

"Don't touch it," Rilex said. "It's going to be hot for a while."

"What did you do?" Eden asked. "How did you do that?"

She sounded frightened and Rilex held up a hand to quiet her. He reached into the leather pouch that he wore and drew out what looked like a small pebble. Jacob knew what it was from his time with Vyker. He should have suspected that Rilex would use that astounding capability to break through the locks, but until that moment he didn't think that it was possible. Now as he looked at the newborn star in Rilex's hand he felt suddenly humbled by the experiences that he had had after leaving Earth and that he had come into the company of a species so breathtakingly powerful that they literally controlled the starlight and yet so heartbreakingly rare that Rilex was only one of a few left living of his kind and few, if any, on Earth knew or believed that they had ever existed.

Rilex held the small stone in his palm and gently blew on it. The stone began to glow, weakly at first and then increasingly brightly until it was almost painful to look at it.

"This," Rilex said, "is a newborn star. I come from an ancient species, one far older than human or Denynso. When our kind still flourished, it was our responsibility to nurture the stars until they were ready to be put into their positions in the sky."

"You destroyed the lock with a star?" Eden asked incredulously.

"Yes," Rilex said, reaching carefully into the lock pad to withdraw the small stone he had put there. "Even these young stars are astoundingly powerful. Their glow is far more than just light."

Rilex slipped the two stones back into the pouch and turned his attention to the door.

"I'll go first," Pyra offered. He stepped toward the door and rested his hand on the handle. He glanced back over his shoulder at Eden. "Are you ready?" he asked.

Eden nodded and Pyra pushed the door open. The first thing that Jacob noticed was the cold rush of air that washed over them. It was biting, almost painfully cold and it smelled sharp. Pyra stepped beyond the door and a bright light burst on overhead.

"Automatic lights," Eden murmured. "He doesn't want any contact with switches."

Jacob looked around the space, noting the vibrant metal surfaces and pristine floors. Nothing was out of place and it seemed that little had ever been done in the room if anything at all.

"It's a clean room," he said. "It's designed for total lack of contamination."

"But if he didn't want it contaminated, he would have a prep station right inside the door," Eden pointed out. "There would be a place to put on a suit and shoe covers and get properly sanitized before stepping in here. There wasn't any of that. The door goes straight from the abandoned hospital ward into here."

"So, it's not really a clean room," Rilex said.

"No," Pyra said. "It's a front."

Eden nodded.

"But for what?" she asked. "What is Ryan hiding in here?"

They spread out through the room unconsciously, each taking a small section and examining it carefully. The space was uncomfortable for Jacob, too perfect. He agreed that Ryan was hiding something with this room and that they needed to find it. Jacob ran his hand along the edges of the table set up in the middle of the room, then crouched down to peer into the cabinets built into the base. The doors opened to reveal only unopened packages of laboratory and medical supplies lined up neatly along the shelves. He picked one up and glanced at the date of manufacture stamped on the bottom.

"These packages are years old," he said. "Nobody has touched them."

"Here," Pyra said from across the room. They all hurried to him and saw him touching a small dial on the wall. "What is this?" he asked.

"It's a thermostat," Eden said. "It measures the temperature inside the room."

"If there's no light switch because he doesn't want there

to be contamination, why would there be a thermostat?" Pyra asked.

"There shouldn't be," Eden answered. "The clean rooms upstairs don't have thermostats. Their temperature is centrally controlled, like the locks."

"But could that be why there is one?" Jacob pointed out. "The door lock wasn't activated by the master controls. Maybe the temperature down here isn't controlled by the central system, either."

"It still doesn't make sense," Eden said. "A thermostat in a room that is designed to look like a clean room doesn't make sense. If this room hasn't been used, why would he add it? What's the point of putting an inaccurate detail in a room that was going to go untouched?"

"If this is a front," Rilex said, "Ryan might have designed it to look like this to throw off anyone who might accidentally stumble into it but that wouldn't be surprised by another clean room in the laboratory. It is extremely unlikely that anyone who works in the laboratory would find it. They are too familiar with the building and wouldn't go looking for anything. If someone was going to find it, they would be outsiders. They probably wouldn't know what to look for so they wouldn't notice something like an out-of-place thermostat."

"Then why put it there?" Jacob asked. "If this room serves no purpose but appearance, why bother adding something that wouldn't be there?"

"It's another front," Pyra said.

Jacob saw Eden look up at him strangely.

"Another front?" she asked.

"You've noticed that there is a thermostat here, but what haven't you noticed isn't here?" he asked.

Jacob looked around and it suddenly occurred to him.

"Doors," he said.

Pyra nodded and Eden's eyes widened.

"Why would he have a clean room to front for nothing," she said.

"Exactly," Pyra said. "This thermostat will show you what Ryan's hiding."

"How?" Eden asked, then her lips parted in a silent gasp. "The cold," she said in nearly a whisper. "It's so cold in here. Give me something that heats up."

Rilex reached into his leather pouch and brought out one of the stones he had held earlier.

"This should still be warm enough," he said.

Eden took it from him carefully and touched it to the front of the thermostat. Almost instantly the numbers on the screen began to change. Suddenly the screen went red and there was a loud scraping sound as the wall sank back several inches and then slid sideways out of the way, revealing a rectangular doorway cut into the wall. As soon as it was open Jacob felt slightly warmer air coming into the room, carrying with it the sound of low, agonized groans.

5
____

A light came on above them automatically just as it had when they stepped into the clean room, but instead of being such bright, intense white light that it had a blue cast to it, the light was red. The effect was eerie, but it was only the groaning that Jacob could focus on as they continued into the slightly warmer, larger space. It took a few seconds for his eyes to adjust to the light, but when it did Jacob could see that the room they were standing in was curved, the dark outline of a window running along the center of the wall.

The groaning seemed to be surrounding them, coming from behind the wall, and he rushed up to it to try to see through the window. It was dark beyond the glass, but as soon as he lifted his hand to instinctively touch the window, a light came on, on the other side. The red glow from inside the room where he was standing made the image through the window clear and he immediately felt his stomach turn.

"No!" Eden gasped.

She had seen the same thing as Jacob had: a row of cold metal tables, tilted at an angle, with battered-looking hybrids strapped to each one. They had been stripped of their clothing and the straps that held them in place on the tables were cutting into their skin as they fought against the gravity that was trying to pull each of them down onto the floor. Some of the creatures groaned and occasionally cried out, while others hung heavily from their straps in a way that told Jacob that they might have already succumbed to their injuries. Each had black cords attached to their temples and necks, and what looked like small screens in front of their eyes.

"It's like Creia," Pyra muttered.

"What?" Jacob asked.

The warrior was standing at another section of the window, staring through at several other hybrids, all in the same position as the ones in front of Jacob.

"Our king," Pyra explained. "He was captured and held prisoner by Ryan and several Valdicians. This is what happened to him."

"What is it?" Jacob asked. "What is happening to them?"

Pyra shook his head.

"I don't know, but this confirms Eden was right. Ryan did this."

"We have to get in to them," Eden said. "We have to help them."

Jacob expected Pyra to protest, to resist as he had the first time that Eden asked for help. Instead, he nodded. They started moving around the edge of the room, trying to find a door that would lead them into the torture chamber. Jacob finally found it and called the others over. Unlike the other doors throughout the building, this one didn't have a lock pad. Instead, it featured only a simple lock that kept the doorknob still. Pyra didn't hesitate before planting his heavy boot into the center of the door, crushing it beneath the pressure of his foot. They streamed into the space and Jacob rushed up to the first table. He looked at the screen in front of the hybrid's eyes and saw horrifying images flashing across it in rapid succession.

He pulled the screen away from the creature's face and saw it go limp. From the other side of the room he heard Eden's voice.

"Here," she said, "It's here."

Jacob, Pyra, and Rilex ran over to her and found her standing at the side of another of the silver tables. A smaller hybrid was strapped in place, the positioning of the straps doing little to conceal the fact that this creature was female. The reality hit Jacob hard and Pyra seemed to have the same reaction. It was easier to think of these hybrids not as true living beings, but as crafted weapons. Even if he was to embrace that they were alive, he wanted to think of them only as men. Now that he was confronted with the reality that this hybrid, one who fought in the same battle as the others, his perception of what was happening shifted. He understood that they were still a threat, but in the same breath he wondered if they were the only ones threatened by their existence and what they were trained to do.

The creature lying on the table seemed to strain against the straps that held her to the table, her fingers twitching and reaching. Eden noticed this and reached down to inter-twine her fingers with the creature's.

"Save them," the hybrid said. "Please. Find them and save them."

"Who?" Pyra asked. "Who do we need to help?"

"The others," the hybrid moaned. Her voice was getting weaker as she spoke and her eyes were barely open. "Save them."

A low click behind them told Jacob that they were no

longer alone in the room. He turned and saw two tall, cloaked figures walk slowly into the room. The bound hybrids groaned more loudly, those who were still capable of moving strained against the straps that held them, the fear making the air sharp and buzzing around them. Pyra and Rilex rushed the two creatures and in an instant Rilex was off his feet, held in the air by some unseen force. Jacob ran around the side of the tables, getting behind the cloaked creatures. He aimed a kick directly into the center of the creature's back, startling it enough that it stumbled and Rilex fell to the ground. Its hood fell away, briefly revealing its face. Jacob could see Rilex's face change as he looked up at the being that had held him above the ground. He looked as though he were staring through time, witnessing something that he knew but couldn't quite understand.

Jacob leaned down and grabbed onto Rilex, helping him to his feet through the stunned stillness that had come over him. Pyra had the other creature in a tight clash, the two of them thrashing against each other's strength as the warrior slammed the cloaked creature to the ground. Out of the corner of his eye Jacob could see Eden rushing from table to table pulling away the screens that were in front of the hybrid's eyes. As soon as they were freed from the images, the creatures strained harder against their binds. Some hung completely limp and Eden shook them, trying to revive them, though some were far beyond any help that she would be able to give them.

"Help them," another of the hybrids said. "Save them."

"Save them," another said.

Soon the room was filled with the sound of the hybrids' pleas for their help. The words seemed to taunt the cloaked creatures, creatures that Jacob could only assume were members of the Valdicians that Pyra had mentioned when talking about their king. They became agitated, looking around at the hybrids and demanding them to be quiet. One held up a hand toward a panel on the wall and all the hybrids cried out in pain. Rilex was fueled into action, throwing himself toward the creature so that he wrapped his arms around its waist and slammed it to the ground. Eden continued her way around the room, working now to release the straps that held them in place. The three men fought the Valdicians, combining their forces until the two lay in a mound in the corner of the room. Jacob stood, panting at the exertion, and turned his attention to the hybrids.

Eden had managed to release several of them, but they were still attached to the cords at their necks and temples. Jacob carefully pulled these cords away from one of them, cringing when a narrow stream of blood trickled across its skin from where the cords had attached.

"Go get Ciyrs," he said to Eden. "Tell him that we need him down here."

"Wait," Pyra said.

Eden turned burning, streaming eyes toward her mate, a determined expression steeling them.

"No," she said. "We have to save them. Aren't you seeing what I am? Can't you see that they are no threat to us?"

"I know," Pyra said. "But if these were Valdicians, there are more. They are Ryan's servants. Last night Jonah and Oro told me how they got here. They said that the Valdicians took over the ship when they were redirected to Penthos. Ryan communicated with them and told them that we were at the mercy of the hybrids here and would never make it to the planet to help them."

Eden looked stung.

"Why didn't you tell me?" she asked.

"I didn't want to scare you," he said. "You seem to have forgotten that you are my mate, Eden. You are the most precious thing to me beyond my son. No matter what's going on around us, you are always going to be my first priority. I will always do whatever I need to do to protect you and to keep you safe."

Eden stepped up to her mate and he leaned down to kiss her.

"Come with me," she said. She turned to Jacob. "Stay with them, please. Do what you can for them."

They headed out of the room and Jacob turned back to Rilex. He was crouched at the side of the two Valdicians, pushing the hood back so that he could look into its face.

"Rilex," Jacob said. "I'm going to look for another room. Wait here for Ciyrs. Try to get the cords out of as many of them as you can."

The pleas to save the others were still reverberating through his mind and Jacob knew that he had to do what he could for them. There was more to this hidden section of the building and he needed to find it. The Valdicians had come from a door on one side of the room, and a gut reaction sent Jacob to the other end of the room. Just as he thought, he found another door mirroring the position of the first. It opened easily beneath his hand, telling him in Ryan's arrogance he hadn't even bothered to add a lock this far into his compound. The air in this section of the building was warmer still and Jacob felt the tightness of his skin begin to relax.

At first it seemed like there was no sound in this room, but the longer that he stood just inside the door the more that he became aware of a low humming sound punctuated by an occasional chirp like that of medical equipment. The light didn't come on automatically as it had done in the other two rooms and Jacob returned to the first room to pick up the lightstick that Eden had dropped when attempting to help the captive hybrids. He stepped back into the room and adjusted the lightstick to its full vibrancy. The light created a halo of glow around him, but didn't illuminate the walls, indicating that the room was far larger than he had originally thought. He walked to one side until the light he held touched the wall ahead of him. The bottom of the wall looked like a brushed metal trough that rose several feet off of the floor, but beyond that was glass much like the windows from the previous room.

It took only a few moments for him to realize that it was not one continuous window, but rather segments of glass that divided the wall into different compartments. Jacob took a step closer and drew in a sharp breath at what was contained behind the piece of glass just in front of him. Behind him he could hear the heavy footsteps of Pyra, Eden, and Ciyrs coming back through the clean room and into the torture chamber. He barely registered as they called his name and couldn't open his mouth to respond to them. Instead he had been struck silent by the image of a pale woman wearing nothing more than a white sheath seemingly suspended in a standing position as she slept just beyond the glass.

6

"Jacob!" Eden's voice called, growing louder as she came into the room.

She stepped into the light with him and Jacob heard her gasp as she saw the woman in the glass tube in front of them.

"What is this?" she asked breathlessly.

Jacob shook his head.

"I don't know," he said. "I think it's 'the others'. I need more light."

Eden ran out of the room and came back with a lantern. She walked around the edge of the room, illuminating the glass tubes along each area of the wall until she finally found a control panel embedded in it. She spread her hand and touched it to the screen and immediately overhead lights flooded the room. Jacob turned off the lightstick and tucked it into the bag at his hip. He felt horror roll through him as he turned slowly in the space, taking in ten tanks that lined each side of the room.

"This is how Ryan was keeping Aegeus," Eden said.

"But why them?" Jacob asked.

He stepped up to the nearest tank and noticed a small screen on the wall beside it. A series of words and numbers seemed to indicate who this person was and vital details about her, but they were written in a shorthand that Jacob didn't understand. He stepped over to the next tank and noticed something different about her that made dread sink into his belly. Moving on to the next tank only confirmed his suspicions.

"Oh, god," he said, his eyes falling onto the woman's rounded belly. "They're breeders."

Eden's hand came up to cover her mouth and she shook her head.

"He said that he was splicing DNA into adults," she said.

Jacob shook his head.

"He had to get the adults from somewhere. He told you that he was doing breeding experiments."

"He's continuing the experiments of his ancestors," Eden said. "They started the program after they took everyone from Penthos." She was pale and visibly trembling as she stepped up closer to the glass and rested a hand on it. "These are human women," she said. "They aren't hybrid."

"Get Pyra and the others," he told her. "They need to see this."

Eden didn't argue. She turned and rushed back into the chamber where Jacob guessed the men were working to free the survivors. He continued along the row of tanks, doing what he could to check each of the women for signs of injury or distress. When he reached the center of the end of the second wall, he felt a pain tighten in his chest and his stomach drop. He pressed his hand to the glass in front of him, his eyes frantically moving along the face of the woman inside. Jacob knew that face. He knew each of the curves and the softness of her lips. He knew the long, dark eyelashes that brushed her cheeks and the delicate paleness of her skin.

"Phaedra," he whispered. Tears formed in his eyes as he pressed closer to the glass, wanting to get beyond it to the woman who hung there, oblivious to his presence. "How did you get here? What happened to you?"

A moment later Eden, Pyra, Rilex, and Ciyrs streamed into the room followed by two other warriors. Jacob stayed close to Phaedra's tank, needing to protect her.

"We have to get them out," Eden said. "We can't just leave them here. Ryan's gone. They'll die here."

"And even if he wasn't, leaving them in his hands may be worse," Rilex said.

He stepped up to one of the tanks and ran his fingers along the band of metal that differentiated it from the one beside it, but Ciyrs held up his hand.

"We have to be careful," he said. "We don't know what he's already done to them."

Jacob turned back to Phaedra's tank and rested his hand on it again.

"He's right," he said. "Ryan could have them on medications to keep them sleeping. If we wake them up too quickly it could cause serious damage."

"We can't take too long," Pyra said. "We have to get out of here if any of us, including them, are going to have any chance of survival."

"The wounded from the battle will need more rest," Ciyrs said. "They can't carry on yet. They are still recuperating from the healing, especially Jem. We'll need to be here for another night at least."

Pyra nodded.

"See if you can find out what Ryan has them under and how to save them. I'll start a patrol around the entrances to the hospital and start the women collecting as many supplies as they can."

Jacob reached up and touched the screen that contained the information about Phaedra. He hoped that it would tell him something about how to release her. No sooner had his fingers touched the screen than a light inside the tank turned on and Phaedra's eyes snapped open. Jacob gasped and looked around the room. The lights in all of the tanks were illuminating one right after the other, and the women inside were waking. The troughs at the bottom of the wall made a mechanical grinding sound and a conveyor within it began to move slowly. After a few seconds, he saw small square packages appearing on the conveyor, apparently coming out of the wall where the trough attached.

The women moved simultaneously, bending their knees and reaching down to take the packages off the belt as it pulled in front of them. They didn't seem aware of the others in the room with them even though their eyes were open. Once they had the packages, the women sat on the bottom of their tanks and opened the packages, unpacking food that they promptly began to eat in synchronized, systematic movements. After a few moments, the belt began to move again, bringing other containers to the women.

"Phaedra," Jacob said, trying to get her attention. She didn't respond, but reached forward to put her hand through the gap at the bottom of the wall to pick up the container on the belt. "Phaedra," he said again.

When she didn't respond, Jacob crouched down and touched his fingers to the back of her hand. The simple contact seemed to startle her out of the daze that was holding her. Her eyes widened in fear when she saw him and she pulled her hand back, pressing herself to the back of the tank as far as she could go. She whimpered and the sound triggered the women around her, bringing all of their attention to Jacob and Rilex. A few of the women cried out as they all tried to make themselves as small and inaccessible as possible. Those with swollen bellies wrapped their arms around them protectively, guarding the tiny lives within them even though Jacob knew these were not children that had been created in love or that these women would be able to raise on their own.

"Phaedra," he said again, "don't be afraid. It's me. It's Jacob. I'm not going to hurt you. You're safe now."

Phaedra's tense, frightened expression relaxed and she slid closer to the glass. Her hand lifted to touch the window in front of her.

"Jacob?" she asked.

Jacob aligned his hand with hers on the glass and offered her as much of a smile as he could through the fear that was controlling him.

"How do I open the door?" he asked. "How do I get you out?"

Phaedra shook her head.

"I don't know," she said. "They don't let us out very often. When they do, they put a code into the screens."

Jacob stepped back and looked at the glass again, trying to determine how much of it was the actual door.

"Are you attached to anything in there?" he asked.

"Yes," she said. "When feeding time is over it will put me back to sleep and suspend me again. You only have a few more minutes."

"Is there anything in there that could hurt us? Gas or electricity?"

"No," Phaedra said.

Jacob nodded.

"Move back against the wall and crouch down," he said. "Don't look back."

Phaedra did as she was told and Jacob moved back several steps before running up and kicking the glass. It cracked, but didn't shatter. He repeated the assault twice more and finally the glass fell away. He saw Phaedra wince as the shards of glass rained down on her, but she remained where she was crouched.

"Ciyrs," he called. "Come here."

The healer rushed up to him and Jacob repeated what Phaedra had told him. Ciyrs climbed up into the tank and carefully helped Phaedra to her feet, keeping her as far back as possible to prevent her from stepping on the broken glass with her bare feet. He examined her and discovered a set of thin rubber strands connected to the back of her neck.

"Take a breath," Ciyrs said.

As Phaedra did as he asked, the healer pulled on the lines, removing them from her skin. She cried out slightly, but then seemed to give a sigh of relief when she realized that she was no longer attached to the tank.

"Hand her to me, Ciyrs," Jacob said.

"I'm going to pick you up, alright?" Ciyrs said to Phaedra.

She nodded and he scooped her up effortlessly. The glass crunched beneath his feet as he crossed the tank and carefully handed her out to Jacob. Jacob gathered her close to his chest and carried her to the center of the room, wanting to get her as far from the tanks as he could.

"The others," Phaedra said softly. "The others. Please, save the others."

The words were the same as the hybrid's and they sent a chill into his heart. He looked over at Pyra and the other warriors.

"Break the glass," he shouted. "Get them to the back of

the tanks and break the glass. Hurry. They only have a few minutes before they'll be put back to sleep. Ciyrs, get the lines out of them and help them out. Be careful. These are breeders. Some of them are pregnant."

Jacob tucked his head down against Phaedra's and started out of the room amid the sound of glass shattering all around them. He had had enough. He didn't want her to have to see the tanks again. Now that she was in his arms, he wanted her to know that she was safe.

7

"What are you doing here?" Jacob asked Phaedra as he ran his fingers along her skin to check for any glass that might have embedded in her when he broke through her tank.

Phaedra looked at him through eyes so green it was as though they had been chipped from emeralds and rested on the soft creamy velvet of her face.

"I could ask you the same thing," she said. "You were gone. You've been gone for five years. Your mother told me that you joined an expedition in Europe."

Jacob felt the anger burning inside him again. Someone had questioned his disappearance. Phaedra hadn't believed them. She had asked. It was his own mother who had let herself believe that what the company had said was true.

"I didn't," he said.

"Then what happened?"

Jacob looked down at her delicate hand in his and knew that he couldn't explain it to her right then. She was already dealing with too much. She only needed to know that he hadn't left her on purpose.

"I'll explain it all later," he said. "Tell me why you're here. How did Ryan get you?"

Tears were shimmering in Phaedra's eyes.

"I came for you," she said, her voice strained with emotion.

"You did?" Jacob asked.

"I know we broke up a long time ago, but I couldn't stop thinking about you. I know that it doesn't make any sense, but when I heard that you had just joined up with some other excavation and left without coming back to say goodbye to anyone, I knew that it wasn't true. I knew that something else was going on. Nobody would listen to me. They said that you didn't need to say goodbye to me."

It sounded challenging and almost painful for her to make that final confession and he saw her look away slightly as if trying to control her emotions before she looked back at him.

"I would have said goodbye to you," he said. "I never would have left without seeing you again."

"It had been three years," Phaedra protested.

"I never stopped thinking about you," Jacob said. "I didn't want to walk away from you. I regretted it the second I did it."

"Then why didn't you come back?"

"I was too afraid to. The things that I said to you. The things that you said to me. I didn't think that there was any chance that you would..."

"That's why I came for you," Phaedra said. "When I heard that you were gone, I knew that there was something wrong. It just wasn't right. I couldn't get in touch with the company controlling the excavation or even any of the other members of it. It was like everyone had just closed up and weren't even going to admit that you were ever with them." She drew in a breath and let it out slowly. "So, I came here."

"Why?" Jacob asked.

"I remembered that you had studied here and that you still had contacts with some of the people who worked here. I thought that maybe they would have something to do with the excavation and would know more about where you were supposed to be. I went to the History and Anthropology departments first, but none of them would talk. Then I came here. I couldn't remember what you had done here, so I just walked around talking to whoever I found. No one would listen, until..."

Her voice trailed off.

"Until you found Ryan."

Phaedra winced at the sound of his name and nodded.

"He agreed to talk to me. I didn't remember him as someone you knew or who you had worked with, but by that point, I felt like I would have talked to anyone who would listen to me. It had been more than a year since you disappeared and no one had heard anything from you. I wanted to know where you were and if you were alright. It just didn't make sense to me that you would go away like that without even so much as a letter to let someone, anyone, know that you were safe."

Jacob's heart was beating faster in his chest, but he didn't want to express too much of the emotion that was coursing through him. He didn't want to betray what was going through his mind if she wasn't feeling the same things. It was possible that she was only thinking of the friendship that they had had before their brief but intense relationship three years before he left for the excavation when she came to the University trying to find out more about his disappearance. There was something in her eyes, though, that told him that there was more to her determination than just the time that they had once spent together.

"Why?" he asked.

She stared back at him, words that she wanted to say to him hovering there just beyond the glaze of tears that hadn't dissipated since he had freed her from the horrible tank. He saw her lips part and then close again as if she had started to respond to him, but then rethought the words before she spoke them. She started again, but Pyra stalked into the room, startling her.

"What *is* he?" Phaedra asked nervously.

Jacob realized that even though she had been a part of the breeding program for more than three years she wasn't familiar with any of the other species that had been used in the experiments. Somehow that made the situation even more horrifying.

"That's Pyra. He's a Denynso warrior."

"Is he...safe?" she asked.

Jacob could understand why she would ask such a question. Pyra was imposing and did little to try to be less intimidating for those who encountered him. After what she must have experienced as a part of this program, he could only imagine that seeing someone as large and stern as the Denynso leader would be frightening for her.

"He can be loud and is a fierce warrior, but he is above everything the leader of his kind here and those who have joined him. He will do anything to protect them."

"And you've joined him?" Phaedra asked. "Is that where you've been?"

Jacob shook his head.

"I've only known Pyra since returning to Earth. I'm not formally under his leadership, but I consider myself his ally."

"Returning to Earth?" Phaedra asked, sounding shocked. "What do you mean?"

"Ciyrs has informed me that the wounded will need at least one more day to recover from their injuries and the healing process. We will have to stay here until they are ready to get to the shuttles and leave. For now, it's time to get some sleep. We have guards positioned throughout the area and will trade shifts during the night. Men, be prepared for your shift when it arises. Jacob, I'll need you to stand guard at the stairs."

The warrior looked at Jacob with significance in his eyes, reminding him that the others crowded into the two other emergency chambers still weren't aware of what they had discovered downstairs or the women now sheltering in this chamber. It was a testament to the power that Pyra held over these people and the utmost in trust that they gave to him. They were willing to go where he told them and do as he asked without question. While it was unnerving in a way, it was also a comfort to Jacob, reassuring him that the group would be safer and more controlled no matter what decisions they had to make moving forward.

Jacob looked down at Phaedra and she gave him a faint smile.

"Thank you for coming for me," she said.

"Thank *you* for coming for me," he replied.

Phaedra slid down and turned to lie on her side. The position made her hair fall away from her back, revealing the skin to him. Once smooth and beautiful, her back was now marred by deep scars along both shoulder blades. Jacob couldn't withhold the gasp that escaped his lips and Phaedra turned to look over her shoulder at him.

"What's wrong?" she asked.

Jacob shook his head.

"Nothing," he managed to say, offering a tremulous smile.

She settled back down to sleep and Jacob left the chamber, stopping to extinguish the lanterns as he went. He took a deep breath as he left the room, trying to rid his mind of the awful images that the scars had conjured. They were deep and long, standing out against the perfection of the rest of her skin boldly and unapologetically. It filled him with a combination of grief and anger, and he felt like he didn't know how to move forward.

Finally, Pyra approached him, giving Jacob something else to think about to distract him from his torment.

"There has to be more down there," Pyra said. "These women are only part of what Ryan was doing."

"I know," Jacob agreed "There has to be more to the breeding facility than just that room. Whatever else is down there is the cornerstone of what's going on here."

"And on Penthos," Pyra added. "We need to find out what we can. It might help us wipe out Ryan and his army once and for all."

"I'll go back down there," Jacob offered. "During my guard shift I'll see what I can find out."

"There might be more Valdicians," Pyra said.

"I'll bring my weapon," Jacob said. "They won't get past me."

"I'll come with you," Rilex offered as he walked up to them.

Jacob nodded and they started toward the stairs.

"If you need us," Pyra said, "yell. We'll come as fast as we can."

Jacob glanced back over his shoulder at Pyra and nodded once more before he and Rilex began down the steps.

8

———

"What do you know about the Valdicians?" Rilex asked when they reached the door to the false clean room.

"Nothing," Jacob admitted. "I'd never heard of them until today. Why?"

Rilex let out a sigh and shook his head as if he wasn't entirely sure what it was that he wanted to say.

"I'm not sure," he finally said. "There's just something about them. I don't know what it is, but it's been bothering me since I first saw them. I feel like..."

"Like what?" Jacob asked.

"Like I've seen them before. But I know I haven't. There were no Valdicians before I came to Earth and since being here, there have been no invasions or alliances with such a species."

"Did you read about the Nyx 23 mission?" Jacob asked.

"Some, but the sources that I read never mentioned the Valdicians by that name. They would only refer to the enemy army or the enemy species."

They walked through the clean room and observation

room for the torture chambers before stepping back into the breeding facility. The machines were still making their low humming and beeping sounds, the rhythm somehow more ominous now that the tanks were empty. It was as if the machines were taunting them, telling them that it wasn't over. It didn't matter that they had freed the women. It didn't even matter that they had released the survivors of the battle. There were more.

Jacob crossed the room and found another door. Like the one leading into the breeding room, this one was unlocked and he was able to open it easily. It led into a long, narrow hallway lined with doors. Together he and Rilex began opening the doors on either side. As they forced the doors open they found empty chambers that looked like a cross between examination rooms and small efficiency apartments. At the end of the corridor they found a door that was larger than the others and didn't feature the same narrow window. This door had a lock pad beside it and Jacob hesitated.

"It might be linked to the same controls as the first," Rilex suggested.

Jacob tried the door and found it unlocked. He gave a sigh of relief. He had had enough of Rilex's starlight for now. The last thing that he wanted them to do was bring attention to their presence in the secretive section of the building, which is exactly what would have happened with the vibrant light and explosive sound.

When he opened the door, Jacob found himself standing in an office. The rich leather and dark décor of the space stood in stark contrast to the pristine cleanliness and bright white and metal of the rest of the facility. He crossed to the desk and sat in the massive chair. This had to be Ryan's office for when he was spending time in his hidden facility.

That meant that this would be where they could find out any information that might be available.

"Look at these," Rilex said from the far side of the office.

Jacob looked up from the drawer that he had opened and saw the other man standing beside the wall, his hand rested on what looked like a handle embedded in it. Rilex took hold of the handle and pulled. A section of the wall came toward him and he took a few steps backwards to open it the rest of the way. The movable section of the wall was comprised of shelves from the top to the bottom, each lined with files. Rilex turned and pulled on the next section of the wall, revealing another movable set of shelves, it, too, filled with files.

Rilex took one of the folders off a shelf and opened it.

"What is this?" he asked.

Jacob stood and walked over to him.

"It's a file," he said. "It holds papers and information. This is how offices and hospitals and such would keep their records organized before everything started being kept on computers."

"So why aren't these on computer?"

Jacob shook his head and took another of the files from the shelf. He opened it in his hands and sifted through some of the papers. He checked the date on the top and noticed that it was from several years before. He checked another and found that it was more recent. The next was from only a few months before, the next nearly 80 years old. He couldn't understand the organizational method or what the symbols and numbers on the front of each of the files meant.

"Some of these are from long before Ryan was alive," he said, "but there still would have been computers. Why would he go to the effort of taking all these notes and keeping all of this information by hand?"

"Did you see the screens beside each of the tanks?" Rilex asked.

Jacob nodded as he took out another of the files and opened it.

"I didn't understand any of the codes on them," he said. "I thought that they might tell us something, but they didn't make any sense."

Something suddenly occurred to Jacob and he looked up at Rilex.

"They didn't make any sense to us," he said. "Maybe that's the point. Even the most secure and encrypted computers can be hacked if someone knows what they are doing. That means that any information that someone keeps on a computer system, especially one that is in this close of proximity to a research university, is vulnerable to someone else seeing it. If someone didn't want what they were recording found..."

"They wouldn't put it in a computer," Rilex said. "They would write it down and put it in one central location."

"Exactly," Jacob said. "Ryan's experiments are something that he doesn't want anyone to know about. He's gone to extensive lengths to prevent people from finding out what he's been doing. He keeps these files so that he's the only one that can read them."

Jacob's eyes scanned over the top page of the file and then he flipped to the second page.

"We need to go talk to Pyra and Eden," he said, gathering as many of the files he could hold in his arms.

Rilex grabbed a few others and they hurried out of the office and back down the hallway. Jacob's blood was rushing in his ears and his breath was tight in his chest. Suddenly he felt like he had uncovered the reason that he had been drawn here with the others, and what he needed to do.

They found Eden pacing outside of the emergency chambers, gently bouncing Lysander in her arms as she tried to calm the baby to sleep.

"Where's Pyra?" he asked as he approached her.

"He's patrolling the rest of this level," she said. "None of us had gone to the other side, and he wanted to make sure that we are really safe staying here until Ciyrs says that we can leave. Why?"

"We went back down into the breeding facility and we found something that I think both of you need to see."

Eden nodded.

"Let me bring Lysander back in to the women and we'll go find him."

Jacob, Rilex, and Eden crossed the large space carefully, unsure of what they would find as they went. They found Pyra inside what looked like another of the emergency chambers, going through boxes of supplies from one of the shelves. Jacob spread the files out across the floor and explained what they had found to Eden and Pyra. He flipped open one of the files and pointed to the papers inside.

"This is all the personal information about one of the women that he brought into the breeding program. It's not just a few little details, it's everything. Her address, her contact information, her birthdate, where her family lives, her medical history. Everything."

"I would think that he would want to know as much as he could about the women who he was using to breed," Pyra said.

"But there's more," Jacob said. "These papers," he said, pulling out a few sheets from one of the folders. "They have dates on them that are after the medical record sheets from here. This is a lease for an apartment and utility bills. This one is letters supposedly written between this woman and her family. It's just like what the excavation company did about me and the others when we went through the portal. They didn't want to explain to our family that we just disappeared and they had no idea what happened to us, so they made up new lives for us. Ryan was doing that for the women that he put into the program."

"I don't think I'm following," Pyra said. "Why would he need to do that?"

"I didn't have a choice when I went through that portal," Jacob said. "I just disappeared and they had to cover their asses. It's the same thing. These women had no choice. If they had volunteered to become part of the program, their families would already know what was going on and that they were a part of something, even if they didn't know exactly what it was. There wouldn't be any reason for Ryan to fake things like a new apartment for them to live in or letters to the family. The only reason that he would do that is that the women came into the program involuntarily and he didn't want anyone looking for them." He looked down at the files and picked up one. He had been debating with himself whether he was going to show them, but decided that he needed to. "I found this," he said, offering it to Eden. "It's from almost two years ago."

Eden took the file from his hand with a quizzical look.

"What is this?" she asked.

Jacob gestured at it.

"Read it," he said.

Eden opened the folder and looked at the first few pages.

"What the hell is this?" she asked. She looked up at Pyra. "It's about me. He started a file for me."

"In case you came back with my blood," Pyra said. "He was going to force you into the breeding program."

Eden nodded.

"That's why he was so happy when he found out about Lysander. We had handled the breeding aspect for him. We already had what he thought that he was going to have to force out of us."

"None of the women knew," Pyra said. "They didn't know what he was doing to them."

"They don't know anything about the program," Jacob said. "Phaedra didn't even know what you were. If they knew about Ryan's plan, she would be familiar with the different species that he was using."

"We didn't know."

Jacob turned sharply and saw Phaedra standing at the doorway to the chamber. He stood and crossed to her.

"Phaedra," he said, taking her hands. "What are you doing here?"

"I couldn't sleep," she said. "I looked for you at the stairs, but I couldn't find you."

Jacob led her toward the others.

"This is Phaedra," Jacob introduced.

"We didn't know anything about what was going on," Phaedra said without further greetings. "He took me captive when I came here to talk to him about Jacob. I don't even know what happened. I was here talking to him, and then I woke up in a cage. I didn't get much of an opportunity to talk to the other women here, but when I have they've told me similar stories. None of them knew what was happening when they were taken either."

"What's been happening to you?" Eden asked. "What has Ryan done?"

Jacob felt Phaedra step back slightly and shook his head.

"I don't think that she's ready to talk about anything right now. We just got her out. Give her some time."

He felt intensely protective of Phaedra as emotions that he had struggled to keep hidden within him made themselves strongly and undeniably present again.

"We need to tell the others," Pyra said, standing. "These women were slaves. Ryan didn't just start creating new beings. He stole other people and forced them to become his incubators. He's no better than the Covra."

"He's worse," Eden said. "They were only forced to hold eggs inside them. These women were impregnated so that they would carry hybrid children that were likely taken from them soon after birth to be experimented on and trained as weapons, or used for further breeding."

"He held them like he has Aegeus. They aren't a part of this willingly. They don't even know what's happening. We have to protect them."

9

———

Jacob watched as Rilex, Eden, and Pyra gathered the files off the floor and stormed out of the room back toward the emergency chambers before turning toward Phaedra. Her face had relaxed into an expression that was more peaceful than he had seen her since finding her. She looked more like the woman he had loved so deeply and lost so painfully years before now that the edge of pain and fear had eased from her expression.

"They'll help them," Jacob reassured her. "He'll make sure that they get away from this place."

"What will they do?" Phaedra asked. "They don't have homes or families any longer."

"I don't know," Jacob admitted, "but there will be a way. This is over now."

Some of the fear came back and she held his hands more tightly.

"No, it's not Jacob," she said. "It's not over. It's just beginning."

Phaedra's eyes stared into Jacob's and he could finally see the emotions there that he had been seeking. He couldn't deny what was happening within him any longer. Jacob pulled her forward gently and released her hands so that he could touch his to her hips. Still wearing nothing but the thin sheath that she had been in the tank, Phaedra's body felt warm and soft against his.

"What happened to us, Phaedra?" he asked.

"We were on different paths. We wanted different things," Phaedra said. "You wanted to focus on your career."

"I wanted you," Jacob said.

"I wanted you, too," Phaedra admitted softly. "It broke my heart when you left."

"I didn't think that you were ever that committed to us," Jacob said.

"Because we never slept together?" Phaedra asked. "That didn't mean that I wasn't in love with you. I was just..." she looked down at her hands rested on his chest.

"Waiting for the right moment," Jacob said softly. "I know."

They met each other's eyes again and Jacob leaned in to tenderly brush his lips across hers. Phaedra returned the kiss softly, but then suddenly pulled away. She looked at him with tears sparkling on her cheeks and ran out of the room back toward the emergency chamber. Jacob followed and found her standing near the steps, her back turned to him. He could see her shoulders trembling with the force of her crying. The glow from one of the lightsticks sitting on the steps sent up just enough illumination that he could see the scars in her skin.

Jacob stepped up behind her and wrapped his hands around her waist. He felt Phaedra tighten beneath his touch and turned her gently to look at her.

"What is it?" he asked.

"I can't do this, Jacob," she said.

"What do you mean?" he asked. "I thought that you came to look for me because…"

"I did," she said, cutting him off, "but things have changed. It's not the same anymore, and I can't pretend that it ever will be."

"Of course it won't be," Jacob said, trying to pull her closer. "It will be better."

Phaedra shook her head and stepped back from him.

"You don't understand," she said weakly.

"Then make me understand. Tell me."

"You saw my scars," she said.

Jacob nodded.

"Yes. I didn't want to ask you about them."

"Ryan made them," she said. "Before he put me in the breeding program I was part of his early experimentation with DNA splicing."

"DNA splicing?" Jacob asked.

"He learned to isolate the DNA of different species and splice it onto the DNA of adult creatures. Though the bred hybrids are stronger and allow for training from a young age, but splicing lets him transform adults so that they are ready for warfare faster. That way he could have a force of disposable soldiers available that could tire out the enemies or handle smaller operations while his hybrid special forces handle the more challenging missions."

"How did you find out?" Jacob asked. "I thought that you said you didn't know anything about the program."

"I didn't when he first imprisoned me. All I knew was that he was keeping me captive and that I saw others come and some I never saw again. When he chose me for the splicing project I decided I was going to try to figure out what was happening. I was going to escape and help the others." She lowered her eyes again. "He made sure that didn't happen."

"What did he do to you?" Jacob asked, already feeling disgust crawling up his throat.

"In the early stages of his experiments he was working on a particularly rare form of DNA. He didn't have much of it available to him, and what he did have had been preserved a long time ago. He injected several of the people he was holding captive and then just waited for the effect to set in."

"What happened?"

Phaedra sighed heavily, looking away as if she didn't really want to confront the memories that she was reluctantly bringing forward so that she could tell Jacob.

"Two of the men died within a few days. One changed only slightly. I am the only one who changed as much as I did."

"What changed?" Jacob asked hesitantly.

"I grew wings," she said.

"Wings?"

"It took a few weeks, but they grew in right over my shoulder blades. Soon they were almost as long as the rest of my body. He kept me chained by the ankle so that I couldn't try to fly. I don't even know if I could. If I had been able to..."

Her voice trailed off and Jacob drew close to her, kissing her on the forehead and then holding her close to his chest.

"Where are they now?" Jacob asked.

He didn't really want to know. He knew deep within him that he didn't want to know any more of what she suffered, but somehow, he knew that he must know everything to truly do what he was meant to do for Phaedra and the others. He braced himself against what he was going to hear next.

"Ryan didn't want me to have them," she said. "He didn't want a woman to have such powerful features."

"But there are female hybrids," Jacob said. "At least one."

Phaedra shook her head.

"It was a punishment," she said. "He said that it was because he only wanted the male soldiers that he created to have the most powerful features, but I never believed it. He didn't want me to have them. He wanted to punish me for finding out about the project and wanting to escape, so he cut them off. Part of the experiment was to see if the splicing experiment made any impact on my ability to withstand pain."

She didn't have to explain what she meant. Jacob knew and he didn't want to hear the words come from her lips.

"You're safe now," Jacob murmured to her. "I'm here. I'm not going anywhere again."

Phaedra shook her head again and pushed away from him.

"It's not that easy," she said. "I can't just go back to my life."

"You're not just going back to your life," Jacob told her. "I'm here now. We can have the life that we talked about."

"That I talked about," Phaedra said. "You never wanted to."

"I'm talking about it now," Jacob said softly.

"You shouldn't," Phaedra said. "We can't have that life."

"Of course we can. This will be over soon. We'll leave and start again. I can give you that life."

"No, you can't, Jacob." She sounded aggressive and almost angry now, and Jacob took a slight step back. "I wasn't in that tank for no reason. After the splicing experiment, he moved me into the breeding program. I'm pregnant, Jacob."

The words burned through Jacob and he felt them settle into his heart. He tried to respond. He tried to say anything he could to her, but nothing would come. He felt his lips part and stuttering sounds emerge, but he couldn't bring himself to express anything that was happening within him.

"I don't know what type of hybrid this baby will be. I only know that part of its DNA was taken from my wings. I haven't let myself think about it very much. I've always known that as soon as it is born, it will be taken from me and brought to the nursery unit to be raised and trained. There was no reason for me to think..." her words choked off and she took a few seconds to compose herself. "It's my child," she said. "My egg manipulated with hybrid DNA." She paused and stared at Jacob. "Please say something."

He still couldn't speak and after a few silent moments Phaedra gave an exasperated sigh and pushed past him, disappearing back into the emergency chamber. Jacob felt like he couldn't move or breathe. For a moment, it had seemed like his life was falling back into place for the first time since his disappearance. It had been horrible and tragic the way that he had found himself back under the hypnotically lovely and comforting gaze of Phaedra's emerald eyes, but Jacob felt that he could take that horror into himself and transform it into something beautiful for her, a life that would be worthy of her. It was the only thing that was getting him through what he had seen and experienced, and what he feared might lie ahead, but now everything had dissolved around him, falling to his feet like the shattered glass.

The wall of the corridor slammed against his back before he realized that he had turned and slid down to sit on the floor. He pulled his knees up toward his chest and rested his head forward onto one of them, trying to let the frenetic thoughts swirling through his mind process and organize themselves. The pain within him was palpable and he didn't know how he was supposed to move forward. For so many years his heart had been devoted to Phaedra, even when he was stubborn and wouldn't allow himself to admit how much he truly loved her. When he was on the frozen planet it was often thoughts of her that would keep him pushing through the snow and biting wind, and yet in other moments it was the thought of losing her that would make him nearly give up and surrender himself to the elements. He had finally found his way back to her but now she was scarred from years of unimaginable torture and carrying a child crafted purely out of hatred and desire for power and vengeance. Could he withstand watching her through her pregnancy knowing that it wasn't his child that she was carrying? Could he handle seeing the hybrid creature that she would bear and raise it alongside her? Would he be able to love her like he would have before he knew, or was she right and they would never be able to have the life that they had envisioned?

10

"When we get outside, everyone needs to move as quickly as possible," Pyra instructed. "Warriors, carry what women you can. Those of you who are traveling in Jonah's vehicle, go with Oro and Azrael. Everyone else, come with me. We need to get to the transportation bay before anyone finds us. If you encounter anyone who puts up a threat, be ready to fight. We'll come back together on Penthos."

Jacob watched Pyra turn back to Jonah who stood at the door to the closet. There were still several people inside that and one other of the chambers and Jonah's posture spoke to the protectiveness that he felt for them.

"Are you sure that you won't come with us?" Pyra asked.

Jonah shook his head.

"I need to stay here," he said. "There's too much I need to know. Besides, someone needs to be here for these people. They can't be alone."

"They should be coming with us," Pyra argued.

"They've experienced so much suffering, Pyra," Jonah

said. "Their minds and bodies are broken. The last thing that they need is to be in the middle of a war."

"We'll come back for you when it's over," Pyra said.

Jonah extended his hand and Pyra grasped it, pulling him in for a brief embrace.

Jacob was tucking a final pack of rations into his bag when he noticed Phaedra sitting in the far corner of the room. She hadn't spoken to him again in the nearly two days since she revealed her pregnancy to him, and the silence had been brutal. He closed his bag and crossed the room to her.

"Phaedra," he said, but she wouldn't look up at him. "Phaedra, please. Talk to me."

"Is there anything for us to talk about?" she asked quietly.

"Yes," he said.

"Then talk."

"It's time to leave," Jacob said. "We're going to the shuttle."

"I'm not going," she said.

"You can't stay here," Jacob told her.

"Of course I can. I've been here for years."

"You aren't a prisoner anymore, Phaedra."

Her hands touched her belly through the shirt that had replaced the light dress she had worn when he found her.

"Yes, I am."

"You aren't and I won't let you be. You can't stay here."

"All of these people are," she said, gesturing to the others still sitting around the room who had either chosen to say behind with Jonah or were still recovering from injuries and couldn't travel but were well enough that they didn't need Ciyrs with them any longer. "Why shouldn't I?"

"You're safer with me."

"It's better this way, Jacob. I'll leave here and just start over."

"You don't think that Ryan will come after you? That he'll find a way to bring you back?"

"I'll handle that if it happens."

Jacob felt panic rising within him. For the last two days he had been thinking about her, struggling with the thoughts that kept him from getting more than a few hours of sleep and that distracted him from anything else. Jem and Angela were his friends and he would be there alongside them to protect Uoria and everyone who had been threatened, but Phaedra was his reason and he wouldn't let her slip away again.

He walked to the door of the chamber.

"Gyyx, could you give me a hand?" The warrior nodded and came to him. "Will you carry Phaedra? She's traveling with me."

"No," Phaedra protested. "I'm staying here."

"You can't," Jacob said. "You'll be safer with us. Gyyx, please."

He knew that Phaedra would resist him if he tried to carry her and that the warrior was powerful enough that even if she struggled against him, Gyyx would be able to control her until they got to the shuttle. Gyyx hesitated for a moment, but Jacob looked back at him with pleading in his eyes and the Denynso seemed to understand the importance of his request. He leaned down and scooped Phaedra off the ground, carrying her across his shoulders as they left the chamber and began up the stairs toward the hallway above and the dangerous path to the transportation bay.

∼

Phaedra slammed her hands against the window as she watched Earth get smaller and smaller into the blanket of darkness around the shuttle. Tears stung on her cheeks and she felt her hands shaking. Behind her the door to the pod opened and she whipped around to see Jacob standing just inside. The door closed behind him and he took a step toward her.

"How could you do this to me?" she asked.

"I had to protect you," Jacob said. "You should be with me."

"Jacob, I don't want to be protected. Ryan destroyed everything that I ever could be and I will never be able to escape it. I will always be his prisoner."

Jacob swept her into his arms and pulled her close to his body. She felt herself melt into his touch, wanting desperately to believe that the emotion she heard in his voice was real, that there was an escape from the torture and the darkness that had defined her existence since the day that she walked into the University and encountered Ryan. Jacob leaned close to her, sliding his hands down her arms until they grasped hers.

"You are mine," he whispered, "You always have been."

Jacob's lips brushed against her ear and the sensation rippled through Phaedra. Those words carried far deeper meaning than she could have ever fathomed, but before she could say any more to him, Jacob released her hands and she felt his fingers peeling the shirt away from her shoulders. She didn't resist the insistent, dominant touch and a moment later she heard it drop to the floor beneath them. He slowly pulled aside the thinner shirt she wore beneath to reveal the curve of her neck.

Phaedra felt her body trembling as Jacob finally touched her again. Her skin was hot and tingling with the anticipation of more. She could hear her breath escaping her lungs in slow, tremulous waves as she tried to control the nearly overwhelming desire that was coursing through her. Jacob's teeth nipped at her skin but the gesture that had once felt playful now seemed primal and possessive, as if he were overcome by need that had built up within him for the years that they had been apart. She couldn't resist it. She didn't want to. Phaedra tilted her head to offer her neck and felt him bite down more aggressively. Though slightly painful, the bite was followed by the soothing touch of his tongue and Phaedra gave a little cry at the intoxicating blend of sensations.

That sound seemed to touch something deep within Jacob, breaking him from any control that he had managed to maintain. He turned her quickly in his hands, forcing her backwards until she pressed against the wall. Now that he had gotten her into this position, primed and ready for the attention that he promised to lavish on her with the smoldering look in his eyes, his movements slowed again. Phaedra ached for him to touch her, to kiss her, to give her everything that he had left her longing for when he had disappeared from her life so long ago. Jacob stood against her, the pressure of his hips on her lower belly confessing his desire without the need for him to say a single word. His eyes were closed and he seemed to be concentrating on his breath as if to bring himself back under control.

Phaedra wanted to break through that control, to shatter the wall that had always been between them. She longed to savor every touch that he could offer her, to finally experience with him what they had never allowed themselves to, but what she had dreamed of in the long, empty nights without him. Many times they had come right up to that invisible barrier that kept them at once at a distance and yet unable to escape one another. Years of longing, of wondering and fantasizing, of missing him and finding peace and strength in her memories of him, had built inside her and Phaedra was ready to release it. She ached to offer herself to him and hope he was ready to accept it.

Lifting her head from the wall she touched her mouth to the front of his neck, at the same time reaching behind his head to draw the leather band from his hair. His thick hair slid over her hand like silk and she ran her fingers through it luxuriously. He had never had hair like this when they were together and the change was almost unbearably sexy. She continued to enjoy the feeling of the smooth strands on her fingers while trailing small, slow kisses toward the soft dip between his collarbones. When she reached the tender spot, Phaedra let her tongue just glaze across the surface of his skin. Jacob grunted and nudged her forehead with his to make her straighten.

"Phaedra," he said through labored breath.

"Yes," she replied, voicing her consent as much as responding to him.

Jacob brought his hands to the front of her shirt and then brought them down to the hem, lifting it so that he could run his knuckles along her skin. The cold air washed against her, bringing relief from the burning heat that his touch created.

There was no point in fighting anymore. None of the reasons that had ever kept them apart mattered any more. Phaedra could see it in his eyes and feel it in the heartbeat that was seeking her through his chest. Jacob slowly removed her shirt and let it drop from his fingertips onto the floor. She wore nothing beneath it and she could see Jacob's eyes darken when he saw her breasts.

Jacob dropped down to his knees and took her hips in

his hands. He captured one hardened nipple between his lips and drew it into his mouth. Phaedra gasped and buried her fingers in his hair, at once wanting to pull him away to relieve the intensity of the sensation and hold him in place to lose herself in it even further. His mouth moved up and his tongue trailed languidly along her skin until they were face to face again. Jacob caught Phaedra's mouth in a deep, exploring kiss. As timid and brief as their first kiss had been, this kiss was intense and completely consuming. Her lips opened willingly beneath the guiding pressure of his and her tongue welcomed his into her mouth. Their tongues tangled together as the heat between them built to a feverish pitch.

They both sank to their knees, their hands roving over each other's bodies as they shattered the barrier between them and sought all of each other. Jacob wrapped his arms firmly around her waist and brought her down to the floor so that she lay on her back, her head rested on her shirt. Her body trembled as he stretched himself over her.

He was rocking his hips against her, drawing whimpers from her lips as she felt his throbbing erection nudge against her core. Phaedra parted her legs to allow his hips to settle in between them. The position increased the intensity of the feeling that his cock created and Phaedra felt her mouth water at the thought of touching him. She brought her hands frantically to the bottom of his shirt and gathered it in her fingers to reveal his skin. Jacob sat back and removed the shirt, catching her hand and touching it to his chest so that she could feel the rippling of his muscles. He came down on top of her and she sighed at the feeling of their skin touching. She reached down to push her pants off of her hips and Jacob sat back on his knees again to help her remove them.

Jacob paused long enough to look down at her, his eyes grazing across her as if taking in every inch of her and committing her to memory so that he would never be far from her. Phaedra felt lush, beautiful, and feminine in his gaze. The spread of her hips and the fullness of her breasts were no longer a tool to be used, but desirable and fulfilling to the powerful man who hovered over her.

Jacob grasped her damp panties and removed them in one quick movement, following their progress with his mouth until it settled at the apex of her thighs. Phaedra writhed against the cool floor, willing herself to maintain her control. His tongue delved into her wet, waiting folds and flicked across her taut, sensitive pearl. It was a sensation that she had long forgotten, putting the deep pleasure behind her as something she would never be able to enjoy again once she was in Ryan's clutches. She cried out, arching against Jacob and grabbing onto his hair as she pressed her hips further into his mouth.

Jacob's slow, torturous licks were a sharp contrast to the speed and fever with which he had gotten her into this position, but she didn't want to rush him any further. She craved every second of the pleasure as she closed her eyes to savor the sensation. Jacob's tongue swirled gently across her, occasionally dipping inside of her to taste her silky fluids until she felt like she was spiraling toward oblivion. Just as the pressure that was building throughout her body was threatening to take away all her control, Jacob moved his mouth away from her. Phaedra started to protest, but quieted when she saw him sit back on his knees and start to untie the fastenings at the front of his pants.

The muscles in his arms tensed and moved beneath his gold-tinged skin as he released the ties, opened the fabric, and eased the pants off. She could feel his eyes on her face, but her gaze was locked firmly on him as Jacob pushed his pants to his knees. He pushed her legs further apart and moved forward to get the rest of the way out of them.

His body was even more breathtaking than she had ever imagined, even in the privacy of her thoughts. The V-shaped muscles over his hipbones defined a flat, chiseled stomach, and a trail of dark hair led from his navel down to an erection that was impossibly thick and hard. She craved touching him, wrapping her fingers around the delicious-looking shaft and feeling its strength in her hand.

Jacob flattened his palm against her chest and drew it down between her breasts, over her stomach, and back into her core. He stopped just before touching her and gazed down into her eyes before turning his hand so that the heel of his hand rested on her belly and the pad of his thumb dipped between her hot, wet folds massage her clit again.

Jacob looked at her a moment longer as if to confirm the sincerity and desire in her eyes, not wanting to push her any further than she was willing to go with him. She gazed back at him, wanting to express everything that was in her heart but not able to bring any words to her lips. It seemed to be enough, because Jacob leaned down to brush a kiss across her lips and then, still staring into her eyes, pushed into her. Phaedra cried out at the feeling of him sinking deeply within her, stretching her body to accommodate him and cradle him as tightly as she had dreamed of for so many years. Jacob silenced the sound by capturing her mouth with his, crushing her lips tightly and delving his tongue in to further their connection.

He kissed her slowly, exploring her mouth as he held his body still within her. Her walls were tight, almost painful as his incredible size pressed against them. She brought her hands to his back and tenderly stroked the muscles, letting the smooth feeling of his sweat-damp skin calm her. As her body began to relax around him, Phaedra bent her knees to draw her legs up beside his hips. This new position sent him deeper and for the first-time Jacob reacted, closing his eyes and growling deep in his throat.

Running her fingernails along his back, Phaedra gave herself over to the kiss and to the feeling of his body nurturing hers. Her hands dipped along the muscular curve on his back, then onto his butt so that she could grip the firm muscles there. She pressed her nails into his skin and pulled him harder and deeper into her body. Jacobs hips rocked slowly at first, and then built into a steady pace, each thrust sending a wave of pleasure over her. The long buildup made the sensations more intense and Phaedra already felt herself rushing toward climax.

Breaking their kiss, Phaedra cried out his name and dug more deeply with her fingernails. Jacob growled again and quickened his pace. He pounded into her so hard Phaedra could barely catch her breath, but she didn't want him to slow down. Jacob was claiming her with every deep drive and she wanted to relinquish herself fully. Soon he began to grunt with each thrust. His pace built greater and greater intensity until Phaedra felt Jacob slam forward in one final, hard push. His head fell back and he roared with his release, the sound and the feeling of his cock pulsing within her sending Phaedra crashing over the edge into her own earth-shaking orgasm. Her body contracted around him, the muscles through her legs, hips, and stomach tensing almost painfully before releasing into a series of tremors that clutched him, drawing him further into her where she wished that she would never have to let him go.

Their bodies started to cool and Jacob lowered himself carefully on top of her so that he could kiss her languidly.

Finally, he rested his head down on the pile of clothes beside her and they drifted to sleep.

A few hours later she woke gradually to find him looking peacefully into her face.

"I love you, Phaedra," Jacob whispered.

Phaedra felt emotion welling within her and closed her eyes against the tears that were pooling there.

"I love you, too," she said. "I always have."

Jacob slid to his side and ran his hand down her body to rest on her belly. He touched it tenderly, staring down at it almost as though he could see the baby growing within her. Suddenly he leaned down and touched a kiss to the slight swell there. He murmured something that she couldn't hear and Phaedra laughed softly.

"What did you say?" she asked.

"I told our child that I can't wait to meet him and that I love him already."

"Our child?" Phaedra asked timidly.

Jacob looked at her and nodded.

"Yes," he said. "It doesn't matter how this child came to be or what he will be when he's born. I love you, which means that I love this child. We will raise him together and give him the family that Ryan would never have permitted him to have. He doesn't have that power over you and together we'll make sure he never has it over anyone else again."

Phaedra rested her hand to her belly and the other to Jacob's cheek. This was everything that she thought she would never have when she no longer allowed herself to dream. Finally, she could breathe. Finally, she could live.

UNTITLED

To be continued...

THE ALIEN UNCOVERS

1

___

Samira felt a hand wrap around her wrist and pull her out of the stream of people moving from the stairwell toward the emergency chambers. For a brief moment she resisted, worrying about those who had been wounded in the brief but intense battle that had just occurred in the corridor above, but then she heard Ty whispering her name and turned to see him standing in the doorway of a small room down a narrow hallway to the side of the stairs. He smiled at her and gestured for her to come with him into the room. She took another glance at those being carried or helped into the chamber where Ciyrs would attend to them and then allowed Ty to guide her into the room with him.

She turned toward her mate and offered him a smile. As she did he pulled her closer and she rested her hands on his chest, catching the sparkle of the ring of her finger in her gaze. In that moment, she remembered. He wasn't just her mate. He was her husband. The thought filled her with excitement and joy and she rose up on her toes to press a kiss to his lips. She could taste the sweat of his exertion in the battle there and her happiness was slightly dampened. As she lowered back down and looked slightly away, Ty tucked his finger beneath Samira's chin and lifted it up so that she was looking into his eyes again.

"How could this be happening?" she asked him softly.

"You knew what was happening with Ryan," Ty told her. "You knew that there was conflict with Eden."

"I didn't know it was anything like this," she argued. "I couldn't have imagined that coming here for our wedding would have turned into this." She glanced away and then back at him. "We missed our wedding day."

"No, we didn't," Ty said. "We had our wedding. We got through the ceremony. We're married. They can't take that from us."

Samira felt her lips turn up slightly into another smile. Ty was right. Even though they had tried to completely destroy the day by invading the wedding and kidnapping Lysander during the ceremony, the Valdicians hadn't been entirely successful. They had been able to get through the entire ceremony which bound them in marriage, sealing their full and total commitment to each other with the kiss that the hooded creatures had broken with their sudden and horrifying appearance.

"I'm so happy that we're married," she told him. "It means more to me than you could understand."

"I do understand," Ty said. "Bonding for the Denynso is a precious and unshakable connection. It is something that we wait for throughout our entire lives. It is the most important and most meaningful of relationships that we will ever experience, and even though it is not exactly the same among humans, I can only imagine that the emotions that you feel regarding marriage would be as strong. I am proud to be able to give that to you. I'm proud to be the first Denynso warrior to marry."

"Even though your wedding day and the first days of your marriage turned into this?" Samira asked.

"I'm a warrior, Darling. This is the life that I have always led and the one that I expect to always live. Every other day of my life has been defined by war. I've either been preparing the warriors for a battle, engaged in battle, or helping the men recover from a battle, since I was old enough to be out of my training."

"But this was our wedding," Samira said. "This is supposed to be such a beautiful and celebratory time in our lives, and instead of us being able to celebrate with the people who matter the most to us, we ended up in a fight that none of us expected and none of us could have been prepared for. I feel like we put our friends and family in so much danger."

"No, Samira," Ty said, taking her hands and bringing them up to his lips to kiss them tenderly. "You can't think that way. People came from Uoria who had never left the planet at all, much less traveled so far across the galaxy to get to Earth just so that they could witness us getting married. It was an incredible journey for them and truly speaks to how much they care about us and about our marriage. What's happened here isn't our fault. This was all happening long before we planned to come here. Long before we even met. If it hadn't happened when we were here for our wedding, it would have happened at another time. It might have even been worse. You can't give Ryan even more power by not feeling the joy that we should at being married."

Samira nodded.

"You're right," she said. Her heart swelled as she looked

into Ty's eyes, the sight of the color that had once shifted from their natural shade to the deep, rich orange that indicated that he had found her, now completely solid, an unchanging tangible reminder of the connection that they had. "I love you so much and I am so happy that we got to experience this together."

"I only wish that we had been able to get to the reception," Ty said.

"Why is that?" Samira asked.

"I had made you a special wedding cake as a surprise," he said.

"You did?" Samira asked.

Ty nodded.

"Of course, I didn't know anything about human weddings but I wanted you to be a part of the planning and I wanted to do something special for you to show you that I really did care about the wedding and wasn't just doing it because you wanted to. So, I asked Zuri and Eden about weddings and they told me about the cake. They said that it was an important part of the reception and I figured that that was the best way that I could contribute something that was meaningful to you, but also a part of me."

Samira felt tears stinging in her eyes.

"That's so sweet," Samira said. "Thank you. I wish that I could have seen it. I'm sure it was beautiful."

"It was," Ty agreed. "Besides that, it was delicious."

He looked so disappointed at the thought that they hadn't been able to eat the confection that he had created that Samira couldn't help but laugh. Though Ty described himself as a warrior now, Samira knew that that was not how he had always been defined. Though he had trained as a warrior when he was young just as most of the men within the clan did, it had been clear that he was not destined to fight the way that the others did. Part way through his training the Denynso King had identified him as a nurturer, one of the Denynso specifically born to take care of the others within the clan. He had left his training early to become the apprentice of the nurturer of the time. Samira also knew that it wasn't a shock to the others of the clan that Ty would not be the warrior expected of most of the children born into the village. His father had been different, too, though he had died when Ty was still a very small child.

It wasn't until he was an adult that he learned it was not just his talents for baking and cooking that set him apart from the rest of the men in his clan. His blood was not pure Denynso, though no one other than Creia knew it. It was something that they hadn't spoken much about, but it was this very reality that gave Ty the amazing gift of being able to control things with his mind. It had been instrumental in saving the lives of several of those he fought alongside, but it had also made confronting the creatures that had now become their enemies even more difficult.

"I promise when we get back to Uoria you can make me another wedding cake and we can celebrate."

"But it won't be a wedding cake anymore," Ty said. "Would that make it less important to you?"

Samira shook her head.

"Of course not. Anything that you make for me will be special. And then we can enjoy it even more knowing that we are safe."

2

———

Pyra stood back and watched as more injured were brought into the third emergency chamber. There were enough bedrolls and blankets for them to lie on, but some had simply dropped to the floor when they got inside the room and were now scattered throughout the space awaiting the attention of Ciyrs or Elianna. His mind was reeling from what had just happened and his eyes struggled to focus on the makeshift bed that he had just created for Jem. He still couldn't believe that he was seeing the young warrior before him. The Denynso leader and everyone else in the clan had thought he was gone, assuming that when he threw himself off the branch in the reflected realm beneath the Denynso compound on Uoria, that he had tumbled through some unknown space to his death. They had suffered through the loss of him and the emptiness that it had left in the clan for so long now that it had simply become a part of their daily living.

Now, though, he was watching as Jem's face contorted in pain and Ciyrs desperately attended to the deep wound in his torso. Pyra was incredibly thankful that the healer was with them. Though he didn't have all the supplies and amenities that he would in his clinic on Uoria, the items that he had brought with him in his kit would allow him to perform some basic procedures and healing on them. He wished that he could be closer to Jem. He wished that he could be right beside him, helping him alongside Ciyrs. Though he didn't understand what was happening or how the young warrior returned to them, in that moment he didn't really care. All that mattered to him was that Jem was alive and had come back to fight alongside them as they struggled to survive the labyrinth of the medical wing and the laboratory. He didn't want to let him out of his sight again, too afraid that if he did Jem would slip through his fingers and they would never have the chance to find him again.

One of the men who had arrived with Jem came to Jem's side and offered his assistance to Ciyrs. Pyra watched as they worked, feeling disconnected from everything that was happening around him. The only other time that he could remember when he felt more helpless than he did at that moment was when he watched Eden give birth to their son, not being able in any way to help her get through the pain or to ensure that their baby would come into the world safely. In those moments, he had feared for Lysander and for Eden, but there had been a sense of completion as he listened to the baby's first cries. Pyra was freed from the feeling of helplessness by the new sense of responsibility and awe that filled him when he first saw Lysander's tiny face. Right now, Pyra couldn't anticipate the feeling disappearing. He didn't know what the completion of this situation would be or when it would come. There was likely far more ahead of them that they would have to face and it was his responsibility to be strong for everyone who followed him. It didn't matter how he felt or what he was worried about. As the leader of the Denynso warriors, he had to be emotionless and think not of himself, but only of how he would lead everyone else through whatever they would face.

Suddenly his concentration on Ciyrs's efforts to heal Jem were broken by the sound of Eden calling his name. He turned to see his mate rushing toward him.

"Pyra! I need your help."

Pyra crossed the room toward Eden, reaching for her hands as she approached. Her eyes were wide and bright with fear and her delicate hands felt slightly tremulous in his.

"What is it?" he asked.

He felt a sense of panic within him that he fought to keep down. It was not tradition for the leader of the Denynso warriors to feel that level of fear, and it would be unacceptable for him to show it. The room around him was filled with his followers and allies, suffering from injuries that ranged from minor scratches and cuts to those so grievous he feared they may not all survive. The frantic way that she approached him meant that there may be something else happening that he hadn't noticed in his effort to get Azrael into the temporary infirmary, but that may be even more serious than the horror that he was already witnessing.

"We need to go downstairs," Eden said, tugging on his hands in an effort to pull him out of the room and to wherever she wanted to lead him.

"What do you mean?" Pyra asked. "We're safe here."

He knew that this was the only place in their surroundings that would keep them secure. These rooms kept them together and gave them supplies and tools that would help them to defend themselves. It would take time for the injured to recover and while that time passed, they needed to stay there. Eden shook her head.

"No, it's not about us. When I was leaving the hall one of the hybrids that was on the floor grabbed me. It said I needed to save them."

"Save who?" Pyra asked.

He felt immediately suspicious. There had been times when he had encountered enemies after battle that tried to distract the warriors with pleas for help or false claims of help. These moments were dangerous and put everyone at serious risk. Hearing that one of the hybrids that they had come up against in the hallway had gotten Eden's attention put him on edge and began to replace the fear that he was feeling with defensiveness and anger.

"I don't know. It didn't say. It just pleaded with me to save them and said 'downstairs'. Those stairs that lead down, the ones that we noticed earlier, it must have been talking about those. We need to go down there."

Pyra squeezed his mate's hand, trying to relay the emotion that he was feeling, hoping that he was able to convey his reservations to her without having to speak or to communicate with her through his mind, but she continued to stare at him desperately and pull on his hands to guide him out of the room. He held his place and gently pulled her back so that she couldn't get further from him.

"Eden, we can't do that," he told her.

"Why?" she asked, her voice strained with the emotion that she was feeling.

He could see the pain in her eyes. Pyra knew that she was struggling with what she had seen and that it was deep within her to do whatever she could to help the hybrid who had called out to her. It hurt him to see her go through that, but he also knew that he couldn't let her relent to the emotions that the hybrid hoped would control her. He had to use his training and knowledge as a warrior to protect his mate and his child, as well as everyone else who had, willingly or unwillingly, fallen under his leadership.

"That hybrid was created as a weapon specifically for the purpose of fighting against us. Anything that they say to you is just as dangerous as them fighting against you."

"How do you know that?" Eden asked, sounding more desperate, but also now showing some of the fire and abrasiveness that she had had when he first met her. "It was lying there dying. It was asking for help."

"Exactly, Eden," Pyra said. "It was dying. It was taking the last chance that it had to find a way to hurt you. It couldn't do it itself, but it could lead you downstairs where others might be waiting."

"If there were others waiting down there, why didn't they come up when we were spending the night here? Why didn't they hear the battle and come reinforce them?"

Pyra had been accustomed since he first took his place as the leader of the Denynso to others following him without question and giving him respect purely by merit of his station and his size. When Eden first came to Uoria she had been impressed by neither. She had come out of the ship defensive and feisty, resistant to him acting as her escort and guard, and willing to stand up to him in a way that both shocked and aroused him. She had softened considerably in their time together, especially since becoming a mother, but being back on Earth and in the laboratory where her torment by Ryan had started, was beginning to reveal that layer of her again. In any other situation, it might have amused Pyra to experience the fiery woman he had fallen in love with again, but now it only frustrated and worried him.

"I don't know the military techniques that Ryan has taught them. Just as the Denynso has methods and maneuvers, so do these hybrids. Those that were up in the hallway with us had the commands to go up there and fight us. Those downstairs might have been given orders to stay down there until we got there."

"These aren't the Denynso. They have no reason to fight against us except that they were told to. I don't think it was trying to manipulate me," Eden protested. "I really don't, Pyra. It was asking for help. It was desperate. I know that there is something that we need to see downstairs."

"We aren't going downstairs," Pyra said, adding more volume and intensity to his voice to tell her that he was finished with the conversation and that he had made his final decision.

Pyra released her hands and started to walk around her, back into the infirmary so that he could check on the wounded and offer his assistance in whatever way he could. Eden, though, wasn't ready for the conversation to be over. She wasn't satisfied with what he had said, and wasn't going to simply let it go. Showing no hesitation, she stepped in front of him and pulled herself up to the fullest size that her small stature could afford her. Her vibrant orange eyes seemed to spark with the energy that they held and her red hair tumbling around her shoulders made her look wild and ethereal at the same moment. Even though she was tiny compared to him, the sheer strength of her presence and the bond between them held his attention and kept him in place.

"What if there really are people down there who need our help?" she asked.

"There is no help that we can offer them," Pyra insisted. "They are an enemy army, whether they are confronting us in battle or lying in wait for us. We are going to stay right here in these emergency chambers where we are safe and have the supplies that we need to get us through. You are going to stay here and take care of the baby."

Eden straightened even further, nearly rising up onto her toes as she tilted her head back so that she could look into his face. Pyra couldn't help but look at his son strapped to her chest with the makeshift sling she had created for him. He was sleeping peacefully, the warrior blood in his veins keeping him calm even in the aftermath of the battle. It was as if, as long as he could hear his mother's heartbeat, he felt secure and would rest calmly.

"The Klimnu were our enemy army, but we helped them when they needed us. The Denynso have no alliance with the Eteri or the Irisa, but we have helped and connected with both."

"We helped Maxim," Pyra argued. "He is not Klimnu."

"There was a time not too long ago when you wouldn't have argued that," Eden said. "You were ready to kill him, but you changed your mind."

"I'm not going to change my mind this time, Eden."

Pyra was still haunted by the way that he had treated Maxim on Uoria when the younger man accidentally came into contact with the flowers that contained the toxin that started his transformation from Mikana to Klimnu. It had been horrifying at the time, infuriating as much as it was terrifying. They had fought so hard against the Klimnu, battling seemingly endless against the gruesome creatures that had declared themselves the greatest enemies of the Denynso. He had nearly lost Eden to these creatures. Elianna, Leia, and Zuri had all suffered at the skeletal hands of the Klimnu. They were the reason they thought they had lost Jem. He had sacrificed himself to destroy the last two by throwing himself off the branch in Loralia's realm. Seeing Maxim change so rapidly had proven to Pyra that their confidence at the end of that battle had been premature and their celebration next to futile. The Klimnu could come back at any time. It had taken the birth of his son and a fierce admonition from Creia to show Pyra how wrong he had been in that situation and since then he had learned to respect Maxim deeply. Now that he was in the presence of Maxim's father, he was even more remorseful.

That didn't mean, however, that he was going to let his defenses down completely and abandon his determination to stand up against those who threatened his kind or his alliances. It was different with the hybrids. They were not victims of a forced transformation like Aegeus or just another species that was in conflict with the Denynso. They were ready-made weapons, crafted specifically for the purpose of attacking and destroying the Denynso and anyone who was with them. He couldn't just relent because one of the creatures had asked for help.

"You don't have to," Eden said. She stepped back from him and pulled the baby away from her body as she started across the room toward where some of the women had gathered as they waited to hear news about their mates and friends. "I already have." She removed the sling from around her chest and held Lysander carefully toward the Zsilvia. "Zsilvia, will you please take care of Lysander for me?"

Zsilvia looked slightly startled, but held out her hands to take the baby. She glanced in Pyra's direction, but he didn't catch her eyes. At this point he knew that there was nothing that he could do to stop Eden. She was determined and he could only hope that whatever she had wanted to show him wasn't dangerous enough to put her at serious risk.

"Yes," Zsilvia said as she cradled Pyra's son to her chest.

"Thank you," Eden said and stalked out of the room.

For a brief moment he considered following her, at least for long enough to see where she was headed, but then he changed his mind. He could only trust that she wouldn't go into a truly dangerous situation alone. He watched until she disappeared and then turned back to the room. His eyes fell on the man who had arrived with Jem and who had assisted Ciyrs in the beginning of the young warrior's healing. Distrust and suspicion flared within him and Pyra strode fiercely toward him.

3

"Who are you?" Pyra demanded in a low, rumbling voice.

"I'm Jacob," Jacob, looking somewhat unsure of what the Denynso was asking him.

"Who *are* you?" Pyra asked again, more aggressively this time. "You just showed up here with Jem without any explanation of who you are or where you came from or how you found him."

Rilex watched the exchange cautiously at first, but when he heard the fierceness in the massive warrior's voice he crossed the room to Jacob's side. Though they had not created much of a bond since coming together, he felt a sense of protectiveness toward Jacob now that they had found themselves thrown into the battle with these unknown creatures. They were among strangers and he felt a sense of connection, the circumstances drawing them closer together and driving him to defend him.

"What's going on here?" Rilex asked as he looked up into Pyra's face.

"You," Pyra said, his voice becoming angrier as he spoke.

"The two of you, and that woman, showed up here with no explanation."

Rilex immediately hated the way that the warrior was speaking to them. He had been alone and under the command of no one for many years, and even before that he had been among the highest ranking and most respected of his kind. To be spoken to like an inferior was offensive at best and enraging at worst.

"Who are you to ask who we are or our intentions?" he asked.

"I am Pyra, the head of the Denynso, and the leader of this group," Pyra said angrily, his shoulders straightening further as he presented himself.

Rilex felt Jacob tighten beside him and knew that the man was having much the same reaction to Pyra as he was. It was arrogant and pretentious of Pyra to simply assume that his name or his station would strike fear into their hearts and instantly demand their respect and admiration. Though Rilex had read about Pyra and the rest of the fierce, violent Denynso, he didn't feel that he was entirely prepared for what he confronted when he met them. Pyra was rougher, more agitated than he had expected, yet exceeded what he had envisioned with the control that he maintained and the fearlessness with which he had fought. Neither earned him Rilex's unquestioning faith and obedience.

"You may lead the Denynso and even those who have joined you, but we came here of our own volition and without any expectation of loyalty or leadership," Rilex said, trying to keep his voice steady.

"Are you rejecting cooperation with us?" Pyra asked, the threat evident in his voice though he had lowered the volume now.

"We are rejecting nothing," Rilex said defensively. "We

came here. We joined you and fought alongside you in a battle that was not our own. But this was not our intention when we came to Earth. It was never in our plan to encounter a battle or to join an army. We aren't rejecting cooperation with you, but we also don't owe you anything, particularly a promise of following you as our leader."

"Do you have a problem with my leadership?" Pyra asked.

Pyra stepped up closer to him, but Rilex didn't waver. He simply lifted his eyes further to look into at his face. He tried to decipher the emotion in Pyra's glare, to understand what he was feeling as everything happened around him. Even though the Denynso were known for being the most fearsome and brutal of warriors throughout the universe, Rilex had never heard them described as cruel or unfeeling. He knew that even with the aggression and ferocity that controlled him, Pyra had to be experiencing his own emotions toward the sudden battle and the aftermath they were all suffering. It wasn't just anger at the attack or fear of what could happen next. It was the desire to fight, the need for violence and blood, and the determination to eliminate everyone who had threatened him and the people who followed him. A lack of loyalty toward him from Rilex and Jacob wasn't confusing to Pyra and was likely immediately considered a threat. Without them giving their loyalty and committing to his leadership, he felt out of balance and unable to keep the situation around them under control. Rilex felt the need to break the barrier between them, at least enough to reassure the warrior without compromising himself.

"I have no problem with you leading anyone who is willing for you to lead them, but I am not. I have no leader. Not anymore. That doesn't mean that I'm against you or that

I will resist simply for the sake of resisting, but if I agree not to stand in the way of your leadership of those who have pledged loyalty and allegiance to you, you must agree not to stand in the way of my not being led."

"If you refuse to be loyal to us and to allow my leadership, how can I know that I can trust you? How do I know that you won't betray us?"

"I fought alongside you," Rilex repeated. "Being loyal does not have to mean pledging yourself. To truly trust is to acknowledge that a person has no ties and yet knowing that they will still stand beside you. I am nothing but loyal to Jem, yet he is in no way my leader. I don't think it's too much to ask the same of you."

"Jem was dead," Pyra said.

Rilex felt his body stiffen at the sound of the words. They were abrupt and startling, uncomfortable in their raw reality. He had known since soon after meeting Jem that his kind back home on Uoria had no idea of his fate when he disappeared, that they most likely assumed that he was gone forever. Actually hearing someone who had known him better than perhaps anyone express the grief they had felt when they thought him dead solidified the thought and made it painful. It took Jem out of the abstract, the imaginary place where Rilex had put him in his mind so that he only existed on his jungle planet. He had come from nowhere and had no past. It was easier that way, less painful than admitting that there was more to him than the time he had spent isolated on the planet where he found himself after transferring through the portal, that he had a home planet, a family, and friends who thought of and missed him. Thinking about Jem that way was too close to thinking of his own suffering and what he had gone through after transferring through the portal in his own stream so long before.

He started to speak, hoping that the right words would come to him. Before he could speak, however, Eden ran back into the room and up to Pyra.

"I need you to see something," she said.

Pyra turned to look at her, a blend of thoughts swirling in his eyes that told Rilex he didn't know what exactly to think or feel about what his mate was saying to him.

"I told you not to go down there," Pyra said.

Rilex took a step back away from them. This didn't involve him. He didn't need to know what was happening between them and there were others who needed him in that moment. The Denynso healer gestured at him from across the room and Rilex strode over to him.

"Could you please go to the other emergency chambers and find as many blankets as you can that aren't being used. The wounded are going to need to stay warm after their healings."

Rilex nodded and started out of the room and down to the next chamber. Inside was utter confusion, people swarming throughout the space trying to understand what had happened and seeking out information about those who had been injured. Some still didn't know who had been carried into the infirmary and others were struggling to prevent concerned friends and partners from going over there.

"You have to give Ciyrs space," one of the women said as she tried to hold another back. "You know that he can't have everyone in there with him while he's trying to heal them. I'll be going back in there to help and I will make sure that he's alright. Please just stay here, get some rest, eat, and trust us to take care of them."

"Elianna, please," the struggling woman pleaded.

"No," the woman she had called Elianna insisted. "You can't go in there. There is someone in there helping Ciyrs. We're doing everything we can."

"Who is that?" the woman asked. "Who is it?"

Rilex rushed toward her, the desperation in her voice cutting through him.

"His name is Jacob," he said.

"What?" Elianna asked.

"His name is Jacob," Rilex repeated. "The man who is in there helping the healer. He's human."

The woman looked at him, her teary eyes blinking as if she was trying to clear them so that she could look at him more fully.

"You," she said. "You came here with Jem."

Rilex nodded.

"I did," he affirmed. "My name is Rilex."

"This is Zuri," Elianna said. "I'm Elianna. Ciyrs, the healer, is my mate."

"Hello," Rilex said.

It felt like an awkward greeting, strange in the tense situation.

"How did you find him?" Zuri asked. "Where did you find Jem?"

The question didn't sound accusatory as it had when it was coming from Pyra. Instead it was soft, filled with awe and with the slightest hint of gratitude, as if the tall blond woman had no other place to direct her thankfulness at seeing the lost warrior again and so gave it to him as the first person she directly encountered who she had seen near him. Unlike the defensiveness and tension that he had felt when dealing with Pyra, Rilex felt a wave of compassion toward the woman.

"Jem is fine," Rilex reassured her. "He is injured, but Ciyrs is caring for him and he will recover, I'm sure of it. He has always been healthy and strong since I have known him. Though I haven't had much opportunity to spend time with him since we met, I can tell you that he's strong and brave." He paused and searched Zuri's eyes for any sign of comfort that he might have given her. "And he loves his home and all of you. He's desired to come home for as long as he's been gone, but didn't know how to return. Just know that he didn't mean to be away from any of you or for you to worry about him. Returning to all of you is the reason that we're here now."

"I don't understand," Elianna said. "How did you get here? Where has he been if not here?"

Rilex took a breath and looked at Elianna.

"You should go in with Ciyrs," he told her. "The wounded need all of the care and help that they can get. I'll tell Zuri all I know and she can tell you later."

Elianna nodded her agreement and rushed out of the chamber toward the infirmary so that she could assist Ciyrs in caring for the wounded. Rilex turned back to Zuri and saw her staring at him with reluctant hopefulness in her eyes. He gestured for her to follow him toward the back corner of the chamber where they could hear each other more easily. Zuri settled onto a low cushion and Rilex reached up to a shelf above her to get a bottle of water. He offered it to her and she took a long, grateful swallow.

Rilex watched as she tried to calm herself. He was still struggling to wrap his mind around their sudden and deep entanglement in the situation. When he first learned of the trouble on Uoria and knew that he needed to get to Jem if he was able, he thought that it might take some time to get to him. He didn't imagine that he would find them escaping from the museum so soon, or that in an instant they would be thrown into a confrontation that would put all their lives at risk. It had been his intention to notify Jem of what he had found out about Uoria and about Ryan. He thought that he would help the warrior find a way to get back to his planet so that he could help his kind.

Now he found himself fully involved in the conflict and he didn't know what he should think about it. He was conflicted about their involvement in what was obviously a complex and intense war. At once he was concerned about their involvement, unsure of whether he should interfere with long-standing tensions, but also compelled to stand up and fight beside them. In a way, it felt like joining this fight was a way that he could continue to protect his kind even from this unimaginable distance. He knew that he had made the right decision when he chose not to return to his stream with Vyker and Galadriel and instead remain on Earth where he could continue to do the work he had been doing since he had first arrived. At the same moment, however, it hurt him to know that even as he breathed and lived, his kind was long decimated. The stars that hung above them were reminders of them, secured into place by a treasured gift bestowed on the world long ago, protecting the shimmering balls of light from falling when the creature that made them died. Rilex had to remind himself that that was only the reality in this stream, in this existence. Vyker, Galadriel, and the others were safe and alive in their stream, and if he needed to, he would be able to get to them. They were taking care of his kind, fulfilling the role that he had once held. Being a part of this fight could be his way to continue that role here and show his honor and respect for the life that he had left behind.

When Zuri finally seemed to have settled down enough

that she would be able to listen to him, Rilex began to explain how he came to know Jem. He wasn't sure how much he should tell her, if he should wait until he was able to explain himself to more of them at once. He didn't want it to seem like he was being secretive, or to cause any panic or upset among the already distressed group, but he also knew that there was no way to explain Jem's sudden reappearance without fully explaining himself and his kind, as well as the portals that had transported them across the streams. Rilex told her the story in the most basic of terms, knowing that in her state she would likely not remember much of what he had said and that later he would need to tell it all again. When he finished, he paused, giving her the opportunity to process what he had told her so that she could ask any questions that she might have.

Zuri lifted her eyes to him and seemed to peer into him, evaluating whether he was telling her the truth. Finally, she nodded.

"Thank you," she said quietly.

"For what?" Rilex asked.

"For bringing him back to us safely. I'm not Denynso, but my mate, Ero, is, and I have come to love them dearly. Jem was very important to all of us and we've grieved him since he disappeared. Thank you."

Rilex shook his head.

"I didn't do anything," he said. "It was Angela who gave him the confidence to come to Earth so that he could try to make his way home. She is the one who kept him strong and made sure that he got here."

"Do you really think that he is going to be alright?" Zuri asked. "We couldn't bear to lose him again so soon after he got back."

Rilex nodded.

"I know," he said. "I'm going to go check on him. I can look in on Ero, too, if you'd like me to."

"Please," Zuri said. "I haven't seen him since we went up into the hallway."

"I'll check on him," Rilex said. "The best thing that you can do right now is stay here and take care of yourself. Those of us who weren't injured need to be as strong as possible to help the others."

"This isn't over, is it?" Zuri asked.

Rilex shook his head as he stood.

"No," he said.

She nodded subtly as if resigning herself to the reality of what lay ahead of them. Rilex left her and wove his way back through the rest of those clustered in the room. He opened the door to the infirmary and almost immediately a large form stepped in front of him

"It's alright, Gyyx," Ciyrs called from across the room. "Let him in."

Rilex stepped around the enormous warrior to get out of his imposing shadow and then looked at him.

"Zuri wants me to check on Ero," he said. "Could you direct me to him?"

The warrior Ciyrs had called Gyyx seemed to release some of the tension in his shoulders when he heard the familiar names. He nodded and gestured to a man propped against the wall.

"That's him," he said.

"Thank you."

Rilex walked over to Ero and crouched down beside him.

"My name is Rilex," he said. "I just spoke to Zuri and she wanted me to make sure that you are doing alright."

Ero was far smaller than the other Denynso warriors

and had a softness to his looks that told Rilex there was something different about him, but he couldn't determine exactly what. He looked at Rilex and shrugged.

"I could be better," he said. "I should have been able to get around that hybrid. It shouldn't have been able to get me."

"You can't think that way," Rilex said. "Remember that all they have ever been trained to do is fight."

"So have the Denynso," Ero said.

It was the first time that that thought really sank in for Rilex. As much as they had been talking about the hybrids as weapons that had been born and raised to fight, it wasn't until this moment that he made the same parallel with the warriors. He remembered reading about them, learning that these warriors were the most fearsome, most skilled, and most powerful in all the universe because it was their destiny and their duty. It was all they knew. If a Denynso man was born to be a warrior, that was the defining characteristic of their entire existence. They fought because it was their responsibility to fight, but it was also their craving. If he had learned of them when he was in his stream, when he was fighting the battles that had faced him there, he wouldn't have thought there a difference between the warriors and the hybrids that they had just fought in the hallway. They would have seemed the same to Rilex, compelled by the same force, after the same goal. Now, though, he knew that that wasn't entirely true.

"They aren't the same," Rilex said. "The hybrids were crafted as individuals. The Denynso were born. You have families and bonds that tie you together and that give your life meaning beyond the wars. Yes, you are born to be warriors, but warriors aren't weapons. Weapons are instruments, warriors are so much more than that. When the hybrids fight, it is because to them there is nothing more. They don't know a life without training, battle, and violence. They have no love, no friendship, no family, nothing to define them. You can go home after a battle and find solace in Zuri and in the others of the clan. They can't. It's different."

Ero nodded, looking comforted by Rilex's words. Rilex patted his leg and then stood, making his way back over to Jem. He was resting more quietly now, the tension that had been in his muscles when he was first brought into the infirmary gone as the treatments that Ciyrs gave him eased his pain and kept him relaxed. His eyes were open again now and he offered a weak smile when he saw Rilex approaching.

"It's good to see you," Rilex said as he came to the side of the bed that Pyra had crafted for Jem.

He crouched down, his eyes drifting involuntarily to Jem's chest. The deep wound that had been caused by the shard of glass was concealed by the blanket that covered him, but Rilex saw no blood seeping through, which reassured him.

"It's good to see you, too. I'm glad you weren't injured in the battle."

"I'm sorry you were," Rilex said.

Jem shook his head.

"I'm sorry that I got you into all of this. I didn't know that anything was happening."

"I know you didn't, Jem," Rilex said, wanting to reassure the warrior without being condescending to him or making him feel as though he thought differently of him now that he had been injured. "This wasn't something that any of us could have expected, but I'm glad that we were here for it."

"You are?" Jem asked.

"Yes," Rilex said. "It wasn't what you thought that it was going to be. But as soon as I found out what was happening on Uoria, I knew that you would be a part of it as soon as you could be. This is where they were. Your kind needed you and you were here for them."

"But you got involved in something that you have no part of. These aren't your people and Ryan has no issue with you."

"You got involved with Vyker, Galadriel, Angela, and Jacob when you had absolutely nothing to do with what was happening to them. You offered yourself to their service with nothing to go on but knowing that they needed help. All they had to do was tell you what they were going through and you were right there for them. You didn't ask questions or try to justify anything. I am honored to do the same for you."

Jem smiled, but then his eyes flickered over Rilex's shoulder as if seeing someone that was approaching. Jacob appeared at his side and Rilex shifted slightly to give him space.

"How are you feeling?" Jacob asked, his eyes scanning over the blanket covering Jem in much the same way that Rilex's had.

"Tired," Jem admitted. He shifted his weight as if to get more comfortable, but winced slightly as the exertion either exhausted him further or caused him new pain. "Ciyrs's healings are phenomenal, but they take a lot out of you."

"So, he's healed you before?" Rilex asked.

Jem nodded. The revelation was uncomfortable for Rilex in a way that he couldn't quite understand. He knew that Jem had been involved in wars before, and that meant that he was likely to have been wounded, possibly even more severely than he was now. Hearing it, though, forced

Rilex further into accepting the reality that was Jem's existence before he met him the night Galadriel arrived back on Earth.

"This isn't the first time that I've been wounded in battle," he said, confirming Rilex's unpleasant thoughts. "It will likely not be the last." He chuckled more to himself than to the others, almost as though he was reacting to a memory that had suddenly come to his mind. "And Ciyrs will be there again."

As if the conversation had taken all of the energy that he had summoned, Jem's eyelids started to droop and his head turned slightly to one side.

"You rest," Jacob told him, lowering his voice so that he didn't jostle the warrior out of his impending sleep. "When you are ready, I'm sure Angela will be beyond relieved to see you."

Jem was already nearly asleep, but he gave a slight nod. Jacob waited until Jem's breath was even and deep, and then turned to Rilex. He gestured for Rilex to follow, and Rilex climbed to his feet to comply. He didn't want to leave Jem's side, especially now that the intensity of the injury seemed to be pulling him back into sleep, but there was something in Jacob's eyes that told him there was something important that the younger man needed to tell him.

"I need you to come with me," Jacob said. "Eden found a door downstairs and it's locked."

4

Samira ran her hand down the side of Ty's face, her heart starting to tremble in her chest as the adrenaline of the battle that they had just fought melted into the desire that she felt for her new husband. Talking about their wedding and his words about their marriage had only intensified what had already been on her mind since she realized that they were alone together in the room. She pushed all thoughts of the battle out of her mind and focused on her husband in front of her. She didn't want to think of anything else but him.

"You know," she said, running her fingertips along the side of his neck. "All this talk about our wedding day has me thinking about something else."

"What?" Ty asked her.

Samira smiled up at him mischievously.

"Our honeymoon," she said.

"What is a honeymoon?" he asked.

"Of everything that you learned from the others about human weddings, nobody told you about honeymoons?" Samira asked.

Ty shook his head.

"No. I don't think that anyone mentioned that word. What does it mean?"

Samira pulled up a little closer to him. She was much taller than the other human women who had come to live on Uoria with the Denynso, but the massive size of the Denynso men still left her considerably smaller than Ty. She felt small and delicate in his arms, a feeling that she hadn't had the opportunity to feel very often in her life, and one that she loved.

"A honeymoon is a trip that newlywed couples go on to celebrate their marriage," she told him. "Usually it happens right after the wedding and the couple goes somewhere special together to spend some time alone. The wedding night is particularly special."

Her voice had dropped to a soft whisper, but she knew that Ty heard every word that she said to him. His body was already responding to her and she felt her stomach trembling at the feeling of his erection hardening against her.

"I know that we missed our actual wedding night," Ty said, "but maybe I can make it up to you."

He ducked his head down and caught her mouth in a tender kiss.

Samira parted her lips, welcoming his tongue into her mouth and sighing at the incredible taste of him. She wished that she had had the opportunity to taste the cake that he had baked for her, for their wedding. In the days leading up to the ceremony she had dreamed of feeding him a bite of their wedding cake and then tenderly eating a piece from his fingers. Though she hadn't known that it would be a cake that he had created especially for her, she had fantasized about the way that the sweet icing would taste in contrast to his skin as she licked it from his fingertips. Her hands wrapped around Ty's neck and then slid around to the front of his shirt, working their way down the laces and pushing the neckline open so that she could slide her hands beneath the fabric and touch his smooth, chiseled body.

After a few passionate moments, she pulled her mouth away from his and moved it down to the side of his neck. She kissed along his neck as she ran her fingers along the muscles of his sides. The taste of his mouth on hers and the feeling of his body promising her all of the pleasure that she had been aching for since before they left Uoria washed away everything that the battle had put into her mind and she surrendered herself to the bliss of just being with Ty. He was nothing short of irresistible to her. She wanted to touch every inch of his body and feel the warmth of his skin against hers.

Unable to hold back her craving for him any longer, she let her mouth progress further down until it found his collarbone, pausing only for a few seconds to dip the tip of her tongue into the soft spot between the bones. She then moved to his chest, gradually letting her fingers leave the path that they had been following and trace along the deep groove of the muscles at his hips until she reached his waistband. She looked up at Ty, wanting to express her intention and desire to him, and to see his in the rich orange depths of his eyes. Instead of saying anything to her, Ty rested his hands on her hips and moved back a few steps so that his back rested against a set of shelves along the wall. Once in place, he brought his hands to the front of his pants and released the ties that held them closed. Samira continued to stare unwaveringly into his gaze as she lifted her hands to join his. Her touch encouraged him to move his hands away and allow Samira to open his pants the rest of the way. Ty's delicious-looking, impossibly hard shaft sprang out into her hand and Samira's breath caught in her throat. She felt her mouth water as her palm glided along his warm, velvety skin and discovered the trickle of slick fluid that had slid from the slit at the tip.

Samira drew her fingers up and down his hard length several times, her arousal rising as she watched his breath deepen and his head fall back against the shelves behind him. Finally, she felt his hand cup behind her head and ease her down so that she could lean forward and run her lips along the head of his cock. Samira wrapped her hand more tightly around the base and parted her lips so that he slipped into her waiting mouth. Ty felt and tasted even more luscious than he looked and Samira moaned, bringing her body forward so that she could draw him deeper across her tongue.

Ty didn't hesitate to show her exactly what he wanted. His hand tightened slightly and he guided her gently, rolling his hips slightly in conjunction with the movements until she assumed a smooth, steady rhythm. There was nothing forceful or controlling about the way that he was leading her. Instead the dominance was thrilling, and made Samira want him even more. Ty's eyes closed and she heard a groan from deep in his chest. She rewarded the sound by adding her hand, stroking him with each long suck so that there was never a part of his engorged cock she wasn't touching. Craving even more of him, Samira increased her intensity and Ty released an even louder groan and pressed his hips closer to her. He thrust his hips more quickly and started to pull away from her, but Samira grabbed his hips and held them tightly to prevent him from moving away from her. He gave in to her insistence and continued to roll his hips as she sucked him until suddenly she felt him tighten and heard him cry out just as he spilled into her mouth. Samira sighed and swallowed luxuriously, letting her tongue glide around him softly to remove every drop of the delectable streams and stroking him slowly to ease him down from his climax.

Samira straightened and found Ty smiling lazily at her. As soon as their eyes met the intensity returned to his expression and he reached forward to guide her head toward him again and crush his mouth to hers. He kissed her deeply but without urgency. He was still recovering from his orgasm and it would take time for his body to be ready for her again, but Samira didn't need to rush him. She wanted every moment, every delectable second. His mouth moved slowly across hers as he started to rebuild the arousal within his body. She felt Ty's hands move along her body and find the bottom of her shirt. He inched the hem of her shirt up out of her waistband and slipped his hands beneath it so that he could flatten his palms onto the sides of her ribcage. Samira felt his thumbs brush along the underside of her breasts and drew in a breath at the incredible power of just that simple contact.

The kiss ended and Ty pulled her shirt off over her head, tossing it aside. She mirrored him, pulling his shirt off and letting it fall to join hers on the floor at their feet. His hands returned to the dip of her waist and she felt her skin shiver under the warmth of his skin. Her body eased forward so that her breasts crushed against him. It was a slight taste of what she had been needing, and it only increased the desire that swelled within her chest and belly. She took a step back away from him and released the button on her pants, taking hold of her zipper and guiding it down. Ty's eyes watched her hungrily and she moved slowly, letting each of her suggestive movements tantalize him further. Finally, she was standing bare in front of him and she saw him stepping out of the pants that had fallen to his knees.

Samira took another step back so that Ty could see her fully and ran her hands down along her own body. She didn't move her eyes away from him, wanting to see his reaction to her exploring herself, suggesting to him what he could be doing to her. Her breasts felt full and succulent in her hands and she felt the hardened peak of one nipple beneath her palm. Samira gave a slight squeeze and saw Ty's nostrils flare slightly. Biting into her bottom lip, Samira ran her fingertips down along the center of her belly until it reached the quivering flesh between her hipbones.

Her fingers had just dipped into her folds when she saw Ty's hand run down his belly onto his hardening cock. He stroked slowly, watching her cautiously swirl her fingertips into her peak. A shudder of pleasure rolled through her and Samira sighed. Ty was fully hardened again and he reached out to cup her butt with his other hand, squeezing gently. In one swift movement, he turned her around so that her back was to him. His hand moved around to her belly and he pulled her back against him so that Samira could feel the pressure of his erection nudging against her. They turned around until she was facing the shelves.

Ty's hand flattened on the middle of her back and guided her forward so that she leaned with her hands gripping one of the shelves and her hips pushed back toward him. The cool air of the room rushed along her hot, wet core, but the vulnerable feeling only increased Samira's excitement and she pressed her hips back with more insistence. Ty's hand left her back and she heard him lower to his knees on the floor behind her. An instant later she felt his tongue delve between her thighs. Crying out at the intense feeling, Samira rose up onto her toes. Ty grabbed onto her thighs and eased her legs further apart. His hand slipped between her thighs and flattened in the valley between her hipbones so that he could guide her hips back even more until her back was nearly flat.

The position opened her to Ty and he took the invitation enthusiastically. His tongue played across her and she sagged forward, feeling her control disappear. She released the shelf with one hand and reached back to bury her fingers in his thick white hair. Her head dropped back, giving herself over completely to the sensations he was creating in her.

Just as Samira was spiraling toward oblivion, Ty stopped and climbed to his feet. Ty ran his fingernails lightly down her back from her neck to her hips, giving her an unusual, but intoxicating feeling. A moment later she felt him reverse the trail with his tongue. His hands came forward to cup her breasts in his palms, and then one traveled down her stomach to the apex of thighs so that he leaned over her, fully engulfing her with his presence. He applied pressure with his fingertips as he swirled them into her swollen clit. An instant later he was inside her and she was gasping for breath, struggling to control the overwhelming experience as he filled her. The familiarity of him within her was breathtaking and brought tears to her eyes. Though it was not the first time that she cradled him with her body, it was still indescribable to feel as though she was welcoming him, accepting him as their bodies came together to worship each other as they were crafted to do.

Instead of withdrawing and plunging into her again immediately, Ty pressed close and rolled his hips just enough that his hard length nurtured her while keeping her hips nestled tightly back into him. He leaned forward to cover her body with his and kissed her shoulder tenderly before bringing his lips to the soft place just beneath his ear.

"Turn around," he whispered in her ear and carefully withdrew from her.

Samira turned to face him and Ty swept her into his arms. She tucked her hips against his and wrapped her legs around his waist so that she was completely in his hands. Their mouths met again, their tongues tangling as he guided her around and lowered himself to his knees on the floor. He rested her back onto their clothing and then fell forward so that he came down over her. Ty kissed his way down her body until his mouth closed over one breast. Though she would have liked for him to pause there longer, teasing her nipple with his tongue, Samira's disappointment disappeared as he continued down her body and positioned himself between her legs. He dipped his head and ran his tongue through her folds again.

He ran his tongue along one side of her core and then the other, seeming to purposely avoid her clit. When he had traced all of her folds, he finally reached her intensely sensitive peak. One flick of the tip of his tongue caused her back to arch and her thighs to tremble. She knew she wouldn't be able to control herself much longer when he stopped and rose back up to stare down into her eyes. He groaned deeply as he eased into her again.

Samira bent her knees so that just the tips of her toes touched the floor, opening herself to him completely. Ty reached down and cupped one hand around her hip, holding her tightly so he could thrust into her faster and harder. She clung to him, digging her fingers into his back and letting the sounds pour out of her with abandon as they gave themselves over to each other and let their bodies meld and their hearts reach toward one another. Ty tucked his head down into the curve between Samira's neck and shoulder, further increasing his intensity until she could feel herself climbing toward climax. His sounds deepened into primal grunts that belied his generally gentle, quiet nature. He sped up more until he suddenly slammed into her with one hard, intense thrust. She felt him throb as he filled her, then Ty grunted and drew in a strangled breath.

Samira cradled him close as he released the tension in his hips and began to slowly roll into her with greater focus. The depth pushed her over the edge so that she crashed around him, and Samira wrapped herself around his body, holding Ty as close as she could as she lifted her hips to meet each of his gentle strokes and rode out her climax. When they were both fully satisfied, Ty guided her back down to lie on the floor and dipped his head. His mouth covered one breast and his tongue lightly traced around the nipple before he moved over to the other to lavish the same passionate, adoring attention. She tenderly licked sweat from his shoulder and wrapped her legs around the backs of his thighs to keep their connection as close as possible.

She didn't know how long they had been lying there, enjoying the warmth that radiated off of them, but finally they both knew that they had to drag themselves from the blissful peace of one another and return to the reality of what awaited them outside of the chamber. Ty groaned as he pushed away from her and then reached down for her hands. Samira offered them to him and reluctantly let him pull her up off the floor. He gathered her against him for a final kiss before they both reached down for their clothing and started to redress. Samira watched Ty as he guided his pants up, wanting a final glance at his immaculate body before it was concealed away from her again. When he had tied them into place, she relented and pulled her own pants on, leaning back against the shelves for balance as she straightened a cuff that had twisted. She was lowering her foot back to the floor when her hand slipped and hit a box.

The box tumbled from the edge of the shelf and fell, scattering slim metal files across the floor. Ty crouched down to look at the files as she finished dressing and she noticed a strange look on his face as he glanced at several of them.

"Did you look at these?" he asked.

"No," Samira said, smoothing her hair. "What are they?"

"They look like the file that Jonah found in the examination room upstairs," he said.

"Do they have names on them?" Samira asked, lowering to her knees and reaching for one of the files.

"Yes," Ty said. "Etan, Grayson," he said, stacking the files in front of her as he read off the names. "Brendan, Amelia, Emerie."

Samira felt her chest tighten as she looked at the file in her hands and saw the name etched on the front. Her eyes lifted to Ty and she held the file out to him.

"Rain."

5

Ryan hissed as the Valdician finished stitching the long gash along his arm and started wrapping it tightly in a bandage. His body stung and burned with the injuries that he had sustained in the laboratory and each time that one of his servants dressed one, the anger within him increased. This wasn't the way that this was meant to turn out. This was not how his plan was supposed to unfold. He was supposed to have Pyra in his grasp by now, with Eden and their offspring a bonus, not sitting in his safe house being mended and wondering what his next step should be. The attack by so many of their kind and by creatures that he didn't even recognize had been unexpected, something that was outside of his control, and Ryan hated to ever feel like he wasn't in control.

The only solace that he had as the creature turned to another of his injuries and began to clean it with the stinging, harsh-smelling liquid, was that the hybrids had been released and the battle had begun. The thought of the swarm of hybrids taunting the rogue group, forcing them through the maze that he had created with the locks in the laboratory building, and then ushering them onto the unintended battleground brought a hint of a smile to his lips even through the grimace of pain. The look on the faces of the people on Penthos had made even the wounds and the frustration at the fracturing of his plans worth it, at least for a moment. The shock in Maxim's eyes when Ryan told him that his father was still alive and the promise of a war on Penthos that they would never be able to win filled him with a sense of vengeance and justice. He had been waiting for so long for this moment to happen, so long to finally bring down Uoria and achieve the goals that his ancestors had had so long ago. Soon he would have all the DNA that he could ever want and would be able to craft an army that no one, not even the mighty Denynso or the mercenaries that fell into step so willingly behind them, would be able to defeat.

A sound behind him brought Ryan's attention from the section of the wall where he had been staring, trying to distract himself from the suffering of the stitches and disinfecting wash. Another Valdician had stepped into the room with him and was now standing just inside the door, seeming on edge as if he wanted to be ready to escape the room at an instant's notice if he needed to. Ryan stared at him expectantly, but the creature didn't say anything. Nervous sounds came from the recesses of the black hood that he wore, sounding like he was trying to get words out but couldn't quite form them.

"What is it?" Ryan finally demanded. "If you came in here when I specifically asked not to be disturbed, you must have something important to say to me, so get it out."

The Valdician took a step toward him, then retreated back to the space that he had assumed when he first stepped inside.

"The battle is over," he finally said.

Ryan stood, excitement bringing him to his feet.

"It is?" he said. "That went faster than I had even anticipated. My hybrid's training must be..."

"They were defeated, Sir."

Heat burned across Ryan's face and he felt his hands begin to shake.

"Excuse me?" he said.

"The hybrids, Sir. They were defeated. There were very few survivors."

"And the rogues?"

"They were all alive when they left the hallway."

"The hallway?" Ryan asked.

The Valdician took another step back away from him and Ryan knew that he had something else to tell him that would infuriate him even further.

"Yes," the Valdician said hesitantly. "The main front hallway of the laboratory."

"What do you mean, the main hallway?" Ryan asked. "That is not where the battle should have been fought. How did they get there? The locks should have kept them on the predetermined path and brought them to the meeting room."

"They discovered the medical ward."

Ryan felt a surge of anger within him. Spots danced in front of his eyes and he felt violent urges rushing through his veins.

"How did that happen?" he asked.

"My contact doesn't know," the Valdician said. "He could only tell me that the entire group is now in the abandoned wing." He hesitated for another few moments. "Eden found the breeding facility."

Fury burned painfully in Ryan's belly, threatening to

burst out of him. The ancient medical building had been concealed within the laboratory since long before even Ryan was alive, containing the core of the experiments that his family had been carrying on for so long. It was him, however, that revolutionized the space, creating the breeding facilities and outfitting them with the most advanced technology that existed, technology that he developed himself or modified into exactly the purpose he needed so that he could carry through with his experiments without being detected. He didn't understand how Eden could have uncovered the building that had been forgotten for decades, but even finding the medical ward didn't explain how she got into the breeding facility. The lock on the door to the facility wasn't attached to the master controls of the rest of the building and the code to the facility was only known by him.

Ryan slammed his fist into the wall, feeling the bones in his hand crunch, but not caring. He was too infuriated to care. His hatred for Eden was reaching a delirious peak and he felt himself losing grip on the control that he had forced himself to maintain when he was within close enough proximity to finally destroy her. He thrashed angrily around the room, knocking items off the shelves and table as he let out roars of anger. Suddenly he noticed that the Valdician who had come into the room to tell him of the battle was still standing in the same place just inside the door.

"What?" he demanded, taking a long stride toward him. The creature didn't say anything and Ryan stepped up closer to him. "What?"

"Eden brought some of the others into the breeding facility with her," the Valdician said. "Several arrived after you left the laboratory."

"Who?" Ryan asked. "Others from Uoria?"

"Some of them," the Valdician said. "But there are three who are not any of the species from Uoria. Two are human."

"Are they from the settlement?" Ryan asked.

The Valdician shook his head.

"My contact says that they do not fit the records of any one from that settlement. They do not seem to have traveled from Uoria with the others."

"So where did they come from?" Ryan asked.

"None of us knows."

"You said that there were three who were unaccounted for. What about the third?"

"That's the thing," the Valdician said cautiously. "My contact isn't sure."

"What do you mean he isn't sure?"

"The man doesn't fit with any of his species recognition references, except for one, but it's impossible."

"Why is it impossible?"

"None of us have ever seen this species before," he said.

"There are many species we haven't seen," Ryan argued.

"But we know that those species are real, that they do exist."

"I don't understand what you're trying to tell me," Ryan snapped. "Why don't you stop speaking in riddles and just tell me what it is about this man?"

"If the recognition references for my contact are correct, this is a species that hasn't been alive for many, many years. It is a kind that you searched for, for many years, but never thought that you would never find. One with no name."

Ryan's eyes widened and the anger that he had felt drained away.

"No name," he said.

The Valdician nodded.

"If it's true..."

Ryan smiled, no longer caring that the battle had been lost or even that Eden had uncovered the facility. If what the Valdician contact still at the laboratory said was accurate, it changed everything. He had hungered for that species ever since he taken up the legacy of his great-grandfather, but no matter how extensively he had researched, no matter how far he sent the missions out into the galaxy to search, he was never able to find any of them. Over the years, he had relented to the fact that this species was gone, eliminated from existence generations before. He would never find them. Now, though, there was suddenly a chance that everything he had put into his searches, all of the time and energy and resources that he had devoted to uncovering this species was not in vain. He could be close to capturing a species of unimaginable power, one that carried potential for his hybrids that none could fathom.

"Should we prepare to go back to the laboratory, Sir?" the Valdician that had been working on his injuries asked. "We could stop them."

Ryan thought for only a moment before he shook his head.

"No," he said, then turned away, returning to his chair. "No. We'll keep going as planned. I'll orchestrate the war on Penthos from here and allow the hybrids to continue their duty at the laboratory. The Valdicians there have my instructions and can regroup."

"What about the breeding facility?" the Valdician asked. "What about what Eden and the others uncovered? Aren't you concerned that she will reveal you?"

"Eden?" Ryan asked with a scoff. "No. She thinks she is far more intelligent than she truly is. She might have found the facility and they could have defeated the first wave of hybrids, but they won't get out."

"And if they do?"

"Eden fancies herself a Denynso now," Ryan said. "She isn't thinking about the Earth authorities or what it would mean for them if she did reveal what I was doing. All she cares about is Uoria and the creatures that she has aligned herself with. There's nothing that she can do. No matter what they think that they have found, they will never be able to break down the entire program. They have only uncovered one small piece. What I have accomplished goes far beyond anything that they know now or will ever know."

Ryan settled back down into his chair and looked around him at the aftermath of his violent reaction to Eden's discovery. Laughter started bubbling up in his throat and tickling the backs of his lips. It escaped and poured out into the room, reverberating off the walls as the two servants began to move slowly around the space, cleaning up the wreckage and returning the room to the way it had been. Soon it would be like it had never happened. Soon his mind could restructure the minutes that had passed, manipulating them into what he wanted them to be so that when he looked back he could tell himself the story that he wanted to tell, just like with everything else.

6

———

"Have you seen Jonah?" Ty asked Oro.

The warrior looked at him and shook his head.

"Not since the battle. What's wrong?"

"I just need to talk to him."

"I'll let him know if I see him."

Ty walked back out of the room and shook his head at Samira, who stood in the hallway holding the files that they had found in the smaller room.

"Try the other chamber," she told him.

Ty walked into the first of the three rooms and scanned everyone crowded into the space until he found Jonah. He crossed to him and touched his back to get his attention.

"Can you come with me for a minute?" he asked.

Jonah looked at him strangely as if he was unsure of whether he should go along with the Denynso. After a few seconds, he relented and followed Ty out of the chamber and back to Samira.

"What is it?" Jonah asked.

"There's something we need to show you," Samira said.

She took a few steps backward in the hallway that led away from the emergency chambers and Ty followed, holding his lightstick so that Jonah could see what she was holding in her arms.

"We found these," Ty said, picking up one of the files and holding it out toward Jonah. "It looks like the file that you found in the examination room."

Jonah took the file from Ty's hand and examined it. Ty could see his eyes grow wider as he read the name on the front. He reached for another of the files and read its name before lifting his eyes to Ty and Samira.

"Where did you find these?" he asked.

"I'll show you," Ty said.

He started down the hallway and guided Jonah into the room where he had brought Samira when they first left the battle. He had craved her so intensely when they got back down into the basement that all thoughts of the battle and the dire situation that surrounded him had disappeared into the passion that he felt for his new wife. There was a sense of guilt, as though his need for her was just a confirmation that he wasn't made to be a warrior. Now that they had these files, though, he knew that he couldn't think of that guilt any longer. Whatever the reason they had been in that room, it had enabled them to find these files and bring them to Jonah. Ty didn't know why, but these files were important. They had something to do with the one that had Jonah's name on it that they found in the examination room above them, and Ty couldn't rid his mind of the suspicion that there was a strong link between them and what had been happening to them even before they left Uoria for Earth.

"These are all members of Nyx 23," Jonah said.

Ty nodded.

"I thought so," he said. "I recognized Rain and a couple of other names. What are these?"

"They're just like mine," Jonah said, pulling a few more of the files from Samira's arms into his hands and reading their names. "They're medical files. These are the records the doctors kept for everyone involved in departments that involved intergalactic travel. Especially then, when there was far less known about traveling such far distances from Earth for long periods of interaction with the different environments and the effects that it might have on the human body, anyone who was involved in research, exploratory, or humanitarian efforts had to be kept to very strict health regulations. Before and after every mission we underwent examinations and tests to ensure that we were healthy enough to travel, and then that we hadn't suffered any serious effects from the trip."

"Why would your files be down here? Wouldn't they store them with the rest of the patient files for the doctor?" Samira asked.

Jonah shook his head.

"There was a specific doctor who worked with the Nyx 23 crew. Like I said, it was a clandestine mission. The entirety of the department wasn't involved and there was a possibility that what we were doing wasn't entirely legal."

"What do you mean?" Ty asked.

"Since we were technically affiliated with the University even though we weren't an academic department, we had to have approval of the larger department head any time that we were going to do a mission, especially when it would require experimental technology. When we first uncovered the uninhabited planet and started suspecting that there was an illegal prison colony, it was not a popular idea."

"Not everybody believed it?" Samira asked.

Jonah shook his head.

"No. Some of the original team thought that we were overreacting and seeing things that just didn't exist."

"How did you find the planet in the first place?" Ty asked. "You said that it was uninhabited. What brought your attention to it?"

Jonah paused as if thinking about the question.

"I don't really remember," he said. "I know that someone brought it up, pointing out that it was a decent-sized planet that hadn't been properly classified."

"Classified?" Ty asked. "What does that mean?"

"There was an initiative for a while that aimed to identify all of the planets in this galaxy and classify them based on a variety of different criteria," Samira explained.

"Why?" Ty asked.

"The goal was to establish better security protocols throughout the galaxy and prevent things like the prison colony from happening," Jonah said. "The intergalactic cooperation agreements were still fairly new and some of the governing bodies decided that it would be easier to control the movements of anyone living or visiting in the galaxy if there was a compendium of information about each of the planets. That way if there was suspicious activity near any of the planets, there would be greater justifiable cause to control movement and bring sanctions."

"How did they classify Uoria?" Ty asked.

Jonah shook his head.

"We didn't even know that Uoria existed," Jonah said.

"Nobody on Earth was aware of Uoria until 50 years after the Nyx 23 mission disappeared," Samira said.

In the back of his mind Ty remembered that Rain had mentioned that, but it seemed so strange to him that only a little more than one hundred years before, the people of

Earth had no idea that his planet existed and now they were building alliances and fighting to preserve the safety and security of both planets. Even as the thought moved through his mind, something occurred to Ty. He shook his head.

"Yes, they did," he said.

"What do you mean?" Samira asked. "I can show you in the history books where they describe the discovery of Uoria by the human teams."

"Uoria didn't need to be discovered," Ty told her, feeling slightly defensive. "Look at the number of species that came here from Uoria. All of our kinds have existed on Uoria for far longer than 50 years. The people of Earth *discovered* nothing. They might have realized that the planet was there, but them becoming aware of it didn't change anything for Uoria, except for introducing humans. And I would have very little faith in what your history books would say."

"Why is that?" Jonah asked.

"Because if I did, I would assume that you were dead."

Jonah looked struck and he fell silent, obviously unsure of how to respond.

"Why did you say that the people of Earth did know about Uoria before they...became aware of it?" Samira asked.

"The first hybrids," Ty said. "The picture that Eden said she remembered from Ryan's office. Think about it. Those were Denynso. When the Nyx 23 team disappeared and the Earth military went to Penthos, they said that they freed the prisoners, but Ryan told us that his great-grandfather was the Valdician general and that he aligned with a rogue military leader to start the breeding program to create weaponized hybrids. They didn't free the prisoners, they brought them back to Earth with them. The military knew that they had members of a species that they had never known before."

"At least some of them did," Samira said, her voice telling Ty that the same realizations were gradually becoming clear in her mind. "Whoever aligned with Odan had to trust some of the members of the team. He couldn't pull off transferring all of the Denynso prisoners to Earth on his own. At some point those people had to question who these people were and where they came from. Somebody had to know."

"They also had to know what the Valdicians had done to us," Jonah said. "The military only went to Penthos because of us. Odan would have told them that they had sabotaged our ship. They knew all along."

"What if they knew before?" Ty asked.

Jonah's eyes snapped up from the file in his hand and met Ty's orange gaze. The nurturer's words felt like they were ricocheting through his brain, bouncing off of each other until they were a buzzing blend of sound in his ears. *What if they knew before?*

"What is it, Jonah?" Samira asked, obviously noticing the expression on Jonah's face.

He couldn't answer. He wanted to say something, but he couldn't come up anything. He didn't think that he could take the thoughts that were trying to form in his mind and turn them into words that would properly express what he was feeling and wondering. Leaning forward, Jonah gathered up all of the files that Ty and Samira had found. Not knowing if they would follow, and not knowing if he even cared if they did, he headed out of the small room and toward the stairwell that would lead him up to the abandoned medical floors above.

Jonah hadn't taken his own lightstick out of his bag

before leaving the room and by the time he stepped into the stairwell he was engulfed in total darkness, but it barely slowed him down. Though he had been in this building countless times before, when he was with the others, traveling in the glow of the lightsticks and focusing on trying to understand what was happening with each step, he hadn't felt the familiarity. Now that he was in the darkness, unable to depend on anything else, the memories of the space were flooding his mind. He was no longer navigating an abandoned, outdated structure entombed within the newer building. As he moved through the blackness, the time fell away and he was walking through the space again just as he had before he left. The air around him no longer felt stagnant and forgotten, but was again filled with the energy of the days when it was the medical center of the University.

He let his feet climb the stairs as quickly as they would go, his hand running across the wall to feel for the doors as he reached each landing. He counted as he went until he knew that he was back at the floor that contained the old examination rooms. The door slammed behind him as he stepped out into the hallway and for a brief moment he wondered if there were other hybrids around that could have heard the sound and were now coming at him through the darkness. The compulsion to get into the examination room where he had found his file overrode any hesitation that he felt and he continued down the hallway, pacing his footsteps until he knew that he had gotten back to the room.

Even though they had broken the door to get inside, they had closed it again as much as they could when they left the room to go further down into the building and for a brief moment he wondered if he had imagined the pristine examination room. Maybe his imagination had taken over and he hadn't truly seen the room as it had been, but a memory becoming real before his eyes. He felt for the door and pushed it open. Just as he had so many years before, he stepped into the room and walked toward the bed. When he felt the edge of the bed on the front of his thighs, he lowered the files he carried to it and reached into his bag for one of the lightsticks he had packed before they left Uoria. That day felt a lifetime behind him and as he activated the stick, surrounding him with the light, the reappearance of the untouched examination room pulled it even further away.

7
____

"Everybody out," Ciyrs demanded as he stalked into the center emergency chamber. "Go into the other chamber. Find another room. Out."

Rilex watched as those who had gathered in the chamber exchanged confused glances, but started out of the room toward the other spaces in the basement. They streamed into the first of the emergency chambers and then into some of the other small rooms along the hallway that led away from the first. He knew why the healer was doing it, he didn't want them to know about the hybrids or the women that they had found, but watching the group fracture and disperse throughout the huge basement was uncomfortable. The closer they were together, the safer they were going to be. Even though they hadn't seen any Valdicians or hybrids in the basement, he knew that they could never be completely positive that there weren't others creeping closer to them through the honeycomb of rooms, alcoves, and hallways that made up the basement.

When everyone had left the chamber Ciyrs ran out again and Rilex followed him back down the stairs toward the hidden torture chamber that they had discovered. He could hear the groans of the surviving hybrids and had to fight the emotion building within him. In that moment it didn't matter to him that these creatures had been the ones raging against them in the hallway. They were still alive, still individual living beings that were being tormented just beneath the feet of their own wounded. It was obvious that they didn't have any compulsion within them to fight. They didn't feel any hatred against the Denynso or any that were with them. They were fighting because they had no other option. They didn't deserve disdain. They deserved rescue.

"Take the most alert first," Ciyrs ordered. "They have the best chances for survival. Bring them up to the emergency chamber and make sure that you shut the door. We can't have anyone seeing them. Not yet."

Rilex stepped into the room and saw that the woman who had pled with Eden for help was struggling to sit up. He came to her side and placed a hand on her shoulder.

"Don't," he said soothingly. "Don't try to move. We're here to help you."

"What about the others?" she asked, sounding as though just forming the words was taking every bit of energy that she had within her.

Rilex moved a matted piece of hair away from her forehead and looked down into her face.

"We found them," he reassured her. "We found them and we've gotten them out of their cages."

"Will they be alright?" she asked.

"Our healer will do everything that he can, and I will help him as much as I can. Jacob will as well. Right now I want to help you."

"There's no reason," she said, her body seeming to weaken as she laid back.

"Of course there is," Rilex said, feeling worry building up inside him. "Of course there's a reason to help you. You'll be alright."

She shook her head.

"No," she said. "There's no reason to help me. I'm finished. Please help them. Let me go."

There were tears in her eyes, but there was also still a flicker of life behind the exhaustion and pain. She was still there, and he wasn't going to let her slip away. Rilex swept one arm under her legs and one around her back to scoop her up against his chest.

"That's not good enough for me," he said. "You're not finished. Not yet."

Holding her closely against him, Rilex carried the woman out of the torture chamber and back through the room's false clean room toward the stairs that led up into the basement. He checked that there was no one in the hallway before ducking into the chamber they had emptied. Eden had gone in front of them and laid out pads and mats to create a row of beds along the walls, and Rilex brought the woman to the first one. He rested her down onto it and Eden rushed to her side, dropping down to her knees beside her and draping a blanket across her. It wasn't until the blanket concealed her that Rilex processed that she had been unclothed, her bare body exposed to the cold and the disrespectful eyes of the Valdicians. The thought made Rilex even angrier and he had to stand and turn away from her to regain control of himself.

"Take care of her," he told Eden. "I'm going to go back to help more."

"What about them?" the woman asked weakly.

"I told you that we found the women in the cages," Rilex tried to reassure her. "We already got them out."

"No," the woman said. "*Them.*"

She shuddered when she said it, as if it was horrifying just to get the word out.

"Who?" Eden asked.

The woman's eyes widened and Rilex realized what she was asking.

"The Valdicians," he said.

The woman recoiled at the sound of the name and Eden inched closer to her protectively. Rilex took a step toward her again.

"They're dead," he told her. "The two that came into the room when we found you are dead. I promise they won't hurt you again."

"There are more," the woman said tearfully.

"We know," Rilex said. "They still won't hurt you again. I will make sure of that. You're safe now."

"Safe," the woman said experimentally as if tasting the word on her lips.

He realized it might be the first time that she had ever said it, or felt that it could apply to her. Eden touched the woman's hand compassionately. There was a connection between the two that was tangible. Though this woman's experience was at a different extreme than Eden's, both had been victims of Ryan and understood the vile, grotesque nature of this man. Rilex left the two, knowing that he would be back to her, but also that he was needed downstairs. They had more people to move out of the horrifying rooms down there into the new infirmary, and the woman's confirmation that there were more Valdicians only reinforced that they needed to do it as quickly as possible.

Ciyrs watched Pyra carry another woman into the room, quickly followed by Jacob.

"Is that all?" he asked.

Pyra nodded.

"All of the survivors," he said.

"What did you do with the dead?" he asked.

"We had to leave them where they were," the Denynso leader replied. "There's nowhere to bury them right now."

Ciyrs nodded and turned back to those lying on the beds along the walls. The women had only had minor injuries and others seemed physically uninjured, but were visibly pregnant and traumatized by what they had been through. The hybrids, however, were grievously injured, some so severely Ciyrs feared that even his healing and the help of the other men wouldn't be able to save them. Rilex was sitting beside the first of the hybrids that they brought in, his back rested against the wall as he stared straight ahead rather than looking at her. Ciyrs crossed to them and knelt beside her.

"What is it, Rilex?" he asked.

"I don't want to leave her," the other man asked.

"Why?" Ciyrs asked as he noticed her eyes were closed and she seemed to be sleeping fitfully. "Did something happen?"

"Look at her," Rilex said. "What did he do to her?"

"I don't know," Ciyrs said. "All I can do is try to help her, and if I'm going to be able to do that, I need your help. I need you and Jacob to check on the others. Review their injuries and identify the ones who are in the worst condition so that I can start the healing on them first. There are healing ointments in my bag. If there are minor injuries, clean them, coat them with the ointment, and then cover the area."

Rilex hesitated, but Ciyrs looked at him intently and finally the man climbed to his feet and started to the next bed and the man who lay there, groaning in pain. Ciyrs checked each of the woman's injuries, carefully cleaning the blood from them so that he could evaluate their severity. He was moving the blanket away from her breasts when the woman's eyes snapped open and she gasped, starting to move as if she was trying to scramble away from him but didn't have the energy to get away. Ciyrs made quieting, soothing sounds and pressed his hand to her thigh to try to hold her still.

"It's alright," he said. "I'm trying to heal your injuries. Please lie still."

"Who are you?" the woman asked nervously.

"My name is Ciyrs," he said. "I'm a Denynso healer."

"Denynso?" she asked, sounding slightly in awe.

"Yes," he answered, using the distraction of the conversation to let him peel away the blanket so that he could look at her other injuries.

"I came from a woman who was part Denynso," she said. "I'm not as big as Ryan wanted me to be."

She said it as though it was a failure on her part, an excuse for the way that he had treated them.

"Do you have a name?" he asked.

He hated the way that the question sounded coming out of his mouth, but he wanted to know more about her and didn't know if Ryan would permit the creatures that he created to have something so personal as their own identity. Just as he suspected, the woman shook her head. She looked embarrassed and glanced away. He didn't push her. He didn't need to have something to call her. For now all that mattered was stabilizing her.

After several minutes of treating her injuries, Ciyrs knew

that all that was left was the actual healing. He wished that Elianna was there to handle this part for him. His mate was nearly as powerful as he was, capable of handling even some of the most serious of injuries and ailments. He had purposely kept her in the infirmary with the wounded from the battle so that she could continue managing their needs. He was more experienced with healing and knew that he would be able to move more quickly, which was what these people needed. The healing itself, though, was so personal, so intimate that it often made him uncomfortable to perform it on a woman.

"Close your eyes," he instructed. "Just relax."

When she complied, he rested his hands on her chest, allowing the healing power to flow through him and out of his hands into her. She gasped, her back arching slightly as the healing started to set in. He could see her skin start to flush and her breathing became deeper. Ciyrs moved his hands along her body as quickly as he could while still putting enough focus into the healing. Finally, her body fell limp and she went into the deep sleep that generally followed the intensity of being healed. He drew the blanket up over her body again and moved on to the next of the injured hybrids.

The more he worked, the more intense the sick feeling in his stomach became. The fresh wounds from the battle and injuries from the cords that had been attached to their heads when they found them were only the beginning of what he was discovering on their bodies. Each showed signs of wounds and mistreatment that stemmed from many years before, as if each had been through a lifetime of systematic torture that began long before they swarmed the hallway in battle. He had finished the healing on the final of the hybrid survivors when he heard a whimpering sound coming from the first woman he had healed. Rilex rushed past him toward her and Ciyrs followed, intrigued by the man's strong reaction toward her as much as he was drawn to check on her and how the healing had impacted her.

The woman's eyes were fluttering open and closed as Ciyrs got to his knees beside her and rested his hand over her heart to check its rhythm. Her eyes opened and the fear in them seemed to soften slightly when she saw Rilex beside her.

"Is she alright?" he asked.

"She is doing better," Ciyrs confirmed. "I wouldn't say that she is fully healed yet. Her injuries were extensive, but it wasn't just her body that was wounded. Her mind and heart have been damaged. They will need to heal as much as her body before she will be truly recovered."

"Thank you, Ciyrs." the woman said, looking at Ciyrs. Her eyes moved to Rilex and the healer saw their gazes lock. "And thank you. Thank you for coming for me."

Rilex nodded, looking as though he were unable to speak for a moment. He touched her hand briefly and Ciyrs saw his expression change.

"What happened to you?" he asked. "Why were you in that room?"

The woman hesitated for only a moment.

"Reprogramming."

"What does that mean?" Ciyrs asked.

"We have been trained since before we were able to walk to succeed in battle. Our lives have been defined by mock battles so that we were prepared for when Ryan would finally use us."

"Mock battles?" Rilex asked.

"He would select us randomly and put us through drills

and challenges to test the skills that we learned in our training."

"He pit you against each other?" Ciyrs asked.

"Yes," the woman said without hesitation, her voice sounding as though there was no other option. "If we did well, we returned to the living quarters. If we failed, we went through reprogramming. The screen showed us what we did wrong and what we should have done. The cords underscored it."

Ciyrs shuddered at the description. It was the straightforward, simplistic way that explained the systematic torture that truly emphasized the horrific nature of what Ryan put them through. Not giving more detail into the torture that they went through as a means of restructuring their behavior and further pushing them into methodic violence that defined them only highlighted the brutality of their existence.

"Never again," Rilex said. "That will *never* happen to you again. I will never let anyone hurt you again."

Ciyrs felt the meaning in the words, understanding that there was something in them that went far beyond just his commitment to protect all of those who had been so hurt by Ryan.

"Thank you..." the woman said, her voice trailing off as she seemed to realize that she didn't know what to call him.

"Rilex," he said. "What's your name?"

Ciyrs felt his heart squeeze slightly at the question. He didn't want to hear it again. He didn't want to have to think about her reality again, but he knew that he had to face it.

"She doesn't have a name," he said, hoping to free her from the pain and embarrassment that she clearly felt at the admission. "Ryan didn't allow them."

Ciyrs could see the fury and indignation on Rilex's face,

but the man controlled his reaction carefully. He slid closer to her head and moved a piece of hair away from her face as he had seen Eden do earlier.

"Choose one," he said.

"What?" the woman asked.

"Choose one," Rilex said. "Choose a name."

8

Maxim slammed the door to the shuttle behind him and Elise rushed up to input the code to secure the locks in place. He stalked across the open room, wiping blood from his eyes as he let his thoughts circulate his body, mentally checking for any injuries beyond the small cuts and bruises he knew he would have. The drums were gone and he could no longer hear them in his head. They had been replaced by the sound of fighting and he tried to shake it out of his ears. He didn't want to hear it anymore. He didn't want to have to think about it. What Kyven had told him about the hybrid who had helped him in the quarry had stuck with him throughout the brief but fierce battle they had just endured outside of the shuttle and it was hanging heavily over him now. He crossed the shuttle toward the infirmary, leaving the crew behind him.

"Tell me about Mhavyrch again," he demanded as he entered the infirmary.

"Maxim!" Kyven gasped when he came to the side of his bed "Are you alright?"

"I'm fine," Maxim said "Nothing serious. Their army was small. We were able to get them back fairly quickly. I think they were scouting us more than anything. They want to intimidate us and to gauge how we were going to respond to them."

"Let me look at your hands," Elon said as he approached.

Maxim looked at the human medic, uncertain if he could trust him. He hadn't forgotten the way that he had spoken to them when he started treating Nylek and Kyven.

"I've spoken to him, Maxim," Avery said from behind him, making Maxim turn. "I know that my apology doesn't take away the way that he treated you, but I hope that in time you will learn to trust us."

Maxim nodded toward the pilot.

"Thank you, Avery," he said.

He looked at Elon and gave a slight nod of permission. The medic turned Maxim's hand over to examine his palm and wrist, and then checked the other.

"Are you hurt anywhere else?" he asked. "Is the blood on your face yours?"

"Some of it may be," Maxim said. "Not all of it."

Elon took a small stack of cloths from a box on one of the shelves built into the wall of the infirmary and placed them on a rolling metal table that he drew up beside Maxim. He took one of the cloths and use it to wipe Maxim's hand. Maxim gritted his teeth at the sting of the wet cloth in the cuts on his skin and turned back to Kyven to distract himself.

"What do you remember about Mhavrych?" he asked.

"I told you everything that I remember," Kyven said.

Maxim saw his brother glance to Emerie at his side.

Kyven's mate adjusted her hand in his as if to hold it even more tightly and shook her head.

"I don't know anything else," she said. "I only got a glimpse of him and I was so scared that I don't even know if I could tell you what he looked like. All I know is that he gave us the ball of light that saved us from the Meldor."

"He saved me, too."

The sound of Nylek's voice from the bed across the infirmary was almost startling in its weakness and Maxim stepped up to the bed, Elon following him so that he could continue to clean off Maxim's hands and arms. The Denynso warrior looked smaller, almost as though whatever he had encountered out in the desert had drawn some of his very being out of him. Some of the color had returned to his face, however, and even though he sounded strained, Maxim felt a sense of relief just to hear him talking.

"What happened?" Maxim asked. "How did he save you?"

"I'm not sure," Nylek said. "It was dark and I had gotten myself off track. I meant to get to the rest of you in the quarry, but I must have deviated from the path because I ended up away from shuttle and never encountered you. The attack came out of nowhere. There was nothing around me for them to hide behind, so they must have just been stalking me in the darkness, staying enough out of the glow of my light that I wasn't able to see them even though they were close enough to ambush me without me even realizing they were coming."

"How many of them were there?" Maxim asked.

"I don't even know," Nylek said. "I'm so embarrassed to even admit it."

"There's nothing for you to be embarrassed about," Maxim said. "You did what you could. None of us are prepared to fight these creatures. We don't know what they are or what they are capable of doing. The fact that you were out there alone in the dark and are still alive is..."

"A miracle?" Kyven added.

Maxim nodded, the word even more meaningful now.

"How did you find out his name?" Maxim asked.

"I heard it when he was fighting off the hybrids that had attacked me. One of them screamed it. I assumed that that was his name."

Maxim couldn't understand what was happening. This man had stepped in to save one of their group twice now, but hadn't remained long enough to justify his actions or even explain who he was. Could he really be trying to help them without the other hybrids knowing what he was doing, or was this just another of Ryan's ploys, setting them up for something more that he had planned for them?

Rain ran her fingers along the control panel, hoping that something would look familiar to her. The door to the control room was closed behind her and each time that she got a glimpse of it out of the corner of her eye it was as if she was back in the StarCity that brought her to Penthos the first time. The last time that she had seen a door closed that way was seconds before she found Etan as the ship plummeted toward what she knew now was Uoria, but what they thought then was a desolate, unknown stretch of ground.

Even after so many years she could still see Etan's face clearly. She wished that she couldn't. She wished that that image had faded away and that she could put it behind her so that she didn't have to suffer the questions that moved through her mind incessantly each time that she thought of him. Her hand wrapped around a handle embedded in the control panel and she pulled it experimentally. A hatch beside her opened, revealing another complex set of controls. Rain let out an exasperated sigh. Though she knew that it had been more than 115 years since the last time that she had been on Penthos, it wasn't until this moment that she felt the years that had passed. Encountering the species that lived on Uoria, falling in love with Lynx, even hearing the women tell her that their disappearance had been a heavily-covered element of their education from the time that they were young children. None of it had made her really feel the impact of the years that she had been locked in place by the Covra. This technology, however, made those years crash down around her.

The door to the control room opened and Rain tensed for a moment before realizing it was Lynx who stepped inside the room with her. Relief washed over her and she rushed toward him to gather him in an embrace.

"Are you alright?" she asked, stepping back away from him to make sure he hadn't been injured in the battle.

"I'm fine," he said. "What are you doing in here?"

"I couldn't stand by the window and watch you fight," she told him. "It was already bad enough that you had made us all stay here in the shuttle when you went back to the quarry to help Kyven. I wasn't about to just stand by again. I thought maybe if I could figure out how to operate the shuttle, I would be able to use it to go to Uoria for the others, but the technology is too hard. I can't figure it out."

"Why haven't you asked Avery?" Lynx asked.

"I did," Rain said, trying not to let the question offend her. "My first thought was that he could either bring some of us to Uoria or he could teach me how to do it."

"What did he say?" Lynx asked.

"Apparently when the shuttle came to Penthos it was damaged. Just like with our ship when we were redirected from here to Uoria, this ship was sabotaged and directed here. The main controls had been deactivated so even if Avery had tried to steer the ship rather than going and hiding in the panic room, he wouldn't have been able to."

"So the shuttle won't work?" Lynx asked.

"Not right now," Rain said. "But that can't just be it. There has to be something that I'm missing. When the Star-City crashed into Uoria, it was far more violent than the crash here. The ship itself started to fall apart. The weapons that the Valdicians had thrown into the ship and attached to the outside actually started to destroy it once they disabled the communication and navigation systems and led the ship to Uoria. Once we were over the planet, the ship started to come apart and we actually felt it crashing. That's not how it was with this ship."

"I'm not following you," Lynx said.

"We didn't crash here," Rain said. "The ship was redirected here, but then we landed. It was fairly controlled and nothing seemed to break off of the shuttle when it happened. The main controls, though, are no longer working. That means that there were measures put into place to deactivate the control system and override any navigation once we were at a particular point in the journey. Now that we're here, those measures are still in place, which means that the navigation system still isn't working."

"But the ship itself isn't damaged."

"It doesn't appear to be," Rain confirmed.

"So if you could just find whatever the Valdicians did to the controls and remove it..."

"I should be able to get the shuttle moving again." She took a breath as she examined another cluster of buttons on the wall. "I wonder if that thought even crossed Etan's mind," she said, more to herself than to Lynx.

"What?" Lynx asked

She looked at him for a moment and then took a step toward him.

"It still doesn't make sense," she said. "Why did Etan kill himself?"

"He knew that the ship was going to crash," Lynx said. "You already told us that. It was in his journal."

"I know that his journal said that he knew the Valdician plans, but that doesn't explain why he decided to kill himself rather than trying to reclaim the shuttle. As the pilot, he knew how to operate the StarCity like nobody else did. I could have taken over if I had to, but my knowledge of the technology was basic compared to his. I know that we tried to reconnect the communication systems and tried basic navigation, but I don't remember him going to any further lengths to try to defeat the sabotage and take the ship back. Why?"

"Maybe he knew that he wasn't going to be able to and was worried that if he tried, he would cause something even worse to happen and none of you would have a chance to survive."

Rain shook her head, moving on to another set of switches and buttons.

"It doesn't make sense," she repeated. "The information that he had about the Valdicians. It wasn't much. A couple of pages that he snatched from an office on Penthos. It wasn't enough to justify what he said in his journal. He knew too much. There was something going on that we still don't know, and it made him kill himself before we landed. I want to know why." She pushed another handle and an empty drawer opened. "But first, I need to know what happened to this ship and how I can fix it so that Athan and I can get back to Uoria."

"Why Athan?" Lynx asked.

"Maxim and Kyven are needed here, but we need the weapons and the army that is building there. Athan is our connection to the Mikana and to everything that Maxim and Kyven's father left behind."

9

C iyrs stood in the center of the room, surrounded by the women and hybrids, listening to the rhythm of their breathing and hoping that the worst was over for them. Eden came to his side and he wrapped his arm around her shoulders to give her a brief hug. The fact that through saving her life he had manipulated her DNA to make her Denynso and linked their minds in a way that was usually reserved only for mates made them closer than the others in the clan, and he was glad for the few quiet moments that he was getting with her beside him. It was comforting to have her with him, even though he could feel the emotion radiating off of her and knew that she was suffering with each moment that she stood in the laboratory building. Deep within her, Ciyrs knew that Eden blamed herself for what was happening. If only she had made a different choice when she worked with Ryan before coming to Uoria. If she had given in only once to his advances or gone another direction and revealed to the governing bodies of the University what Ryan was doing to her, or what he had asked her to do on her journey to Uoria, he might have been stopped.

"You can't think that way," Ciyrs said.

Eden glanced up at him, but didn't question what he meant by the statement. Even though Ciyrs rarely communicated with her through their thoughts, she knew that he could still read her face and knew her well enough to anticipate what she was thinking.

"But, maybe I could have stopped him," she said. "If I had done something different. If I had been nice to him, maybe he would have told me what was happening and I could have stopped it, or if I had told the University what I knew that he was doing, they could have investigated."

Ciyrs turned toward Eden and leaned forward slightly to look at her intently.

"Eden, listen to me. There is nothing that you could have done. If you had been nice to him, you would have been swept up into this and probably would have become a part of the experiments. You wouldn't have had the opportunity to stop him or to tell anyone what was happening. If you had told someone, they wouldn't have believed you. Even if they did, they wouldn't have had anything on him other than the way that he was treating you and asking you to get Pyra's blood. They wouldn't have been able to do much to him, and if they did, what would have happened to these people? Besides, if you had done anything differently, you wouldn't have ended up on Uoria. You wouldn't have met Pyra, and you wouldn't have had Lysander. We never would have found the human settlement or connected with the Mikana. You're right, you could have done something different and it wouldn't have ended up like this, but that wouldn't have been a good thing. It would have been a tragedy."

"I just feel so helpless," Eden said. "I wish that there was more than I could do for them."

"I know," Ciyrs said. "So do I. For now, we've done what we can. We'll keep watching them and I'll perform healings as needed. They seem to be responding well and that's all we can hope for right now."

Behind him Ciyrs heard the door open and turned to see Pyra come inside. His eyes scanned the room and Ciyrs saw the warriors' leader's jaw twitch. He stalked toward them and wrapped an arm protectively around Eden.

"What kind of leader could do this to his followers?" Pyra growled.

"He's not a leader," Eden said. "Ryan is an owner and a dictator. He doesn't see any of these people as living beings."

"Are these women all pregnant?" Pyra asked.

Ciyrs nodded.

"Yes. They're all in different stages."

"What are we going to do for them?" Eden asked.

"I don't know," Ciyrs said. "I'm not familiar enough with human pregnancies to really help them, but I will do everything that I can for them."

"Ciyrs, have you noticed Jacob?" Pyra asked.

Ciyrs glanced across the room toward where Jacob sat on the floor beside one of the women they had rescued from the breeding facility. He recognized her as the first woman that Jacob spoke to in the room and the one that he took from the room first. The human man was leaning toward the woman, speaking to her quietly and occasionally touching her gently. It was far more familiar and intimate than the way any of them were speaking to the other women, and it struck the healer as strange.

"Does he know her?" Ciyrs asked.

"It would certainly look that way," Pyra replied. "How do

you think he knows her?"

Ciyrs shook his head.

"I don't know. He didn't tell me anything about her."

"Do you think that we're going to be ready to leave tonight?" Pyra asked, apparently pushing the questions about the man who had arrived with Jem away.

Ciyrs looked around the room and shook his head adamantly.

"No," he said. "Even the wounded from the battle will need more time to heal and get stronger before we can think about trying to leave. The surviving hybrids and the women might need even longer."

"We don't have the time to keep waiting. We need to get to the shuttles and to Penthos. The longer that we wait here, the higher the chances that more of the hybrids or Valdicians will find us, and the more danger the others are in. We need to move."

"They are not strong enough," Ciyrs insisted. "If we try to leave too soon, they will not make it. Moving too quickly is going to be more dangerous than waiting. We must stay here. For at least one more day. Maybe more. I already told you that."

Pyra looked frustrated, but Ciyrs wasn't going to back down. He had already told the warrior leader that those in the infirmary needed more time, and the need was even more pressing now that they had the hybrid survivors and the women to care for.

"You're probably right," Pyra said, "but I am going to tell those who aren't injured to start collecting supplies. The more prepared we are when the wounded are ready, the better."

Pyra turned sharply and left the room with Eden close behind him. Ciyrs scanned the room a final time to make sure that no one there needed additional help. When he was satisfied that they were resting comfortably, at least for the moment, he decided it was time that he take a break and get something to eat. He didn't know how long it had been since he had rested or eaten, but he was starting to feel hazy with fatigue. As he stepped into the first chamber, Elianna rushed up to him and he gathered her in his arms.

"Have you rested or had anything to eat?" he asked her, worried that she was doing the same thing that he was and neglecting herself as she cared for the injured.

Elianna nodded.

"Some," she said. "I've been in the infirmary most of the time. What is going on in that other chamber?"

Ciyrs hesitated. He wanted to be able to tell his mate what was happening. He wasn't accustomed to having to hide things from her. Usually she was his greatest source of comfort and his confidante. He shared everything with her and let her support and guide him when he didn't know what to do. This time, though, he was under orders from Pyra not to talk about the surviving hybrids or the breeding facility. They didn't want to frighten any of the group or give them anything else to worry about until they knew what was to be done with these people.

"I can't tell you right now," Ciyrs said. "I'll let you know as soon as I can. Don't worry. I'm safe. You just take care of yourself and keep doing what you can for the men in the infirmary."

Ciyrs felt himself sway slightly and Elianna grasped him by the arm.

"You need to sit down," she said. "Have you even slept since we got here?"

"I don't remember," Ciyrs said.

Elianna started guiding him toward the corner of the

room next to a set of shelves. He settled onto a mat and she handed him a box of rations and a bottle of water.

"Eat," she told him. "Whatever's going on can wait. Everyone will need our healer no matter what happens next."

Ciyrs accepted to food and eagerly began to eat, feeling hungrier as the food touched his tongue. He had finished the rations that Elianna brought him and was downing the water when something in the corner of his eye caught his attention. Placing water back on the shelf beside him, Ciyrs turned toward the glimmer of reflection he had seen. Aegeus was standing in front of a piece of reflective metal, staring into the hazy image of himself. The healer watched as the man lifted one skeletal hand and touched it to the side of his pale, slimy face.

There was a time when Ciyrs would have felt nothing but disgust looking at this man. He was Klimnu, his appearance exactly like the countless other creatures that had proved themselves the most lingering of enemies of the Denynso. They had been the grisly and vicious enemies of the Denynso king Creia, and had continued to engage in violent conflict with the clan until they finally defeated them the day that Jem disappeared, taking the last two of the army with him as he dropped off of the reflected branch into the sky. It wasn't until they saw Maxim's skin begin to dissolve away and mimic the appearance of the skin that they had all become horribly familiar that they learned the Klimnu were gruesomely mutated Mikana. They had been originally changed from the beautiful, intelligent species into the disgusting beings by a toxin on Uoria, but it was the greed, arrogance, and violence of a small group of them that had sealed their fate, effectively dividing the species into two.

Aegeus had never intended to be Klimnu. A Mikana warrior who had been a part of the mysterious Order and fought vehemently against the corruption within his kind that bred the Klimnu, Aegeus was a casualty of Ryan in many ways. His family had thought him dead for many years, with his sons Maxim and Kyven suffering throughout life with all of the questions that came from never knowing what had happened to their father. In reality, he had been captured by Ryan's servants and brought back to Earth where Ryan forcibly transformed him into the creature that he loathed so deeply. For years he had been keeping Aegeus prisoner, strengthening his aggression and using him in his experiments with the ever-present threat that Ryan would destroy his family and then eliminate his kind in his quest to control the galaxy.

Where there had always been disdain and hatred toward these creatures, Ciyrs now felt compassion. He could see the agony in Aegeus's eyes as he saw his fully mutated self for what might have been the first time in the years that he had been held captive. Putting the empty rations box aside, Ciyrs stood and crossed the room to Aegeus. The man tensed as Ciyrs approached, still hesitant to trust anyone after his years of torture. The healer could see the compulsion to fight in Aegeus's eyes. He was struggling not to lash out against Ciyrs and the other Denynso that surrounded him.

"I can help you," Ciyrs said.

Aegeus looked up at him through the reflection in the mirror. His expression was difficult to decipher due to the mutation of his face, but Ciyrs knew that he was thinking about what the healer had said, unsure of whether he could believe or trust him.

"Why would you do that?" Aegeus asked.

"You aren't Klimnu," Ciyrs said. "This isn't who you are.

You are a Mikana warrior, the father of two men. What happened to you isn't your fault."

"You can really reverse it?" Aegeus asked.

His voice crawled across Ciyrs's skin, reminding him of all the times that he had heard the creatures taunting them in battle. This time, however, it wasn't disgust at the voice itself, but at what made that voice come out of Aegeus's mouth. He nodded.

"I can," he said. "I have to warn you. It will take time and may be very painful."

"I don't care," Aegeus said. "It can't take nearly as long or be nearly as painful as what I've been through here. I will suffer anything for the chance to not be this way."

"You're sure?" Ciyrs asked.

"There is no reason to live if I have to be what I hate the most and stay separated from my family. Please. Help me."

Ciyrs nodded and looked around the room.

"We shouldn't do it here," he said. "The last thing we need is so many people swarmed around you."

"I heard one of the men talk about other rooms down here," Aegeus said. "Would one of them work?"

Ciyrs nodded.

"I don't need anything but a place for you to lie down and space for me to put my supplies. We'll bring blankets from here and I can get my bag from the infirmary. Are you ready?"

"I don't want to wait any longer," Aegeus said. "I want to be back to myself as soon as possible."

"I can't guarantee that you will be by the time that we leave here. You have been fully transformed for so long now that it will take extensive treatments to return you to your normal state. It might take several days of treatments."

"I will endure whatever you need me to."

"Alright," Ciyrs said. "Let's go then."

They gathered the supplies that Ciyrs needed and met in the hallway in front of the emergency chambers. Together they started down the dark hallway leading further into the basement. Ciyrs stopped when he reached the far end of the hallway and found another set of emergency chambers much like those that they had taken over on the other side of the basement. He briefly considered telling the others about the rooms, but then changed his mind, acknowledging that keeping as many of them as close together as possible was going to keep them safest. Having privacy was also going to be important for Aegeus as he went through the challenge of his treatment. It would be better to let everyone stay together, at least for now. If they had to stay in the laboratory building for much longer than they intended, they might spread out into these chambers, but until then it would be beneficial for everyone not to disrupt them any further.

Once they were inside, Aegeus laid out the blankets that he had brought with him and placed a pillow at the top, readying a bed for him to rest on as he received his treatment. He took a breath, glancing down at his body as if reminding himself one more time what he had gone through so that when the treatment began he would have a reminder that it was worth it.

Ciyrs lowered his supply bag to the floor and gestured to the blankets.

"Take your shirt off and lay down," Ciyrs said.

He waited while Aegeus did as he asked and then reached into his bag for the container of special herbs that he had tucked there after using them on Maxim so long before. He never thought that he was going to have to use them again, had hoped that he would never encounter a situation when he would need them. Now, though, he was thankful that he had them.

"What are you going to do?" Aegeus asked.

"I am going to give you something to drink to help keep you calm. I'm afraid it won't completely take away the pain, but it will help to relax you. After that I will have more herbs for you to take that will start to absorb the toxins in your blood. Then I will apply an ointment to your skin and perform the healing. I must warn you that my skin touching yours would be very painful and cause serious damage. With the ointments, I should be able to keep my hands on you for a few moments at a time without damage, but it will likely still hurt."

"I understand," Aegeus said.

Ciyrs took a bottle from his bag and offered it to Aegeus.

"Swallow this," he said.

Aegeus complied and handed the bottle back to Ciyrs. Within a few seconds the healer noticed that the man's muscles began to relax and his breathing became slow and even. Ciyrs watched him relax as he mixed more herbs and added them to thick nectar he had made when in his clinic. When the tincture was complete, he offered it to Aegeus, who swallowed it down without a moment of hesitation. After handing the bottle back to Ciyrs, Aegeus rested back on the pillow, closing his eyes as if preparing himself for the treatment that was to come.

Ciyrs opened the container of herbs that he had used with Maxim and carefully coated his hand. He remembered the way that Maxim's skin had burned and seized when he touched it after he had begun to change, and he didn't want to put Aegeus through the same agony. He didn't ask if he was ready again. There was no reason. It was better to just get started. Checking his hands a final time to make sure that they were fully covered in the herbs, Ciyrs reached forward and began to smear the blend onto Aegeus's pale, grisly skin. As soon as his hands touched him, Aegeus grimaced and tightened, but Ciyrs didn't stop. He had to apply the herbs and the faster that he went, the sooner it would be over. As soon as his upper body was fully covered, Ciyrs carefully removed the rest of his clothing and covered his legs. Finally finished with that stage, he covered Aegeus with a blanket so that the herbs could begin to work.

Several minutes passed with only the sound of Aegeus's hissing breaths in the air when he suddenly spoke.

"Tell me about my sons."

The question sent a shock through Ciyrs. He carefully drew the blanket back away from Aegeus's chest and covered his hands with a thick layer of the herbs again, preparing to perform the first healing treatment.

"What do you want to know?" he asked.

Aegeus's hands gripped the blankets on either side of him, bracing him against the pain that he knew was coming, and shook his head.

"Anything," he said. "I just want to know about them."

Knowing that hearing about the sons that he hadn't seen since they were children would comfort and distract him, Ciyrs started talking.

"They are grown," Ciyrs said, "and strong. Maxim has a mate named Ivy, she is human."

As he spoke, he reached forward and pressed his hands to the center of Aegeus's chest. The man's eyes squeezed closed more tightly, but he didn't make any sound. Even though Ciyrs knew that this part of the healing was the most painful, Aegeus endured it in silence, strengthened by hearing about his sons and thinking of the possibility of being with them again.

10

____

"Pyra, can I speak with you?"

Jonah led the tremendous Denynso toward the room where Samira and Ty had found the files and closed the door behind them.

"What is it?" Pyra asked. "We are getting ready to leave and I need to ensure that everyone is prepared."

"That's actually what I need to talk to you about," Jonah said. "I won't be leaving with you."

Pyra's expression fell and he looked at Jonah more intently.

"What do you mean?" he asked. "The wounded will be strong enough to leave in the next day. We have to get to Penthos. Maxim, Rain, and the others are waiting for us there."

"I know," Jonah said, "but there is something going on here that I need to investigate further."

"What did you find?" Pyra asked.

"Samira and Ty found a box of files in this room. They are the medical files for all of the members of Nyx 23 from before we left."

"The medical files?" Pyra asked.

"Like the one of mine that I found in the examination room upstairs. They are complete and untouched since the day that they were filled out for the mission. I went back upstairs to the examination room and looked around. I thought that nothing had been changed when I first saw it, but I wanted to look at it more thoroughly. Absolutely nothing has changed. The supplies in the cabinets are completely outdated. They are the brands and styles from when we were here. The others said that the hospital was still in operation for years after we left before it was shut down and sealed off. If that room had been used at all after I left it, there would be supplies that were newer. That just confirms that when my examination was over that day, they closed that examination room and never used it again."

"But why would the files be down here?" Pyra asked.

"I don't know," Jonah said. "The examinations were done in secret because of the nature of the mission. That means that the doctor who performed them could have kept the files after each one and put them down here. He must have just overlooked mine."

"What do you think that means?" Pyra asked.

"I'm not sure yet, but that's why I need to stay here. It has to mean something. There has to be a reason why that room is still in that condition and wasn't used after I left, and why the files for the team are separate from the rest of the patient files from that time. I can't help but think that it's not a coincidence that all of that is happening in the same place that Ryan chose for his breeding facility. And if that's true, this is much deeper than we thought. I need to try to find out what's going on."

Pyra looked tense.

"We should all stay together," he said. "We aren't as

effective if we aren't together. The conflict is waiting for us on Penthos. That's where we need to be."

"Ryan has called out Maxim, Kyven, and the Denynso. You have your army. There are many of my crew that aren't around anymore. They didn't have anyone to stand up for them then, and I owe it to them to stand up for them now. I need to know what happened. This is my fight."

Rilex walked carefully back into the room with the women and the surviving hybrids, not wanting to make enough sound to disturb any of them. He expected to see Ciyrs checking on them, but the healer wasn't there. Instead Eden was using a cloth to carefully bathe one of the women. Another of the women was sitting up against the wall, cradling Lysander in her arms. They had found clothing stored with the emergency supplies and seemed far more comfortable now that they were dressed in more than just the thin gowns that they had been wearing when they first found them.

"He's so sweet," the woman holding Lysander said.

Eden smiled at her and nodded.

"He is the most wonderful thing that has ever happened to me. There's nothing that can describe what it's like being a mother."

Rilex saw the woman give a tremulous smile and a tear slide down her cheek.

"I won't get the chance to know," she said sadly.

"Of course, you will," Eden said, dipping the cloth in a bowl of water beside her and drawing it down the other woman's arm again.

Rilex was impressed at her incredible tenderness and

the way that she was able to balance attention for both women while also keeping her eye on her baby.

"Ryan won't let us keep our children," the woman said tearfully. "I won't even be able to see him. When it's time for him to come, Ryan will bring me to the delivery ward and put me to sleep. By the time that I wake up, my baby will be gone."

Rilex stepped up to the woman and crouched down in front of her. She looked nervous, but he gave her a comforting smile

"Ryan has nothing to do with you anymore," he said. "He can't get to you. We will protect you now. When it is time for you to have your baby, it will be in the way that you choose, and then you will be a wonderful mother."

Eden looked up at Rilex and smiled at him warmly. He returned it and then stood, making his way toward where the hybrid woman slept. He settled down beside her as he had earlier, not wanting to disturb her from her sleep. As if his presence itself had roused her, she opened her eyes and looked up at him. A hint of a smile touched her lips and he felt something tremble within him.

"Hi," he said quietly.

"You're here," she whispered.

Rilex nodded and she started to sit up. He reached for hand and helped her until she was reclined against the pillows on her mat.

"How are you feeling?" he asked.

"Better," she said.

"Does anything hurt?" he asked.

"Something always hurts," she said, "but it's not as bad now. I can move. I can breathe."

"I'm glad," Rilex said.

They fell into a comfortable silence for a few moments

and he felt the urge to touch her face. He resisted, however, all too aware of what physical contact had meant for her throughout her life.

"Is this all of the women who were in the breeding facility?" she finally asked.

"Yes," Rilex reassured her. "I told you that we found them and rescued them."

"But did they all..." her voice trailed off as if she didn't want to finish her sentence and was hoping that he would understand what she was asking.

"They are all alive," Rilex told her. "Some are close to delivering their babies, but none are seriously injured."

She sighed with relief and nodded. Rilex hesitated for a moment before speaking again.

"How did you know about the women?" he asked.

"What do you mean?" she asked defensively.

"They have names," Rilex said. "They weren't born here. They were chosen specifically for the breeding part of the experiments. You were born here. Made here. If the women aren't even permitted to see their babies when they're born, why would Ryan allow his hybrids to know about the human women that he brought here?"

The woman looked stung and Rilex felt guilty for pushing her so hard. She had been through enough and he shouldn't have delved into something so difficult for her so soon. He wanted to apologize to her, but she straightened slightly and stared directly into his eyes, showing more confidence than he had seen from her since the first moment he looked at her.

"I tried to escape," she said.

Rilex drew in a breath, feeling his body start to shake as images of what she must have suffered when Ryan found her flashed through his mind.

"He didn't kill you," he said, genuinely surprised that Ryan's first reaction when he found one of his creations defying him wasn't to simply destroy it.

"I wish that he had," the woman said.

Rilex shook his head, fighting the sickness in his stomach and the tears in his eyes. He gingerly rested his hand over hers and didn't feel her resist or try to pull away, but also didn't feel her try to return the touch. It was enough for that moment. It had to be enough.

"I'm glad that he didn't." He knew that there was more to that story, but it wasn't the time to hear it yet. She would tell him in her own time. Instead, he tried to offer her another smile and eased slightly closer to her. "Have you chosen a name yet?" he asked.

She shook her head.

"I wouldn't even know how to begin choosing one," she said. "I haven't heard many names in my life. I don't know what it should be."

"It can be anything that you want it to," Rilex said. "This is your chance to be whoever you want to be. Ryan doesn't have control over you anymore. You've escaped. You're free. You can choose to be called whatever you want."

The woman looked into his eyes again, her hand moving very slightly against his.

"Would you choose for me?"

11

———

Maxim felt the ship tremble beneath his feet and reached for Ivy, who grabbed his hand and coiled against his side.

"What was that?" she asked with fear in her voice.

"I don't know," Maxim said. "They might have weapons and are attacking the ship now rather than waiting for us to come back out."

"Maxim!"

A shout from the front of the shuttle brought Maxim running from the room he was sharing with Ivy, his hand moving to the sword at his side as he went.

"Maxim!" the shout came again and Maxim recognized it as Lynx's voice.

The warrior met him in the front chamber of the shuttle, his face high with color and an excited smile reflecting in his eyes that told Maxim he had been wrong about the assault from the hybrid army in the desert outside.

"What is it, Lynx?" Maxim asked, still tense from being startled.

"She did it," Lynx said. "She did it!"

"Who?" Maxim asked. "What did she do?"

Lynx had started across the shuttle and Maxim followed, confused by Lynx's excitement. The warrior led him along a narrow hallway that he hadn't been in yet and then turned into a room. Maxim noticed Athan and Rain in the room before he recognized that it was a control room.

"Rain," Lynx said by way of explanation. "She figured out how to use the shuttle."

"What?" Maxim asked. "Avery wasn't even able to make it work again."

He stepped up to the control panel where Rain was standing and watched as she pressed a few buttons, bringing up an image on the screen ahead of her. She pointed to it, indicating an area of the shuttle on the blueprint that had appeared.

"That's because he is only familiar with this type of technology," she said.

"I don't understand," Maxim said.

"I was upset because I'm not familiar with the transportation technology that has developed since I left Earth," Rain said. "I thought that that was keeping me from being able to figure this thing out. Then I started thinking about the StarCity and what I learned from Etan before we left."

"You knew how to fly the StarCity?" Maxim asked.

"Yes. Back then every crew had a pilot, but there was also another member, one who wasn't identified in the mission logs or even known among the other crew members, who was familiar with the ship and how to operate it. They might not be as extensively skilled with it as the actual pilot, but the point was for them to have enough knowledge that they could take over operation of the ship should something happen to the pilot at some point during the mission. That's why I went into the control room during the crash."

"Because you thought that Etan just wasn't controlling the ship."

"Right. I knew that something was going wrong. He had already confirmed that the ship wasn't operating properly and that we had lost communication and navigation, but during the crash the ship went totally out of control. It felt like he wasn't even trying. So, I went into the control room to do my duty. That's when I found him. I tried to get the ship back under control and on track, but I couldn't. It had been too severely sabotaged."

"What does that have to do with you being able to operate this one?" Maxim asked. "Like you said, this technology is far more advanced than the technology in even the StarCity."

"That's right," she said. "But sometimes advanced doesn't always mean better. Some of the advancements that had been integrated into the StarCity were simple, but extremely effective and efficient. Jonah and I used those advancements and some of the prototypes of further technology that was under development when we left to design the vehicle that he brought to Earth."

"So, you were able to use that knowledge to figure out how to operate this shuttle," Maxim said.

"Not exactly," Rain told him. "The Valdicians haven't changed very much since they first brought Nyx 23 to Uoria. They utilize essentially the same weapons to disable the ship so that they could redirect it here rather than letting it get to Earth. What they didn't expect, though, was that there would be safeguards. I thought about what Avery and Elon had said about the panic room. There was no such thing as a panic room in the StarCity. That came to be after Nyx 23 disappeared. That got me wondering whether they would have put other forms of safeguards into place. It turns out that they did."

"Wouldn't Avery know about those?"

"Maybe if he knew what he was looking for. The team that designed this ship created several levels of protection to help prevent a ship from being taken over again. Some of them are pretty obvious. So obvious that it was fairly easy for the Valdicians to use their same weaponry to get past them. That's when I decided to take a glimpse at the blueprints and I noticed this."

She pointed at the image of the blueprints again.

"What is that?" Maxim asked.

"The StarCity was called a city for a reason. That ship had everything that we needed to give us a pretty high quality of life while traveling, even if we were traveling far distances. The only reason that we were able to use it for a clandestine mission was that one of the department heads who agreed with our perceptions about Penthos was also a part of the developmental team and thought that it would be the ideal vessel to bring us to the planet safely. Everything that you would think of as being a part of a normal city on Earth was in the StarCity, with one exception."

"What?" Maxim asked.

"A miniature."

"A miniature?"

Rain turned to him, a smile like he hadn't seen on her face in quite some time making her eyes sparkle and her cheeks flushed like Lynx's.

"A miniature," she repeated. "The team that designed the StarCity worried that the sheer volume of the ship would be excessive and too difficult for most people to handle. They were concerned that if something went wrong, the team wouldn't remember all of the different elements of the ship so that they would be able to fix it. To be honest I think they might have also been worried that people would get lost in it and not be able to describe in the ship where they were for the others to find them. To help prepare for all of that, they built a scale model and put it in the center of the ship. A lot of the pieces that Jonah and I included in our vehicle came from the wreckage of that miniature."

"I still don't understand," Maxim said.

He was starting to lose his patience. Ivy was still in the bedroom and he wanted to spend the time that he could with her before the next battle began.

"The Valdician weaponry was completely unknown to anyone at the time, so there was no way to develop protective measures against it. When they started adding these types of measures to new ships, however, in response to the Nyx 23 mission disappearing, they did everything that they could possibly think of to prevent the same thing happening to another ship."

"And that meant looking back at the plans for the original ship," Maxim said, realization starting to clarify his mind.

"Exactly," Rain said. "The StarCity that we rode on our mission was the only one of its design that was ever made. According to Avery, the team that designed it immediately scrapped it in favor of smaller, more efficient war machines as soon as the team didn't return. I'm sure the goal was always to go back to the StarCity design for long-distance research and recognizance as well as luxury use. They would be perfect for galactic suspension so that people could spend a year living in far space or for alternative communities. Apparently, though, they never returned to the concept and instead went in the direction of the ships that the human women used to get to Uoria. The hijacking of the shuttle that had Leia on it, though, evidently brought back some bad memories of the mission disappearing and they started designing new ships with more extensive modifications for safety. They brought out the original plans for our ship, thinking that they would be able to identify the vulnerabilities of the ship and fix them in the new designs."

"But by now nobody is alive that remembers the details of the ship," Maxim said. "At least that they know of. You can't just take basic plans and build off of them, especially if they were experimental in the first place."

Rain nodded.

"The same thing occurred to me, and that's when I asked Avery if there is a core to this ship."

"Is there?"

"He didn't know. Apparently they don't do as much training with pilots for pleasure cruises that they do for experimental or research trips from Universities and the military. He knows how to operate the ship and the basic emergency procedures, but since they don't really expect a tourist ship to get involved in a war, they didn't brief him on the more complex details of the ship, such as..."

Maxim looked more closely at the image on the screen.

"The miniature," he said.

"Yes. For the first time since the StarCity, they put a miniature inside the ship. They must have seen it in the original plans and thought that it had some more elaborate purpose, so they added it to the designs for this ship and ones like it. Like you said, though, the people who designed the original StarCity aren't around anymore and the team scrapped the project when Nyx 23 didn't return. They didn't add the necessary details to the designs, which means that there is one very impactful difference between the miniature that was in our ship and the one in this ship. This one is functional."

Maxim was shocked by the revelation.

"It's functional?" he asked. "What do you mean, functional?"

"It is, in every way, a tiny version of the bigger ship. Everything within it is completely operational. Once I realized that the miniature was there, Athan was able to help me examine it and find the areas of the main ship that had been impacted by the Valdician's weapons. We realized that they had only compromised one aspect of the navigation system, but that there were measures in place to easily override that. We fixed the components that were broken, overrode the system, and now we're back in action."

"How could the Valdicians not be ready for something like that?" Maxim asked. "After all this time, they tried to use the same attack as they did?"

"The Valdicians do as Ryan tells them to. Remember he is the legacy of their general from generations ago. As misguided as it may be, they respect him. They will do as he orders. To him, the Nyx 23 mission was a tremendous success, so why would they need to use a different type of attack to bring us here? It's actually fairly elegant if you ignore the arrogance. He can't imagine that anyone would be as smart as him or as powerful as his creatures. They were able to disable the most impressive ship ever designed at its time, so why wouldn't they be able to do it again? He couldn't wrap his head around the idea that somebody thought ahead of him."

A rush of renewed hope flowed over Maxim.

"When can you leave for Uoria?" he asked.

Rain smiled.

"As soon as you want me to."

"What needs to be done before they leave, Maxim?" Athan asked.

"We don't know how long it will be before everybody on Earth makes it here, or you get back. Those of us who stay here are going to need at least basic supplies to get us through until then."

"Those of us who stay?" Elise asked from the door as she stepped inside the control room. "What do you mean? Why wouldn't we all leave this horrible place?"

Maxim hadn't realized that she was listening and felt irritation taking away some of the lightness the hope had brought. He turned fully to the flight attendant, wanting to make sure she heard every word that he would say to her.

"We are here because Ryan wants to destroy anyone who opposes him and bring the universe under his control. He took my father. He has threatened my family and those dear to me. He is threatening the life of every being in existence. I am not running away from this. You are the mate of a Denynso warrior. You shouldn't even be thinking of running away, either."

Elise looked stung, but she didn't say anything. She squared her shoulders and turned away from Maxim, leaving the control room and disappearing into the rest of the ship.

"Athan, you'll go back to Uoria with Rain," Maxim continued without hesitation.

"I can stay here and fight, Maxim," the older man said.

"I know you can," Maxim said. "I don't doubt you. But we need the weapons and the army that are waiting for us there. I need you to be there to gather the ranks and make sure that they bring along what we need. I have to stay here. I need you to act in my stead."

Athan nodded.

"I would be honored," he said.

"Thank you, Athan." He turned to Rain. "I want Nylek and Kyven to go back with you, too. They need more time to heal and they can do it better there than here. Avery and his crew can stay there, too, we'll bring them back to Earth when this is all over. I am also going to send Ivy with you. Bring her to my mother."

"There's no way that Ivy is going to leave you here," Rain said. "She's going to insist that she stays here."

"She can't," Maxim said. "She needs to not be here during this. I need you to bring her to my mother and leave her in her care. I'll start preparing now. You'll be ready to leave within the hour."

He left the control room and headed directly back to the room where he had left Ivy. She was sitting on the bed, her hand rested protectively over her belly as she watched the door expectantly. It was that image that reinforced to Maxim that he was making the right decision sending her back to Uoria with Rain. The thought of being without her was excruciating, even if was only for a few days. He knew, though, that she and their baby would be safer on Uoria. If she was in the Mikana kingdom with Ellora she could be under the care of the midwives. They would ensure that her pregnancy was progressing properly and keep her healthy and safe, away from the war.

Maxim lowered himself to his knees at the side of the bed and leaned forward, wrapping his arms around her waist and resting his head on her belly. He knew that she would protest. She would be just as reluctant to leave his side as he was to watch her leave, but he couldn't relent.

An hour later Maxim walked into the abandoned compound, the bags on his back heavy with weapons and supplies he had taken from the ship. Behind him bodies littered the sand and sweat glided down his face from the exertion of the fight that left them there. The shuttle had nearly not escaped the sudden and fierce assault of the hybrid army that swarmed just as the men were climbing down into the desert. Two had tried to force past them into the ship, but they had managed to hold them back long enough for the door to close and Elise to activate the locks. If they had gotten in, all would have been lost.

Maxim could still hear Ivy's sobs as he turned away from her and walked out of the ship. He had to close himself to the sound, push it so far within him that he wouldn't be able to touch it. She was safe now, already gone from his sight in the sky and on her way back to Uoria and to the protection of his mother. When everything was over, he would be back with her. They would welcome their child together and create the life that he had dreamt of since the moment that he first saw her standing by the stone wall in the human settlement. She was different then. Uoria had changed her. He had changed her. But she had changed them as well.

Until he was able to be with her again, he couldn't allow himself to think of her or of their baby. He could think only of war. His father had left footsteps ahead of him and now it was time for him to rise up and let them guide him so that he could complete what Aegeus had intended to do so many years before.

12

Jem knew that he should be sleeping, trying to get as much rest as he could before they left the safety of the basement to try to get to the vehicles that would bring them to Penthos, but he couldn't. His mind was moving too quickly, overwhelmed with all of the thoughts that wouldn't stop moving no matter how hard he tried to quiet them and rest. The war that awaited them on the distant planet that he had never even heard of hung heavily over him. It felt like a painful, unchanging reminder of everything that he had missed during his time that he was away from Uoria.

Angela stepped into the room carrying a box under one arm and smiled at him softly. She sat beside him and placed the box on the floor in front of him before placing her hand on his cheek and turning his face toward her to rest a kiss to his lips.

"I brought us something to eat," she said, indicating the box. "I'm sure you're hungry. I don't think I've seen you eat anything since the bar."

Jem shook his head.

"I'm not hungry," he said.

"What's wrong?" she asked.

"Did I make the right choice coming back?" he asked.

Angela looked at him quizzically.

"Why would you ask that?"

"So much happened while I was gone. I keep hearing names that I don't know. They told me that the Klimnu traveling with us is Maxim's father. I don't know who that is, Angela."

"Why didn't you tell them that?" Angela asked.

Jem shook his head again and stared down at the floor in front of him. He didn't want to look at her and let her see the pain in his face.

"They didn't even realize that I wouldn't know," he said. "They met him after I left Uoria. He's not the only one. I keep hearing names that I've never heard and about people they've met, places they've gone, that I don't understand. When I left, the Denynso had never gone outside of the compound. Now I know that the warriors have not only left the compound but found other settlements, other species that we didn't know about. They've formed alliances and relationships. There are new bonds and wars. I feel like I don't even know them anymore."

"That's not true, Jem," Angela tried to tell him.

"It is," Jem argued. "It's like they didn't even recognize that I was gone. Now that I'm back, I've just melded back in and they expect me to know what's happening."

"They more than recognized that you were gone," Angela told him. "You haven't heard what they've been saying about you. They missed you so much, Jem. They love you. You are a part of them. If they haven't told you about something that they've done or explained something to you, it's because you are such an integral element of their lives that they don't want to think about the time when you weren't around. They just want to pretend that you have always been there."

Jem looked at his mate and felt warmth fill him. It was hard for him to face everything that he had missed since being gone and trying to find his context within the clan again, but he knew that she was right. He was born Denynso. Nothing could change that. It didn't really matter what had happened in the time that had passed since he disappeared from that underground realm and moved through the unknown portal. What mattered was that he was back now and he would give everything he had to protect his kind and those that they trusted.

Angela gave him a gently suggestive smile and opened the box in front of them.

"Why don't you try to eat something," she said. "It will make you feel better."

She took what looked like one of the cupcakes that Ty had baked when he was trying to help Ero show Zuri how much he loved her, but smaller.

"What is that?" he asked.

"Apparently when they were packing the emergency rations for these chambers, they decided that people stuck in some form of disaster might have cravings for sweets. This is a cupcake designed specifically to stay fresh for more than one hundred years."

Jem's face contorted.

"How did they do that?" he asked.

"Don't worry," she said. "They were perfected by the deep space travel research department to be taken on extensive missions with them. It just so happens that they last a lot longer than they originally thought."

"So you've had one?" he asked.

Angela nodded and took the cupcake out of its wrapper.

"These were my one request when I signed up for the excavation mission," she said. "I didn't go to this University, but I was friends with some of the people in the research department that worked on these. I might have nearly lived off of these when I was a poor University student and they let me be the test subject for some of the early recipes for these."

Jem could see a veil of memories in her eyes and felt he same tug of emotion that he always did when he thought of Angela's life before he met her. He tried to not dwell on it. He tried to focus on life now and not let himself imagine what her future would have been like if she hadn't signed up for the excavation, or if she had chosen to stay close to the main dig site rather than going to the cave to explore with the others and fallen through the portal that took her away from her stream on Earth in the same way that the portal had taken Jem from Uoria.

Angela smiled and broke the cupcake in half, revealing a creamy white filling. She dipped her finger into it and then put it in her mouth. Jem's stomach clenched as she sucked the cream from her fingertip and smiled at him. Placing the halves of the cupcake back into the box, she reached forward and peeled Jem's shirt away from his body. There was still a dull ache where the deep wound had been, but Ciyrs's healing had taken strong effect and the gash was nearly healed.

Angela gathered more of the cream out of the cupcake and trailed it down the center of Jem's chest, following the curves of his deeply chiseled muscles and glazing his nipple. He let out a long, growling breath as she leaned forward and swept the sweetened cream away from his skin with her tongue. Even when the cream was gone, she continued to swirl her tongue along his chest. Losing himself in the sensation of her warm mouth on his skin, Jem brought his hands to her shirt, bunched it at her waist, and then waited until she sat back, away from his chest so that he could remove her shirt. Jem released the hooks on the back of her bra, revealing her breasts to him, and groaned at the smooth fullness of them as she drew in a breath. He dipped his thumb into the cream filling of the cupcake just as she had and coated one taut pink nipple. His mouth closed over her breast, his tongue flicking across her skin as he sucked away the sweet cream, savoring the delectable contrast of the cream with her warm, salty skin.

Angela's eyes drifted closed as she bit down on her bottom lip and arched back to press her breast deeper into his mouth. Jem's hands smoothed down over her hips to grip her butt tightly, pulling her closer to his body so that he could kiss his way to the other breast and repeat the attention there. Her hands moved to the front of his pants and she worked them open so that she could pushed them down off of his hips. Jem's already surging erection sprung free from the thick fabric and he groaned as Angela wrapped her hand around the shaft eagerly. He loved the way she sighed at the feeling of him against her palm and ran her fingertips along the ridges as if greeting them. She flattened her other hand in the center of his chest and guided him carefully to lie back on the floor so that she could straighten his legs and remove the rest of his clothing. He closed his eyes and let himself relax as she dipped her fingers in the cream again and set to work painting his chest.

Angela created patterns against his skin and then

promptly followed them with her tongue. She worked her way gradually from his chest down his belly and he pressed his hips up toward her, but she seemed to purposely avoid touching his cock. Instead, she started a trail of kisses down the deep muscular V of his hips and along one inner thigh to his knee before moving to follow the reverse trail up the other thigh and along his hip until she reached his belly again.

By now Jem's breath was rough and ragged as he struggled to control himself. The powerful sensations that Angela was creating in him were making the tension that had been within him melt away. He was no longer thinking about the battle or the war that awaited them on Penthos. He wasn't thinking of the time that he had spent away from Uoria or the future that could have been if neither of them had found the portals. He was fully in that moment, wanting only to give himself over to the experience and savor the pleasure of Angela. She straddled his legs and leaned forward to brush her full breasts across his erection, teasing it and tempting it to twitch and rise toward her. She was still nuzzling him as she dipped her head down and licked from his belly up to his chest in one smooth glide of his tongue, pausing to bite playfully into one of his nipples. Her movement brought her breasts away from his erection and instead stroked her belly along it. Jem felt the silky drops from the tip spread onto her skin. He wrapped his hand around the back of her head.

"Suck me," he growled, suddenly filled with an intensity and dominance that he hadn't felt since the days before he had completed his bond with Angela.

Angela moaned slightly and rose up on her knees. He watched her slide out of her pants, moving from one knee to the other so that she could get as bare as he was. Her body was luscious and irresistible. His need for her was deep and primal, and he lifted his hips toward her. Angela took the invitation, positioned herself between his thighs and opened her mouth to take him fully in. The tip of his cock touched her throat and then slipped in deeper as she wrapped her lips around the base of his shaft. Jem released a loud groan and let his hips fall back to the ground as his head tilted back and he squeezed his eyes closed.

Jem's hand clutched at Angela's hair and he used the grip to guide her into a smooth, fast rhythm. She didn't resist the guidance, and instead seemed to respond eagerly to it, relaxing her mouth so that he could move her in the pattern that was most desirable to him. Jem lifted his hips as he guided her to thrust into her mouth with each glide of her mouth. He could feel himself racing toward orgasm, but didn't want to stop. After a few moments, he forced himself to withdraw from her mouth and took her by the shoulders. He pulled her up his body so that she sprawled on his chest and their mouths met. As they kissed passionately, he positioned her thighs on either side of him. Jem wrapped his hand around the base of his cock and held his shaft steady so that he could circle the tip at her opening.

Her back arched and Angela let out a moan of pleasure. She circled her hips into him, gradually lowering herself so that he slipped inside her. Finally, she settled onto his hips, enveloping him completely. She was still tight and he felt her hugging him with her hot, slick walls. With each circle of her hips, she relaxed, taking him deeper. Jem grabbed her hips and led her to roll them so that they stayed close even while he massaged her walls. She whimpered and moaned, her body arching slightly as if she were trying to pull away from the intensity of the feeling, but Jem only pressed deeper into her and nurtured her to a shattering climax. She screamed out as her body closed tightly around him and drew him deeper. In an instant Jem's control shattered and his cock throbbed explosively. Jem released his hold on her hips and thrust up into her hard and fast until finally she screamed again and then collapsed forward onto him, her sweaty body trembling against his.

Their breathing slowed and her body fell still, but Jem stayed inside her. The feeling of her cradling him with a body crafted specifically for him was comforting and intimate, and he ran his fingers down her back and tenderly kissed her shoulder. The world around him started coming back into focus and Jem could hear the voices of some of the other men discussing their preparations for the next day. Soon he would be off of Earth and on a shuttle, that would bring him away from the life that he had lived since his disappearance. He knew that he wouldn't be going straight home to Uoria, but rather to a planet that he couldn't even envision. Suddenly, though, he didn't feel as disconnected from the war that was raging there. Angela's words had clarified his thoughts and brought calm to his heart. He knew now that the time away from Uoria and the Denynso didn't make him less a part of them or uninvolved in the battle that was looming ahead of them. It had only increased his compulsion and drive to fight.

Outside the laboratory, the night was calm and dark, its peaceful stillness acting to conceal the tense, almost frantic energy that boiled within. Around them everyone in the basement started to wake and ready themselves to leave. Jem cradled Angela closer, wanting just another few seconds of the quiet that she created around him before they left. Everything was changing. Jem could feel it within him just as strongly as he had felt the need to get back to Uoria. It was as if everyone who was aligned with the Denynso had joined the same rhythm. They drew in their breaths together and released them as one, preparing in every moment for when they would stand alongside one another again.

UNTITLED

To be continued...

LORALIA & BANNACK'S STORY

1

"Are you alright?" Loralia asked as she watched Bannack pull another box from the top of the shelving unit and place it on the stack that he was creating on the floor beside him.

"I'm fine," her mate responded brusquely without looking her direction.

Loralia struggled with her urge to tune into Bannack's emotions, to let herself feel what he was feeling. It was a capability that she had been born with, one that she had never realized set her as far apart from the rest of her kind as it did. This was a gift not from the Irisa who had raised her and who she thought was the only species whose blood ran through her veins, but from the mysterious father, the Eteri who she had never known and who she had only just seen for the first time. This was something that had always been a part of her, a way that she went through life and how she understood those she encountered. It had been the way that she knew that she was able to trust the Denynso when they entered her underground home and how she had known that the same could not be said for the gruesome, skeletal creatures that had invaded before and forced her into hiding. It wasn't until she had bonded with Bannack and gotten used to life outside of the loneliness of the reflected realm that she learned not to use it with every interaction.

There were some moments when this gift had brought great value, such as when she was able to comfort Eden about the health of the child she had been carrying within her and tell her that she would soon bear a son who would be strong and powerful like his father. There were also moments, too many moments, when she felt that she was intruding in the lives of those around her and suffered intense emotions and thoughts she didn't want to have within her. She discovered that she and Bannack couldn't communicate with each other through their minds in the way that the Denynso could usually do with their mates, even those born from other species. It was then that she began to question this way of exploring the world and learning from others, and soon after taught herself not to reach out in that way, to give others the privacy that their emotions deserved and connect with them on their level first.

At this moment, though, she craved the clarity that came from when she was able to detect exactly how her mate was feeling. He seemed closed and angry, lost in his own thoughts as he followed the instructions that Pyra had given him as they all worked to prepare for when they would leave the laboratory building and head for Penthos. He took another box from the shelf and placed it on the stack. Apparently satisfied that he had taken enough, he reached down and scooped the entire stack into his arms. He carried them out of the room and she knew that he was bringing them back to the section of the emergency chamber that

Pyra had designated as the central location where they would gather all the supplies for the trip to Penthos and the conditions that they might face there.

Loralia stood in the room where Bannack had left her, waiting for him to return. She didn't want to walk away without knowing what was going through his mind. With everything that they had been facing since arriving on Earth, she knew that he was under a tremendous amount of strain. He was struggling with something and it was drawing him away from her. Loralia knew that she couldn't let that happen. She couldn't simply walk away and allow the tension and pain that was pressing in around them fracture the bond that had held them so closely on Uoria. Finally, he came back into the room and stopped short when he saw her still standing there. They stared at each other for a few moments before he went back to the shelves and started pulling more of the boxes down.

"What are those?" Loralia asked, wanting to start a conversation between them just so she could hear his voice.

Bannack glanced over his shoulder at her. The expression on his face was angry at first, but then softened before he turned back to the boxes.

"Food," he said. "Whoever built these chambers really must have thought something terrible was going to happen and that a lot of people were going to seek refuge down here. There's enough food and supplies down here to last for months."

Loralia took a step toward him, trying to offer him a smile.

"But isn't that a good thing?" she asked. "We didn't expect any of this to happen, so we didn't prepare for it. We didn't have any food or supplies or anything to bring back to Penthos with us. What's down here will sustain us while we're here and then after we leave. That's a wonderful thing."

Bannack's arms fell to his side and he gave a deep sigh.

"Yes," he said, sounding more exasperated now than angry. "Of course, it's a good thing that the supplies are here for us to use, but doesn't it make you sad that they are?"

"What do you mean?"

"What type of world is this? What type of suffering and disasters did the people who lived at this time have to see and expect for them to go to this extent to prepare for something terrible to happen? This isn't just a few supplies and some rations to carry them through bad weather or to protect them for a day or so. These supplies were put here to keep people going for long stretches of time. They wanted to make sure that every person who might have been in the hospital at the time was able to come down here and survive whatever horror was going on outside. What could they have been so afraid of?"

"I don't know, Bannack," Loralia said. She could feel the emotion tightening in her throat now and was glad that she had kept her mind blocked to what he was feeling. She didn't think that she had the strength right then to endure what he was obviously going through. "Maybe it just gave them comfort to know that there was enough down here to support them if something did happen. This was a hospital. People would come here in their most difficult times. Maybe it was just reassuring to know that once they were here, they were safe."

"Or maybe it haunted them," Bannack said. "Maybe they thought about it constantly, the fact that there was something happening on the horizon that was so terrifying they needed to build up the walls around themselves and prepare to scramble for survival. They knew that it could happen so quickly. In an instant, the life that they thought that they were living could be over."

"But they never had to use them," Loralia said, taking another cautious step toward her tremendous mate. "All these supplies are still sitting here, which means that nothing ever happened that made them have to come down here and use them."

"Not yet," Bannack said.

Loralia reached forward and took hold of Bannack's arm so that she could turn him around to face her.

"What's this all about?" she asked. "Why are you thinking about this so much?"

"We came here for a wedding," he said.

Loralia nodded.

"I know," she said. "We saw it."

"We also saw the Valdicians swarm the ceremony and kidnap Eden and Pyra's baby."

"But they got through the wedding. Samira and Ty are married now."

"I know," Bannack said. "That's what's bothering me."

He turned back and started pulling the boxes down from the shelves again.

"I don't understand," Loralia said. "Why does it bother you that Samira and Ty got married? That's why we came here. That's what they wanted."

"I know," he said.

"Then..."

"Because we aren't," Bannack snapped, startling her into silence. Loralia took a slight step back, giving Bannack the space that she felt he needed. "We aren't like them. We didn't go through a ceremony together. We haven't been tied, Loralia."

"I know," she said. "But we are bonded. Our relationship is just as strong as their marriage."

"Not to your kind," Bannack said.

"I'm the only one of my kind," Loralia answered.

"You know what I mean," he said more gently now, turning away from the boxes to look at her. "When we first bonded, you told me about the tying ceremony that the Irisa used to bind mates. I asked you if you would go through that ceremony with me."

"And I agreed," Loralia said. "When the rest of my species died out, I didn't think that I was ever going to have the opportunity to have such a ceremony. I didn't know that I would ever love anyone or have the chance to promise my life to another. When you asked if I would do the tying ceremony, it meant more to me than I could ever tell you. It felt like you really did love me and cared about what I would want for our relationship."

"Of course, I love you," Bannack said. "That's the point. We haven't had our ceremony yet, and we have no way of knowing what's going to happen tomorrow. Just like these people didn't. They spent their time preparing for a disaster that could strike them at any time. They didn't know if it would be years in the future or the next day, but they thought about it. They prepared for the future by thinking about how they would survive something terrible that happened to them. That's not how I want to prepare for the future."

"How do you want to prepare?" she asked.

Bannack finally turned toward her fully and took a step to close the space between them. He took Loralia's hands in his, engulfing hers completely in his palms, and stared into her eyes. The deep orange of his gaze still brought a tremble to her belly and she couldn't help the smile that curved her lips. It was the perfect expression of their connection, the visual representation of the unbreakable bond that they shared. She remembered the way that his eyes looked when they first met and the flickers of orange that she saw in their first early glances. She didn't know what it meant then, didn't know that each of those flickers of orange was his heart telling Bannack that he had finally found the woman that he had been waiting for his entire life.

"I don't know what's going to happen tomorrow," he said tenderly. "I don't know if we're still going to be sitting here in this basement or if we will try to get to the shuttles. I don't know if we'll make it back to Penthos or if we never see the stars again. I don't know. What I do know is that if there is a future, I only want to share it with you. I don't want the future to come without us being completely ready for it, and that means being fully and completely bound to one another. I want us to have our tying ceremony."

Loralia felt her heart rise in her chest and butterflies fluttering in her belly.

"You do?" she asked.

Bannack nodded.

"I always have."

"I know that we are already bonded and that the connection between us is unshakable, but it really is important to me. It wouldn't be just for us. It would be a way for me to honor everyone who I have lost and the futures that they never got to have." She drew in a shaking breath, glancing down at her feet and then back up at him. "It would honor my mother...and Azrael."

2

───────

Bannack was still shaking slightly from his conversation with Loralia when he lowered his second load of boxes to the stack in the emergency chamber. He hadn't meant to be so emotional. This wasn't the time for that. There was too much to be done and too much danger still lingering all around them for him to allow his mind to wander that way, to think so much about himself rather than the rest of the group. He had held the idea of the Irisa tying ceremony in his heart since she had told him about it, and hadn't forgotten the way that Loralia's eyes shimmered and the soft glow around her intensified just slightly when she talked about it that day when they were standing in the underground village that she used to share with the members of her kind before they were destroyed by the unexpected plague. He had known since then that he wanted desperately to give her that experience. She had offered herself to him and to the Denynso form of bonding so willingly and without question, and Bannack had only fallen more deeply in love with her.

The thought of them being able to engage in the tying

ceremony together had been made seemingly impossible soon after when Jem disappeared and the Denynso decided to leave the compound and tour Uoria in the way of the old Denynso kings. As much as he loved her and wanted the experience for them, the warrior devotion within him had taken over, reminding him that he had responsibilities and duties to his kind that he had to attend to first. He wanted comfort and peace before he gave her the ceremony that she wanted and deserved.

Now he was facing even more conflict than they had before, but had witnessed Samira and Ty marry. Rather than it seeming that their celebration had been marred by what was now happening around them, their union seemed to have strengthened them and made them even more confident in their convictions against Ryan and his army. Now Bannack felt like he wasn't protecting Loralia by waiting for the ideal moment for them to have their ceremony. Rather, he was hurting both of them, preventing them from being able to experience something that would be more than just a cherished moment in their lives, but something that defined them.

There would be no perfect moment. There would never be a time when there wasn't danger on the horizon or questions in the backs of all their minds. Even when the war was over, he knew that they wouldn't ever be able to put it completely behind them. The Denynso carried every battle with them, no matter how swift the victory or total the destruction of the enemy. It was what made them and what continued to build them. This would change them in ways that would linger with them always. The reality was that every moment that he spent with Loralia, no matter what was happening, as long as he knew that she was breathing and that he would hold her in his arms again, was as close to perfect as he had ever experienced. The only thing that could make his life better would be to know that they were fully committed to each other in the ways that both of their hearts had prepared to be committed since they were children.

Thinking about it, however, had only seemed to make not being able to have it even more difficult. There was so much happening around them that he couldn't even begin to think about when the conflict might end. It could take only a few days to destroy the enemy army and eliminate Ryan once and for all, or the war could continue for months, or even years like the conflict with the Klimnu.

"Could everyone please gather for a moment?" Pyra shouted.

The room fell silent and the group drifted closer to him. Bannack felt Loralia come up behind him and slip her hand into his. The touch was soft and tender, and Bannack wrapped his grip around it.

"Is everything alright, Pyra?" Eden asked, stepping up to her mate.

"I think it's time that I let everyone else know what's happening," he said. "I've hesitated to share this information with some of you because I didn't want to cause any more upset or fear, but I don't think that there's any other option at this point." He drew in a breath and looked around at them. "Ryan's tyranny goes deeper than any of us expected. We have recently uncovered disturbing evidence of the experiments and breeding program. As a result of this, our number has increased significantly, as has the pressing urgency with which we must leave. Ciyrs has informed me that the wounded are responding well to their healing and we should soon be ready to leave."

"What did you find, Pyra?" Azra asked.

Pyra took a deep breath and looked out over the group. It was almost as if he had been hoping that he wouldn't have to explain what he had told them, and that he would just be able to move ahead with the conversation, but now he knew that he was going to have to tell them. Bannack listened as the warrior leader described the facilities that they found on the floor beneath them and the people that they rescued. He felt his stomach turn as Pyra told of their injuries and what the hybrid woman had told them about Ryan's torturous retraining techniques.

"What will we do with them?" Zuri asked. "We can't just leave them here. They can't take care of themselves."

"I know that," Pyra said. "That's why it's more important than ever before for us to leave as soon as possible. We need to get them away from here and figure out how to get them the care that they need. For now, we need to decide how everyone will travel. We still have the shuttle that we rode from Penthos, unless it has been commissioned for another trip. Jonah and Oro brought a vehicle that can accommodate several people. Jonah has informed me that he will be staying here."

There was a ripple of gasps and protests through the group, and Pyra held up a hand.

"He has his reasons," he said loudly. "He is staying here to continue with his own mission, and as much as I would like him to be with us, he has my support."

"I will stay with him."

The voice was weak and unfamiliar, and when Bannack turned toward the door, he saw a strange man step inside the chamber. He was no longer wearing the dark hood, but Bannack knew that he was one of the hybrids that had fought against them. His defenses immediately surged forward and Bannack felt himself wanting to rush at the man, take out everything that was still built up within him. Loralia's grip tightened on his hand and he knew that she had tuned into him, was feeling what he was and was stopping him from doing anything. He knew that meant that she must be getting overwhelmed by everything that was happening around them and needed this connection to help her understand. The moment gave Bannack the chance to breathe and remind himself what Pyra had just told them about the hybrids and what they had been through. He relaxed and stepped back toward Loralia.

"You shouldn't be up yet," Ciyrs said to the man.

He shook his head.

"I'm fine," he said. "I feel better than I have in a long time. That's why I'll stay here with Jonah. There are others who aren't ready to leave yet. They need more time to heal and they'll need help. I will stay here and take care of them."

Pyra nodded.

"Thank you," he said. "I'm sure that Jonah will appreciate all of the assistance he can get." He turned toward where Rilex was standing. "Do you know of any others who will stay?" he asked.

"I haven't spoken to all of them," Rilex said, "but I know that there are several who are still is poor condition, and others who are unwilling to leave. That isn't all of them, though. The woman who first called to Eden is very eager to leave. She wants to get as far from the facility as she can. She is willing to go anywhere with us."

Pyra nodded again.

"So be it," he said. "Continue to prepare. We will leave tomorrow night."

∼

The group was dissipating under Pyra's command and Loralia watched as several of them walked toward the back of the chamber, revealing Azrael standing across the room from her. He was still looking up toward Pyra, giving her the opportunity to look at him for several long seconds, evaluating him without him noticing. She wished she knew what he was feeling, but somehow, she knew that he had blocked himself off long ago and wouldn't permit her to read him the way that she could others. Her eyes traced his tall, muscled body and the wings that hung low at the sides of his body. They were torn and broken, showing the scars of countless conflicts, and Loralia felt a sudden pull toward him. It seemed to have settled into her mind and heart that this was truly her father. Rather than the man who had raised her and taught her all that she knew about using the skills and capabilities given to her by her Irisa blood, it was actually this man who had created her. Something swelled inside her and she strode toward him.

"Did you know about me?" she asked as she approached Azrael.

The man turned toward her, seemingly startled by her sudden appearance beside him as much as the question.

"Yes," he answered without hesitation.

Bannack walked up behind her and placed his hand on her back.

"Are you alright?" he asked.

Loralia nodded.

"Loralia," Azrael said carefully, "can we go somewhere and talk? I would very much like the opportunity to meet you officially."

Loralia nodded, not trusting herself if she tried to speak at that moment. They turned and she guided him back toward the room where Bannack had been gathering supplies. It was still empty and she led Azrael inside, silently relaying to Bannack that she didn't want anyone else to come in. When Bannack took his place at the door, Loralia turned back to Azrael.

"Did you know about me?" she asked again.

Azrael nodded and took a step toward her.

"I did," he said. "I knew about you before your mother did, and I have loved you since that moment."

Loralia's heart ached, but she wasn't sure why. There were too many emotions flowing through her, too many questions and possibilities, too many moments that could have been but had been shattered before she was ever able to live them.

"Then why?" she asked. "Why did you go away?"

"I didn't want to," Azrael said. "I wanted to marry your mother and raise you as a family. I wanted us to be together, but it was too dangerous."

"I don't understand."

"I know you don't," Azrael said, "and I wish that there was something that I could say or do that would help make it easier for you."

"Nothing about this is easy for me," she said.

"It isn't for me, either. I've waited your entire life to meet you."

"You have?" Loralia asked.

"Of course, I have. You and your mother have been the most precious things in my life since the moment that I knew that you were coming. You have only just found out about me, but I have missed you and waited for you for years. Most of it I never thought that I would see you. I thought that you had died with the others."

Loralia's head hung as she felt a pang of longing for the

family that she had lost when she was younger, leaving her completely alone until she met Bannack.

"Why did you go?" she asked. "Why did you never come for me."

"I told you," he said. "It was too dangerous. Your mother and I wanted to be together. We had our life planned and I couldn't wait to see you. The times were complicated then, though. The Irisa were dying and the Valdicians were destroying the planet along with their allies. We intended for her to go into hiding along with the others and stay safe there until the conflict was over, then we would be back together. I was trying to protect you by staying away. I didn't want to do anything that might put either one of you in any more danger than you already were."

"And then?" Loralia asked.

"I waited. I waited for as long as I could and then I came for you. I searched. I went back to the entrance to the underground settlement and searched, but I couldn't find it. I looked everywhere, but the blocks that had been put on the entrances were too strong. They kept me from finding them. I couldn't get to you. I never stopped thinking about you. Never. Then I heard that the Irisa were gone and it felt like my soul had been taken from me. I thought that you were gone. I had already lost your mother. I couldn't bear the thought of never getting to even meet you."

"They are gone," Loralia said. "All of them. I'm the only one who survived."

Azrael nodded.

"I know," he said. "Do you know why?"

Loralia shook her head.

"I never got sick the way the others did. There was nothing I could do, and then they were all gone and I was alone."

"The Irisa became very ill when the Valdicians came. You do not have pure Irisa blood in your veins, and that is what kept you alive. There is enough of me within you that it prevented the illness from taking you."

"So, in a way, you have protected me my entire life."

Loralia could see a mist of tears in Azrael's eyes and the resistance and anger that she had felt for the large winged man when she first saw him melted away.

"Will you tell me about your mother?" he asked, his voice sounding soft and choked. "Was she happy?"

Loralia nodded.

"Yes," she said. "My father..." she paused and took a breath, "the man who I thought was my father, loved her very much. He loved both of us."

"I'm glad," Azrael said. "I wouldn't want for her to be alone and without love." He hesitated briefly. "She never told you about me?" he asked.

Loralia shook her head.

"No," she said. "But don't be angry with her. I know that she would never hurt me, and I believe that she never would have hurt you. I only remember him, but I know now that she wasn't always with him. There was a time when she waited for you, but when you didn't come back, or when she was told that she wouldn't be allowed to leave and go find you, she might have been afraid of what it would mean to raise me alone. She knew that I wasn't going to be like the others."

"You don't have wings," Azrael said.

Loralia nearly laughed but she didn't know why. She shook her head.

"No," she said. "I never have. But there are things about me that are different. The color of my eyes. I glow. It's faint, but it's there. And..." she hesitated.

"And?" he asked.

They stared at each other for a few seconds and she suddenly felt a strong rush of emotion wash over here. There was fear and nervousness, excitement and joy, sadness and longing. The strongest, though, was an overarching feeling of love. Loralia gasped slightly.

"You can feel," Azrael said softly. "You can read others."

Loralia nodded.

"I think that I always knew," she said.

"Always knew what?" Azrael asked.

"My mother loved the man I believed to be my father. They were very happy together until the end. No matter how happy she was, though, there was always something else there. I could always feel the emptiness within her. There was a faint haze of sadness over everything that she felt. I knew that there was something that she was missing, something that was so deep within her that she didn't even want to touch it, much less share it with anyone around her. Now I know that that was you."

Loralia took out her compact and heard Azrael give a slight gasp, like he was looking at something from his past. She touched the back and felt a small lip of metal. Tucking her fingernail beneath the lip, she opened the hidden compartment of the compact and withdrew the fine, delicate fabric from inside. When she held it out toward Azrael, tears pooled under the man's eyes and then trickled down his cheeks.

"This was hers," Loralia said. "She gave it to me when I was younger, but never told me why. I've had it with me my entire life."

Azrael nodded and reached for the fabric. She draped it over his fingers and allowed him to examine it lovingly for a few long seconds. The delicate strip of fabric unfolded and he ran his fingertips along it.

"This was for our tying ceremony," he said, so softly that Loralia barely heard him.

"She never told me why she had it, but I knew that it wasn't from her and my..." her voice trailed off again and Azrael shook his head.

"It's alright, Loralia. That man was there for you when I wasn't able to be. He gave you what I couldn't and ensured that you and your mother weren't alone. I will always be grateful to him for that. He was your father, but I hope in your heart you know that I am, too, and that I love you."

"I do," Loralia said. "As much as there was a part missing from my mother, I knew there was a part missing from me as well. I'm glad to have found that part."

She stepped forward and offered her arms to Azrael. For a moment, he looked at them as if he didn't remember what it meant to embrace someone, as if the years of being hardened by fierce battles and bloody confrontations while longing for the only family that he would ever create had taken from him any memory of showing affection. Soon, though, he opened his arms as well and took her into them, holding her close to his chest and resting his cheek against the top of her head. Loralia felt him relax, as if finally holding his child after so long removed a lifetime of tension and pain from his muscles.

When they parted, Loralia turned and walked over to Bannack. She took him by the hand and led him back across the room.

"This is my mate," she said, "Bannack. Bannack, this," she gestured toward Azrael, "is my father."

Loralia saw Bannack's eyes widen, but he reached forward to grasp the Eteri man's hand in greeting.

"Hello," he said. "It's nice to meet you."

"It is very nice to meet you," Azrael said. "Thank you for taking care of my daughter."

Something flashed in Bannack's eyes as he glanced at Loralia and then back at Azrael.

"I love Loralia with everything that is in me. I was born to be her mate and to take care of her as her mate, but I would like very much if I was able to give her the union that she dreamed of. If you would give me permission, I would be honored to have a tying ceremony with your daughter."

Loralia's heart felt like it was soaring. Her eyes filled with tears as she saw the first smile touch Azrael's lips.

"I can think of nothing that would make me happier than to give you my permission and witness your binding," he said.

3

———

Bannack woke before Loralia the next morning. He lay beside her, holding her close and enjoying the warmth of her body molding so easily and comfortably to his. Her breaths were long and soft, sounding peaceful and content. As he listened to them, images began to form in his mind. He thought of the delight on Azrael's face the night before when he had formally asked his permission to become tied to Loralia. He saw the emotion in her eyes and the smile that seemed like it would never go away. Things had fallen into place in a way that Bannack could never have expected, but that were beyond perfect. He could see the years that were lost between Azrael and Loralia, and even though they were beginning to bridge them, there would be nothing that would ever fill those moments that they had never gotten to have together. Bannack wasn't willing to let that happen for him and Loralia. They had been waiting long enough and he didn't want to wait anymore. He wanted them to have their tying ceremony as soon as possible.

Easing away from Loralia as carefully as he could so that

he wouldn't disturb her, Bannack crossed the room where they had slept and went to the emergency chamber where he knew that he would find Ty and Samira. Ty was sitting on the floor in the partial light of two lightsticks that had been positioned in opposite corners of the room to cut through the almost tangible darkness of the room. A box was on the floor between his legs and he was sifting through its contents, occasionally taking items out and putting them to either side of him. Bannack could hear faint whispers coming from Ty's direction and realized that Samira was lying on the mat beside him, but was talking to him softly.

Bannack approached them cautiously, not wanting to startle them. Ty looked up and saw him.

"Hey," he said, starting to stand up. "Is everything alright? What's wrong?"

Bannack held up his hand to disarm the other Denynso. Though Ty had been the nurturer of their clan since he was old enough to take on his role, over the last year he had experienced and changed so much that Bannack now couldn't consider him as anything but another warrior. It was that warrior spirit that brought the tension into Ty's shoulders and made his eyes wider with anticipation now. Bannack lowered down to sit with him.

"Nothing's wrong?" he said. "Don't worry. There's just something that I needed to talk to you about. Both of you, if that's alright."

Bannack looked to his side and saw Samira sitting up. She nodded.

"Of course," she said. "What do you need?"

"I've asked Loralia to have a tying ceremony with me," he said. "It's the Irisa version of getting married."

Samira's eyes lit up and she grinned at him.

"That's wonderful!" she said. "I'm so happy for you."

"Congratulations," Ty said.

"Thank you," Bannack said. "But that's not it."

"Alright," Ty said. "What else?"

"With everything that has happened, it has proven to me more than ever that we never know what tomorrow is going to bring. With all of the battles that I've faced in my life and the horrors that I've seen, I never thought of that. It took thinking that I could lose Loralia to really realize that life isn't something that I am guaranteed. I can't just look ahead into the future and know that I will be granted something that I want. Then I saw her with Azrael last night and it hit me that he missed her entire life. I don't want to even begin to know what that's like. I don't want any more time to pass without giving her the union that her kind revered." He took a breath. "But I also know that this visit was supposed to be about you getting married. Your wedding didn't turn out the way that you wanted it to and you never even got a chance to celebrate your marriage. I want to have our ceremony when we leave here, on the ship before we get to Penthos. I know that not everyone will be together, but I don't want to wait any longer. I needed to talk to you about it first, though."

Samira slid closer to Bannack and tilted her head to look into his eyes.

"Our wedding is over, Bannack," she said. "We are married. That's why we came here. No, it didn't turn out the way that we thought it would, but that doesn't change that Ty is my husband, and that's all that I care about. I can tell you how much it meant to me that Ty was willing to go through a human wedding when he had no idea about the traditions and it held no real meaning for him. He did it to please me and to make sure that I felt completely bonded to him. That is what you want to give Loralia. You want her to know that you love and respect her, and that it is not just the beliefs and traditions of your kind that matter. That is an amazing and wonderful thing. I would never ask you to wait even a second longer than you wanted to, to give that to her or to have that for yourself."

"Listen to me, Bannack," Ty said. "I have known loss my entire life. There has never been a moment that I felt I was promised. That's why I asked Samira to marry me and that's why I'm telling you now that if you want to marry Loralia, in whatever way that means for her, that you shouldn't wait. I would never ask you to not do what makes you happy for me. In fact, I can't think of anything that would make me happier than to witness this with you. Ryan might have stolen some of our wedding from us, but you can't let him take yours from you. He can't have that power."

"Thank you," Bannack said. "I can't tell you how much that means to me."

"Is there anything that we can do to help you plan it?" Samira asked.

Bannack nodded

"I can use all the help I can get," he said. "I don't even know where to start."

"We should be safe, shouldn't we?" Gyyx asked as they gathered at the door to the basement, readying to leave. "Now that we've uncovered the breeding facility and know that the hybrids were made as slaves and freed some of them, we shouldn't be in any danger. They should recognize that we aren't a threat and let us through."

Loralia saw the hybrid woman that stood close beside Rilex shake her head. She knew now that these people had no names and it created an ache of sadness inside her. It didn't matter how or why they had come into existence. Everyone deserved a name.

"What do you mean?" Pyra asked.

The woman looked uncertainly up at Rilex, her face showing that she didn't know if she should continue. Loralia understood exactly what the woman was experiencing. She remembered what it was like the first time that she saw the Denynso come down into her home beneath their compound, and then the first time that she had encountered Pyra. It was incredibly intimidating, and she hadn't even posed a threat to them. The fact that this woman was standing amongst them, willing to speak at all, showed a courage and strength that was truly amazing.

"Not all of the hybrid army are slaves," she said. "Some of us were born here and have no identities outside of what Ryan made us into. Others were stolen and manipulated with his experiments to turn them into the hybrid creatures that they are now. There are others, though, who believe in the same things that he does. They think that he is the savior of the universe and the ultimate leader who will bring them to an existence of glory and power. They gave themselves willingly to the program and allowed Ryan to transform them. They are not slaves. They fight because they want to destroy. They stand with the Valdicians and believe wholly and completely everything that they or Ryan says. They might not use them or even remember them, but they have names. They are extremely dangerous. Even more now that you have found and freed us."

Pyra straightened and Loralia saw his jaw tighten. He gave a single nod and lifted his head slightly as if looking out over the rest of the group.

"When we get outside, everyone needs to move as quickly as possible," Pyra instructed. "Warriors, carry what women you can. Those of you who are in the worst condition will be traveling in Jonah's vehicle, go with Oro and Azrael. That is closer to here and will be easier to get to. Everyone else, come with me. We need to get to the transportation bay before anyone finds us. If you encounter anyone who puts up a threat, be ready to fight. We'll come back together on Penthos."

Loralia gripped Bannack's hand tightly beside her. They had been anticipating this moment, but now that it was here, it was more frightening than she had thought it would be. Though the basement was not the most comfortable or ideal of lodging places, it had proved safe and now they were leaving it and making themselves completely vulnerable again. The hybrid woman's words were chilling, but Loralia couldn't push them out of her mind. There had been a brief moment of reassurance when they learned of Eden and the men rescuing the hybrids and the human women. It had seemed that maybe they weren't in the danger that they thought they were, and perhaps they could get out of the laboratory and to Penthos without incident. Once there, they might even be able to resolve the situation quickly. Now, though, she knew that this wasn't the case. The hybrid army was just as dangerous as they originally thought, perhaps even more so. Soldiers who fight because they are forced to will never be as fearsome as those who fight because their heart and mind are in the fight.

Pyra said goodbye to Jonah, and Loralia gave the man one more look before starting toward the exit. She was worried about him staying behind without the assistance of the rest of them, but she knew that it was the right thing for him. He had to understand why his file was still in that examination room, and what it meant for them. He had already been through dangerous, stressful times, and she knew that if there was anyone outside of the warriors who was prepared to handle this challenge, it would be Jonah.

She was lifting one of the bags of supplies that she would carry when she felt a hand touch her back. She looked up to see Azrael standing behind her.

"I am going to travel in the shuttle with the rest of you," he said.

"Shouldn't you be in the vehicle that you came in?" Loralia asked.

Azrael shook his head.

"That needs to be for those who are in the most need. I'm fine. I can make it to the transportation bay. Oro knows how to use the vehicle and will make sure that they get to Penthos safely."

Loralia nodded.

"You're right," she said. She paused for a moment, unsure of how to express what she was feeling. "Thank you," she said.

"For what?" Azrael asked.

"For being here," she said.

"I had to come," he said. "I have fought alongside Creia before. As soon as I learned that they knew you, though, I knew that there was nothing that would keep me from this conflict. I thought I had lost you before, and when I learned that I hadn't, I wasn't going to put myself in the position of possibly losing you again. I haven't had the opportunity to be your father, but I have always loved you and wanted to be there for you. This is my way of taking care of you, and all those who have helped you, now that I can."

Pyra stepped up to the front of the group and looked out over them. His eyes touched each of them as if he were taking inventory of those he had with them so that he could make sure that they all got to their destination safely.

Without another word, he opened the door to the stairwell and they started up through the levels of the abandoned medical wing and toward the world beyond.

The building was still and quiet as they made their way through it. Loralia could feel the tension of everyone around her. They were filled with anticipation, ready for more of the hybrid army to ambush them. There were hints of distrust in the air around her and Loralia knew that there were some of their number who were not as willing as others to simply believe that the hybrids were held against their will and didn't want to fight. It would take time for them to relent and Loralia only hoped that it wouldn't influence their power against Ryan.

It seemed like hours had passed before they got back into the hallway where they had fought just days before. There were still streaks of blood on the floor and walls, but their color had darkened as they dried, making it easier for her to overlook them as they passed by. The doors were ahead. All they had to do was get down the hallway and past those doors, and they would be on their way, beyond the maze where Ryan had tried to imprison them, and another step closer to reuniting with the others.

Bannack squeezed her hand and Loralia returned the squeeze. They gave and received comfort through the touch even though they didn't speak, and knowing that Azrael was nearby made her feel even more secure. The entire group moved down the hallway as a single unit. They stayed vigilant as they moved through the aftermath of the battle in the near-darkness of the hallway toward the darker outline of the doors ahead. When they finally reached them, Pyra, Oro, and Ty stood shoulder-to-shoulder across them. They paused only for a moment before crashing through the doors and bursting out into the night.

The air rushed over Loralia and she filled her lungs with it, thankful for the freshness and the cool touch that was a refreshing and reassuring contrast to the conditions of the basement. Just as Pyra had ordered, as soon as they got out of the building, they started running. It felt like chaos for a few seconds, everyone trying to understand where to go. They all moved around the corner of the building toward where Oro had told them the vehicle waited. They were nearly at the back of the building when Loralia suddenly felt Azrael stop beside her. His hand reached out for her and she felt a pain shoot through her chest as she felt what she knew he was feeling. There was anger and vengeance in the air around them that she knew wasn't coming from any of their group.

"Stop them," she said to Bannack. "Make them all stop and get up against the building."

Without questioning the command, Bannack spread it to the people in front of them and start guiding the group toward the stone wall of the building. Soon they were all crowded in the deeper shadows and Pyra made his way toward Loralia.

"What is it?" he asked.

Azrael lifted a hand to quiet him.

"They're here," he said. "I can feel them."

"Where are they?" Pyra asked.

Azrael shook his head.

"I don't know, but they're close. We need to be careful."

"What do we do?" Pyra asked.

Azrael's wings twitched and he looked toward where Ariella stood close by Oro. He gestured at her to come closer.

"We need to try to find the army," he said. "They are somewhere close by here."

"Are your wings strong enough?" Ariella asked.

"Yes," Azrael said. "You stay close to here, I'll go further in each direction." Ariella nodded and Loralia saw Azrael turn toward Pyra again. "Everyone needs to turn off all of their light sources. Stay as close to the building as possible until we get back."

"Where are you going?" Loralia asked.

"We're going to see if we can identify where they are." He looked around to each of the people standing close by. "Be ready," he said. "Have your weapons in hand. They could be only steps from here, and if they are, they could be here in moments."

Loralia stepped back to let Azrael and Ariella walk out of the shadows close to the building. In an instant, they rose up off the ground, their wings lifting them above the building so that they could scan the ground. Loralia watched their silhouettes against the starlight. They moved gracefully and silently, occasionally disappearing out of view as they moved further over the buildings. After a few moments, Azrael lowered to just above them.

"I can see them," he said. "Those who are going in the vehicle with Oro, come to the front and follow me. The rest of you, stay here until we get back. They are all gathered on the other side of the building, but they could move at any moment."

Part of the group separated from the rest and Azrael rose up into the sky again to guide them toward the vehicle that was waiting. A nervous silence settled into the group as all seemed to be listening for any sign that the hybrids or Valdicians might be coming closer. The time passed slowly until finally they heard the roar of an engine and above them a flash of light streaking across the sky told them that the vehicle was safely off the ground and on its way toward

Penthos. A few gasps and laughs of relief broke through the silence and Loralia felt hope rise in her chest, but then Azrael and Ariella appeared above them again.

"They're coming," Azrael said. "They heard the vehicle and they are on their way. We're going to have to hurry."

"Which direction?" Pyra asked.

Ariella gestured in the other direction.

"If you go that way, you are less likely to encounter them," she said.

"That's the opposite direction as the transportation bay," George protested. "We'd have to pass by five more buildings and through an open courtyard."

"The army is coming this way," Azrael said. "You can go the longer way, but there is no way of guaranteeing that they won't change direction, or that there aren't more waiting for you in other areas of the compound. The shorter direction will bring you right into the path of the army, but it will get you to the transportation bay faster. Make your choice, but make it quickly."

An argument rose throughout the group, but Pyra quickly stopped it.

"We go the short way," he said. "Prepare to fight."

4

———

The journey from the doors of the building to the transportation bay changed from controlled to chaotic in seconds. They were moving through a small courtyard behind the laboratory building when several of the hooded creatures stepped out of the shadows and came toward them. In an instant the group fractured, spreading out across the open space to fight. Bannack looked up and saw Azrael soaring in the air above them. He reached into his bag and pulled out a blade.

"Azrael!" he yelled.

The Eteri man looked down at him and Bannack tossed the weapon up into the air. Azrael dipped down and caught it before swooping back up so that he could evaluate what was happening below. He dove down suddenly, bringing the blade back and burying it in the back of one of the hooded beings. The creature fell instantly, his arms falling away from where they gripped Ty. The Denynso drove his own blade into the creature's throat, finishing him, and kicked the body aside. Bannack took his own weapon into his hand and surged forward into the fray, forcing himself between the creatures and smaller members of the group that they were attacking. He heard a scream behind him and turned to see the hybrid woman who had told Pyra she would come with them, being dragged away by one of the other hooded creatures.

Rilex seemed to see the situation in the same moment and they both ran for the woman. Bannack leapt toward the hooded person, knocking the creature to the ground as Rilex swept the woman into his arms and pulled her away. Bannack could hear the woman's frantic breaths, but when he looked at her, there were no tears on her face.

"You," the creature hissed at her, trying to scramble away from Bannack. "You are a traitor. Traitor!"

Bannack stomped down on the man's throat, silencing him instantly. He looked at the woman.

"Are you alright?" he asked the hybrid woman.

She clung to Rilex, but nodded, glaring down at the body of the creature on the ground at Bannack's feet.

"I have her," Rilex said. "I'll make sure that she gets to the shuttle."

Bannack nodded and ran back toward the rest of the group. Azrael had lifted another of the hooded creatures into the air by its throat and Bannack watched him pull away the hood that covered its head. A sickening creature that looked like a grisly blend of Klimnu and Covra hissed at him.

"I should bring you back to Ryan," it said in a voice that made Bannack's skin crawl. "He could restore your wings. He could give you your strength back and make you more powerful than you could ever have imagined."

"I don't need Ryan," Azrael said through gritted teeth. He rose up higher into the sky until Bannack could only see the dark shape of them against the sky. "My wings don't need restoration," Azrael said. "Each wound has only made me stronger."

Azrael took his other hand and grasped the creature's head. There was a chilling crack and the hybrid fell from Azrael's grip into a heap on the ground. The winged man looked down at Bannack for a moment before flying away again. Bannack felt someone pull on his back and turned to see Loralia.

"Come on," she said. "The hybrids and Valdicians are under control. Pyra wants as many of us as possible to continue toward the transportation bay. We need to find a pilot and get into the shuttle. Can you carry one of the women?"

"Of course," Bannack said.

They ran across toward the others that had separated out from the main conflict and Bannack scooped one of the women onto his shoulders so that they could move more quickly. They had run a few yards when he reached down and swept Loralia up as well, holding her close so that he could both protect her and make sure that she got to the transportation bay as quickly and easily as possible. Behind them he could hear the sounds of the final gasps of the battle. He wondered how many of the hybrids had escaped and what would happen to those who survived.

Clouds had started to roll in, obliterating the glimmer from the stars so that they moved through almost complete darkness as they approached the transportation bay. When they finally reached it, George input his code into the keypad and they waited, barely breathing, until the click within the door told them that the code had worked and the lock had released. The human man pulled the door open, washing them with light as if the building itself were reaching out to protect them.

"Is there anyone here?" Zsilvia asked.

"There are always people here," George told her. "Shuttles and experimental ships leave and arrive at all times, and they need maintenance day and night. At this time there will only be a skeleton crew, but there has to be someone who can help us."

They streamed into the building as quickly as they could and as soon as the door closed behind them, a wave of relief passed over Bannack. It wasn't over. He knew that it wasn't. But they had survived the laboratory and made it to the transportation bay. They were closer to leaving Earth behind. George led them down the hallway toward the bay where they had left the shuttle when they first arrived. That felt like a lifetime ago. He could barely remember the sense of excitement and energy that had filled them when they first got off that ship. Now it seemed like they had always been embroiled in this horror.

In sharp contrast to the crowd of people that had greeted them when they arrived, the bay seemed empty and silent. The same shuttle that they had ridden to Earth was still sitting in its place. It looked larger and more beautiful than when they had first seen it and Bannack couldn't wait to get inside again. He saw George looking around, rushing through the expansive bay looking for someone who might be able and willing to pilot the ship for them. The original pilot who had brought them to Earth wasn't there and none of them had the skills necessary to bring them on this mission, and their only hope was that they would find another pilot who would be willing to go against regulations and head out on a mission that was both dangerous and unpredictable.

Behind him Bannack heard the door to the bay open and the rest of the group rush inside. He turned and saw

Pyra carrying a hooded creature in his arms and another of the warriors supporting another as they came inside. Rilex and the hybrid woman came in last and Bannack could see the worry etched on her face.

"We need to get them inside," Pyra said.

Bannack rushed up to him.

"Are these…" he started.

"The Valdicians were trying to drag them back to the torture chamber," Pyra said. "These were slaves. We freed them."

George finally reappeared with a man behind him.

"Pyra," he said. "This is Fredrick. He is willing to pilot the ship for us. He doesn't have full licensure from the University yet, but he knows how to operate the ship."

"And he understands what he's facing?" Pyra asked.

"I do," Fredrick said.

"Very well," Pyra said. "Thank you."

Within moments Fredrick had opened the shuttle and they were inside, storing the supplies they had brought had aboard and choosing the passenger rooms where they could rest. Frederick had headed for the control room and everyone rushed to get into their pods for the ascent. Bannack could hear the various systems of the ship starting up and closed his eyes, awaiting the sinking feeling of the massive shuttle rising up off of the ground and soaring out of the bay.

The wait for the pods to open was excruciating. Bannack knew that he didn't have much time and as soon as the lid to the pod lifted, he climbed out. Loralia stepped toward him and he rested a kiss to her lips.

"Wait here," he said. "Take a bath. Rest. Have something to eat. I'll be back."

"Where are you going?" she asked.

He shook his head at her, a soft smile on his lips.

"I'll be back," he said. "Don't worry."

He gave her another kiss and left the passenger room, heading directly toward the room where he had seen Samira and Ty go when they got inside. Ty was coming out of the room as he approached.

"Let's get started," Bannack said.

"Does she know?" Ty asked.

"Not yet," Bannack said. "I want it to be a surprise. But the trip will take less than a day. We don't have much time to get everything into place."

Ty grinned.

"I can handle the food. Let me find the kitchen and see what is available there and in the rations that we brought with us."

Samira came out of the room and took Ty's hand beside her.

"I can work on decorations and getting a room set up for you. If it's alright with you, I can tell some of the other women and we can work together to set it up and then get Loralia ready."

Bannack nodded.

"Thank you for your help," he said. "I want this to be as perfect for her as possible. I know that this won't be anything like what she would have imagined when she was younger, but I want to do everything that I can to show her how much I love her."

"It will be amazing, Bannack," Samira said. "What will matter most to her is that you even thought about her and want to do this for her."

She smiled at him and hurried away. Bannack took a breath.

"I'm going to go talk to Azrael," he said. "I asked his permission to have the ceremony."

"Why?" Ty asked.

"He's her father," Bannack said. "I know that he never got to see her until now, but he has been thinking about her since then. I'll never have the opportunity to meet the man who raised her. The least I can do is show respect to the man who's the reason she's here."

"That's true."

"Now I need him to tell me about the ceremony and what I need to do to prepare for it."

"Good luck," Ty said. "I'll do whatever I can with the supplies that I find." He started in the direction of the ship's kitchen and then turned back toward Bannack. "Do you know if there would be a cake at the celebration after the ceremony?"

He looked so hopeful that Bannack couldn't help but laugh.

"I don't know," he said. "But why don't you go ahead and make one? This isn't exactly a traditional ceremony, so I think that it would be alright to have a few unique things just for us."

Ty smiled again and turned away, walking faster as he made his way back toward the entrance to the ship so he could find the kitchen. Bannack drew in a steeling breath and made his way down the hallway, hoping that he would find Azrael. He finally found him standing in one of the lounges, staring through the window at the sky as it zoomed past them.

"Azrael?" he said, hesitating at the door to the lounge.

Azrael turned to look at him and gave a faint smile that didn't extend to his eyes.

"Hello, Bannack," he said. "Please, come in."

Bannack stepped inside and walked up to the winged man.

"I wanted to say thank you for giving me your blessing to have the tying ceremony with Loralia," he said.

Azrael nodded.

"Of course," he said. "I am so happy to know that my daughter has found love. I can only hope that she has the lifetime of happiness with you that I had hoped to have with her mother."

"I do, too," Bannack said. "And I don't want to wait any longer, which is why I need your help."

"What can I do for you?" Azrael asked.

"I want to have our ceremony before we reach Penthos," Bannack said. "I know that it's very short notice and that it won't be everything that it could have been if we took longer to plan it, and maybe did it when we get back to Uoria, but I don't want to go to sleep again without doing this for her."

This time Azrael's smile reached his eyes and they brightened. He reached out and took Bannack by the shoulders, staring into his face as if memorizing his expression in just that moment.

"I will do anything that I can to help you," he said. "Aside from the time that I spent with her mother and bringing Loralia into existence, it will be the greatest honor of my life to give my daughter to you and create one family."

5

———

Loralia couldn't relax. She knew that Bannack had told her that she should stay in the room and try to get some rest, but every time that she tried to sit down, the energy and anxiousness inside of her made her stand and continue to pace around the space. When she heard the door to the room open, she whipped around, ready to confront him about leaving her alone for so long since they boarded the ship. Instead, she saw Samira and Eden coming toward her. Eden held something folded in her arms while Samira carried a small bag in one hand. They both smiled at her, but she didn't know why.

"Come with us," Samira said, reaching for her hand.

"Why?" Loralia asked. "What's wrong?"

"Nothing's wrong," Eden said. "We are here to help you."

"Help me with what?" Loralia asked.

She felt confused and nervous, but she let the women take her hands and guide her out of the room and down the hallway toward another room. When they got inside, Samira closed the door behind them and Eden guided her toward the edge of a large bathtub in the center of the room.

"When I was carrying Lysander, you were there to help me. You told me that I was going to be alright and even prepared me to hold a son in my arms. That was one of the most important moments in my life. Now I want to help you with one of yours."

"I don't understand," Loralia said.

Samira walked to the edge of the tub and started the water. As it filled, she drew small bottles and containers out of the bag that she carried. She sprinkled and poured various liquids and powders into the water until a sweet, fresh fragrance filled the air and the bath turned a delicate shade of pink. Eden stepped up to Loralia and helped her undress, then guided her down into the tub. The water around her was luscious and Loralia couldn't resist the soft moan that slipped from between her lips. She rested her head back against the side of the tub and felt one of the women releasing the ties in her hair that held it high on her head. The silver mane tumbled down and she looked up to see Eden pick up a brush and begin to run it through the long strands.

For the next several minutes she let the women help her bathe, carefully washing her hair and pouring the sweetly scented water over her skin to wash away her sweat and the dust from the basement. By the time that she emerged from the water she felt clean and refreshed for the first time in as long as she could remember. Eden and Samira dried her off carefully and then led her back to her pod chamber. Samira unfolded the cloth that they had brought in with them, showing Loralia a beautiful champagne-colored dress. Loralia gasped and ran her fingertips along the delicate, silky fabric.

They dropped the dress over her head and let it fall over her body. It grazed her skin softly, hanging slightly too large.

"I had this at the house with the other women," Eden said. "When they came to the laboratory, they brought my bags with them and it was in there. It's a little too big, but we can fix that."

There was a soft knock on the door and then Leia stuck her head in.

"Come in," Samira said.

Leia was carrying a large bag that she lowered to the pod. She reached inside and withdrew what looked like a handful of ribbons.

"Will these work?" she asked.

Samira nodded.

"They're perfect."

She took the ribbons from Leia's hand and came back to Loralia. Tucking the end of one of the ribbons beneath the narrow straps over Loralia's shoulders, she drew the ribbon down so that it crossed over her shoulder blades. Samira brought them together, tightening the straps so that the dress fit more securely. The three women worked for a few more moments to gather her hair into long braids woven with the ribbons, then brought the braids up to pin them in place on her head. When she was finished, Leia reached into the bag again and withdrew what looked like flowers. She brought them to Loralia and rested them in her hand. Loralia touched them, realizing that they were crafted out of pieces of stiff paper that had been carefully colored with ink.

"I made them for you," Leia said. "I'm sorry I wasn't able to make more, but I didn't have much time."

Loralia shook her head.

"They're beautiful," she said. "Thank you." She looked up at the women surrounding her. "I still don't understand," she said. "What is this all about?"

Samira looked over Loralia's shoulder toward the door.

"I think that there's someone here to explain it to you."

Loralia turned and gasped when she saw Bannack standing in the doorway. He had bathed and wore fresh clothing, but it was the look in his eyes that took Loralia's breath away. The women walked away from her silently, each gently touching her back as they went, and disappeared out of the room. When they were gone, Bannack entered the room slowly and came up to her.

"You look incredible," he whispered.

"Thank you," she said. "So do you."

Bannack looked down and then back up at her.

"I have loved you since the moment that I laid eyes on you. Even longer. From the moment that I came into existence, you were within me. My heart and soul have been waiting for you since then and it was the greatest blessing of my life when I finally found you. I know that I struggled to admit it for far too long. I never deserved for you to forgive me or to love me. I never deserved for you to overlook my behavior and offer yourself to me, but you did. You are my everything and I have devoted myself to trying to be the same for you. There is nothing that I wouldn't do for you, nothing that I wouldn't give to protect you. I once asked you to become tied to me the way that your kind has always done. You agreed then, but I want to ask you again now." Bannack lowered himself to his knees and took her hand in his. "Loralia, my mate, my life, will you please honor me by tying our hearts, our hands, and our souls together?"

Loralia laughed through the tears that were streaming down her cheeks.

"Yes," she said. "Yes, of course, I will."

Bannack wrapped his arms around her waist and pulled

her in for an embrace before climbing to his feet. He began to guide her toward the door to the room.

"Everything's ready," he said.

Loralia felt her heart leap.

"Now?" she asked.

Bannack nodded.

"Can you think of a better time?" he asked.

Loralia shook her head.

"Never."

They walked through the ship to the soft sound of singing from deep within it. As they walked it grew louder and finally Bannack opened a large door to reveal a lounge that was filled with a soft glow. As she stepped inside she realized that the glow was coming from lightsticks that had been tucked inside more of the paper flowers, allowing the light to pick up the color from the ink and carry it into the room. Smaller versions of the flowers were strewn across the floor, creating an aisle that led to Azrael where he stood on the far end of the room.

The rest of the group was lining the aisle, each holding another of the paper flowers, each created with different ink so that the lights created a flow of color through the dimness of the room.

"How did you do this?" she asked, the emotion in her throat making her voice soft and fragile.

"I had a lot of help," Bannack admitted.

Loralia felt him squeeze her hand and they started up the aisle together. They were a few steps from Azrael when she noticed the braided cloth rested across his hand. The primary piece of it was the length that her mother had given her when she was young.

"Some of the women gave pieces of their clothes for the braid," Azrael said. "If your mother and I had been able to use the piece that she gave you, it would have been our families that would have contributed the other pieces. These are your family. They love you and so do I."

Loralia felt herself trembling with the emotion that was overtaking her. With everything that they were going through, she couldn't believe that everyone had come together to do this for her. Bannack reached forward and rested his hand to Loralia's arm and she did the same. Azrael took the braided cloth and wrapped it around their arms, binding them together. He tied the length tightly, then placed his hands over the knot. His eyes closed and he began to speak. Loralia heard words falling around her that she hadn't heard since she was a young child. They were in the ancient Irisa language that had been spoken only by the elders and on special occasions, a language that had always filled her with an emotion that was difficult to describe.

She closed her eyes and felt herself taken away by Azrael's voice. She could feel herself in her home again, surrounded by the family that she had lost. She could see her mother again and feel her soft fingertips on her cheek. Their voices joined with Azrael's as the blessing rained down around them.

When it was finished, she opened her eyes and looked at Bannack. He was gazing back at her with tenderness in his deep orange eyes. Around them the rest of the group cheered, applauding like they had at Samira and Ty's wedding. Bannack leaned forward and kissed her. She breathed in, taking in the kiss, his touch, the words of the blessing still lingering in the air.

"Should we go celebrate?"

Loralia looked toward Ty.

"Celebrate?" she asked.

"Ty has put together a bit of a party for us," Bannack said.

"What did he do?" Loralia asked.

"I'm not sure," Bannack said, "but I'm pretty sure that there is a wedding cake involved."

Loralia laughed and kissed Bannack again as Azrael released the tie from around their arms. Even with the braid gone, she could feel the impenetrable link between them. They had been bonded since they first came together, but now it wasn't just the traditions of the Denynso that stood behind them. For the first time in many years, she felt like she was a part of her own kind again, and everything that she had lost had, in a way, been returned to her.

6

Bannack carried Loralia to the pilot's private chamber where they would spend the first few hours of their union until they arrived at Penthos. He brought her into the room and lowered her to her feet. She watched him return to the door and close it, locking it behind them so that they were in their own private world together. Even through the thick door she could still hear the party faintly and wondered if any of those celebrating their union had even noticed that they were gone. She didn't mind. She longed for the time alone with Bannack. He walked back toward her and Loralia met him, reaching up for his mouth and drawing him closer to her with a deep, intense kiss. Despite the intensity, there was no urgency in the way that they connected to each other through the kiss and explored each other's mouths with their tongues. As desperately as Loralia wanted to touch him and be touched by him, she was also lost in the luxurious pleasure of his kiss. She furthered the sensation by tucking her hands beneath his shirt and savored the warmth of his skin as she rested her palms on his chest.

Bannack pulled away from their kiss just long enough to remove his shirt and toss it aside, giving her free access to his smooth skin and chiseled muscles. He wrapped his arms around her waist and drew her even closer to his body so that she could feel the rhythm of his heart and hear each labored breath. The emotion emanating off of him was intoxicating and she wished that she could crystallize this one moment so that she never had to lose this amazing feeling.

One hand glided up her back to rest at the base of her head, holding her steady as he pressed deeper into their kiss. Loralia let her fingers trail down his chest, enjoying the feeling of his muscles beneath his skin and the pattern of his breathing. Each measured breath told her that Bannack was feeling the same nearly overwhelming desire for her that she was experiencing for him.

Loralia's fingers reached the waistband of his pants and she slowly traced them along the fabric, teasing his skin. She felt his muscles tremble beneath the suggestive touch and she took a step further, resting her hand on the front of his pants, beginning to guide the ties out of place.

"Is this alright?" she asked softly, at once teasing and not wanting to do anything that was going to ruin the beautiful moments that were forming around them.

Bannack nodded.

"Yes," he whispered back.

Loralia pulled the end of the cord and released the ties until the sides of the fabric separated. Once open, she slid her hands into the front of his pants and around his hips, then guided the fabric down so that they fell to his ankles. Bannack shifted his weight to step out of the pants and kick them away. Just that quickly, he was fully bare, his erection standing out proudly from his body and making Loralia's mouth water. She ached to run her fingers along the delicious-looking shaft, but before she could touch him, Bannack tightened his arm around her waist and swept her off her feet and against him. He carried her backwards across the room and then lowered her to the bed. He gently came to rest on top of her, one hand supporting himself beside her to prevent his massive body from crushing her far smaller frame. His lips played across hers as he seemed to be trying to slow their progress, guiding them into a more gradual pace so that they could enjoy each other more. The hand that was around her slid out and she felt Bannack flatten it to the side of her ribcage and then draw it down the side of her body. He moved slowly, keeping a constant level of pressure on his hand as if trying to memorize the curves and swells of her waist, hip, and thigh before returning to her ribs and running the pad of his thumb along the underside of her breast.

Loralia hated the loss of his warmth and weight on her when he pushed back and sat on his knees, but was immediately consoled when he reached forward to run her fingertips down the center of her chest. She arched into the touch, wanting to subtly present herself to him without pushing him into a faster pace. Bannack reached the bottom of her dress and grasped the fabric, guiding it up her body until he could sweep it off over her head.

The cool air of the bedroom brushed over her skin and contrasted with the warmth of his fingertips, creating a shiver that rolled across her. Loralia saw Bannack's eyes lock on the delicate panties that she wore, and heard a soft grumble in his throat. He lifted one of her legs and rested it on his shoulder, turning his head to kiss his way from her knee to the arch of her foot, then back, continuing past her knee so that he leaned completely forward, pressing his shoulder into her thigh as his mouth touched the skin above the front of her panties. She could feel his breath through the thin fabric and whimpered softly. His tongue dipped just beneath the waistband, brushing at the skin just above her peak. Her hips tightened and lifted slightly, offering herself to him. Bannack lowered her leg back to the mattress, positioning it so that it was partially bent at the knee and opened further.

Loralia lifted her hips toward him again to offer her permission for his touch and express her need for more. His fingers tucked around her panties and guided them down off of her so that she was fully exposed and vulnerable to him. He was gazing down at her with a hunger in his richly orange eyes that made her body quiver and her heart beat faster.

Bannack touched a single fingertip to the center of her chest again. She knew that he could feel the rhythm of her breath and the tremble of her heartbeat. Staring down at her as if drinking in the look of her body, he drew his finger down slowly. He let it follow the natural dip down the center of her torso, pausing momentarily at her navel and then traveling over the softness of her belly. He reached the valley between her hipbones and stopped, lifting his eyes to hers. Loralia drew in a breath and Bannack continued. Finally, the pad of his finger swept lightly over her hyper-sensitive pearl, discovering the wet heat that was waiting for him. She gasped at the sudden intense sensation and he drew his finger down further so that he could gather some of the smooth, silky fluid her body was offering him. His finger glided easily through her arousal, and he spent a few intoxicating moments exploring her most intimate curves and folds.

Loralia needed more of the incredible feeling and drew

her thighs up to grant him fuller, unrestricted access. Bannack took her invitation eagerly, delving his finger into her. She cried out and arched briefly off the mattress, savoring the feeling of him exploring her in such an intimate way, but also craving him to be fully inside of her. Bannack leaned forward and kissed her belly, causing his breath to ripple down her body so that it joined the incredible sensations his was creating within her with his hand. After a few moments, Bannack withdrew his finger and sat back up on his knees. Their eyes remained trained on each other as he reached for her hand and brought it up to touch him. Loralia bit her bottom lip and wrapped her hand around his erection. It was warm and impossibly hard against her palm as she settled her fingers around it as far as they could reach.

Bannack released a sound that was somewhere between a groan and a long exhalation as he continued to hold her hand against his cock. She began to stroke him, bringing her hand from the base up over the head, and then giving a subtle twist before bringing it down again, and his head fell back. His hand fell away so that she had complete control and he could indulge himself fully in the sensation of her nurturing him. Bannack rested his hands on either side of her ribs and pulled Loralia up so that she was sitting with her legs bent on either side of him. She continued to stroke his cock, reaching forward with her other hand now to stroke his chest. The pad of her thumb swirled over his nipple and then she ran her hand down his chest to reach his erection so that she could wrap it firmly around the base, gripping it as she continued to stroke the rest of the shaft with her other hand. Bannack tucked his hands under Loralia's hips and lifted her so that he could guide her forward and across his lap. She took her hands from his erection and wrapped her arms around his neck. He brought her slowly down onto him, controlling her progress as she settled onto his hips. Loralia gasped as he filled her, gradually sinking into her until she felt like she couldn't accommodate any more, yet so perfectly fulfilled as she welcomed him into the body that was crafted specifically for him.

She brought her head forward to tuck against Bannack's shoulder and rest her lips against the side of his neck. They took a still, quiet moment as they both breathed in the first moments of being interlocked in this perfect, indescribable pleasure, his cock touching the curves and ridges within her in a way that sent shivers of delight radiating from her core throughout her body.

Bannack cupped his hands around Loralia's hips and she felt him guide them to roll against his body. The movement allowed him to stroke deeply within her without sacrificing the tight connection of their bodies, drawing moans of pleasure from her lips as she released all of the tension into her hips so that he sank even more deeply into her and his hands could lead her more easily. Loralia kissed along Bannack's neck and ran her hands up and down his back as she surrendered herself to his body and the love that he was expressing to her with each press that filled her.

Bannack's intensity grew and he gripped her hips harder, grinding them lustfully against his body so that his pelvic bone massaged into her clit, adding even more incredible sensations. Loralia felt her body stretching to hold him, her walls surrounding him in a passionate embrace that she had never experienced before she met him. After a moment, his grip relaxed and Loralia felt Bannack ease her off his lap so that he could lay her back onto the bed. He tucked his hand beneath her hips to gently guide her over onto her stomach. She bent her arm in front of her and rested her head on it, turning it just enough that she could watch him coming forward to stretch his body over hers. The return of the delicious, surrounding weight of him pressing down onto her made Loralia feel protected, safe, and wanted, further illuminating her deep love and burning desire for him.

Bannack slipped one of his arms beneath her chest and he filled his hand with her breast, kneading it gently as his other hand glided down her other arm to tightly interlace his fingers with hers. She tightened the hold as she felt Bannack push forward, entering her again. The new angle was even more intense and sent a new wave of dizzying pleasure throughout her body, causing her to cry out and raise her hips up into him. Bannack's head settled onto her back between her shoulder blades. She felt his tongue glide across her skin, seeming to bring her back into her body so that she focused on more than just each deep thrust.

Suddenly Loralia felt his weight shift as Bannack pushed back on his knees and held firmly to her hips. This increased his leverage so that he could slide his incredible shaft even deeper into her. Loralia moaned and arched her lower back slightly, lifting her hips to him to meet each stroke as he replaced the slow, tight rhythm with hard, intense thrusts. His upper body fell forward over her and she felt him lift her chest up against him. She turned her face and saw him close to her. Their eyes met and his groans became deeper and more primal. Bannack's pace quickened, each insistent thrust driving him so deeply inside her it nearly hurt, riding the delicate, exquisite edge between pain and pleasure that only fanned the growing fire in her belly.

Each stroke was gradually building the delicious pressure she craved through her hips, thighs, and stomach, and she squeezed her eyes closed as she moaned his name and whimpered blissfully. That little sound seemed to push Bannack over the edge. He thrust into her with one more hard, impaling movement and she felt his cock throb deep within her. This incredibly intimate moment dissolved the pressure that had built within her body, causing it to cascade down around her in an earth-shattering climax. She gave a strangled cry as her body clenched around his and began a pattern of strong spasms that met each of his pulses in perfect rhythm. She imagined her body milking him, drawing his enraptured cock deeper and closer as he filled her, and she tucked her head down against the mattress to scream out as the image caused another wave of pleasure to crash over her.

They remained like that for a few delectable moments, seemingly suspended in time, before Bannack finally came to rest on top of her. He remained that way only for a moment, then turned so that he didn't put too much pressure on her and positioned them so that they could lay side by side. He curved his body around hers, molding to her back and holding her close with his hand pressed to her ribcage. Loralia could feel the rapid rhythm of his heartbeat against her back and each deep breath pressing his belly to her skin. Bannack kissed her shoulder and the side of her neck softly as their bodies cooled and their breathing normalized. Loralia smiled and brought her hand up to rest over his. His fingers intertwined with hers and he moved his hand up to rest over her heart, giving a sigh as if the feeling of her heartbeat brought him the same type of deep fulfillment that she felt.

"I love you," he murmured tenderly to her.

"I love you," she whispered back.

Somewhere ahead of them in the darkness of space Penthos waited for them, but Loralia wasn't afraid. Even as they hurtled toward it and the war crafted for them, she felt stronger and more prepared for anything that she would face than she ever had. She and Bannack were together now, bound together by their own love and by the history and culture of their kinds, and together they would stand up against everything that had happened to themselves, their species, and their allies, and protect the future that still lay ahead.

UNTITLED

To be continued...

THE ALIEN'S GLIMPSE

1

Rain felt her hands trembling as they drew closer to the shape of the planet in the distance. It had been so long since the first time that they had traveled from the desolate planet of Penthos to Uoria, but the feeling was far different this time. When the Nyx 23 mission was first overtaken, their ship sabotaged so that they had no control over its navigation or communication, they were traveling from one unknown planet to another. The existence of the planet that would come to be known as Penthos had been only just identified and they knew nothing about it. The planet that she now knew as Uoria hadn't even been identified. The very concept that it existed wasn't debated, there was simply no knowledge that the planet even existed.

In the moments that they were falling toward Uoria during their first journey, Rain hadn't had the opportunity to watch as the ground came closer and closer beneath the ship. Instead she had been frantically trying to get to the control room, wanting to try to fulfill her responsibility to reclaim control of the ship. It was Etan, though, that had taken her focus away from the controls. She knew now that there was nothing that she could have done, even if she had stepped over Etan and grasped the controls. The ship had been taken out of their power and no matter what she had done or tried to do, there would have been no way that she would have been able to reclaim the ability to pilot the ship. The weapons that the Valdicians had used to disable the StarCity were impenetrable and any efforts that she had tried to put forth to override what they had done would have been completely futile.

Just as much as there was nothing that she could have done about the sabotage of the Valdicians, there was nothing that she could have done to help Etan. He was beyond anyone's help by the time that she had found him, destroying himself before he had to watch as the rest of the crew that he was supposed to lead, guide, and protect suffered the catastrophic crash. In those moments, it had felt nearly hopeless. Rain had never been one to allow herself to completely give up any hope that she might have, no matter what the situation. She had always been determined and almost aggressive in her pursuit of what she wanted. As a child, she had been told that she wouldn't be able to fulfill the dream that she had for herself to be a part of the elite research and paramilitary department that she dreamed of joining. She had been told that she wouldn't be able to handle the education or the training that it would require just to earn a place in the program, much less be a part of any of the missions. There were times when it was only her hope, her dedication to herself, that kept her going. Too many times she had felt alone and like she had no one who cared if she managed to accomplish anything that she had set her mind to doing. In those times, she could only rely on her own mind to push her through.

It had been hard to hold to that hope when they were hurtling toward the unknown, seemingly empty planet below. She didn't know if they were even going to survive the crash. What they might find if they did barely even crossed her mind. She could only hope for her next breath, one right after the other, hoping that she would be able to take in another breath, hoping that when the ship finally did crash that she would either survive it or die quickly, hoping that if she did survive she would know what she should do next. Though it had been a struggle, it had been her hope, the same determination that she had always had, that had brought her from breath to breath and kept her going as they went through the rest of the fall, crashed into the planet, and began the new life that waited ahead of them on their new planet.

Now the hope inside Rain was stronger and she felt more confident as they approached Uoria. The power of the ship beneath her hands almost felt like a vindication, redemption for that horrific day. She could control the descent of the ship now. She knew what waited below them and what she would do when they finally rested on the ground again. It restored her faith in herself and invigorated her against the battle that they had left and the war that lay ahead.

When the surface of Uoria was close enough, she set the signal for those aboard to secure themselves in their passenger pods. She knew that not everyone would be able to follow that instruction. Those still in the infirmary would have to simply lock their beds into place, secure belts across their bodies, and hope that they remained in place. Rain took one hand away from the controls to secure her own hardness so that it held her tightly to the pilot chair. As the belts clicked into place, cuffs emerged from the base of the chair and locked around her legs. Another secured around her chest. The pressure was reassuring in that she knew they would protect her as they landed. At the same time it was frightening, reminding her that she couldn't move, that she was stuck in place until the ship was fully landed and the built-in restraint system released. The thought that she was completely unable to move, to get away from the chair even if she wanted to, made anxiety rise in her stomach and squeeze in her chest. If something was to happen and the sabotage by the Valdicians came back into effect, there would be no way for her to save herself or anyone else in the ship.

Rain took a breath and tightened her grip on the controls. She didn't know if everyone had made it into the passenger pods, but she couldn't wait any longer. They were too close to the surface of Uoria to continue moving forward. She needed to start the descent. She felt the slight sinking feeling as the ship started to move down. It would only be a matter of seconds, but it felt like an eternity as she willed the massive machine to bring itself down. She hoped that she was close to where she had intended them to come down. Though it would have seemed appropriate for them to land in close to the same spot as the original crash, this would have been too far from the Mikana kingdom or the human settlement. Instead, she had planned for them to come down in between the two, close enough that they would be able to get to the kingdom quickly and be only a brief trip to the human settlement as long as the Denynso had done as they asked and brought the small vehicles Athan had revealed to them back to the kingdom from the orchard in the compound.

She wished that Lynx was with her. She would be more comfortable with him beside her, reassuring her with just his presence. But she took comfort in knowing that at least this time everyone in their pods would be protected. Many of the deaths that occurred when the StarCity crashed were among those who were working in the ship, moving around the various rooms and systems rather than securing themselves before landing. Of course, the pods had been different then. They were nowhere near as strong and effective as the ones in the ships now. Rain's mind was still filled with horrifying images of exploring the far-flung wreckage and finding bodies tangled in the remnants of destroyed pods, some killed by the shattered shells of the very pods that were meant to protect them.

The planet was coming closer. It was just ahead. She braced herself and continued to guide the ship down. There was no landing platform to support the ship, meaning that they would have to land straight onto the ground, which would be a far less comfortable landing. Finally, the bottom of the ship touched down and Rain felt the rumble of the impact go through her. She held her breath, waiting for the ship to settle and tell her that the journey was over. Seconds later the ship fell still and the breath streamed from her lungs. The restraints released, enabling her to remove the harness that she had locked into place and stand from the chair. She had done it. They were back on Uoria.

2

C reia paced back and forth across the entrance gate to the Mikana kingdom. He felt like he had been walking there for hours, but he couldn't bring himself to stop. Mina had received communication from Nylek informing her that they were on their way from Penthos, and while it was a relief and a comfort to know that they were coming, she had said that his voice was weak. The Denynso king knew that this meant that the warrior was injured, and he was worried about what they had endured already.

"They will be here when they get here," Theia said as she approached, holding out a cup toward Creia. "You are going to exhaust yourself. Remember, you are not fully recovered yet."

"I want to be here when they arrive," Creia said. "I need to see them." He took the cup from his mate and took a long sip of the sweet nectar. "Thank you," he said, leaning down to give Theia a kiss.

She swept the sides of her robes around her, shuddering

against some chill that Creia didn't feel. Seeing her reaction, though, brought his attention even harder to the horizon. The empathetic skills of his mate were unparalleled. Though she didn't have the same abilities as Loralia, allowing her to know what they were feeling and experiencing their emotions as if they were her own, Theia was able to sense the energy of those around her, especially when they were at their extremes. The chill that she was feeling now was likely the pain and intensity that the group was feeling now as they approached. Finally, he saw dark figures in the distance. They moved as an amorphous unit, sometimes appearing to be one and other moments separating so that Creia was able to identify the individual figures.

The numbers that he saw didn't make sense. There weren't enough of them. There should have been far more with them. Creia felt the wind whipping across his face before he realized that he was running. There should have been pain as his feet hit the ground and his body pushed harder than it had since before his imprisonment, but there was nothing. The intensity of the worry that coursed through him was enough to mask anything that he might experience. He might suffer later, but for now he had to get to them. He needed to know what was happening.

As he approached he saw that the group was working together to carry two of the men. One was Nylek, the other Kyven. He scanned the faces of the others in the group, but didn't see Maxim, Oro, Jonah, or many of the others that he expected would be with them.

"Creia!" Ivy shouted as they drew closer.

"Ivy," Creia said, reaching for the human woman. "What's happening? Where is everyone?"

Ivy shook her head. She appeared drawn and breathless,

and Creia was immediately even more worried about Maxim and the others.

"We are the only ones who are here," she told him. "The others are still on Penthos, and on Earth."

"On Earth?" Creia asked, horrified by the revelation. "They didn't make it to you?"

Ivy shook her head again.

"No," she said. "Oro, Jonah, Azrael, and Ariella used the vehicle that Jonah and Rain designed to get to Earth to assist the ones that Ryan had captive there, but they haven't returned. Maxim, Zyyr, and the others are still on Penthos. They have been able to keep the hybrid army back, but the conflict will only get worse. They need all the help that they can get. They need the army and weapons from here."

"We need to get these men to the clinic," Rain said, gesturing to the two men being carried. "Is Rey in the kingdom?"

"Yes," Creia said, "he's there, so are the doctors. What has happened to these men?"

"Nylek was attacked by a group of hybrids. Kyven was injured by a creature who lives under the ground on Penthos. We've done everything that we can to treat them, but they are still weak. They need more food, water, and treatment. We brought them back here so that they would be in less danger. This is Elon," Rain said, gesturing to the unfamiliar man in the group. "He is a human medic. He was on the shuttle when we were traveling toward Earth. He's been helping take care of the men."

Creia could hear tension in Rain's voice, but he didn't question her. For now, they needed to get the men to the Mikana clinic. He reached forward and swept Nylek into his arms, freeing the smaller man from the burden of trying to support the massive warrior. They started back toward the kingdom as fast as they could and as they approached, Creia called out to Theia.

"Get the doctors," he called. "Tell them to get to the clinic. These men need help."

They rushed through the gate and into the kingdom, heading directly toward the clinic that rested in the center. He carefully lowered Nylek to one of the beds and turned to watch them help Kyven into place. Out of the corner of his eye he saw Athan back out of the clinic and start running toward the homes at the back of the kingdom. The Denynso king backed away as the doctors came into the room and headed for the two wounded men, then turned to Ivy.

"How is Maxim?" he asked.

Ivy nodded.

"He's well," she said. "He's gotten through the battles without serious injury."

"That's good to hear. I am surprised to see you here instead of with him there."

Ivy looked down, her eyes brimming with tears.

"He sent me here," she said. "He wants to keep me safe."

He knew that there was more to it than just that Maxim didn't want her on the dangerous planet. She had already been engaged in battle with them. He knew that she was capable of taking care of herself, or could at the very least remain out of the way. Maxim needed her like the Denynso needed their mates, and Creia couldn't imagine him sending her away without a good reason. Before he could ask anything else, she looked back up at him, her eyes suddenly clear and stern.

"Did you gather all of the supplies that he asked you to?" she asked.

Creia nodded.

"Most of them," he said. "We brought the vehicles from

the orchard and have some supplies from the Denynso compound. Ellora hasn't given us permission yet to go into the war room to get the weapons that Maxim described. She doesn't want to even talk to us. It's like she's trying to ignore that the war is even happening."

"She can't do that," Ivy said. "Maxim needs those weapons. We aren't going to be able to get through this with just the supplies that they have. Even when the others arrive from Earth, there aren't going to be enough weapons or rations to support them. She can't just not allow them to get what we need."

"I can do as I please."

Creia saw Ivy whip around to face Ellora where she stood at the door to the clinic. The woman looked angry and drawn, but there was a sadness in her eyes that was impossible to ignore.

"Ellora," Ivy said, taking a step toward her.

"Where is my son?" she asked.

Creia stepped out of the way so that she could see Kyven lying on the bed further into the clinic. She immediately pushed past him, rushing to the side of the bed and leaning over her son. She took his head and reached forward to touch the side of his face.

"Kyven," she said softly. "It's Mama. I'm here."

Kyven's eyes opened and smiled at his mother.

"I'm alright," he said. "I'm healing. It wasn't serious."

"It *was* serious," Emerie said from the other side of the bed. "The Meldor nearly killed you, and we don't know what kind of toxins it had on its claws. That's why Maxim sent you back here."

"I should be there with him," he said. "I should be fighting alongside him, not lying in this bed."

"You can't be there with him," Emerie said. "You aren't in

any condition to be fighting. You need to recover, and when you do, you can be of good use to him."

"Listen to her, son," Ellora said sternly. "She's right. You might want to be with your brother and I'm sure that he wants you to be with him, but if you are injured, there's no way that you are going to be able to give him the support that he needs. You will be in more danger and you will put the rest of them in danger as well. If you stay here and focus on recuperating, you will be strong enough to fight, though I wish that you wouldn't."

"Why?" Kyven asked, shifting as if trying to sit up. "Why shouldn't I fight?" Emerie touched her hand to his shoulder and laid her mate back down onto the bed, but Kyven kept staring at his mother intently. "It's like you don't want us to win," he said. "You don't care what's happening to all of us."

"I do care, Kyven," Ellora said, "but I have already lived so much of my life suffering the loss of my husband. I don't want to lose you and your brother as well. All of this has happened before. There has been struggling and fighting for your entire life, and there will continue to be in all parts of the galaxy, in all parts of the universe throughout the rest of time. You don't have to be a part of it."

"There will be fighting," Creia said, stepping forward, "but it won't be like this. There is so much more happening than has ever happened before. There is so much more than any of us have ever known. This isn't a grudge, Ellora. This isn't something that we are fighting just for the sake of fighting."

"How do you know that?" she asked. "You just came here. I have never seen you before now. How am I to know that I can trust what you have to say about this war? We were peaceful until your kind showed up here. We hadn't seen war since the battle when Aegeus died. Then your warriors came here and suddenly everything has fallen apart around us."

"Don't talk to him that way," Kyven said. "This is not Creia's fault. He didn't cause this. If it hadn't been for the Denynso, we never would have learned what we have. We wouldn't have found out the extent of what's happening, and things would be much worse very soon. Besides, Papa..."

Athan stepped up to the side of the bed with a sound that silenced Kyven.

"You should rest now," he said. "The doctors will take care of you and Emerie will bring you something to eat soon. Ellora, you should go back home for now. They need good food and drinks to restore their strength."

Creia saw Ellora look down at her son with questions in her eyes. It was obvious that she knew he had more to say and he waited for her to ask, but she didn't. She straightened slowly, releasing Kyven's hand as she went, and then looked at Athan and nodded.

"Alright," she said. She lifted her eyes to Emerie. "Come to my house later and get food for these men."

"I will," Emerie said.

Creia watched as Athan carefully place a hand in the of Ellora's back and guided her away from the clinic. He turned back to Kyven and looked down at him.

"What were you going to say about your father?" he asked.

"He's still alive," Kyven said. "He didn't die in that battle."

"Are you sure?" Creia asked.

Kyven nodded.

"Ryan told us himself. At least until then, he was still alive."

"He's been holding him all these years?" the king asked.

"Yes," Kyven said. "They captured him during that battle and he has had him since. I can't imagine what he's been doing to him."

"I can," Creia said, his mind immediately flashing back to the horrific time that he had spent captive by the Valdicians, his very thoughts controlled by Ryan as he was forced to stare into the screen attached to his head for hours at a time. Starved and tortured, he had barely lived, and he had been held only a brief time. "Did he say that he would keep him alive?" he asked.

Kyven shook his head.

"No," he said. "He wants me and Maxim, though. Maybe if we're able to keep fighting and can resist him, that will keep him alive."

"If he wants you and Maxim, Aegeus isn't safe. He knows where you are and that he can get to you. That's enough to make it no longer necessary for him to keep your father around. If he decides that Aegeus has become too much trouble, or that he doesn't need him anymore, or even just that he wants to be as vindictive as possible, he will kill your father without a second thought. We need to get to him as quickly as we can if we want to keep him alive."

"The group needs rest for tonight," Kyven said. "We can't simply go back."

"I know," Creia said. "There is still preparation to be done, but now that you are all here, you can help. We'll do everything that we can to gather what we'll need, and then we'll go back. We can only hope that Maxim will be able to hold them off on his own until we get back, or that the rest of the group will make it to Penthos in time to help him. This has to end."

He started toward the door to the clinic and heard Kyven call after him.

"Where are you going?" he asked.

"I need to go talk to Ellora," he said. "Maxim gave instructions for what we needed to do to get ready for this war. I remember fighting alongside your father when we were young. I know the importance of the weapons that he collected. He wouldn't have done that if he didn't know that something was going to happen, if he didn't have a plan already in motion. She needs to let us access to war room."

"No," Kyven said. "Don't."

"Why not?" Creia asked. "We don't have time to wait for her to decide that she is going to accept what's happening. We can't give the power of the future of the galaxy to her and her denials."

"I know," Kyven said, "but she won't listen to you. Let Athan talk to her. She doesn't trust anyone like she trusts Athan. Give him time. Do whatever else you can to get everyone ready, but let him talk to her."

"Alright," Creia said, "but I can't just give them endless time. We have to prepare. We have to get to them."

He turned and left the clinic, walking out into the growing evening with too much energy and anticipation to even think about sleeping. There had to be something else that he could do. Until they were on the ship heading back to Penthos, he wouldn't be able to allow himself to stop or to rest.

3

Jonah stepped into the infirmary as quietly as he could. He didn't want to disturb anyone who was sleeping inside. Though they had made the decision to stay on their own, he felt strangely responsible for the wounded hybrids and pregnant women who remained in the infirmary. Before Pyra left he had helped the women move into the original infirmary, joining them all together so that they could be safe and secure together. It made Jonah feel more comfortable knowing that they were in the same space, protected simply by merit of being closer to one another. Being out of sight of others was when they were in the most danger, and it was important to him that he do everything that he could to help keep them as safe as he could while he was alone with them on Earth. He didn't know what he would be able to do for them if further danger did arise, but for then he could at least offer his presence.

Everyone inside seemed to be resting comfortably and he stepped out, closing the door as gently behind him as he could. He went back into the chamber where he had slept since they first arrived in the abandoned medical building and settled onto his bed. The others had been gone for only a few hours, and the reality of the situation was beginning to settle in for Jonah. He had been completely confident about the decision that he was making when he told Pyra that he was going to stay behind to look further into the medical files while the others went to Penthos, but now it was truly sinking in that the rest of those from Uoria had gotten onto that shuttle, leaving him behind to handle whatever might happen on his own. Though he knew that they were doing what they needed to do just as he was doing what he needed to do, it was also unnerving to know that he couldn't just turn to them if something else happened.

Jonah's hand settled onto the stack of medical files beside his bed and he felt a slight shock of energy move through his palm, reminding him of why he had decided to stay, of how pressing it was for him to remain behind so that he could try to understand what could have happened so many years before that could have had an impact that was still lingering now. He didn't understand what it could possibly be that would make the doctor not just leave his file behind, but to close the door to the examination room and apparently walk away, leaving that space untouched and unchanged even as the rest of the medical building continued to operate and was then closed down. Why didn't anyone open the door? Why didn't anyone question why the doctor never used the examination room again? Why didn't they look at it or take the things out of it when they were closing the medical building down in preparation to build the new section of the hospital.

A thought suddenly occurred to him and Jonah sat up straighter. The new building. Why would they build the new building around the old medical facility? Eden and the other human women had told him that they had planned to replace the old University for several years before they actually got started on the construction. All the other buildings were completely leveled so that they could build the new facilities in their places. They even built a new research hospital on the other side of the campus, establishing a much larger and more advanced facility for medical research and treatment for people who studied at the University as well as the other programs that used the campus as their headquarters, such as the department that bore Nyx 23. It didn't make sense that of all the buildings that they would keep, they would choose to preserve an old, outdated hospital ward that they would seal completely within the laboratory so that it wasn't just inaccessible, but fully forgotten until now.

The thought brought a strange feeling to Jonah's stomach. He knew that this was so much more than they could have imagined. The further that they thought that they went, the closer that they thought they were getting to finally laying the conflict to rest, the more and more it seemed to unravel, revealing further and further layers. He thought of those who had left the basement on their way to the transportation bay so that they could get to Penthos. He hoped that they had made it and were on their way, but he knew deep in his chest that there was a possibility that they hadn't survived the short but treacherous journey from the laboratory building to the vehicles that would take them off of Earth and back to the nearly barren planet. There was also a possibility that they had gotten part of the way there and then encountered the Valdicians or more of the hybrids and were captured, taken prisoner and forced into another area of Ryan's compound of torture. This, Jonah thought, was likely a far worse possibility than even a brutal and bloody death in battle.

Jonah looked down at his hand on the files again. He needed to understand what happened, not just for him but for every person whose name appeared in these files. Their lives had all been taken, stolen from them, by something. Even those of them who had survived no longer had the lives that they thought that they were going to, and no longer had the potential to do what they thought they would do or be with the families, friends, and partners with whom they imagined they would spend their lives. He could still remember what it was like as they were preparing for the Nyx 23 mission. It had been the most thrilling time in his life, so filled with hope and anticipation. The entire reason that he had joined the department was so that he would be able to make a difference. Even though the program was designed primarily for research and recognizance, he had felt deep within him that it was going to give him the opportunities that he desired to really make a difference.

Nyx 23 had been the first chance that they had to do something truly impactful. They had done seemingly endless research and gone on a few missions, but none of them carried the weight and significance of what they had planned for the then-unknown and unnamed planet that they knew was harboring an illegal prison colony. This colony had been such a severe and blatant breech of the intergalactic agreements that at that time had only recently been made. Jonah had been one of the first people to start suspecting that the colony existed. The planet had seemed unoccupied, and according to the government and even the rest of the department itself, it was. In fact, when it was first found and identified as an inhabitable planet, some companies put in applications to receive permits to establish and build it as a tourist attraction. Jonah's department had been instrumental in tying these applications up so that they wouldn't be able to go through until after they made their mission. The last thing that they needed was for tourist companies to arrive on a planet that was being used illegally by a cruel and vicious species to imprison another.

Despite the severity of what was happening on what was now known as Penthos, and the horrors that they knew that they might face when they arrived, there had been such hope and even excitement when they prepared to leave. This was their chance. They were going to get to do something that not only helped others, but that changed the perspective of the entire galaxy. They might even be able to be the ones who decided how the planet was utilized after the prison colony was emptied and destroyed. Because so many of the original department hadn't believed what they were saying when they told them their suspicions about the prison colony, Nyx 23 was developed in secret, and the plan for the mission had to be made away from the rest of the department. At the time, the goal was to protect their plans and their mission from others who would be able to stop them. Now, though, he wondered if they had truly made the right decision by remaining so secretive. By concealing everything that they were doing they ensured that they were able to put the mission together and leave without interference, but it also meant that it took longer for anyone to take note of the fact that they were missing, and then once they did realize that the crew and the experimental ship were gone, they had little information to go on in an effort to find them. Even the skeleton mission control that remained on Earth only knew that they were traveling to the planet now known as Penthos. They would have no way of knowing what happened to them, just as the crew itself had no way of imagining what they would encounter when they left Earth behind.

Remembering the hope and determination that had filled him in the days leading up to their mission reassured Jonah that he had made the right decision staying on Earth rather than returning to Penthos. It wasn't a decision that he made because he was afraid or that he didn't want to be involved in the conflict that was threatening not only his kind but those who had freed them from the horror of the Covra. Instead, this was a decision that was made by a heart and mind still linked tightly to the past. It was as if he was getting another opportunity to make this right. He couldn't save the lives of those who had already been lost, but he could save their memories. And for those who were lingering on, and who they had met along the way, he might be able to save their futures.

The anger coursing through Ryan was so intense that he couldn't even bring himself to express the violence that burned in his veins. He sat in his chair, his hands gripping the arms until his knuckles ached and the wood cut into his palms. He could sense the presence of the Valdician man standing close behind him, but he didn't turn to look at him, and the creature said nothing. Finally, he brought enough control into himself that he was able to speak.

"How could they allow them to leave?" he asked.

"They fought," the Valdician replied.

"There should have been chaos," Ryan said. "The anger and the energy of the battle should have made the Klimnu insatiable. The Denynso wouldn't have been able to tolerate it and they would have killed him. All hell should have broken loose."

"They're healing him," the Valdician said.

"Healing him?" Ryan asked.

"The Klimnu is nearly whole again. The Denynso healer has been working with him."

"That would be excruciating."

"I suppose after what you've put him through, he was able to tolerate it."

"Reprogram the survivors," he said. "I want full forces on Penthos. Maxim and Kyven must be destroyed."

There was a moment of hesitation and Ryan could feel that the Valdician was trying to come up with a way to tell him something. Ryan's grip tightened on the chair further and he felt his heart pounding even harder in his chest.

"Kyven is no longer on Penthos," the creature said. "And there are no survivors to reprogram."

"What do you mean?" Ryan asked.

"The ship was able to escape from Penthos."

"How is that possible?" Ryan roared, the control that he had been able to maintain shattered by this revelation. "Their ship was sabotaged. How would they be able to navigate it?"

"The one they call Rain is from Nyx 23. She remembers the first attack and was able to overcome it. They headed back toward Uoria."

"They've gone for reinforcements," Ryan said.

"We believe so," the Valdician said. "They brought those who had been wounded in the battles with them, including Kyven."

"And there are no survivors from the battle when they left the laboratory building?"

"There were survivors," the Valdician clarified, "but they

didn't get back inside the building. Pyra and his followers took them and brought them to the transportation bay with them. I can only assume that they are on the ship headed for Penthos now."

Ryan began to laugh, the sound bubbling between his dry lips so that they cracked, but the pain and faint taste of blood only made him laugh harder. The sound filled the space around him, reverberating off the walls. The Valdician didn't react. He stood completely still in his place by the door until the maniacal laughter stopped.

"They think that they are so powerful being able to escape, but they are running scared. They are so terrified that they have to go gather up as many others as they possibly can just to try to stand up to us. They are desperate and they have only seen a few of the army. When they are faced with the full forces, there is nothing that will bring them to victory, and it will be all the sweeter that we can destroy all of them at once and leave their bodies to be forgotten on Penthos forever." He paused and laughed again. "At least those that I don't want to use for myself."

"What instructions should I give to those still on Earth?" the Valdician asked. "Should I prepare them to go to Penthos?"

Ryan thought for a few moments, then shook his head.

"No," he said. "Send them to the other facility. When the battle on Penthos is over, there will be a lot of work to do and I want to be as prepared as possible."

"Very well, Sir," the Valdician said.

Ryan heard the creature leave the room and settled back into his chair again. For days, he had been staring at the same wall and now the surface seemed to be changing, the plain white surface seeming to swirl into color as it formed the images that inhabited his mind.

4

———

The music was still blaring around the small lounge, fueling the celebration for Bannack and Loralia's tying ceremony that was still going strong even long after the couple had slipped away. Rilex felt like he might have been the only one who had noticed that they left. The others were too invested in enjoying the party, lost in the music, dancing, and delectable food that turned the ship's lounge into an experience that was more festive than anything that Rilex had experienced since he left his own stream. The music around him was just as unusual. It was like nothing that he had ever heard and he wasn't sure that he was enjoying it as much as the others.

Rilex stood toward the back of the lounge, watching the celebration as it continued on in front of them. They laughed and danced, savoring the treats that Ty had created as they celebrated the union between Bannack and Loralia. The longer that he watched them, however, the more he wondered if it was only the tying ceremony that had filled them with such mirth and excitement. While he knew that all of them, particularly those who knew and loved the couple, were excited and happy to see the ceremony, and were touched by the lovely surprise that Bannack had created for her with the help of some of his friends and Loralia's father, he felt like it wasn't just their union that was keeping this party going for as long as it was.

According to those who had already made the journey, they had only a matter of hours between leaving Earth and arriving on Penthos where they were to reunite with the rest of the group and face off against the hybrids and Valdicians on the battlefield. This brief time would have been better used sleeping, eating, and restoring their minds and bodies than it was in the loud, energetic party. Even knowing this, though, Rilex still hadn't left the room. It was like he was drawn to the room, kept in place by the energy of the people who filled it. He knew that he should be resting. He should be eating the nutrient-dense rations that they had brought with them from the emergency chambers. He should be trying to prepare his mind for what they were going to face when they reached Penthos. Yet he couldn't bring himself to pull himself out of the protective, reassuring barrier that the party seemed to create. They weren't just celebrating the love and union of the Denynso warrior and his mate. They were also celebrating the very fact that they had made it onto the ship. After the torment and fear of the laboratory building, they had made their way out and though they were now on their way toward what was likely to be an even more challenging conflict, it was a step to have come this far, and one that filled them with excitement and joy.

Even as he was watching those around him dancing and enjoying themselves, there was something missing for Rilex. He hadn't seen the hybrid woman who he was so drawn to since they had gotten to the celebration after the tying ceremony. Though she had been there during the ceremony, and walked alongside him to the adjoining lounge were Ty, Jem, Leia, and Samira had worked together to design the celebration for Bannack and Loralia, she seemed to have disappeared in the time since. He could understand why she might not want to be there. Even he had known these people for longer than she did, and with the life that she had had, she would have no way of understanding what was happening around her or why everyone was filled with the joy, excitement, and hope that the tying ceremony had given them.

The thought made Rilex wonder if the hybrid woman even understood the concept of love or sharing life with another person. This made his heart tighten painfully as the depth and extent of the pain and destruction that Ryan had caused became even more clear. The horrific physical conditions and torment that these hybrids suffered was awful enough. But, delving into the emotional suffering and loss that they had experienced simply by merit of coming into existence was intolerable.

Rilex swept his eyes across the lounge and felt his breath catch in his throat. As if his thoughts of her had summoned her to him, the hybrid woman stood just inside the door to the lounge, alone and looking around the room uncertainly. It was obvious that some of the women had taken her under their wings, showing her the tenderness and consideration that she so desperately needed. She had bathed carefully, washing the blood, dirt, and sweat from her skin and hair, and her hair had been brushed so that it lay thick and soft down her back. The front was pulled back away from her face, and when she turned to look to the other side of the room he saw that that portion of hair had been braided and styled so that it twisted around and in on itself before resting in the center of her mane. The dress that she wore was delicate, the long sleeves and layer that covered the soft pink fabric thin and ethereal.

She was breathtaking and Rilex felt himself pulled toward her. He couldn't resist her, even if he told himself that he shouldn't have these thoughts for her, that she would never be able to understand what he was feeling or that she was made to feel the same way. None of that mattered to him, he just needed to be close to her. Keeping his eyes locked on her, he crossed the room carefully. He didn't want to startle her, but the way that she looked around the room made him hopeful that maybe she was looking for him again.

He was a few steps from her when she turned back and their eyes met. Something close to a soft smile touched her lips and she glanced down as if unsure of what she should feel or even if she should be there. Before she could get frightened and leave, Rilex stepped up to her.

"Hello," he said.

She looked up at him and he saw a soft blush of color across her cheeks. It only worked to make her more beautiful and appealing.

"Hello," she said softly.

"You look incredible," he said.

Though the music was still loud around them, he kept his voice low, wanting to create a private space around them and show her that he was focused only on her. He wanted her to know that she mattered and that, for the first time in her existence, she had a voice.

"I don't understand why they wanted to do this," she said.

"Don't you like it?" Rilex asked.

She hesitated, but then nodded.

"I do," she said. "It feels wonderful to be clean. I can't tell you how long it's been since I was able to take a bath or wore clean clothes." She reached up and ran her fingers through her hair. "They brushed my hair."

"You are beautiful," Rilex said.

"Thank you," she said.

"Would you like to dance with me?"

He wasn't sure about asking her, not knowing if she knew what he was asking or if she would even be willing to accept his touch. She hesitated for a moment, looking around at the others.

"Is that what they are doing?" she asked.

"Yes," Rilex said. "They're celebrating."

"I've never danced," she said.

"That's alright," Rilex said. "It's not difficult."

He reached for her hand, carefully tucking his fingers beneath hers so that hers rested lightly against his skin. It was a soft, fleeting touch, but the light contact of their skin would be enough for him for now. He didn't want to push her, to attempt to force her beyond what she could tolerate in these first moments and days of freedom.

She relented to the touch, allowing Rilex to guide her a few more steps forward until they were just at the edge of the center area of the room that the others had taken over as their dancefloor. The woman stood still and Rilex stepped up to her. He rested his hands to her hips, taking his time with every touch so that he could gauge her reaction and be prepared to step back if he needed to. As his hands settled onto her, though, he could feel her relax beneath the touch. He took another step forward so that their bodies were only a few inches apart. After a few moments, the woman lifted her hands and let them rest on the fronts of his shoulders. Her hands were trembling slightly, but he saw less fear in her eyes and more soft, awe-filled questions as she began to explore thoughts and emotions that she could never have even fathomed.

5

———

"Ellora," Athan said as he stepped into the kitchen.

Ellora wouldn't turn around. She didn't want to face him right then or deal with anything that he might have to say. Instead, she focused on preparing food for those who had traveled from the distant planet to return to Uoria. Though she didn't want to know more about what they were facing on that planet or the plans that they might have for returning, she could see that they were in need of sustenance that would help them to recover from whatever they had suffered in the time that they were away, and prepare them for what they might need to do moving forward. She could only hope that she could somehow convince them that they needed to let this go, to stop the horror that had been carrying on for much too long.

"Ellora," Athan said again.

His voice made Ellora's muscles tighten. Though he had been a treasured and trusted part of her life, as close to a member of her family as she could ever want, he was also a painful reminder to her. Every time that she heard his voice say her name, she could only think of the night that he appeared at her door to tell her that her husband was gone. Aegeus had been precious to Athan as well, but as soon as she had heard this news, Ellora felt like something within her had closed. She wasn't able to feel the empathy that she knew that she should. She hadn't been able to reach out to him, to comfort him, or even to fully accept the comfort and support that he had tried to offer her. As much as she would have liked to rely on him more for herself, it was too painful. When she looked at him, she saw the eyes that had seen Aegeus after she had. When he spoke, she heard the voice that he had heard after he had heard hers for the final time. When he reached out to touch her, she could only think of the last time that she felt her husband's touch and didn't want to replace it with his.

"Athan, I don't want to talk about this," she finally said, knowing that he wasn't going to back down or leave her alone until she spoke to him.

"You have to," Athan said.

"Excuse me?" Ellora asked, turning toward him.

"You can't pretend it isn't happening, Ellora," Athan said. "You've spent years refusing to talk, and you don't have that option anymore."

"And who are you to tell me what I'm allowed to do or what I have to do?" she asked.

"There was a time when you would have trusted me completely," Athan said. "You would never have dreamed of turning me away or refusing to talk to me."

"That was different," she said, turning back to the pot on the large black stove and stirring it absently.

"How?" Athan asked. "How was that different?"

"That was when I knew that what was happening was inevitable and that there was nothing that I could do to make it any different. I knew what was going on and why, and could see the reason behind it."

"Could you?" Athan asked. "Did you really understand what was going on?"

"Of course, I did," Ellora replied, even though she didn't even trust the words coming out of her own mouth. "I always trusted that Aegeus knew what he was fighting for."

"And did you know what that was?" Athan asked.

Ellora poured the vegetables that she had chopped into the pot and sprinkled in some of the fragrant herbs from a canister on the counter beside the stove.

"He never gave me all of the details, you know that, but when he told me that he needed to go fight against the corruption in the Order, I knew that what he was doing was right. I knew that he knew what he was doing, and that no matter what he was facing, he was doing what was right for the Mikana, and for Uoria."

"And do you believe that now?" Athan asked.

Ellora fell silent. She wasn't sure what she should believe any longer. It had been so many years she couldn't remember everything that her husband had told her about the struggle that they were facing or what he wanted to accomplish when he went into battle.

"I don't know," she said. She looked at him sharply. "Why are you still a part of the Order?" she demanded. "How could you continue to serve the group that was so corrupt Aegeus went into battle against them and lost his life?"

Athan took a step toward her, shaking his head.

"You don't understand, Ellora," he said. "The Order is something far beyond each of the people who make it up. It is something that stretches beyond us, beyond the Mikana. It has always been and always will be, and until my death, I will serve it. I was chosen when I was a child. It wasn't my choice, and I don't have the choice of whether to continue."

"But you can betray them?" she asked coldly.

"What do you mean?" he asked, his voice falling softer now that she seemed to have broken through a barrier that had existed silently between her and the Order since he found out about the mysterious organization that her husband served with unwavering loyalty and devotion.

"You gave the vehicles to the Denynso and their team," she said. "You allowed Maxim, Ivy, and Kyven into the tunnels. Don't think that the members of the Order who remained here don't know what you did. They have already been here to question me."

"What did they ask?" Athan asked.

"They want to know where you are," she said. "They want to talk to Maxim and Kyven."

"Why would they want to talk to them?" Athan asked. "They aren't a part of the Order."

"I know," Ellora said. "That has always been one of the greatest comforts and reassurances of my life, but now I'm not as sure."

"Why?" Athan asked.

"Why weren't they chosen?" Ellora asked. "Their father, their grandfather, his father before him. They have all been in the Order. How could Aegeus's sons not be chosen?"

Athan shook his head.

"I don't know," Athan replied. "I always expected that if Aegeus had any sons, they would be accepted into the Order immediately. None of us, though, not a single one of us, knows how the Order is built. We don't know who makes the appointments or why."

"But how is that possible?" Ellora asked. "How is it

possible that none of you know who selects the members or determines what the Order does? I know that there is a hierarchy. Even Aegeus said that the corruption was in the upper levels of the Order. If it is that clear, how can you not know?"

"It isn't that simple," Athan said. "Yes, there is a hierarchy. There are those who are leaders within the Order and who are respected to guide and provide structure, as well as uphold the laws and regulations. Many of those were the ones who had become corrupt and who Aegeus wanted to eliminate. Even within that hierarchy though, it isn't the end. It's well-known within the Order that there is more than just those on Uoria that we know and who we encounter in our operations. I can only assume that it is those who we never see who make the decisions."

"They didn't choose Maxim and Kyven," Ellora said, starting to feel desperate and worn. "They left them alone. Why do they need them now? What could they possibly want with them now?"

There was something in Athan's eyes. It burned there, waiting to be spoken and yet pushed away.

"What is it, Athan?" she asked.

"Ellora, your sons are brave. They are stronger than you know. It's in their blood. They might not have been chosen by the Order, but that doesn't change who they are. From the moment that they came into existence, it is has been within them to do what they need to do to protect the things that matter to them, and to do what is right. I know you don't understand, but what they're doing right now is exactly what they should be doing."

"The war ended," Ellora said. "After the battle when..." her voice trailed off and she drew in a breath to calm herself and steel against the emotions threatening her control, "when Aegeus died, everything went quiet. I didn't hear about any more battles. It was done."

"It wasn't done," Athan said. "This has never ended, it just went quiet. It's come back now, stronger than ever, and it's Maxim who is leading. Even Pyra, the strongest and most powerful warrior in all the galaxy, has given his trust and loyalty over to Maxim. They are leading together. You should be proud of him, not resisting what he's doing."

"I can't lose anyone else," Ellora said. "There's nothing that could make me willing to offer up my sons."

"Even for the safety of the galaxy? Of the entire universe?"

"The galaxy can continue without me losing anyone else that I love."

The inexplicable emotion flashed over Athan's eyes again and Ellora focused on it. There was something there, something that he wasn't saying, but that she needed to know.

"What is it, Athan?" she asked again. "Tell me."

The man took another step toward her. It was a movement that was both comforting and intimidating. At once she felt like he wanted to be closer to her to provide comfort and reassurance, but also that he may be closing her in, blocking her in so that he could control her movement when he finally spoke.

"You haven't lost anyone you love," he said.

"How could you say that?" she asked, angered at Athan's words. "I lost my heart, my love, my life."

"You haven't lost anyone," Athan repeated. "Aegeus is alive."

His voice trembled slightly when he said it, and Ellora thought for a moment that she had misunderstood him. She had to have misunderstood him. There was no way that what she thought he had said could possibly be true.

"What?" she asked breathlessly.

"Aegeus is alive," Athan said again. "At least I hope that he is."

"What does that mean?" Ellora asked.

"Shortly before we left Penthos to return here, we found out that he is still alive, but I can't promise that that is still true. That's one of the reasons why it is so important that we get what we need and get back to the planet and the others as quickly as possible."

"I don't understand," Ellora said.

The revelation had overwhelmed her and she was feeling dizzy. Blackness crept into the edges of her vision and small points of light burst in front of her eyes. She felt herself shaking and the strength in her legs slipping away. Reaching for one of the chairs at the table where she had sat with Maxim and Ivy when they first visited, Ellora took a few steps across the floor. She dropped into the seat, but continued to grip the back to stabilize herself.

Athan lowered himself into the seat across from her and dipped his head down to look into her face.

"Aegeus didn't die during that battle. He was captured and brought to Earth to be used in experiments by a man named Ryan. He has been held captive ever since. Now Ryan is after the others, but Maxim and Kyven especially."

"Why?" Ellora asked.

"He is working to breed a master race of soldiers that have the powers and capabilities of every species he can find. He wants to take over Uoria and use his soldiers to then conquer the universe. Maxim and Kyven stand in his way. It is their destiny to unify the planet."

"How?"

Athan shook his head.

"They'll fight."

"My husband is alive?" Ellora asked.

"I hope that he still is," Athan said.

"Did you know?"

"No," Athan said. "I promise you, I didn't know. I thought that he died that day, just as you have since then. I had no idea what he was planning to do during the battle, or what happened to him after. If I had known that he was still alive, no matter where he was or what was standing between us, I would have found him, or died trying. You have to know that."

"I do," Ellora said, nodding. She took a breath. "And now it's our chance."

6

Ivy felt butterflies fluttering in her stomach as she approached the small, low building at the edge of the village. She didn't know what to expect when she stepped inside. Maxim had described this building to her before they left, telling her that this was where she would find the care that she needed. He assumed that she would first go to Ellora and tell her of the pregnancy before she went to see the midwives, but Ivy hadn't been able to bring herself to have the conversation with her. Ellora seemed tense and on edge from the moment that they arrived, and Ivy hadn't felt ready to share the news with her. She had been wary of her since they met, though she had begun to warm to her, Ivy was still hesitant and she didn't know how Ellora would react to finding out that her son had conceived a child in a time of war. Ellora didn't even want her sons fighting. Ivy couldn't imagine how she would feel about her grandchild being involved even before its birth. She knew, though, that she needed to find out as much as she could about the pregnancy now, and perhaps then she would be better prepared to tell Ellora.

Taking another breath, Ivy glanced around to make sure that no one saw her standing outside of the midwife building, then gently knocked on the door. A moment later a woman who appeared many years older than Ellora opened the door a few inches and peered out. She stared at Ivy questioningly for a few seconds and then her eyes widened. She opened the door further.

"You are Maxim's partner," she said.

Ivy nodded.

"Yes," she said. "My name is Ivy."

"Is Maxim home?" the woman asked.

"No," Ivy said. "He didn't return with us." She noticed the woman's face change as a flicker of fear went across her face, and she held up a hand to reassure her. "He was safe when we left," she said. "He chose to stay so that he could continue to fight, but we needed to come back to Uoria. Before we left, he told me to come here. Are you Opaline?"

The woman nodded.

"I am," she said. "Does that mean..." her voice trailed off, but her eyes lowered along her body to rest on her belly.

Ivy nodded, not wanting to say it and risk someone being nearby and hearing her. She was still guarding the secret vehemently, holding it close as if it somehow kept her closer to Maxim. Protecting this secret was a form of connection between them, something special and precious that, at least for the time, was just for them. She knew now that she had to share it with the midwife. She needed to know more about the child that was growing within her so that she could ensure it was safe and healthy, and could protect it as best as she could.

Opaline's face lit up and she opened the door the rest of the way so that she could reach out and take Ivy's hand. She guided her into the building and shut the door behind her.

"Come with me," she said. "Let me look at you."

Nervousness filled Ivy as she followed the older woman through the front room of the building and into a smaller space toward the back. She remembered when Eden was pregnant and neither the Denynso nor the Mikana were able to help her because she was human. It wasn't until Rey, the king of the Mikana kingdom, stepped forward and confessed that he had assisted his mother and grandmother with human births that she had had the help she needed to bring Lysander safely into the world. The thought of what she went through made Ivy worry now. She didn't know if there had ever been a Mikana baby born to a human woman and what that meant not only for her pregnancy, but also for her child.

As they entered the smaller room, Ivy hesitated. Opaline turned to her and tilted her head quizzically.

"Are you alright?" she asked.

"You know that I'm human," Ivy said, part-statement, part-question. "Will that make a difference?"

Opaline shook her head, a knowing smile on lips lined by time and emotion.

"I have delivered many, many children. I helped Ellora bring Maxim into the world."

The revelation filled Ivy with a sense of peace and trust. It made her happy to think of the same woman who saw her love in his first moments being there for the first moments of her baby's life.

"Rey was able to help Eden when she gave birth," Ivy said. "He knew what to do when none of the Denynso did."

"And you think that he learned those skills alone?" Opaline asked with a bigger smile. "Come along, now. Lie down here and let's see what we can find out about this precious new baby."

Ivy nodded and took the few steps to the elevated bed in the center of the room. The room didn't have any of the equipment and machines that she would have expected to see if she went to the doctor during a pregnancy on Earth. She reminded herself that the midwives in the Denynso compound didn't have any of the equipment, either, and that even midwives on Earth often forewent the machines and equipment. The love that she had found in Maxim and the life that she was even still just beginning to build was nothing like she would have ever expected. She would have to change the way that she thought of everything and her expectations for the future in everything that she did, but as she settled onto the table and lifted her shirt to allow the midwife to see her belly, she knew that she was absolutely willing to do it.

Opaline came up beside the bed and looked down at Ivy's gently swollen belly. It seemed like it had gotten larger in just the short time since she had told Maxim, and Ivy knew that she wasn't going to be able to keep it hidden from the others for long. She resolved to tell Ellora after she left the midwife, hoping to share as much information with her as she could, and then find a time to tell the others. She didn't want the news to become a distraction to the others, but at the same time she also didn't want them to feel as though she were purposely concealing it from them because she didn't want them to know, or she didn't care enough about them to include them.

"Do you know how far along you are?" Opaline asked.

Ivy shook her head.

"I don't," she said. "Maxim said that Mikana pregnancies aren't the same as human ones."

"He's right," Opaline said. "They aren't. But that's

nothing to worry about. I'm sure that you will be just fine. Both of you."

Ivy glanced around again, still somewhat concerned about the lack of equipment even though she already knew that it wasn't there.

"Is there any way that you will be able to tell if the baby is healthy, or when it might be born?" she asked.

"You're worried that I'm not a doctor," Opaline said.

Even though the words were almost accusatory, the woman said them with a softness that showed her understanding and compassion.

"I'm sorry," Ivy said. "I just don't know what to expect. This is my first baby. To be honest, I never even really saw myself as a mother."

"Really?" Opaline asked.

Ivy shook her head, resting her hands on the sides of her belly as if to protect the little one growing inside from the words that she had just said.

"I've always concentrated on my career. It was just really getting started when I came here to assist my mentor, George." She gave a short laugh. "He actually wasn't too happy to see me. I had originally told him that I wasn't going to be able to come, but then I got the opportunity to, so I came to surprise him. Even after I came, I thought that this was just going to be a brief part of my life. I was going to finish up what I could do here, and then go back to Earth and keep going with my career. I wanted to eventually have my own laboratory and work on my own projects. It never occurred to me that there would be anything beyond my work."

"But then you met Maxim," Opaline said.

Ivy couldn't resist the faint smile that touched her lips at the mention of his name. He had been the most unexpected development of her life. Uoria had been nothing like she anticipated, but it had been discovering Maxim that had surprised her the most. She had fallen so deeply in love with him so quickly, and even though she had wanted to go back to Earth, she knew as soon as she met him that she would never be able to be without Maxim. Now she couldn't even imagine leaving Uoria permanently. She could easily adapt to life on Uoria and even continue to do more research. He, however, would never be able to live happily on Earth.

"I did," she said, "and I love him more than I could ever explain. It is only because of him that I can imagine being a mother. I thought that my work would be the only thing that mattered to me in life, and now I know that I have more than that. I'm just worried that I'm going to do something wrong or that I'm not going to be ready when this baby comes.

"You don't need to worry," Opaline said. "I can see it in your eyes. You are made to be a mother, and as soon as this little one arrives, you will know what to do. It will come to you."

"But how do we know when it will arrive?" she asked. "Have you ever helped a human woman through a pregnancy with a Mikana baby?"

She knew that the question was futile. This was unknown.

"I haven't," Opaline said. "But I know enough of the signs for both to be able to care for you throughout the pregnancy and until you deliver. We'll have to be careful, but together we can bring this baby into the world safely and happily. Now let me examine you."

As Ivy began to undress in preparation for the examination, her mind wandered back to Maxim. She wished that he could be there with her. She longed to be back on Penthos with him. Even though he had made it clear that he didn't want her returning to the battlefield even when the others came back, she couldn't imagine staying on Uoria without him. Eden had fought alongside the men while she was pregnant and hadn't been questioned or stopped. Ivy only wished that the others would see her as strong as they saw Eden, and as capable of taking care of herself and her baby while she continued to be a part of the efforts of the others. It was a thought that she would never have had before she left Earth for Uoria, or even in her first weeks on the planet. Being a part of a war wasn't something that she would have ever envisioned herself doing, but now all she wanted to do was be back on Penthos with Maxim, fighting to protect the family and the life that had become all that mattered in the world to her.

7
———

Maxim tucked his arms under Zyyr's and ran backwards with all of the strength and energy that he could build in his muscles. The sun was beating down on his back with vicious intensity and he could feel it searing through the fabric of his shirt painfully. The heat brought sweat down his face that stung in his eyes and mixed with the blood on his arms and chest. He could feel Zyyr trying to help him get him across the deep, stinging sand. The warrior's heels dug into the sand, forcing him backwards a few inches for every step that Maxim took.

He could still hear the voices of the hybrids that were marching away from the site of the brief but intense battle that they had just waged. The few that had survived were carrying the wounded, but Maxim hadn't seen any compassion in the assistance that they gave. It was almost as though they were already dead and their fellow hybrids were merely bringing them back to wherever they had been sleeping on the planet. Maxim got through the gate to the inner compound and released Zyyr so that he lay back on a cushion on the floor.

"Are you alright?" he asked.

The warrior nodded.

"I'll be fine. Thank you for getting me in here."

"What hurts? What did they do to you?"

"My leg," Zyyr answered. "I think it might be broken. One of them had a club that they hit me with. It brought me to the ground and took the wind out of me, but I don't think that there's anything serious but the bone. That will heal."

"But it will take time," Maxim said. "We need to stabilize the bone and then you're going to have to rest. You aren't going to be able to fight anymore."

Zyyr struggled to sit back up, an almost frantic look on his face.

"I have to," he said. "Nylek, Kyven, and Athan are already gone. There aren't enough of us left to help you if there's another attack. You can stabilize the bone, but I have to fight."

"Zyyr," Maxim said. "You can't. There's no way that you can safely go back out onto the battlefield. You will be an easy target. I know that you want to fight, and I appreciate your dedication, but I have to make sure that you stay safe as well. Ryan wants to destroy all of us. We can't give him the satisfaction of making that easy for him by putting ourselves in danger. The others are coming. We just have to stay strong and resist the hybrids until they get here."

Finally, the warrior seemed to relent. He rested back, his eyes closing and the color draining from his face as if the pain of the injury to his leg was settling in. Maxim rushed further into the building to get the bag of supplies that they had kept from the ship when the others left. He brought it back into the front room and called out to Lynx and Elise. When they came into the room, he gestured for them to come closer. He knew that speaking too loudly would only make the warrior feel more anxious, which could worsen his pain and even make it more difficult for his body to heal properly.

"I need you to find something that I can use to stabilize his leg," he told them. "Then find me as many rags as possible. If you can't find them, bring anything that you can. We need to get the bone in place and secure it so that it can start to heal. I'm going to give him some of Ciyrs's serum to relax him and ease the pain, but it will only last for so long, so we need to hurry."

Lynx and Elise both nodded and hurried out of the room. He knew that both were still struggling being away from their mates and he hoped that helping him care for Zyyr would distract them and help them to keep moving forward. He was particularly concerned about Elise. This was not her world, not the life that she ever thought that she was going to live. She had already been away from Azra for longer than any of them had been separated from their partners, but she had also been thrust into a war that she didn't understand. As they had said when they arrived on Penthos, however, she was the mate of a Denynso warrior. It had been her decision to give her heart to him, and when she made that choice, she was also choosing to give over her life to the Denynso way. By being with them on the journey and having the strong connection with Azra that all Denynso had with their mates, she had made herself a part of the conflict and she had little choice but to go along with it.

Maxim could see the fear and worry in her eyes, but he also knew that she was stronger than she thought. She had already proven herself in the ship and during the first battle with the hybrids. Though he knew that she wasn't going to be like Eden, Leia, or Zuri, or even like Ivy, anything that she could do for them would benefit them and would make

Azra proud. All she needed to do was believe in herself and what she was capable of doing.

Reaching into the bag again, Maxim withdrew a small battle of the calming serum that Ciyrs had created and opened it. They had very little to last them for as long as they were on Penthos, so using it had to be cautious and thoughtful. The pain that Zyyr was clearly in, however, justified the use of as much as he needed, at least through the challenging and potentially excruciating process of putting the bone back into place.

"Are you ready?" he asked.

"Is Lila here?" Zyyr asked.

"I don't think that she should be here to see this," Maxim said. "Drink this."

His eyes moved down to Zyyr's leg, drawing in a breath as he looked at the bleeding wound created by the shard of bone sticking through the warrior's leg. The fact that Zyyr didn't know the severity of the injury was a benefit, and he didn't want his mate to see it and make the situation any more anxious. Zyyr nodded his agreement and allowed Maxim to pour the serum into his mouth before he settled back against the mat. His eyes were still closed and he seemed to tighten them as if squeezing them harder would prevent some of the pain that he knew was coming.

"Just relax," Maxim said. "You'll sleep for a while."

Even as he spoke the mixture of herbs seemed to be taking effect. Zyyr's breathing had become deeper and more even and the tension in his face was releasing. Maxim immediately went to work cutting away the bloodied fabric of Zyyr's pants to provide better access to the injury. He took a cloth and splashed as little water onto it from his canteen as he could while still dampening the surface. He didn't want to waste any of the precious and limited water that they had, but he knew that he had to get the wound clean. He was finishing wiping the skin around the injury when Elise and Lynx came back into the room. Lynx was carrying an armful of pieces of wood and Elise held long rags that appeared to be made out of one of the blankets that they had brought with them from the ship.

"You're going to want to pack that wound with some of the herbs," Lynx said when he saw the full extent of Zyyr's injury. "That will help prevent infection and get it to heal faster."

Maxim nodded and took a container of herbs from the bag.

"We don't have many supplies left," he said. "Maybe we should have kept more before the ship left."

"We'll have to make do for as long as we can," Lynx said. "Ciyrs will be here soon. Hopefully he'll be able to help."

"Hopefully he won't have a reason to."

Lynx and Maxim met eyes and then Maxim looked away, concentrating on spreading the herbs into Zyyr's leg. He couldn't let himself keep going along that train of thought. In this moment, he needed to concentrate only on what he needed to do for Zyyr.

Lynx handed him the first piece of wood and Maxim looked down at it. It appeared to come from one of the pieces of furniture that they had found in the building. Maxim placed the piece beneath Zyyr's leg, then accepted one of the rags from Elise. They worked as quickly as they could and soon Zyyr's leg was fully bound and properly supported. Elise left the room and came back a few moments later with Lila. She held another blanket in her arms and Maxim could see the streaks of tears still on her cheeks. Lila approached her mate's side and carefully knelt down beside him. She draped the blanket over Zyyr and tucked it around him. She had begun to cry again, but the tears fell quietly and she said nothing as she reached forward and ran her fingertips across his forehead, brushing a lock of his thick white hair out of the way.

Maxim stood and walked out of the building. Lila needed this time alone with Zyyr as much as he needed to have her with him as he tried to recover from his injury. Evening was falling outside by the time that he stepped out into the air and the intensity of the sun had dissipated so he didn't feel the pain of it on his back any longer. It was a relief, but at the same time it meant the darkness was growing around the compound that they had claimed for themselves. The darkness was the most dangerous time. When the night came, they could hear the hybrids swarming to the walls of the compound, standing outside with their drums, taunting them, but never trying to get in where they were.

Maxim almost wished that they would. This was not what he had expected when it came to warfare with the hybrids. They knew that these creatures had been bred specifically for the purpose of fighting, and Maxim expected that the clash would be fierce and continuous once it began, but that wasn't what happened. Instead, there were long quiet stretches in between the battles, and when the battles did occur, they were brief. They would descend on them and clash, but within moments they were leaving, dragging their wounded with them. There had been few casualties, and when there were, the survivors often left them lying in the sand until the next battle, then brought them with them much like they did the wounded.

Maxim couldn't help but wonder about this approach to the war. When they had first arrived on the shuttle and Ryan confronted them, the hybrid army had appeared on the horizon. Their numbers had been expansive and Maxim had assumed that they would send as many of them as they could with each encounter. As soon as the fighting had begun, however, the army has dissipated, leaving only a few behind to engage with them. It was almost as though they were toying with them, tormenting them to make the conflict difficult beyond the physical fighting. With each wave of battle, they were breaking them down further, sending in fresh soldiers to replace the dead and wounded so that they were always at their strongest while Maxim and the rest of the group were growing more tired and worn with each passing hour. He wondered if this was the way that Ryan had planned it, knowing that if there was one tremendous battle the hybrids may not be able to withstand the tactics of the Denynso, but that if they simply kept pushing, kept attacking in brief but intense waves they would be able to break them down until they were completely vulnerable.

The thought was infuriating. It only illuminated who Ryan was, demonstrating that he was cruel and weak in everything that he did. Maxim had to remind himself that the others were coming. It didn't matter what the hybrids did. Soon those who had gone back to Uoria would return with supplies and a bigger army, and those who had been on Earth would join them, bringing with them the most powerful of the warriors and new insights into Ryan and what he was capable of doing. All Maxim and those still in the compound on Penthos had to do was survive. They just had to linger on, keeping the hybrids back long enough for the reinforcements to arrive so that they could battle them face-to-face.

As Maxim thought, he found himself wandering deeper into the compound than they had been. When they moved into the compound after the ship had left, they chose the first large building that they found to be their shelter. It seemed that it had once been living quarters, filled with aging furniture and dilapidated remnants of those who had once lived on Penthos before Nyx 23 arrived. Now that he was moving further into the compound, however, Maxim was seeing more of what Rain had described to them. Her memories of the space that they had infiltrated in an effort to free the prisoners and eliminate those who had built the illegal, vile prison colony had been vibrant and detailed, and Maxim could see the skeletons of those memories now. After the more than one hundred years that had passed since they had walked this ground, the abandoned buildings had begun to dissolve away under the power of the sun and the stinging of the sand that rose up when the rare but powerful wind blew.

The memories that Rain had shared were on the very edge of his mind as he walked through the rows of buildings. Part of him wished that he could have seen what she did, had been there to witness the colony as it had been. Maybe he would have been able to see something that the others didn't when they arrived. Maybe he could have changed what happened. If he had, though, Nyx 23 never would have ended up on Uoria, the Denynso wouldn't have started the exchange program with Earth, and he never would have had Ivy. Nothing would have been the same. This was his chance. This was the time to resolve the past and protect the future.

A large building rose up in front of Maxim and he stepped up to the door. The wood was old and dry from the heat and the sun, but a thick lock was still in place, preventing him from being able to open it. Maxim took a step back and aimed a hard kick right beside the latch. The wood cracked and another kick splintered it, enabling him to push the door the rest of the way open. Stale, hot air rushed out and Maxim took a step back to let the years flow out and rejoin the breath of the planet. When he stepped inside he saw that he was in a building that was far more elaborate than the other buildings he had seen. The furniture was larger and held faded padding that was absent from the furniture in the other locations, and the walls of the front room held massive frames with what looked like the remains of artwork. Time, heat, and brutally dry air had shriveled the art, leaving only shrunken pieces of paper that became powder beneath Maxim's fingertips when he touched them.

Maxim continued through the building, moving toward a door on the far end of the room. When he stepped through it he found himself in what he could only guess was the office that Rain had described. Unlike anything that Maxim had seen before, this space seemed like a small fortress of its own. The furniture here was more severe, including the heavy desk that sat toward the far wall. Maxim approached it cautiously, unsure of whether the office was truly still slumbering like the rest of the compound or if there were traps just waiting to lure him in. Finally, he reached the side of the desk and touched his hand to the surface. It felt warm beneath his fingertips and it was almost as though he was able to feel the energy of the creature who once sat behind it. Maxim walked around to the back of the desk and pushed the large chair behind it out of the way, not willing to sit in the same place that once held one of the Valdicians that had been the root of all the horror that they were now facing. He crouched down to examine the desk more closely, discovering a large drawer along the front.

Remaining cautious, Maxim took hold of the pull at the

front of the drawer and eased the drawer open. There were stacks of papers, files, and books inside, seemingly protected from the severe environment of the planet by the desk. Unlike the art that once decorated the walls, the papers inside the drawer were still in good condition, the words on them clear and legible. Maxim pulled everything out of the drawer, placing it on top of the desk so that he could look deeper into the drawer. He ran his hand along the piece of wood at the bottom and felt his fingertips hit something hard in the back corner.

Drawing the object out, Maxim looked down into his palm. The faint light streaming through the single window wasn't enough for him to clearly see what it was and he was beginning to feel strangely vulnerable and exposed in the building, as if there was someone there watching him even though he couldn't see them. He stood and gathered all of the papers from the drawer into his arms, then went back through the front room of the building and out into the night. The uncomfortable feeling immediately dissipated and he looked up at the sky, scanning the expanse to see any sign of the ships coming back. The stretch of stars was still. He would have to continue to wait, at least for now, for the others to come.

Maxim made his way back across the open expanse of the compound quickly. He couldn't hear the hybrids outside of the stone wall of the compound, but the silence was nearly as unsettling as the sound of the drums that had become their constant companion. When he arrived back to the building where they had settled, he could see a slight glow around the edges of the windows on the side. He hurried inside and found Zyyr sitting up, his back leaned against Lila behind him as she cradled his head against her chest and ran her fingertips through his white hair. His face was still paler than it usually was, but there was a slight smile on his lips as his mate comforted him. Lynx sat on the floor a few feet away with Elise leaning against the wall across from him.

Tucking the papers and journals in his arms closer to him, Maxim reached up to adjust the makeshift curtains that they had created to block the windows. Though the hybrids hadn't yet stepped inside the boundary of the compound, he didn't put it past them, and if they did he didn't want for them to be able to see the light that would betray their location.

"What's all that?" Lynx asked when Maxim turned around.

"I'm not sure," he answered. "Where's Avery?"

"He's in the back room," Lynx replied. "I think he may be sleeping."

Maxim nodded and settled onto the floor. He wasn't sure why, but he didn't feel ready to share the information that he had discovered with the human pilot of the ship that had brought them to Penthos. Though Avery had offered his assistance to the rest of the crew when they confronted him, he had still hidden in the panic room when he knew that the ship was going down. It was what he had been taught when preparing to pilot what he thought was a leisure trip, but the fact that he had done it, leaving those who were aboard at the mercy of the Valdicians that took over the ship soon after they left Uoria made it difficult for Maxim to trust the man completely. Avery had promised his service to them, and even commanded Elon, the human medic from the ship, to cooperate with the crew after the women found them hiding away, and Maxim had accepted it willingly. Despite this, though, he couldn't just consider this man one of them, a true part of what they were going through. The other two men had gone to Uoria with the others to make sure that the injured handled the journey safely. For now, Avery would have to remain on the outskirts of those who had remained behind. He would share with him what he could, but there were things that Maxim knew that he needed to keep close until he felt ready to make them known to the still-unfamiliar man. Even he didn't know what these papers held and he would wait until he did to make decisions about how to move forward with them.

Maxim placed the stack in his arms onto the floor and divided it into loose papers, files, and journals. The division was primarily arbitrary, achieving little but giving him some sense that he was doing something. The truth was he didn't know what he should do with what he found in the drawer in the office. Finding them had made him feel as though he were in a strange position. He was still in a moment of potential, not knowing what discoveries might be contained within those papers. As long as that potential remained intact, there was still the chance that he would be able to use it to make a difference in what was happening around them. As long as he left the papers unread and the journals unopened, he still had the hope that he had found some form of valuable information tucked away in the desk, waiting as the decades slipped by to be found so that he could use it to resolve the chaos that had befallen the planet again.

Everything would change the moment that he opened the journals, rifled through the files, or read the papers. Once he delved into them, he would know what he had found and if they made any difference. The potential would be gone and he would have to face whatever it was that he found hidden away in those words, even if they meant nothing to him. Even if they meant nothing to the planet, or the war, or the people who had already suffered so much on the dusty, searing surface of Penthos had had returned for vindication.

Maxim took one of the loose papers first, scanning his eyes over what looked like a list of names. He picked up one of the journals and opened it. He had flipped through several pages when he slammed his hand to the open page, his heartrate increasingly slightly at what he saw.

8

Rilex barely even heard the music around him as the woman gradually relaxed more and more in his arms and they danced at the edge of the others. Everything around them disappeared and he only cared about the strange but beautiful creature that he held close. Soon it seemed like some of the others were starting to drift out of the room, ready to take advantage of the time that they had left on the journey to get some rest. The woman stepped back away from him and glanced down at the floor as if she didn't want to meet his eyes. He didn't know if she was embarrassed by the closeness that they had discovered, or if this was something that she had been taught, a lingering reminder of the regimented, torturous life that she had led until they found her. He could only hope that it was the former. Time would make their interactions easier and more comfortable for her, but he didn't know if she would ever be able to get over the scars that were left from what she had gone through when she was still under the control of Ryan.

"I should go," she said so softly Rilex almost didn't hear her.

"Why?" he asked.

"People are starting to leave."

"So?" Rilex asked. "I'm still here. I'm not going anywhere. Unless you want to go somewhere."

The woman looked slightly startled.

"Where?" she asked.

There was nervousness in her voice that made Rilex's stomach turn. He wondered how many times she had been told where to go, and how often it had gone horribly for her when she went along with the command. He slid his hand down along her arm until it rested against hers, again not latching on or forcing the touch any further than she wanted it.

"You are safe with me," he reassured her. "I might not know what will happen or what we are going to be facing when we reach Penthos, but what I can promise you is that I will do everything in my power to protect you. You will be safe when you are near me and I will never put you in a position to get hurt again. I just meant that we could go to one of the lounges if you wanted to spend some more time together. If you would rather just go to one of the bedrooms by yourself to rest..."

"No," the woman said, cutting him off. "I'd like to go to the lounge with you."

Rilex smiled and nodded. He could feel her hand close slightly around his, not quite holding it yet, but transferring more of her touch to him than before. They started out of the room, leaving behind the remnants of the party that was still going on, and headed toward the nearby lounge. As they stepped into the lounge Rilex tried to imagine what the room would have been like if they had been on one of the leisure cruises that this ship was used for. He knew that it was designed to use for any type of transportation and had been used frequently for transport of researchers and teams between planets, but there were characteristics of the ship that made it clear that its purpose was not purely academic. This room had obviously been designed for comfort and relaxation, not something that would be a priority when it came to a school, scientific, or military mission.

As they walked further into the room to stand by the massive window that covered nearly the entire wall, Rilex imagined the happiness of those who would stand in this very position when they were on vacation, gazing out into the open space without a worry or a concern marring the view. It would be purely luxurious, the only thought in the mind of the person standing there likely being whether they should stand there for a few minutes longer or return to their room to sleep until whatever pleasures awaited them the next day. That thought made him wonder about the passenger pods and if any change would be made for those who had paid the premium price for one of the trans-galactic journeys rather than boarding the ship for work. Though they were fairly comfortable, he couldn't imagine them being the only place for sleep for those on the trips that could last weeks at a time.

"What are you thinking about?" the woman asked.

Rilex chuckled in embarrassment. He hadn't meant to lose himself in the thoughts that were running through his mind and forget that he was standing there with her. He turned toward her and gestured toward the window.

"What do you think of all this?" he asked.

Her eyes narrowed at him.

"What do you mean?" she asked.

"I was thinking about what it would be like to go on a vacation, just to be so peaceful and carefree."

"A vacation?" the woman asked.

Rilex realized that it wasn't a word that she would have any reason to know.

"It's when people travel just for fun. They go somewhere and relax, spend time with their loved ones, see things that they don't see when they're at home."

"I can't even imagine something like that," she said.

"Neither can I," Rilex said with another soft laugh. "I never took one."

"Can I ask you a question?" the woman asked.

Rilex nodded and looked at her.

"Of course," he said. "What would you like to know?"

"What are you? I mean, how did you get here?"

She seemed flustered and even embarrassed by the question, but Rilex understood. For someone who was created like a product rather than crafted out of the love two people shared, it was a completely normal and expected concept that she would wonder at the origin of others she encountered.

"I came here by accident," he told her. "I traveled through a portal in my home and ended up on Earth."

"Couldn't you just return there?" she asked. "Didn't you know how to?"

"No," he said. "It wasn't just that I had traveled to another place. I was many, many miles, but also many, many years from the home that I knew. Though I knew that it was possible because I had been doing it my entire life, it wasn't something that anyone here understood. I couldn't tell anyone what had happened and had no way of reaching out for help. I was stranded. I had no choice but to just assimilate and start a new life here."

"You said that you went through a portal," the woman said. "Why couldn't you just go back through it?"

She was asking the question in a way that told Rilex that she didn't truly understand what he was telling her or even what she was asking, but that she was trying. He wanted to encourage her, to reassure her that she was allowed to use the new freedom of thought that being away from the facility afforded her.

"Unfortunately, it doesn't work that way. The portals don't just go from one place to another and back. I'd never used the one that I did to bring me here, and I didn't know where it would bring me if I attempted to go back through it. There was a chance that it would bring me somewhere that I still didn't know and didn't know how to leave. Some of the places that the portals bring are extremely inhospitable. My only hope was that one day those from my stream would figure out what had happened to me and come for me. I settled in and started a new life here while I waited."

"And they never came."

It wasn't a question, but a statement, an illustration of her immediate, resigned reaction to any situation. No matter what was happening, or what the possibilities that the situation held, she was quick to believe that nothing good could come out of it. She would never believe that there was hope, even after she was rescued. As much as he didn't want to consider it, he knew that deep within her, she was likely still scared, still worried that at some point she would be back in Ryan's possession and that her life would be even worse than it had already been.

Rilex took a half-step toward her.

"They did," he said. "It took far longer than I expected, but they came. The son of my best friend, the man who I was trying to help when I went through the portal, ended up here with a human woman who traveled through the portals."

"But you didn't go back with them," she said.

He shook his head.

"No. I could have. They offered to bring me back, but I chose to stay here."

"Why?" the woman asked.

"I had work that I needed to do here. It had been so long, I had made a life here. I was accustomed to it. Everything back in my own stream had changed so much, I didn't have my same place there any longer."

She shook her head and turned her head to look out of the window at the blackness around them.

"I would have gone back," she said. "If I had a home somewhere, nothing would keep me from it."

"I did have a home," Rilex said. "I had two homes. My home there, though, wasn't the same as it had been. I wouldn't have been able to just go back and keep going as if I had never been gone. I had a home here. Over the years I had learned to live here and had been doing important work that would ensure the home where I was born and the home I had chosen were protected and wouldn't be destroyed."

"Destroyed by who?" the woman asked.

Rilex felt a chill roll down his spine. He wished that he hadn't said that. He didn't want to explain any of this. It was something that he had put behind him and now that he thought there was a chance that it wasn't fully behind him, he was terrified. Putting voice to it would only make it real, and he wasn't ready for that. Instead, he tucked a finger beneath her chin and turned her face toward him.

"Have you chosen a name yet?" he asked with a smile.

She shook her head.

"I asked you to choose one for me," she said.

"Why?" Rilex asked. "Don't you want to decide what others call you?"

"Does anyone choose their own names?" she asked.

"No," Rilex said, "but you aren't just anyone."

"I know," she said, "but I don't know if the words that I would use to describe myself would be anything I would want others to call me. You choosing something for me would let me know how you see me, and how others might as well."

It was a bold and forward request, but one that Rilex felt honored to accept. He could feel himself drawing closer to her, something within her calling out to him at just the sight of her and the feeling of her presence near him fulfilled an ache that he had likely always had but had only just come to know. He wanted to reach out and pull her into his arms again. He wanted to touch her skin and feel her heartbeat. He had to be patient, to take his time and give her time and space to grow and learn to be herself within this new and strange context of life.

"There are so many things that I could name you if I wanted to describe you," he said. "I could call you Beautiful, or Wonderful. I could reach into my heart and my past and name you Starlight. But none of those would honor you properly. You deserve a name that is yours and yours alone."

"And what is that?" she asked. "What will you name me?"

"Severine," he said without hesitation. "It means traitor."

It was a word that had stayed with him after it fell so bitterly from the lips of the other hybrid on the battlefield at the University. He had meant it as a cruel and vindictive insult, but the truth was that it was the kindest thing he could have called her.

"Severine," she said, sampling the feeling of the name in her mouth and its sound in her ears.

"When he called you that, he embodied you like nothing else could. You were everything that you were trained not to be; strong, courageous, powerful in your own right. To be called "Traitor" for the rest of your life will be a lasting reminder that you saved them all."

9

———

Jonah put the file in his hands aside again and picked up another one. He felt like he had gone through each of these files a thousand times already, but no matter how many times he looked at them, he still didn't understand what he was seeing. The information contained within them didn't make sense. He remembered the examination that he had undergone prior to the mission very clearly. He knew exactly what they had gone over with him and the tests that they said that they performed, yet the information that was contained within the files didn't correspond to what he remembered. Some of the tests and vitals that they had done weren't accounted for, while others that they didn't do were recorded with details that he knew hadn't actually been taken.

He put the file down and opened another, laying it beside the other so that he could compare them side-by-side, then opened his own and reviewed it against the others as well.

"I just don't understand," he muttered to himself. "The

height and weight are off. Not by much, but they're still wrong. Why would they do that?"

He read through the test results again.

"I know that I didn't have this test, but there's results."

The sound of his own voice in the silence of the room was uncomfortable and he fell quiet again. It was like just hearing himself talking without the benefit of someone responding underscored the fact that he was largely on his own. As soon as that thought moved through his mind, he knew that it wasn't accurate. Though there were others who were still in the basement with him, he knew that this journey that he was taking, the path that he was on as he tried to unravel the mystery of the files was his own. None of them knew what he had been through and wouldn't be able to help him. He wouldn't ask them to. They had gone through enough and were facing their own troubled and complicated journeys moving forward. They had already been forced into a war that meant nothing to them. They didn't need another fight that wasn't there placed at their feet.

He ran his fingertips along the series of numbers that was supposed to be the results of a test that he remembered taking, but knew that they weren't the results that he had gotten. Jonah sifted through the rest of the files and pulled one out. He flipped it open and read the same results from it. After a few seconds, he closed the file and turned it to check the name on the front to make sure that he had chosen the right one from the stack. He had selected it because he distinctly remembered the day after he had gone in for his examination when he sat down for lunch with Brandon and discussed their test results. This particular test had been presented to them as largely experimental. It wasn't one that they had undergone before for any of their missions, but the doctor had told them that they needed to go through it now because of specific environmental concerns regarding the area of space where Penthos resided.

As with nearly everything else that had to do with the department, none of them had questioned anything that the doctor had told them that they needed. As he looked back on it now, he cringed at how pliable they were, how willing they were to simply go along with whatever was said to them, whatever was expected of them, without question. It was as though they never even thought about themselves and what they were actually giving themselves over to, they were too wrapped up in the idea of what they might accomplish or who they might one day be. Now Jonah knew that he would never be that trusting or selfless. He would never be able to simply agree with what someone said without questioning what that meant for him and how it might turn out if he went along with it. Though he was happy to support and assist those who had come to mean so much to him on Uoria, he did so with caution, evaluating each step and each order before he followed it.

Jonah reviewed the test results another time. It was as though he thought that if he looked at them enough, he would be able to make the results change so that they better fit with what he thought that they should say. He knew that they didn't properly record the results that he had gotten on the test, and also didn't correspond with what Brandon told him that he had received. Though he knew that there was always a chance that Brandon had lied about his results, Jonah knew that when he looked at his own file he didn't see the proper series of numbers. Even if his numbers did even vaguely correspond with his results, Jonah knew that there would be no reason for Brandon to lie about his own results. The true purpose of the test and what the results meant was something that was never revealed to anyone on the team. They only knew that they were undergoing a new, experimental test that would ensure that they had some undefined characteristic that ensured they would properly withstand the environment of Penthos. Since they had no understanding of what the results even meant, there would be no reason for Brandon to try to fabricate his own results.

It was obvious to Jonah that the results were changed purposely, but why? What would be the reasoning behind putting the team through a strange experimental test, telling them their results without giving any explanation of what those results meant, and then changing the results when they recorded them in their files, especially if those files were just going to be hidden away for no one to see? He stacked the files carefully and tucked them against the wall so that they wouldn't be disturbed and then gathered his bag and his lightstick and started back up into the abandoned medical ward again.

This wasn't the first time that he had entered the derelict hospital since the others left, but Jonah still didn't know what he expected, or even hoped, to find when he explored the examination room. The glow of his lightstick filled the empty hallway and he let it fall on each of the closed doors as he went. He wondered why they had bothered to fill the rooms with the useless equipment before sealing up the hospital. Why didn't they bring it out with them when they left the building for the last time? Or if they weren't ever going to use it again, why didn't they just leave it in place in its original rooms rather than taking the time and effort to divide it into the abandoned examination rooms and then close the doors, almost as though creating tombs for the remnants of the era?

Jonah's thoughts wandered again to the strange reality of

the abandoned hospital. He couldn't understand why the ancient medical ward was still there. It didn't make sense. The rest of the old University had been demolished, yet this, the most outdated and unusable building of all of them, had remained so that it could be used as the lost and forgotten skeleton of the new laboratory building. He wished that he could return to the buildings that he had spent his time in when he was studying and working at the University. Walking through the hospital had given him a taste of his previous life, yet reminded him blatantly and painfully of how long it had been. These were not the floors where he last stepped before he climbed onto the ill-fated ship, but those that were had long-since been destroyed. It was a sad feeling to think that he had walked along those hallways so filled with anticipation and even excitement, not realizing that it was the last time that he was ever going to see them. It was a foregone conclusion that within a few weeks, they would return and simply walk along the same path back to the department rooms. Instead, he had moved along that familiar path, the images that he was seeing passing through his eyes and into memory.

Without fully knowing why, Jonah turned away from the crumbling hallway and started back down into the basement so that he could go back up the stairwell and into the corridor above. He stepped out into the corridor and was immediately struck by the energy that filled the space. It was as if he could still feel what the rest of the group had felt when they were making their way down the corridor and out into the open space around the building. It suddenly struck him that he didn't really know what had happened to them in the time between them leaving him in the basement and them getting out of the building. He could only hope that it had not been as difficult as the last time that they were there. Ignoring the nervousness that made its way down the back of his neck and into his stomach, Jonah made his way toward the stairs that they had climbed to go through the laboratory building. He wove through the floors of the building, trying to remember what doors they had used, until he finally found his way back to the room behind Ryan's lab.

Jonah hesitated in the backroom. He didn't know what might be inside the room, if even Ryan himself could be waiting for any that might return. For a moment, he considered turning back around and heading back to the basement, but he knew that he couldn't. He had to go beyond just the basement and the medical ward if he was going to understand what happened. His hand felt almost electrified as he placed it on the doorknob to the lab and pushed the door open. As soon as he stepped inside he was struck by the cold, still feeling, and sharp, unnerving scent of the space. He looked around and knew immediately that they had not been the last ones who had walked through that room.

There had been chaos in the lab the last time that he had been inside. The conflict with Ryan had tossed the entire space into complete disorganization and left the surfaces covered with blood, chemicals, and other remnants. Now the entire lab was back in its original pristine condition. If anything, it was more organized and cleaner than it had been before. He could smell the cleaners used to wipe away all reminders of them and feel the chill of the temperature having been turned down to accommodate a delicate experiment.

The Valdicians had been here. They had come to the lab after the group left to repair what they had done and bring the room back into the condition that Ryan expected. Jonah couldn't imagine that they would have done something like that out of any sense of kindness or affection for Ryan. Instead, it was more likely out of a sense of responsibility, obligation, and even fear.

He walked to one of the tables and ran his fingers along the surface. It was cold but dry, telling him that the room had been restored well before, likely only briefly after they had captured Ryan. Most likely they had come into the room to free him and been commanded to fix the damage that had occurred, as if Ryan believed that he could pretend that it hadn't happened if he didn't have to look at it. He was leaning down to look under the table when he heard a slight gasp from across the room.

Jonah stood up sharply and looked toward the door. He hadn't thought to look at the main door to the lab when he first stepped in and now noticed that it was standing open a few inches, revealing a figure standing in the hallway just outside of the lab, a halo of golden yellow glow at its feet.

There was a tense moment when both stood completely still, aware of the other, but unsure of what to do next. Finally, Jonah took a step forward and lifted his lightstick up above his head to shed more of the light toward the figure so that he could see it more clearly. When it did, he could see that the figure was a woman, her hand rested on the doorknob. She looked both startled and confused, but unafraid.

"Hello?" she said.

"Hello," Jonah replied.

Her head tilted slightly and Jonah wondered if there was something about his voice that sounded different to the people of Earth a century after his own time and that had struck this woman strangely. She took a somewhat hesitant step toward him, crossing the threshold of the lab. Her hand slid across the wall beside her and her finger pressed into a dip on a silver metal panel. In an instant, the room filled with a blinding white light. After days with nothing but the glow of the lightsticks and the light from the small lanterns in the basement and the hospital, the illumination felt like it was exploding in his head. He grasped his temples, pressing against the pain that he felt in his temples and crumbling forward with the shock. It took several moments for his eyes to acclimate to the bright light and for him to be able to open them again. When they did he found that the woman had disappeared. He rushed around the table to the door and looked out into the hallway. He could see the faint remnants of her light moving around the corner at the far end of the corridor and felt an uncomfortable sensation in his belly, wondering who this woman was and why she had come to Ryan's laboratory in the middle of the night when the building was locked and no one else was supposed to be there.

10

———

Nylek winced as he made his way around the perimeter of the room, trying to convince his legs to move normally and willing the pain in his body to go away. The treatments he had received on the ship had effectively begun to heal his wounds, but not receiving a healing from Ciyrs had left him feeling weaker than he ever had this long after being injured, and he could tell that some of the gashes in his skin were still only tenuously healed. No matter what he was experiencing, however, he hadn't wanted to spend more time lying in the bed in the clinic. He felt like he had been trapped in a bed for longer than he ever had, and it made him feel fragile and vulnerable, things that he couldn't stand feeling. As soon as he was able, he had gotten out of bed and left the clinic, insisting that he go to one of the homes in the kingdom for the rest of the time that they were in Uoria. He would have preferred to be back in his own home in the Denynso compound, but he knew that the journey was too far, and by now nearly everyone who had remained in the compound when they left for Earth was now in the kingdom with the Mikana.

Elon and the Mikana doctors didn't seem confident that he would be well enough to return to Penthos with the others when the ship left, but Nylek refused to accept it. Until they had boarded the ship again and were gone, he wouldn't admit that he wasn't able to go with them. For now, he would keep walking, keep moving to start rebuilding his strength and encouraging his injuries to heal further.

The door behind him opened and he saw Mina step inside. She looked startled to see him out of bed and held a stack of blankets toward him.

"I brought these for you," she said.

Nylek looked at his mate, feeling his body and his heart burning for her. It had felt so long since he had left her behind in the compound so that they would be able to communicate with Creia while they were gone. He had missed her so desperately, but since he had returned to Uoria injured, she had seemed skittish and unsure around him. It was as if she didn't know if she should get close to him or if it might hurt him further.

"Mina," he said. "Please. Come here."

"I shouldn't," she said. "You should be resting. Without Ciyrs..."

"I don't need Ciyrs," Nylek insisted. "I'm healing just fine on my own. I just need you."

"You need to rest," she said. "Just get back in bed. Get some sleep."

He could hear the emotion and tension in her voice, and knew that she was struggling seeing him wounded after being apart for so long. Of course, he had been injured before, but that had been as a result of battles that she understood. She knew what they were facing and the dangers that they would experience while fighting. When he left Uoria with the others, though, she didn't know what he was going to encounter or what he would have to do. It was bad enough that he came back hurt, but she also knew that he hadn't returned with everyone else, and that the encounter wasn't over. His mate couldn't stop worrying about him because the situation hadn't yet come to an end and they had no way of knowing what else they were going to have to face.

Mina turned and started back out of the room, but Nylek followed her. He got to her in the hallway that led away from the bedroom and out of the house. Without saying anything, Nylek wrapped one arm around her waist and swept her up against his chest, crushing his mouth down on hers. Mina didn't resist but gave herself completely into the kiss, wrapping her arms around his neck and opening her mouth to allow his tongue to slip through her lips to massage against hers. The hesitation was gone, replaced by passion and need that told him his mate had missed him with the same fire that he had missed her during the time that they were away. He no longer cared about the pain that still lingered through his body. All he cared about was feeling her and reconnecting with her now that they were back in each other's arms, at least for the time.

Nylek led Mina back into the bedroom and kicked the door behind him. His mouth continuing to play across hers, he turned and lowered her to the bed. He stepped back and stared down at her as he peeled off his shirt and tossed it to the side. Mina stared up at him, her eyes widened in awe of the sudden kiss and her lips slightly swollen and red with its passion and intensity. He undressed as Mina watched him, revealing himself to her completely and purposefully. She watched him with a blend of emotion in her eyes. There was a powerful, slumbering hunger that he knew was reflected in his own eyes as well, but there was also something softer and more tender. Nylek could see her gaze settle on the lingering bruises and scars of his wounds, but she didn't wince or try to look away. Instead, she focused on them, following them like she wanted to know everything that he had gone through when he was away from her.

He could see Mina's eyes roving across his body, taking him in as if memorizing every inch of him, committing to memory the new injuries that had changed the landscape of the skin that she already knew so well. They had completed their bond years before, but his passion and love for her had never changed. He still craved her with every breath and felt the flutter deep within him when he thought of her. She was the greatest aspect of his life and the most precious companion he had and would ever know. He stepped forward and reached for the waistband of her skirt. He eased it down over her hips, revealing only the thin, gauzy panties that she wore beneath. Growling deep in his throat, Nylek removed the rest of her clothes almost frantically, tossing them aside as fast as he could. He wanted to run his fingertips over every inch of her and feel her smooth curves against him. When he was gone he had dreamed of filling his hands with the softness of her nearly every night. Now that she was stretched out in front of him, nothing separating them, he wanted to show her everything that had filled his mind in those long, dark moments.

Nylek forced himself to slow down. As much as he wanted her, it had been too long and he had wanted her too much for him to simply rush through and make it end too quickly. He reached forward and placed his hands on either side of her ribs, then ran his hands down along the deep curve of her waist. Applying gentle pressure, he ran his palms around the full swell of her hips and then up her belly onto her breasts. The warm, familiar lushness of her body filling his palms made his body tremble with anticipation of the pleasure they would soon enjoy. He allowed his thumbs and forefingers to gently squeeze her nipples, feeling them harden beneath them. Mina arched slightly into the touch and he saw her eyes flutter closed as her lips parted. She was no longer resisting him or trying to avoid the need that she felt for him. Instead, she was soft and compliant beneath him, just waiting for Nylek to guide her as he reclaimed his life and pushed aside the injuries to show her that he was still just as strong as when he had left her side.

He drew in another long breath to keep himself calm and slow. He had to constantly remind himself not to move too quickly, to let himself enjoy everything that was to come and to savor every second of it. Memories of the taste of her brought him to his knees at the edge of the bed and his hands to her thighs so that he could ease them apart. They parted easily and willingly, and Mina's body opened to him. Nylek could already see how wet she was and the warm, musky smell of her body was enough to drive him nearly to the edge of what control he had. She was ready for him, waiting for him, but he still wasn't willing to let this end yet. There was so much more that he wanted to explore with her now that he was back with her and they had nothing but time to explore and enjoy each other. This was purely about them and he had every bit of privacy to indulge himself in every detail that his beautiful Mina offered. It was a gift that he wasn't going to take for granted.

Resting one hand lightly on her belly to hold her in place, Nylek ducked his head down and drew his tongue through her folds, moaning at the taste of her as it filled his mouth and reached into him to begin fulfilling the empty ache within him. Mina gasped and reached down for him, but he eased her hand away from his head, wanting her to relax and simply enjoy the attention that he was giving her. He licked her again, pausing for a moment to flick the tip of his tongue across the sensitive pearl of flesh. It began to come forward with his coaxing, further intensifying the sensation that he was creating for her. Nylek brought his other hand down and carefully eased one finger into her body. He felt himself melt slightly at the softness of her hot, wet walls closing in around it, and pressed it deeper until the heel of his hand rested against her pelvic bone.

He moved his finger gently within her as he continued to trace through her core with his tongue. He didn't want to leave any of her untouched or neglected. Nylek applied slightly more pressure against her upper wall, exploring the pattern of ridges until he found the smooth, slightly softer spot that he knew would push her to the brink of her control. It was a spot that he had discovered in the long afternoons and blissful nights that they had spent together, and one that he loved to touch and nurture, bringing whimpers to her lips and tightening the muscles through her hips and thighs. He rubbed his fingertip onto it a little harder and heard Mina draw in a sharp breath. Her body was starting to tremble and he knew that her own control was close to shattering. Nylek rose up over her and took her hands in his. He pushed them back and pinned them on the bed on either side of her head. Mina gasped slightly, but he could see her chin lift and her mouth open as if seeking him. Continuing to exert every bit of control that he could, he slowly stretched out across her. Gradually their bodies met so that their skin melded and she was fully enveloped in him. Nylek slowly lowered his mouth back to Mina's and brushed it slowly across her lips. She whimpered softly and parted her lips further. He dipped his tongue briefly into her mouth, allowing it to glide across the inside of her bottom lip, seeking out his mouth.

Nylek lowered his mouth to hers and offered a deep, languid kiss. He could taste all of the kisses that he had missed while he was gone, all of the words that he didn't hear, and all of the moments that they hadn't been able to share. After a few moments, he ran his hands down her arms and along the sides of her body, then wrapped one arm around her waist so that he could pull her closer to his body. In one smooth, controlled movement, he rolled both of them over so that she lay on top of him. The new position caused the warmth of her core to nestle against his erection. It was a promise of what was to come and he could feel the intensity of his desire for her increasing even further. Nylek reached for her legs and tucked his hands around the backs of her thighs so that he could pull them gently and cause her to straddle him. Mina pressed her hands to his chest to push herself into a sitting position, putting her body on display just for him.

In that moment, it seemed that Mina had found her confidence and was no longer intimidated by his injuries or by the unknown conflict that he had experienced. Neither of them expected what had happened when they agreed to help Creia. Nylek hadn't been part of the group of warriors who had gone to Earth or who was still in the Mikana kingdom. When he agreed to travel with them as a connection between those on Earth and those remaining in Uoria, particularly the King and Queen, he expected the journey to be primarily exploratory. There was always the chance of violence any time that the Denynso were involved in anything. Their reputation as fierce and aggressive warriors extended throughout the universe, and they had fought countless species and battles. The sudden brutality that they encountered, however, had been far outside of what he thought that he was going to experience, and he knew that it had been horrible for Mina to relay the messages that he sent through her to Creia. She was a distant witness, knowing what was happening and yet separated enough from it that she couldn't do anything about it or even be completely sure that she really did know what he was going through. To tolerate it, she had built up a barrier, closing off the emotions that she had been feeling so that she was able to handle the responsibility that had been presented to her. It kept her locked away from him, unable to reach what she was really going through and commiserate with him for his own suffering.

Now Mina had seemed to break through the barrier that had been made in her mind. She had broken free of the distance that she had built up in her mind and was ready to connect with him fully again. She lifted her hips, moving them forward so that her hot, wet core slid along his hardened length. Reaching forward, she wrapped her hand around his cock and held it in place so that she could slowly roll her hips against it. The sensation was nearly overwhelming and he dug his fingertips into her hips.

"You're so close," she whispered.

Nylek nodded, biting into his bottom lip to keep himself from toppling over the edge.

"I could just slide inside you right now."

Mina leaned forward, causing the taut peaks of her breasts to brush across his chest, and brought her mouth close to his ear.

"Please," she whispered, the warmth of her breath trailing along the side of his neck.

Nylek turned his head so that he could claim her mouth with his. As they kissed passionately, their tongues tangling, he used one hand to adjust their bodies until the tip of his erection just settled against her opening. He held her hips more tightly and then lifted his just enough that the very tip entered her. They both drew in breaths and he could feel her trembling. Pressing herself back, Mina sat up again. The new angle allowed her to sink down onto him until her hips rested on his. Nylek groaned as their bodies completely melded. They both paused, the sound of their breath, audible in the silence of the room around them, and cherished the feeling of coming together again.

Mina sighed softly and began to move her hips. She rolled them slowly but deliberately, ensuring that their bodies never parted while still guiding his engorged cock to massage her walls. The slow, steady darkness that had settled around them and now sent shadows through the room felt like it was cradling them, protecting them from the world outside as they worshipped one another and gave thanks for the bond between them.

After a few moments of simply treasuring the sensation of being enveloped fully inside her, Nylek pressed a hand to the small of her back to stabilize her, and then sat up to tuck her close into his lap. He leaned forward to rest his mouth to the soft dip at the front of her neck, and then rested his head against the front of her shoulder. Mina wrapped her legs tightly around his hips and her arms encompassed him, one coming around his shoulders and the other cradling his head as he nestled into her neck. Though she was smaller than him, as a Denynso woman she was far larger than the human women who had come to Uoria and found their mates. In that moment, he was blissfully grateful for it. Her size enabled them to wrap their bodies around each other fully, melding to one another in a way that wouldn't be possible if she were much smaller. She felt strong and lush in his arms, yet sweet and feminine. They remained in this peaceful position for several long seconds. The closeness of their bodies enabled their breaths to synchronize and soon Nylek felt like they were truly one. He tightened his hips to press into her more deeply and she rocked her hips to return the sensation to him. Nylek needed more. He couldn't be satisfied with just this any longer. He slipped his hand in between them and pressed the pad of his thumb to her peak. He applied gentle pressure and began to create small circles.

Mina's pace increased slightly in response to the touch and he met each rock of her hips with a lift of his own so that he sank more deeply into her with each thrust. Nylek filled her completed, fitting into her body in a beautiful, perfect way that reminded him with each long stroke within her body that she was crafted specifically for him. He had waited for Mina his entire life and had known the moment that he met her that they were intended to be together for the rest of their existence. It was only her. It had always been her, and would only ever be her. Neither could ever love another and their lives would be forever designed around their devotion to each other.

Nylek could hear murmuring coming through her chest and he drove into her until they became louder, faster, and more desperate. Finally, she reached forward and her hand gripped onto his back. He felt her arch, her body squeezing down around him as she cried out. The sound of his name tumbling from her lips with such abandon broke every semblance of control that he had left. Nylek lifted her up with one final, impaling thrust and he felt himself pulse before he poured into her. Each of her tight, hard spasms milked him, drawing him further into her and pulling out the hot streams that filled her.

When they both seemed to have relaxed and calmed enough to move, Nylek embraced her and rolled her onto her back. He came down over her as he continued to slowly stroke into her to extend the delirious pleasure of the aftershocks of his orgasm that rolled through him. He stared down at her, his hand absently brushing along the hair around her forehead, and felt a smile come to his lips. There was nothing that he could say at that moment that would even begin to express everything that he was feeling or the gratitude that he had just to be back with her. Even if they weren't able to remain together for long, even if he was able to recover enough to get back on the ship and return to Penthos with the others, he had these moments that he could hold on to and think of when he was away. All he could do for now was watch as her eyes fluttered closed and the soft smile on her lips relaxed slightly. When she was fully asleep, he rolled on to his side and allowed himself to fall asleep, feeling as though he were able to really rest for the first time since he had been away from her.

11

———

Ellora felt the muscles in her jaw twitch as she opened the door to the war room and looked around at the weapons that her husband had compiled. She didn't know how long he had been collecting the arsenal or how long he had been planning the war that he had hoped would ensue after the battle, but now it didn't matter. Gone were her hesitations about the conflict that her children and the rest of Uoria was facing. Gone was the fear and the bitterness that had been controlling and guiding her for the years since she thought he died. This was for Aegeus now. She reached forward and took down one of the largest swords that she could manage. It felt heavy and meaningful in her hands, speaking to her in a way that she couldn't explain. Behind her she heard Athan come down the steps and into the hidden space.

"What are you doing?" he asked.

"What does it look like I'm doing?" she asked.

She lowered the sword carefully to the surface of a table and reached for another, working to systematically remove the weapons from the room so that she could bring them up to the house and prepare them for travel.

"Does this mean that you will support Kyven and Maxim now? That you won't stand in the way of the war?"

Ellora turned and shoved a sheathed blade into Athan's hands.

"I will never be able to get back the years that were taken from me that I could have spent with my husband and that he could have spent with his family, but I want to destroy whatever took them. If Maxim needs weapons and an army, then I will get them for him."

Athan nodded and accepted another sword that she handed him before stepping up to the wall and gathering several into his arms. She watched him carry them out of the room and heard his footsteps climbing the stairs back up into her house. Tears of fury were stinging in her eyes, but she didn't want to give into them. She had already shed enough tears after Aegeus disappeared. The time to cry was over and she didn't want to give the creatures that had stolen him even a second longer of the satisfaction of her tears. It was her time to fight.

An intense compulsion burst in her chest and she stormed out of the war room and up the stairs. Out of the corner of her eye she saw her husband's symbol and resolve dried the tears from her eyes and settled the beating of her heart so she felt completely calm and under control. She was determined in a way that she hadn't felt in so long. No longer was she living in a shadow or surviving just for the sake of Maxim and Kyven. The blood seemed to be running through her veins again and she was thinking clearly for the first time in years.

Without saying a word to Athan, she lowered the weapons that she had brought up from the war room to her kitchen table and then left the house, starting toward the barely-used hatch that Maxim and Ivy had used to emerge from the Order tunnels when they first arrived back in the kingdom. This was her time, her chance to stand up and show that she had the strength and the ability to protect her home, her family, and her husband, and that had to start with confronting those who put him in the position in the first place: The Order.

There was a time when Ellora would never had even considered entering the tunnels that ran beneath the kingdom and were the stomping ground of those chosen for the Order. She knew that she wasn't even supposed to know that the organization existed, and once it was known that Aegeus told her of the Order, she wasn't supposed to know anything of their operations. She had always followed that as closely as she possibly could. It was an honor for Aegeus to have been selected for the Order. Though she didn't know what the organization did or even why it existed, she knew that it was extremely selective and the fact that he had been chosen to join them was incredibly meaningful. She didn't want to do anything that would disrespect him or the others, or put the organization at risk.

Now, though, she no longer cared. It didn't matter to her that she was never supposed to go down into the tunnels or that she didn't even know what she would find there. If Ivy, a human woman who had been on Uoria only weeks when she arrived at the kingdom, could walk through them and emerge without harm, Ellora was confident that a lifetime in the kingdom and the strength and power of Aegeus in her heart would get her through. As long as she found the leaders of the Order and was able to confront them, she didn't care what else she discovered in the hidden, unspoken world beneath her feet.

Ellora took a breath and dropped down through the hatch so that she could climb down into the tunnel. The colored lights burst on above her and she felt immediately exposed, but instead of it making her feel vulnerable, it was as though the multicolored glow above her was announcing her arrival. She stalked down the tunnel, not knowing where it was leading. When the path turned or forked, she let her heart guide the way. Suddenly she heard fast footsteps and harried voices in the distance. Above her the light in the ceiling glowed red and she stood her ground, wanting for whoever it was who was coming toward her in the tunnel to find her. She wasn't going to hide. She wasn't going to apologize for her presence in the tunnels. It was their turn to explain themselves.

A moment later she could see the darkness ahead of her dissolving away as the lights in the ceiling turned on in sequence, announcing the approach of whoever was in the tunnel with her. She knew that they could see her light now and soon they would be able to see her face. Her fingers twitched and she wished that she had brought one of the swords with her. For now, the small dagger that she had tucked into her boot would have to suffice. The rhythm of her heart quickened, but not out of fear. She was beyond fear. This was excitement, a thrill at getting closer to a truth that had always been kept away from her and dangled just out of reach, though in the back of her mind she had hoped she would discover it.

The footsteps drew closer. They were only yards from her now and she knew that it was only a matter of seconds until they would see her face and know exactly who had invaded their private world. Ahead of her the light in the ceiling turned yellow and then white. Three figures came into view and she felt her stomach twist. They paused, not drawing near enough to trigger the light segment just ahead of her so that a bar of darkness remained like a wall in between her and the men now glaring at her across it.

"Ellora," one of them said. "What are you doing here?"

"Malcolm," she said, barely able to get the name past her lips. "You are a part of this?"

"Ellora, you shouldn't be here," Malcolm said. "You don't belong down here."

"Yes, I should be here," she said angrily. "I should have come down here long ago. How dare you keep this from me? How dare you not tell me?"

"I don't understand," Malcolm said. "Tell you what? You of anyone should know that I wasn't allowed to say anything to you about the Order or that I was a part of it. The only person who was permitted to let you know that he was a member was Aegeus."

"Don't you dare say his name," Ellora spat. "You are never allowed to say his name."

"I don't understand," Malcolm repeated. "Why are you so angry? Why did you come down here?"

"Why am I so angry?" Ellora asked. "My husband was bound to serve an organization whose origin he didn't know and whose purpose he didn't fully understand. He discovered extensive corruption among the hierarchy that was meant to be the most honorable and powerful of all Mikana, and when he fought against them, he was taken from me, from our children. I have suffered for years wondering what happened to him and trying to explain to boys who were rapidly turning into men why their father was just gone. I came down here to confront them, these creatures who claimed lives for themselves that never belonged to them, used them, and then tossed them away. I came down here to see what could possibly be so important that it would justify how grotesque the Order really is. Then I find that my brother has been a part of it all along."

"I couldn't tell you, Ellora," Malcolm said.

"Is that why you stopped talking to us? I married Aegeus and you just left my life. It was like you never even existed."

"It was just too hard," Malcolm said. "I hated having to lie to you. I knew Aegeus and it was too difficult to balance being in the same family and being in the Order together."

"So, you chose the Order," Ellora said accusingly.

"I had no choice. You don't understand."

"*You* don't understand," Ellora said. "Not telling your only sister who you really are isn't hard. What's hard is losing the love of your life. What's hard is raising two boys alone and hoping every moment that they wouldn't realize that they didn't have any masculine influence and lose all of what of their father was within them. You could have been there for them, Malcolm. You could have been there for Maxim and for Kyven, helped them deal with the loss of their father."

"You did fine on your own," Malcolm told her.

The comment was meant to be encouraging, but it only enraged her further.

"I shouldn't have had to!" she screamed. "I *never* should have had to."

"You don't understand," Malcolm said again.

"Then tell me," she said. "Explain to me what could possibly be so important about the Order that you could turn a blind eye to corruption, violence, and death."

Malcolm opened his mouth as if to respond, but no words came out. Instead, his eyes widened and seemed to focus on something over Ellora's shoulder. She began to turn, but she felt a hand clamp around her wrist and another clasp the back of her neck.

"What do you think you're doing down here?" a voice hissed into her ear.

Ellora fought out of the grip on her neck and turned, finding a man with a dark red mask standing close behind her.

12

———

"I'm so sorry that I missed that," Ciyrs said in his mind, transmitting the message to Elianna in his thoughts.

His mate was on the ship with the others while he had taken the vehicle that Oro and Jonah had brought from Uoria so that he would be able to take care of the wounded and the pregnant women during the journey. The strange car was traveling far more quickly than he had anticipated it moving, and they found themselves ahead of even the large transport vessel from the University. Being away from Elianna during this journey was difficult for him even though it was only for a few hours. He hated that they weren't near each other and that he had no idea what she was going through. Now she was communicating with him through their thoughts, giving him a harsh reminder that she was far away from him and that if something did happen, he wouldn't be able to protect her.

"It was so beautiful," Elianna said. "It was so unexpected. We got onboard and I think we all just kind of expected that we were going to spend the next few hours getting some sleep. At least the rest of them were, I knew that I was going to have to be in the infirmary with the injured."

"The injured?" Ciyrs asked.

He didn't know what she was talking about. The whole reason that they were in separate vehicles was that Pyra decided the most wounded and the pregnant women should travel in the faster vehicle with Oro and Ciyrs rather than trying to make it all the way to the transportation bay to travel in the larger ship. He knew that she was going to be offering support to those who were in better condition, but he hadn't thought that any of them were bad enough off that she would need to be in the infirmary throughout the entire journey. The thought made him uncomfortable, as though he was failing even further in his responsibilities.

"Pyra brought the hybrid survivors from the battle."

"What battle?"

"We encountered the hybrids and the Valdicians," she said. "There were injuries and we saw them dragging away some of the hybrids. All we could think was that they would be put through the same things as the ones that we rescued from the breeding facilities. They brought them to the ship and I've been working on healing them."

Ciyrs drew in a breath and reached into his bag for one of the bottles of water that he had brought with him from the emergency chambers. He longed for a sip of something cold after days of the warm, still water from the basement. He shook his head, needing to get the thoughts of the wounded who were now on the ship out of his mind. There was nothing that he could do about it right now and he had to trust in his mate that she would be able to use the skills that he had given her through his first healing with her and the methods that he had taught her to stabilize and heal them as well as possible until he could get there to help her.

"Why did he do the tying ceremony on the ship?" he asked, trying to redirect the conversation back to the ceremony between Loralia and Bannack that Elianna had contacted him to describe. "I know he had mentioned something about a tying ceremony when he first met her, but I thought that they would wait until they were back on Uoria to do something like that."

"I think that's what she thought, too, but something changed his mind. I was in the infirmary and Samira came in and told me that I should take a break and have a bath."

Ciyrs laughed, then glanced nervously at the women who had finally fallen asleep across the furthest back section of the vehicle. He didn't want to disrupt their rest, assuming that it had been a long time since any of them had really been able to sleep deeply, knowing that they were secure and safe.

"That sounds pretty amazing right now," he said.

The sound of Elianna's laugh in his mind was refreshing and brought a bigger smile to Ciyrs's lips.

"I have to admit that it didn't take a lot of convincing. I felt bad leaving the wounded just so I could take a bath, but they were resting and I knew that there wasn't much more than I could do for them in that moment."

"It's alright," Ciyrs told her. "You can't always think of others. Sometimes you have to think about what you need, too. You can't be a good healer if you don't. Did you enjoy your bath?"

"More than I think I have ever enjoyed a bath in my life," she said, then paused. "Well, no." She paused again and Ciyrs felt like he knew what she was thinking about in those moments of hesitation. "The first bath that I took after getting out of the Covra prison. That was the best bath of my life."

"I bet it was," Ciyrs said, wishing that he could rid himself of the thoughts of that dark, horrific time that lingered in his mind.

"Anyway," Elianna said, obviously wanting to get away from the thoughts just as he did. "After I took the bath, Eden brought me some of the clothes that I had with me for the wedding and told me to put them on. I don't know what I was expecting, but somehow I just couldn't imagine that they were going to bring me to one of the lounges and Loralia and Bannack would surprise us all with their tying ceremony."

Ciyrs laughed again, but he felt a tug of pain in his chest. He knew that that ceremony was one of the most important events in Bannack's life, and he hated to have missed it.

"I really do wish that I had been able to be there to see it," Ciyrs said. "I know that was really important to both of them."

"I know," Elianna said. "And I'm sure that they were sad that all of us couldn't be together, but it was something that they felt like they needed to do. It was amazing to see Azrael officiate for them. I know how hard it was for Loralia when she first found out who he was, but it's obvious how much he loves her, and she seems to be really growing close to him."

"That's wonderful," Ciyrs said.

Suddenly he heard a small gasp behind him. He turned and saw that one of the human women was writhing in her sleep, her face contorted slightly as if she were either afraid or in pain.

"What is it?" Elianna asked, recognizing that his thoughts had turned away from the conversation that they were having.

"One of the women," Ciyrs said. "She's restless."

"I hate to think of what they're going through," Elianna said. "After everything that they've already suffered, they shouldn't be traveling like this, and they definitely shouldn't be going somewhere like Penthos."

"I know," Ciyrs said, "but I understand why they wanted to come with us. Would you want to stay in the facility where Ryan kept them? I know that some of them chose to remain there with Jonah, but if it was me, I would want to be as far away from all of that that I could possibly get. I would always be afraid that Ryan would come back and that I wouldn't be able to get away."

"But you know that it is very possible that Ryan will show up on Penthos with the rest of the hybrid army. We could be bringing them right to the most dangerous place they could be."

"No," Ciyrs said. "Even if he does come to Penthos, they won't be alone. They'll be with us, and we'll protect them. I just don't know what will happen to them from there."

"I don't either," Elianna said.

He was about to respond when the healer heard the human woman let out a sharper, louder cry. He turned to look at her and saw that she was now sitting part of the way up, her eyes open and wide as she clutched at her belly. She took a gasping breath and looked up at him frantically.

"What's wrong?" Ciyrs asked the woman, speaking out loud now as he leaned across the seat where he sat to get closer to her.

"It hurts," the woman gasped.

"What's going on, Ciyrs?" Oro asked from the front of the vehicle where he was piloting. "Is everything alright?"

The woman groaned loudly and another of them woke beside her.

"Astrid," the second woman said. "What is it?"

"It hurts," Astrid said again.

"What hurts?"

"My belly," Astrid answered. "It really hurts."

"You can't be in labor," the other woman said. "You still have more than a month to go."

"What's your name?" Ciyrs asked.

The woman looked at him briefly before turning her attention back to Astrid.

"Zadie," she said.

"What's happening?" Ciyrs asked.

Astrid curled around herself, crying out again and wrapping her arms around her belly tightly.

"She seems to be having contractions," Zadie said. "But she shouldn't be."

"Why?" Ciyrs asked.

"What's wrong?" Elianna asked in his mind.

"One of the women may be in labor, but another said that she shouldn't be."

"Is something wrong with her?" Elianna asked.

Ciyrs repeated the question to Zadie, who was now pressing her hand to Astrid's forehead. By now the other woman were starting to rouse and Ciyrs felt like he was losing control of the situation.

"It's too early," Zadie repeated. "She still has weeks to go before she should be delivering."

Ciyrs relayed the information to Elianna.

"How do they know?" Elianna asked. "She is carrying a hybrid baby."

Ciyrs repeated this to Zadie, who looked at him sharply.

"Do you honestly believe that Ryan left anything up to fate?" she asked angrily. "He knew every detail of everything that he did. We weren't people to him, we were living machines. He followed the development of our babies from the moment that they were conceived and knew with almost perfect accuracy when they would be born. Astrid shouldn't be ready to give birth now."

"I can't stop it," Astrid gasped.

"You'll have to deliver the baby," Elianna said.

"I've never delivered a human baby," Ciyrs said. "I've only been present for one birth, and I didn't manage it. I'm going to need your help."

Zadie looked at the other women.

"You need to stay calm and give us as much room as you can," she commanded. "If you can, get into the seats further up. Astrid needs space."

Ciyrs helped two of the women climb over the seat to sit in front of him and then climbed over into the back section where Astrid lay. She was soaked in sweat now and tears had pooled under her eyes. She gasped again, her back arching with the shock of the contraction, and Zadie reached to guide her back down.

"You need to try to relax," she said. "We can't stop the contractions now. The baby is coming and you have to help it."

"I can't," Astrid said in a tremulous voice. "I can't."

"Yes, you can," Ciyrs told her. "You are ready for this."

Astrid's eyes opened and she looked into his with an insistence that chilled his blood.

"Please," she said.

It was the only word she said, but he knew that it carried with it far more meaning than the single syllable implied. Her fingers had weakly gathered her skirt up her thighs and over her knees, and when he looked down he saw blood spreading across the blanket beneath her. Suddenly her hands fell away from her legs and he saw her eyes roll back in her head.

"What's happening?" Elianna asked. "Ciyrs, what's happening?"

"She's bleeding," he said. "She's not responsive."

"You have to get the baby out," Elianna said. "Now."

The urgency in Elianna's voice jolted Ciyrs into action. He pushed her dress the rest of the way up Astrid's legs and pressed on her belly, allowing Elianna's voice in his mind guide him through urging the baby out of the woman. Zadie cradled Astrid's head in her lap, stroking the sides of her face as she spoke softly to her. Ciyrs worked as quickly as he could and finally a tiny baby emerged into his hands. He gathered him close to his chest and reached for one of the blankets, draping it over the frail, shivering frame. In his arms, the tiny child let out a weak cry just as Ciyrs looked up and saw the dark outline of a planet building on the horizon.

TBC

To be continued...

RILEX & SEVERINE'S STORY

1

R ilex felt too warm and comfortable to want to come out of the sleep that had unexpectedly taken him over only a few short hours before. He had thought that he was going to stay awake throughout the entire journey from Earth to Penthos and hadn't felt any of the fatigue that the others seemed to show when they got onto the shuttle. As he stood with Severine staring out of the window of the lounge at the calm, peaceful space beyond, however, he had started to feel the tiredness settle into the muscles throughout his body and his eyes grow heavy until they had sat down into one of the large reclining seats positioned in the lounge and fallen asleep.

Just thinking of her name sent a thrill of excitement through Rilex and settled a warm, comforting feeling into his belly. He could still barely believe that the beautiful hybrid woman had chosen him to select her name for her. It was such a meaningful decision, and the fact that she had allowed him to make it for her felt intimate and precious in a way that he had never experienced. He couldn't yet put voice to the hope that he held in his heart, the hope that someday, hopefully someday soon, they would be able to extend that intimacy and trust and move forward into a relationship that went beyond the simple and somewhat tenuous bond that had begun to grow between them.

He heard a soft murmur and wrapped his arms more tightly around Severine, who cuddled close to his body in the large, thickly cushioned chair. The sweet sound made him relax even deeper and he hesitated in opening his eyes for a few more seconds. He knew that as soon as he opened his eyes he was going to have to come back into reality. For now, as long as he kept his eyes closed and his arms cradling her, Rilex could pretend that this was reality and that it would continue on for as long as he wanted it to. Severine shifted in his arms and let out another cooing sound as she gradually came out of sleep. Wanting to see her sleeping against him, even if only for a few seconds, Rilex opened his eyes and looked down at her. They were curled around each other in the seat, her head rested forward on his chest as he held her, and his head leaned above hers.

He didn't remember falling asleep this way. Instead, they had stood at the window talking until they both moved back toward the chair and sat in it. It was a gradual and natural movement, as if both of them were experiencing the same thought in the same moment. Their conversation had flowed just as naturally and by the time her voice quieted and her head rested back against the seat, he felt like he knew her on a new level, a level that confirmed both his deep and undeniable attraction to her, and his disgust and hatred for Ryan. Rilex had listened to Severine talk until the words stopped and watched her as each blink became longer, till finally her eyes stayed closed and her face softened in sleep. He remembered watching her for a few minutes, wanting to make sure that she was truly resting, but then his own eyes closed and he fell into a sleep that was deeper than any he could remember having in his recent memory.

Their bodies had moved toward each other during the night until they were lightly intertwined. It was as if they had been magnetized to each other by something that existed inside of them and recognized itself in the other when they were finally vulnerable in sleep. Now they were both coming out of that sleep and it was up to them to become aware of what was happening between them and decide how they were going to allow themselves to respond to it.

Rilex watched as Severine's eyes briefly squeezed closed more tightly and then her long eyelashes lifted off of her cheeks and she let out a sigh as she stared across his chest at the window ahead of them. After a few moments, she raised her gaze to his. He offered her a soft smile, hoping that it would start to fill the space that existed between their minds even as their bodies remained closely linked. Severine stared back at him nearly expressionless. She blinked several times and then her eyes narrowed questioningly.

"What is it?" he said quietly.

He knew that no one else on the ship would be able to hear them even if he spoke to her normally, but something about the situation made him feel as though he should keep his voice low a quiet, almost as though he didn't want the words to get far away from them. This was something that he had never felt before. He couldn't explain what he was experiencing when he looked into Severine's eyes or felt the warmth of her skin through her clothing. Rilex had left his own time and planet before he had found the mate who he could share his life with, and when he came to Earth, this type of relationship had been the furthest thing from his mind. By the time that he had come to terms with the reality that being on Earth and away from everything that he knew was the life that he would be living from now on, he was already too engrossed in his study of the HM-1313 wall and its meaning to even consider that finding a partner was something that he would ever have the opportunity to experience. It wasn't something that he ever thought about. Had someone asked him about it, he would have told them that he didn't have the space in his life for another person. In truth, after being torn from the life he had known and the people who had meant everything to him, he didn't have the space in his heart for one.

Now, though, he didn't feel that way. Suddenly it seemed that there was always space, but it was waiting for him to find Severine. She continued to look at him with her haunting eyes and then shook her head slightly.

"I wasn't sure if all of this was real," she said.

"What do you mean?" Rilex asked.

"I thought that it was a dream," she said. "I haven't been that comfortable and slept that well," she sighed, "ever. I was afraid that when I opened my eyes, all of this wouldn't be real."

"All of it?" Rilex asked.

Severine nodded, the gesture causing a strand of her gold-streaked hair to slide over her shoulder and settle against the gauzy fabric of the dress that she still wore.

"The fact that I was free from Ryan." She looked around them at the lounge where they had rested. "This ship. Everything out there." She finally turned and looked at Rilex again, a new softness and tenderness in her eyes. "You."

Her voice had dropped slightly and Rilex thought that he detected an underlying layer of emotion, but he didn't want to create something in his mind that wasn't truly there.

Instead, he shook his head and carefully brushed the strand of hair back around her shoulder so that it fell with the rest of her mane.

"No," he said. "It wasn't a dream. You are really free, and you always will be. We are really here, on this ship, out in the vastness of the galaxy. I am really here with you."

Her lips curved into a smile and Rilex felt a tug in his belly. He wanted desperately to kiss her. It was a compulsion, a need unlike any he had ever had. He had been attracted to other women before he came to Earth, but never had he experienced an absolute, overwhelming desire just for a kiss. He licked his bottom lip, hoping to ease the need, but it didn't go away. He lifted his hand to cup around the base of her head, holding it steady, but he paused before he could bring his mouth to hers. She had been through so much already. She had had experiences like no one could imagine and a life that no one else but those who had gone through the same thing could ever even begin to understand. The concept of love, even just the simplest gesture of a kiss, was something that was beyond her understanding of the world and she might not yet be ready to venture there yet. He didn't want to push her and risk causing her any more hurt that she had already had in her life. She wasn't ready. She may never be ready. But he would have to be patient and simply hope that one day she would be and that he would know.

Rilex's hand was sliding away from where it rested in her hair when footsteps alerted him to someone coming into the room. He turned to look over the back of the lounge chair and saw Jem.

"Rilex," he said with relief in his voice. "There you are. We've been looking for you."

"Is everything alright?" Rilex asked, afraid that something had gone wrong somewhere in the ship and that they were in danger.

"It's fine," Jem reassured him. "We're almost at Penthos. Everyone needs to prepare for landing and get into their passenger pods. We should be arriving within the half hour."

Rilex nodded.

"Thank you," he said.

Jem returned the gesture and rushed away from the door. Rilex looked down at Severine, the strange feeling between them somewhat strained now. It felt like neither of them quite knew what they were supposed to do now that they were being forced out of each other's arms and back into the reality around them. Severine sat up and twisted to stretch her back, then climbed off of the chair and stood. She put back on the shoes that had fallen from her feet while they slept and looked down at him with a hint of a smile.

"Thank you," she said.

"For what?" Rilex asked.

Severine drew in a breath and let it out slowly, seeming to enjoy just that most basic and intangible demonstration of freedom and relief.

"For everything."

She turned and walked out of the lounge. Rilex assumed that she was going back to the room where she had gotten prepared for the party. He wished that he could stay with her to make sure that she got to her passenger pod safely, but he had his own preparations to do before they landed and very little time to do them in. He stood from the chair and took a final look out of the window at the expanse of space rushing past them. Even though he couldn't detect them in the vast blackness around them, he knew that they were soaring through a tremendous blanket of stars. He knew those stars. He had seen each and every one of them long before, and being among them at once reminded him of everything that he had lost, and everything that he had gained.

2

———————

Severine felt like she wasn't quite touching the ground as she left the lounge where she had spent the last few hours with Rilex and started back toward the room where the women had helped her get ready for the celebration of the tying ceremony. It was a strange feeling that she had never experienced before, but one that she hoped would linger. She knew that she had to take off the dress that she wore and brush her hair out of the lovely style that they had created for her, and she wanted to hesitate as much as she could. If she could have her way, she wouldn't ever change or let this evening end. It was all too incredible, too perfect to let go. She felt like she and Rilex were hovering just on the edge of something amazing, though she wasn't entirely sure what it might be, and there was a part of her that wasn't sure she wanted to go any further. She didn't know what could possibly be waiting for her beyond that edge and she didn't feel ready to tip over it and find out. Instead, she wished that they could simply stay where they were, savoring the new and thrilling feelings that were appearing inside of her. It was like she was opening from within. She had always felt like there was only darkness and emptiness within her, and never guessed that there could be anything beyond that. Rilex, though, had gone beyond the hybrid exterior that she had been afflicted with by merit of Ryan's creation of her, and reached that darkness. Now it was breaking, revealing more within her than she ever could have guessed that she had.

Her heart filled as she thought of the name that he had given her. *Severine. Traitor.* A name was something that she never had and would never have been given if she had remained in the torture chamber under the control of the Valdicians, or, far more mercifully, been left to die in the corridor after the battle. Those who were born in the facilities were considered disposable, not worth the time, energy, or emotion of an identity of their own. It was only those who had offered themselves into Ryan's program and sacrificed their bodies to the DNA splicing that had names and were allowed to be called by them. Even those who had been stolen and forced into the experiments lost their names when they entered the laboratories and were taught swiftly and severely not to use the names that they once had. To have a name was validation and resistance, it was proof that she was more than just a living machine created for the purpose of war. When she had first asked Rilex to give her her name, she thought that he might give her something beautiful and melodic like what she had heard the other women called, but he hadn't. Instead, he had named her "traitor", taking the word that was spat at her by the angry fellow hybrid after they fought their way to the transportation bay, and turning it into a badge of honor. Though it wasn't what she had expected, he had been right. It was perfect and she was proud to carry it.

The chamber where she had been transformed from the

battle-worn hybrid to the woman who had entered the cele-bration was empty, giving Severine the chance to remove the dress gradually and reluctantly. She didn't want to relin-quish the touch of the airy fabric against her skin and the feeling that it gave her to wear it, but she knew that she had to. She hadn't yet decided what she was going to do when they arrived on Penthos and the others went back into battle, but she knew that she wouldn't be able to stay in the blissful, dreamlike state that she had been living in for the last few hours.

The women had offered her fresh clothing to wear and it was waiting for her on a low seat at the side of the room. She stepped into it and looked into the mirror that she had used hours before to see herself in the dress. It was the first time that she had seen a mirror, the first opportunity that she had had to see her reflection fully. There had been a few times when she had caught the hazy outline of herself in the brushed metal tables or the glass of the chambers, but it wasn't until the women had brought her to stand in front of the mirror in the ship that she had really seen herself. She didn't know what to think of herself or the way she looked. She knew that she didn't look like the other women, but for the first time it didn't seem strange. Instead, she felt unique and different. As she looked at herself in the slim-fitting pants and shirt, she wondered if she was beautiful. It wasn't something that she would have ever considered before, but now that she knew what it was like to have Rilex's eyes on her, she couldn't help but wonder what he saw in those moments.

Once she was dressed again and had tied her hair back behind her head, she left the room and started toward the passenger pod she had ridden in as the ship took off. She was nearly there when she heard frantic voices in the hallway in front of the passenger chambers. She recognized one of them as Eden, but the other was too muffled by tears for Severine to know who it was.

"I don't know what to do," the crying woman said. "I couldn't help him."

"You did everything that you could," Eden said. "You know that."

"But I'm a healer," the woman said, telling Severine that this must be Elianna. "I'm supposed to be able to help people and keep them safe."

"You weren't born a healer," Eden said. "You are only a healer because of the care that Ciyrs gave you. He was destined to be a healer at birth and even he wasn't able to give her what she needed. Sometimes that's just what happens. It isn't possible to save every life."

Severine turned the corner of the corridor and saw Elianna bent forward, her face in her hands as she sobbed. Eden was standing beside her, cradling her baby son in one arm and rubbing Elianna's back with the other, trying to comfort her. Severine felt awkward standing there. At once she wanted to know what was happening. They were talking about a life that was lost under Ciyrs's care, and she knew that the Denynso healer was in the vehicle with the most severely wounded and the pregnant women from the breeding facility. She wanted to know who it was and what had happened to them. At the same moment, she knew that this was a private conversation and that she shouldn't be interjecting herself into it. She was starting to turn away, planning to find another passenger pod for the landing, but she heard Eden call out to her.

"Hello!"

Severine knew that it was only she and Rilex who knew the name that he had given her, but she had still expected to hear it come out of Eden's mouth at the end of the greeting. When it didn't, she questioned whether she should tell her, but decided against it, knowing that this moment wasn't about her and that she shouldn't try to take it over. She turned back to Eden.

"Hello," she said. She took a cautious step toward them. "I'm sorry for interrupting."

Eden shook her head and wrapped her arm around Elianna protectively while also seeming to try to take a step toward Severine.

"No," she said. "You aren't interrupting. I'm happy to see you. How are you doing?"

Severine nodded.

"I'm feeling better," she said.

"Good," Eden said. "Did you have fun at the reception?"

Severine nodded again, uncomfortable at the way Eden seemed to be ignoring Elianna. She looked at the healer who had taken care of her when they were still in the basement and brought her back from the brink of the death that nearly took her first during battle, and then during the retraining at the hands of the Valdicians.

"Is she alright?" Severine asked.

Elianna lifted her face and looked at Severine.

"One of the women gave birth in the vehicle," she said. "It was too early and she didn't survive."

Severine felt her breath catch in her throat. They had just managed to get out of the horrific conditions of the hidden facility. The woman had tasted only a few days of freedom, and now had lost her life far away from everything that she had ever known. She would never have the opportunity to see her family again, to explain to them why she had suddenly disappeared from their lives. She would never be able to hold the child that she carried or experience the peace of knowing that that child would not live the life of an experiment or a weapon.

"Who was it?" Severine asked when she felt like she could speak through the painful tightness in her throat.

"Her name was Astrid," Elianna told her.

Severine nodded. Though she hadn't had much opportunity to interact with the breeding women, she had heard the name. If she thought hard enough, she could vaguely see the face of a woman with thick blond hair and thin, chiseled features. She didn't know if that was truly the woman that they were talking about or just a composite of the details that she had gathered about the women from the brief times that she had been able to see them, but she chose to believe that it was her. She deserved to be remembered, even if it was only by others who had lived a captive life as she had.

"What about the baby?" Severine asked.

The other two women seemed only concerned about Astrid, and while Severine was sad at the loss of the woman, she was thinking about the innocent child who had been born into the world too soon, and who now had no one.

"Ciyrs says that the baby survived the birth and seems to be doing well, but is very small. One of the other women has tried to feed it, but she hasn't produced milk yet. They hope to express milk from the mother, but since the baby came so early, she hadn't yet produced enough."

"The baby will need formula," Severine said. "If it is to survive it will need care very soon."

Elianna nodded.

"He doesn't know if the baby is strong enough to live. For now, it is breathing and has good color, but none of the other women know what else they can do for it."

"Is it a boy or a girl?" Severine asked.

"What?" Elianna asked, seeming thrown off by the question.

"The baby," Severine said. "You keep calling the baby 'it'."

Severine hated the dismissive way they were speaking about the child. It didn't matter how it had come to be or even how long it might live, this was a living being and deserved to be shown some form of respect and dignity.

Elianna shook her head.

"Oh," she said through her tears, wiping her cheeks as if she were trying to get control of her emotions. "I don't know. Ciyrs didn't tell me. He just said that a baby had been born and that the mother died in childbirth. He didn't mention if the baby is a boy or a girl."

Pyra came down the hallway and rested one large hand on Eden's back. He looked at Elianna, but she was fighting to keep the tears from continuing to fall and he seemed to recognize that she didn't want to talk about what was happening.

"The ship will be starting its descent in just a few minutes," he said. "We need to get into our landing pods. Elianna, they need you in the infirmary."

Elianna nodded and started away from them without another word. Severine watched as she went, wondering what was being done in the infirmary to protect those who were undergoing care and those helping them while they were landing. She was sure that a ship of this magnitude, designed for exploration, was properly equipped to handle situations when there would be passengers and crew in the infirmary, but it still made her uncomfortable to think of any of them being in danger, particularly those who had already been through so much. Eden and Pyra turned toward the passenger chambers and Severine followed, splitting away from them and going into the chamber where she had traveled when they first left Earth. She climbed into her pod and adjusted the harnesses before reaching up to grasp the handle on the lid and pull it down into place.

As soon as the lid clicked closed, Severine squeezed her eyes closed and took several long breaths, willing herself to remain calm. She hated the tightness of the pod. She hated the feeling of being strapped down inside of it. Though she knew that this was the way that the others were traveling as well, and that the shell of the pod, its surrounding padding, and the tight harnesses were designed to protect her during the potentially hazardous ascent and descent portions of the voyage, it felt far too much like the experiments and reprogramming that she had been forced to undergo in the facility. Too frequently she had been closed in spaces that prevented her from going where she wanted to or even moving when she needed to. The harnesses reminded her of being strapped to the cold metal tables of the reprogramming unit, while the lid of the pod made her mind go immediately to the screens that the Valdicians would move into place in front of her face and force her to watch for days on end.

Severine kept her eyes closed as she felt the slight sinking feeling of the ship starting to lower down. Her mind moved back through the years, dredging up memories that she hadn't wanted to dwell on since she packed them away in the darkest recesses of her thoughts. She knew what she had to do. It was the only choice. The nervousness and fear disappeared as a feeling of sadness that she couldn't quite explain settled in.

3

———

Rilex felt the slight shift in pressure as the ship landed and heard a long, slow sound that was like a release of air, almost as if the machine itself was relieved that they had finally arrived on Penthos. He hesitated before opening the harnesses that held him still in the passenger pod. He didn't know what to expect when he finally climbed out of it and stepped out onto this unknown planet. Like many of the other people aboard the ship, he had never been to Penthos and knew nothing about the foreign planet. He didn't know what it would be like to step out onto the ground of another land and be expected to instantly acclimate as he threw himself into the war that was equally unknown.

They had no way of knowing what those who had remained on Penthos had gone through in the time that Azra, Ariella, Oro, and Jonah had been on Earth, and what was happening with the hybrid army that they knew was on the planet with those who had been left behind. He had heard those who had arrived from Penthos talk about their unexpected arrival on the planet after leaving Uoria on the way to Earth, and about the hybrids that had surrounded the ship as Ryan's image taunted them on one of the ship's screens. Rilex knew that they were there, and that they were likely fighting against those who had stayed when the others had climbed into the stowed-away vehicle and flew to Earth to find help. Knowing that, though, didn't change the questioning feelings that were building in the back of his mind.

Rilex's thoughts about the hybrid army and the war itself had changed, and he wondered if they had changed for the others as well. When they were still on Earth, hunkered in the basement trying to decide what to do, he knew that they all felt a sense of anger and even hatred toward the hybrids that had attacked them. They saw them as powerful, living weapons that had been created not to think or feel, but only to fight and destroy. When they thought of going to Penthos and fighting the war that had broken out there, they thought of fighting those hybrids and preventing them from eliminating the group that had come together from both Uoria and Earth to defeat Ryan. That wasn't how Rilex thought of it any longer. These hybrids weren't weapons. They were living, breathing, feeling creatures that had been given an existence that none of them could imagine. While Severine had told him that there were some who had actually offered themselves into the experiments and took joy and fulfillment in the opportunity to fight, Rilex now knew that this was not the case with most of them. These were not just machines that happened to have heartbeats. They were people and they didn't deserve what was happening to them. There was obviously still reason to fight, but that reason had shifted in his mind and in his heart. He no longer felt that they were fighting just for themselves anymore.

The lid to the pod opened slightly and Rilex pressed it

open the rest of the way. He climbed out and walked toward the main area of the ship where the others were gathering. As they collected in the open area, he looked around for Severine, hoping to find her among the faces that were closing in tightly around him. He had expected that she would have taken the passenger pod beside him as she had when they first left Earth, but by the time that he came to the passenger chamber to get into his pod, all of the others in the chamber were already taken and she wasn't in any of them. He hoped that she had found one where she would feel safe, but he wanted to find her before they left the ship. He didn't know if she knew anything about Penthos and he didn't like the idea of her being alone on the planet even for a moment. After the conflict with the other hybrids and the Valdicians when they were trying to get to the transportation bay, he knew all too well that Severine wasn't safe near the other hybrid creatures. He wanted to be close enough to her to protect her if they tried to take her again.

It seemed that everyone had gathered in the area, waiting to be told what they were going to do next, when he finally saw Severine. Her face was drawn, the sparkle that had begun to appear in her eyes when they were sitting together in the lounge now gone. Rilex started toward her, trying to make his way through the group to get to her, but she stepped away. He continued toward her, but she stepped behind others, gradually disappearing further into the group so that he couldn't get to her. Suddenly he felt himself swept up among the others and was forced back further away from her as the group closed in more tightly toward the front of the room. Rilex turned and saw Pyra standing on something that made him tower even higher over the rest of them. He was looking out over them sternly, seeming to check each face and take inventory of them to make sure that all but those limited to the infirmary were there. They hadn't yet planned what they were going to do when they finally made it to Penthos, and now that they had arrived it was time for them to come together and determine what steps they would take next.

Pyra held his hands out in front of him and the silence rippled through the group until they all stood quietly, staring up at him expectantly. When he knew that he had all their attention, Pyra lowered his hands to his sides.

"The others have already arrived," he said. "We landed as close to them as we could safely, but it is still a short ways off. They haven't yet left their vehicle and are waiting for us to make the next move. We will need to send out scouts to rendezvous with them and then we can plan a mission to locate Maxim and the others."

There was a feeling of hesitation in the group, but Rilex took a step forward. He held up his hand so that Pyra would notice him among the others.

"I'll go," he said.

Pyra looked at him questioningly as if waiting for him to say something else.

"Are you sure, Rilex?" he asked.

Rilex nodded. Those in front of him parted, letting him move up through the crowd until he was standing directly in front of the Denynso leader and could see that he was standing on top of one of the boxes of rations from the ship's supply room. That image was strangely impactful for Rilex, dissipating the thoughts that he had had when they were in the lounge that told him that the ship was primarily designed for comfort and relaxation. The box of rations was an undeniable reminder that this ship was designed for those traveling far into the galaxy for missions that were potentially dangerous and could leave them sailing through space for long, even indeterminate, stretches of time.

"Yes," Rilex said, nodding at Pyra.

"You know that the hybrids are out there. There is an army waiting for us."

"I know," Rilex said. "That's why I think that I should be the one who leaves the ship first to go to alert the others of our arrival and guide them back to the ship."

"I don't understand," Pyra said.

"The hybrids were created and trained for a specific purpose. They were sent to Penthos to confront and destroy Maxim and Kyven, along with the Denynso. I'm not a part of that group. Ryan doesn't know me. He doesn't know my species. It doesn't mean that the hybrids won't attack when I go out there, but they wouldn't have reason to plan as massive an ambush on me as they would any of the warriors or the more recognizable of your allies. They wouldn't want to waste the energy or the resources on an attack on someone they haven't been trained to recognize."

Pyra stared at him for a few moments, his dark orange eyes holding something that Rilex couldn't decipher, and wondered if even Pyra knew exactly what he was experiencing. It was something close to gratitude and surprise, but also uncertainty and resistance. Finally, he nodded.

"Alright," he said. "Rilex will go to the vehicle where Ciyrs and Oro will meet him. They will then return here and we will determine what we should do from there."

"I'll go with him."

Rilex turned toward the voice, shocked and thrilled that Severine was offering herself to go along with him on this mission. He thought that maybe her seeming to try to get away from him through the crowd was a misunderstanding and that she really did feel what he was and want to be with him. As she stepped forward, however, Rilex's heart fell into his stomach. She kept her eyes focused squarely on Pyra, not even glancing at Rilex for a moment as she stepped through the crowd.

"That could be very dangerous," Pyra said. "You have already had hybrids attack and try to drag you back to the Valdicians. They might do it again."

"They might," Severine agreed without hesitation, "but I know more about them, the training that they've gone through, and their fighting techniques than any of you ever will. It is unlikely that that they know what happened in the facility on Earth. They would have no reason to be suspicious of me. If I walk close enough behind Rilex, it will to any of them look like I have taken him hostage. They will have no reason to attack if they think that I have already gotten him under control."

Rilex hated the way that the words sounded in his ears. They not only confirmed that she wasn't volunteering to go along with him because she wanted to spend time with him, but also the type of training that she had had to endure.

"Thank you," Pyra said. "We appreciate your help."

Rilex knew that Pyra didn't know the name that he had given to Severine and waited for her to offer it to him, but she didn't. Instead, she gave a terse nod and turned back to move back through the crowd toward the passenger pods.

"I'll help her gather the supplies that she'll need," Eden said, giving Rilex a glance before leaving Pyra's side and moving through the crowd toward where Severine had disappeared.

There was something in the glance that told Rilex Eden could see that there was something that was happening between him and Severine, and he hoped that she would say something to her that would help him to understand the sudden and unexplained change that had come over the beautiful hybrid woman he could feel himself falling so hard for.

"Elianna," Pyra said, bringing Rilex's attention back to the Denynso leader. "Will you please contact Ciyrs and let him know that Rilex and one of the hybrid women is coming?" he asked. "Ask that he wait a few minutes and then release the sight blocks on one of the windows so that he can watch out for them."

"Yes, Pyra," Elianna said.

She moved to the side of the room and turned to face the wall. Rilex could only guess that she was trying to find some quiet and privacy so that she was able to connect with her mate through her mind. It was a capability that astounded Rilex. He had never seen anything like that among the species he had come into contact with and found himself wishing that he could experience that type of intimacy. After a few moments, Elianna came back and nodded at Pyra.

"Ciyrs said that he will be waiting for them," she said.

"How are we to find the vehicle?" Rilex asked. "Where did they land?"

"Turn your face to the sun and walk," Pyra said. "You will come upon them."

Out of the corner of his eye Rilex saw the crowd shift again as Severine approached. She carried a bag over her shoulder and her hair had been swept back so that it was knotted tightly at the back of her head, getting it completely out of the way rather than letting it flow down her back as it had been.

"We should leave," Severine said. "Do you have your supplies?"

Though she was speaking to him, Rilex felt like she was looking right through him. The connection that they had built while they were in the lounge was gone now, replaced by a distinct chill as if she had put a wall between them and was intent on keeping him at a distance from her.

"Yes," he replied.

She gave another terse nod and looked at Pyra.

"We'll have Ciyrs alert you as soon as we've arrived at the vehicle and then we'll head back. If the hybrids attack while we're gone, close all access points and put up all defenses. Do not open the doors for anyone, even us."

"We can't leave you out on a strange planet without any protection," Pyra protested.

"It's better that a small number of us are in danger than they get into the ship and put everyone at risk. If it happens, we will drive them away. You remain inside until you can't see or hear us any longer, and then you get to those who are here as fast as you can. Don't stop. Do what you came here to do."

She stared at Pyra unflinchingly until Rilex finally saw the massive Denynso warrior nod almost imperceptibly.

"I will," he said.

Severine lifted her chin and headed for the door as Rilex fell into step behind her. The strength that she was showing was incredible, and unnerving in a way. When they were talking in the lounge she had seemed so much softer and more delicate, as though she were finally allowing herself to set aside the intensity that she always carried. Now, though, all signs of the tenderness were gone. He couldn't reach her. He couldn't get anywhere near her, even when he was walking along right beside her. She had disappeared somewhere and he didn't know where she had gone. He could only hope that he would be able to find her.

4

———

Severine stepped through the ship door and felt the rush of searing hot air sting her face. The dryness filled her lungs and the sensation created an assault of memories on her mind. She didn't want them. She didn't want to experience any of them or let them take over the thoughts that she was trying to let control her steps. The further she and Rilex got from the ship, however, the harder it became to deny what immediately came to mind as they began to cross the vast desert of Penthos. In the back of her mind she could hear Ryan's voice and the shouts of the Valdicians put in command of the training for the hybrid army. Many of the hybrids that she had trained alongside had been undergoing this type of training since they were just a few years old, while others had given themselves into the training, wanting to be a part of the experiment and join the army that they believed would be responsible for giving complete control and power over the universe to Ryan. Severine didn't fit with either group.

Instead, Severine had been born into the experiments, intended for one purpose but then changed into a soldier later when Ryan's perceptions of her shifted. There had been nothing more terrifying than those first few days of her training, when she was thrown into the intense, often brutal training that expected her to participate in drills and simulations from the moment that she woke up in the morning until her body gave up and she fell asleep at night. Frequently this sleep wouldn't last for long before Ryan or members of the Valdician troops that he used as extensions of himself would appear in the barracks and wake them up to force them through further training experiences to test their ability to respond and to fight when deprived of sleep and unprepared.

Sometimes this training would involve being put into chambers that were then filled with incredibly hot, dry air and light so vibrant it burned the backs of her eyes. They would remain there for hours, brought to the brink of what Severine felt like she could endure. There were many times when she felt like she wasn't going to survive the experience, and they were never told the purpose of the experience, somehow making the intensity of her suffering worse. Now as she took her first steps across the sand of Penthos, she knew exactly why Ryan had subjected them to the blazing heat and blinding light. Those seemingly endless sessions were in preparation for the strenuous conditions of this planet and the battlefield that Ryan knew he would one day use.

Knowing that Ryan had put her through that training to prepare her for the extreme situations that would present themselves when she arrived on Penthos only told Severine that each of the drills meant something very specific. He wasn't just training them to make them into weapons that he would be able to use however he pleased when the chance arose. Instead, he had planned out how he wanted to use them and was training them to develop the specific characteristics that would ensure they could accomplish the goals that they had for them. This thought pushed her even harder. She needed to get to the ship and to the baby who waited inside.

As her steps sped up, she could hear Rilex rushing to catch up to her. She didn't turn to look over her shoulder at him or even acknowledge that he was there. Even when he called out to her, she kept her eyes focused ahead of her and never hesitated in her progress. Anything that she thought that she was feeling for Rilex had to be put aside. It didn't matter what they had experienced or even what Rilex had said. That could never be her life. Her life had been predetermined for her and even if she was no longer in Ryan's hands, that still defined her. Putting Rilex behind her was the only option that she had. She didn't know what was waiting for her now or the type of life that she would have, but it didn't matter. When they left Penthos, Rilex would return to his own life and there was no way that she could be a part of it. Any thought that she ever could have was only a fantasy designed to fool herself. Now it was time to come back into reality, to embrace the path that was already laid down for her and do what she could to redeem herself.

They had walked several yards from the ship when Severine suddenly remembered what she had told Pyra. She paused and waited for Rilex to get to her side.

"You need to walk ahead of me," she said. "If the other hybrids see us, it needs to look like I have you captive."

"Won't they realize that you aren't one of the army who was here already?" Rilex asked. "Won't they be able to recognize that you were one who remained in the facility on Earth? That should tell them that you don't actually have me hostage."

Severine stopped and turned angrily toward Rilex.

"What do you know about how the hybrids think?" she demanded. "What do you know about anything that we do or know?"

"You aren't one of them," he said.

"Of course, I am. I always have been. I always will be. Nothing is going to change that. Right now, you should be thankful for that because it means that I know how these soldiers were trained and what they are most likely to do if they do decide to attack. I also know that they are much less likely to do that if they think that you have been taken hostage and I am forcing you to give me intelligence about the others on the planet. And to answer your question, no, they aren't likely to recognize that I stayed behind on Earth when they were brought here. We have no names. No friends. No family. No connections. They would see me as just another soldier. There's no differentiation."

Rilex seemed like he wanted to say something, but hesitated. Instead, he stepped in front of her and walked along with her close behind. Severine hated to admit what she had. She knew that it didn't apply to all of them. In her mind, she knew that she would be able to recognize some of the soldiers and remember some of the times that she had encountered them, and she would hope that there were some of them who would feel the same way about her. In reality, she knew that few of them would. They had been raised as solitary beings with no sense of connection among them. Without names or relationships, there was nothing to differentiate each other, and no reason for them to need to identify each other as separate entities. All that mattered was the maneuvers and drills that they were taught to run, and the efforts to get rid of the dead after a battle or bring survivors back for retraining. Those were the only circumstances when it would matter for any of the hybrids to recognize or acknowledge the others.

Severine could almost feel eyes on her as they made their way across the sand, but she didn't know if she was genuinely sensing the army that had been sent ahead to Penthos watching them as they made their progress toward the vehicle that was waiting for them, or if it was just the knowledge that they were there, the understanding that the soldiers were finally on the battlefield for which they had been crafted and honed, that made her feel so obsessively aware. She knew all too well that if they wanted to be, the hybrid soldiers would be impossible to perceive. They would be implementing the skills that they had learned to keep them totally concealed until they found the right moment to attack.

Just as Pyra had told them, they had turned toward the sun and started walking to make their way to the vehicle, and the further they walked, the brighter the light seemed to become. It wasn't the pure light of the sunlight on Earth. Instead, it was a darker orange light that soaked into them and obliterated everything ahead of them so that it looked as though they were walking ahead into a wall of flame. Severine wanted to look down, to look away from the burning light, but she had spent too much time looking down already. She was going to keep her head up even as she walked back toward a life of control.

Finally, the horizon ahead changed and she saw the dark outline of the vehicle appear. Rilex quickened his steps and she followed suit until they were moving more rapidly toward the vehicle, hoping that Ciyrs was doing as they had asked and was watching out of the window for them. They were within a few feet of the vehicle when Severine heard a series of clicking and buzzing sounds as the locks and protective shields released, and then a door at the side of the vehicle opened. Ciyrs looked out at them and gestured for them to get inside. Compared to the ship that they had just left, the vehicle looked miniscule and Severine didn't like the idea of getting inside knowing how many others were in there. She knew, however, that she had to complete what she had offered herself into, and what she knew that she needed to do.

Rilex climbed into the vehicle first and then Severine followed, perching on the edge of the seat and sliding fully in before closing the door behind her. The interior of the vehicle was small, but not as cramped with the number of passengers as she thought it would be, which offered some sense of relief as she climbed her way over the seats toward the back where she could hear women's voices talking frantically. A few of them immediately recoiled when they saw her, showing a fear that she was sure the appearance of one of Ryan's hybrids usually warranted for these stolen humans. It was obvious that they hadn't registered that she was one of the hybrids that had been in the infirmary with them and that they needn't fear her. Ciyrs, though, held up a hand as he appeared beside her.

"Don't be afraid," he said. "She is with us."

"Where is the baby?" Severine asked, trying to avoid looking at the figure lying across the floor, a blanket draped over it.

A woman whose name Severine didn't recognize turned toward her and Severine saw the bundled baby in her arms.

"Here," the woman said.

"I had her hold him while I waited for you," Ciyrs said. "He seems to be doing well. He's small, but he's been breathing and the women say that his color looks good."

"It's a boy?" Rilex asked.

There was something in his voice that Severine tried to block out of her thoughts and she looked at the woman, holding her hands out toward her.

"Give him to me," she said.

The woman looked resistant, slightly tightening her grip on the baby.

"Why?" she asked.

"He needs special care," Severine said. "Do you know how to care for a hybrid newborn? Especially one who was born prematurely?"

The woman's face dropped and she shook her head. Severine briefly regretted the way that she had said it, knowing that her words had immediately brought to mind the babies these women were carrying and the concerns that they likely had about caring for the children that they never thought they would see, much less have the opportunity to raise. The emotion quickly left her, though, as she reminded herself that she needed to get them back to the ship as she had promised Pyra and then move on. She held her hands out toward the woman more insistently and finally she rested the bundle in them. Severine drew the baby toward her and looked down into his tiny face. She could see that he was several weeks early and knew that he would need careful care to get him stronger and help him survive.

Holding the baby close to her, she climbed back over the seats and positioned herself near the door to the vehicle. She looked back at Ciyrs.

"Let Elianna know that we arrived and then get ready. We need to get back to the ship."

Ciyrs nodded at her and relayed the message to the women, instructing them to prepare for the trip to the ship. From the front of the vehicle Oro reassured Ciyrs that he would carry the most wounded and Rilex offered to carry another. Ciyrs confirmed that he would be able to carry others, and that those who were not carried would be strong enough to get the short distance to the ship where they would be more comfortable. Severine waited for them to gather closer to the door before opening it and stepping back out into the brightness of the sun again. Now that she had the rest of the group out of the vehicle and they were moving back toward the ship, she was less concerned about how they looked. If the hybrids were going to attack, how close she walked to them wasn't going to stop them. Now her concern was the baby in her arms. The small amount of milk that he got from his mother's body wouldn't be enough to sustain him for long. She needed to get him to the ship as quickly as she could and find the proper supplies. She knew that Ciyrs did everything that he could to help the baby when it was born, but there were things that even the healer didn't know.

The journey back to the ship seemed longer than the way to the vehicle and every few seconds Severine found herself glancing down into the little child's face to make sure that he was still breathing. Finally, they got close enough to the ship that Pyra opened the hatch and she barreled her way into the ship and through the crowd that still filled the open area where she had left them. She tucked the baby as close to her chest as she could and bent her head down over him as she went, wanting to protect it from even the prying eyes of those who had remained in the ship. She could hear the voices of some of the women calling after her, but she ignored them. Just as she had with Rilex, she had closed herself off to them and had to resist the urge to even look at them. They couldn't be a part of her any longer, either.

Remembering what she had seen of the ship during her

brief time on it and the direction that she had seen Elianna go when Pyra told her that she was needed in the infirmary, Severine rushed through the bright, pristine corridors and seemingly endless doorways until she came upon the infirmary. It was far larger than she would have expected, but she found comfort and reassurance in that, knowing that she wasn't going to have to share a small space and limited supplies with others who might interfere with her care for the baby.

The severely wounded who had been restrained to the infirmary gasped and shouted at her sudden appearance, but she ignored them. She rushed through the room toward one of the supply cabinets and started sifting through its contents, occasionally putting a carton or bottle aside. When she finished, she swept everything she had collected into her bag and then went to another cabinet where she took out a blanket and several sheets. Finished there, she left the infirmary and headed toward the kitchen and the storage rooms attached. By the time that she had gathered everything that she need, Severine could barely hold it all, but she supported the baby carefully with one arm and kept him pressed to her with the blanket and sheets so that he would remain warm and secure.

Wanting to be as far away from as many of the people as possible, she crossed the ship again and returned to the lounge where she had passed the trip from Earth with Rilex. She placed everything that she carried onto one of the seats and then laid out one of the blankets onto the seat where she had slept before resting the baby down on top of it. He was squirming now, his little face starting to redden. She knew that he was preparing to cry, likely from hunger, and went to work with the other supplies that she had gathered to make a batch of the thick, nourishing formula that was given to the babies in the breeding facility. Though she had found a bottle in the infirmary, she knew that the nipple was far too large for the infant's tiny mouth. Instead, she filled a large eye dropper with the formula and then gathered the baby back into her arms, tucking the dropper into his mouth. He drank deeply and Severine felt reassured by his eagerness.

"That's it," she whispered. "Eat. Get strong." She touched a kiss to his head. "We're both going to need to be as strong as we can now."

Behind her she heard the door to the lounge slide open and footsteps come inside. She glanced in their direction and saw Rilex standing there. She had hoped that he wouldn't come looking for her and now that he was standing there staring at her, she had a sudden surge of anger and frustration. She didn't want to see him. She didn't want to look at him a second longer. As she turned away, she saw him taking another step toward her.

"Severine," he said.

"No," she said, whipping around to face him. "Don't call me that."

"But that's your name," he said in bewilderment.

Severine shook her head.

"That's not my name," she said. "It never has been. It is just something that you call me. I have no name."

"You do," Rilex insisted. "You do now."

"Nothing's changed. I haven't changed. This is who I am, who I always have been, and who I always will be."

"I don't understand," Rilex said. "I thought you were trained to be a soldier. Are you planning on rejoining the army?"

Severine's eyes closed and she felt her shoulders sag under the weight of the situation that was crashing down around her. She felt like she had already offered so much of herself to Rilex during their time in the lounge. It was too much. She never should have told him so much, or felt like she was in a place that justified that type of openness and vulnerability. It had put her in this place, leaving Rilex feeling as though she owed him even more of an explanation of herself and her life than she had already given him.

"No," she said.

"Then what?" he asked. "Because this isn't who you are."

"Yes, it is," Severine insisted, settling the now-sleeping baby back onto the chair and tucking the blanket tightly around him to keep his tiny, vulnerable body warm. She looked back at Rilex, knowing that she had to tell him everything if he was ever going to understand, even partly, why she had made this choice, even though there was a large part of her that didn't feel that it was a choice at all. "I was not always a part of the army," she said. "When Ryan created me, it wasn't as a soldier. I was first designed to take care of the babies born into the program. The breeders never have the opportunity to care for their children. They are taken at birth and the breeders are returned to the facility for recycling."

"Recycling?" Rilex asked, his voice registering the horror that she knew it should even though to her this was just another element of the life that she had lived.

"They were put through a regimen of nutrition, supplementation, and exercise to rebuild their body, then put back into the breeding rotation."

Rilex cringed.

"How many times did this happen to these women?" he asked.

"Some of them as many as 10 or 15. Most didn't survive that long, though."

"Didn't survive?" he asked.

Severine shook her head.

"No. Ryan might be very intelligent and know a lot about the experiments that his family started generations ago, but what he does know doesn't outweigh what he doesn't, and that is far more dangerous. When he started combining the different species into hybrids and attempting to use them as the incubators to breed the new generations, he didn't always know what to expect from their pregnancies or births. When these women would have complications, he wouldn't know what to do. More often than not, they would simply die."

"And he would have more at the ready."

Severine nodded.

"But it was always frustrating to him to have one of the creatures that he had built die, especially if the baby died along with her. It wasn't that he mourned the loss of their lives. When they died, all he saw was all of the time and work that went into that hybrid, and the fact that his progress was set back by her death. That's the main reason that he started capturing human women and using them. While the babies themselves remained hybrids and were often not related to their carrier at all, which could make some differences in the pregnancy, the fact that the breeders were human gave Ryan an extra degree of control. It made it easier to guess the length of the pregnancy and created less eventful and dangerous births."

"So, you weren't used as a breeder?" Rilex asked.

"No," Severine told him. She could see the relief in his eyes. "It was just my job to take care of the babies when they were born. I was there when the breeders delivered them, and then I took them to the nursery facility and took care of them. Ryan had done research into the milk of the females of each of the species that he used in the breeding experiments so that he could identify what was in it. Then he isolated each of the components and found a way to synthesize them."

"What does that mean?" Rilex asked.

"It means that I was able to take the ingredients that he developed and make formulas to feed the babies that were specified for their nutritional needs based on the different species that made up their DNA. That way they got everything they needed to develop the characteristics that Ryan wanted in them."

"With intelligence and ideas like that, I can't even imagine that good that he could have done if he had wanted to."

"Well, he didn't," Severine said. "He doesn't care about anything or anyone but himself and what his family started. He didn't care if the babies were comfortable or happy. All that mattered to him was that they stayed alive and grew up."

"But if you were designed to take care of the babies, why were you in the battle?"

"When he decided that enough babies had been born that he wanted to focus on training them, the breeding program shut down. I was supposed to turn my attention to raising them and preparing them for their training."

"What happened?"

Severine's spine stiffened and she squared her jaw. That was enough. She wasn't going to go any farther now.

"I made a decision," she said. "I was punished for it by being sent to the war program."

"That doesn't mean that this is all that you will ever be," Rilex said. "That's over now. You aren't a soldier anymore.

You have your own life to live. It's yours to do with as you please."

Severine scoffed and walked back over to the baby, holding her hand in front of his face to make sure that he was breathing properly.

"I will never have my own life," she said. "I never did. I never would have even existed if it wasn't for Ryan and the experiments that he wanted to run. I shouldn't have existed. And the things I've done..." she let her words trail off, not wanting to give any more voice to the thoughts that had broken through the block she had tried to put up and were now attempting to make themselves known. She shook her head. "This baby is innocent. He doesn't deserve to go through anything that I ever did. He didn't ask to be created or to be born, and he didn't ask for the only mother that he would ever have to die bringing him into this world. He needs someone to take care of him. I don't need a life for myself, but I can do everything that I can do to give him one."

5
———

Rilex felt his heart drumming in his chest. He could hear the desperation in Severine's voice no matter how hard she was trying to conceal it, and he felt just as much desperation to be back in the blissful, peaceful space that they created in the lounge after the celebration. They had seemed so close. They were just on the edge of something incredible, and now it was slipping through his fingers. He didn't want to lose her. She was so unexpected, so amazing, and even though he had known her only for such a short time, he didn't want to think that he wasn't going to have her with him when all of this was over.

"I don't understand why that has to change anything," he said. "You can take care of him and still live the life that you have earned. We can still..."

"Please, Rilex," she said, shaking her head slightly as she looked at him. "Don't. Please don't say anything."

Not knowing what was going to happen or even if he was making the right decision, Rilex took the few long strides to close the space between them and swept her to him with one hand around her waist. He didn't wait to gauge her reaction or even to look at her before dipping his head forward and catching her mouth with his. Her lips were taut at first, parting slightly if only in pure shock at his action, then began to soften. Rilex leaned deeper into the kiss and for a moment he thought that Severine was responding to it, returning the kiss and perhaps even rethinking her resistance to him. All too soon, though, she pulled away and stepped back from him, her hand coming to her mouth as she touched her lips as if to block more of the kiss. She shook her head at him, then turned away, putting her back to him and staring at the dark shield that had been set into place over the large window as though hoping her stare would be intent enough to see through it and out onto the planet beyond.

Hurt and discouragement cut through Rilex and he felt himself stumble backward a few steps, unwilling to take his eyes away from her, before he turned and stalked out of the lounge. He didn't know what he should be thinking or feeling, and part of him felt guilty for even attempting to bring Severine away from what she knew too quickly. He wondered if he should never have tried to begin with, if he should have simply kept his eyes and his heart away even as he felt the emotions growing.

He was making his way back to the main chamber of the ship when he heard someone call his name behind him. Rilex turned and saw Jem coming down the hallway toward him.

"What is it, Jem?" Rilex asked.

"Pyra wanted to talk to you," the warrior said. "We should be leaving to go to the others shortly."

Rilex nodded.

"Alright," he said.

"Is something wrong?" Jem asked.

Rilex hesitated, not knowing if he wanted to get anyone else involved in what was happening with Severine. The genuine look of concern in Jem's eyes, however, convinced Rilex that it might benefit him to get another perspective on the situation. He explained it to Jem, telling him everything that he could without letting all of the emotions that he was experiencing take over. When he was finished, Jem nodded.

"In the Denynso, finding his mate is the most important thing that any warrior hopes for in his life. It is also one of the most terrifying. We know that our mate was intended for us from birth and that bonding with that person will create an unbreakable link that will strengthen and enrich us. We also know that when we bond, we are giving ourselves over to something that is so much bigger and more powerful than anything that we have ever known or been. While our bond is meant to be for life and we know that we will never love anyone but our mate, we know that there is always a chance that our mate will be taken from us, and that we will live the rest of our life alone, empty, and longing. That is a level of vulnerability that many aren't ready to experience when the time comes for them, and are too afraid to accept no matter how deeply they know that this is what was meant for them. Loving someone is the greatest thing that any of us are ever called to do and it can be hard to answer that call, especially when it comes when you don't expect it."

"Like you and Angela?" Rilex asked.

Jem laughed softly.

"Absolutely, but probably more so for her than for me. I knew the instant that I saw her that she was my mate, and I have loved her every moment since then. She, though, hesitated. She had a life on Earth before she went through that portal and part of her was still stuck in that life. Even though it had been years, she struggled with accepting that what she thought her future was going to hold for her wasn't an option any longer. It was even harder for her to accept that what the future did hold was me. It was like that for many of the warriors. Pyra and Eden. Ero and Zuri. Ty and Samira. Gyyx and Leia. Ciyrs and Elianna. Zsilvia and George. Even Bannack and Loralia. They all found each other when they didn't expect to and had to learn each other. Some struggled far harder than others. It wasn't easy for them to accept that they were falling in love with people who were so different from them and that they didn't understand. Zuri even left Uoria and went back to Earth, and Ero had to go after her. These people have been through the unimaginable. Severine probably doesn't even know what it is that she is feeling or that she should be allowed to feel that way. Give her time."

Jem's words sank in and Rilex felt a greater sense of calm coming over him.

"Thank you, Jem," he said. "Could you tell Pyra that I'll be there in just a few minutes?"

"Sure," Jem said.

Rilex waited until the warrior had disappeared around the corner before hurrying back to the lounge where he had left Severine. He needed to apologize, to let her know that he understood and that he would be there for her whenever she might need him. When he stepped back into the lounge, however, it was empty. Severine and the baby were gone, and so were her bags. Rilex ran out of the lounge and to the infirmary, wondering if she might have gone to gather more supplies for the baby. Elianna was attending to one of the wounded when he rushed in and looked up at him, apparently startled by his sudden appearance.

"She's not here," one of the others said before Rilex could even ask Elianna if she had seen Severine.

Rilex turned toward the voice and saw another of the hybrids, a larger man, sitting on another bed with a large bandage wrapped around his head. He took a step toward the bed.

"What?" he asked.

"You're looking for the woman with the baby, aren't you?" the hybrid man asked.

"Woman with the baby?" Elianna asked, coming toward Rilex.

"Yes," Rilex said. "I am." He turned toward Elianna. "You haven't seen her?"

"Not since you two left," she said. "Ciyrs said that she took the baby. I had hoped that she would bring it here so that we could look over it and make sure that it was alright, but I haven't seen her."

"She left," the hybrid man repeated. "She's gone."

"Where did she go?" Rilex demanded.

"She came here just a few minutes before Elianna came, took a few more things, and left. It looked like she was getting ready to go out onto the planet."

"Alone?" Elianna asked.

"She was trained for the environment," the man said. "If she wants to go, there is nothing to stop her."

A sick feeling surged into Rilex's throat. He knew what the hybrid man had said was true. There was nothing to keep Severine from leaving the ship and heading out onto Penthos, and once she did, her training meant that she would be able to move across the unhospitable terrain with much more confidence than the rest of them. But going out onto the planet also meant that she would be completely exposed to the hybrid army that would soon know that she was no longer one of them, if they hadn't yet realized it.

Without saying another word, Rilex ran back through the ship, gathered his bag and the weapons that he could carry, and started out of the ship. Pyra tried to stop him before he went through the door, but Rilex ignored his calls. He knew that the Denynso leader remembered their first conversation, and that Rilex was with them only by his own choice. He would do what he wanted to do without concern for Pyra's plans or orders.

Outside the ship the sun seemed even more intense than it had when they first went toward the vehicle. It was sliding lazily across the sky like thick liquid, growing brighter and harsher as it went as if it knew that the day would soon die and it wanted to give off as much intensity as it could before it was over. Rilex narrowed his eyes and looked down at the sand, squinting against the pain of the light refracting from the grains as he looked for her footsteps. He could see the paths that they had made as they headed toward the vehicle, but then another, narrower path that led in the other direction. He followed it, running alongside it as not to kick up any dirt that might disturb the prints ahead, and looked up as frequently as he could bear to try to see her.

If the hybrid army was watching, he knew that he was totally vulnerable to them now. There was no one else with him to help him detect an attack or to fight with him should they come, but he didn't care. All that mattered to him was finding her and making sure that they didn't bring her back into captivity. There was nothing about his feelings for her that he could deny now. She was everything and he wasn't going to stop trying to protect her.

Suddenly ahead of him Rilex heard a scream. He pushed his steps harder and faster, forcing his feet deep into the sand to make himself move toward her as quickly as he could. His hand moved to the long blade on his hip and he drew it out even as he continued across the desert, wanting to be ready for whatever he would encounter. Several yards away he saw a small cluster of hooded creatures, each clutching at Severine as they tried to get a grip on her. She was holding the baby tightly to her with one arm and slashing at them with her own weapon with the other. One of the creatures lunged for her and Severine took a step back, falling to the sand with another scream.

Rilex let out the loudest shout that he could and surged toward the group with his blade thrust ahead of him. The sound seemed to startle the cloaked creatures enough that they turned toward him, giving Severine the chance to release herself from their grip and begin to scramble away. Rilex clashed with the hybrids as they rushed toward him. He grabbed for another weapon so that he could attack with both hands, thrashing indiscriminately at them. One ducked his head and rammed it into Rilex's chest, sending him crashing to the sand. Rilex tried to stand, but the hybrid came down on top of him. It held a small but vicious-looking weapon above him, aimed at his throat.

Just before the creature could bring the spiked weapon down, there was a cry and Rilex saw Severine bring a blade down in between the hybrid's shoulders. The creature arched briefly and then collapsed down. Rilex kicked his body out of the way and climbed to his feet, slashing at the nearest hybrid while Severine fought another. Finally, they were both on the ground and he heard Severine calling out to him.

"Come on!"

He turned and saw her gathering the baby off of the sand where she had placed him. She started running and

Rilex followed, glancing back over his shoulder to see the surviving hybrids starting to stand. When he turned back, he could no longer see Severine. Rilex skidded to a stop in the sand and looked around frantically. The footsteps she had made stopped a few feet ahead of him, but he couldn't see her anywhere. He looked back and saw that the hybrids were standing now and had started toward him. He had drawn his blade, preparing to fight them again, when he felt something grab at his ankle.

Rilex jumped to the side and looked down, nearly slashing with his blade before he realized that it was Severine. She was beneath him, her head and one arm sticking out from beneath what looked like a concealed trap door in the sand. He crouched down and she moved out of the way to give him space to slip beneath the door and into the small room beneath. When his feet hit the ground, Severine reached up and slid three heavy bars into place over the door, securing it. She grabbed a torch from the wall and led Rilex through another door. Once closed, she locked that door with several bars as well. Rilex immediately thought of what Jem had told him about how he went through the portal and appeared on the planet where Galadriel and Vyker found him. He had described a mirrored realm beneath the Denynso compound and the hidden hatches in the orchard that led down to it. They sounded very much like the trap door that they had just entered, making Rilex wonder if there was any connection between them, and if there was, which set of hidden doors was created first.

Severine settled the baby onto a pile of blankets and rested her hand on his belly, using it to rock him gently as she made soothing sounds until he quieted and fell asleep. When she climbed to her feet, she gestured for him to follow her and they moved into another room.

"What is this place?" he asked when they stepped inside.

"It's a bunker," Severine said, settling the torch into place in a metal holder on the wall. "Ryan had several of them built throughout the planet."

"Are we safe here?"

"Why did you come?" Severine asked, ignoring his question.

"What do you mean?" Rilex asked, slightly startled.

"I left the ship because I didn't want to be there anymore. I knew that I would have a better chance on my own. If I had wanted you to know that I was leaving or where I was going, I would have told you. I just wanted to be alone."

"Did you?" Rilex asked. "Did you really want to be alone, or did you just not want me near you?"

Severine looked away.

"They're the same," she said softly.

"No, they aren't," Rilex said.

Severine stalked across the room and dropped her bag to the top of a table that was positioned against one wall. She reached in and drew out a book.

"I don't know what you expect of me," she said. "I don't have anything to offer you. I have nothing within me that you would want, that would do you any good."

Rilex felt like she had hit him, and he curled around the pain in his belly. Severine placed the book on the table and took a pencil from where it was tucked in the spine. She drew a single line on the page, put the pencil back in place, and then put the book bag in her bag.

"What is that?" Rilex asked, needing to separate himself from what she had said to give himself time to process it and know how to respond.

Severine glanced up at him and then back at her hands as she closed her bag.

"It's the baby's first day," she said. "I want to keep track so I know how old he is."

A sobering realization hit Rilex and he took another step toward Severine.

"Do you know how old you are?" he asked.

Severine shook her head.

"No," she told him. "All I know is that I am one of the first that Ryan made when he was much younger. Before he even built the facilities that are there now. I grew up in the lab that his family had used."

"I can find out for you," Rilex said. "We can talk to Eden and find out how old Ryan is. We might not be able to find out exactly, but we can at least get close to..."

"It wouldn't change anything," Severine said. "Those years are gone. It doesn't matter how old I am now. I want it to matter to him one day."

Rilex could hear the tears beginning in Severine's voice and his heart called out to her. He didn't want to stay away from her for another moment. He couldn't watch her suffer anymore without telling her how precious she was to him.

"Every year that you've lived matters to me," he said. "And every one that you live from now on will matter to me, too. That's why I came for you. I have been without you up until now and I'm not willing to do it for even another day. Please. Don't push me away."

Severine's back was still to him and Rilex stepped up close behind her. He reached forward and wrapped his arms around her waist, drawing her back gently so that he could hold her. His lips tingled as he dipped his head to touch them tenderly to her skin.

$$6$$

Rilex's mouth touched her neck and Severine sighed into the feeling that had been so strange and unexpected, but was now filling her and breaking down the barrier that she had forced between them. She hadn't wanted to admit those feelings, but now she wanted nothing more than to indulge in them, to give herself over completely and willingly to the unknown that waited just beyond his kiss. Rilex's arms loosened from around her waist and his hands slipped beneath her shirt to run along her back and then across her stomach. Not entirely sure of her actions, but following the urge that was building within her, Severine reached back to wrap her hands around the back of his thighs, holding him closer as he touched her. The adrenaline, fear, and anger of everything that she had been through, and anticipation of what waited for them when the morning came and they had to leave the bunker for the danger of the planet above, translated into a deep, primal need that went beyond the training and torment that she had endured. She offered herself to it and pressed back against him.

Rilex seemed to notice the willingness that she finally had and continued ahead. His lips traveled gradually and patiently along her neck, and the tip of his tongue slipped out to follow the same path, licking slowly as he mirrored the pace of his mouth with his hands along her waist. They traveled up to her breasts and paused briefly over her ribs. Severine took a deep breath and she felt his hands brush along the bottom swell of her breasts. He cupped his palms over her kneading into the lush flesh and coaxing her nipples to tighten beneath his touch. She felt Rilex's mouth slide along her skin up to her ear and she shivered at the feeling of his warm, damp breath rippling along her neck.

"Let me make love to you," he whispered. "Let me show you that you were made for so much more."

Severine's body trembled at the words and she felt her heart softening, opening to him and releasing all of the pain that she had felt so that she could replace it with the love that Rilex was offering her. She nodded and felt him ease her shirt off over her head. The air touched her skin as the shirt dropped to the ground and sent a shiver of anticipation over her skin. He undressed her slowly, his hands moving across her with incredible tenderness as he gradually exposed her body to the air and to himself. She felt revered and admired in a way that she had never experienced, that she never would have thought that she would feel. She wanted to give him the same feeling, to show Rilex how deeply she loved him and how much she wanted to give everything to him. She turned in his hands and carefully removed his shirt, sliding her palms back up over his shoulders so she could fill her hands with the luscious firmness of his muscles. Rilex dipped his head to catch her mouth in a deep kiss. She let her lips part as she released the ties at the front of his pants and opened the fabric. She could feel him stepping out of his shoes as she pushed the pants down over his hips and let them fall away. The hardness of his erection brushed against her palm and she reached forward to wrap her grip around it tenderly. Her hand ran down the length of his shaft and he made a soft, appreciative sound.

They stood still for a few moments as Severine experimented with her touch on his deliciously thick, engorged cock. Finally, he pulled her closer to him and deepened their kiss further, beginning to ease her down toward the ground. She surrendered herself completely to him, allowing him to guide her down to her back on the cool ground. Rilex came down over her, the strength and protectiveness of his presence enveloping her, making her feel loved, beautiful, and above all, safe. Rilex let his mouth play over hers for a few seconds before pushing back so that he could kiss down her body, taking his time as he worshipped every inch of her. His tongue dipped into her navel and she gasped at the unexpected feeling, arching against him as her desire began to spiral out of control. She didn't know what was waiting for her on the other side of that desire, but she didn't want to hesitate, even for another moment, and risk missing anything.

His mouth came to the valley between her hip bones and his tongue traced along each bone and then from one to the other. He lifted his mouth up and blew a stream of cool breath along her dampened skin. The muscles in her belly twitched and Severine felt her hips lift involuntarily toward his mouth. Rilex took the invitation that she seemed to be offering and gently eased her thighs apart. Her body was hot and wet, the sensation feeling strange and unexplainable, but at the same time welcome and empowering. Rilex touched a kiss to the apex of her thighs and then she felt his tongue slide down into her folds. The sensation that struck her was nearly overwhelming and she cried out, reaching down and grasping the sides of his head. He gave another soft, slow lick that introduced her to feelings that she never knew existed. Severine felt like her body was waking up. Sensations and reactions that she had never known and that she would never have expected were blooming within her and she felt herself responding to each of Rilex's touches in intense, enlightening ways that made her feel at once vulnerable and powerful.

Finally, Rilex brought his body back up to stretch across hers and stared down at her. He aligned his body with hers and Severine felt the tip of his erection touch her opening. She instinctively drew her knees up to open to him further, and the movement caused him to slide into her slightly. They both drew in breaths at the sudden, beautiful feeling of their bodies beginning to meld together.

"I love you," Rilex said, meeting her eyes as if wanting her to see the sincerity in them as he spoke those words.

She traced her fingertips over his lips. He closed his eyes and leaned into the touch, parting his lips so that her fingers dipped briefly into his mouth.

"I love you," she said, meaning it more than anything that she had ever said.

Rilex brought his hips forward slowly so that he gradually and gently filled her. He moved without urgency as if he were letting himself savor the feeling of sinking deeply into her for the first time. Severine could feel her body hugging him closely, shaping to him as if she had been crafted specifically to accommodate him. For the first time, she liked the idea of being made for a purpose. Rilex kissed her languidly as his hips started to move. Severine let her body relax and accept the sensation of him stroking within her slowly. Each glide of his thick, long cock massaged her deeply and intensely, and she moaned softly beneath him. The similar sounds that came from Rilex's lips made her feel powerful as she felt his body tremble. There was no rush, no frantic hurry to his movements as he made love to her. She closed her eyes, allowing the delicious feeling of her hot, wet body cradling him and his strong erection massaging deep within her wash away all of the pain, the fear, the anger, and the loneliness that had defined her.

Wanting to surround him more and continue the connection between them, Severine pulled her thighs closer to his body. The new position intensified the pressure of her body on his and she heard him groan deep in his throat. It was incredible to see the delicate, feminine power that she had over him, the ability that she had to leave his strong body shaking and sweating. Rilex quickened his pace in response to her holding him more tightly and her own sounds grew higher and more rhythmic as he drove into her faster but with the same control. Something amazing was happening within her. She could feel the muscles throughout her hips, thighs, and belly tightening and her heart pounding so quickly it seemed that she was teetering on the brink, but she didn't know of what. A few moments later all of the pressure reached a dizzying peak and then crashed. She cried out beneath him as her body contracted hard around him and dissolved in a series of intense, shaking spasms that took over her entire being. Rilex thrust into her a few hard times before she felt his body tightened and his cock swelled within her, then hot streams poured into her.

Sleep had taken over, but Severine didn't know how long she had been resting when the sound of the baby crying woke her up. She groaned slightly as she rolled away from the warmth of Rilex's arms, not wanting to relinquish the bliss that she had found there. As she dropped his shirt down over her head, she looked down and saw Rilex looking up at her with slumbering eyes. His lips curved up in a smile and he reached out a hand to run his fingertips along the top of her foot.

"I'll get him," he said.

He climbed to his feet and pulled on his pants before walking out of the room toward where they had tucked the baby in to sleep when they first got below ground. A few seconds later she heard the cries start to quiet and then Rilex appeared back at the door to the room, cradling the baby against his chest.

"He's probably hungry," Severine said. "There's formula for him in my bag."

Rilex crossed to her bag and pulled out the canister of formula that she had prepared. She crouched down beside the bag and handed him the dropper that she had brought. He filled it with the thick concoction and placed the tube of the dropper in the baby's mouth. The baby's tiny lips closed over it and he started to drink eagerly, calming as he filled his belly.

"He's going to need a name," Rilex said.

Severine smiled and ran her hand tenderly over the baby's little head. The boy's eyes were starting to droop again and soon he was sleeping, his mouth still sucking at the dropper.

"He's going to need a lot of things," she said. "He has a whole life ahead of him and he already doesn't have anything that he needs."

"What does he need?" Rilex asked.

"His mother," Severine answered, feeling emotion tightening painfully in her throat as she thought of Astrid giving her final moments and last breath ensuring that her child at least made it into the world.

"He has a mother," Rilex said, taking one hand from under the baby and running it along the side of her face. He tucked a finger under her chin and guided it up so that she turned to look at him. "And a father."

"He does?" Severine asked.

Her heart was pounding in her chest and she could feel her hands shaking, but she didn't want to let herself believe what he was saying. It was too good. It was beyond anything that she could ever have hoped or dreamed she would experience, and she didn't want to build herself up only to be hurt again. Rilex was gazing at her with pure, genuine tenderness in his eyes, though, and he wasn't withdrawing from her. As she looked at them she realized that what she had thought were paler streaks across the darker depth of his eyes were actually the tails of shooting stars. She remembered what he had said about Ryan not knowing his species and knew that there was so much more for her to learn about him, and all the time in existence to learn.

"Of course, he does," Rilex said. "Another woman might have carried him, but the moment he was born, he was in your heart and you were meant to be his mother. I know that I was meant to be his father, and if you will have me, I would like to do everything that I can to give him the life and the family that he deserves – that both of you deserve."

Severine felt the breath catch in her throat. There were so many things that she wanted to say to him, to express how she felt when she looked at him and when their bodies touched, and now as they accepted this innocent child as their own and built a family for themselves. The words wouldn't come, though. She didn't seem to have the words that would adequately tell him what she was feeling or what she wanted him to know. All she could do is lean forward and touch a kiss to his lips, feeling more gratitude and fulfillment than she could have ever imagined. She pulled back and rested her forehead against his, tucking one arm beneath Rilex's under the baby so that they both cradled him securely between them.

"This is what we're fighting for now," Rilex said softly. "We aren't fighting for any one individual or any one kind. Not for the Denynso. Not for the Mikana. Not even for us as a unit. We're fighting for everyone and for everything. We're fighting for a future."

TBC

To be continued...

THE ALIEN'S MYSTERY

1

———————

Jonah tried to concentrate on the food that was in
front of him, but his mind kept wandering. It had
been more than a day since he had eaten, but now
that he was sitting with the rations on the floor
between his feet, he couldn't keep his thoughts calm enough
to actually bring himself to eat. His thoughts kept
wandering to the woman who he had encountered in the
laboratory when he went upstairs. He had only been near
her for a few moments, but she was etched in his mind and
he couldn't stop thinking about those few seconds and the
way her eyes looked when they met. This wasn't the time for
him to be thinking about a woman. There was already too
much happening for him to let himself get distracted.

He looked around at the corner of the room that he had
set up for himself. When the others had left, he knew that
he had to settle in and create as much of a home for
himself in the basement as he possibly could. There was no
other option for him. He no longer had a home outside of
the University or anywhere that he could go even if he did
leave the basement. For as long as he was going to be on

Earth, he would find his comfort and protection in the walls of the hidden and forgotten emergency chambers. Though many of the group had found the dark corridors and rooms eerie, even frightening, there was something soothing about knowing that this building, these walls, were standing when he was still on Earth. It was hard for him to think about the reality of how incredibly different Earth was since the last day that he was there before stepping onto the ship that would eventually bring him to Uoria. Though he had seen nothing of it but the University itself, just seeing the bright new corridors, rooms, and labs of the building and facing technology and developments that he could never have conceived of before leaving had been startling.

Jonah knew that beyond the grounds of the University the world would barely resemble anything that he remembered from his time there. He had to stop himself from thinking about everything that would be gone and all that he lost when he left and headed on what he thought would only be a brief journey into space. Thinking about that would cause too much pain, too much emptiness for him to continue on with what he knew that he needed to do. Instead, he had to close his mind off to the existence of anything beyond those gates. Instead, he kept his focus totally on the University and this building. It was almost as if he had a sense of camaraderie with the old medical building. They were lingering reminders of a time long since passed. He had breathed within those walls. He had spoken, laughed, and lived in those rooms. He had looked into the eyes of the young receptionists and seen the life that was stretched before them in their gaze. All the years that he had seen waiting there in those eyes had passed, the lives long-since ended. Everything that had happened there, though, kept him connected to the life that he'd had when he was still here.

It was still so hard to think about all the years that had slipped past him while he was on Uoria. He could remember so few of them. Only the fifteen that they had lived between the ship crashing and the Covra locking them, were present in his mind. All of the time that had gone by when their bodies were being used as incubators for the next generation of Covra was blank to him. He could clearly remember the day that the Covra returned. It was like any other day until they swarmed. He knew that he was one of the few people in the settlement who actually saw them when they came back. Most people were caught completely by surprise and frozen in place in the middle of a normal activity or even while they were asleep, as Rain had been. Jonah had tried to fight. He didn't want to face the horror of the Covra again. He remembered the gruesome way that they had killed and the potentially worse way that they had controlled the minds of those they attacked so that they could force them to destroy each other. He would have done anything that he could to stop them, but their invasion had been carefully timed and planned so that there was nothing that he could do. Before he could kill even one of their number, he had been cornered and frozen in place.

What came next was a century of emptiness. One hundred stolen years that took far more from them than just the days and nights that they could have lived. As they hovered somewhere between living and not, on a distant planet, the lives that they should have lived continued on back on Earth. Those years were still going. The days kept slipping by. The paths that they should have followed kept marching forward, but with a gap where they should have been. To all of those who loved them, they were like ghosts.

The memory of them was still there and they kept holding them closely within them, not knowing that exactly as they imagined them was how they still were. The Covra had taken so much from all of them, but also from the people who waited on Earth for them. Jonah struggled with deciding which had suffered more. Those who had stayed on Earth suffered an excruciating loss thinking that the entire team had gone missing somewhere in deep space, never to return. They had gone the rest of their lives not knowing where they had gone or what had happened to them, and never imagining that most of them had not only survived, but had created a new settlement on a distant planet that they didn't even know existed. Not knowing had to be brutal, a torment that they had never been able to escape. Though they had likely never completely recovered from the pain, however, they would have had the chance to process it, to think through it and soothe their suffering by memorializing their loved ones. They had had the opportunity to watch as the story of their family members and friends became a part of the history of Earth and the basis for new regulations and advancements in technology and safety.

For those on the Nyx 23 crew, however, this comfort hadn't come. They had spent fifteen years thinking about the people who were back home and knowing that they had the most horrible thoughts about them. They knew that they had no way of contacting them or letting them know that they had survived. They most certainly had no way of getting back to them. For those years, all they could do was long for them. Then in an instant everything changed. They went from knowing that they had been away from everything and everyone that they knew and loved on Earth for just fifteen years to waking up in the horror of the Denynso and those with them trying to kill off the Covra before they destroyed them all, then discovering that another one hundred years had passed without them knowing. They had never had the opportunity to mourn their loved ones properly or to feel like they had said goodbye. Instead, they were just thrust into the reality that they were all gone and that there would never be the chance, even with a miracle, that they would see them again. Now they had the rest of their lives to think about what they had lost and try to piece together a new existence.

When he was within the building, Jonah could almost pretend that it hadn't all happened. Even with the devastation of the abandoned structure around him, he could tell himself that everything was still as it had been. This slipped slightly when he stepped out of the medical ward and into the newer laboratory that had been built up around it, but only somewhat. Even with the advanced equipment and renovated rooms, the building itself was still old, allowing Jonah to keep his mind focused. The moment, if it ever came, that he left the grounds of the University, though, he knew that he was going to be confronted with the overwhelming reality of life a century displaced from what it could, and should, have been.

Jonah gave up on trying to eat and decided to go back to the emergency chamber that had been converted into an infirmary to check on those who had stayed behind when the others left. He felt responsible for them even though he knew that there was little that he could do for them other than follow the instructions that Ciyrs and Elianna had left. When he walked into the chamber he saw one of the hybrids who had been rescued from the torture chamber in the breeding facility walking slowly from one side to the other.

"You're up," Jonah said encouragingly.

The man turned to look at him and Jonah tried to decipher his characteristics, still trying to figure out what species had gone into creating him. The hybrid gave a hint of what could have been a smile and nodded.

"It hurts," he said. "But I'm willing to deal with the pain to be moving again."

Jonah nodded. He didn't want to think about what this nameless man might have gone through at the hands of the Valdicians that made him so thankful just to be able to walk. He didn't know how long the hybrid had been strapped to the cold metal table, attached to the screen that the hybrid woman had told them was a form of torturous reprogramming. There were no plans in place for what was going to happen to these people when they had recovered or when the time came for Jonah to leave the basement for whatever was next for him. Those who had gotten onto the ship with Pyra or into the vehicle with Oro had escaped from the basement and from the facilities that had been their torment throughout their lives, but those who had stayed behind were still so close to the danger. Jonah didn't know what would happen to any of them and suddenly felt a strong sense of connection with them.

Even though coming back to Earth was returning home for him, it was still foreign and frightening. He could only imagine that it was far worse for these hybrids who had never known anything but the facilities and training that Ryan forced on them. Now they were suddenly away from that captivity and had nothing to tell them what to do or how to live. It must have been at once a relief and sense of freedom, but also an incredible sense of vulnerability and fear.

As Jonah checked the condition of each of the people in

the infirmary he felt himself becoming more and more angry at the situation. These were people whose lives had been stolen from them just as his had been stolen from him. For the hybrids, Ryan had both given them life and stolen it, but Jonah was determined that he would be able to help them claim them. He knew that he had to go back up into the laboratory as soon as possible. He didn't know what he would do or say if he encountered anyone while he was there, but it didn't matter. There were enough people working in the laboratory and enough secrecy around some of the projects that he would most likely be able to go unnoticed. If he was somehow recognized, he would determine what he would do from there. It may even give him the opportunity to get some of the answers that he so desperately sought.

2

The group was still bustling around in the main room of the ship, unsure of what they were supposed to do next, but Elianna could only think about Ciyrs. Her mate had returned to the ship with the others just as planned, but rather than it being a joyous reunion, he had ensured that the wounded and the pregnant women were brought to the infirmary and then disappeared deeper into the ship. She knew that he was suffering, but he had closed himself off from her, not even allowing her to communicate with him through her mind. She stepped into the infirmary and looked around, hoping that he would have returned to check on the patients and possibly lost himself in the treatment of their injuries, but she didn't see him.

Jacob had come to the infirmary and was looking over them, utilizing the skills that he had learned during his training to be a field medic for the excavation team that had led to him going through the portal and disappearing into the unknown. She knew that he could handle it enough for a few minutes, and left the room again without saying anything. The ship was expansive and complex, and the thought that her mate could have gone to virtually any corner of it was intimidating. He had never left Uoria before boarding the ship to bring him to Earth for Samira and Ty's wedding, and somehow the thought of him roaming through the huge ship was more unnerving to her than thinking of him wandering the open of his home planet. In that moment, Elianna was grateful that Ciyrs had closed off the communication between them. She wouldn't want him to hear her questioning him going through the ship. The longer that they had been away from Uoria, the more that the Denynso men had recognized the differences between them and those of Earth.

Strong, powerful, and fearsome, the Denynso were incredible warriors and had designed innovations and resources that astounded Elianna. The technology and transportation that Elianna was accustomed to from Earth, however, weren't their way. She thought no less of them for these differences, and in fact was incredibly impressed by the amazing people who she had joined and now considered her family, but she worried that her mate and the other men would be hurt if they thought that this wasn't the case. The discomfort at him going through the ship alone stemmed not from the thought that he would get lost, but more from the thought that the strangeness of the stark, cold environment would trigger the fierceness within him that dwelled within all of the Denynso. Even though Ciyrs was not a warrior, but a healer, he still had the aggressive nature of the other men and could easily become uncontrollably violent, worsening the emotional turmoil that he was obviously experiencing.

Elianna continued through the ship as quickly as she could without running. If she controlled her steps, she could keep herself calm. That way if Ciyrs did decide to reach out for her through his thoughts, he wouldn't feel her emotions and be further upset. She wanted to find him so that she could comfort him and give him the strength and support that she knew only she could provide for him. It went beyond the love and passion that grew stronger with each day that they spent together, to the sense of destiny and responsibility that had been bestowed on her when she bonded with him. He had been waiting his entire life for the woman who was made for him and from the moment that they came together, she knew that she had been waiting for him as well. It was his love for her that had saved her life after her brutal attack, and that had imbued her with the power to heal that she now shared with him. It was her love for him that would support and reassure him.

She felt like she had gone through nearly the entire ship when she finally walked past a small observatory and noticed Ciyrs out of the corner of her eye standing in the center of the room. She stepped up to his side and joined his gaze at the solid grey expanse in front of him.

"The shields are up," she said, wanting to break the silence in the room as much as explain to him why the observatory was opaque.

"Shields?" Ciyrs asked, not turning to look at her.

Elianna walked over to the small control panel on one wall and pressed the button in the center. There was a low humming sound and the panels that covered the curved ceiling above started to move out of the way. As they disappeared into the seams between the individual panes of glass they revealed a geodesic dome melded together with thick bands of metal between the glass. She came back to his side and they stood silently staring through the glass for several long seconds. In the far distance Elianna could see a cluster of glimmers that looked like stars but that she knew were planets. To one side there was a larger planet with a small moon hovering close by. Though she knew that all of the celestial bodies that she saw were moving rapidly, the entire scene was calm and peaceful, as if everything was still and they were still in it.

"The baby could have died," Ciyrs finally said.

His voice was low, almost too quiet for her to hear. For a moment, she was unsure if he had actually spoken it to her or if it was a personal musing that he hadn't intended for her to hear.

"But it didn't," she said.

"He," Ciyrs said.

"What?"

"He. The baby. It's a boy."

Elianna couldn't help the slight curve of her lips as she thought of the new baby boy that her mate had helped into the world.

"But *he* didn't," she revised herself. "He survived."

"His mother didn't."

The words hit Elianna painfully and she drew in a breath to soften the clenching of her heart.

"I know," she said. "You can't blame yourself for that."

"Of course, I can," he said. "There's no one else to blame."

"That's because there is no blame to be had. Sometimes women die during childbirth. It's horrible, but it happens. It always has. Especially when the baby is coming earlier than it is meant to. Haven't you ever heard of a premature baby?"

Ciyrs shook his head.

"Until we encountered these women, Eden was the only pregnant woman I had ever encountered. The warriors who are younger than me were born and raised in their mother's homes. I was only a few years old when they came along, and had no reason to meet their mothers or see them when they were babies. Mothers and children didn't eat in the banquet hall with the rest of us, and until they were old enough to start their training, they didn't engage with us."

Elianna was astonished. She knew that Lysander was the first of the new generation of the Denynso, and the first baby to be born in the compound in quite some time, but she couldn't imagine a life without ever encountering young children.

"Well, I can tell you that at least in human women, there are times when pregnancies do not continue for as long as they should and the babies are born too soon. A lot of the times when this happens, it's because of something that's wrong in the mother's body."

"Why are you telling me this?" Ciyrs asked.

He sounded frustrated, but Elianna forged forward.

"Because when that happens, the only thing that can be done is to try to save the baby's life. With everything that that woman had been through during her pregnancy, and likely even before, her body probably couldn't handle the stress of giving birth on top of whatever it was that caused the premature labor. It just gave out. You did everything that you could."

"If I had done everything that I could, they would both be alive."

"That's not true, Ciyrs."

"There had to be something else that I could have done to help her. I didn't know what to do. I barely even noticed that there was anything wrong with her. All I was thinking about was the baby. By the time that I had him out, she was beyond my help. She just lay there bleeding and I couldn't do anything to stop it. I was so afraid that the baby wasn't going to live. He's so incredibly small. Much smaller than Lysander when he was born. He barely made any sound. I just tried to keep him warm."

Elianna turned toward her mate and reached out to touch his back.

"Ciyrs, there is nothing that you could have done. You couldn't have prevented her from going into labor, and even if she had been in a hospital, there's a good chance that she still wouldn't have survived."

"How am I supposed to call myself a healer when I could just let a woman die right in front of me and not be able to do anything to help her? I tried. I did a healing on her, but it didn't do anything. The other women said that she had just lost too much blood."

"You are a healer," Elianna insisted. "You were born to heal and to care for people. This isn't the only time that you have seen someone die."

Ciyrs's eyes closed briefly and she regretted the bluntness of her words.

"I know," he said. "I've seen death. I've caused death. I have walked into battle with the sheer purpose of killing as many of the enemies as I possibly could. I watched as they died around me and never once considered helping even a single one of them. I've also watched as warriors were wounded and fell to the ground at my feet. Very few didn't survive. I have saved many lives. I have taken more. Nothing has ever made me feel as helpless as watching that woman die right in front of me. I felt like she was taken from me. I saw her breathing. I heard her voice. She was there with me, getting ready to deliver her baby, and then she was gone. I don't even know if she heard him cry."

"You are a healer. You are not magic. You have the power to help, to heal, and to treat. You have done incredible things. I wouldn't be alive today if you weren't determined to heal me. Neither would Leia. Neither would Zuri or Eden. Lysander would never have been born. Imagine what would have happened to Maxim. That doesn't mean that you will always be able to stop something from happening that has already started. That woman might have been breathing or talking when you went back to her to help her, but the life was already leaving her. She was already gone. She had gathered all of the energy and life force that she had left within her and directed it toward making sure that her baby was born and was a safe as possible. Once that was done, she had nothing else to keep her going. You didn't lose her. You saved her baby."

"Where are you?"

The sound of Eden's voice in her mind was startling, and she pressed her fingertips to her temples.

"Eden?"

"Are you with Ciyrs?"

"Yes," Elianna replied through her thoughts.

"Where? Pyra is trying to find you."

"We're in the observation dome."

"He should be to you in a minute."

Eden's voice left her mind and Elianna looked back to Ciyrs.

"Eden?" he asked.

Elianna nodded. Communicating with Eden through her mind wasn't a frequent occurrence. They had been able to link their minds this way since Ciyrs had saved Eden's life, connecting himself and his mate to Eden while also giving Eden Denynso DNA. Being able to communicate this way was something that was usually reserved only for mates after they had completed their bond, which made the connection among the three of them unique. It was also a fairly sensitive subject for Pyra, who was not linked to them in the same way and was uncomfortable with the closeness that his mate maintained with the healer who had rescued and changed her. To ease this discomfort the two women agreed that they would limit their communication to each other except in the most dire of situations, ensuring that Eden's connection with Pyra remained special and Ciyrs and Elianna didn't feel intruded upon by her hearing their thoughts.

A few minutes later, Pyra stalked into the room.

"We need to leave," he said forcefully.

"Has Rilex returned?" Ciyrs asked.

Elianna noticed that he hadn't asked about the lovely hybrid woman who Rilex had chased or the baby who she had taken with her.

"No," Pyra said.

"Then we have to stay," Ciyrs said. "We can't just leave and head for Maxim without him. All of us came here together. We need to stay together. He might be in danger."

"We don't know Rilex," Pyra said. "I know that he arrived with Jem and that he's been helping us, but how much do we really know about him? He hasn't told us what planet he is from, or even what species he is. We don't know why he was with Jem, other than that he told us that he and some others found him on some other planet. We don't know why he's here helping us or what his motivation might have been to follow that hybrid woman back out onto the planet."

"What's going on?" Jem asked, coming to Pyra's side in the doorway.

The Denynso leader looked at Jem as if still startled at the appearance of the once-lost warrior.

"I came to find Ciyrs," Pyra said.

"I know," Jem said. "Eden told me that you were looking for him. What were you saying about Rilex?"

Elianna saw Pyra bristle slightly.

"He left the ship with that hybrid woman."

"Severine," Jem said.

"What?" Pyra asked.

"Severine," Jem said. "Rilex gave her a name."

"Why would he do that?" Pyra asked.

"Because she's a person," Jem said calmly, the gentle personality that they had all mourned so heavily when they thought he was dead obvious. "She deserves a name."

"That doesn't explain why he followed her back out onto the planet. How do we know that she wasn't some sort of spy that infiltrated our ship and has now left to rejoin the hybrid army and tell them everything about us so that they could attack us more effectively? He could have been manipulated by her and joined them."

"You saw her captive," Jem said. "You saw the torture that she was facing. Ciyrs himself treated her injuries. Your mate tended to her."

"She could still be trying to ingratiate herself with the army with information about us hoping that they will take her back in."

"Why would she do that?" Jem asked. "She might not have seen or experienced anything but the facilities and labs, but she knows about the Denynso. She's heard nothing her entire existence but about the power and viciousness of the Denynso warriors. She has been trained to destroy every one of our kind. Why would she put herself in the position of being vulnerable to us just in hopes that we would keep her alive and bring her here to Penthos?"

"I don't know," Pyra said. "I don't know anything about these hybrids except that they were created by the man who tried to kill my mate and my son, not to mention me and every one of us."

The tension in Pyra's voice was a harsh reminder for Elianna of the dark time on Uoria when Ciyrs discovered that the Klimnu were mutated versions of the Mikana and Pyra commanded that all of the Mikana men were held captive in the meeting hall of the human settlement. She knew in her heart that the Denynso leader was truly a good man. He was devoted to Eden as her mate and was a wonderful father to Lysander. He was passionate about protecting the people he cared about and defending Uoria. Sometimes, though, those emotions overtook his logic and combined with the powerful warrior instincts born into him to create nearly overwhelming aggression and violence that shadowed his ability to make the decisions that he needed to.

"Even you said that they needed to be rescued and protected," Ciyrs pointed out.

"Rilex wouldn't trust someone for no reason," Jem said. "He is anything but easily manipulated. He cares for her. Very deeply. He told me that he was struggling to let her know how he feels about her because she had suddenly withdrawn from him. If he went with her, it's because he wanted to protect her. Nothing more."

Pyra let out a long breath and squared his shoulders.

"We'll wait for a short time longer."

With that, he turned and stalked out of the observatory and back down the corridor.

3
———

Ellora stood her ground as the man in the red mask loomed over her. He took a step closer and leaned his concealed face down toward hers, obviously trying to intimidate her, but she refused to give him the satisfaction of seeing any fear in her eyes. Instead, she straightened up to her fullest height and kept her eyes locked on him. She wished that she knew who was behind the dark red mask, but at the same time she felt that if she did know who was lurking behind the deception of the mask that she wouldn't be able to control the anger that was already burning in her belly.

"What are you doing down here?" the man repeated in the same low growl.

There was a tense, buzzing energy around him that made Ellora's skin prick and the hair on the back of her neck stand up, but she still wouldn't take a step back. She narrowed her eyes at him. The mask continued to taunt her and she couldn't hold back the venom she felt any longer.

"What are you hiding behind that mask?" she asked.

"Are you so afraid that you don't want anyone to be able to see your face?"

"I'm not afraid," the man said.

"Then take off your mask," she said. "If you are so proud of what you have done and aren't afraid of me, show me your face. Show me who you are."

"Ellora," Malcolm's voice said from behind her, his tone low as if he were trying to calm her and lure her back toward him. "Stop."

"No," Ellora said. "I'm will not be afraid of someone who will confront me but is not even strong enough to show their face."

In an instant, the man's hands shot out from beneath his robes and clasped around Ellora's neck. She choked as the pressure of his fingers dug into her skin and blocked her air. As she clawed at his hands with her own fingers and felt him lift her feet away from the floor, she heard Malcolm screaming, pleading with the man to put her down. Ellora kicked as hard as she could, but even when she made contact with the man's legs he seemed to barely notice it, and the longer that he held onto her throat, the more her strength slid out of her, making her kicks weaker. Darkness was creeping into the edges of her eyes and she saw tiny lights bursting in her field of visions. She wondered why Malcolm hadn't come up to help her, and felt suddenly and overwhelmingly alone.

As if the feeling of abandonment and helplessness had reached something deep within her, in the moment just before everything went completely black, her mind went clear. Suddenly she wasn't thinking of the masked man's hands tightening around her throat. She couldn't hear Malcolm's voice or the fierce, growling breaths of the man holding her. In her mind, she saw Aegeus. It was an image that she had fought with herself not to think about for so many years, but that now was clear and vibrant in her thoughts. She could see her husband's face, the details so present she felt as though she could have reached out to touch him. His mouth moved and she could hear his voice in her ears just as loudly as if he were standing right beside her.

"Don't give up, Ellora. Fight for me."

All of the determination and fury that had led her into the tunnels surged back and her eyes snapped open. The man's masked face was close to hers and his hands were still tight around her throat, but she no longer felt like she was under his control. Ellora released all of the tension in her muscles, no longer holding herself up or trying to pry his hands from her throat. She let her hands fall away and went limp, forcing him suddenly to withstand her full weight in his grip. The sudden weight was obviously startling to the masked man and Ellora felt her head snap backwards as she fell toward the ground. She didn't pause to think. She scrambled past the man, climbed to her feet, and started running. The multicolored lights above her head turned on rapidly as she ran through the tunnel, but she felt like she was moving blindly. She had never been within the tunnels and Aegeus had never told her about the subterranean network of corridors with enough detail that would tell her how to move through them. She passed by a few of the ladders that led up to the exits, but she could hear the heavy footfalls of the masked man as he chased her down the tunnel and knew that she wouldn't have enough time to get up the ladder before he caught up with her.

The sound of her husband's voice reverberating through her mind kept her moving forward. She continued to refuse to feel fear or hesitation. Aegeus had always done everything with courage and strength. He hadn't been afraid when he walked into battle or when he faced down the corrupt members of the Order. This was for him.

Ahead of her Ellora could see the darkness of entrances to other tunnels that led off of the corridor where she was running. She kept her eyes focused on one several yards ahead of her, knowing that this was the one that she was going to take. Drawing in as deep a breath as she could, she forced her feet to run harder and faster. Though the man was far larger than she was, allowing for his strides to bring him closer to her with every moment, she suddenly felt like she was pulling away from him. He was getting further behind her, no longer close enough for her to feel like if he reached out toward her she would be able to feel his fingertips touch her back. She knew that she was getting further away from him and that it was her thoughts of Aegeus that were giving her the strength and the energy to continue pushing.

The entrance to the other tunnel was only a few steps away now. Ellora kept pushing, kept running. As soon as she was close enough, she dove into the new tunnel and ran as hard as she could to the nearest void that put her into another tunnel and then another. With every turn, she felt like she might be getting far enough away from the masked man that he might not be able to find her. She paused and strained, listening as hard as she could to hear the footsteps of the masked man. They were no longer loud as if close behind her. She could hear muffled shouting now as he called through the tunnels for her. Ellora paused for a brief moment to try to determine where the man was. She couldn't hear his footsteps any longer and decided it was time to start back toward the entrance that she had used to get into the tunnel.

Ducking back into the last tunnel that she had used, she started back through the labyrinth, occasionally using tunnels that she knew that she hadn't before to try to keep herself off of the same path as the masked man while still moving back in the direction of the entrance closest to her home, closest to the security of the weapons that she had gathered from her husband's war room. There she would be safe. There she would have what Aegeus had prepared to handle the very people who were threatening her now.

She had to keep thinking about him. She had to keep reminding herself that her husband had made this plan so many years before, and even if it had taken her from the time that their sons were children until they were adults to understand it, now was the time for her to stand up and fight the way that she knew would make him proud. Even though Athan had told her that Ryan could have killed Aegeus now that he knew where to find Maxim and the Denynso, if there was even the smallest possibility that her husband was still alive, she had to keep going. She wouldn't stop until she saw his face or they destroyed her.

The tunnels were becoming more complex as she ran and she started discovering doors embedded in the walls. She tried to open a few of them but found them all locked and soon gave up, knowing that pausing to try the doors was taking up time that she should be using to get through the tunnels. As hard as she was trying to keep track of where she was going and focus on moving in the direction that she thought would bring her back to where she had entered, she soon realized that she no longer knew where she was or how she should continue. Her body was growing tired and she couldn't maintain the speed that she had been. Finally, she turned down another tunnel and found that the space was growing more and more narrow the further she went.

After another turn she realized that the lights on the ceiling were no longer turning on and changing colors in response to her presence. Instead there were small white lights recessed in the ceiling that sent faint pools of glow to the ground every few feet. Ellora found the change unsettling. There was a reason that those lights were designed to turn on as the people who used the tunnels made their way along them, and if this section didn't feature those it was also for a reason.

There were no longer other tunnels stemming off of the corridor, which meant that unless she was going to turn around and go back the way that she had come, possibly putting herself right in the path of the masked man, she had no choice but to keep going along the path that she had chosen. Around her the tunnels had fallen silent. She could no longer hear even the sound of the masked man calling for her. As much as she hated the sound of the calls, almost feeling like they were a taunt, not being able to hear them was proving to be worse. As long as she had been able to hear his voice, she had been able to gauge how far away from her he was and which direction he was most likely in from her. Now that she couldn't hear him, though, she felt more isolated and out of control of the situation.

Ellora had been moving along the corridor for several minutes when she saw that the tunnel ahead of her was dark, the lights no longer glowing from the ceiling. She hesitated, unsure of whether she should proceed into the darkness ahead. She glanced back over her shoulder again, considering for a moment turning back and retracing her steps. Something told her to keep going and she turned back, surging into the darkness with greater speed so that she couldn't question herself any further. For the first several steps she still had enough of the illumination from the last light in the ceiling that she could see ahead of her. Soon, though, she could no longer see anything and had to reach to either side of her to run her fingers along the walls and navigate her movements.

One hand indicated a turn in the tunnel and she followed it, continuing to feel along the sides of the corridor as she went. She had followed along two more corners when she found what felt like the edge of a doorway. Ellora paused and felt along the door to gauge its size. As she felt, she found a handle of cold metal. She pushed down on it and felt it resist. Gathering her strength, she pushed down on it with all of the force she had within her and the handle gave, allowing her to push the door open and slip around it into the space beyond.

Beyond the door was just as dark as the tunnel and Ellora couldn't tell where she was or how large of a space it was. She reached ahead of her, ready to use the same technique as she had in the tunnel to evaluate her surroundings, and had taken only a few steps before she felt her fingertips hit a wall ahead of her. She was turning to measure the space in the other direction when she felt an arm wrap around her waist and a hand clamp over her mouth.

4

———

"Their training means nothing. They will never be able to stand up to the Denynso and the Mikana. With us together, no one can defeat us!"

The small crowd gathered in front of the Mikana meeting hall cheered in response to Creia and the Denynso king held one fist up in the air as if in victory.

"But they are hybrids, Creia," someone called up to him where he stood on the top step. "How are we to know how to fight against creatures that are made up of more than one species?"

"More than one species in each hybrid just gives us more opportunity to fight," Creia said. "We'll defeat them as we would any of the beings that make them up. These pieced-together creatures are nothing compared to us. Ryan wanted to make the strongest weapons in existence, but all he accomplished was making half-life's. According to Rain, Azra communicated with Elise from Earth and says that these creatures don't even have names. They are shells, nothing more. They have no hearts, no souls, nothing to fuel them. Everything that they don't have, we do. Ryan thought that he was training them to defeat us, that he was creating soldiers that couldn't be defeated. He didn't know what he was facing. These soldiers are made up of scraps. They won't have any chance when they actually confront us on the battlefield. We will cut them all down and return home before breakfast."

There was another cheer and Ivy felt her heart clench. She couldn't cheer along with the rest of the crowd that had gathered gradually as the king had begun to speak. They all seemed to be swept up in the furor of the huge Denynso and even Rey, the Mikana king, who was generally calm and controlled seemed ignited as he stood beside Creia on the step. Ivy felt like she was getting lost in the buzzing energy of the crowd and it frightened her. The louder the men cheered in response to Creia's fiery statements, the more Ivy's heart pounded in her chest and she felt the desperate urge to get away.

She had come upon the gathering when she left the midwife's home and had been drawn into it the same way as the others, but the longer that Creia spoke, the more uncomfortable she became. She stumbled back through the group, pushing people aside as she went, desperate to get away from them and escape the sound of the king's voice. Finally, she broke through and started to run. She wasn't sure where she was going, but she knew that she had to get away from them. Running through the Mikana kingdom made her ache for Maxim. Though it had only been a short time since she had seen him, she missed him with an intensity that she could have never fathomed. Every step that she took through the kingdom reminded her of the first time that she had come to this place with him. She already loved him when they left the human settlement and started their journey to the Mikana kingdom, but their relationship had changed once they were there.

Seeing where Maxim had grown up and learning more about him had deepened her love for him, but conflict with his mother and the realization that her life was never again going to be what it was when she was on Earth had nearly torn them apart. She still remembered the painful sting of looking into Maxim's eyes and seeing doubt and questions where they had once been such security. It was that brief separation, however, that had cemented their bond and made her realize, fully and completely, that it was him that she wanted. She no longer cared if that meant that she was going to have to give up the life that she'd had on Earth in exchange for a new life on Uoria. All that mattered to her was that she was with Maxim. It was then that her mind switched and she devoted herself not just to the planet, but also to the fight that was building around them.

Now she was running through the kingdom, the darkness around her making it harder for her to know where she was going, the ache within her growing with each step. She suddenly became aware of the sound of footsteps behind her. Ahead of her she could see a small cluster of buildings and she rushed to one, ducking behind it and crouching into the shadows. As she peered around the corner of the building she saw that is was Rain who had been pursuing her and she felt relief wash over her. The building, almost frantic energy of the crowd around Creia had frightened her and she was glad to know that it was someone she knew and trusted that had been chasing her.

Rain approached her, her expression quizzical as she reached for Ivy's hands.

"What is it?" Rain asked. "Are you alright?"

The woman looked into her eyes and Ivy felt like she

was staring back through time. It was still so strange to her to think that this woman had lived more than 100 years before Ivy was born, and yet looked only slightly older than her. Rain's memories didn't stretch the decades that she had been alive, but Ivy still felt like she could see everything that happened around her even during the years that she had spent frozen in place, tucked perpetually into her bed awaiting the saviors who would come and free her, saving her from a horrific fate at the mercy of the Covra. The kindness and concern in Rain's eyes made all of the emotion that Ivy had been trying not to acknowledge rush forward and she felt her chest swell painfully. She shook her head and looked down, watching as tears dropped from her eyes to the ground beneath her.

"How could Creia say those things?" she asked.

"What do you mean?" Rain asked. "What things?"

"You heard him," Ivy said. "You heard what he was saying about the hybrids."

"Yes," Rain said. "They are our enemies. He's a warrior. It is in his nature to feel that type of hatred toward them."

"It isn't that," Ivy said. "I understand that he's going to hate the people who have threatened his kind and want to destroy people he cares about and take over his planet. What I don't understand is how he could be so cruel about all of the hybrids just because they are hybrid."

"I don't understand," Rain said. "You know as much as we do what those creatures are. Ryan made them for the sole purpose of being weapons. They have no names. They have no personality. They are bits and pieces of other species put together so that he could exploit them for their characteristics and abilities."

"What about Lysander?" Ivy asked.

"What?" Rain asked, sounding slightly taken aback by the question.

"Lysander," Ivy repeated. "He's half-Denynso, half-human."

"No, he isn't," Rain said. "Remember Eden was transformed into a Denynso. Her DNA is no longer human."

"She was already carrying Lysander when that happened. He is not pure Denynso."

"And Idella?" Ivy asked.

"Lila's great-grandmother?" Rain asked.

"Yes," Ivy said. "She was one of the first hybrids created in the program. She had a name. She had a family. She wasn't a weapon or a shell."

Rain looked stunned, as if she, like all of the others, hadn't thought about the woman who had, through the love and commitment of her great-granddaughter who had become the mate of one of the Denynso warriors, led them to the Eteri settlement where they found Azrael and Ariella.

"She came from the early phases of the experiment," Rain said. "It was different then."

"How?" Ivy asked.

"The people running the experiments weren't like Ryan. Though they were cruel and vicious, it wasn't to the extent of Ryan. They didn't have the extensive technology and resources that Ryan has. They understood that each person who they brought into their experiments was valuable. They couldn't replace them as easily as Ryan can replace his. Though they still held them and subjected them to horrible conditions, they recognized each of them as individuals. Even so, Idella escaped. She was only part of one level of the hybrid blending."

"So?" Ivy asked. "Why does that matter?"

"Some of the creatures that are in Ryan's army were born to adults that he spliced. Their parents aren't even pure."

"Pure?" Ivy asked, appalled by what Rain had just said. "So, they are like what Lysander's children will be? Or if George and Zsilvia had a child, what their child would be? Or what..."

Her voice trailed off as she stopped herself from saying the words that had been hovering in her mind since she started to run.

"What?" Rain asked, tilting her head so that she could look more fully into Ivy's face. "Or what?"

Ivy shook her head. She knew that this wasn't the time. She had said that she would tell Ellora about her pregnancy before she would tell anyone else.

"Nothing," she said, but she knew that her voice and the expression on her face betrayed her.

"Ivy," Rain said. "What's going on?"

Ivy felt like all of the energy and strength had left her legs. She turned so that her back was against the building and slid down to sit on the ground. Rain crouched in front of her and reached forward to rest her hands on Ivy's shoulders. Ivy pulled her knees close to her chest and rested her hands on her belly. She took a few moments to settle herself and then looked up at Rain.

"I'm pregnant," she said.

Rain's eyes lit up and she smiled.

"That's wonderful," she said happily.

"Is it?" Ivy asked.

The smile melted away from Rain's face and her eyes darkened.

"What do you mean?" she asked. "You're having a baby!"

"But I'm human," Ivy said. "Maxim is Mikana."

"I know," Rain said. "Why does that matter?"

"Why does it matter for the other hybrids?" Ivy asked.

The tears were still falling lightly from her eyes, but she didn't bother to wipe them away. It didn't matter if Rain saw the emotion that she was feeling. Now that she had confessed her secret, she wanted Rain to understand the stress that she was facing.

"Your baby isn't a hybrid," Rain said.

Ivy nodded.

"Of course, it is," she said. "It is not one species. It isn't 'pure'."

Rain winced at the sound of the word that she herself had used only moments before.

"Ivy, it's not the same. Your baby isn't the same as those creatures."

"Why not?" she asked. "The mixed children who were born into the experiments had no choice in what they were or that they were born, just like my baby doesn't. It has no say in the fact that it is being born to a human and a Mikana, and no matter what type species it one day falls in love with, its children won't have any choice in the fact that they, too, will be hybrids. Even if they have a child with a human or with a Mikana, that baby will still be blended. It will never be just one species, and never again in its bloodline will there be someone who can be considered pure. This one decision that I have made, to fall in love with a Mikana and have his baby, has put my entire family on the path of always being seen as hybrid."

"It isn't a decision," Rain said. "You simply fell in love."

"And it isn't a decision for those soldiers, either," Ivy said. "You said that things were different when the experiments first started. That at least the Valdician and the human who started those experiments weren't as cruel as Ryan. How can Creia and the rest of you understand that and yet still see the hybrids the way that you do? Think of what it felt like to find out that you were being used by the Covra as an incubator for their eggs, or when the Covra injected the men with the toxin that let the Covra take over their minds and force them to fight and kill each other."

"It was awful," Rain admitted. "Our bodies weren't ours anymore. They had been taken over by another species and used for their own purposes, even though those purposes weren't what we wanted, and we never would have gone along with it had we been able to prevent it."

Ivy nodded.

"That was only for a time," she said. "You had a life before the Covra and you have a life now. You can do whatever you please and live whatever life you want to now. They don't have control over you anymore and you are willing to fight to make sure that no one else has control over you or anyone else on Uoria or anywhere else in the Universe ever again. Imagine what it's like for the hybrids. Yes, they were bred, born, and raised to be weapons, but they are still alive. They are still people. They have lived their entire lives under the complete control of Ryan and the Valdicians. They aren't able to make any choices for themselves and know that there is not a point at any time in their lives when they can hope for freedom. Is it so difficult to imagine that this is not what they want to do? You think Ryan is horrible for what he wants to do to the Denynso and the Mikana, for wanting to control them and turn them into weapons that he can use to take over the rest of the Universe for his own purposes. How can you not see the horror of what he has already done to the people who he is using to get to them?"

5

———

Severine reached down and placed her hand on the baby's stomach, gently rocking him to soothe him further into sleep. His face looked sweet and peaceful and she felt a sense of calm come over her. Though he was very small and had struggled when she first got him from Ciyrs and the vehicle in which he was born, he seemed to have gotten stronger in even the small time that she had been caring for him and she was no longer concerned that he might not survive. She felt Rilex wrap an arm around her waist and lean down to kiss her cheek.

"When is the last time you had something to eat?" he asked.

Severine thought back, trying to answer him, but realized that she didn't remember the last meal that she had eaten. She shook her head at him and he took her by the hand to lead her out of the room and back toward the room where they had left their bags. He guided her to sit down and brought his bag over, pulling a few containers out and putting them on the floor in front of her. She watched him as he prepared the rations and divided them into collapsible bowls. He looked up at her as he handed her a bowl and she saw the shooting stars in his eyes again.

"Will you tell me more about yourself?" she asked.

Rilex stiffened slightly and sat down in front of her, picking up his own bowl and looking down into it as if hoping that it would tell him what he should say to her. She saw him reach down for one of the packets of food and then put it down and select another before looking up at her again.

"I already told you about myself," he said.

"I know," Severine said, "but there has to be more. You told me that you come from a different time and place, and that you traveled to Earth through a portal, but that's really it. I still don't feel like I don't know much about you."

"Do you need to?" Rilex asked. "I'm here now. I'm with you. It doesn't matter what happened before."

"Of course, it does," Severine said. "Everything that happened to you before right now is what led you to me. If a single one of those things hadn't happened, you might never have gotten here. You might not have found your way to Jem and you might not have been at the University when Eden found us."

Rilex leaned across their food and touched a kiss to the tip of her nose. Severine smiled at the touch and returned it.

"I'd like to think that I would have found you no matter what," he said. "Nothing could have kept me from you."

"If you didn't know that I even existed, how would you be able to find me?"

"The Universe would have brought me to you," he said.

"It did," Severine said. "How?"

Rilex gave a resigned laugh and settled back into place.

"What do you want to know?" he asked.

Severine smiled. She barely knew what to ask first.

"You said that Ryan wouldn't have trained the hybrids to come after you because he didn't know your species. What species is that? You already told me that your home is in a different time and on a different planet. How? Why did you go through the portal? Did they know that you were missing? Did they ever try to look for you? How long were you gone? Who found you? How did they find you? Why did they come back to Earth? Why did you come to the University if you weren't with the original group?"

Rilex laughed again and closed his eyes as if he were trying to let everything that she had asked him process so that he knew where to start. She saw him draw in a breath in preparation.

"My kind is an ancient species, one that no longer exists and hasn't in so long that most have forgotten that we ever existed, and even those who have heard of us think that we are nothing more than a myth."

"I'm sorry," Severine said.

Rilex shook his head and took another bite of the food from his bowl.

"No reason to be sorry," he said. "This is the way that it was meant to be."

"What do you mean?" Severine asked.

"My kind was tasked with caring for the stars. Each of us was given the power to create and nurture stars, and to put them in place in the sky. The first of our stars appeared in the sky when we were born and most often, when we died, the stars that we created fell."

"Most often?" Severine asked.

"Yes. Sometimes when one of the race died, some of their stars would fall, while others remained in place. These were often the most important of our kind, or those who had made a tremendous impact when they were still living.

During my time, the sky had so many stars it was almost as light as daytime at night. Each of those stars meant something. Over time, it was only those stars that lingered that remained. My species was meant to protect the Universe."

"From what?" she asked.

"There are countless threats against existence. If people knew about them, they would spend their lives terrified. My kind was responsible for ensuring that the Universe was always as safe as it could be. There are threats that I can't even explain. When the time had come that we had done what we were meant to do and it was time to pass along the protection to others, that is when our kind disappeared. We left behind the work that we had done to protect existence and the light of the stars. When I left my home, a species had emerged that had put all of existence into more danger than it had ever been. My best friend was the ruler at the time. I was his most trusted advisor. The StarKillers had come and destroyed our temple, tossing pieces of it through all of the streams of existence. We had to retrieve them and restore the temple or the Universe would cease to exist. I was seeking out one of the stones when I accidentally stumbled through one of the portals."

"You didn't know that it was there?" Severine asked.

"No," Rilex told her. "I had gone through one that we already knew about into a stream that I was positive contained more than one of the stones. I was trying to get back when I accidentally found another portal that brought me to Earth."

"And you had no way of communicating with anyone back home?"

Severine couldn't imagine what it had been like for Rilex to suddenly lose everything. He'd had a life that he loved and that he was proud of, and in moments one decision had taken that from him.

"No," Rilex confirmed. "When I arrived on Earth, I didn't even know where I was. I knew that the portals brought us through the different places and versions of the streams, but I had never thought that it could transport me through time. I was suddenly in a world that I didn't understand in a time when my home and everyone I knew and loved had been gone for millennia. There was nothing that I could do to reach out to them, and nothing that they could do to reach out to me. I can only imagine what they thought had come of me."

"The only choice that you had was to make another life."

Rilex nodded.

"I spent the first few years learning everything that I could about Earth and its history, and I tried to find out as much as possible about my kind. I was hoping that I would be able to learn what had come of them so that at least I would have some comfort of knowing the type of life that they had lived. But I found very little. That's when I knew that it was going to be up to me to make sure that what my kind had done and the accomplishments that they had would not be fully forgotten. Some years after I arrived, though, I heard of the HM-1313 wall."

"I heard you mention that," Severine said. "What is it?"

"It was a discovery made during an archeological excavation far in the desert. There was a team who was researching an ancient civilization and some of the members of the team disappeared when they went into a strange cave outside of the research grid. During that excavation, they also found a wall that they hadn't discovered before and that didn't correspond with what they thought that they knew about the civilization that they were researching. They didn't think that there was a connection between the two."

"But there was?" Severine asked.

Rilex nodded again.

"The group that disappeared actually went through a portal in the cave. The wall that they found they gave the label 'HM-1313' and brought it in for research. Even though they knew that there were things about it that weren't in line with the civilization and it was found in a place that didn't make sense, they decided to include it in their under-standing of that people and basically made things up about it to make it fit in with what they had already published about that civilization. But I knew that they were wrong. I started looking into it and realized that it wasn't a wall. It was part of a wall that had once been a piece of our temple."

"The temple that had been damaged by the StarKillers?" Severine asked.

"Yes. It was just one part of the wall, but it was an impor-tant piece of it. I knew that it was my connection to my own stream, but that it also meant my stream, and all of exis-tence, was in danger."

"I thought that you said that by the time that you arrived here, the Universe was already safe."

"I thought that it was. Then I realized that that wall showing up in the desert meant something. I had to find out more about it and do what I could to help. I started researching. I visited the wall and tried to decipher what it said, but it seemed to have been changed from what I remembered it saying. I knew that I wasn't just going to be able to use it to get home and that I was going to need help. It took a few months, but then a woman named Galadriel called me. She was interested in the wall as well and wanted to work with me to find out more about it. It couldn't have been more perfect, but I knew that I couldn't tell her who I was or what the segment of wall really was. Telling her too much could have compromised what needed to be done. I had to let her discover it for herself and just hope that it would work out."

"And did it?" Severine laughed.

"We're all alive, aren't we?" Rilex asked. "We aren't under the control of an overlord?"

Severine felt heat on her cheeks and glanced away.

"Are we?" she asked.

"I'm sorry," Rilex said. "I only meant that the Universe is still going and we aren't under the control of the StarKillers. I sent Galadriel on an incredibly dangerous mission that didn't go the way that I had planned. She ended up going through the portal before I intended her to and ended up not in another place, but another time."

"Did she find the others who had already gone through?" Severine asked.

"No," Rilex said. "Not at first. They had been gone for five years by this time. They had spread out and not all of them had survived. She did, however, find Vyker, the son of my best friend. He's grown now and leading in his father's place. But he was bitter and angry. He didn't trust anyone and felt that he was the only one who would be able to save his kind and the entirety of existence. He wasn't willing to accept Galadriel's help, but she insisted on it. Along the way they encountered the two of the original group that had survived, Jacob and Angela."

"The ones in the University? Who traveled back with us?"

"That's them," Rilex said. "They joined Vyker and Galadriel to continue working to restore the temple. They had lost them when they ended up on the planet where they found Jem. He had been missing from the Denynso compound for some time."

"Missing?" Severine asked.

"He was fighting on Uoria, their home planet, and he went through one of the portals. He and the rest of the Denynso thought that he was sacrificing his life to destroy the final members of the enemy army. When he arrived on the new planet, he didn't know what had happened and had no way of reconnecting with his own planet. They mourned him bitterly, but it was losing him that convinced them to leave their compound and start exploring Uoria, which led them to the humans and the Mikana, the Irisa and the Eteri. It's what brought them here."

"And you?" Severine asked. "That is how the Denynso got to Earth and then to Penthos, but you haven't told me what happened to you. After you found Galadriel, what happened? Didn't you go home?"

"I did. For a time. Galadriel, Vyker, and Jem eventually reunited with Jacob and Angela. When Galadriel and Jem ended up back on Earth, they came to me for help. That's when we found our way back to my stream and to Vyker. I told you that I decided to come back here because there was more work to do. Vyker had our stream under control and didn't need my interference. I needed to come back to the life that I had already built. I knew that they would be alright, and that I could get to them whenever I needed to. Jacob stayed with Vyker and Galadriel, Jem went back to his stream, and eventually Angela joined him there."

"But if Jem made it back to Earth, why didn't he stay and go back home? Didn't he want to go back to Uoria and to his own kind?"

Severine saw Rilex's eyes change. There was a sadness in them now.

"He was afraid," Rilex said. "He could have found a way to get back to Uoria when he was here, but he knew that Galadriel still needed his help. He had sworn his loyalty to them and he knew that he had to stay true to that. The Denynso are known for being the most powerful and fierce warriors in the Universe, but they are also known for their dedication to loyalty and duty. Even if he had known exactly how he was going to get back to Uoria, Jem wouldn't have gone if he felt that Galadriel still needed him and that there was something more that he could do. So, he went back."

"But when he knew that Galadriel didn't need him anymore? When everything was alright again, why didn't he come back to Earth and go home?"

"Like I said, he was afraid. He didn't know how long he had been gone and whether the Denynso would welcome him back. It was easier for him to stay away than it was to face the possibility that he would go back and they would reject him."

Severine felt her heart clench and tears sting in the corners of her eyes. Though she hadn't had much time with any of these people, Jem had been one of the ones who had come to the rescue of the hybrids being tortured by the Valdicians, and the women in the breeding facility. He had helped Ciyrs, Elianna, and Jacob take care of the wounded. He was gentler and kinder than the other warriors, but still a fiery and intense fighter. To think that he had gone through something so difficult was upsetting.

"So how did he end up here? How did you find him again?"

"When I came back here, I started researching the Denynso. I didn't know much about them, but interacting with Jem had made me want to know more. As I researched them I started to see rumors about turmoil that was happening on Uoria and an unethical scientist on Earth."

"Ryan," Severine said.

"I knew that I had to find Jem. Something was going to happen and the Denynso needed him. The only way that I was going to be able to get to him was to go to my stream and then travel to his planet. It was going to be treacherous and there was a chance that I wasn't going to be able to find the right portals to go to the places that I needed to go. When I was on my way to the museum that had the first portal that I needed to go to, I heard that there had been a break-in and the intruders had escaped through the front door of the museum. I immediately knew that it was Jem. It wasn't long before he, Jacob, and Angela got in touch with me and we started to the University."

"How did you know that the other Denynso were there?" she asked.

"We didn't," Rilex admitted. "Our plan was to find a way to get to Uoria and to help them from there. When we got to the University, though, we found the others."

She could see the expression in his eyes become more serious and she knew that he was thinking about something, but wasn't ready to tell her.

"So, Galadriel and Vyker weren't with him when he came back to Earth?" Severine asked.

"No," Rilex said. "He didn't go to them before he came here. Once he returned to his planet, he didn't have much to do with them. They were at peace and he was trying to get on with his life on his new planet."

"So where are they now?" Severine asked carefully.

She knew that Vyker and Galadriel were important to Rilex and that it was difficult for him that he didn't have the opportunity to be with them as he wanted to.

"It's hard to explain," Rilex said. "They are both long-since gone and alive and well. It's hard for me to think about them."

"That's how I feel," Severine said. "At the same time real and not."

Rilex reached across and stroked Severine's cheek with his thumb. She could see the tenderness in his eyes and felt herself melting again. It was incredible the effect that this man had on her. She never could have imagined that he would have taken over her heart the way that he had, and given her the hope for a new life that she now had in front of her.

"Have you thought about his name?" Rilex asked.

Severine shook her head.

"I don't know what name to give him," she said.

"You can name him anything that you want to," he told her. "Why don't you choose something from one of the species that you have in you? Do you know any of the languages for those species? Any of the words?"

Severine knew that the suggestion was coming to her from a place of warmth and love, but it made her uncomfortable. She shook her head.

"I know a few words," she said, "but I don't think that that's a good idea."

"Why?" Rilex asked. "I named you with a word from my language."

"I know," Severine said, "but it's different."

"Why is it different?" Rilex asked.

"You have a heritage," she said. "You can trace your family. You know where you came from, who your parents are. You have a connection to the species that you are and your history. I'm not even sure that I know all of the species that I have in me, and even if I did..."

Her voice trailed off and Rilex looked at her intently.

"Severine," he said. "You have a heritage. You have a history. It doesn't matter where you come from or how you came to be. You should be proud of who you are. You are starting a new family, and that family needs a heritage. You need to teach our son to appreciate who he is and the history that he has, no matter how difficult that history may be."

Severine tried to nod, but her head hung and she looked down into the bowl that still held most of the food that Rilex had put out for her. What he said touched her deeply, but she still struggled to feel the connection to the species that had combined to make her that he so obviously did to his kind. She felt like she had stolen their heritage and history.

"I don't deserve any of that history," she said. "I don't deserve to claim any of the heritage or the pride of those species. I was never intended to be a part of them. I was not born to be someone's child or to continue the line of any family. I am an Other. I am not a part of anything except being a part of nothing."

"Severine..." Rilex started, but she shook her head to silence him.

"We shouldn't stay here," she said, stating to collect the food back into the storage containers. "We need to get back to the ship."

She could sense that Rilex wanted to say something else, but he relented.

"How should we go?" he asked. "Do you think that the others are still up there waiting for us?"

Severine had pushed the attack by the other hybrids out of her mind and now the reality of it came rushing back to hit her. She felt like the breath had been knocked out of her and she no longer wanted to move, but she knew that they had to. They couldn't just stay in the chamber while the others were in the ship or making their way to those who were waiting for them elsewhere on Penthos. They needed to get back to them and figure out what was going to happen next.

"I don't know," she admitted. "They could be, but they could have also gone back to their barracks. We could try to go back up there and walk back to the ship."

"Or?" Rilex asked, obviously hearing the hesitation in her voice that told him that there was another option.

"Or, we could use the network of chambers down here."

"Network of chambers?" Rilex asked. His voice hovered somewhere between interested and quizzical, as if that meant something more to him than she meant it to.

"When Ryan designed the bunkers, he wanted to make it so that we could easily get to them without having to be on the surface. It would let us go between the different bunkers and also move around the planet without being exposed to the enemies. That way we could more easily ambush them."

She hated saying the words. Just thinking about the training that she went through and the horrible things that she had done, and planned to do, made her stomach turn. Even though she knew that she had been forced and tortured into everything that she did, she still felt ashamed of what she had been responsible for in the years that she had been under Ryan's control. Now that she was admitting them to Rilex she wasn't just telling him about the bunkers or the network of chambers that connected them. She was telling him what she was used for, what Ryan wanted to make her do. She felt like she was admitting to him what she might have done to him.

"Who built the network?" Rilex asked.

It was a question that Severine wouldn't have expected

him to ask. She didn't understand why it would matter to him who had actually built them, rather than the fact that they were there at all.

"I don't know," Severine admitted. "We started learning about them during our earliest training and they were already here by the time that we came to Penthos for the first time to run training drills."

"Ryan designed them?" Rilex asked. "They were his idea?"

"I assume that they are," Severine said. "Everything was always Ryan's idea. Why? What is it?"

Rilex looked around at the chamber where they sat as if he was examining it more closely than he had before, trying to find something specific. Finally, he shook his head and looked back at her.

"I don't know," he said. "I just feel like..." he hesitated and looked around again. "This is so familiar, but I can't remember why. It's like something that is so far in my past that I can't reach it anymore."

"Was there something like this on your home planet?" she asked, hoping that she might be able to help him draw the memories forward.

Rilex shook his head again.

"No," he said. "There was no reason for us to go underground. Not to this extent. I don't know."

"I can bring you through the network," Severine said. "It would keep us from having to go up to the surface until we were closer to the ship, but there is a chance that there could be other hybrids down here."

"Why didn't the ones who attacked you follow us down here if they knew about them?"

"I'm not sure," Severine said. "I know that there are some that aren't used as often, even some that were only shared with a few of us. That doesn't mean, though, that there aren't those who do know about it down here, or that we won't encounter them when we get closer."

"Our choice is either to go back up to the surface and be exposed, or to remain down here and have a chance of encountering them and possibly being trapped."

"Yes," Severine said.

"Which do you think would be better?" Rilex asked.

It was still so strange to be asked for her opinions, to be given a choice. She could see the sincerity in Rilex's eyes, though, and knew that he truly wanted to know how she felt about the situation and what she thought that they should do. She drew in a breath, thinking through both options as quickly as she could. Finally, she let out a breath.

"We should use the tunnels."

6

———

Jonah hesitated for only a moment before stepping out of the abandoned medical facility and into the closet at the end of the laboratory building corridor. His hands burned and his arms ached from the effort it took to move the blockade out of the way, but he had known that it was the only option. Jonah had been concerned that the Valdicians and the hybrid army would use the hole in the main corridor of the laboratory building to come down into the basement to access the rest of them, or that they would recognize that they must be in the basement and use the door from the breeding facility to get to them. In the middle of the night, however, he heard loud pounding sounds coming from the stairwell. When they went silent, he climbed the stairs to find that the hole in the wall had been repaired. Downstairs, the door to the facility that Rilex had destroyed had also been repaired and he was unable to open it.

The idea of the Valdicians being so close to him and to the wounded and the women that he had tasked himself with protecting was unnerving. He didn't understand why they would repair the door to the facility without coming up into the basement after them, unless they didn't realize that when Pyra and the rest had left and gotten onto the ship that there had been some left behind. Whether they knew that there were more in the basement or not, he understood why they would go to the effort of repairing the hole in the wall in the middle of the night. The last several days it seemed that the laboratory building had been closed, but now he could hear the faint sound of footsteps overhead, which meant that it was open again. They wouldn't want any of the people who worked inside the building during the day to see the damage and possibly venture down the forgotten stairwell to uncover the facility. It made Jonah wonder what they had done about the damage to the main office and the electrical locking system, or if they would simply allow those working in the building to believe that there had been an intrusion of some kind.

He suddenly wondered about the staff that was meant to take care of the building, cleaning it during the night or acting as security. It occurred to him that Ryan could have influenced those positions as well, ensuring that the people who took those responsibilities would know what he was doing and to protect him. The thought sent a chill down Jonah's spine. What this man was doing was more far-reaching than they even imagined, which made him wonder how much more Ryan was doing that they hadn't even yet considered.

The repaired wall in the main corridor had left his only access point to the rest of the building the closet that Eden had led them to and it had taken Jonah quite some time to remove the barrier that they had built against the door at the bottom of those stairs. Some of the pieces he had simply sent crashing to the ground because they were too large to lift away, and after each he would pause and listen, waiting for any sign that someone had heard and was coming to find out what had happened. When he finally got through the barrier, he traveled through the door and up the stairs into the closet, briefly concealing himself behind one of the pieces of equipment before stepping through the door into the hallway.

It was silent and shadowy when he emerged onto the laboratory floor. The newer section of the builder smelled fresher and cleaner than the basement and he thought of the extensive repairs, improvements, and renovations that must have been made to the building to preserve its new appearance and to keep it relevant to the blinding speed with which science and technology developed within these laboratories.

Jonah didn't know what time it was or even the part of the day. It seemed by his sleep patterns and the atmosphere of the light throughout the building that it was very early in the morning, but he wasn't sure. He hadn't had access to a clock while he was in the basement, and because of the travel, the battle, and staying awake to care for the wounded and the women who were still in the basement, he knew it was entirely possible that he had inadvertently reversed his internal clock and that it was actually the evening hours rather than the beginning of the day. Either way, he didn't see a sign of anyone else in the building and resolved to continue on. He turned and adjusted the equipment inside the closet to conceal the entryway to the stairwell. It was his only option for getting down into the basement again and he didn't want to risk coming back to it sealed back up by the mysterious cloaked team that seemed to hover around Ryan.

He walked quickly toward Ryan's laboratory and grasped

the handle to the door. He pressed down on it, but it stayed stiff. The lock had been replaced and Jonah felt his heart sink. He needed to get back into the lab, and if this door was locked again, that meant that the back entrance was likely locked again as well. He didn't know what to do. Stepping back, he looked at the door carefully, hoping that he would notice some area of vulnerability that he could use to get back into the lab.

"I think that I might be able to help you."

The soft, cautious voice startled Jonah and he took a step away from the door, turning defensively toward the words. His hand had gone instinctively to the weapon at his hip, and he saw the woman coming toward him in the hallway take a step back when she saw him. Jonah dropped his hand and reached out toward her to reassure her.

"I'm sorry," he said. "You startled me. I didn't realize that there was anyone else here."

The woman shook her head.

"It's alright," she said. "I'm sorry, too. I didn't mean to just sneak up on you like that."

"What are you doing here?" Jonah asked.

He didn't mean to sound so aggressive, but he felt on edge and suspicious of everything that he encountered when he was outside of the basement. Though she had been inhabiting nearly his every thought since the first time that he saw her, actually seeing her again had thrown him off and he was unsure of how he should react to her. The woman held up an access chip.

"I got here early for work. I thought I heard a door close and I came up here. It looks like you're having trouble getting into the lab. Maybe I can help you."

She hesitated and Jonah nodded.

"Thank you."

The woman stepped in front of him and touched her access chip to the fixed keypad by the door. There was a low click and she turned the handle, pushing the door open.

"Did you forget your access chip?" she asked casually, glancing to her side to look at him.

Jonah stuttered for a moment.

"I, umm..."

"You know, it was so strange," she said, stepping into the lab. "The other day when I was here all the locks throughout the building had been compromised, but then it seemed like overnight they were repaired. Did you hear anything about that?"

"That is strange," Jonah replied, glossing over her question as he stepped into the lab and closed the door behind himself. "I guess it's good that they got repaired, though. Did you, um, need to get your access chip reprogrammed for the new locks?"

He knew that he sounded awkward, but he realized that if the locks had been replaced he wouldn't be able to come back once she left. She turned around to look at him and he couldn't decipher the expression on her face. It was as if she was at once as suspicious as he was, but also hopeful.

"Are you here in Ryan's place?" she asked.

There was a hint of nervousness in her voice that made it go higher even as she was trying to sound conversational. The sound immediately created a knot in Jonah's stomach. He had heard Eden talk about Ryan and the uncomfortable, unethical treatment that she had faced from the man. Just like Eden, this woman was considerably younger than Ryan and it wasn't beyond his notice that she was beautiful even beyond the lab coat and hair tied up in a messy knot on the top of her head. He wondered if she had gone through the same types of things that Eden had, and the thought of it made him feel sick. He shook his head.

"No," he said. "Not in his place, no."

She nodded, a look of relief crossing her face.

"Do you know what happened to him? Nobody seems to have seen or heard from him in a while."

Jonah didn't know how to respond. He felt like he was in a fragile, vulnerable place. He didn't want to tip himself into a never-ending spiral of lies that he might not be able to keep up with, and that might threaten everything that he was trying to accomplish. At the same time, he couldn't figure out a way that he would be able to even begin to explain to her what was really happening and why he was there.

"He must have had something that he needed to do away from the University," Jonah said, hoping that that was enough for her and that she wouldn't pry any further. As soon as he said it, though, something occurred to him, and he turned back to her. "How do you have access to his lab?" he asked. "I thought that this lab was restricted."

"But you have access to it," she said, her tone saying that she wouldn't tell him anything if he didn't offer the same information in return. They stared at each other for a few seconds before she extended her hand to him. "My name is Aubrey."

He took her hand and shook it.

"I'm Jonah," he said.

She looked at him through slightly narrowed eyes and he got the distinct feeling that he was being scrutinized. Their hands fell away from each other and he immediately felt the regret of no longer feeling her skin against his.

"I work in the main laboratory downstairs," she told him. "I've done some special assignments in cooperation with Ryan and his lab assistants. When he had them, of course."

"When he had them?" Jonah asked, trying not to let his voice suggest that he knew anything about it.

"His female assistants never lasted very long. Eden was the one who was with him the longest, but you must know how that turned out."

"I must?" he asked, crossing to the cabinets at the far end of the room and opening one of them.

He didn't know how long he was going to be able to be in the lab and he needed to make the most of whatever time that he had in case he wasn't able to get back in.

"Well, yeah," Aubrey said. "She left more than a year ago. Supposedly she had some assignment and just decided never to come back. That must be why they chose you. To replace her, right? They wouldn't dare give him another woman after all of the rumors."

"Rumors?"

He closed the first cabinet and started going through the next. He didn't want to sound as though he were disinterested in what she was saying or she might stop talking and force him to leave. At the same time, he was too focused on going through each of the items in the cabinets in hopes of finding something relevant to his mission to really invest in the conversation.

"The reason that the women didn't last long? I know for one that they weren't just rumors. Of course, the powers that be in the University don't care enough to actually listen to what any of us had to say. Ryan is far to well-respected in the scientific community and his family has too much of a tie to the University for them to question him or his integrity unless someone had real evidence to show. He's too smart for that, though. He'd never do anything that could be documented or actually brought up in front of the dean or the department heads. He hasn't had an official assistant since Eden left, but there has to be somebody helping him."

The words stopped Jonah's exploration of the third cabinet and he turned to look at Aubrey. She was standing beside one of the brushed metal tables in the center of the room, one of the tables that Jonah remembered lying on its side, splattered with blood, when they came back to this lab after he, Oro, Azrael, and Ariella arrived from Penthos. She was looking down at her lab coat, her fingers playing idly with the buttons. She glanced up at him when he didn't respond. He could see the intensity of their blue shade and felt his stomach flutter even as his mind started to churn with what she had said.

"Somebody helping him?" Jonah asked. "Why would you say that?"

Aubrey shrugged and pushed away from the table.

"He's still working here, isn't he? He has to be doing something. The types of projects that he works on can't be done by just one person."

Jonah felt his heartbeat increase slightly. What could she have meant by that? Did she know something about the breeding facility or the hybrid experiments? Was there any way that she could be involved, putting him in serious danger as he stood there sifting through the contents of the laboratory cabinets? He tried to subtly lean forward so that he could examine her face more closely, looking for any indication that she might be one of the hybrids that Ryan had created in the gruesome labs hidden only a few floors beneath their feet. Unlike the hybrids that he had encountered when Pyra and the others freed those being tortured in the facility, Aubrey showed no signs that she was anything but completely human, but he didn't know if that should reassure him or make him worry even more.

"What types of projects?" he asked.

Aubrey gave a short laugh.

"Wow. He really does keep things secretive, doesn't he? Don't worry. I don't know any of the specifics of his work. I just know that his projects are always considered high priority and a huge percentage of the grant money that comes into the department is funneled right to him. Even though I haven't personally seen any finished results from any of these projects, some of the progress reports that he's presented have been impressive. I just can't see him being able to take on that much work without an assistant. At least if he's anything like any of the other scientists. It seems like they are heavily motivated while they are still one of dozens working on University-sponsored research projects down in the main lab. They'll take on huge portions of work and be in the lab day and night to get the work done. The minute that they get their own lab and are able to design their projects, though, suddenly they are just too burdened and fragile to do anything on their own and need the department to give them funding to pay for assistants to do the grunt work for them. Besides, look at this place. It's immaculate. Do you really think that there is any leading scientist in this place who would have enough time in his schedule to keep his lab so clean on his own? Especially with all of the equipment that he designs and builds himself."

She gestured at the corner of the room and Jonah turned to look at the strange tube embedded in the juncture of the walls. The curved glass that had been shattered when Jonah first saw the lab was repaired just like the rest of the damage had been. It was as if Pyra, Eden, and the rest had never confronted Ryan there. As if they had never released Aegeus from his chains. Everything had been wiped clean and it had accomplished exactly what was intended, removing any sense of suspicion or even realization that anything had changed from those who might find their way into the room.

"Um..." Jonah started.

Aubrey laughed again and Jonah looked at her sharply, startled by the sudden sound.

"Listen to me," she said. "I'm standing here explaining Ryan to you. I'm sorry. Anyway, I'm just glad that they found an assistant for him that he won't be able to push away with ick-factor." She paused and looked down at her feet for a few seconds. "Well. I guess I should be getting back to my lab. The main lab." She sighed. "One day I'll have my own lab."

It sounded like she was trying to find a way to stall, to stay in the room with him for longer. Jonah gave as much of a smile as he could and she started toward the door. He felt a sense of urgency rise up inside him and he took a step toward her.

"Wait," he said.

Aubrey turned around to look at him.

"Yes?"

Jonah took another cautious step, trying to formulate what he was going to say.

"Can I trust you?" he asked.

Aubrey's head tilted slightly.

"Should you be able to?" she asked.

"I don't know," Jonah said, "but I really need to right now."

"Why?"

"I'm not Ryan's assistant. I don't even work with him. But I need to be able to get back in the lab. Can I use your access chip?"

"Why do you need to be able to get in the lab?" she asked.

Jonah opened his mouth and closed it, unsure of what he should tell her.

"I can't say right now," he finally managed. "But I need you to trust me."

"Am I supposed to trust you, or are you supposed to trust me?" she asked.

"Both," he said. "Look, I know that this sounds ridiculous and that you could get in a lot of trouble for helping me. I need you to trust that I wouldn't ask you to do this if it wasn't critically important. There are literally lives hanging in the balance. Please."

Aubrey looked at him for a few long seconds and then stepped forward, holding the access chip out to him. Jonah smiled and let out a relieved rush of air. He reached out and took the chip from her palm, allowing his hand to rest over hers for a moment longer than it needed to. Their eyes met and he saw hers darken slightly. She licked her bottom lip and then pulled her hand away, looking away as if embarrassed by her subtle reaction to him.

"I've got to go," she murmured.

"Thank you," Jonah said as she stepped out of the door, waving at him as she disappeared.

Jonah looked down at the chip in his palm and then laughed, tossing it up in the air and catching it as it came down. This access chip was how he was going to be able to do what he needed to do undetected. With this chip, he could move throughout Ryan's laboratories whenever he pleased. He tucked it into his pocket and went back to his exploration of the cabinets. He hadn't found anything yet, but now he knew that he could take his time.

Two hours later he gathered every piece of paper that he

had found in his examination of the lab and went to the door to the lab. He opened it carefully and peered out into the corridor. It was empty and quiet, giving him the opportunity to slip out and rush toward the closet. When he was back in the basement, he added the new items that he had found to the collection of evidence that he already had and sat on the floor as he had for the majority of the time that he had spent since the rest of the group had left for Penthos. The new discoveries meant nothing to him, but he kept staring at them, letting the lists and rows of numbers and letters, calculations, and notations roll through his mind in hopes that eventually something would make sense to him.

The day passed slowly as he went to check on the wounded and the women, prepared meals for them, and helped apply new ointment on the worst of the injuries, then returned to his room and continued to stare at the papers and the files that were gradually filling the floor. Finally, the exhaustion dragged on his eyelids and he couldn't stay awake any longer. He lay down beside his collection of information, draped a blanket over himself, and fell into a deep, dreamless sleep.

The next morning Jonah crept out of the closet into the corridor and paused again to listen for any sign that there was anyone else on the floor. Hearing only the quiet, almost imperceptible whir of some internal system of the building, he closed the closet door and rushed straight for the lab. Using the access chip that Aubrey had given him, he entered the lab and returned to the same examination that he had done the day before. Though he felt that he had gone over it as carefully as he could the day before, he was compelled to go over it again, to dig deeper and find anything that may be hidden.

Jonah was crouched on the floor peering into another of the cabinets when he heard the click of the lock behind him. His body tightened anxiously and his eyes shot to the side to look at his bag and the weapon that he had placed on top of it. He hadn't expected that he would have to use it, but he realized now that that had been foolish of him. There had to still be hybrids and Valdicians somewhere, and if they had caught any wind that there were still members of the group in the building, they would be looking for them. He scrambled toward the bag and wrapped his hand around the handle of the weapon, crouching behind one of the tables to watch as the door opened. A pair of high heels stepped into the room and he stood sharply, bringing the weapon up to his side.

Aubrey took a startled step back, nearly going back into the hallway. Jonah placed his weapon on the table and reached out a hand to her.

"I'm sorry," he said. "You startled me."

"Is that going to be our traditional greeting every time that we see each other?" Aubrey asked, resting her hand over her heart for a second as she stepped the rest of the way into the laboratory and closed the door behind her.

"I'm sorry," Jonah repeated. "I thought that you might be..."

His voice trailed off as he realized what he was about to say. She took a few steps closer to him.

"That I might be what?" she asked. "What is it that you are so afraid of?"

"I'm not afraid," he insisted.

Aubrey looked at him incredulously.

"You've tried to pull a blade on me twice," she said.

Jonah shook his head and looked down at his hands pressed to the table in front of him and drew in a breath. He knew that it was unrealistic that he would be able to continue on with his explorations of the lab and the medical facility using this woman's access chip and having her know that he was there without soon giving her at least some form of understanding of what was happening.

"I didn't mean to pull it on you," he said.

"No," she said. "You meant to pull it on these mysterious people that might be threatening lives."

"Not might," Jonah said insistently.

"Then tell me what's going on." When Jonah hesitated, Aubrey walked closer to him and looked at him unflinchingly in the eye. "If there are people in danger and it has something to do with the University, you need to tell me."

Jonah drew in a breath.

"What do you know about Ryan's work? Anything. Anything that you might know about his research or the projects he's been working on."

Aubrey shook her head.

"I really don't know much," she admitted. "To be honest, my access chip shouldn't even open the doors to his laboratory. He has special clearance even beyond the other scientists and only the most authorized of personnel have access. When they repaired the broken locks, though, they reprogrammed my chip to allow access. When I first saw you, I was coming here to see if I could find out anything about where Ryan went."

Jonah was surprised at the revelation, but it was also reassured him in a way. If she had been sneaking into the lab, that meant that she wasn't one of the creatures that Ryan had weaponized or one who was under his control.

"Why?" Jonah asked. She didn't answer and he stared

more deeply into her eyes. "You know something," he said. "There's something about Ryan or the work that he's been doing that has concerned you enough that you thought to come up here and look through his lab. What is it?"

Aubrey hesitated. She looked uncomfortable and unsure, as if she regretted that she had said anything. After several seconds, her shoulders lowered as if she had resigned herself to the reality that they had both made themselves vulnerable to each other and that she might as well keep going.

"The official word of the University is that Eden left on her own, but I just can't shake the feeling that they either aren't telling the full truth, or they don't really know what happened to her. And there are other women who have just disappeared in the last few years, and the only connection any of them had is either that they were coming to the University or knowing someone that was in the University. They never found any trace of them or any indication that something happened to them. That is just far too coincidental to me."

Jonah nodded. His heart was pounding in his chest and he felt like he could hear the adrenaline rushing through his veins. He felt a connection to Aubrey that he hadn't expected to feel with anyone, and now that he heard her voicing her suspicions, the appeal only got stronger. He leaned closer to her and touched his chest, wanting to both keep her attention focused on him and show his sincerity.

"I know what happened to them," he said. "I know Eden and I think I know about the women who disappeared, at least some of them."

Aubrey looked taken aback, but she didn't step away. She searched his face as if waiting for him to laugh, and when he didn't, her eyes widened. Not wanting to risk her leaving without knowing what he needed to, Jonah surged ahead, telling her about Eden, the Denynso, and the time that they had spent on Earth. He withheld the details about himself, thinking that that would be simply too much for her in that moment, and still unsure of how he himself wanted to handle his arrival back on Earth. For now, he wanted to stay anonymous and not have the pressure or responsibility of his true identity on him. He needed to conceal who he really was and why he had remained on Earth while most of the others went to Penthos so that he could protect himself and the integrity of what he was trying to do.

He felt like he had been talking forever, pouring himself out to her until the final words fell from his lips and he felt drained. When he finished, Aubrey was leaning on her elbows on the table, her hands covering her mouth as she rested her chin in her palms. Her eyes were wide and searching, and Jonah expected her to run out of the lab. Instead, she stood slowly and started unbuttoning her lab coat.

"What are you doing?" he asked.

"You are going to need help," she said. "So, I'm going to help you."

I t was late in the evening when Aubrey checked her phone and saw the time. She reluctantly turned toward Jonah, not wanting to leave his side.

"I should be getting home," she said. "I need to be up early in the morning for work."

"I know," Jonah said with a hint of a laugh in his voice.

Their eyes met and she felt the same heat swell up between them as she had at several points throughout the day. She could feel the draw toward him and each time that he looked at her she thought that she saw a flicker of the same attraction in his eyes. It made her not want to leave his side and the privacy of the lab that they had been sharing as he told her more about what Ryan had done and they worked together to find out as much as they could about what he had been doing in that room as they could. She wanted to stay there with him and keep riding the tingling feeling of the attraction growing, but she knew that she couldn't. She needed to get home and sleep so that she could return to her own lab the next day before her coworkers thought that she might have gone missing like the other women.

"I'll try to come up here during lunch and any lulls that we might have."

Jonah nodded.

"I hope you do."

Aubrey felt a tremble through her belly, but she reached for her keys and started for the door to the lab. Her hand had just rested on the handle when she felt Jonah wrap his hand around her wrist. He spun her around, pulling her up against him so that she felt her body crush against his and the warmth of his breath touch her face. The keys fell from her hand and skittered across the polished floor, but she was focused on the feeling of Jonah's body against hers and the velvety darkness of his eyes as he stared into hers with incredible intensity. Suddenly his mouth crashed down on hers, and he held her body tightly against him and kissed her with ferocity.

The kiss took Aubrey completely by surprise and for a moment she barely knew what was happening. Jonah's hands pressed against her back and he pulled her even closer. She could feel the pounding of his heart against her chest as if it was reaching toward her with every beat. Her eyes fluttered closed and she gave herself over to the kiss, reaching up to rest her hands on the back of his neck to make herself feel steadier. Aubrey felt Jonah's tongue teasing at her lips and she parted them, welcoming it into her mouth. His mouth was hot and strong, his taste both comforting and invigorating. She had craved his touch and taste since the moment that she saw him, and had thought that it was never going to be in her reach. Now that he was this close to her, offering her everything that she had wanted, Aubrey was going to give herself to it completely.

Jonah's strong arms wrapped around her and she felt him sweep her up off of the ground. As he lifted her, her shoes dropped to the floor. It was only her shoes, but it seemed like a suggestion, a promise of what was to come, and she felt a shiver move through her. Still supporting her with one arm, Jonah slid one hand down the back of her thigh to guide it up around his hips. Aubrey complied, mirroring the movement with her other leg so that she was wrapped fully around him. They continued to kiss almost frantically as Jonah carried her back across the lab toward one of the tables. She felt as though he were making up for everything that he had lost and showing his gratitude for the years that he had suffered but that brought him to her.

Aubrey felt him lower her onto the table and realized that he had reached around to spread her lab coat across it so that she didn't touch the cold metal. He positioned her so that she sat at the edge and took his mouth away from hers. He brought his hands to the front of her blouse and pulled it out of the hem of her skirt, tearing away at the fabric until the buttons popped and she felt the cool air of the lab brush against her skin. She heard Jonah groan low in his throat as her lavender lace bra came into view. Her body was fuller, softer than she wanted it to be and she was often self-conscious about it, but the way that Jonah looked at her took away the negative emotions and made her feel lush and beautiful. The way his eyes roved over her and the depth of his breath made it obvious that he appreciated everything that he was seeing, and she was eager to allow him more. She wanted him to explore her fully and to allow her to explore him in return.

She slid off of the table and reached behind her hips to ease the zipper of her skirt down, rolling her hips as she guided the fabric down. Jonah pushed the blouse back off of her shoulders as she let the skirt fall away. Giving her another long look, he reached up and took the clip out of her hair, allowing the long strands to tumble free around her shoulders. There was a pause and Aubrey worried for a moment that he was going to stop. She was terrified that the reality was going to hit him and that he was going to walk away from her, leaving her cold and alone in the lab. Instead, Jonah took her by her hips and picked her up, placing her back on the edge of the table and easing her thighs apart so that he could step in between them.

Aubrey brought her fingers to his belt buckle and released it as he pulled the hem of his shirt out of his waistband and started to pull it up over his head. As she moved her hands away from his now-open belt, he pulled the shirt completely off and toss it aside. Jonah cupped the back of her head with one hand and captured her mouth again, kissing her as if he couldn't stand even a few moments without the taste of her in his mouth or the feel of her skin beneath his hands. She continued to undress him as he kissed her, losing herself in the rush of undying need that seemed to surge higher with every passing beat of her heart. Jonah's free hand slipped around her waist and up her back. It touched her bra and she felt him slide it around to cup her breast, then trace the lower swell, taking his time as if to appreciate every second of touching her. When he was finished, he brought his hand around to her back again, coming to the hook of her bra and flicking it open. The lace fell away from her breasts and he peeled it away slowly, revealing her to himself reverently. Cool air touched her nipples and she pressed them toward him in search of his touch.

Jonah rested his hand to the center of her chest and gently pressed her back. He applied light pressure, sliding his hand down between her breasts and onto her stomach. Aubrey arched in response to the touch and her belly trembled with the presence of his hand. Suddenly she felt Jonah's mouth close down over one of her taut nipples. The feeling of his warm mouth suckling her, his tongue sliding around her nipple and each suck drawing the flesh deeper, was so enrapturing that she barely registered his hands coming to the waistband of her the lacy panties that matched her bra and peeling them away. When she became aware of the tug around her thighs, she lifted one leg higher and allowed Jonah to slip that leg of her panties off of her foot, then repeated the process on the other side until she was completely bare beneath him.

After a few more moments of worship, his mouth left Aubrey's breast as Jonah dropped to his knees beside the table. He pushed her thighs apart and Aubrey felt his tongue delve into her folds. She cried out in surprise as the tip of his tongue flicked across her clit. She hadn't expected him to be as confident and forward, and every new touch was enthralling. Her hips lifted up off of the table as she instinctively strained toward the delectable sensation, but Jonah's hand came up to press down on her lower belly, holding her down so that he could continue with his delicious torment. Aubrey's head tilted back and her mouth fell open but no sound came out. All she could do was reach down to grip his thick hair and roll her hips luxuriously against his mouth.

She felt like she was spiraling toward oblivion but instead of letting her tumble over the edge, Jonah gave a final long lick and climbed to his feet. Aubrey lifted her head in time to see him drop his pants to the floor and kick them aside. She drank in the intoxicating sight of his chiseled body, thankful for every moment of work that had gone into crafting his incredible beauty. As quickly and urgently as he had moved up until this moment, now he seemed to have slowed and became meticulous with each movement. He stood straight in front of her and ran his hands slowly from her hips down her thighs as he admired her.

Aubrey felt vulnerable and on display, but in a way that made her feel desired and beautiful. Jonah leaned over her, his chest brushing over her tight nipples and sending a thrill of sensation down through her body until it settled between her legs. His mouth met hers and she felt the slick head of his thick, hard erection nudge against her core. Jonah rocked his hips a few times to tease her sensitive peak, and then settled at her opening. She opened her eyes and met his. She wanted him to see the sincerity and sureness in her gaze as she drew her knees back to open herself to him more. The movement caused him to dip inside her just slightly and they both drew in sharp breaths.

Jonah touched the side of her face and traced his fingers along the curve of her jaw, then along her lips. She kissed his fingertips and he cupped his hand around her face so that the heel of his hand settled against her cheek and his fingers buried in her hair. He let out a breath and she felt him rock his hips forward, sinking into her. Aubrey had never felt so perfectly filled. It was as though her body had been designed for Jonah and she had been waiting her entire life to cradle him this way. The tightness of her body made it so that he couldn't move as deep within her as she would have wanted him to, and she focused on drawing in and releasing breaths to quiet and calm her body so that it could accept him more. He paused for just a moment as her walls relaxed around him and she felt him slide deeper. Her body continued to ease until his hips settled against hers, and she felt his hips starting to move. They rolled just as hers had against his mouth as he had nurtured and coaxed her with his tongue, stroking him deeply within her. She wrapped her arms around his back and gripped him tightly to her, closing her legs around his hips to keep them as closely together as she could manage.

Now that she fully enveloped him, Jonah thrust into her relentlessly, his speed and intensity increasing until his grunts and groans filled the space. She couldn't help but let small whimpers slip past her lips with every hard stroke, and soon her mouth fell open and she released a loud, gasping cry. Suddenly she felt him press as deeply inside her as he could and his deliciously engorged cock pulsed. Aubrey opened her eyes and looked into his face. His eyes were squeezed shut as he bit down on his lip as if to hold back a roar of pleasure. The thought of him spilling into her sent Aubrey tumbling headlong into her own climax and she cried out, pulling him closer to her while savoring the feeling of her body's spasms meeting each of his pulses and drawing him ever deeper inside of her.

Aubrey clung to him as she rode the final waves of her orgasm and then felt the rush slowly draining from her body. As the energy and adrenaline that she had been feeling since the moment that he first touched her started to slip away, it felt as though clarity was returning to her mind. What had she done? She couldn't believe that she had given into her urges like that. She barely knew this man, and even though she had been attracted to him since the first moment that she laid eyes on him in the lab, the reality of his situation made it so that allowing herself to lose herself in her hormones was not only utterly inappropriate, but potentially dangerous. She couldn't do this. She couldn't even pretend to entertain the idea that he would be around for a moment longer than it would take him to figure out what was going on and to arrange to reunite with the rest of the crew. And even if he would...would she want him to? There was too much at stake. For Earth. For the women. For Uoria and its inhabitants. For her. She didn't know if she had it in her to face those kinds of emotions again. Not now. Not yet. Maybe not ever.

She felt Jonah trying to guide her back into his arms as she started to pull away from him, but she shook her head and pushed his hands away from her.

"I'm sorry," she said. "I need to go."

"What?" Jonah asked, stepping reluctantly out of her way as she slid down off of the side of the table and started gathering her clothes. "Where are you going?"

Aubrey wriggled into her skirt as fast as she could and then slipped back into her blouse.

"I shouldn't have..." she stumbled. "This was...." She remembered that the buttons on the front of her blouse had been torn off in their frantic desire for each other, and she reached for her lab coat. "I shouldn't have let this happen." She slipped it on and started buttoning it up to conceal her. "I'm sorry."

Jonah reached for her and grabbed her wrist. She pulled out of his hand and shook her head.

"What's wrong?" Jonah asked. "What happened?"

Aubrey finished buttoning the coat and reached down to scoop her heels and keys up off of the floor. She wanted to get away from him as quickly as she could and didn't want the shoes to slow her down. Her eyes stung as she turned away from Jonah and ran out of the lab, not allowing herself to even glance back over her shoulder at him. She knew that she would never be able to see him again and she didn't want the last moment that she saw him to be with the look of hurt and confusion that would correspond with what she heard in his voice. The door to the lab slamming behind her was deafening as she ran down the corridor, forcing herself to get out of the building before she let the tears fall.

8

than held his torch higher above his head to cast more of the light through the buildings of the kingdom. He swept it back and forth, trying to illuminate as much space as possible. There was a sense of fear in his chest, but he was doing everything that he could to suppress it. He had gone through this much to get back here, he had to keep himself as strong and under control as possible. The further that he walked, though, the more that the fear was building within him.

"Ellora?" he called out in an elevated whisper.

He didn't want to shout and disrupt those who he knew were sleeping in their homes, but he also felt like just walking around the kingdom wasn't enough to look for Ellora. He hadn't seen her since she had brought the weapons up from the war room to her kitchen and then rushed out of the house. Too much time had passed and he was starting to worry about her. She had gone into a frenzy and didn't seem to be thinking clearly when she was gathering the weapons, and he was afraid that that had put her in danger. With her mindset where it was when she found out that Aegeus was still alive and started preparing for the return trip to Penthos, she could have been capable of doing anything.

Having covered all of the main village of the kingdom and not finding Ellora, he started back toward Ellora's house. Maybe he had simply missed her. Maybe she had gone for a walk to work through the thoughts that she had to be facing with all of the new information that was coursing through her brain and then decided to go back to her home to relax for the evening. It was the time of night when she would usually sit down with a cup of coffee and read through one of her favorite books that she kept tucked on the shelf beside her chair in the main parlor of her home. There had been many nights that he had visited her at this time, wanting to sit in the same room with her just so that she would know that she was not alone. She had never asked him to be there or even commented that it helped her, but he could see the look of appreciation in her eyes each time that he walked into the house and then the hesitation when it was time for him to leave.

Athan arrived back at Ellora's house and felt his stomach sink as he saw that there were no lights burning in the windows and no sound coming from inside. He tried the front door and found that it was locked. Walking around the back of the house, he tried the door that she had used earlier and easily opened it. Inside, the home was still and quiet. He held his torch up and let the light fall throughout the kitchen. Immediately the illumination fell across the pile of weapons that she had made on the table and Athan's heart sank. He knew that she was gathering those weapons to bring them to the warriors, the Mikana army, and Creia so that they could learn how to use them and then put them on the ship for the return to Penthos. If she had returned home since leaving, she would have brought those weapons to them, or had one of them come to her home to get them. There was no reason for them to be still be sitting there in the kitchen.

"Ellora?" he called into the house.

Even though he knew that it was futile to call for her, he couldn't help but give it at least one chance. It was possible that she had come home with the full intention of delivering the weapons or having one of the warriors or army come to get them, and then suffered some accident or injury that kept her from getting back into the kitchen. The war room was designed to protect the weapons and the plans that Aegeus had, and no one knew what he could have put in place there to ensure that they didn't fall into the wrong hands. She could have accidentally triggered a defensive system or even fallen victim to one of the weapons that were kept there, and was waiting for someone to find her.

Still calling for her every few steps, Athan explored the rest of the house. He ventured into each of the rooms, examining every inch carefully to make sure that she wasn't there. Finally, he went down into the war room. As he descended the stairs, his eyes fell on the symbol for Aegeus's father and then Aegeus himself. They sent a chill along Athan's spine and his steps quickened. When he got down into the hidden room, he examined each wall and the floor carefully, hoping to detect any abnormalities that might have indicated a trap or defense system, but he didn't see anything. The weapon room was still standing open and he could see that there were still weapons hanging from the walls and sitting on the tables. He knew that she hadn't been there.

Athan rushed out of the house, determined to find her. He could hear voices coming from the opposite direction that he had initially walked, toward the official buildings on the other side of the kingdom from the homes. He ran toward them, at the same time cursing himself for not even considering going to the official buildings to look for Ellora and feeling a lift of hopefulness that this was where he was going to find her. Perhaps she had gone to talk to Rey to find out more about his plans for going to Penthos with the others, or to see Creia to talk to him about training his warriors with the Mikana weapons that were so different from those that the Denynso were accustomed to using. She could have even gone back to the infirmary to see Kyven and check on his condition.

Athan felt silly for the fear that he had been feeling as he made his way toward the voices. It had been ridiculous of him to think only of the section of the village that held the homes and not the other half. When he was looking for her, he hadn't even considered the other half. As soon as he had passed all of the homes and was nearing the orchards, he felt that he had looked everywhere possible. Now he was embarrassed and felt foolish for all of the thoughts that had been going through his mind.

As he approached the meeting hall, he saw a crowd had gathered and Creia and Rey were standing on the steps looking down at them. It seemed that the Denynso king had been giving some sort of speech but was finished now and was instead answering questions from those standing before him. Athan scanned the crowd, but didn't see Ellora's face. He paused for a moment to listen to the questions that were being asked.

"When do we leave?" someone asked.

"As soon as possible," Creia said. "There are still some preparations to be made. We are awaiting the arrival of further reinforcements from the human settlement and the bakers and nurturers are working as fast as they can to prepare food for the journey and for our time on Penthos. We'll work tirelessly until we are ready to leave."

"What will the battle be like?" another asked. "Is there any word about their fighting techniques or how we will organize attacks?"

"We know only a small amount about the fighting approach of the hybrids, but I am confident in the skill of our warriors, all of them from all species. Tomorrow we will begin training drills and continue to train until the preparations are finished. I will provide more information about what we know then."

"What about the weapons that Maxim told us to gather?" the man continued. "He was very specific that we get the weapons that his father had put aside for the war. Has anyone done that?"

Creia nodded.

"I am anticipating receiving those weapons soon," he said. "Ellora and Athan will remove them from the war room and ensure that they are in place for us."

Athan lifted his torch high into the air to catch Creia's attention.

"Creia," he called up to the Denynso king.

The crowd parted to allow Athan to get closer to the steps and he looked up at the Denynso king.

"Yes, Athan? Is everything alright?"

"Have you seen Ellora?" Athan asked.

"No," Creia said. "I haven't seen her since she left the infirmary earlier with you."

Athan nodded.

"Alright," he said. "Thank you."

He started away from the crowd, but Creia called out to him.

"Is something wrong?" he asked.

Athan looked back at him, forcing his expression to remain calm. He didn't want to alarm anyone while he still didn't know what was happening. There was nothing that they could do even if they knew. He shook his head.

"I was just gathering those weapons that you were talking about and I needed to ask her something, but she had stepped out. I'm just looking for her."

Creia nodded.

"If I see her, I will let her know that you are looking for her," he said.

"Thank you. I'm sure that I'll find her somewhere or we'll end up back at her house."

"Would you like me to come with you?"

"No, that's alright. You have planning and preparing to do on your own."

"Will you be ready first thing in the morning to begin training?" Creia asked.

Athan nodded once.

"I will."

He made his way back through the group and started toward the rest of the official buildings, forcing himself to keep his pace casual so that if they were watching him they wouldn't detect the nervousness that was starting to creep back into his mind. He reached the infirmary and stepped carefully inside, not wanting to disturb any of those who were resting and trying to heal. The interior of the building was dark except for small bioluminescent plants positioned along the walls to provide a faint glow that let him just see the outlines of the people in their beds.

Athan backed out of the infirmary and started for Rey's palace before remembering that he was with Creia at the meeting hall. He stood in the center of the courtyard in front of the infirmary and looked around helplessly. All of the fear and the negative thoughts that had melted away when he thought that he would find Ellora in the official buildings suddenly rushed back and he felt like he couldn't breathe. He thought of the ship that they had landed in the openness of the planet outside of the kingdom. Was it possible that she went there? Could her state of mind carried her out of the kingdom and toward the ship, determined that she was going to get to Penthos and Aegeus?

Athan rushed toward the nearest entrance to the kingdom. He saw a man standing beside it on guard, and his chest tightened. Though he hadn't been called up by them, he knew that he had offended the Order, that they knew he had revealed secrets and even given vehicles to the group so that they could travel across Uoria more easily. If the guard had instructions to bring him in, he could consider his life over. He sank back into the shadows and stared at the entrance, debating what he should do next. The guard was stoic, not moving as he protected the entrance in the way that he was commanded. Athan remembered his own long hours standing at the gate on the other side of the kingdom. He was guarding it the day that Maxim had come home with Ivy. That was the first time that he had truly betrayed the Order, and he felt that it was that decision that had taken the rumblings of the war and surged them into full force.

Remembering that moment and how deep he already was, he knew that he couldn't let his fear of the Order keep him from fulfilling his commitment to Maxim, to Kyven, to Ellora, and to Aegeus. Drawing in a breath, he pulled the hood of his cloak up over his head and ran with all of the speed that he could across the open area, past the guard, and through the entrance. He could hear the guard yelling after him, but it didn't matter. By now the Order knew that he was back in the kingdom. If they wanted to, they would come for him. And when that happened, he would handle it.

As he ran into the darkness, thoughts of the last battle that he had fought alongside Aegeus formed vibrantly in his mind. He could smell the damp ground of the battlefield and hear the battle cries of the armies as they approached each other. In his mind he saw Aegeus, walking ahead of him with the warriors at his side. He remembered deeply within him how he felt when Aegeus disappeared, and then when the battle ended and he still couldn't find a trace of his best friend. He thought he was dead. Rather than trying to understand what might have happened, he had simply resigned himself to Aegeus's death and steeled himself for having to tell Ellora. He had given up on him.

As soon as that thought crossed his mind, he knew where Ellora was. The ship had just come into view, but he turned back and ran toward the kingdom with new speed. What he needed to do would put him in extraordinary danger, but he had to do it. He couldn't give up on her. No matter how much danger he was facing, if she was where he thought that she was, it was nothing compared to what she could be enduring. He needed to get to her if she was going to have any chance of survival.

Circumventing the entrance that he had just used to get out of the kingdom, Athan ran along the edge of the stone wall toward the gate that he was guarding when Maxim and Ivy arrived what felt like a lifetime ago. He noticed another guard in place and continued past, not wanting to risk trying to pass a second guard so soon after the first. When he got around to the side of the kingdom, he gathered all of his strength and what felt like might be the last of the energy that he had within him, moved back several steps, and then ran toward the wall. He dug his foot against the stone and felt his body pause for a moment, pulled between falling back to the ground and allowing him to get up and over the top of the wall. Using his thoughts of Ellora and Aegeus to fuel him, he forced himself up and grasped the top of the wall, digging his fingers into the stones on the other side. He took a few breaths and then pulled himself up and over the top of the wall. Dropping down on the other side, he landed and took off running.

His fingers flew as he input the code into the keypad hidden in the stones of the wall and he stepped back to allow the section of ground to sink away, revealing the entrance to the network of underground tunnels that were the hidden lair of the Order.

9

———————

Maxim walked to the entrance to the compound for what felt like the thousandth time and peered out across the seemingly endless expanse of sand. The group from Earth should have been to him by now. He had been waiting for days and Azra had communicated with Elise to tell her that they would be arriving on the planet soon. He was getting more concerned about them as the minutes passed, giving him a helpless feeling that he hated. The papers that he had found in the Valdician office were still in the back of his mind, and the more he thought about them, the more the worry increased until he felt like his stomach was tied in knots. More than ever he wished that he and Ivy could communicate the way that the Denynso were able to. He knew that sending her back to Uoria was the right thing to do to keep her and their baby as safe as possible, but it also made him feel so disconnected from her. The distance was painful and he longed just to hear her voice. He had to remind himself, though, that he had made the decision that he had to and that it would be his efforts here that would ensure that he made it back to her.

Seeing no one on the horizon or any other indication that they might be coming, Maxim turned and headed back to the building that they had claimed as their headquarters. He stepped inside and looked to where Zyyr was leaned against the wall, still recovering from the injury to his leg. Lila came into the room carrying a plate of food and looked at Maxim earnestly.

"Did you see them?" she asked.

Maxim shook his head.

"Where's Elise?"

"She went to get water from the pump," Lila said.

"I need to talk to her."

"To me?"

Elise pushed the curtains that separated the two sections of the building out of the way and stepped into the room. She set a large pitcher of water on the table set against one wall and glanced at Maxim over her shoulder. Her voice sounded like she was hovering somewhere between fear and confidence, balancing both emotions that she had struggled with since they had been on the shuttle. He knew that she wanted so much to live up to what they had told her was now her place: the mate of a Denynso who was involved in this war whether she was prepared to be or not. At the same moment, though, she was still afraid, still unsure of the situation that had swept her up the instant that she fell in love with Azra.

"I need you to contact Azra," Maxim said. "It's been far too long. They should have been here by now."

"You shouldn't panic," Zyyr said. "They had no way of knowing where to find the compound. They could have landed far from here and still be on their way."

Maxim shook his head.

"No," Elise said. "The ships are extremely accurate when it comes to navigation. If they had a pilot that was at all familiar with how to use one of the newer ships, they would be able to see the compound from far enough that they could land within a fairly short distance. Not right beside the compound, but not so far that it would take hours to get here."

Maxim was surprised at the calm with which she was able to say this. He knew where Ivy was and still couldn't shake the worry about her no matter how determined he was to close himself off to thoughts about her. Azra was among the group that was missing on the dangerous and desolate planet, and she was still able to remain in control. She might never walk into battle, but he would never forget that she was fighting just as hard as they were.

"Have you heard from him?" Maxim asked.

"No," she said. "Not since he told me that they were preparing to leave."

"Can you try to reach out to him, please? We need to know where they are."

"They still haven't arrived?"

Maxim turned toward the curtain and saw Avery holding it back as he stood in the doorway. He immediately stepped back and looked toward Zyyr.

"No," Zyyr replied shortly.

Avery scoffed.

"Are you seriously going to keep going with this?" he asked.

"What?" Maxim asked.

The human pilot stepped the rest of the way into the room and held his hands out as if to encompass all of them.

"This," he said. "All of this. You can't honestly think that

I haven't noticed that you have been completely isolating me. I've been forced into my own little corner and totally left out of everything that's been happening. The instant that I walk in the room, you stop talking."

"It's just that you aren't a part of this. You are only here because of circumstances that were beyond your control."

"Don't give me that," Avery snapped aggressively. "You know as well as I do that I'm here by choice. I might have been trapped on that ship because of the Valdicians, but I chose to stay here with you. I offered my service to you and I demanded that the rest of my crew show you respect. I could have gone to Uoria with the others and then taken the ship and gone back to Earth with my crew if I didn't want to be a part of this."

Maxim felt the words hit him in the gut and knew that Avery was completely right. The pilot could have easily rejected them and refused to help them. He could have waited for Rain to repair the damaged navigation system and then taken over the ship again so that he could go back to Earth rather than letting her bring Kyven, Nylek, Ivy, and Rain back to Uoria along with the other two members of his crew. Instead, he had joined them without question and was willing to fight alongside them.

"I'm sorry. You're right," Maxim relented. "I shouldn't have treated you that way. We need all of the help that we can get, and if you are still willing to give it to us, I would appreciate anything that you could do."

He expected Avery to reject him, but instead, the man stepped forward and held out his hand. Maxim took it firmly, meeting the other man's eyes to show his sincerity.

"My opinion hasn't changed," Avery said. "I'm happy to do whatever I can for you. I might not fully understand what's happening, but I know enough to know that I can't abide by what's happened."

"I'm going to go outside and try to contact Azra," Elise said. "He's had his mind blocked, but I might be able to get through."

"Thank you, Elise," Maxim said. He turned back to Avery. "I need you to tell me everything that you know about Nyx 23 and this planet."

He drew in a breath, hoping that Avery could tell him something that would help him understand what was happening.

"To be honest, there isn't much to know. It was such a long time ago and there wasn't much documentation."

"The human women told us that the case was in history textbooks. It's something that is well-known," Maxim said.

"Known about, yes," Avery said. "But there simply weren't many details. When we learned about it in school, we learned the names of the crew and the official backstory for why they left Earth."

"And it mentioned Penthos?" Maxim asked.

"Yes," Avery said. "When the crew originally left, the existence of the planet was still contested. There were many official agencies and even academic groups that didn't believe that it was there. The disappearance of the Nyx 23 crew was the confirmation that it did actually exist. That was when the planet got its name."

"That's right," Maxim said, remembering when Rain and Ivy first confirmed the story in the meeting hall of the human settlement. "Rain told us that the mission was clandestine and that even people within her department didn't know about it. What did they teach you was the purpose of the trip?"

"No real details were ever given," Avery admitted. "The

official backstory is that they were a carefully selected elite group that was on a humanitarian exploration mission."

The explanation didn't sound exactly like what the women had told him, but it was close, reaffirming that the government and University had either covered up what had really happened to Nyx 23, or didn't know.

"How did they explain their disappearance?" Maxim asked. "Ivy said that you mentioned it when they found you in the panic room in the ship."

Avery nodded.

"Some of the newest technology in the ships that has just been released was developed because of what happened to Nyx 23, and there are security measures now because of them and because of the more recent hijackings. They said that the Nyx 23 crew went missing because the ship's security was breached and the navigation was compromised. Crews were sent to Penthos to find them, but didn't recover them or the ship."

"How would they know that the systems had been compromised?" Maxim asked.

"What do you mean?" Avery asked.

"You said that they developed new technology based on the fact that the Nyx 23 StarCity had their security and navigation systems compromised. Since they never recovered the ship and had no communication with the crew after they left Penthos, how could they possibly know that that's what happened?"

Avery shook his head.

"I don't know," he admitted. "We just accepted what they told us because it was a tragedy. You don't question tragedies."

Maxim could hear the regret in Avery's voice. It struck Maxim as incredibly strange that the official documentation of the disappearance of the crew would include information about a ship that had never been recovered and couldn't have transmitted any information back to Earth. There was no way that they would have known what had happened to the ship in order to change future technology or procedures.

"What can you tell me about the crew?" Maxim asked. "Did they explain how they were chosen or any special qualifications that they might have had?"

Even though he had spent time talking to Rain and some of the other humans from the settlement about the time before they left for the mission, Maxim didn't know if he was truly getting the full information from them. It was possible that Avery could tell him something about them that would give him a new perspective.

"It was a fairly large crew," Avery said. "Some of them weren't involved in the actual mission, but were chosen just for the purpose of keeping the StarCity itself operational."

"Rain never mentioned that," Maxim said. "I thought that everyone who was onboard was part of Nyx 23. She said that she was trained to fly the ship."

"She was," Avery confirmed. "She was given that credit. Many of the crewmembers performed duties throughout the StarCity, but at the time that was the largest ship in use. It was an experimental ship style that had never been utilized before and was never utilized again. It needed a larger support structure than could have been provided by just the crew that was chosen from the department."

"Do you know that there was a support crew, or are you just assuming that there was because of the complexity of the ship?" Maxim asked. "Were their names released?"

"No," Avery said. "Only the members of the official Nyx 23 mission were released. The ones who had official positions like Rain and Martin Roe were noted."

"Martin Roe?" Maxim asked. "I don't recognize that name."

"He was the pilot," Avery said.

Maxim shook his head.

"No," he said. "That's not right."

"What do you mean?" Avery asked. "He was one of the most skilled pilots in the transportation department of the University as well as being a part of the department that Nyx 23 came out of, which made him the obvious choice for the mission."

"No," Maxim said again, shaking his head and looking to Zyyr and Lila for backup. "That's not the name that Rain mentioned. She's told us about the pilot. She..." he stopped himself before he revealed the suicide of the pilot as the ship was crashing to the surface of Uoria, not wanting to dishonor the memory of a man that he had never known. "Rain mentioned his name many times. She called him Etan."

"Etan?" Avery asked. "I've never heard that name mentioned. All of the crew lists have Martin Roe as the pilot. It's even his picture in textbooks and at exhibits about the disappearance."

Maxim's thoughts were churning. Why would Rain not know the real name of the pilot? Or could it be that the official crew lists purposely listed the wrong man as the pilot for the Nyx 23 crew? And if that was the case, what had happened to Martin Roe?

10

—————

egeus avoided the reflective doors of the ship's
elevators as he made his way toward the infirmary. He knew that he still wasn't entirely himself
and he couldn't bear the thought of seeing the results of
Ryan's disgusting work again. The gruesome, skeletal
appearance of the Klimnu represented so much of the darkness and evil in his past. The first time that he saw himself
after being freed from the lab, the mutation was unbearable
to look at. He had become everything that he hated. From
the very beginning of his service to the Order and to the
army of the Mikana kingdom he had sworn that he would
give his life to protect the kingdom from their enemies, and
when he saw himself in the tiny mirror in the University
basement he was confronted with the stark reality that a
portion of his life had been stolen to force him to be the
very thing that he had railed against most severely.

He knew that he didn't look the same that he did when
he first looked in that mirror. He had undergone extensive,
painful treatments with Ciyrs in an effort to heal him, and
he knew that he had begun to improve. The transformation

back wasn't complete, however, and he didn't want to see how it had left him. Now, though, he needed to keep going. He couldn't stop.

Stepping into the infirmary, he saw Elianna checking on one of the wounded hybrids. She smiled down at him and nodded reassuringly before pulling a blanket up to cover his chest where she had just had her hands pressed to his skin. As if she could feel his eyes on her, she looked up at Aegeus. He gestured for her and she approached with a concerned expression on her face.

"Are you alright?" she asked in a low tone.

"Where is Ciyrs?" Aegeus asked.

"He's in our chamber," Elianna said, sounding somehow mournful.

"I need him," Aegeus said. "I want to continue my treatment."

Elianna nodded and guided him out of the infirmary. They walked in silence to the chamber and Elianna knocked before opening the door to step inside. He saw the Denynso healer sitting in a chair at the far side of the room, his eyes seemingly locked on something unseen in front of him.

"Ciyrs," Elianna said. "Aegeus is here to talk to you."

Ciyrs' head turned to them slowly and for a moment he looked at Aegeus as if he had never seen him.

"I want to continue with my treatment," Aegeus said, taking a cautious step toward Ciyrs.

"It's not time," Ciyrs said.

His voice sounded dry, almost as though he hadn't used it in years.

"I know," Aegeus said. "I know that you told me that I should wait for a while before another treatment, but I can't. I really need to finish this."

Ciyrs looked back to the space in front of him and shook his head.

"Elianna can do it for you," he said.

"Ciyrs, I don't have even a tenth of the power that you do," Elianna protested. "You can't do this."

He didn't respond and Aegeus saw Elianna stalk across the room to him and crouch down in front of her mate. She grabbed his hands and he adjusted his focus to look into her face.

"I can't, Elianna," he said. "I don't have it in me anymore."

"Of course, you do," she said. "I tried to tell you that that woman's death was not your fault. It has nothing to do with your ability to heal. Look at me. Look into my eyes. I'm alive because of you. Nobody else."

"So am I," Aegeus said, walking closer to them. "I wouldn't have survived much longer in that tank, and I know that I couldn't have lasted as a Klimnu. You saved me. I'm asking you to finish. Please. I haven't seen my sons since they were young children, but I know that I will know them as soon as I see them because they are in my heart. I need for them to be able to recognize me, too."

Ciyrs looked at Aegeus and drew in a breath.

"I don't know if you will ever be able to fully recover," he said. "When I healed Maxim, it was only a small part of him that had transformed, and it had taken hold for only a short time. You have been this way for so many years. I don't know if it is possible to totally change you back."

"Ryan did everything that he could to try to change me completely. I was tortured. I was subjected to violence and anger. I was fed blood and forced to witness atrocities that I will never be able to forget in an effort to allow the Klimnu toxin to take me over fully and steal who I was. I never let that happen. I fought with everything that I had to preserve what was within me, to always remember who I really am. I might have looked like I was fully mutated. He might have been able to take my body and manipulate it, but there was part of me that Ryan was never able to reach. I know that what is inside me will prevail. I will be restored. But I need your help."

Elianna looked at Aegeus and then at Ciyrs.

"Could we heal him together?" she asked.

"It could destroy him," the healer said. "Combining the forces of our healing capabilities would create an energy so intense that it could be too much for his body to withstand. He might not be able to recover from it."

"I'm willing to risk it," Aegeus said. "I will endure anything to have a chance at reclaiming my life."

"Please, Ciyrs," Elianna said. "This is what you were born to do. You are questioning yourself and your worth as a healer. Let this be your chance to prove that you are still what you have always been. There was nothing that you could do for that woman. You couldn't save her life. You can give Aegeus back his life."

Ciyrs turned to look at Aegeus and he drew in a breath, then nodded.

"This will be far more challenging on you than any of the treatments that you have already endured," he warned.

Aegeus nodded, feeling hope rising in his chest even through the sense of dread that came from thinking of the pain associated with the healing he had already gone through.

"I understand," he said. "I am willing to face it."

Ciyrs stood.

"If you're ready, we can get started."

"I'm ready."

Elianna led Aegeus out of the chamber toward one of the elevators and they rode up to the floor above. He knew that this was to isolate them so that no one would hear his cries of pain or come in on the healing. He didn't care what he had to experience. This was his only chance.

A few minutes after they chose one of the small rooms on this floor Ciyrs arrived carrying the kit that Aegeus knew carried the herbs, ointments, and bandages that he would use in his treatments. Elianna gestured toward the couch in the room, but Ciyrs shook his head.

"He should be on the floor," he said.

Elianna gathered cushions from the furniture in the room and placed them on the floor. Ciyrs spread out a sheet that he withdrew from his bag and gestured for Aegeus to lie down. Without hesitation, Aegeus removed his shirt and stretched out across the pallet that they had made for him. He rested his head on one of the cushions and closed his eyes. He could hear Ciyrs and Elianna talking to each other in hushed tones, but he didn't pay attention to what they were saying. His mind had wandered safely away from the room and what he was about to endure back to his home in Uoria, a place that he had thought of throughout his captivity, reaching out to it when he felt himself slipping away so that he could remain grounded, secure in the sights, sounds, and smells of the kingdom, and the touch of those he loved.

Ellora's face materialized in his mind. It had been so long since he had seen her, he knew that she must look different from the last memory that he had of her. That smile was from the morning when he had left for what would be the battle that would bring him to Earth and to Ryan's torturous facility. He knew that she was unhappy that he was leaving. She never liked when he was away, especially when she knew that he was going to fight, but he had been confident. The plan that he had built was broken down into its every detail in his mind and he knew that he would be back home in her arms soon, the steps put into action to bring a close to the corruption of the Order and restore peace to Uoria. Carrying this in his heart, he had tucked a finger beneath his wife's chin and asked her to smile for him. He couldn't leave without a smile and a kiss to bring into him so that he would always have it with him. That was what he carried in his heart now, that final smile as she waved at him from the door, the sound of their tiny sons playing innocently and peacefully inside drifting out to follow him as he crossed the kingdom to where the rest of the army waited.

It didn't matter that she would have changed. There was nothing, not even long years and stressful suffering, that would take the beauty from her face and the love that he had from her from within him. The youth might be gone, but she would still be his beloved Ellora, the most incredible woman he had ever known. He could only hope that she had not forgotten him and that when he saw her again, that she might still love him the way that he loved her.

Aegeus felt Ciyrs and Elianna come to either side of him and rest down on their knees. There was a moment's pause and he heard Elianna draw in a slightly shuddering breath. He knew that she was nervous and worried about the warning that Ciyrs had given. It didn't matter to Aegeus. The risk was by far worth the benefit that he would receive by finally being rid of the Klimnu toxin and being able to live his own life again.

"Are you ready, Aegeus?" Ciyrs asked.

Aegeus kept his eyes closed, but nodded. He focused on relaxing his body fully, knowing that the treatments and healing would flow through his body better and be more effective if his muscles weren't tensed. The smell of the herbs filled his nose and he focused on Ellora's face again. An instant later the pain hit him. It seared across his skin from either side and coursed through his body. He wanted to cry out, to thrash against what they were doing, but he didn't. He forced himself to remain calm and accept the treatment, telling himself that for every second of the pain that he endured, he was another second closer to being himself again.

After a few long seconds of them applying the herbs to his skin, Aegeus heard Ciyrs's voice.

"We're going to do the healing now, Aegeus," he said.

Aegeus opened his eyes, getting one more look at the world through the perspective of the Klimnu, then closed them again.

"I'm ready."

11

———

Samira wrapped her hand thankfully around the cup of coffee that she had dispensed from the machine in the wall and carried it over to the small table tucked against the curved window across the room. She settled onto the thickly cushioned stool on one side and took a long sip of the strong, hot drink, savoring its bitterness as it flowed down her throat and seemed to reinforce her instantly. Across the table Valerie was holding her own cup of coffee, but it remained undrunk as she stared out of the window. It was only darkness beyond, but there was an infinite feeling of the darkness that underscored the depth of space and the sheer distance that they had traveled.

"It's amazing, isn't it?" Samira asked.

Valerie jumped slightly as if she hadn't noticed her daughter come and sit across from her, but then looked at Samira and nodded.

"It really is. I still can't believe that I'm out here. I never would have imagined that I would leave Earth. Especially like this."

"How are you feeling about all of this?" Samira asked.

She was worried about her mother. Though she had seen her do things in the last few days that truly astounded her, she was concerned that eventually it would all catch up with her and Valerie wouldn't be able to handle it.

"About all of what?" Valerie asked.

She turned back to the window and Samira tilted her head at her. She couldn't tell if Valerie was genuinely asking her what she meant, or if she were trying to avoid the conversation, pushing aside negativity as she did so often before they left Earth. It had been one of her most trusted, and yet most horrifying, defense mechanisms. No matter how cruel her husband became or the hardships that she faced, Valerie would simply pretend that it wasn't happening. She could close herself off to it and let it wash over her, not reacting to it and not letting it change anything about her life, as if she could keep it from getting any worse or stop it from being truly real if she just kept going forward. Too many times Samira had seen the brutal results of her stepfather's treatment of her mother as Valerie continued to smile and talk to her as if she were blissfully happy. If she mentioned anything that she had seen, Valerie would look at her as if she had no idea what she was talking about and ask her what she meant. It had gotten more and more difficult for her to pretend in this way as the years progressed, but she kept trying. The more valiantly she tried to cover it, the sadder and more terrifying the situation became. It wouldn't be until Ero came, though, that she would finally be able to break free.

"I'm sorry that this is how this turned out," Samira said, trying to reach out to her mother through the defense mechanism that had become more familiar than her true personality. "I never meant for my wedding to turn into this."

"Into what?" Valerie asked. "An adventure?"

Samira gave a short laugh.

"That's hardly the word that I would use," she said. "I wanted my wedding to be such a beautiful time for both of us. I never thought that anything like this could happen. With the Valdicians invading the ceremony and all of us getting caught up in this war. I'm sorry that you are having to go through it. I never would have put you in this position if I had been able to prevent it."

"Samira," Valerie said, cutting her daughter off as she stumbled to find her next words. "After what I have been through, no war can scare me."

Her voice was even and calm, indicating none of the anxiety or sadness that Samira expected to hear. Instead of seeming fragile and weak, the way that Samira had come to know her mother to be, Valerie seemed more secure and confident in herself than she had been in longer than Samira could remember.

"Why did you stay?" Samira asked. "Why did you just keep dealing with...him?"

She hadn't intended on asking the question but it had tumbled out of her mouth before she could stop it. She started to apologize, but Valerie let out a sigh and gave the faintest hint of a smile.

"You can say his name, Samira," she said. "You don't have to give him that kind of power over you anymore."

It had been so long since Samira had even let the horrible man's name enter her mind and even longer since she had heard it touch her mother's lip. She didn't know if she was ready for it, but at the same time, she knew that Valerie was right. Refusing to utter his name was just another way that they had given over their control and their lives to him, and allowed him to oppress and torment them.

"Were you ever happy with…Randall?"

Her body and mind flinched when she said the name, but Valerie seemed totally unfazed, as if something were protecting her from the impact that those two syllables had once had on her.

"I don't think that I ever really was," Valerie admitted.

"Then why?" Samira asked. "Why did you marry him? Why did you stay?"

Valerie shook her head, as much at herself as at Samira.

"When I look at you with Ty, I see myself with your father. He was the most incredible man I ever knew. I know that you don't remember much about him."

Samira shook her head.

"Randall never let us talk about him," she said. "He even forced you to get rid of all of your pictures of him. I don't even remember what he looks like."

Samira felt a painful tightness in her throat at the memory. Even though she had never had the opportunity to know her father, she sometimes found herself missing him in an inexplicable way, as if she were mourning the idea of him.

"A lot like you," Valerie said, a misty quality to her voice now.

"What was his name?" Samira asked. "I hate that I don't even know that."

"It's not your fault," Valerie said. "You were just a baby when he died. His name was Martin."

"Martin," Samira said, testing the name and letting it cover up the name of her stepfather in her mouth and her heart. "How did you meet?"

"We actually met at a museum," Valerie said. "He loved science. I guess that's where you got it. I never understood what he was telling me about, and I rarely understood you, either."

Samira laughed.

"If you don't like science so much, why were you at a science museum?"

"Truth be told, I had a crush on my best friend's older brother at the time. He was a science major in the University and I was trying really hard to impress him. I figured that if I could understand some of the science stuff that he was prattling on about every time that I ran into him at her house, that maybe I could sweep him off his feet. Or convince him to sweep me off of mine."

"What type of science was he majoring in?" Samira asked, taking another sip of her coffee.

"See, that was the problem," Valerie said. "I just figured that if someone was a science major, they were majoring in science in general."

Samira nearly spit her coffee across the table and had to reach for a napkin to cover her mouth as she laughed. The sound of her mother's laugh joining hers was like light rushing into her and filling her. She hadn't heard her mother laugh in so long it was likely what she thought was a memory of it was just something that she had created to soothe herself.

"That would be a pretty broad major," Samira said.

Valerie nodded, still laughing.

"I realized that once I visited the museum," she said. "As soon as the woman at the information desk asked me what discipline of science I was interested in learning more about, I knew that I was in trouble."

Samira laughed harder.

"What did you tell her?" she asked.

"I didn't," Valerie said. "I ran into the exhibits and got

lost. I was staring at a hologram of deep space that was supposed to show a series of suspected planets and the future plans for those planets about an hour later when I met your father. He made a comment about the high-rise hotel complexes being a strange choice for the first thing to build on a newly-colonized planet."

"That is strange," Samira said. "Why would they build hotels if there was nothing else on the planet for the tourists to see?"

"That's exactly what he said," Valerie said with a softer note in her voice.

"What did you do?" Samira asked.

"Started crying," Valerie said matter-of-factly.

"Oh, no!" Samira said. "Why did you start crying?"

"Because I was so confused, and felt so incredibly stupid, and I just knew that there was no way that I was ever going to land that boy who I had a crush on."

Samira laughed again.

"I guess that didn't really matter much for long."

"No, it didn't," Valerie agreed. "I spent the rest of the afternoon walking around the museum with Martin, and then he bought me dinner and explained all kinds of things that I would never remember, but that I know I found utterly fascinating then. From that day on, he was what I thought about. He never made me feel like I was less than him for not understanding the things that he loved. Instead, he showed interest in the things that I cared about and made me feel special and unique for my own skills and abilities. I never felt more beautiful and appreciated than when he was around me. We could literally sit around the house doing absolutely nothing together, and I was happy. I just needed him around. What was even more wonderful than that, was that he felt the exact same way about me."

Samira sighed dreamily. Valerie had never been allowed to talk about Samira's father to her when she was growing up, and now that she was hearing these stories that she had never known, Samira was feeling even greater longing for her father, along with a sense of gratitude that he had made her mother's life as beautiful as he did for the time that he was able to.

"I just don't understand," Samira said. "If he was so amazing and made you feel so good, how could you fall in love with someone like Randall?"

"I never loved Randall," Valerie said. "That's the first time that I really admitted that to anyone. Even myself. The truth is, though, that when your father died, I died, too. You were an incredible joy to me and to your father, and we loved you more than any child had ever been loved, but when he was gone there was an emptiness in me that I couldn't seem to make go away. I thought that things would get better. I thought that I would get through the grieving process and the pain would ease, and eventually I would be able to go on with my life. That just never happened. So, one night I went out to a bar and I met Randall. He told me I was pretty and asked me to dance. It was the first time since your father that I had gotten any attention from a man. Looking back on it now I know that that is because I had kept myself completely locked away from everything and everyone after he died. This was the first opportunity I had to have someone look at me with any semblance of the feeling that your father did, and even though the look that Randall gave me was nowhere near emotional, I latched onto it. I hoped that having a man in my life again would make me feel better about myself and help me to get through. Instead, he took a broken woman and just broke me even further. He had recognized the hurt in me from the moment that his eyes fell on me, and he took advantage of it."

"I just don't understand why you let him do it," Samira said. "The first time, why didn't you just walk out and not go back?"

"I wish that I could tell you when the first time was," Valerie said. "Maybe then I would have a better idea as to why I didn't just walk away. The reality, though, is that it happened so fast, I didn't even have a chance to process it. It was as if I had been living half-awake and by the time that I woke up, I was already living with him and he was treating me so badly that I didn't feel like I was worth saving. It's so much harder to want to save someone who is already dead inside."

"I think that you were worth saving," Samira said through the tears that were now sliding down her cheeks. "I always have."

"I know," Valerie said. "I'm sorry that I couldn't have done better for you."

"It's not your fault," Samira said. "You didn't do anything wrong."

"When you grew up, you looked and acted and thought so much like your father. Like Martin." She said the name as if it tasted cool and sweet in her mouth after all of the years when she had been forbidden to say it. "I was so proud of you. I knew that you would have a life ahead of you. I honestly didn't know the things that he did to you."

"I know that you didn't," Samira said. "I know now."

"I said that I felt like I was half-awake after your father died. Well, when I realized the situation that I had gotten myself, that I had gotten us, into, I feel like I went back to sleep. I had to. It wasn't until Ero came that I started to wake up. That first time, when you were staying at Zuri's and you came to get your things? There was a short time after that when Randall actually let me breathe. I thought that things were going to get better and that I might be able to endure the rest of my years. All too soon, though, I could see it in him again. If you hadn't come back here to get married and Ero hadn't confronted Randall again, I don't think that I would have survived much longer. That was the moment when I woke up, completely and totally."

"I am so proud of you," Samira said. "Leaving him must have been so hard."

"Harder and scarier than the thought of staying with him," Valerie said. "But I had to do it. If I had let you walk out of that house that day without me with you, that would have been it. I never would have seen you get married. I never would have had the chance. But I did, and I'm here. That's how I've known that I could do this. Nothing is more horrifying than fighting a battle against someone who is both the person who is supposed to love you, and the enemy whose fight against you that you don't understand. With this war, there is a reason to fight and the enemy that is against us is clear. There are lives to save and people to free who never deserved the fate that they were given, but who do deserve another chance. I got that chance, and I will do anything in my power to give one to someone else. I am braver and stronger now than I have ever been, and I know that I am ready for whatever is waiting for us beyond this ship.

12

———

"Where's the baby?" Pyra asked as he stepped into the sleeping chamber.

Eden smoothed an extra blanket across the bed, thankful for the private chambers that were far more comfortable than the pods that she'd had to travel in on previous trips. Though she and Pyra still had to use a pod during the ascent and descent of the ship, having access to the ship's officer quarters meant that they had more space and amenities to enjoy during the rest of the flight, and now as they continued to wait for Rilex to return so that they could leave to connect with Maxim.

"He fell asleep with Zsilvia, so I decided to let him nap for a little while with her."

"So, we have some time to ourselves," he said.

Eden nodded and fluffed the pillows. Though she knew that they would be leaving the ship soon and didn't know when they would return, making the bed helped remind her that they would eventually be able to return. Knowing the soft, comfortable bed was waiting for them helped to reassure her and keep the reality of the war that waited outside at bay.

"We should," she said.

"I feel like we haven't gotten any time to be alone together in far too long," he said.

Eden felt a tremble in her belly as she heard her mate's footsteps come up behind her. Pyra's hands cupped over her breasts, filling his palms with her pliant flesh and kneading into them through the thin shirt that she wore. She could feel her nipples tighten in response to his touch and she sighed, enjoying the touch from her mate that it had been so long since she had been able to enjoy. Her body was shivering with desire and anticipation, but Pyra was moving with a slow, almost torturous precision as if he wanted to take full advantage of every second that he had with her. His hands left her breasts and ran down along her ribcage and into the dip between her hipbones. They paused at the waistband of her skirt.

Pyra brought his hand back down between her thighs and nestled his fingers into the wet heat of her core. They moved masterfully over her, showing her with every tender circle and increase of pressure just how much he knew her and her body. It was comforting and reassuring, making her feel safer and more secure as he reminded her of the powerful bond that they held between them. Her breathing was labored and she could feel herself shaking as he leaned her forward and his tongue stroked up her back. She gasped, rounding her back toward him in search of more of the feeling. Pyra guided them both back toward the bed and swept her up into his arms. He lowered her to the mattress so that she sat in the center and then climbed up to sit behind her. He positioned his knees on either side of her, cradling her back against him as he used his hands to press her knees apart.

She was completely swept away by the feeling of his skin on her back and the scent of him surrounding her. They filled her senses and took away everything else so that she didn't care about anything but what she was experiencing in his arms. Eden reveled in the brush of Pyra's fingers over her tightened nipples, along her ribs and onto her belly, and then down to her inner thighs. Her body was hot and aching for him, and she knew that he was well aware of how much she wanted him, but he took his time. He let each of his touches on her body linger, gently guiding her through controlled, increasing levels of pleasure.

Eden writhed as her mate's huge, strong hand explored her slick folds, his fingertips swirling over the taut, hyper-sensitive pearl at her peak with an intimate knowledge of her that was unlike anything that she had ever experienced. The touch was intoxicating, reminding her of how extremely the existence of Pyra had changed her life, and building intense pressure throughout her hips, thighs, and stomach. Pyra held her firmly around the waist with his other arm, offering her strength and stability as he brought her closer and closer to the brink of her control. She felt her body tightening as the sensations reached the edge and she resisted the oblivion that waited just beyond. She didn't want to give up the pleasure that he was giving her or to have to return to the reality that would press down around her.

"Relax," Pyra murmured into her ear. "Enjoy it. Let me bring you there."

At the urging of his words, Eden released her control, letting go of her hesitation and handing all of her trust over to him. The pressure of Pyra's fingertips increased slightly and he slid down until two fingers entered her. Eden felt like the world dissolved around her as her walls clenched down on his fingers and then released into a cascade of rippling tremors. The series of frantic, shuddering spasms pulled his fingers deeper into her and tore a gasping cry from her chest. She arched into the feeling and finally collapsed back into his arms, gasping for breath as she let the waves of pleasure roll over her.

Pyra groaned deep in his throat and slowly withdrew his fingers. He turned her around in his arms and then eased her back so that she lay on the mattress staring up at him. The fresh bedding that she had placed on the bed felt cool and it was soothing against the fiery flush of her skin. She turned her cheek to touch it and let out a long exhalation. Without a word, Pyra gently parted her legs again and settled his hips in between them. For a moment, he simply hovered above her. His eyes were locked on hers and she felt closely, tightly connected to him. The tip of his engorged cock brushed her core and he rocked his hips slightly to massage through her still-trembling folds. She rolled her hips in response, causing him to slip down and nestle at her opening. Pyra groaned at the suggestive touch and he pushed forward so that he filled her in one deep stroke.

Eden's mouth fell open and moaned as she reached up to wrap her arms around him. He paused where he was, pressing fully into her and giving her body a chance to stretch around him before he started to move. Pyra rolled his hips so that his hard length massaged her, nurturing her intensely and powerfully. She felt like he was taking care of her and was instantly overwhelmingly grateful for him. No matter what she was facing, no matter what they went through, as long as he was by her side she felt like she could surmount anything.

The world around Eden was reduced to purely sensory experiences. The masculine smell of Pyra's body blended with her own musky and clean sweat. The warmth of his skin and pressure of his body on hers stood in delicious contrast to the soft blankets and deep, cradling pillows. Around her the sound of Pyra's heartbeat and deep breath combined with the comfort of the bed to create a surrounding bubble from which she never wanted to emerge.

After a few more long, deep strokes, Pyra wrapped his arm around Eden's waist and settled back on his knees so that he could pull her up an into his lap. She wrapped herself happily around him, holding him as close as she could with her arms around his shoulders and her legs around his waist, and allowed him to guide the movement and pace of her hips. The rhythm and feeling of her clit massaging against his pubic bone was dizzying and soon she felt herself building up toward another climax.

Eden ran her fingers through Pyra's shock of thick white hair and gazed into his eyes. Their color was a testament to the connection between them, the unique link that proved that they were made for each other, destined to be together from the moment of their births, and that made them insep-arable. He was set aside only for her, as she was set aside only for him, and there was nothing and no one that could part them. It was a sense of security and strength that was indescribable. These moments when they were so close together, their bodies melded into one, only intensified their bond. This was more than the passion of their bodies. They were joined together to a place that transcended the moment and each of them as individuals.

Pyra's fingertips dug into her as he rocked her hips harder. He leaned forward and caught her nipple in his mouth, suckling at her breasts to muffle the sounds that she could feel pouring out of his throat. Suddenly Eden felt him lift his hips to drive into her with a hard thrust and his cock pulsed, spilling into her as her body responded with its own intense contraction. This orgasm was even more intense than the last and when her mouth opened, no sound came out. Her back arched and she clung to his shoulders. Pyra rested his hands on her lower back and drew her forward into his arms so that he could embrace her. She tucked her head into the curve of his neck and tenderly kissed along his shoulder.

They stayed as they were for several more minutes, Pyra still buried deeply inside Eden as they kissed and stroked each other's sweaty skin. She never wanted to move. As long as they stayed just as they were, nothing else existed. She could continue to just enjoy him and pretend that there was nothing else waiting for them outside of the ship.

When their breath had returned to normal and their heartbeats had slowed and normalized, Pyra rolled to his hip and then lowered her down to the mattress so that they lay beside one another. Eden reached up and ran her fingertips along the side of Pyra's face. He turned and touched a kiss to her palm, then rested his hand on her hip. She didn't want to speak, she didn't want to shatter the peaceful, beautiful energy that they had created between them, or to bring back the anxiety and stress that she knew that her mate had been suffering. But she knew that she had to.

"What do we do now?" she asked softly.

Pyra let out a long exhalation and ran his hand along her hip and into the dip of her waist.

"I think that we need to leave," he said.

"What about Rilex and Severine?" she asked. "You heard what Jem said."

He nodded subtly, looking down at the bed briefly.

"I know," he said. "I heard him and I know what Ciyrs said, too, but I don't think that we can wait any longer. We've been here for long enough as it is. Maxim has been waiting for us. There's no way to know what type of danger that he might be facing, and we're just sitting around the ship waiting for one person to come back."

"Two," Eden reminded him.

"What do you think is going to happen with them?" Pyra asked.

"What do you mean?" she asked.

"The hybrids that you rescued and the pregnant women. What will happen to them? They might have been captive, but that was the only home that they had."

"Not the women," Eden said. "Remember what Severine said. They were captured and forced into the breeding program. They have homes and lives that they had to leave behind."

"Do you think that they will be able to go back to them?" Pyra asked, lifting up to lean on his elbow. "We don't know how long they've been gone, and now that..."

His voice trailed off and Eden narrowed her eyes at him.

"Now that what?"

"They're all pregnant," he said. "Even though they're not in the facility anymore, they are still being forced to carry those babies."

"Why does that matter?" Eden asked, mimicking his position. "Do you think that their families won't accept them because of what they've been through?"

"I don't know," Pyra said. "I don't know how their families would react. Some of them have been gone for years, and their families might have moved on."

"Would you move on from me?" Eden asked.

She felt emotion tightening her throat painfully as she thought about the possibility of Pyra turning his back on her if something were to happen. She knew that she was fortunate to not have been captured and used as one of the breeders, and that there was always a chance that something could happen that would take her away from Pyra. Encountering the hybrids and the situation with Jem had only proven that to her even more poignantly.

"That's different," he said.

"Why?" Eden asked. "What if he had captured me when we were in the University? What if one of the Valdicians takes me prisoner while we are fighting? Would you just give up on me?"

"Of course, I wouldn't," he said. "We are bonded together. There's nothing that can take us apart."

"So, you would only stay loyal to me because of our bond?" she asked. "Only because you are Denynso and are linked to me as your mate?"

"You are Denynso, too," he told her.

"But I wasn't always," Eden said. "I was human when I went to Uoria and we first completed our bond. You knew then that I didn't have the same link that you have to me. When the Klimnu attacked me and Ciyrs was trying to save my life, did you only stay beside me because of our bond?"

"I stayed with you because I love you," he said.

"And there are people who love these women," she said. "Humans may not have the destined bond with mates the way that Denynso do, but their love is still strong and they still have loyalty. Just as you would have wanted me to remain by your side when I was still human, I know that these women will hope that their families will remain by theirs now."

"Then it is up to us to help them get back to their families when all of this is done."

"And the hybrids?" Eden asked.

"They don't have families or homes," Pyra reiterated. "There's nothing out here for them."

Eden climbed out of the bed and crossed the room to her bag to take out fresh clothing. Her mind was spinning as she struggled to understand her mate's perspective and reconcile it with her own emotions.

"Nothing but us," Eden said. "Rilex and Severine are obviously connected. I don't know if she can understand that yet, or if he has admitted it, but the only reason that he would follow her is if he loved her. We can't just abandon them, Pyra. Aegeus has been tortured in the same way, and you were willing to accept him."

She turned and saw Pyra get out of bed and start to dress as he spoke.

"Aegeus was somebody before he was Klimnu," Pyra argued. "He's not a hybrid."

"The hybrids are people, too, Pyra. They were forced to be what they are just as Aegeus was. Why don't you understand that? Why do you just want to throw them away?"

She could hear the tears in her own voice, and Pyra seemed to hear them as well. His face softened and he took the two long strides across the room to her. He reached up and cupped her cheeks with his massive hands, tilting it up to look at her.

"I do understand, Eden," Pyra said. "I know that they didn't choose this, but that doesn't change that I don't know what the future holds for them. It's not that I want to throw them away. It's that they aren't mine to throw away. I don't have control over their lives, and I shouldn't. They've been through enough and had enough of someone else controlling them and dictating to them who they are and the lives that they are going to have. I don't know what's right for them. They need to make that choice, and I don't know what our place is when it comes to helping them make it."

Eden felt her heart swell and a smile broke through the tears.

"All we can do is be there for them," she said softly. "I don't know what's right, either. I don't know if any of them have even fully processed that they are free now and that they have those choices. I don't know if they even understand what having choices is. What I do know is that we've been doing exactly what Ryan wants from us. We've been afraid. We've been scared of these hybrids and have been focused completely on them and protecting ourselves."

"The hybrids are still a threat," Pyra said. "They attacked us at the University and there have been attacks here on Penthos. They even tried to drag Severine back when she was trying to get to the transportation bay."

"I know," Eden said. "I'm not saying that all of the hybrids are safe. She told us that some were once humans and they volunteered to be spliced with DNA from other species so that they could be a part of the experiments. I understand that the hybrid army still represents a massive threat to us, but what I'm saying is that they aren't the only threat that we need to remember. They aren't what started this war. We need to remember that it's Ryan who is at the center of all of this. He created this and it's him who we need to defeat. That goes for the hybrids, too. As much as we have to stand up against him, they do, too. As long as they remain afraid of him, as long as they don't claim the life that is theirs to live, they are feeding into his final mission. He wants nothing more than to control the Universe and make every living being do his bidding. It's what makes him feel powerful and keeps him going."

"So, we take that power away from him," Pyra said. "Every hybrid that we take out of his control and who rises up against him is another crack in the armor that he's built up around him, another piece taken out of him. The more that we take from him, whether it's you, Lysander, Aegeus, Maxim and Kyven, or the hybrids, the weaker he gets."

"Exactly," Eden said.

"Then it's time," he said, crossing to the mirror on the wall at the side of the room and sculpting his hair into the tall, sharp mohawk that marked his readiness for battle. "Rilex and Severine will be fine. He is strong and has faced more than this in his time. Severine is courageous and knows this planet better than any of us. They will make it back here and we will reconnect with them later. For now, we need to get to Maxim and the rest. It's time to do what we came here to do."

TBC

To be continued...

JONAH & AUBREY'S STORY

1

———

Jonah felt like he had been staring up at the ceiling for hours, trying to will his body to go to sleep. Without the benefit of a clock or even a window so that he could see the movement of the sun, he was still struggling with keeping track of the time, and he hoped that he hadn't wasted the entire night staring into the darkness rather than getting the sleep that he needed. His mind was stuck firmly on Aubrey and what had happened between them in the lab. It was entirely unexpected, and yet the desire and need had been building inside of him since the first moment that he saw her.

In his mind, he knew that that was all that it was. It was a sudden, powerful attraction unlike anything that he had experienced since he had left Earth that was combined with hormones unaddressed for far too many years. Intensified by the sheer magnitude of the situation that they were facing, the urge had just been too much for him to deny. In his heart, though, he questioned if that was really all that pushed him into Aubrey's arms. He felt something for her beyond just the immediate attraction. He couldn't explain it, but he knew that there was something more that wouldn't be there if she had been any other woman.

As much as being with her had been absolutely incredible, thinking of it forced Jonah to think about the abrupt way that she had left immediately after. He could still taste her on his lips and feel the burn of her skin on his when she had jumped up from the table and rushed out of the lab, apologizing to him and telling him that what had happened between them had been a mistake. He hated that she felt that way and didn't understand what could have caused her to change so quickly. She had seemed as in need of him as he was of her when he first kissed her, and offered her lush, beautiful body to him willingly and enthusiastically. As soon as their bodies had cooled and their minds had cleared, though, her thoughts seemed to have completely changed and she ran away from him as fast as she could, barefoot and half-dressed beneath her lab coat.

He knew that he wasn't ever going to see her again. This upset him not just because he already missed her even though he truly barely knew her, but also because it meant that he was on his own again. She had helped him immeasurably by giving him her access chip and had been a valuable pair of extra hands as they were going through the lab trying to find anything that might be helpful or illuminating. It was her presence, though, that mattered to him the most. Even though he wasn't able to tell her everything about himself or even what he was really doing in the lab, just having her there with him had been encouraging. He could bounce ideas off of her and she would give him feedback that clarified his ideas and in small ways that would likely be imperceptible to her, helped him to understand this new version of the world that he had left behind.

That was all gone now. He was back to being alone on

this journey. But that was how he had intended it when he first began, and what he committed to doing. When he told Pyra that he was going to stay on Earth rather than going to Penthos with the rest of them, he had done it with the full knowledge that he needed to handle this part of the quest for himself.

Trying to tear his mind away from Aubrey, he instead thought about his investigations of the lab. He had gone over it so many times. Each time that he explored it, he tried to go deeper, to think of places where someone might hide something, or different ways that he could look at the space or the things that he found within it so that maybe he could find something that would be of some use to him. As many times as he had been through it, though, he hadn't found anything that really helped him, at least that he understood, and he was getting frustrated at himself. It seemed like he should be able to understand this better. He should be able to break through whatever barrier was standing between him and figuring this out, but he just couldn't. Everything was at a distance from him and no matter how hard he looked, and how hard he tried to decipher the information that he did have, nothing was speaking to him.

He knew that he had to move on from Ryan's lab if he was going to have any chance of finding anything else. He had exhausted that space and what little he had found there was stacked among the rest of the information that he had, undeciphered and relatively meaningless. He didn't know where to go from here. When he first found the patient file and the pristine, strangely preserved examination room, he felt like everything was laid out in front of him and all he needed to do was piece it together. Now it was as though he had stepped up to a wall and had nowhere to turn. He wondered if he was really ever going to be able to do anything beneficial by staying here in the basement and returning to the lab and the abandoned medical facility over and over in search of something that he couldn't even identify, or if he should have just listened to what Pyra had told him and gone to Penthos with the rest of the team. They were readying themselves to fight a war that could change the future. Maybe it was time that Jonah put his focus there and put the past behind him.

2

———

"Aubrey?"

Aubrey jumped slightly and turned to look at the lab assistant beside her, who was staring at her through narrowed eyes.

"What?" she asked.

"Are you finished with those calculations yet?" he asked in a tone that was just a touch too snide for her to be able to tolerate in her current state of mind. "I need them for the next step in this experiment."

"I'll get them to you when I get them to you," Aubrey snapped back at him, wondering how long she had actually been staring blankly at the blinking cursor on her calculator and holding her pencil poised over the sheet in front of her.

"And when do you think that's going to be?"

Aubrey slammed her pencil down on the paper, turned off her calculator, and started unbuttoning her lab coat.

"After I get a cup of coffee, stuff my face with a cheese Danish, and take a walk through this beautiful spring weather. How's that sound?"

She tossed her goggles onto the cart beside the door and

stalked out of the lab, finding some level of satisfaction in Jamie's creative muttering as she left. As soon as she had stepped out of the lab and approached the door to the courtyard, however, any hint of amusement that she had gotten from her brief taunt of her annoying coworker was dashed. Instead of the bright sunny morning that had greeted her when she stepped outside for her first coffee break of the day that would have been perfect for a mind-clearing walk around the grounds, hard streams of rain dashed across the glass and outside the clouds were so dark that she could barely see the building on the opposite side of the patio space. It seemed that the weather had heard her complaints that the day was simply not appropriate for how she was feeling and decided to change to better suit her mood.

Rather than crossing the courtyard as her shortcut to the cafeteria, she went the long way, walking down the maze of hallways past smaller labs and reading rooms. Inside she could see the rows of white-coated scientists, assistants, researchers, and technicians leaned over their projects, fully immersed in what they were doing as if there was nothing else in the entire world that mattered. She wished that she could focus on her work the way that they were. The project that she was supposed to be working on was one of the biggest that the University had taken on in years, and it really did need full focus and commitment from everyone on the team. Unfortunately, she just didn't have it in her to put herself into her work.

She couldn't get her mind off of Jonah. What had happened between them in the lab was impetuous, and impulsive, and incredible. No matter how spectacular it was, or how much she wanted him, though, she knew that it was a bad decision on her part, one that she should have been able to avoid if she had simply taken the time to think it through. Instead, she had let the draw that she had felt to the mysterious stranger and the tortured reality of the mission that he was on take over and compel her into something that was reckless and potentially disastrous. Jonah had far too much happening in his life to have someone coming in and messing with his thoughts and emotions, distracting him from what he needed to be doing. He also had obligations on another planet, responsibilities that she couldn't even begin to fathom, that he would have to attend to when he was finished with what he needed to do on Earth. It wasn't a position that she should have put either of them in.

Even beyond those barriers, though, Aubrey had the sense that Jonah wasn't being entirely honest with her about himself or what he was doing. He had explained that the rest of his team had gone to another planet to confront Ryan and the army of hybrids that he had created, but he hadn't been entirely clear on why he had remained behind on Earth. He simply told her that there was more work to be done here and that he was tasked with finding out more information about the experiments and Ryan's facilities. When she listened to him, however, there seemed to be more to it than that. He was holding something back from her and not giving her the full story, and that alone was enough to make their encounter a terrible decision. She couldn't handle another dishonest relationship. She just didn't have it in her.

As she reached the cafeteria and started filling the largest cup she could with coffee so dark it very well might have been motor oil, her thoughts went to what Jonah had told her about Ryan and the things that he had done. She knew that the scientist, as highly respected as he was, was eccentric and not known for treating the women he encountered as he should, but she never could have imagined that he would have been involved in the types of unethical and cruel experiments that Jonah had described. She found it difficult to wrap her head around the idea that just below the floors of the laboratory was a subterranean complex used for breeding, creating, and enslaving weaponized creatures pieced together from a variety of species, some that she hadn't even heard of. At the same time, she remembered the way that he had often spoken of the inadequacies in the military and how if they focused more energy not on the weapons that the armies were carrying, but what was carrying them, victories would not be so hard to obtain. Not *who*, but *what*. It struck too closely to what Jonah had said for it to be purely coincidental.

The more that she thought about what Ryan was doing, she more her stomach turned. She thought of the brief time that she had spent as his assistant in his lab. During that time, she had never known exactly what type of projects they were working on, or the objective behind the individual tasks that he had her complete. No matter what they were doing, though, she had always felt like he was scrutinizing her, examining her in everything that she did. The things that he said to her were completely out of line and unprofessional, and deep inside her she was ashamed that she had never done anything about it. Like the other female assistants had undoubtedly done, she had just swallowed everything that she wanted to say to him and tried to ignore his advances, telling herself that she had far too much to lose to offend one of the most influential scientists in the community. When she finally couldn't take it anymore, which took a far shorter time than she would have hoped her strength would have carried her, she still hadn't told her superiors what had happened. Instead, she told them that she was more interested in the projects being handled elsewhere and felt that her skills and knowledge could be better applied in that work. Now that she knew what he was capable of and could think more clearly about the things that he had said to her, she wondered if she might have become another of the women lost to the experiments if her request hadn't been put through and she hadn't been reassigned.

Aubrey knew then that she couldn't just pretend that she didn't know what Jonah had told her. She had to help in any way that she could to unravel what was happening and bring Ryan to justice, even if that meant doing some digging on her own.

3

———

Jonah took the depleted lightstick down from where he had anchored it on the wall in the stairwell and replaced it with a fresh one. The new stick spread light that was far brighter and more intense than the glow from the dying stick, filling the entire space and allowing him to see much further in either direction than he had been since he had taken to keeping a lightstick in place on the steps. It was reassuring to him to have the light there rather than having to bring a stick with him whenever he wanted to climb the stairs. It allowed him to go up to the closet whenever he wanted to, and gave him a greater sense of security than he felt when he had darkness both ahead of and behind him and only the faint light of a smaller stick that he would carry with him.

He felt like what he was doing was arbitrary. He had just been going through the motions, fulfilling basic tasks in the basement since Aubrey left him in the lab. Though he was doing what he needed to do to keep the human women and the hybrids that were still down there protected, he had done little to continue his mission of understanding what had really happened to the Nyx 23 mission. He suddenly felt himself missing the rest of the crew and the settlement that they had created on Uoria. It was a strange position to be in. He remembered the earliest days that they were on the foreign and unknown planet, grappling with the idea that their ship was completely destroyed and they had no way of either contacting those still on Earth or getting back home. It had been a sad and terrifying thought in a way that he would never have been able to put into words. It wasn't something that anyone would be able to understand or to empathize with unless they themselves had experienced it.

As he thought about Rain and the long days that they had spent together building the vehicle that they hoped would someday be their salvation, he couldn't help but realize that it was through that work and the dedication that they had given in the years that they were on Uoria, when they went from being stranded to re-envisioning the planet as their home, that they had created the salvation for many. He couldn't abandon that now. Too many lives had been lost or sacrificed, and none of them knew what might be coming next. He had to keep going. No matter how much he might be struggling or how frustrated he was getting, he had to keep pushing himself to understand what had brought them all there. So far there had been so many links that they uncovered. They already knew that Nyx 23 and the hybrid army were connected, but there had to be more. It couldn't be so simple as how Ryan explained it, even if the disturbed scientist believed that it was. If it was, there would be no reason for the examination room to still be as it was, or for Jonah's file to be inside. He couldn't help but believe that there was so much more to the link between the Nyx 23 mission and the hybrid experiments than they had even imagined.

He suddenly remembered the power cells from the vehicle that he and Rain created. When they uncovered the vehicle after so many years of it sitting abandoned in their hidden workshop, it wouldn't work. The power cells had been depleted and he wasn't able to get the vehicle started. Once the cells had some time in the sun, however, they were rejuvenated. They remembered how to work and were able to keep going with even more vibrancy than before. Gripping the depleted lightstick tightly in his hand, Jonah ran back down into the basement to get his bag and another lightstick to guide his way. All he had needed was a reminder to restore his strength and motivation.

His bag over his shoulder, Jonah climbed back up into the abandoned medical facility. He had been thinking about the other examination rooms and the furniture and equipment that filled them, but it hadn't occurred to him until then that each room had a different type of equipment or furniture inside, filled up to the ceiling and then the door locked. It didn't make sense for someone to go to that much trouble to arrange the items that way. The building was supposed to be demolished, but was preserved covertly for reasons that Jonah still didn't understand. If whoever had decided to keep this building in place knew that no one else would know that it was still there, why would they put forth that much effort? Why not just dispose of the furniture and equipment, or leave it in place the way that it was when they cut the center down?

Jonah knew that he needed to get into those rooms and explore inside of them. The reason that they had been filled and locked might just be information that he had been searching for to help him solve this and possibly save lives he still felt could be in danger.

When he got to the first door in the hallway, Jonah tried

the doorknob, knowing that it was locked but still wondering if there was a possibility that it might have been opened since they found this abandoned floor. Placing his bag on the floor, Jonah pulled out the tools that he had put inside before leaving the basement. When they first explored this part of the building Samira had mentioned that the contemporary hospital utilized metal doors that sank fully into the frames to allow for faster and easier maneuvering through the rooms. Jonah was thankful that these were not like that, but simple, more traditional doors. This allowed him to fit the end of a crowbar into the gap between the frame and the door and smash it with the end of a hammer. It was a crude approach, but proved highly effective as after the fourth blow the door started to warp and soon Jonah was able to smash the locking mechanism and pry the door fully open.

Once inside, he took the lantern from his bag and settled the lightstick he carried inside to multiply the light, then placed it on a shelf bolted to the wall just inside the door. The chairs inside were stacked so close to the door that Jonah could barely take a step all the way inside. He looked around them, trying to identify how many might be in there, and resigned himself to removing them one by one rather than maneuvering through them to reach the back of the room. He set to work taking the chairs out of the room and setting them in the waiting room, resisting the urge to arrange them in the way that he remembered they once were when this medical facility was still in operation. He had removed several when he heard a crashing sound coming from the waiting area. His muscles tightened and his ears pricked up defensively. Bracing himself, he stepped out of the room and closed the door behind him to block the light so that it would be more difficult for whoever had invaded the space to tell the direction that they should be moving.

Jonah crept down the hallway and into the waiting room. Suddenly a bright light burst in his eyes and he squinted, lifting his hand to shield them while also trying to see who was standing there.

"Jonah!" he heard Aubrey's voice gasp.

"Aubrey?" he asked.

The light lessened as Aubrey lowered the sleek metal lantern that she carried to the ground by her side.

"I don't know what to say," she said. "I barely recognize you greeting me without a knife in your hand."

Jonah slowly withdrew his hand from behind his back, revealing the weapon that he had been holding in anticipation of a clash with the Valdicians or members of the hybrid army. Aubrey's eyes fell on it and he saw them sparkle. Her lips twitched and finally she let out a short laugh.

"Well, I'm glad to see that you're consistent," she said.

Jonah slipped the weapon back into its sheath at his hip and took a step toward her. His heart had leapt when he saw her, but now that he had gotten over the initial surprise, he was concerned, not only that she had uncovered how to get into the medical facility, but also that she had come down here without any idea that he was there, meaning that she was willing to go exploring through the building completely alone and vulnerable to whatever dangers might still lurk there.

"What are you doing down here?" he demanded. "It's not safe for you."

"You told me that you were able to get up into the laboratory building through a hole in the closet wall. I wanted to know more about what was going on and to see if what you told me was true."

"You didn't believe me?" he asked, feeling stung by the revelation that she questioned him and that she hadn't asked him about it, but rather took it upon herself to see if she could find out about it.

"I barely even know you," Aubrey said.

"I think that we've gotten past the barely knowing each other stage, don't you?" Jonah snapped.

Aubrey looked taken aback and he regretted being so snide with her. He took another step toward her.

"I'm sorry," he said. "It's just that it might be incredibly dangerous down here. Even I don't know where Ryan's little minions are or if they even know that I'm still here. Besides, if anyone saw you going through that closet, it could compromise everything."

"No one saw me," Aubrey insisted. "It's the middle of the night."

Jonah realized that he had, in fact, lost track of time.

"Regardless, you shouldn't have come down here. Especially not without knowing if I was here. You shouldn't be in a place like this alone. You need to go."

"Absolutely not," Aubrey said.

Jonah straightened and tilted his head at her as if stunned that she would defy him.

"Excuse me?" he asked.

"I'm not going anywhere," she said. "Who are you to tell me what I can and can't do, or what is safe for me?"

"I'm someone who has actually experienced the dangers that are down here and know what these creatures are capable of. You didn't even know that any of this was happening a few days ago, and now you think that you can just come down here and be perfectly fine? And what? You're going to miraculously find something that I've missed over and over again, and everything's is going to wrap up neatly?"

"No," Aubrey said, taken aback by his intensity. She hadn't known that he was going to be down here when he resolved to come into the medical facility, but if she had known she wouldn't have thought that he was going to react this way. "I – I'm sorry. I just – "

She didn't know how to finish the sentence. She turned

away from him and started through the pile of chairs that she had accidentally knocked over when entering the space so that she could go back upstairs.

"Wait," Jonah said and she turned back to him. "I'm sorry. I shouldn't have said that. I just know how dangerous this can be, and I don't want you to be put into that."

"I want to be in that," Aubrey argued. "Now that I know what Ryan has done and what's going on, I can't just sit around and pretend that I don't. I have to do something about it. I started doing some research into the history of the University and I found out that this medical facility isn't even supposed to be here."

"I know," Jonah said. "It was supposed to be torn down when the rest of the old buildings were removed and replaced with the new laboratory facility."

"Exactly," Aubrey said. "So why is it still here? Who made the decision to keep it, and why did they? It doesn't make any sense to keep a building that is totally outdated sealed up inside another building, especially when nobody knows about it."

"That's why I'm here," Jonah said. "When the rest of the team was here, we found this building accidentally. We were trying to get away from Ryan and the Valdicians, and Eden remembered the closets at the end of the hall and how strange they were. She figured out that they each correspond to a flight of stairs in this building. That's how we broke through from that closet and ended up down here, and then went further down and found the basement."

"Do you have any idea why the old medical ward was preserved?" Aubrey asked. "It was closed and set for destruction more than a hundred years ago. What use could it do to anyone?"

"The basement itself is where we found the entrance to

Ryan's facility," he revealed. "That's where we found the human women that I told you about."

"But Ryan wasn't even alive when this medical ward was in operation," Aubrey said. "He couldn't have influenced them keeping it. It was already here when he came to work here."

"The experiments were started by his great-grandfather," Jonah said. "He could have had something to do with it."

"I don't know how," Aubrey said. "How would a scientist influence keeping an ancient medical ward in place so that a new lab could be built around it rather than letting it be torn down? Especially without anybody knowing about it? What would be the purpose?"

"I don't know," Jonah said. "That's something that I'm trying to figure out. Maybe if we can find out why this building was kept, and by who, we can better understand what's really happening. This isn't just Ryan. It's so much bigger than him and even his family. I just don't know how."

Aubrey felt a tug in her belly and a rush of warmth across her cheeks as she looked into Jonah's eyes. The attraction to him was undeniable, but she was still conflicted. There was something about him that made her feel slightly off-balance. He wasn't giving her all of the information, even though he was sharing so much with her, and that made her worry about what it could be that he was hiding. If he was willing to tell her about the horrors that he had already seen and what he knew Ryan was capable of doing, what could be so serious that he wasn't able to tell her? She knew that she needed to concentrate on what needed to be done and not him or what had happened between them, but that was going to be hard. She forced herself to look away from him, instead scrutinizing the chairs that were placed haphazardly throughout what looked like it had once been the reception area of the medical ward.

"So, why did you come down here today?" she asked.

Jonah cleared his throat softly and gestured toward the corridor that led off of the room.

"When we first came here we found all of these examination rooms locked, but if you look through the windows in them, you can see that each one of them is filled with a different type of furniture or equipment."

"Really?" Aubrey asked. "That's strange. Why would whoever wanted to keep this building around bother with putting everything away in the rooms and locking them up if they didn't intend on using it, or didn't think that anyone knew that it was here?"

"That's exactly what I was thinking," Jonah said. "I came down here to see if I could find anything."

"Like what?" Aubrey asked.

"I figured that I would know it if I found it," he said.

Aubrey nodded.

"Did you find anything yet?" she asked.

"No. I'm still working on getting these chairs out of the room. They used to be in here anyway, so I thought that I might as well put them back."

Jonah chuckled quietly, but the comment struck Aubrey.

"How do you know that these chairs used to be in here?" she asked.

Jonah hesitated just for a moment before answering her.

"Well, I'm assuming that since this was a hospital that this would be the waiting room, and these look like chairs that would be in the waiting room of a hospital, don't they?"

Aubrey looked down at one of the wide wooden chairs with its rigid arms and plastic-covered, muted multi-colored floral cushions. She knew that he was exactly right, and admonished herself for being so suspicious.

"They do," she agreed. "Can I help you move the rest of them out of the room?"

Jonah nodded.

"I would appreciate that," he said. "I feel like every time that I get one out, it just regenerates."

Aubrey smiled as she picked up her lantern and brought it with her across the waiting room toward the corridor. It created an eerie glow down the long-forgotten hall and she felt a chill go down her spine. Something about this place was off even beyond just still being there when it wasn't supposed to be, and part of her wished that she could just leave. She had come this far, though. If she hadn't wanted to be a part of this, she could have just pretended that she had never met Jonah, never heard what he had told her, and just gone back to work. She had come here, and by doing that she had committed herself to helping him. There was no turning back now.

They kept working for what felt like hours, until finally most of the room was cleared of the large chairs. As they emptied, they revealed a row of low shelves positioned along one wall. Each was packed tightly with boxes marked with a complex-looking symbol. Aubrey leaned down to examine it more closely.

"Do you recognize that?" she asked.

Jonah shook his head.

"No," he said. "I don't think I've ever seen it."

"Me, neither."

"Should we see what's inside?" Jonah asked.

Aubrey shrugged and scooted back a few inches so that Jonah could grab one of the boxes and take it from the shelf.

He set it on the floor in between them and used his knife to open the seal on the top.

"Oh, so that has another purpose other than threatening me," Aubrey said.

Jonah looked up at her with a smirk and tucked the blade back in his sheath before prying the box the rest of the way open. He reached inside and pulled out a small, dark bottle. He looked at it for a few seconds and then handed it to her. Aubrey took it and examined the bottle.

"This is old," she said. "I've never even seen bottles like this."

Jonah reached into the box and pulled out another.

"The whole box is full of them," he said. He stuck his finger in the open mouth of the bottle. "They're all empty."

Aubrey set reached forward to push aside one of the flaps of the box so that she could peer inside.

"All of them?" she asked.

"Yeah," Jonah replied.

He turned and pulled another box down from the shelf. He opened it and revealed that it contained the same old, empty bottles. A few boxes later, the bottles appeared newer, but were still empty. Finally, Aubrey was able to read the name of the chemical.

"Izalux," she muttered.

"What?" Jonah asked.

She looked up from the aged label and shook her head.

"I feel like I've heard that name before."

"Is it something that's used in the lab?" Jonah asked.

Aubrey shook her head and looked back down at the bottle, trying to jog her memory.

"No," she said. "I know all of the chemicals that we have in stock. This isn't something that we have around. I just feel like I've seen it before, though." She let out an exasperated sound. "I just can't place it." A thought occurred to her and she put the bottle back in the box. "Why don't we go to the library tomorrow when it opens and do some more research?" she suggested. "We might be able to identify what this chemical is and what it's used for. That might tell us why there are so many empty bottles of it here."

Jonah looked hopeful at the thought of learning the purpose of the chemical, but unsure of going to the library with her.

"I don't know if I should go with you," he said, sounding nervous. "Do you think that you could just do the research yourself and I'll come back down here and work on emptying another one of the rooms so that we can see if there's anything there."

"What's wrong?" Aubrey asked.

"Nothing," Jonah said, sounding unconvincing. "I just think that we should maximize our time by doing both things at once."

"And I think that it's a better idea for us to find out more about this building and about whatever this chemical is before we spend any more time digging around through it."

"The bottles are empty," Jonah said.

"That doesn't necessarily eliminate the hazard," Aubrey said. "As a scientist, you should know that. There are some chemicals that we use in the lab that are so volatile that if one of the empty canisters were to be dropped on a hard enough surface with anything around it, it with explode with such magnitude that it could kill people with the shrapnel. If neither of us know what this chemical is or what it's been used for, we can't take a chance."

Jonah continued to stare at her for a few long seconds before his expression relaxed and he relented.

"Alright," he said. "I'll meet you in the lab tomorrow morning."

"Do you think that it's safe to keep going there?" Aubrey asked. "Could the people who are working for Ryan come back there?"

"I don't think so," Jonah said. "If you've noticed that Ryan's missing, that means that other people have, too. Like you, the people working here wouldn't think twice seeing me in the lab. They'd just assume that I am there representing Ryan and working on a new project, but knowing that Ryan himself isn't there is going to make people pay more attention. They would notice too easily and too quickly if they saw the types of creatures that are helping Ryan lurking around his lab. Besides, with Ryan not here and the people who he is after already on Penthos, there isn't really a reason for them to go back to the lab. If there are still Valdicians or hybrids here, they're waiting somewhere else."

Though she knew that Jonah hadn't intended them to be, the words were chilling. Aubrey was unnerved by the reality that all of this could have been happening inside the laboratory where she worked every day, and she had no idea.

5

____

The next morning Jonah paced through the lab nervously, trying to come up with some excuse that would prevent him from having to go the library with Aubrey. Though he knew that it was a good idea to do some digging into the history of the medical building and the University itself, as well as trying to identify the chemical that they had found, the idea of leaving the laboratory building to go to the library was more intimidating than he expected it to be. He knew that he was going to be anxious leaving the building. It was too real. It was too much of an acknowledgement of everything that he had gone through. As soon as he heard her suggest that they go to the library, however, the reality of it came crashing down on him and he felt like the world was closing in around him.

He had taken one of the empty bottles from the boxes in the examination room and he kept sweeping it off of the surface of the brushed metal table so that he could look at the label, trying to bring forward any memories of the mention of this particular chemical and its purpose, then setting it back down. He had specifically chosen the table that he had shared with Aubrey, hoping that he would be able to fill his mind with thoughts of this new piece of the puzzle rather than memories of her delectable naked body writhing and eager beneath him.

As if the thoughts of her had lured her to him, the door opened and Aubrey stepped inside. He noticed that she had a bag across her chest and was carrying a bundle of cloth beneath her arm.

"Good morning," she said.

She smiled and held the bundle out to him.

"Good morning," he said back, but didn't reach for the cloth.

She pressed it closer to him and Jonah finally took it out of her hands.

"What's this?" he asked.

"Well," Aubrey said, "it's just that it is pretty obvious that you have spent some time on another planet." She gestured toward the clothes that he was wearing. "Unless you want everyone to notice you and start asking questions that you might not be ready to answer right this second, you might want to put these on so that you blend in a little bit better. Besides, I'm guessing that living in a basement hasn't given you much opportunity to freshen up. These will probably feel pretty good."

Jonah smiled as he unrolled the bundle to reveal two sets of fresh clothing. He selected one and set it aside, then tucked the other into his bag. He had no way of knowing how long he was going to be staying in the basement and it would be nice to know that he had an extra set of fresh clothes when he needed them.

"Thank you," he said. "I really appreciate it."

Aubrey nodded and he headed for the back room of the lab to change, knowing that they were not in a place that would make dressing in front of her appropriate. When he emerged from the back room wearing the contemporary clothes, he saw a small smile of appreciation curve her full lips.

"Are you ready?" she asked.

He drew in a breath. She had no idea just how poignant that question really was. He gave a single nod that he hoped was convincing and crossed toward the door. They walked along the corridor and down the steps toward the main hallway. Jonah felt a shudder roll through him when he stepped into the space, the sight of a man walking casually along the polished floor, unaware that he was stepping where there were pools of blood just a short time before, seeming to underscore the brutality of what he had experienced there.

"Are you alright?" Aubrey said to him quietly, drawing slightly closer to him.

He had spared her many of the details of the battle, but she knew enough to understand that it was difficult for him to simply pass through this space as if nothing had occurred. But it was what he had to do. He couldn't let that continue to control him or stop him from doing what he needed to do. He forced out a breath and looked at her.

"Yeah," he said. "I'm fine."

Finally, they reached the front door to the building and Aubrey pushed it open. Reminding himself that he had been outside the laboratory building when they were coming from the vehicle, Jonah followed her out into the sunlight. The warmth of the light fell on his skin and he turned his face toward it, giving himself a moment to just enjoy it. This was the first time that the Earth's sun had touched his skin in more than 115 years. Though he knew it was essentially the same as the sun of Uoria, it was somehow different and he felt it invigorate him. He let himself look around, taking in the world surrounding him. The differences were blatant and he felt a hint of the mourning feeling settle into his chest. He wondered if he had known when he stepped onto the StarCity what was going to happen, what he would have done in those last moments on Earth. What would he have wanted to look at one more time? What would he have wanted to remember the most?

When he was at the University the library was in the center of the grounds, and now as Aubrey led him, it seemed that it was in essentially the same position. As they approached he could see that the building was several times larger than the one that he had frequented during his time here. Then he felt like the library was tremendous, but the new monolithic structure in front of him dwarfed it. The sight was both exciting and humbling as he contemplated the incredible increase in knowledge that went into the growth of the institution.

Aubrey touched her new access chip to the keypad outside of the library and they walked inside. Jonah wanted to explore everything that he saw, but Aubrey immediately grabbed onto his elbow and guided him across the large atrium at the center of the library toward a stairwell leading down. They followed it quickly and then went through a door to another set of stairs that led further down into the building.

"Great," Jonah said. "Back into the basement."

Aubrey gave a short laugh.

"The best stuff is always in there," she said.

Jonah smiled and there was a brief moment of energy between them, but Aubrey looked away, breaking it. She led him across a small room dotted with chairs and tables, and stopped in front of a desk beside a closed door. A severe-looking woman looked at her over the rim of her glasses and Aubrey offered a wide smile.

"Hello, Cecilia," she said cheerfully. "I just need to do a bit of research."

Aubrey slid an identification card across the desk toward her and Cecilia picked it up, scrutinizing it as if she had never met Aubrey, though she clearly had.

"Aubrey," the woman said in the tone that a disappointed parent usually uses with their misbehaving children. "You know that these stacks are restricted. Authorized faculty only."

"I know," Aubrey said. "I have authorization to access the restricted area."

"Yes," Cecilia said, "but what about your...friend."

She said it like she was discussing something decidedly distasteful, but Aubrey broke into a crystalline laugh that was almost startling in its glaring inappropriateness.

"Oh, Cecilia," she said through the fake laugh. "This isn't my friend! This is my husband."

Jonah turned toward her in surprise at the sound of the word, but then turned back to Cecilia with a forced smiled, knowing that he needed to go along with it.

"I didn't know that you were married," Cecilia said.

There was an edge of suspicion in her voice, but Aubrey wasn't to be bested. She looped her arm around Jonah's and rested her head on his shoulder.

"Oh, yes," she said dreamily. "Newlyweds. We didn't have a big wedding. We just kind of ran off and did it. We couldn't wait another minute."

She looked up at Jonah and when he looked down at her she pressed a quick kiss to his lips before turning back to the woman whose mouth was now screwed into an expression that said that she was still displeased, but more because she was going to have to let Aubrey through rather than turning her away.

"Well," Cecilia said shortly. "Congratulations, then."

"Thank you," Aubrey said.

"Thank you," Jonah added.

"So, we can go on through?" Aubrey asked.

Cecilia pressed a button on the desk in front of her that released the locks on the door and waved her through. Aubrey gave another wide smile and grasped Jonah's arm more firmly so that she could lead him through the door. Jonah's lips were still tingling with her kiss when the door closed behind them and she released his arm to walk into the slightly musty stacks of aging tomes.

"There are some computers in the back with scanned files and some books that they don't have hard copies of, but most of what we want is going to be in these books."

"I'm your husband now?" Jonah asked. "Have things changed that much since I was on Earth?" He made sure to put a teasing lilt in the question, but he was genuinely curious about what had just transpired with Cecilia.

Aubrey looked up at him quizzically as if she didn't remember what she had said, then jumped slightly.

"Oh, that. This is a restricted area. Only specific people are allowed to come in here, and Cecilia is a stickler for the rules."

"I gathered that," Jonah said. "Did you know that you say 'oh' a lot?"

"I never noticed that."

"So, if this is a restricted area, why did Cecilia let me in?"

"Did you know that you say 'so' a lot?" Aubrey asked.

Jonah laughed.

"No, I never noticed that."

Aubrey reached up and grabbed a large book from the shelf above her head.

"Well, you do. Anyway, there is a little bit of a loophole in the rules about the restricted area. Only authorized faculty is allowed in here, but they are allowed to bring spouses with them to help with research."

Jonah tilted his head at her.

"Why is that?" he asked.

Aubrey lugged the book over to one of the small tables set up in the center of the room and clicked on the green lamp that flooded the surface with light.

"Because spouses are supportive and encouraging, and far less likely than other people who work in the University to steal the work that you're doing and sell it to competing groups."

"That makes sense," Jonah said.

Despite the purely functional explanation behind it, Jonah liked the way that the introduction had sounded, and he couldn't help but smile as he selected another book from the shelf and settled at the table across from her.

A few hours had passed and the stacks of books that each had gone through had grown into teetering piles at the edges of the tables when Jonah leaned back and massaged his tired, burning eyes. It had been a long time since he had spent this much time reading.

"Alright," he said. "I think that we should take a little bit of a break. I need to go back to check on the others."

Aubrey's eyes snapped up from the book that she was reading.

"The others?" she asked. "What do you mean?"

"In the basement," Jonah said, lowering his voice even though he didn't think that Cecilia could hear him.

Aubrey's lips parted and she leaned toward him conspiratorially.

"I thought that they all left with the rest of the team and went to the other planet," Aubrey said.

"Most of them did," Jonah said. "But there are some who are still here trying to recover. A couple of the hybrids were in pretty bad condition and there were some of the pregnant women who didn't want to leave."

"I'm going with you," Aubrey said. "I want to meet them."

Jonah started to protest. He didn't think that it would be a good idea for her to go down into the basement with him. It was too dangerous, and would bring her too close to finding out the secrets that he had been trying to keep. As soon as he started to form the words, however, he stopped. Aubrey had already done so much. He had no choice but to let her continue.

6

———

Aubrey drew instinctively closer to Jonah as he led her down through the floors of the old medical ward and into the basement. As eerie as she had found the abandoned hospital when she was only in the waiting room and the first of the examination rooms, these floors were far worse and the chill that had settled into her when she heard that there were still victims of Ryan in the basement sank further into her bones the deeper they went into the building.

When they reached the basement, Jonah reached into the bag that he carried and pulled out what looked like a narrow tube. An instant later, it began to glow, shedding a faintly green light around them, reminding her of the strange-looking lantern that he'd had in the examination room and the light in the stairwell. She wished that she had her lantern with her at that moment so that they could have illumination that actually cut through the damp darkness rather than just butting up against it as his did.

"What is this place?" Aubrey asked.

"Remember in that book about the history of the

University it mentioned that some of the older buildings were outfitted with emergency chambers to provide shelter and supplies in the event of a disaster? These are the ones built for the hospital."

Aubrey had seen pictures of these chambers only minutes before when they were in the library, but her mind still had a difficult time reconciling those pictures with what she was seeing now. The century that had passed since the medical ward had been shut down in the massive renovation of the University complex had not been kind to the basement. The pictures that were taken of the chambers at the time that the book was written, decades after the building had actually been built, were hopeful and reassuring. Bright lighting and grinning images of the then-president of the University and the head of the department that had designed the emergency chambers standing inside one of them presenting one of the supply kits made them look almost inviting. These pictures could have been in a brochure meant to lure prospective students and faculty by advertising the amenities of the University, including the well-equipped chambers that stood fully prepared for the possibility of an emergency, disaster, or attack.

When she looked at the basement around her now, though, there was none of that hope. The light was gone and the chambers looked cold and frightening. She couldn't imagine staying here any longer than a few minutes, much less days on end.

"Why would you stay here?" she asked. "It's miserable down here."

"We had no choice," Jonah told her. "The Valdicians and army were ready to attack at any moment and we had nowhere else to go. We were happy to find this place. At least we were protected and had food, water, and clothes."

Aubrey felt a wave of guilt at her reaction and quieted, allowing Jonah to guide her the rest of the way through to a partially closed door. He knocked on it and then opened the door the rest of the way. As soon as she stepped into the door, Aubrey felt her heart tighten painfully and her hand came up to cover her mouth. The room was cluttered with makeshift beds and on each was a person who looked at the same time happy to see Jonah and drawn to the point of fragility. Jonah came to her side and gestured at her.

"Everybody, this is Aubrey. You can trust her. She's...a friend of mine."

One of the women waved at her, but even as she offered a smile, Aubrey could see her cradling her obviously swollen belly a bit tighter. A man with features unlike anything that she had ever seen looked at her for a few long seconds as if he was going to say something to her, and then turned away, walking to a set of shelves in the corner and pulling down a box that he set on a table and started digging through. Aubrey took hold of Jonah's wrist and pulled him back out of the door into the hallway.

"They can't stay here," she said.

"What?" Jonah asked.

"Those people. You. You can't stay here anymore."

"I told you," Jonah said. "This is our only choice. We don't have anywhere else to go, and it isn't safe for us to try to find someplace else."

"It isn't safe for you to stay here," Aubrey insisted. "I know that you are doing everything that you can for them, and that you want what is best for them, but this isn't it. They need a safer more comfortable place and better care."

She saw Jonah tense and felt the compulsion to reach out to touch him and reassure him.

"Until Pyra comes back for me, we have to stay here.

This is where I can do the research and investigation that I need to do, and where we know that we have what we need to survive."

"Jonah, these people have been tortured. The women have been kidnapped and forcibly impregnated. The hybrids have been held against their will. They can't just stay here and hope that they will survive, or that something else won't happen. You know that at any minute one of those women could go into labor, or the Valdicians could come up from the facility to find you. Ryan could come back. You should go to the police."

"No," Jonah said swiftly and fiercely. "We can't do that."

"Why?" Aubrey asked. "They could help you. They could help them. What Ryan has done is criminal and he should be held accountable for it."

"He is being held accountable for it," he said. "He is facing exactly what he wanted. He's getting the war against the Denynso and the Mikana that he has been planning for, and he will get the destruction that he deserves."

"The police can prevent any of that from having to happen," Aubrey said, trying to convince him. "No one has to be hurt. No one has to die. They can take him into custody and handle it so that his victims can move on."

"Move on to what?" Jonah asked. "What do they have to move on to? These hybrids have never had anything else but this facility. The human women have their own struggles to deal with and challenging decisions to make. If we call the police, that's it. The investigation is over and I will never have the opportunity to find the answers that I've been looking for. We might never know the truth. Please. Just give us the chance to handle this. You might not understand it, but it is what's best."

Aubrey could see the sincerity and determination in his

eyes and knew that she was never going to be able to change his mind. No matter what she thought, she also knew that she couldn't bring herself to take these answers from him.

"Alright," she said. "I won't call the police."

Jonah's face seemed to melt with relief and he reached out to take her by the shoulders.

"Thank you so much," he said.

"I still don't think that they should stay here," she said. "This place isn't going to get them healthy or protect them for much longer. They need somewhere better, and I know the perfect place."

In her mind, she could see her grandmother's sprawling home, the number of rooms inside the centuries-old mansion far exceeding the number of guests or visiting family members that she would ever have. She knew that the home itself would be ideal for providing shelter and comfort for these people and for Jonah, but it was more than that that made her confident that the home where she had spent her summers when she was growing up would be the perfect choice. Though she didn't yet fully understand why, seeing the people inside that room made her feel as though she might have just put herself on the path of solving a long-standing family secret.

7

———

"I don't think that moving them is a good idea," Jonah said. "Where could we possibly bring them that they wouldn't be detected?"

"Leave that to me," Aubrey said. "Just make sure that they are ready at midnight and I will come back for you. Moving in the dark is going to make it much easier to get them there without anyone noticing." She tilted her head to catch his downcast eyes. "Alright?" she said.

Jonah let out a sigh. As hesitant as he was to put the group through any more stress or anxiety than they had already faced, he knew that what Aubrey had said was right. He did everything that he could to make sure that they were eating enough, were comfortable, and were getting the treatments that Ciyrs and Elianna had prepared for them, but there was only so much that he could do in the basement. This environment wasn't good for their bodies, and knowing that they were so close to the facility where they had been kept and tormented wasn't good for their minds. They needed to be somewhere else where they could be safe and really get the type of care and support that would help them to recover and prepare for the new chapter ahead of them.

"Alright," he said.

He saw Aubrey straighten and give a single nod.

"Good. I have to go now, but make sure that they are ready when I get here. Meet me at the closet." She pushed up the sleeve of the light green summer-weight sweater that she was wearing and unlatched the watch from her wrist so that she could hold it out to him. "Take this," she said.

Jonah took the narrow black leather band and tucked it into his palm, closing his fingers over it so that he couldn't see the face. If he had, he might have just stood there staring into it. She would never be able to understand the meaning behind that simple gesture. To Aubrey, she was offering him a way to make sure that he was in place and ready to meet her when she arrived to help move them out of the basement. To Jonah, however, it was so much more. She had given him back his connection to his world. Though there was something relaxing and even freeing about being on Uoria where there was no concept of structured time, it also sometimes made him feel like he was spiraling out of control. In his life on Earth, time and precision were everything. Suddenly being in a place where he wasn't able to keep track of the time made the years that he was losing to the foreign planet seem to go by more quickly, slipping past like water through his fingertips. They were there only for a moment, but he couldn't hold onto them as they past, leaving their lingering mark on him. The crew only knew how long that they had been on Uoria before the Covra came because some had counted the nights that went by and were able to mark the passing of the years. This watch grounded him again.

For the rest of the day Jonah did as much preparation

as possible. He gathered all of the tools and supplies that he could fit into his bag and the bags left in the chambers, and talked the wounded and the women through the idea of leaving. Just as he had been, they were reluctant and nervous about leaving. Though he understood exactly what they were thinking, he couldn't let them see the questions in his eyes. He needed to stay strong for them and make them feel confident so that they would be able to take these first few steps. By the time that he left to climb the stairs to meet Aubrey, Jonah had almost convinced himself as well.

Aubrey arrived just as Jonah opened the closet door. She was carrying two large bags over her shoulders and had a determined expression on her face.

"Do you have everything ready?" she asked.

"Yes," Jonah answered. She stepped toward the door, but he didn't move out of the way. Instead, he met her eyes. "Thank you for doing this," he said. "I really appreciate it." He paused and drew in a breath. "All of us do."

"Of course," Aubrey said.

Jonah turned and led her down the steps and into the basement. Those who had remained behind were grouped in the middle of the chamber, the supplies that they were going to carry sitting around them. Aubrey stepped toward them and set the two bags on the floor.

"I brought fresh clothes for you," she said. "You'll be more comfortable and if someone does see us, you will stand out less."

Some of them looked hesitant, even unsure of what she meant, but one of the hybrid men came toward her, his jaw set and his eyes clear and strong.

"Thank you," he said simply to Aubrey.

It was the first time that Jonah had heard this man speak

and his voice was like a low, driving wind. Aubrey nodded and reached down to pick up one of the bags.

"This is men's clothes," he said. She gestured toward the other bag. "This is women's."

The hybrid man rested the bag on a table and began to pull out articles of clothing. He looked at them with a hint of awe in his eyes, as if he had never imagined something as simple as being able to choose the clothing that he was going to wear. Finally, he selected a pair of pants and shirt, and left the chamber for one of the smaller rooms so that he could dress. Empowered by watching one of his own, the other man approached the table and chose clothing. Jonah followed the last one out of the emergency chamber to allow Aubrey to help the women dress. A few minutes later, she opened the door again. The women looked more assured and secure now that they were out of the thin, gauzy white shifts that they all had been wearing since they found them in the breeding facility.

"Is everyone ready?" Aubrey asked when they had gathered their bags.

"I think so," Jonah said.

"Then let's go."

They started up the stairs and Jonah could feel the bodies of the hybrid men tense as they approached the main hallway. He knew that they were feeling much the same reaction that he had had to it, but from a different perspective. Recognizing this only made their suffering more of a reality for him, and Jonah reached out to rest his hand on the back of the man who was walking closest to him. The man tensed and pulled away from him slightly at first, but then seemed to realize that he was offering him comfort and not trying to hurt him. Jonah felt the man's shoulders relax and he turned to look at him with appreciation in his eyes.

"What do you want to be called?" Jonah asked.

He had remembered what the hybrid woman who had called out to Eden said about them not having names, and knew that that was no longer acceptable. When they walked out of the laboratory, it was final. They were leaving behind the tortured existence that they had always lived and what it represented, and he didn't want them to take even one step outside under the weight of being nameless.

The hybrid man looked at him strangely, as if he didn't fully understand why Jonah was asking him, and shook his head.

"What do you mean?" he asked.

Jonah paused in the hallway and the rest of the group slowed and stopped around him so that they were distributed along the corridor. Aubrey looked impatient as she glanced between them and the front door, but Jonah didn't relent. He looked toward the second man.

"How about you?" he asked. "What name do you want?"

The man lifted his chin, showing that a grisly scar that began on his cheekbone wove its way down his cheek, over his jaw, and onto his neck. Jonah could see worn, prematurely-aged hands clench at his sides and then stretch.

"Mordecai," he said.

The name sounded rich and rumbling in his deep voice, perfectly fitting this powerful-looking man.

"Hello, Mordecai," he said. "I'm Jonah."

He reached his hand toward the hybrid man, but Mordecai didn't move. Jonah realized that he had likely never seen anyone shake hands and didn't understand the greeting. He reached forward and took Mordecai's other hand. He lifted it and placed it against his hand, wrapping his fingers around it. Mordecai looked up at him and his lips curved in a small smile. He wrapped his own fingers around Jonah's hand and Jonah shook it.

"Hello," Mordecai said. "Hello, Jonah."

Jonah turned to look at the other hybrid man again.

"And you?" he said. "Have you chosen? What do you want people to call you from now on?"

He waited for several long seconds and then the man spoke.

"Gannon," he said.

Jonah repeated the greeting the same greeting that he had with Mordecai.

"Hello, Jonah," Gannon said.

Jonah turned and gestured at Aubrey, whose face had softened and who had turned to face them fully.

"This is Aubrey," he said, wanting to introduce her again now that these me had names to offer her in return.

"Hello, Aubrey," both men said.

"Hello," she said.

"I'm Maeve," one of the women said, sounding as though she had just found her voice.

"Linnea," another said.

"Sable."

The others began to speak and the rest greeted them until their names fell around them like snow, cleansing and refreshing against the darkness. They started toward the front door again, but Jonah stopped after only a few steps. He could feel the tingling on the back of his neck like someone was watching them. He turned toward the feeling and saw the corner of a dark cape disappear around the edge of a doorway behind him. He took a step toward him, but behind him heard the crash of a door slamming and a scream pierce through the stillness of the hallway.

Jonah spun around and saw Aubrey struggling against one of the Valdicians who held her around her waist as he dragged her toward the office. He ran toward her and immediately another three of the cloaked creatures swarmed out into the corridor and rushed toward the two hybrid men, one breaking away from the other two to move toward the nearest woman. Without hesitation, Mordecai took a long stride to Jonah and reached for the weapon at his hip. In one motion, he pulled the weapon from its sheath and spun around to bring it into the throat of the figure behind him. The Valdician stumbled back and lifted his hands to the blade. Galvanized by Mordecai's action, Gannon dug his elbow back into the stomach of the creature who held him, knocking him to the ground. Jonah slammed the heel of his hand into the face of the Valdician who was dragging Aubrey, causing him to drop her to the floor. She scrambled away and climbed to her feet.

"Get the women out!" Jonah shouted at her as the Valdician stood again and came toward him.

Aubrey reached out and took Sable's hand, pulling her across the hall toward her.

"Get out," she said. "Go through the door and run. Go to the parking lot." Jonah heard a clinking sound that he assumed was Aubrey handing the woman the keys to the car. "Get the rest of the women in the silver van and lock the doors. Don't unlock them until you see us."

Jonah continued his fight with the Valdician, soon rendering him unconscious on the floor. He kicked the cloaked figure aside and rushed toward where two were pulling Mordecai's arms. He was nearly to him when Gannon grabbed Jonah's blade up from where Mordecai had dropped it and ran directly at one of the Valdicians, planting his foot in the man's stomach. As he fell, Gannon dropped down onto him so that one knee burrowed into his belly and he flattened his palm against the man's forehead. He forced the man's head back and looked down into his face.

"Never again," he growled.

Jonah kicked away another of the Valdicians and tugged Mordecai away as Gannon drove the blade into the prone creature's chest. He looked around to make sure that all of the women had made it out before running toward the door. He burst out and looked over his shoulder to see both hybrid men run out into the warm, star-filled night.

Aubrey drove like they had run, pushing them along the nearly empty streets with the city at their back. Soon their surroundings began to change and thick trees built up around them until it seemed that they were driving directly through a forest. The van was filled with an electric energy, but none of them spoke. Each was lost in their own thoughts, trying to process what had just happened and what was to come. It seemed that they had been driving most of the night when Aubrey finally turned off of the main road onto a long, meandering driveway. Jonah watched through the windshield as the trees ahead of them opened and he saw an imposing, sprawling home rise up from the horizon. Candles were glowing in the windows and on the front porch, and as they approached, he saw the door open and the silhouette of a small figure appear against the backdrop of yellow light from inside.

The van stopped and Aubrey ushered all of them quickly out and up the stairs to the porch. The silhouette stepped forward and Jonah saw that it was an elderly woman wearing a long dress that reminded him of the clothing that his mother wore when he was still on Earth. The thought brought a pang to his heart and he pushed it away.

"Come here," the woman said, her voice heavy with concern and urgency as she reached her arms out for Linnea.

Linnea allowed the elderly woman to take her into her arms for a brief hug and then place her hand on Linnea's back to guide her into the house. She then reached for Mordecai, squeezing him to her a little tighter before ushering him into the home. Soon they were all inside and the tremendous wooden door closed securely behind them.

"Nana," Aubrey said, stepping into the older woman's arms and resting her head to her shoulder.

"Aubrey, my love," she said, stroking her hair lovingly.

Aubrey stepped back and looked at the group. One by one she introduced them to Nana, explaining that this slight woman was her grandmother, the woman who had cared for her during the summer when she was out of school and when her parents were traveling, which was frequent. It was obvious that Aubrey adored Nana, and Jonah felt another longing for his family. He realized sadly as he watched Nana greet each of them tenderly that he had felt the absence of his family and missed them more since he had been on Earth than he had even when he was on Uoria. Being back in the same areas where he had once lived and knowing that everyone he had ever known and loved while here had long-since gone was far worse than being on a distant planet where he could pretend that everything was the same back home and had simply gone on exactly as it had before he left.

"All of you are welcome here," Nana said. "You will be safe."

Jonah felt his body relax and a long exhalation stream from his lungs. His back touched the door behind him and he slid down until he sat on the floor. Drawing his knees up to his chest, Jonah rested his head forward on them. He could feel tears streaming out of his eyes, but he couldn't put a name to the emotion that he was feeling.

"I'll help our new guests settle in," Nana said. "I've already called my personal doctor and he will be here shortly to check on them. He said if any of them are in need of further care than he is able to provide here, he will arrange to bring them to his office." Her voice changed slightly as she seemed to turn to the group that had been rescued from the laboratory building. "Come with me. I have bedrooms prepared for each of you. Relax in a bath and have something to eat. My home is yours."

When their footsteps faded out of the room Jonah felt Aubrey ease down to sit beside him. A moment later her hand was on his back and he felt her head rest on his shoulder. For a moment she just sat there, breathing with him, and then she turned and touched a gentle kiss to his temple.

"It's going to be alright," she said softly. "They're here now. No one knows where to find us."

"Us?" Jonah asked, tilting his head to look at her.

"Of course," she said. "You're staying here, too. You can't possibly think that I was going to bring them here and let you go back to the basement by yourself."

"I need to be there to continue my work."

"You need to be here to stay safe," she said matter-of-factly. "I can bring you to the University to do whatever you need to do. You already have the access chip. You can do whatever you need to do, except for go into the restricted area of the library, and if you need to do that, you can just tell me and I'll come with you."

"Are you sure?" he asked.

The question was heavily loaded, and he could see that she recognized it. She nodded.

"Yes," she said. "I want you to stay here. I went as soon as I left you this afternoon and bought everything that we could need. There's plenty of clothes, food, everything. You should go take a shower. Relax. All of this will still be waiting for you in the morning. You can deal with it then. For now, you need to take care of yourself. You have a lot of people who are relying on you." She paused and swallowed. "I'm relying on you. We need you to be at your best. The fight isn't over, Jonah. It's just time to take a break for a little while."

She stood and reached down. Jonah took her hands and let Aubrey help him off the floor. He wanted to kiss her. He wanted to draw her into his arms and lose himself in her, but he knew that he couldn't. Instead, he let her lead him up the broad staircase and into a beautiful suite.

"This is amazing," he said.

"This was my room when I lived here," she told him.

"Then you should be staying in it," he protested.

Aubrey shook her head.

"No. You need it. There's a full bathroom through there," she said, pointing to a door opposite the bed, "and those doors lead out onto a balcony. There's clothes in the closet and the dresser for you. Everything that you need for a shower is in the bathroom. Enjoy it. I'll see you in the morning."

Before he could say anything more to her, Aubrey backed out of the room and closed the door behind her. Jonah looked around, taking in the soothing white carpet, plush white bedding, and gauzy white curtains flowing in a breeze coming in through the open window at the front of the room. The thought of a shower was irresistible. He removed his shoes and tucked them under the bed, then removed his clothes before going into the bathroom.

The hot water on his skin when he stepped into the shower stall was intoxicating. It fell on him from three showerheads positioned around the walls ensuring that the massaging stream touched all of him even as he stood in the middle. He luxuriated in the feeling of the water beating into his skin and washing away the sweat, dirt, and stress. He hadn't felt a shower like this since before he left Earth. The shower facilities on the StarCity had been designed to replicate those in homes as much as possible, but they always lacked the intense pressure that he appreciated in a shower. Once they crashed on Uoria, the showers they were able to build from the materials they could salvage were adequate, but never enough to give Jonah the truly clean, relaxed, and renewed feeling that he had always enjoyed from showers. He had gotten used to baths in his home or bathing in the river on the hottest days, but now that he was standing in this shower he felt like he never wanted to get out of it.

Aubrey had thoughtfully stocked the shower and by the time that he had finished, Jonah felt thoroughly and blissfully clean. The shower had furthered the release of stress that his tears had begun, and he felt like he could lie down and sleep endlessly in the clean, soft bed.

Jonah stepped reluctantly out of the shower and onto the bathmat. His feet sank into its padding as he reached for one of the impossibly soft towels that were stacked on the shelf ahead of him. The fibers were like silk on his fingers and he couldn't help but let out a small groan of pleasure as he ran it across his body to dry his skin. He had become accustomed to drying on the thin cloths that they had on Uoria or laying out in the sun to let its warmth dry him when he bathed in the river, but there was joy and comfort that came just from the simple pleasure of being able to dry himself with a thick, plush towel and then wrap it around his waist so that he could step back into the bedroom.

When he did, he was surprised to find Aubrey sitting on the bed as if waiting for him. She looked away when she noticed that he was only wearing a towel, and stood.

"I'm sorry," she said. "I thought that you would get dressed while you were in there. I'll wait outside."

"I didn't bring any clothes in there with me," he said. "It's alright. Don't worry about it. Did you need something?"

Aubrey turned toward him and slowly brought her eyes up his body to meet Jonah's eyes. He could tell that she was struggling to focus on what she wanted to say to him rather than looking at his exposed body, and the thought brought a thrill of happiness to his belly.

"I just wanted to talk to you," she said. "I think that we need to clear some things up."

"Sure," Jonah said. "What do we need to clear up?"

Aubrey let out a sigh and looked down at her hands as she played with her fingers as if to distract herself.

"I know that things started between us kind of strangely, and then I probably made it much worse by the way that I reacted after that first...time in the lab."

Jonah saw a slight hint of color flare on her cheekbones as she looked up at him and it only made her look more beautiful. He was struggling to resist her. The time that they had been spending together had made him even more aware of the attraction that he felt for her, but also the feelings that were growing within him, and it was getting harder not to tell her how he felt.

"It was unexpected for both of us," Jonah said. "I don't think that either of us really thought it through very much."

"Yeah," Aubrey said, nodding and looking nervous. "That's just it. I should have thought it through. I can't let myself make bad decisions."

"What do you mean?" Jonah asked, trying not to let himself feel the sting of her words.

Aubrey sighed and let her hands drop to her sides.

"A couple of years ago, I thought that I had found the greatest guy in the world. He was fun and friendly. Intelligent and interesting. Attractive. When we met he made me feel like I was the most beautiful woman in the room and that he was only interested in what I had to say. We talked for hours. I couldn't believe how much we had in common and how much he thought like me. It was like I had literally designed the ideal boyfriend and he came walking into the room. He even spoiled me like a princess for the first few dates. After that, though, he started asking me to pay for things and borrowing money. Suddenly, he didn't have all of those interests and passions that we had talked about, and he didn't seem to want to do any of the things that we had planned. Then I found out that he had been stealing checks from me and had even hooked up my credit cards to his utility bills, credit card bills, and even an automatic draft for his rent. When I confronted him about it, he completely blew up and said that he didn't understand why I was making such a big deal out of it since my family had so much money. That's when I realized that he had spent weeks researching me before we *happened* to meet. He had been scanning all of my social media, talking to my friends, even reading newspaper clippings about my family. He knew that my grandmother is well-off and decided that he was going to seduce me into becoming his very own piggy bank."

There was an emotion to those last words that told Jonah that they hurt her deeply and he realized that the full, gorgeous body that he had been craving ever since he last tasted her made her feel uncomfortable. He instantly hated the man who had made her feel that way and desired feverishly to wipe away any of those thoughts from her mind.

"Aubrey..." he started, but she shook her head.

"It was only when this was all over and I had started the process of pressing charges on him that I found out that he was married. The whole time. I guess that explained why he never wanted to spend the night at my place, huh?" She looked down at her hands again and he saw her swallow hard before her brilliantly blue eyes snapped back up to his. "So, you see, I can't trust myself, especially when I feel myself getting swept away by someone so quickly. I put myself and the cooperation between us in a terrible position by throwing myself at you that day."

"I agree," Jonah said. The breath caught in Aubrey's throat and Jonah could see her eyes welling up with tears. He took a step toward her and shook his head. "Don't misunderstand me," he said softly. "I enjoyed every single moment of that. It's just that that isn't the way that I would have wanted our first time together to be."

He was directly in front of her now and he reached up to brush a strand of hair that had fallen out of her braid away from her face. He leaned forward and touched a kiss to her lips, increasing the pressure as he let the towel fall away from his body and guided her back to lie down on the bed behind her.

8

Their kiss was slow and languid, but Aubrey could feel it sliding through her entire body. A few moments later, Aubrey felt Jonah slide off of her and the loss of his delicious warmth and weight on her body left her feeling cold. She remained lying on her back, but ·reached her arms up for him, but instead of coming back down to stretch out on top of her again, Jonah took her hands and gently pulled her up into a sitting position facing him. His eyes were locked on hers and his hands were sure and steady as they took her braid from her shoulder and released the elastic band that held it. He tossed the band aside and used his fingers to tenderly ease her hair loose, allowing the silky strands to flow around her shoulders.

Jonah stroked her cheek with the back of his fingers and Aubrey felt herself trembling, the reaction an unusual combination of nervousness and intense desire. She had been with him before, and yet she suddenly felt completely inexperienced and vulnerable in his hands. Again, Jonah lowered his mouth to hers and as he tenderly coaxed her with his lips and tongue, Aubrey felt his hands come to her thighs and the hem of her dress. She hadn't thought of how he would react to this dress when she had put it on, but now she was happy that she had selected it. It gave him faster, smoother access to the tender skin of her thighs and she didn't resist as he eased the fabric up her legs until it pooled at her hips. She lifted slightly to allow him to slip it out from under her and he continued to bring it up her body. Jonah hesitated when he got the dress gathered at her ribcage and she ran her eyes up his beautiful naked body to meet his gaze. Jonah looked back at her through dark, slumbering eyes, his lips wet and reddened by their kiss, and she knew that she had to have more of him.

Without saying a word, Aubrey raised her arms above her head. Jonah smiled softly at the invitation and slipped her dress off. He held it out to his side and let it fall from his fingers onto the floor beside the bed as if he wanted her to see the gesture and process exactly what it meant. Again, she was in front of him in nothing but her lace bra and panties, and her nervousness increased. The last time that she had been in this position they were both fueled by a blazing passion that dulled her insecurities and let her give in without, as Jonah had put it, thinking it through. Now, though, they were moving deliberately and purposefully, and she felt self-conscious. She could feel Jonah's eyes traveling over her barely covered body and she instinctively brought her arm over her breasts and the other to wrap across her belly. He looked down at her arms and used one hand to gently guide them out of the way.

"You don't need to cover yourself," he whispered, "You are beautiful." Aubrey felt shy and looked away, but Jonah caught her face softly and turned it back so that she looked into his eyes again. "It's just me," he said. "I want to see more of you."

Aubrey felt Jonah's hands slide around her waist to her back and stop at the hooks on the back of her bra. The pressure around her ribcage released as the bra fell loose. It was a sensation that she could never remember being aware of before, but he was moving with such precision and care that it seemed she was more aware, more present in each moment than she ever had been. Jonah eased the pale pink satin straps down her arms slowly, allowing the lacy cups to remain over her breasts until the last possible second. She moved her arms just enough to get them out of the straps, but the cups remained in place. Jonah ran one fingertip along one scalloped edge and then the other, bringing a delightful chill to each swell. Finally, he dipped his fingers into the cups and removed them. The cool air of the room brushed across Aubrey's nipples, causing them to tighten even further, and she drew in a breath, filling her lungs with the scent of the room and of him.

Jonah made an appreciative sound in his throat as he gazed at her, much like the sound that he had made in the lab. That time, the groan had been one of primal need. This time it was a sound of worship and she felt suddenly proud of her body. Before now her body had created contention and embarrassment in her life. It had made her uncomfortable even when she was alone, and caused her to make decisions that she was often ashamed of later. The way that Jonah's eyes drank her in and the reverent way that he touched her, however, gave Aubrey the sense that her body had become an object of desire and emotion in a new, thrilling way. She craved allowing herself to truly give herself over to it and discover more about the pleasure it was capable of achieving, and providing.

Aubrey's belly fluttered as Jonah led her carefully down onto the bed so that her head rested on the pillow. It was a subtle maneuver, and yet it felt as adoring and erotic as the flick of his tongue or the smooth glide of his fingers. He moved slowly and without any sense of urgency, making her tremble with each feathery touch on her exposed skin as he leaned over her. His chest brushed against hers and the warmth of his fresh-smelling skin made a soft moan escape her lips. Jonah nuzzled into the curve of her neck and shoulder, and Aubrey tilted her face against his as Jonah brought his mouth to her ear.

"Sex should be like a thunderstorm," he whispered, his voice low and rumbling, and his breath hot against her neck.

Aubrey straightened her head to allow him more access to her skin and her eyes drifted closed.

"First the clouds roll in across the sky. That is the anticipation, the desire. You know that something is coming, and you feel like you can barely catch your breath."

Jonah touched his lips softly to her neck, then moved them to her mouth. His kiss was deep, but slow. At first, he touched only his lips to hers, occasionally changing the angle and pressure of the kiss. Soon, though, she felt the tip of his tongue brush across her bottom lip and Aubrey's breath caught. She could feel the tension building throughout her body, fogging her thoughts and making her heart race.

"Then the rain comes," he said, barely taking his mouth away from hers. "It is gentle at first, just enough to break the tension of the anticipation," he whispered. He pulled away from her so that he hovered over her and flattened his palm in the center of her chest, running it down onto her stomach as he spoke. "But as the drops fall, you know it's not enough. You want more."

Jonah's tongue touched the underside of her jaw and

glided down, creating a long, slow trail along her neck. He continued down her chest and along her stomach. In her mind, she could see the rain falling, the gliding of the droplets seeming to mirror his movements. He continued his delicious torture by moving his mouth over slightly each time his lick returned to her neck so that each discovered a new, trembling area of skin. He had done only this, but Aubrey felt like her body was coming alive, responding to him like it never had to anyone else. It was as though she had never experienced such a touch and each sensation was more and more intense. The tip of Jonah's tongue dipped into her navel and Aubrey gasped. Her hips lifted involuntarily off the bed as if in search of him, but he only blew a soft, cool stream of breath onto her belly.

"Not yet," Jonah whispered.

He blew another stream of air onto her skin and Aubrey relaxed back down against the mattress. When she was lying flat again Aubrey felt Jonah's mouth move lower on her eager body. He repeated the process much as he had when he traced her from her neck to her stomach, this time running his tongue from her navel down to the waist of her panties. When he had created several slick paths, he glided his tongue along the lacy edge to one hipbone and then to the other. Aubrey buried one hand in his hair and opened her eyes so that she could look down at him. Jonah lifted his head and gazed at her for a moment. He didn't look at all hurried, but serene as if enjoying every moment of the attention that he was lavishing on her as much as she was enjoying receiving it. He turned to press a kiss into her palm and then he rested his head for a moment on her stomach.

A moment later his mouth came to her breast and he kissed along the swell of the underside and then along the top before finally coming to rest on her nipple. The sensitive peaks tightened even harder in response to his touch and Aubrey felt him draw the taut pink tip between his teeth and then wrap it with his tongue. It was as if he wanted to taste every inch of her, and Aubrey was more than willing to indulge him that pleasure. Jonah mirrored the attention on the other breast and then drew his body up hers to settle beside her.

Aubrey reached out for him and found his thigh. She ran her hand along his soft skin, relishing the feel of his hard, sculpted muscles beneath it. Jonah lowered his mouth to her ear again, gently nipping at her earlobe, and then soothing the playful pain with a tender kiss.

"The thunder comes softly at first," he whispered, "Just a few gentle rumbles." He rested his hand on her lower belly and drew it down slowly, finally reaching her thighs. She held them closely together, but Aubrey felt him ease them apart. "Sometimes they are so gentle that you barely even notice them."

The backs of his fingers ran lightly over her core through her panties and Aubrey knew that he could feel the warmth of her body. He traced the pattern of the lace, the light touch escalating her arousal even further.

"You just have to be patient, though. Soon they will get stronger. They will get more and more intense the longer that you wait."

Jonah bit her earlobe again and she felt him grasp the waistband of her panties with his fingers to drag them down off of her hips. Aubrey lifted them to allow him to remove the damp lace. Her thighs closed again, but he tucked his hand between them so that he caught it, and pressed them apart again. He let out a breath just as he ran his hand up her tender inner thighs and dipped his fingers into her folds. Aubrey cried out at the feeling and gripped the sheet beside her. Jonah drew his fingers through her core and then paused, focusing their touch on the taut, sensitive pearl at her peak. She whimpered, the sound like a high sob in her throat, as her body gave into the sensations that he was creating in her as it never had before. She clutched his thigh, digging her fingertips into his muscle as he stroked her with tender, patient skill. Jonah swirled his finger into her, gathering her silky fluid as he went so that he could explore her easily. There was no sense of a rush in his touch. She didn't feel as though he were trying to push her or even that he cared about anything but the pleasure that he was giving her at that single moment. He wanted to know her. He wanted to understand her body and connect with it on a deep, intimate level.

Moaning low in his throat, Jonah let his finger dip down and slide into her. The touch was powerful and Aubrey's back arched off of the bed. His name tumbled from her lips in a gasping cry and she gipped his leg harder. She sought calm and control in his strength, feeling herself slipping away into a blissful oblivion but wanting to hold on for a little longer. His mouth played against her neck and she could feel his breath become more ragged as her hips writhed against his hand.

"Aubrey," he whispered, as much an exhalation as it was her name, "you are so wet. I want to be inside you. I want to feel you."

"Please," she murmured, running her hand up his thigh toward the erection that she was craving. "I want to feel you inside me."

Jonah growled in his throat, but put his hand over hers to stop its progress in the middle of his thigh.

"No," he whispered, "Not yet."

Dizzying tension was building through her belly, thighs,

and pelvis, and Aubrey found herself struggling to control her breath. She closed her eyes, wanting both to prolong the feeling and to let herself give it over completely. Jonah continued to nurture her, bringing his fingertip back up to stroke her clit again and send shivers through her body.

Jonah lifted the hand from his thigh and drew it up until it cupped his surging erection. As soon as she felt the velvety, engorged hardness against her palm, she felt a mind-shattering orgasm crash over her. Jonah continued to stroke her as her body contracted and released in a series of tremors that tore screams from her chest.

Jonah's hand left her body and in an instant, he was stretched over her. His cock plunged into her to meet the spasms of her climax with deep, hard strokes, pushing her over the edge of another wave of her climax. She opened her eyes as she came back down out of the delirium and he rolled his hips in a rhythm that was both passionate and tender, intense and soulful. She moaned and writhed beneath him as he made love to her. His eyes never left hers as he moved within her with strength and control that contrasted with the abandon that she was feeling. Aubrey ran her hands indulgently along his back, reveling in the feeling of his muscles shifting and tensing beneath his skin, and the sweat creating delicious slickness.

Aubrey lifted her head to kiss him and felt Jonah's pace quicken. He moved at a fast, even rhythm until his mouth pulled away from hers to let deep sounds pour from his throat. A moment later she felt him drive into her with a final hard thrust and growl as he began to pulse. She could sense him spilling into her and her heart swelled. When the pulses eased and his body relaxed, Jonah rested down onto her and tucked his head against her chest.

She was beginning to fall asleep when she felt Jonah lift

his head to look at her. Aubrey opened her eyes to look down at him.

"And by the way," he said. "I was the one who threw myself at you."

He kissed the center of her chest and laid his head down again, not seeming to care about being jostled by her laughter.

9

Cecilia looked less than pleased to see Aubrey and Jonah when they arrived at the library the next day, but she didn't argue with them when Aubrey showed her identification card. Jonah struggled to withhold a laugh as they walked through the door and back into the stacks.

"I have the feeling that she doesn't like you very much," he said as Aubrey sat down at the same table as she had before and tucked into the same book.

She glanced up at him with a smirk on her sweet lips.

"And I have a feeling you're right. Did you bring one of the bottles with you?" she asked.

Jonah nodded and sat on the chair next to her, pulling his bag into his lap so that he could take the bottle from it. He had wrapped it in one of the towels from the bathroom to conceal it, feeling strangely protective of the bottle and the mystery that it held. There had to be a reason why dozens of these empty bottles were hidden in the examination rooms in the old medical ward, and he felt the compulsion to guard it from those who might not want that reason uncovered.

He placed the bottle on the table in front of her and tucked the towel back into the bag. When he looked up, Aubrey was staring at him.

"What?" he asked.

She tilted her head and continued to stare at him.

"Are you alright being back here?" she finally asked. "After what happened last night?"

He had been trying not to think about their escape, but he was thankful that she cared enough to ask him. At the same time, he wondered how she could seem so calm, so unfazed by the conflict.

"I'm fine," he said. "They aren't going to want to be seen. The last thing that Ryan wants is for anybody to know what he's been doing. As long as other people are here, we're safe. Are you alright?"

Aubrey looked to the side as if she was thinking through the question and trying to decide how to respond. He wished that he hadn't asked her. Every time that he thought about them he felt like he was staying tied to that basement and giving Ryan more of the control that he was so determined to take back. Suddenly Aubrey's eyes widened and her mouth opened slightly. She looked at Jonah and then swept the bottle off of the surface of the table into her hand. She scrutinized the label and then looked up at him again, her smile full now.

"I know what this is," she said. "I remember it."

"You do?" Jonah asked, his heart leaping slightly in his chest. "You've seen it before?"

"I haven't just seen it," she said. "I've used it. When I was working with Ryan, this was the one chemical that I had never used before. I remember that for the first few days that I worked with him he had me doing simple little processes with basic compounds and ingredients that didn't seem like they had any purpose. It felt like I was just combining different things and then putting them aside. I had done more interesting things in my high school chemistry class. But he never let me clean them up or get rid of the products of the combinations, and then I realized that he was actually collecting them and taking them somewhere with him. Every few days he would change the processes that I was doing so that I was making a few different products. I had been his assistant for a couple of weeks before he brought me a bottle of this and containers with materials in them that he wouldn't tell me what they were. I don't think it even occurred to him that I would figure out that they were combinations of the products that I had made over the first days with him."

"Did you ever find out what you were making?" Jonah asked.

"Starlight."

Jonah felt a shiver move over his skin at the word.

"Starlight?" he asked.

Aubrey nodded.

"I was making artificial starlight. He never explained why or what he was going to use it for, but every day, he brought me another bottle of this chemical. The bottles looked newer than this, but still pretty old, like they had been in storage for a lot of years."

"Maybe that's why we haven't been able to find out anything about it," Jonah said. "Is Izalux even produced anymore?"

Aubrey shook her head.

"I don't think that it is," she said. "I've gone through these books and done some research online, and all I've found about it is that listings for when it was first formulated. It was apparently patented, but the person who formulated it never presented any formal work to the scientific community and it never hit the larger market. It stopped being produced a few years after it was formulated."

"When was that?" Jonah asked.

"More than a hundred years," Aubrey said.

The words burst in Jonah's mind. One hundred years. What could that mean?

"Do you know who formulated it?" Jonah asked.

Aubrey shook her head.

"Nobody does apparently," she said. "The company that took out the patent was only known as Orion. It never recorded the name of any individual within it or the purpose behind the company other than developing this particular chemical. Since then, the company hasn't done anything else and it doesn't seem to be active anymore."

"Why would they design such a complex and potentially powerful chemical if they had no intention of it actually being used for anything?" Jonah asked.

Aubrey shrugged.

"Maybe they didn't realize how strong it was going to be, or they had plans for it, but it didn't turn out the way that they thought, or didn't do what they thought it was going to do."

"Then how did Ryan get his hands on it?"

Aubrey shook his head.

"By now both of us are fully aware that Ryan is capable of things that are beyond explanation."

Jonah looked at the stack of books that was sitting on the table. Even though they had figured out what the chemical was and how Ryan used it, there were still questions.

"I think that we should bring some of these books back to the house with us," Jonah said. "The longer that we're here, the more suspicion that we'll cause. I'd rather nobody start following behind us and trying to find out what we're researching."

Aubrey nodded.

"You're probably right. We can check these out with Cecilia."

Jonah gathered as many of the books as he could up into his arms and followed her out to Cecilia's desk, the thought of artificial starlight tumbling through his mind.

10

———

"Hi, Honey," Nana said as Aubrey walked into the kitchen.

Aubrey dropped her bag to the floor and massaged her shoulder, relieved to have the weight off of it, then sat in one of the chairs at the small table that her grandmother had put in the kitchen when Aubrey was a child.

"Hi, Nana." She drew in a breath of the rich, savory smell that was filling the kitchen. "That smells good. What is it?"

"Lasagna," Nana said. "I thought that everybody might like something a little different for dinner. They seem to be ready for more variety. I just hope that they like it."

"I'm sure they'll love it," Aubrey said. "You make the best lasagna in the world. Besides, they've loved everything that you've made for them. After two weeks of mostly soups and stews, though, I think that they'll enjoy something more substantial."

"I don't know what they were eating when they were in that horrible place, and I didn't want to make them sick."

Aubrey dug her fingers back through her hair and then let them drop weakly back to the table, feeling too tired to do much else.

"I know," she said. "And I know that they appreciate it."

Nana turned away from the pot on the stove to look at her. Her eyes narrowed with concern.

"You look awful," she said.

"Thank you."

"What's wrong?"

"I'm just exhausted," she said. "The project at the lab has ramped up so I'm getting there early every morning, staying late every evening, and then spending hours with Jonah doing research."

"Have you found out anything else?" Nana asked.

Aubrey sighed and leaned back in her chair.

"No. We were so excited when we found the Izalux bottles and I remembered what they were used for, but we just hit a wall after that. No matter where I look, I can't find anything that's useful. It's like the company produced a whole bunch of the stuff, shut down, and that's it. Nothing else. No explanation for how it was developed, why it was developed, or why they stopped developing it. Especially no explanation for how Ryan got his hands on it, or why in the living hell he was having me work on the base for making artificial starlight."

"And still no sightings of Ryan? No idea where he is?"

"Apparently, he just disappeared."

"Well, I doubt that," Nana said. "Where is Jonah?"

Aubrey gestured over her shoulder.

"He hasn't slept well the last few nights so he went upstairs to get a shower and try to get a nap before supper and yet some more research. I hate seeing what this is doing to him. It's like every day that he keeps working, he's losing a little bit of his soul."

"What do you know about Jonah?" Nana asked.

She had filled a small bowl with the thick, rich sauce that she had made for the lasagna and brought it over to Aubrey with a plate of crusty buttered bread.

"What do you mean?" Aubrey asked.

She glanced up at her grandmother as she tore off a chunk of the bread and dipped it in the sauce. The taste reminded her of her childhood and brought soothing warm to her belly.

"Well, he knows about your family. He knows about your work at the University. He's met me. He's even living here. What do you know about him?"

It felt like a strangely invasive question and Aubrey wasn't sure how to answer it. She took another piece of the bread and swirled it through the sauce, watching as butter melted off to create ribbons of pale yellow in the warm red pool.

"I know that he only just recently returned to Earth after being on Uoria. He came back here to keep digging into this situation with Ryan and has been hiding in the University basement to protect the people who were rescued from the facility."

"Are you sure that that's why he came back to Earth?" Nana asked.

"What are you asking?"

"There was an article in the newspaper a few weeks ago about a wedding for a young woman who worked in the University named Samira."

"I've heard the name," Aubrey said. "I've never met her, though. What does that have to do with Jonah, though?"

"The article mentioned the novelty of the fact that the majority of the bridal party and many of the guests were originally from Uoria, and among them were people from Earth who were participants in an exchange program from the University."

Aubrey nodded.

"Yeah. That program just got started a little more than a year ago. An artist, a writer, a professor, and a couple of scientists went there to educate the Denynso about human life on Earth, and to bring back information about them in an effort to promote closer relationships between the two species."

"So, is Jonah one of the people who traveled from the University to be a part of the program?"

Aubrey wasn't sure how to respond. It wasn't something that she had thought about until that moment. From the way that Jonah had talked about Uoria, it seemed that he had spent far more than just one year there, and he didn't seem to know enough about the Denynso to seem like he had spent that much time with them. After a few moments of silence, Nana stood from the table and walked out of the kitchen. She returned with a blue-bound book in her hands. She sat back in the chair opposite Aubrey and slid the book across the surface of the table toward her.

"Here," she said. "I want you to have this."

"What is it?" Aubrey asked, picking the book up.

The cover had no title and the long blue ribbon that hung as a marker between the pages was frayed and faded at the end.

"Just read it," Nana said. "I think that you might find it interesting.

Aubrey looked into her grandmother's eyes but didn't

find any answers to her questions. She stood, put her bag over her shoulder, and started toward the stairs with the book held to her chest.

11

———

Jonah was standing on the balcony, enjoying the warm breeze on his face as he stared out over the lushness of the green trees beyond the mansion's back lawn. Every few moments there was a flicker of light as a firefly shot through the sky. He heard the bedroom door close inside the room and he turned to see Aubrey.

"Hey," she said. "I thought that you were going to lie down for a little while."

"I tried," he said. "I just couldn't get my brain to quiet down."

"I can understand that," Aubrey said.

He noticed the book that she was holding and gestured at it.

"What's that?" he asked. "Did you bring that home from the library?"

Aubrey looked down at the book and then back up at him.

"Oh. No. Nana just gave this to me. She told that I might find it interesting."

"What's it about?" he asked.

"I don't know."

Aubrey's voice sounded strange and the expression on her face looked like she wasn't fully there in the moment with him. He took a few steps toward her.

"Is everything alright?" he asked. "Did something happen at work?"

Aubrey shook her head.

"No," she said. "No, everything's fine. It's just…" she hesitated and looked back at the door to the bedroom and then back at him. "It's just that Nana was acting really odd just now. I went in to see her in the kitchen and she started asking me all sorts of questions about you and how much I know about you."

"Why would she do that?" Jonah asked.

He felt a prickle of nervousness on the back of his neck. Something had struck him as unusual about Nana the first moment that he met her, nothing intimidating or off-putting, just unusual. Now she was asking questions about him and it was making him anxious.

"I'm not sure," Aubrey said. She placed her bag on the bench in front of her vanity and looked down at the book in her hands again. "She was trying to find out how long you've been on Uoria and why you came back to Earth."

"I told you that I'm here because of what Ryan's doing."

"I know that," she said. "And that's what I told her."

"She doesn't believe me?"

"I don't think it's that. I don't know. She just gave me this book and told me that I should read it."

"Then let's have a look."

Jonah perched on the window seat and gestured for her to come sit beside him. Aubrey complied, but when she sat down on the pastel pink and green cushion, she hesitated.

Her hand was rested on the closed cover of the book and she was staring down at it as if she wasn't sure that she wanted to open it.

"Do you want me to open it?" Jonah asked.

Aubrey hesitated for another second and then nodded. Jonah took the book carefully from her lap and held it in one hand. He took the cover in the other and opened it. As soon as he saw the title written across the cover page in stark black script, he wished that he had never touched the book. He struggled to control his breath, not wanting the panic to be obvious to Aubrey, but he felt like the world was beginning to crash down around him.

"*Silenced Voices: The Story of Nyx 23*," she murmured. "Why would she give me this? I learned all about this mission when I was in school."

She slid the book out of Jonah's hands and started flipping through the pages. Suddenly she stopped and pointed to one of the pages.

"Penthos," she said. She looked up at him sharply. "That's the planet that you said that the rest of your crew went to. I hadn't even made the connection." She looked back at the book. "Wow," she said softly. "That's eerie. Can you imagine? Going to some desolate old planet that's been abandoned for more than a hundred years and knowing that some of the last people who ever set foot there were never seen again?"

She shuddered slightly, but Jonah didn't say anything. His mouth felt dry and his throat was tightening. Words were trying to force themselves up, but he wouldn't let them escape. He couldn't. He had already gotten himself so deep, and he couldn't think of anything that he could possibly say that would bring him out of it.

"I don't think that this really has anything to do with

what we're trying to do," Jonah said. "She probably just gave it to you because the team was from the University where you work."

He tried to reach for the book, hoping that he would be able to get it away from her and prevent her from reading it. At least until he was able to figure out a way that he could tell her the truth.

"I've worked there for a long time, and I went to school there," Aubrey said, resisting him taking the book from her hands. "Why would she wait until now to give it to me?"

She turned the next page and Jonah heard a sharp intake of breath. He looked down at the page and saw pictures of the crew splashed across it. His own face was smiling up from the center row, his eyes filled with the anticipation and honor of the mission ahead of him. He remembered when that picture was taken. They were told that these images of them would be used by the media when they came back to Earth successful and triumphant. They had believed in the leader that had arranged the mission and planned the pictures. Each of them envisioned the welcome that they would receive when they got back and it was finally revealed that they had freed a prison colony and brought greater peace to the Universe.

Now the pictures were used to memorialize them.

He could feel Aubrey shaking beside him and hear her short, shallow breaths. Her eyes were locked on the picture and even when he said her name, she didn't look away from it.

"I remember these pictures," she said. "They were in my textbooks when I was in college. I've seen this face a hundred times before, but I didn't recognize it. I didn't recognize you."

"Aubrey," Jonah said.

Aubrey shook her head and stood up sharply. Not looking back at him, she ran from the bedroom, taking the book with her. Jonah sat on the window seat for a few still moments. He felt like he was in shock. In one moment, everything was going well and he was even starting to open his mind to the life that he might be able to have, and in the next, everything shattered. He knew now that it was just a matter of time before everything that he had been working so hard for fell apart. He had to work faster and make the most of whatever time he had left before Aubrey revealed them and the secrecy that had protected the crew and all of the work that he had been doing would be gone.

Jonah picked up two bags and filled them with as much as he could get into them, and slipped out of the room and down the stairs into the entryway. When he was sure that it was quiet and still, he ran across it and out of the front door, not stopping until he was back up the long driveway and on the main road again. He knew that Mordecai, Gannon, and the women would be fine. They were in good hands and Nana was going to make sure that they got the continued medical treatment that they needed. She would ensure that they figured out what they were supposed to do next.

Though it had seemed like they had been driving for hours the night that they escaped from the basement and came here to Nana's house, over the time that they had been staying there Jonah realized that it was nowhere near as far as he had estimated, no more than ten miles. Undaunted by the distance after the years that he had spent trekking Uoria, Jonah tightened the straps on his bags and started walking back toward the University and what he hoped was still safety that he could maintain in the basement.

12

———

"Why did you give me this?"

Nana looked up from the needlepoint that she held in her lap. Her eyes fell on the book and she looked at it as though she didn't remember giving it to Aubrey.

"What, Honey?"

"This. Why did you give me this?" Aubrey demanded again, holding the blue book out for her grandmother to see.

"I told you. I thought that you would find it interesting." Nana made a few more stitches in the elaborate picture that she was making before speaking again. "Did you?"

"Did I find it interesting?" Aubrey asked incredulously. "Are you serious?" Nana looked up at her again with an expression that balanced between surprise and concern, and Aubrey felt the anger that had built up inside her slip away into a distant, hollow feeling. "You knew, didn't you?"

"Yes," Nana said.

"For how long?"

"From the moment I saw him," Nana admitted.

"How?"

"That book was my mother's most prized possession. She protected it like nothing else for her entire life. I spent so many evenings sitting with her reading and looking through the pictures."

"Why was it so important to her?" Aubrey asked.

"I didn't know. I always had the feeling that it was something much more precious than just a book, but when we looked at it, she didn't say anything. We just read it and looked at the pictures. Sometimes she would run her fingers along one of the pictures. I knew that it meant something, but I didn't ask."

Aubrey felt her interest perk even higher.

"One of the pictures?" she asked. "Which one?"

Nana held her hand out for the book and Aubrey gave it to her. She sat on her knees beside Nana's chair and watched as her grandmother opened the book to the page of pictures. Her heart clenched again at the sight of Jonah's younger, less care-worn face smiling up at her. Nana pointed to another picture on the page and Aubrey felt like she was looking back in time, seeing her great-grandmother's hand touch that face.

"Thank you, Nana," she said, taking the book from her lap again.

Aubrey stood and headed back up to the bedroom. She was already speaking when she walked through the door, but her words cut off abruptly when she saw that the window seat was empty. She walked out onto the balcony to see if Jonah had gone back outside, but he wasn't there. Stepping back into the bedroom, her eyes scanned the space and she realized that his bags were gone. Panic rose in her belly. He was gone. He had left. She rushed out of the room and back down the stairs.

"Nana, I have to go," she called toward the study where she had left her grandmother.

Aubrey ran to the front door, pausing only long enough to grab her car keys from the small silver bowl on the table beside it. Her feet barely touched the ground as she ran to her car and jumped inside. This couldn't be it. It couldn't be over yet. She had to understand. Her tires squealed as she pulled away from the house and drove down the driveway as fast as she could while safely following the curves of the road. There was only one place where Jonah would go, and she couldn't let him just walk into another ambush alone.

13

———

Jonah's steps had fallen into a rhythm. The sound of his feet crunching on the gravel beneath his boots filled the quiet around him and kept him company as he continued his way toward the University. The only light around him was the moon filtering through the trees, but he found the darkness soothing, reminding him of the walks that he would take along the river on Uoria. Again, there was a part of him longing for the planet and the settlement that they had built there. It had been his home for so long and it held all that was familiar to him.

Suddenly brighter lights washed over the ground in front of him and Jonah could hear the roar of an engine approaching from behind. He took a few more steps off of the edge of the road to allow the vehicle more space, but it sidled up beside him and paused. Squinting through the spots in his eyes that came from the bright headlights, he realized that it was Aubrey's car. The window rolled down and as his vision cleared and his eyes got more accustomed to the light, he could see her leaning out toward him.

"What do you think you're doing?" she asked.

"I'm going back to the basement of the laboratory building," he said. "I'm going to stay there for the rest of my time on Earth."

"The rest of your time on Earth?" Aubrey asked.

Jonah thought that he heard a touch of sadness in the question, but he didn't want to allow his mind to entertain that idea. He nodded, turning back to look down the dark expanse of road in front of him rather than continuing to look at her. It made his heart ache and he couldn't stand another moment of it.

"I'm going back to Uoria," he said. "As soon as I resolve everything here, I'm going back. We have a settlement there."

"You can't go back to the basement," Aubrey said. "The Valdicians know that you were there. They're going to be watching the laboratory building. There's nothing that they can do to me while I'm at work, but they won't hesitate if they see you there at night. Especially alone."

"It's my only option," he said. "I need to be close to the medical ward. There's more there for me to figure out."

"Get in the car," Aubrey said.

Jonah hesitated, but when she demanded he get in again, he complied, walking through the bright beams at the front to slide into the seat beside her.

"Alright," he said when he had shut the door.

"I want to know what's going on," she said. "The truth this time."

Jonah laid his head back against the headrest. His time was up. He couldn't keep up with the secrets any longer.

"You might as well turn the car off," he said.

Aubrey did as he said without question and Jonah let out a long breath. He needed a few more seconds just to come up with the right words to get started. Finally, he opened his mouth and the words started to tumble out. He told her everything that he could think of, every detail that he could remember. Jonah didn't know how long he talked, but by the time that he finished and let the interior of the car fall silent, the first glimmers of color from the earliest morning light were appearing around the bottoms of the trees.

"Why didn't you tell me?" Aubrey finally asked.

Her voice was powdery, as if she felt the same level of exhaustion that he was feeling now that he had drained everything out of himself with the story.

"I didn't know how to," he said. "It's not something that I could really put into words."

"You just did."

Jonah nodded.

"I know."

"Did you not tell me because you had a wife that you left behind?"

Jonah's heart sank at the trembling in her voice and he turned his head to look at her.

"No," he said, shaking his head. "I didn't have a wife. I never had a wife. I've never loved anybody like I..."

His voice trailed off and he felt heat come to his cheekbones at the unexpected confession he had begun to make.

"Anybody like what?" Aubrey asked. "What were you going to say?"

Jonah licked his suddenly dry lips.

"I've never loved anybody like I love you."

"Jonah," she started.

Jonah adjusted his body in the seat so that it faced her and reached for her hand. She allowed him to take it, but it shook slightly in his grip and her eyes were wide with surprise.

"Aubrey, when I saw you for the first time, I experienced something that I never have. I immediately felt like I knew you. I wasn't looking into the eyes of a stranger, but the eyes of someone my heart had always loved. It nearly destroyed me when you ran away from me in the lab. I didn't understand how you could not be feeling the same thing that I was."

"I was," Aubrey admitted. "I felt it from the very beginning, and it terrified me. I didn't know who you were or what you were doing in the lab, but I couldn't stop thinking about you. I felt something so strong for you, but I didn't want to admit it, not even to myself."

"Why?" Jonah asked.

His heart was trembling now and he needed to hear more from her. He needed more confirmation, more support for everything that he had felt for her.

"I told you what I went through with my boyfriend a couple of years ago," Aubrey said. "That wasn't the first time that someone had lied to me or tried to take advantage of me, but I had decided that it was the last time. I wasn't going to let it happen again. I was going to focus completely on my career and that was it. Then you came along. I didn't want to be in that place again. I didn't want to give someone else the opportunity to hurt me."

"I would never hurt you," Jonah said.

"But you did," Aubrey said. "You didn't tell me the truth about who you are or why you are back on Earth."

"Ryan really is doing everything that I told you that he is," Jonah said. "That really is why the rest went to Penthos. I only stayed behind to solve this part of it."

Aubrey nodded.

"I know," she said.

"I'm sorry. I just didn't know what to do or what to say. I

was already so deep. I felt so alone and then you were suddenly there. I wanted you with me. I appreciated your help, but I also just wanted you there beside me. I loved hearing your voice and seeing you smile first thing in the morning when you would get to the lab. I relied on being able to look at you to get me through the hard moments when I wanted to give up. I knew as soon as I met you that I should have been honest with you, but then everything happened and you left. I didn't think that I was ever going to see you again. When you came back, I was so thankful. I was so happy to see you again, and so scared that I was going to lose you again if I told you the truth."

"You should have trusted me," Aubrey said.

"And you should have trusted me," Jonah said.

Aubrey nodded.

"I should have." She intertwined her fingers with his. "I do now. With everything in me. I'm just sorry that I was so close to wasting the time that we have left together."

Jonah felt a bolt of fear go through him.

"The time that we have left together?" he asked.

"You said that you are going to finish what needs to be done here and then go back to Uoria." Jonah started to protest, but she held up a hand to stop him. "No," she said. "I understand. Really, I do. Everything here must be so different from how you remember it, and you don't really have a life here anymore. Your life is there now, and I can't blame you for wanting to go back to where you are comfortable, especially after everything that you've faced."

"Do you want me to go back?" Jonah asked.

Aubrey tilted her head and him and shook it slightly.

"Don't you want to?" she asked.

"I've been looking for a reason not to," Jonah admitted. "Maybe you can give me one."

"How?" Aubrey asked, genuinely expressing her desire to know what he needed of her to stay on Earth rather than going back to Uoria. "What can I do to give you a reason not to go back so soon?"

"Marry me," Jonah said. "Let me actually be your husband."

Aubrey gave a short laugh, her smile and eyes wide as she processed what he had just asked.

"Marry you?" she asked in surprise. "Jonah, we haven't even known each other..."

"I know," Jonah said. "I know that this probably seems really fast to you, but not to me. I've been waiting for you for more than one hundred years. This doesn't seem too soon to me at all."

Aubrey looked astonished. Her eyes sparkled and her mouth opened and closed a few times as she seemed to try to speak over her smile. Finally, she nodded.

"Yes," she said. "Yes, I'll marry you."

Jonah climbed out of the car and ran around to her side as fast as he could. She was standing outside of her door when he got to her and she jumped into his arms. He buried his face in her hair and drew in a deep breath of her, filling himself with the scent and presence that he thought that he was never going to have again. Her heart was pounding in her chest and he concentrated on the feeling, immensely grateful for every beat, every breath that she took. He pulled his head back so that he could look at her.

"What are we going to tell Cecilia?" he asked.

Aubrey drew him into her arms again, her laugh filling the world around him.

Jonah's hand was steady as Aubrey slipped the heavy gold band onto his ring finger and then turned his hand to touch a kiss to where the gold rested on his palm. She looked radiant in the simple satin gown, the delicate pink shade so soft it was nearly white, and tiny, fragrant blooms woven into her hair. They stood in the backyard of the mansion, those from the basement, Nana, and the staff who had been caring for them since their arrival gathered around them. It had been only a few days since his proposal in the car on the side of the road, but neither of them had wanted to wait a moment longer than they had to. There was too much uncertainty ahead. They found security and strength in the certainty of each other.

"...in sickness and in health, as long as you both shall live?"

Jonah looked at the officiant and then into Aubrey's eyes, knowing those words had never carried more meaning.

"I do."

UNTITLED

To be continued...

THE ALIEN'S LAIR

1

Ellora struggled against the hand over her mouth. Her fingers clawed at its skin, but it didn't relent. The ground beneath her feet disappeared and she started to kick, hoping that she would be able to make contact with whoever it was behind her and they would let her go. Finally, she heard a door close and the cold stone of a wall on her cheek as the person who held her pressed her to it.

"I'm not going to hurt you," a man's voice said into her ear. "Be quiet and I'll be able to help you get out of here."

Ellora didn't know if she should trust the voice. She didn't know if there was any reason why she should believe that this person would help her and wasn't just another of the Order who were trying to capture her. She struggled again and the man held her tighter.

"I knew your husband."

With those words, Ellora fell still. Her body went limp and the arm around her waist softened and gradually moved away, but the hand over her mouth stayed in place. The man's mouth came to her ear again.

"I'm going to let you go," he said. "I need you to stay quiet. Don't say anything at all. I will explain everything to you, but you are going to have to trust me. You are just going to have to listen to what I have to say and be willing to do what I need you to do. Can you do that?"

Ellora nodded and felt his hand come away from her mouth. Just as she had agreed, she stayed quiet.

"Good. I'm going to take your wrist. Follow me. You'll be able to see in just a minute."

Ellora felt the man take her wrist and let him guide her through the darkness. The wall that she had been pressed against was close enough that her shoulder brushed against it and she found comfort and security in it. Suddenly it fell away and she felt him pull her through a door and close it. A bright white glow started and grew quickly and soon Ellora could see the man in front of her holding a lantern. He put it at his feet and the light shined up on his face. He was younger than her, but there was something ancient in his eyes that looked like pain and secrets. There was something strange about his appearance, but she couldn't quite place it. She knew that he wasn't Mikana, and he didn't look Denynso, either. There was a vaguely human quality about him, but something in her told her that he wasn't human, either.

"My name is Mhavrych," he said.

"I'm Ellora," she said.

"I know," he said. "I told you. I knew Aegeus."

"I never heard him mention you."

"He wouldn't have," he said. "Of everything that he couldn't tell you about the Order, I am the greatest secret." He hesitated and Ellora saw his face harden even further. "Even the rest of the Order doesn't know about me. They only know what I am trying to protect."

"If they know about what you are trying to protect, how do they not know about you?" she asked.

"The Order believes what the Order believes," he said. "They think that they are the only ones who can save the Universe, when they don't even know what they are protecting it from."

"I don't understand," Ellora said.

"I wouldn't expect you to," Mhavrych said. "Not yet. But I don't have the time to explain it to you now. Your husband knew things that no one else in the Order did, and that is what caused what happened to him. I spent many years fearing that he was dead because of me."

"He's not dead," Ellora said, as much to convince herself of it as she was telling him.

"I know. I've seen him."

Ellora's eyes widened and she took a step toward Mhavrych as if being close to him would somehow bring her closer to Aegeus.

"Where is he?"

"When I saw him, he was on another planet. He was enslaved by a man named Ryan and was among an army of strange blended species that he had created. I thought that I was going to be able to help him, but before I could free him, Ryan moved him again."

"To Earth," Ellora said. "He brought him to the facility where he has been breeding hybrids. There are many people who are after him, now. One of my sons is still on Penthos facing the army."

"Penthos," Mhavrych said, nodding. "That was where I was when I saw him. It was only for a brief time and I didn't even have the chance to speak to him.

"What were you doing on Penthos?" Ellora asked.

Mhavrych stiffened slightly.

"I have work there," he said. "It has to do with what I am protecting."

"For the Order?" Ellora asked.

Mhavrych shook his head.

"From the Order," he said. "There was a time when the purpose of the Order was to protect the Universe and all that exists within it, but as your husband discovered, corruption was extensive within the ranks. Though there are still members who believe in the original mission and fight hard for it, there are others who have been so influenced by the corrupt members that they no longer remember what they are meant to do."

"I need you to tell me what you are protecting," Ellora said. "I lost my husband to this for many years and I'm not willing to give up fighting to be back with him."

"I wouldn't ask you to," Mhavrych said. "I still need his help. I need the help of everyone who has been fighting Ryan. He is the final link to what I have spent many years trying to guard. I tried to help them. I saved a warrior named Nylek from the hybrids and a couple named Kyven and Emerie from an animal who lives deep within the planet."

Ellora felt her heart jump.

"Kyven?" she asked.

Mhavrych nodded.

"Yes. He was trapped beneath the ground in a cavern with a creature known as a Meldor. Its weakness is light. I was able to get it away from them long enough for them to get out of the cavern."

"Kyven is my son."

She could see Mhavrych straighten and nod slightly.

"He looks like Aegeus."

"He looks much more like me," Ellora said. "It's my son Maxim that favors his father."

The man looked at her earnestly.

"What I need to do has greater importance that I can even explain. Aegeus knew. He understood the danger of the corruption within the Order and the threat that it held not just for Uoria, but for everything. I need you to help me."

"I will do anything that I can," Ellora said. "But they've already caught me. They know that I'm down here."

"We can get out," Mhavrych said.

He led her to what looked like an old wooden chest in the corner at the far end of the room. Ellora watched as he drew a key from the bag at his hip and used it to open the chest. Inside there was an old, dirty cloth sack.

"What is that?" she asked.

"This is what I have been protecting," he said. "If we can get out with this, we have a chance to finish what your husband started."

2

____

Severine cradled the baby to her chest and wrapped it tightly with the cloth, securing him to her so that she was able to carry him more easily. Behind her Rilex was finishing gathering all of their supplies. She knew that he had an element of excitement about going through the network of chambers and tunnels that were beneath the surface of Penthos, but she still felt a sense of nervousness. It had been so long since she had been in the tunnels and the memories of the times that she had spent there were still strong. Even though Ryan had proclaimed that these tunnels were meant to be their home and keep them safe when they weren't in battle, they had never felt truly safe. They were only permitted to go into them after they had already gone through extensive training and drills, going until their bodies couldn't handle it any longer and they began to collapse into the searing hot sand. She didn't want to walk through them again. She didn't want the chance of encountering the army. But she knew that this was the best way. Going back up to the surface would expose them and put them in more danger. This section of tunnels were rarely used and she knew that chances were, they weren't going to encounter any of the hybrids as long as they moved quickly.

Ready, they started out of the chamber and down the tunnel that led them back in the direction of the ship. The further they went, the more reassured she was that they weren't going to encounter any of the rest of the army. Around them the bunker looked old and abandoned. It was as if the last time that she had been down in them during her training was the last time that anyone had used them. It was a strange sensation walking through the tunnels that were once so tightly crowded and feeling that it was only her, Rilex, and the baby who were down there.

They had been traveling for several minutes when the tunnel branched off. Rilex slowed in front of her and looked both directions.

"Which way?" he asked.

Severine searched back in her memories, trying to remember the last time that she was in this area and where they should go that would bring them back in the right direction. It seemed that she had been here before, but that she didn't remember the branching of the tunnels. She shook her head.

"I don't know," she admitted.

Rilex looked in both directions and pointed at one.

"This way," he said.

"Why?" she asked.

He shrugged and shook his head.

"I don't know," he admitted. "I just feel like this is the way that we should go."

She nodded. That was enough for her. They turned and started down the tunnel. They had only taken a few steps when they started to notice more signs that this area hadn't been used in quite some time. Remnants of clothes and blankets had seemed to break down into the ground, and canisters of what looked like rations were so eroded that they could no longer read the labels. Rilex held his torch up higher as they walked and she knew that he was trying to shed as much light through the tunnel as possible so that they had as much awareness as they could about what lay ahead.

The light touched a curve in the tunnel and she could see that it opened into a small chamber that was similar to the storage rooms that they had used in the newer bunkers to hold their weapons and rations. As soon as they stepped inside, however, she could see that this room had not been used to store the items that she would have expected. Instead, a skeleton encased in tattered cloth lay in the middle of the floor.

Severine gasped and stepped backwards, trying to get away from the image of the body lying in the storage room. Rilex, on the other hand, strode forward directly toward it. He took the light of the torch with him and she felt the chill of the darkness settle around her. She stepped into the room with him, needing the light. Rilex was crouched down beside the skeleton, carefully touching the fabric that clung to it.

"These are old," he said. "This body has been here for more than 100 years, at least."

"Who is it?" Severine asked, knowing full well that there was no way that he would be able to identify the person, even if he had known it when it was alive. "Can you tell if it's a man or a woman?"

Rilex moved a piece of the fabric aside and it fell from the ribcage. Severine could see that the person was lying on its stomach, its arms tucked under it and its face down. As the fabric fell away from its ribs, she could see that there was something under it. Rilex seemed to have seen it at the same time and gently moved the bones to reach for it. He pulled it out and turned toward her, a book in his hands.

"What is it?" she asked, her voice tremulous.

Rilex settled onto his heels and gingerly lifted open the cover. Dust rose from the pages as if they were disintegrating right into the air with his touch. Rilex stared at the pages and the words that it contained with such intensity that Severine felt like he was no longer in the room with her, but somewhere else with only the book. He turned the pages slowly at first, and then faster, moving through them like he was desperate to find out what was on the next page and the next. Ignoring the discomfort that came from the skeleton, Severine stepped closer to him and crouched down, touching her hand to the baby's back to hold him close.

"What is it?" she asked.

She reached out to rest her hand on Rilex's arm and felt him jump beside her as if she had struck him. He looked at her for a few seconds and then back at the book. His hand touched it almost reverently before his eyes slid back up to her and met hers. Deep in their recesses she could see the streaks of the shooting stars and noticed them flash brighter.

"This is something from long ago," he said. "Something that I would never have thought that I would find. Not here."

"What does it mean?" Severine asked.

Rilex let out a long breath and glanced at the skeleton.

"You said that you wanted to know my origin," he said. "The origin of my kind."

"Yes," Severine said. "Is that what that book is about?"

Rilex nodded.

"It is linked to it," he said, "but from long before me. This happened in a different time and a different stream than my life, but it is as inextricably connected to it as you are. "

"I want to know," Severine said. "Tell me."

Rilex shook his head and closed the book, tucking it close to his chest.

"Not now," he said. "It's a long story and one that I won't be able to tell you now. We need to keep going and get back to the others."

"The others," Severine murmured.

Those words had hit her suddenly and unexpectedly, carrying with them more meaning than she would have expected them to. She felt a hint of a smile come to her lips.

"What?" Rilex asked.

She looked up at him, realizing that he had heard what she said even though she thought that she had barely uttered the sounds.

"You said something."

"The others," she said.

Rilex nodded.

"We need to get back to them," he said. "They might still be waiting at the ship for us, but they might also have started toward Maxim and the rest of the crew that remained here."

"No," Severine said. "I know that. It's just the words...the others."

"What about them?" Rilex asked.

Severine ran her hand along the newborn's back as he cuddled against her chest. She could feel his sweet, peaceful breaths as he slept comfortably with the sound of her heartbeat keeping him comfortable and relaxed.

"You said that I should be proud of where I came from and the heritage that I have, whatever that is. "

"You should. However you came to be, that is what made you and what brought you here to save the lives of countless others and to be the mother of this child...and the partner for me."

"There's that word again," Severine said. "Other. I feel like that's us."

"What do you mean?"

"You know who you are. You are sure of yourself and your heritage. You share the culture and the history of that species. Even Eden and Pyra's son will know his heritage clearly. He will know that his mother was human before he was born and that his father is Denynso. I know that they will make sure that he knows about both sides of his culture and what created him. Even if he lives out his entire life on Uoria and only interacts with the humans who live there with the warriors, he will still know that he has part human blood and what that means. That gives him a sense of connection and acceptance with both kinds. It isn't the fact that he has both species in him. That isn't what matters. What matters is that he knows about those cultures and is taught about them by people who willfully and purposefully gave him life. When he is asked who or what he is, Lysander will have a strong sense of identity. That isn't the way it is for me or the rest of the hybrids that Ryan created."

"Your identity is each of the species that create you," Rilex said. "You are each of them. All of you are. You are Mikana, and Denynso, Eteri and Irisa. You are everything that went into creating each of you, so you belong to each of those species."

"But we don't," Severine said. She could see the desperate look on Rilex's face, as if he was grasping for anything that would reassure her and make her feel stronger and more connected to something. She shook her head, smiling in a way that felt more genuine than she remembered in any other situation than when she first heard Rilex confess his love for her. "We don't belong with any of them. And that's alright. I'm not saying that as a bad thing or that there is something wrong with it. I've just realized that. You helped me to realize it.

We are different. But that doesn't mean that we need to try to assimilate ourselves into a world that we don't know, no matter what that world is. As much as each of the species that were used to make us shouldn't have to feel as though they are forced to claim us or accept that we are a part of them just because there is some of their DNA in us, none of us should feel as though we are forced to accept that any one species is what we are, or that we are a pieced-together conglomerate of multiple species. We have identities, and those identities come from what we are. Not the pieces of us. Not the histories of the people who are those species. Not the hope that one day we will fit in with someone or somewhere. We have identities because we are individuals, and those identities are separate from anything else. We aren't Denynso. We aren't Mikana. We aren't Eteri. We aren't Irisa. We are the Others."

The expression on Rilex's face softened and she thought that she saw the sparkle of tears in his eyes. He nodded.

"You're right," he said. "You are individuals and you should be respected for that. I think that the Others is the perfect way to describe you."

Severine leaned forward to kiss Rilex, capturing his mouth and feeling the smile against her lips. For the first time, she wasn't ashamed that when he looked at her he saw that she wasn't like everyone else. She knew that he thought that she was beautiful, but she hadn't felt that way. She had only thought of what each of her characteristics represented. Now she felt proud not just of the way that she looked, but also what that meant. It no longer mattered to her that Ryan had created her for such a cruel purpose. He didn't have claim on her any longer, and the greatest revenge that she could have over him would be to appreciate who she was, devote herself to enjoying the life that she had in front of her now, and reclaim others from his grasp.

3

————

than could sense the change that had come over the tunnels as soon as he got into them. There was a heaviness in the atmosphere that went beyond even the tension that usually hung in the air when the Order was preparing for conflict. The feeling settling over him made him even more uncomfortable and he feared for Ellora's safety at a new level. Carefully closing the access ramp to prevent anyone from the kingdom finding it and venturing down into the tunnels, Athan started toward the center of the network where he would be able to access the side tunnels that would bring him to the entrance where he assumed Ellora had gone inside. It was the rarely-used entrance tucked into a home rather than in the ground or the wall around the kingdom as they usually were, but it would bring her down very close to the main meeting rooms as well as dark, scarcely-seen rooms that he didn't want to think of her encountering.

Moving quickly, Athan rushed through the changing colors of light. Suddenly he could hear other footsteps in the tunnels with him. For a moment, he felt a sense of hope thinking that it might be Ellora, but the longer that he listened to them, the more he recognized that they were too heavy, too loud to belong to the small woman. This meant that this was one of the men of the Order running through the tunnels, which told Athan that they had not only discovered that Ellora was in the forbidden area, but that they were now chasing after her. If they got their hands on her, she would be in incredible danger, and he had to do whatever he could to prevent that.

Taking a steeling breath, Athan turned in the direction of the footsteps and ran toward them. If he was able to find the man who was running through the tunnels, he would have a better chance of finding out what had happened with Ellora and possibly where she might be so that he could find her. Athan had only gone a few more yards when a figure turned the corner ahead of him.

"Malcolm!" Athan exclaimed.

The younger man skidded to a stop in front of Athan and looked at him with a frantic expression in his eyes.

"Athan," he said. "Where did you come from?"

His tone sounded suspicious and Athan knew that he needed to redirect that feeling so that he could get as much information from him as he could. Athan was momentarily stunned. He hadn't expected to encounter any of the members of the Order and hadn't prepared himself for what he might say if they questioned why he had come down into the tunnels, especially considering that the higher-up members of the hierarchy were likely preparing serious discipline for his betrayal of allowing Maxim and Ivy into the tunnels and then giving the vehicles to them to use.

"I heard from the Leader," Athan finally said. "He said that he wanted me to get down here as quickly as possible, that there is an intruder."

He knew that Malcolm wouldn't question instructions from the Leader, particularly if Athan kept them vague enough that it seemed he was too frantic to provide thorough information. Malcolm nodded, immediately going along with what Athan was saying.

"There is," he said. "It is Ellora."

"Aegeus's wife?" Athan asked.

For a brief moment, he thought that he might have gone too far in his questioning. Everyone knew of his closeness with Ellora, particularly because he had been the closest friend and confidante of Aegeus prior to his disappearance.

"Yes," Malcolm said, some of the suspicion finding its way back into his voice.

"I just don't understand why she would come down here," Athan said, trying to add an edge of anger to his own voice to counteract the tone of the younger man's words. "There's nothing here for her. What does she think that she's going to find down here?"

It seemed to work and Malcolm gave an almost imperceptible nod.

"I don't know," he said. "She came down here angry and confronted me, then the Leader found her."

Athan felt himself tense.

"He did?" he asked. "What did he do?"

"He picked her up off the ground. I don't know what he planned to do with her, but by his tone I know that he was infuriated. I don't know for certain that she would have survived much longer down here if she hadn't outsmarted him and escaped."

As soon as he said the words, Athan could see Malcolm's face pale slightly. Even though the Leader was not nearby, he wouldn't want to think that the man in one of the highest ranks of the hierarchy within the Order had heard him utter what could be thought of as even close to an insult. It would be completely unacceptable for Malcolm to say that the Leader had been outsmarted, no matter how true it was. Athan remembered a time when there wasn't such tension and darkness in the Order. Though the hierarchy had always been there and there had always been swift and fierce punishments for those who didn't follow the guidelines of the Order once chosen, it hadn't been this brutal. There hadn't been the overhanging sense of fear and hesitation that seemed to control everyone now. It had been building steadily before Aegeus disappeared, and Athan knew that it was because of that that he had made whatever plans had led to him going missing from that battlefield, presumed dead for so many years. Though after that battle it had seemed that relative peace had returned and the Order had largely returned to the way that it once was, in recent months it had begun to descend again and Athan could see the corruption again taking hold.

"What did she do?" Athan asked.

"She forced him to release her," Malcolm said. "She released all strength and tension in her body and he wasn't able to hold her. The moment that she hit the ground, she scurried away and she's been loose in the tunnels since."

"And you don't know why she came down here?" Athan asked.

"She said that she wanted to know about the Order. She demanded that we tell her what we do and why because she wanted to know what was so important that her husband was willing to die for it, and that she had to give up the years that she could have spent with him. What did she mean by that?"

Athan realized that Malcolm didn't know that Aegeus was alive. Though she had been hasty in her decision to come down here at all, at least she had thought through it enough that she hadn't revealed her husband was still alive. He knew how difficult that was for her. He had seen it in her eyes when he first told her. In that one instant, her entire world crashed down around her, and the rubble of the world that already had, was rebuilt into something beautiful and tenuously hopeful. She had felt betrayed and honored, horrified and delighted, afraid and empowered. It was everything that she had ever felt about her husband's disappearance on top of her all over again, but now with a wash of joy at the thought that she might one day soon be able to look into his face and hold him in her arms again.

"Aegeus died many years ago," Athan said. "I can only guess that when she looks at her grown sons that they remind her of how much time has passed and that she could have spent that time with her husband rather than raising Maxim and Kyven alone. She must realize now that Maxim and Ivy are together and Kyven has Emerie that they won't be with her any longer. She will soon be on her own and she can't help but imagine what it would have been like if she had been able to live out the rest of her life with Aegeus the way that she had always planned that she would."

Malcolm nodded again and looked behind himself as if expecting the Leader to come around the corner or for Ellora to run past.

"You don't know where she is?" he asked, his tone slightly lower now as if he were trying to inspire confidence in Athan just in case he really did know where to find the missing woman.

Athan shook his head.

"No," he answered honestly. "I don't know. But I will help you look for her. What should I do with her if I find her?"

He didn't want to commit to doing anything for fear that the insincerity would betray him.

"Bring her to the center meeting room," he said. "I know that the Leader will want to see her as soon as possible."

Athan nodded and Malcolm turned sharply, taking off running again. Taking a few deep breaths to calm the shaking inside his body, Athan started in the opposite direction. Now that he knew that the men were looking for her, it was more pressing to find Ellora as quickly as possible and get her out of the tunnels. He tried to imagine what was going through her mind when she took off from the Leader. He had been making his way through the tunnels for his entire adult life, and he still sometimes found them complicated and confusing to navigate. The thought of her being alone in them without any idea as to where she was or how she should make her way back in the direction that she needed to go was terrifying. It would be far too easy for her to accidentally loop back around and end up right back in the same hallway where she first encountered the Leader, or to even come upon the rooms and meeting centers that were hidden throughout it. Just as dangerous, though, would be if she didn't find these at all, but rather wandered deeper into the complex of corridors. Many of those corridors hadn't been in regular use for as long as Athan could remember, and the deeper that she went, the more likely she was to find the ones that led into dead-ends and large rooms that on their own were enough to disorient her. She could get lost in them and by the time that any of them found her, she would have long died from lack of water and food.

As he moved down the corridor as quickly as he could, the lights flashing over head to mark his progress, Athan tried to think of where she might have gone. He couldn't imagine that Aegeus had given her any details about the underground network or the corridors themselves. If he had, she might have some way of knowing how to make her way around, but that would mean that she would have either found her way out already or that they would have found her. It was much more likely that she knew that there was something underground and that now she was essentially running blindly through the lair, hoping that she happened to stumble upon the ladder that would lead her back up and out of the hatch.

He didn't want to encounter any other members of the Order. Malcolm was young and still saw him with the respect and reverence of being one of the elder members of the hierarchy. He either wasn't aware of Athan's recent transgressions, or was too intimidated by his age and station to take issue with them. The other men who were of his age and station, and even some younger ones, however, were not as forgiving as Malcolm. They would not hesitate to turn their attention from finding Ellora to capturing Athan if they saw him, and then neither of them would be safe.

As if his thoughts had lured them toward him, Athan could suddenly hear the voices of some of the other Order members coming quickly down the corridor toward him.

"And you just let him go?" one demanded.

"I'm sorry," Malcolm said. "I didn't realize it was so important."

"The Leader was very clear about Athan's betrayal of the Order. He said that if he was to set foot down here, he was to immediately be brought in front of the Panel for sanction."

"What are they going to do to him?"

"He told outsiders about the Order, allowed them down into the tunnels, and gave them hidden technology to use for their own purposes. I can't speak for the Leader or the rest of the Panel, but I can't imagine that they will treat him gently. The members of the Order know that being chosen for this organization is not just a tremendous honor, but a responsibility unlike anything else that they might encounter. We are expected to uphold our duty to protect the Order and everything about it for our entire lives, even if that means giving up our lives. Athan knew what he was doing. The moment that he made the decision to give that information, he forsook himself and his claim for a future. No matter what happens to him, he can only blame himself."

Athan took off running. He didn't know where he was going or what he might encounter, but he knew that he needed to get away from the men who were coming his direction. They wouldn't hesitate for a second to drag him in front of the Panel and sacrifice his life. None of them understood what was really happening, but it didn't matter. Even if they did, they were so controlled by the Order and the men who had corrupted it that they likely wouldn't be able to make a choice for themselves to help Athan. Even if they knew about Ryan and what was happening on Penthos, even if they knew that Aegeus was alive, they wouldn't be able to process it and recognize the incredible importance of them allowing Athan to live, even if they didn't cooperate with him. In fact, there was a chance that if they knew that Aegeus was alive, they might do anything that they could to find him so that they would be able to bring him, too, in front of the Panel.

Not for the first time since finding out that the man who was once his best friend was still alive, Athan thought back to the moment that he realized that Aegeus had disappeared from the battlefield. It was easiest then to think that he had died, even though it was the most painful experience of his life. He couldn't think of anything else that could explain him being completely gone. Now, though, he had to wonder how he had gone from the moment that he was walking into the battle to Ryan's clutches. He could only assume that it was somehow linked to the Order, but even that didn't make sense. If they had found out that Aegeus knew what was happening within the Order, they would have handled it on their own. He couldn't understand why they would have given him over to a human on Earth to be a part of breeding experiments rather than punishing him themselves. The thought of the motivations that might have caused it sent a chill down Athan's spine and he forced himself to run faster and harder, putting the voices of the men at his back and putting more focus on finding Ellora.

4

Rilex peered around the corner, holding his torch up so that he could fill it with as much light as possible. Now that they knew for certain that they were not the only people who had come into this tunnel, he was more on edge and focused on checking every area before they walked into it to make sure that they weren't wandering into a dangerous trap. He glanced back over his shoulder to see Severine. She was gazing down at the baby wrapped close to her chest, murmuring something to him as he wriggled.

"I think he's hungry," she said, glancing up at Rilex. "We're going to need to stop so that I can feed and change him."

Rilex didn't like the thought of pausing again, even for a few moments, but he knew that he didn't have an option. The baby needed to be properly cared for in order to stay safe and healthy, and if he were to keep pushing them to go further even when he needed care he would soon start to cry, alerting the hybrid army of their presence. It was important that they stopped and made sure that he had the care that he needed so that he could keep sleeping comfortably as they traveled.

"We need to find somewhere off of the tunnel to stop," he said. "I don't want to be so exposed."

Severine nodded and they continued on, Rilex letting the light of the torch run across the walls as they went so that he could find any small chambers that might lead off of the tunnel. They had gone on for a few moments when he saw a dip in the wall and paused. Gesturing for Severine to stay where she was, Rilex took the several steps needed to bring him to the doorway and leaned in with the torch. He didn't see anything and stepped further inside. The light from the flame of the torch washed across a bare dirt floor and curved dirt walls. This stood apart from the other chambers where they had been that had a smooth stone floor and walls that made them feel much more like true rooms and not just dugout sections of the ground. When he was confident that there was nothing in the room that would pose a danger to them, he stepped back out into the corridor and gestured for Severine to come with him.

Rilex tucked the torch into the dirt so that it stood independently and helped Severine spread a blanket out onto the ground so that she could settle onto it with the baby. He watched as she carefully untied the cloth from around her waist and over her shoulders, rested her hand on his back, and eased him away from her so that she could lay him down on the blanket. Rilex wished that she would give the tiny child a name. He knew that it was something that was still somewhat foreign to her. Even though she had known that she and the other hybrids didn't have names and had felt that there was something missing about them because of it, and though she now had a name that was carefully selected for her, it still wasn't something that she fully understood. When she looked at the baby, she thought more about the mother that he had lost in the first moment of his life and the care that she was going to need to give him to ensure he stayed safe even in the difficult world into which he was born. Though he could see the affection in her eyes, he knew that she hadn't yet come to the place in her thoughts where she understood the value of naming the baby. Perhaps she had. Perhaps she felt that naming him would give her an even stronger connection to him, would make their relationship somehow more real, and she didn't feel ready to accept that. For someone whose entire life had been defined by pain, heartache, and loss, the thought of building a strong link with not just one, but two people in such a short time would seem overwhelming to her. Bonding with Rilex was one thing. She knew that he was an adult and that the relationship that they had was by their choice. He loved her and was capable of declaring that love for her and making the decision to remain with her no matter what situation they were facing, or the life that they might have to build together.

The baby was different. This was a newborn child who did not truly belong to her. She had claimed him in a moment of desperate protectiveness without thinking about the potential consequences. In her mind, she was the one who was best suited to caring for the baby after his birth mother died. After all, she had been assigned to the nursery in the breeding facility and had been tasked with caring for the hybrid babies when they were born. Rilex wondered if it was now settling into her mind that she didn't have any real right to take the baby with her when she left the ship and that there might have been other arrangements that should have been made for the child. Though there was no father who could have taken him, one of the other human women might have had further claim to him than Severine did. Rilex didn't think that that was what was really bothering Severine, though. He knew enough of her by now to know that it wouldn't matter as much to her if someone else thought that they had more claim on the baby than she did because of the emotional turmoil that it might cause to that person to see him taken from them. Instead, she worried about herself and the impact that it would have to have him taken from her. She already loved this baby and she couldn't bear the thought of acknowledging their bond more than she already had and then having him taken from her.

Her hands moved swiftly but gently as she changed the baby and then brought him back up to cradle him as she reached back into her bag and pull out the bottle that she had made for him. Rilex watched as she mixed the various components of the formula that she had created and nestled the rubber nipple into the baby's mouth. The tiny child immediately calmed as he drank and soon Rilex saw his eyes relax and close. He drank deeply for a few more seconds and then fall into a quiet sleep. Severine looked down at him, stroking his cheek as she tenderly rocked him. The baby continued to take sips occasionally, but his face was peaceful and his body soft and trusting in Severine's arms. Finally, she looked up at Rilex.

"Could you hold him for just a minute?" she asked.

There was tense, tight emotion in her voice and he didn't want to push her. He reached his arms toward her and Severine rested the baby into them. He pulled him closer and cradled him so that his head rested in the crook of his elbow. The tiny child let out a sigh and snuggled into him, and Rilex felt his heart swell.

"Severine, I was telling you the truth when I said that this baby has a family. He has a mother in you and a father in me. I believed it when I said it then, and I believe it now. It doesn't matter what else is going on. That will pass. This will all end and we will have a life ahead of us. We will pass that life together and he will be with us."

"Will we?" she asked.

"What do you mean?" he asked.

"Who was that body, Rilex?" she asked. "Who died down here?"

"I don't know," he answered.

"You said that it had something to do with your origin and why you ended up on Earth."

"Yes," he said. "It does, but I only know that because of the book that I found it holding. I don't know who it was or why it had the book. I don't even know when it died or how, except that it has been many years. I can tell you that I think that it was a man."

"And he was holding the book?" Severine asked.

Rilex nodded.

"Yes. He was lying on his stomach and his arms were tucked under him, so it looked like he was holding the book to his chest. I think he knew that he was dying and didn't have any chance that he was going to get out of the tunnels, so he wanted to do whatever he could to protect the book. He didn't want anybody to get their hands on it."

"Why?" Severine asked. "What could happen if someone found it? Who is it that they don't want to find it?"

He knew that she was trying her best to pull the information that she wanted from him, but he couldn't reveal it. This wasn't the time. They had enough to think about and enough that they needed to overcome. They didn't need something else hanging over them, especially something that he didn't know how it connected with this planet or the war that was building above them, if it connected at all. He knew that there would be a time eventually when he needed to explain it all to her, but for now he would continue to hold it within him. Even as he thought this, though, he couldn't get his mind off of the skeleton that lay alone in the room deeper in the bunker. He wished that he knew who the man was and what had brought him into the tunnels. His presence there proved to Rilex what he had questioned when he first followed Severine down into the chamber where they first hid. Ryan couldn't have designed and built these tunnels. That man had been lying there for at least one hundred years if Rilex had interpreted the condition of his clothing correctly, which was decades before Ryan was even born. It was far more likely that these had been in place when the prison colony run by the Valdicians was in operation, well before the Nyx 23 crew came and were then sent to Uoria. That meant that Ryan was either told about them or found them on his own and decided to use them for his army. As much as Rilex wanted to know who the man was, who was now lying on the ground, protecting the book with his last breaths, he also wanted to know who had created these bunkers and what that meant for the man who had died in them. Had he known why they were created and that was why he came down here? Had he been on the planet for another reason and discovered the tunnels accidentally, but then wasn't able to find his way out? Or had he been found when he was on the planet and forced down into the bunkers for the purpose of ensuring that he would die down there and never be found?

Now that they had found the man, Rilex wondered what they should do about him. He felt strange leaving him lying there, especially after taking the book that he had been holding, but he didn't know what other choice he had. He, Severine, and the baby needed to get through the tunnels and back to the ship, and he couldn't put additional stress on them by trying to transport the body with them. It would be better to leave him where he was and return for him when he had a better chance to investigate him thoroughly and try to find out who he was and what he might be doing there.

5

———————

Maxim took the papers that he had found in the office and laid them out so that Avery could look at them with him. Until then he hadn't thought that the human pilot would have anything of interest or value to add to his investigation and understanding of the papers. He hadn't been involved in the conflict until they found him in the panic room within the ship and didn't have all of the details that the rest of them did. Now, though, he realized that it was that very characteristic that made Avery valuable. He didn't have the closely focused perspective that those from Uoria had about the situation. While they were focused on everything that Ryan had done and the painful impact that his actions had had on them then and that he continued to have on them with every passing moment, Avery only knew the facts about the crew and Penthos that he had learned throughout his life, and the information that they had told him. This took the emotion out of it for him so that he was better able to see the details and intricacies that they overlooked. If it hadn't been for him, Maxim may never have heard the name

Martin Roe, and while he still didn't know the significance of that name, he knew that he would and that it meant something.

As they crouched by the papers, Maxim noticed Avery rubbing around one of his fingers as if there was something that was missing from it. Avery noticed that Maxim was watching him and let his fingers fall away from his other hand.

"Sorry," he said. "I'm used to having a wedding band there."

Maxim wasn't sure what to say. He didn't understand the significance of the statement. While the Mikana used many of the same terms as the humans to describe their relationships, they didn't have wedding bands. He didn't know what it would mean that Avery usually had one but didn't now.

"Did you lose it?" Maxim asked, unsure of what else he was supposed to say.

Avery shook his head.

"Not exactly. My wife and I got divorced. It was a couple of years ago, so I should be used to it by now, but I always used to spin my ring around when I was thinking hard about something. I guess it was just habit, because I still do it. "

"Divorced?" Maxim asked.

Avery looked at him quizzically.

"Your kind doesn't have divorce, I'm guessing?" he asked.

Maxim shook his head.

"I haven't heard the term."

"It means that we ended our marriage," Avery said, a hint of regret in his voice.

"We can do that," Maxim said. "It doesn't happen very often, admittedly."

Avery nodded, a distant look in his eyes.

"That must be nice," he said. "I never thought that I was going to be one of those people who get divorced. I always thought that there must be something wrong with them or that they weren't good at being in a relationship. Maybe they were selfish and self-centered and didn't know how to take care of a marriage, or maybe Sarah and I were just so much more in love than any of them ever were so there was no way that we were going to just stop loving each other and get divorced." He let out a laugh that sounded as though he were completely disbelieving of his own misled thoughts as much as he was trying to connect with Maxim through sharing the situation. "Of course, then I did become one of those people. And you know what I figured out?"

"What?" Maxim asked.

"That those people aren't any different than any other people. These are the same people who love their spouses as much as I loved Sarah when we got married, and think that they are going to be better at being married, and will nurture their marriages, and will love each other so much that there will be nothing that will take them apart. There is no difference between people who get divorced and people who don't. The ones who don't just happen to have found a relationship that will work while those who get divorced didn't."

"I guess it's a good thing that you learned that," Maxim said.

Avery nodded with long sigh.

"It's the one good thing that came out of it," he said with another laugh. "I have to admit, though, there are a lot of times when I really miss being married. It's not so much that I miss her. Everything that happened was enough to make it so that I never wanted to be with her again. But we've come to a point where we are fairly comfortable with each other. It's been long enough that we aren't really angry with each other anymore and can even have a conversation that is almost pleasant. That's really nice."

"But you want somebody at home with you," Maxim said.

Avery nodded and reached forward to shuffle through the papers on the floor between them as if he were starting to feel uncomfortable with the conversation.

"I'm away a lot because of my job, of course. There are months at a time when I'm only on Earth long enough to go home, take a shower, and repack my bags, but then once I'm done with those tours, I have a month or two when I'm only working for a few days for short trips, or even completely off. It would be nice not to have to go home to a totally empty house. I have some friends and all, but that doesn't replace a wife. I guess I can't really expect many women to be interested in a husband that misses a good chunk of the year while he's piloting a leisure ship."

"You never know who you might meet," Maxim said.

His mind immediately went to Ivy and his longing for her became more intense. He had never expected her. Before the Denynso arrived at the Mikana kingdom and brought the men back to the human settlement, he never thought about having a partner. He was dedicated to training to be in the army and to watching over his mother to make sure that she was coping without his father. While other men his age were starting to find their wives and thinking about the families that they were going to build with them, it wasn't something that was a priority to him. Then he saw her and everything changed. In that first moment that he saw Ivy, a feeling came over him that was totally different than anything that he had ever experienced. It wasn't just that he found her beautiful or that he was intrigued by this young human woman who had just recently arrived from Earth to assist with scientific research on Uoria. Instead, he felt a draw to her that was both undeniable and indescribable. It was as if in that very first second that his eyes landed on her, his heart knew that it was meant to love her, that she was there his entire life and he had just had to find her.

"Are you married?" Avery asked.

Maxim shook his head.

"No," he said. "We aren't married, but I have a partner. You met her. Ivy."

Avery nodded.

"Yes," he said, seeming to remember the brief introduction that Maxim had given him to Ivy after they found the men in the panic room. "I remember her. I'm sorry that she went back to Uoria. I know that you would rather have her here."

Maxim nodded.

"I would," he said. "But she needs to be there. She needs to be safe. One day, when this is all over and everything has become peaceful again, I plan on marrying her and having our life together. We've been preparing for war nearly since we met, and though I wouldn't give up even a second of the time that we have had together, I'd like to know what it's like to just live. I want to be able to decide where we're going to settle down and then just have a normal life together. I want to be able to go to sleep with her not being afraid of what might happen in the middle of the night or what we might have to do the next day. It might not seem like much, but it's everything to me."

He saw Avery hesitate slightly as if he had something on his mind and then the human pilot looked up at him.

"Can I ask you something?" Avery asked. "It's something that I probably should have asked you when I first met you, but there never seemed to be an appropriate moment."

Maxim glanced over his shoulder to where Lynx, Zyyr, and Lila were sitting in the corner. They all had expressions on their faces that told Maxim that they were feeling the same sense of wariness about the question that he was. They had shared his hesitation at including Avery, but hadn't questioned him when he agreed to make the man a part of it. He knew that he had to be cautious with the way that he approached Avery's questions so that he could balance making sure that he remained involved effectively and that the rest of the group stayed comfortable.

"What do you want to know?" he asked, looking back at Avery.

"I know that the ship got redirected by people you are calling Valdicians when it was meant to go to Earth."

"Yes," Maxim said. "We were supposed to be going to Earth to join others who are already there, the ones who should be here soon."

Avery nodded.

"Why?" he asked.

It was a simple question, but one that held heavy meaning. Maxim knew that they had been vague about what they were facing and had given only the most basic of information so that the human men from the crew could understand at least some of what was happening. They had chosen not to give details and to avoid describing what was happening both on Earth and back on Uoria, and now Avery wanted to know more. Maxim knew that they had come to a crossroads. This man had already offered his loyalty to them twice and had already faced serious danger without even knowing what he was doing or why. He remembered what it was like when Creia admitted that he had kept so much vital information from his own people, not revealing the true origins of their compound or even that he knew that the Klimnu who were their most hated enemies had once been Mikana and that they had vowed their revenge on him and his kind because he had refused to help them when they mutated. He knew the feeling of betrayal and pain that came from finding out that his father was still alive and that he had spent his entire life agonizing over the moment that he left home for the final time. It was painful for everyone involved to discover that they had been kept in the dark, especially after they had already been fighting. If Avery was going to put himself in danger and give of himself to help them, he deserved to know why.

Maxim glanced at the rest of the group again and saw Zyyr give a small nod as if acknowledging the position that they were in and giving his approval for Maxim to tell Avery what he needed to know. Maxim took a breath and started to speak. As he told him everything, his mind traveled back and he felt like he was reliving some of the moments from the past several months that brought them here. He could feel the burn of his skin where the toxins started to mutate him into a Klimnu and Ciyrs wrapped his bare hand around him. He could see the pain in Ivy's eyes again as they struggled to stay connected during the dark moments when they had been torn apart by her resistance to being on Uoria and his determination to follow through with what he knew that he needed to do. He could hear the pain in Rain's voice as she revealed who the humans were and told them of crashing on the planet after their failed mission to what would later come to be known as Penthos. It was strangely cathartic to pour out the entire story, and yet Maxim could feel himself instinctively holding back, struggling against what he was saying as if there was a part of him that still wanted to protect himself and the rest.

6

———

A very listened as Maxim gave him all of the details that he had needed to hear and delved deeper than he had wanted to admit that this went. Though he knew that the situation had to be extremely serious to justify the intensity of the response from the multiple species now scattered across three planets who all seemed fully devoted to this cause, he hadn't expected anything like what he was hearing. His mind hadn't totally processed what it meant when the woman who they introduced as Rain told him that she had been a part of the Nyx 23 team. It was as if she had said the words, he had attempted to understand and believe them, and then his mind had simply rejected it, putting it into the corner recesses so that there was just enough aware-ness of the reality that he was willing to be a part of what they were doing, but not enough that he had to feel the full impact of it. Now, though, he didn't have that. The protection that he had built up around himself had been shattered and now he was forced to hear everything that they had gone through and everything that had been happening around him, without him, or anyone else, knowing it.

When he was just a child, Avery had been in awe of the ship pilots who traveled far into space to bring passengers to the far planets that he only dreamed of ever seeing. He wanted to be like them, to do something more than just filling another office. The first longing of his heart had been to be a part of the military as his grandfather had, but health problems had prevented him from being able to fulfill the position that he envisioned as his own. Then he found this role. It had seemed like the perfect compromise. Though his primary function would be to bring wealthy leisure travelers on long cruises through space, he would also have the occasional opportunity to participate in exploration, immigration, or military maneuvers when more ships were needed. This meant that he would have the chance to serve the way that he intended to, if only briefly.

Now with everything that Maxim was telling him flooding his mind, Avery couldn't help but struggle against the feeling that what he had been so dedicated to his entire life wasn't what he thought that it was. He thought that he knew what was happening in the Universe and the detrimental events that had caused such a surge in his desire to be a part of the military or at the very least, the academic ventures that would further research distant planets, species, and situations to help prevent more tragedies like Nyx 23. He felt empowered and informed when he learned about the changes in the technology that was used for the ships, technology that was supposedly inspired by what happened to the Nyx 23 crew. He felt as though his missions that he had taken had brought important information and that he was honoring those who had been lost by helping to prevent the same thing from happening again.

Now all he felt was lied to. He had committed himself because of what he thought that he knew, but now it was obvious that virtually none of what he thought he knew was actually true. Listening to Maxim was only confirming things that he had begun to question and he was starting to feel sick to his stomach. He thought back to when he and Maxim had talked about the technology in the ship and the panic room that were supposedly designed partly in response to the disappearance of the Nyx 23 crew. Knowing that that technology had been put in place as a protective measure had always made him feel safer and almost as though they were refusing to allow those who were responsible for the disappearance to continue to win so many years later. It was almost a feeling of vindication. It had never occurred to him that those changes couldn't have actually be made as a response to Nyx 23. Though additions such as the panic room were valuable additions after the recent hijackings of ships, it wasn't logical to think that they would have anything to do with Nyx 23. The official word was that no one knew what had happened to the ship and the crew that it carried after they left the planet that would later be named Penthos. That meant that they would have no idea what would have happened to the ship itself and if that had anything to do with why they went missing. It had never occurred to him that this official word could have been a lie or a misdirection.

Avery felt like he was drowning by the time that Maxim finished what he had to tell him. There was so much that he should have known, so much that he should have been able to change but had never had the opportunity to. He felt guilty in a deep way that he never had before. It was as if he thought that by merit of his desire to protect Earth and the Universe on its own should have somehow given him greater insight into everything and he should have been able to detect something as horrific as had been happening. In his heart, though, he knew that he would have had no way of knowing. He wasn't a part of the University and had no real connections to the military outside of his occasional appointment as pilot. He, like everyone else, had been completely blind.

Maxim stopped talking and looked at Avery expectantly. The pilot opened his mouth to respond, but nothing came out. He shrugged and shook his head, letting out an exasperated sigh.

"I don't even know what to say," he finally managed to get out in a soft, almost apologetic voice. "I had no idea that it was that serious."

"No one did," Maxim said. "That's the problem. This has been going on for more than a century without anyone having any idea that it was happening, so no one was able to stop it."

"What I don't understand is why it took that long."

Avery looked over Maxim at the Denynso warrior propped against the wall.

"What do you mean?" Maxim asked.

Zyyr groaned slightly as he pushed himself up to sit straighter and Lila ran her hand comfortingly along his forehead.

"Why did it take so long?" the warrior repeated. "Like you said, this has been going on for more than a century. More than 100 years and no one knew that it was going on? It doesn't make sense."

"Why not?" Lila asked.

"The children," Lynx said, his voice sounding as though the thought had suddenly occurred to him. "There should have been children."

"Right," Avery said. "The Valdicians and the humans from Earth came together more than 115 years ago and decided that they were going to start this breeding program so that they could create a master race of weaponized hybrids. I can accept that they might not have started the actual breeding element immediately. They might have taken some time to find the perfect place to have their facilities and to build what they might need. They might have done some planning to decide exactly how they were going to handle the breeding itself. This could have taken a while. I could even imagine that it might have taken a couple of years, but even that means that the first children born into the program would have been born more than one hundred years ago."

"So why hasn't there been an intergalactic war with these super soldiers?" Maxim asked.

Avery nodded, knowing that the Mikana man was starting to follow his though process.

"The first generation wouldn't have been the super soldiers like you describe them," Lila pointed out. "Remember," she glanced at Zyyr, Lynx, and Maxim. "Idella? My great-grandmother? She was one of the first born into the program."

"Your great-grandmother?" Avery asked, startled by the revelation.

The delicate-looking woman nodded.

"Yes. She was born into the breeding program during one of the first waves of children. They didn't just breed all of the women at one time. Instead, they staggered it so that there would be new babies born every few months over the course of several years."

"That would ensure that they weren't overwhelmed by a sudden influx of babies," Avery said.

"Exactly. The point, though, is that Idella was only a blend of two species, the Mikana and the Eteri."

"Eteri?" Avery asked.

"The winged men and woman who went to Earth with Jonah," Maxim explained.

Lila nodded again.

"She was only those two. That would hardly be considered a master race."

"What happened to her?" Avery asked.

"She escaped," Lila said. "She fell in love and they escaped the facility together and returned to Uoria."

"If she had remained, she would likely have been bred with another species."

"Exactly. They would have blended in another species with her so that the child had the three species in it. There were probably other children born in the same waves who were made up of other combinations so that they would then be able to breed those together to make a truly powerful hybrid. That's at least two generations, and then those would need to become adults before they would be able to be soldiers."

"Even then," Avery said. "They would have become active by now. It's been 115 years. The first children would have been born within five years. That would mean that by now there should have been a full-blown army that would have emerged, but there hasn't been. Where did they all go?"

"And why is Ryan talking about the hybrids like they are his creation and he is still training them up?" Maxim asked.

Avery shook his head, thoughts racing through his mind now.

"Something stopped the program," he said. "They might have had a decade or two of babies born and a few combinations, but then it stopped. They never got the army that they wanted. That's why Ryan is as rabid about this as he is. His family started something and then never finished it. The children that were born into the program never reached the point of actually being the weapons that they intended."

"So, what happened to them?" Maxim asked.

"I don't know."

Just as he said it, Avery noticed something out of the corner of his eye. He reached forward and pushed aside a few of the papers on the top of the stack. Two sheets of what looked like extremely aged paper stood out against the others. While none of the papers were new and all seemed to have been there for many years, these were obviously considerably older even than those. He picked them up cautiously and brought them closer so that he could look at the words on them. It was in a language that he didn't recognize and he turned it to show it to Maxim.

"Look at this," he said.

Maxim looked at the page and Avery could see his eyes scanning the words the way that his had. He shook his head and glanced at Avery.

"I don't understand that language," he said. "Do you?"

"No," Avery said. "I don't recognize it."

"It looks like a list of some kind. Like a recipe."

"Or a spell," Lila said.

"A spell?" Maxim said.

"Idella taught me that there are a lot of things in this Universe that we don't understand. The way that things work now weren't always this way and some of the ancient ways have disappeared. There were books in her house that were filled with what she said were spells from long-gone people."

Maxim held the paper out to her.

"Do you recognize this?" he asked. "The language or the symbols or anything?"

Lila evaluated the paper for a few moments and then handed it back to Maxim.

"No," she said. "It doesn't look familiar."

Avery kept staring at the paper and the strange symbols scrawled across it in ink that seemed to be gradually fading away with years. It looked familiar in a vague, distant way, but he didn't know why. He was reaching for the page again when Elise walked back into the room.

"They're on their way."

7

———

Azra stepped up behind Pyra and watched as his lead adjusted the weapons that he wore a final time. It still struck the Denynso as strange to see the warriors all armed so heavily. They were accustomed to going into battle with nothing more than their massive bodies and their in-born skill and lust for war to fuel them through their clashes. When they did have weapons, it was generally small blades or hand-hewn weapons that fit with their own personal skill. It wasn't until they were trapped on Earth in the basement of the laboratory building that they had begun to use larger weapons generally relied upon by the other species. They had taken everything that they could from the emergency chambers as well as from the floor of the corridor after the battle with the hybrids, resigned to the fact that they didn't know what they were facing when they encountered the army in the corridor, and that that would be even truer when they finally made it to Penthos to reconnect with the rest of the group.

Eden stood close beside Pyra and he saw her glance back over her shoulder, her eyes scanning over the entire group behind her as if to make sure that everyone who was coming with them had made it to the main lounge of the ship and were ready to finally step through the hatch and onto the surface of Penthos. Azra could feel the energy of everyone around him. Though no one was speaking, the whole area seemed electrified as if they were thinking the same thoughts together and sending the emotions of those thoughts out into the space around them. This is what they had been waiting for. They had been preparing for this moment since they swarmed the laboratory, even before for those who had already been on Earth when the members of the group that had been redirected to Penthos escaped and came to help them. That moment seemed a lifetime behind them after everything that had happened since. He barely remembered the horror of learning what Creia had been going through on Uoria and the plans that Ryan had for them. Now, though, they were finally on Penthos and ready to join back with the rest so that they could bring this situation to an end.

As he stood there, Elise's voice reverberated through his mind. He had been purposely blocking her out of his thoughts, preventing them from being able to communicate, for most of the time that he was on Earth. He didn't want her to worry about him or to be distracted by thoughts of her, which would have kept him from being able to do what he knew he needed to do. It had been painful for him to stay so disconnected from her. Even though they had had to be apart since soon after they completed their bond because of the obligations of her career, it felt different to be apart by force and to not even be able to communicate with her. When she first told him that she was going to have to keep going with her travels rather than staying with him, at least until the end of her contract, Azra was devastated. He wanted it to be like the other Denynso warriors and their mates. As soon as they had completed their bond, they started their lives together. Now, though, he was grateful that she had been on the ship when it was redirected from its path to Uoria so that she could pick up the group that was coming to Earth to help them. Having her there meant that there was greater understanding of the new passengers and what was happening.

Then, though, at least he was able to communicate with her occasionally. He could check in on her and the rest of the group and find out what was going on. When he recognized that he needed to cut off the communication it felt like he was impossibly far away from her. Now he was finally headed to her and he was going to be able to see her again. His heart felt like it was going to pound out of her chest just thinking about being able to see her and touch her again. As excited as he was, though, he was also nervous. He didn't know how she was going to react to everything that was happening around her and the terrible situation that she was now involved in, whether she was going to be coping well or if this was showing her just how serious her decision to be his mate was and what life with him would mean. If that was the case, she might be struggling with it and may even want to leave him as soon as she had the opportunity, returning to the life that she had before she met him and putting him and their relationship behind her.

It would be easy for her to put him aside if that was what she wanted, but the same couldn't be said for him. Now that his heart belonged to her, there was nothing that would get it back. He was fully and totally entwined with her and always would be. Even if she walked away from him and he never saw her again, he would never stop missing her or longing for her. He would always love her and crave her, and the desperation to be near her would never dissipate. There would never be another woman in his life and he would live out the rest of his days alone. Azra couldn't bear the thought of not having her in his life and could only hope that she would still want to be with him when this was all over. All he could do was reassure himself that she was still there. She could have chosen to go back to Uoria with those who left Penthos. She could have made emergency contact with Earth and had them send a shuttle to retrieve her. She didn't do either. Instead, she had chosen to remain on Penthos with Maxim, Lynx, Zyyr, and Lila and was in the compound waiting for him. It had been her choice to remain with him for this long, so maybe that would continue to be her choice.

The sound of the hatch opening was deep and slow. Pyra felt as though he had been standing watching it gradually slide open for hours, the opening revealing the planet in front of them little by little. Though he had seen much of it through the windows of the ship, it was different looking at it without the thick glass between himself and the desert beyond. The entire planet looked dry and desolate. He couldn't imagine anyone or anything able to survive on the hot surface even though he knew that this was the planet where the illegal prison colony had been run by the Valdicians and the prisoners, many of them Denynso, had been kept for a period Pyra didn't know how long. He knew that they had lived there and thrived enough that they were able to leave the planet and go to Earth to be a part of the breeding program, but that didn't provide him with any reassurance. Spending any length of time on this planet seemed like torture in of itself. He couldn't imagine the

Valdicians voluntarily committing themselves to living there for as long as they did.

When the hatch was finally open, Pyra drew in a breath and reached down beside him for Eden's hand. She took it and offered it a squeeze. Even though it was tiny in his, fully enveloped by his grip, the presence of it made him feel stronger and more prepared for whatever they were going to face when they walked out of the ship. Out of the corner of his eye he saw his mate look up at him and he glanced down at her. She smiled at him and for the first time he noticed just how much she had really changed since the first moment that he saw her when she walked down off of the shuttle onto Uoria. There had been no affection in her eyes then. In fact, the bright green, that was now a beautiful orange, was sharp, shallow, and filled with suspicion and distaste. There were moments when he saw something that he would have described as hatred if she had known anything about him or had reason to hate him as the warriors did the enemies that they encountered in battle.

Pyra hadn't felt any of those negative feelings when he first saw Eden or when Creia declared that he was to be her guard and protector for the entire time that she was to be on Uoria. Though she seemed to get angrier and more aggressive with each passing moment that they spent together, Pyra only became surer that she was the woman that he had been waiting for his entire life. Just as this fiery redhead showed sharp aggression with each moment that he was with her, Pyra himself was feeling more intense and more violent than usual, wanting to kill any man who got close to him, even his brothers. The feeling, though, accompanied by sexual arousal unlike anything that he had ever experienced, though, wasn't about anger or dislike for this woman. Instead, it was his body's way of telling him that he was rapidly approaching the moment when he would meet the mate that was intended for him from his birth. The aggression and violence was meant to keep other men away from him so that they wouldn't approach his intended mate, while the powerful arousal acted as a further reinforcement of the knowledge that he was going to meet the woman with whom he would share his life so that he could differentiate this level of violence and anger from the viciousness that was naturally inborn in the warriors and that had given them the reputation of being the most fearsome warriors in the Universe.

Looking back, Pyra knew that it wasn't fully instant dislike for him that had caused Eden to act that way when they first met. Instead, she was being controlled by her emotions toward the same horrible man who had created the hybrid army they were preparing to wage war against. Ryan had been her boss at the University laboratory and when she refused his advances, he had planned what he thought was the perfect vengeance. He demanded that she go to Uoria and collect the blood of the most powerful Denynso warrior so that it could be used for his weaponry development. His thought was that if she succeeded, he would have access to the material that had eluded him and that would help him to move forward with his grisly efforts, and if she failed, which was far more likely, she would be killed in punishment and retaliation, and he wouldn't have to deal with her any longer. What he didn't know was that she would arrive into the guardianship of the very warrior whose blood she was meant to illegally collect, and that that warrior, Pyra himself, would love her ferociously from the first second that they were near each other.

She was so different then, and yet still the woman he loved so much. He had seen some of her softness when she stood before Creia and confessed to the mission on which Ryan had sent her. She wasn't a part of the University program that the King was planning, but rather an independent scientist sent to the planet under the guise of collecting plant materials for biological projects on Earth. That made her more vulnerable, and Pyra could see the nervousness on her beautiful, freckle-sprinkled face as she told Creia what Ryan had asked her to do and handed over materials that he had given her. Pyra knew that she feared for her life. It was not an illogical fear. It was well-known throughout the Universe that no one was permitted to possess the incredibly powerful blood of a Denynso warrior, and anyone who was to attempt to collect it would be punished swiftly and severely. Even though she was terrified of what the Denynso King was going to do with her now that he knew that she had admitted that she had come to the planet with the intention of doing what Ryan had asked, at least initially, Eden had stood before the King courageously and gave him all of the information that she could. It was a show of tremendous bravery and her desire to make sure that Ryan would not have control over the Denynso in as much capacity as she was able to prevent.

Pyra still saw that bravery now, but the harsh, sharp edges that had defined her pretty face had softened. It was a strange development, an odd change that had come over her in a way that he didn't think that it would come over anyone else. The other human women who had found their way into the lives of the Denynso men and their homes in the compound had become noticeably harder since their time on the planet. They were still feminine and beautiful in a way that was so different from the Denynso women, but the challenges and turmoil that they had experienced since committing to being a part of the clan had taken some of the tenderness from them and given them a tangible strength that made them seem more grounded and capable of handling the challenges ahead without being controlled by their fear or emotions. Eden, on the other hand, seemed to be the opposite. When Pyra looked at her then he had seen steeliness and thick walls that had developed over the years of mistreatment by Ryan. She had been virtually emotionless with the exception of anger and frustration, and was always quick to temper. She seemed nearly fearless. Over the time that she had been with him, though, those edges had smoothed. Her transformation into being Denynso and then into a mother had suited her, and now he could see more layers within her than he had ever been aware that she had. He had finally seen her cry and heard her laugh from the depths of her soul. He had seen her look truly happy and held her as she broke down with deep, tearing pain that pulled sadness and feeling of betrayal from within her chest. Though she was still courageous, even more so probably now that she was truly aware of what she was capable of accomplishing, his beloved mate was a calmer, more peaceful, and more comfortable creature who he couldn't wait to share the rest of his life with when they were finally able to put all of this behind them.

As he thought back to the first day that he saw Eden, Pyra's mind traveled to Creia. Both King of the Denynso and Pyra's father, Creia had once been revered as he was as the most powerful and fierce warrior in all the Universe. Now he was seen as a strong, loyal, and fearless leader who protected his compound and his people with everything in him. It was he who was responsible to making sure that every child born into the clan knew their destined position in life, and though it was Creia's wife and Pyra's mother Theia, who was responsible for the actual training of the warriors, Creia was their unquestioned commander, even above Pyra himself when it came to leading and controlling the army.

Pyra knew that Creia held a tremendous amount of faith and respect in his oldest son. He had chosen him as the leader of the warriors when he made the decision to no longer enter battle himself, and it had been he who had agreed to allow the warriors to leave the compound where they had all spent their lives in order to explore the planet in the way that the Kings had done for generations before. He had even humbled himself by admitting that he had been wrong for not telling the warriors the complete truth about their planet and their clan, and asking for their forgiveness. Pyra knew how difficult that must have been for him. He himself had had to ask his father to forgive him when he had acted irrationally with the Mikana men and allow his father to guide him in how he was going to repair the damage that he had done and move forward to earn back the respect and trust of his own kind as well as the other species on Uoria.

The thoughts of his father and King brought painful tightness to Pyra's chest and throat. Creia trusted him. He had sent him out into the Universe with the faith that he would take care of those who followed him and make sure that they were well protected. He was waiting on Uoria, knowing what they had faced in their time on Earth, believing that his son would do what he was supposed to do to handle the situation and restore peace. Pyra could only hope that he would be able to live up to what his father expected and hoped of him. Never before had he questioned himself or wondered if he was going to be capable of handling the challenge that was in front of him. He was the fiercest of the warriors, the most dedicated and aggressive, and the first to storm into battle, always confident of the victory that they would achieve. Now that he was looking into Eden's face and seeing his son's tiny head rested against her chest, however, Pyra felt a flicker of nerves and could only hope that he would be able to protect them and make Creia proud.

8

R yan leaned on the counter and stared down into the sink, watching the water swirl around the sides and down the drain. Even when it was gone, he continued to stare at it, as if there was some sort of wisdom in the lingering traces of the water against the shining metal of the sink. Finally, he looked up into the mirror and glared at his reflection. The dark depths of his eyes seemed flatter, some of the lustrousness gone. There were questions in them that he wouldn't put voice to. If he did, he would be admitting something that he didn't want to admit even to himself much less to any of those around him. The Valdicians stayed with him under the belief that they were far closer to his equals than the hybrids that he had created, but Ryan knew that they were anything but equal to him. Though he descended from them, he was far above them as they were now. There was a tremendous difference between the powerful creatures that his great-grandfather had led and who had joined with the humans to start the breeding. Ryan blamed the men that descended from them for the lack of characteristics that he had. If they had focused on breeding for the special features and abilities of the different species, he wouldn't have been born with nothing to differentiate him from the other men that he encountered every day. Instead, they had diverted from this goal and instead allowed themselves to be controlled by what they thought was love, but what Ryan saw as only weakness.

By the time that his father was born, the youngest child of a grandfather who had married three times, his bloodline was already diluted. He then married a human woman and Ryan was born, devoid of all of the characteristics and features that he knew he should have inherited. All his life he had heard about the incredible intelligence and military power of his Valdician ancestors. They were a vicious and powerful species, rivaled only by the Denynso in their strength. He had watched the banked memories of his great-grandfather living through him as he traveled the Universe and took over planets, battling species for dominance and establishing their control everywhere that they stopped. There were few places that they had not been successful in conquering, and it was the experiments that were going to fill that gap and bring their success rate to completion.

Though no one had ever told him, Ryan knew even then that things had changed for the Valdicians. He knew that they weren't the same creatures that they had once been, and part of the aggression and determination that flowed through their veins was their desire to reclaim what they had once been. He never knew what had happened to the intimidating group that his great-grandfather had built. By the time that he was old enough to be a part of the experiments, the program had faded to nearly nothing and the Valdicians seemed weaker and in need of guidance. That was when Ryan decided that he was going to give that guidance. It didn't matter that his family had achieved only part of what they had set out to do when they planned the breeding program. That was when he had learned about the true history of the Valdicians, and in turn, himself. Hearing what had happened to them and why they had become what they were when they encountered the humans of Nyx 23 had filled Ryan with an anger and disgust that ignited his desire for power and revenge even more. He couldn't tolerate what had happened to them. They still hadn't fully recovered, even with the extensive care that he had been giving them, but soon they would. Soon they would return to what they once were and he would be right there beside them, leading the group that was now beholden to him.

He was ready to take what they had started, piece the program back together, and bring it to its full glorious potential. Then it would no longer matter if he seemed nothing more than human. He wouldn't be controlled by the limitations of the original program. He would create the hybrids in the way that was right for him, ensuring that they were the most fearsome and had the most complex collection of skills and features that he could possibly achieve. Soon he would raise up an army that would conquer the Universe and put it under his control, starting with the source of the greatest anguish from his family's past...Uoria.

The longer he stared into his own eyes, the more Ryan became aware of the tearing sensation within him. It felt as though there was something inside him that was pulling in two directions, ripping him apart, though no one on the outside was able to see it. He didn't know how to describe it, and even if he had wanted to reach out to those around him and explain to them what was happening in his mind and his heart, he wouldn't have been able to. He didn't understand it himself, no matter how intense the pain or how deep the hollow that seemed to be forming low in his belly and spreading through his body. It seemed that the worse this tearing feeling became, the more ferocious the drive to complete his goals reared. The two feelings were at once dueling with each other and encouraging each other to build and grow. Ryan could feel his hands shaking on the edge of the counter and his teeth gritting down on each other so hard his jaws ached.

"Sir?"

Ryan turned away from the mirror sharply, immediately experiencing the strange feeling that the reflection of his face was still there and he was staring at himself now as he looked out of the bathroom and toward the door to his bedroom. He strode away from it, leaving it at his back and pretending that he could no longer feel the imagined gaze burning into his skin.

The bedroom door was standing open a few inches and he could see the slightly shifting shadow of one of the Valdicians standing partially inside the room.

"I've told you that you are never to come into my room without knocking," Ryan said sharply.

The shadow stepped back a few inches, but the door remained open.

"I did knock," the voice he recognized as Stellan said back nervously. "I knocked several times, but you didn't respond. I was concerned about you. I apologize."

The man was starting to back out, but Ryan took a long step toward him to stop him.

"It's alright," he said. "I was taking a shower. I must not have heard you knocking. Is there something wrong?"

He saw the man's eyes briefly lift to his hair and Ryan could feel that the thick lock of hair laying on his forehead was already nearly dry. He wondered how long he had been standing at the counter in front of the mirror, so lost in his own thoughts that he hadn't heard the Valdician man knocking at his bedroom door.

"The hybrid woman who escaped took one of the new babies and started across Penthos."

"One of the new hybrid babies was born?" Ryan asked. "There were no births scheduled for at least three weeks."

"I know that. One of the women delivered early. She didn't survive the birth."

"And the child?" Ryan asked.

"He was alive when he was taken from the vehicle on Penthos."

"Where are they now?"

"They started in the opposite direction of the compound, but they were followed."

"Who followed them?"

Stellan seemed to hesitate, but Ryan couldn't tell if it was because he didn't want to say what he needed to, or if he was just trying to come up with the right words to express himself.

"The man I was telling you about," he said. "The one they call Rilex."

Ryan stiffened at the sound of the name. Though the intelligence that they were able to get from Earth and now Penthos was limited, he had heard enough from the Valdicians who had come in contact with the group that was helping the Denynso to suspect that this man was something that he had never expected to encounter. He had thought about it. He had dreamed of it since he first learned about the true origin of the Valdicians, but had been told so many times that it was never going to happen. That species was gone, long dead, so there was no use in hoping that he would be able to find one so that he could exact the ultimate of vengeance. This man, the one they called Rilex, if he was what the Valdicians were saying that he was, was even more valuable to him than Pyra's blood. Having control over him would mean the ability to have control over all of the Universe.

"Where did they go?" he asked.

He was moving through the room now, pulling out fresh clothing and getting dressed. He had intended to go to bed and try to get some of the sleep that had been eluding him for days, but now any trace of the exhaustion that had been pulling on him was gone and he was filled with an almost frantic energy that fueled him to get back to the room downstairs where he could sit in the chair that seemed to help him think, to give him a connection to what was happening around him a way that he didn't get elsewhere. There was no real reason for it, but he didn't question the one semblance of peace that he could find in the chaos, even if it was still tenuous at best.

"Three soldiers went after them, but they said that they disappeared."

"Disappeared?" Ryan asked. "How could they just disappear?"

"From what they describe, I think that they went into the far side of the tunnels."

Ryan felt the tearing feeling increase as if his blood was beginning to boil and he couldn't control the blend of anger and fear that was welling up behind the indescribable emotion. There was a reason that no one went to the far side of the tunnels. He had only brought a few of his creations there when they were first beginning their training, but he had given them express instructions that they were never again to mention the existence of the tunnels or to venture into them. He believed that he had them under his complete control, that it wasn't just their bodies that he had made, but their minds as well. By crafting them from conception and controlling their every breath after, Ryan believed that he had made it so that the hybrid army that he had made was never going to be able to think for themselves. They were to be like living machines, doing, thinking, and responding exactly as he taught them.

Now he felt the weight of the reality that this wasn't the case. He knew that there was going to be some variance in how each of the hybrids acted and that there would be some moments when they didn't do exactly as he would have wanted them to. Even machines sometimes had glitches and simply needed some repair work to operate properly. He thought that he managed that with his reprogramming strategies. He never would have thought that one of his hybrids, particularly one of the earliest that he created, would break free of the hold and not only escape the facility, but return to the forbidden sections of the tunnels. He thought that they would have left her mind by now.

"What are they doing in the tunnels?" he asked, trying to keep all of the emotion out of his voice and not reveal anything that was going through his mind.

"I don't know," Stellan said. "The intelligence there reports that the three that were chasing them didn't go into the tunnels and they haven't been seen since."

"And the rest?" Ryan asked.

"Those who left on the ship still haven't returned, but all from Earth are on Penthos now. They have not yet reconnected."

"Then ensure that they don't."

9

Pyra felt the sand pulling at his feet as they walked across the desert. It was a different feeling than he had ever had. Even the badlands behind the Denynso compound or the wide, open areas of Uoria didn't have this deep, sucking feeling as he moved across them and he wondered how long it took for those who had been held in the compound to get accustomed to it. He wanted to shake his head to rid himself of those thoughts without anybody around him noticing. He didn't want them to know the thoughts that were going through his mind. Like it had always been, he wanted them to trust that he was focused completely on the task at hand and had complete faith and confidence in their performance. It was that confidence and security that would help them to feel stronger and know that they were able to do what was called of them.

The weapons that he was carrying weighed heavily on him and he wondered if he had made the right decision by arming himself so much. Though bringing along the weapons that they had found in the emergency chamber and that they had stolen from the dead in the corridor was meant to make all of them feel more prepared for whatever they were going to face in the battle against the rest of the hybrid army, it was having the opposite effect on Pyra. He was accustomed to fighting only with his hands. Even the small weapon that he did have was generally left hanging in his house on Uoria, and when he did use it was only the occasional accompaniment to his combat. Never before had he questioned his ability to take down whatever enemy was before him with only the strength of his body and the skill of his hands to rely on. The more weapons that he added, the more it felt like he was forgetting what he was born to do and what he had always done when he walked into battle. It felt like he was hiding and trying to compensate for the uncertainty that he was feeling regarding these creatures. There had been plenty of times when he had gone into battle with a species that he wasn't familiar with and whose characteristics and abilities he didn't know. In those instances, he had been almost excited at the prospect, invigorated by the thought of the new challenge and the accomplishment of destroying yet another type of creature. With each new fight, they learned new skills and were better prepared for the next fight.

It wasn't the same this time. Rather than feeling excited about the idea of discovering the varied skills and abilities and challenging his one in-born prowess, Pyra felt thrown off by the idea that these creatures were not just one species but several, and that many, if not all, of them had Denynso blood in them. This was disturbing to him on more than one level. He was well aware that this meant that the hybrids were strong and fearsome. More unnerving to him, though, was the feeling that he was turning against his own kind. With every passing moment he was more determined, more driven to tear down the army that was standing against them. The more that feeling welled up within him, though, the more he was aware that within them was the same blood that pumped through his veins, and that meant the same intense, all-consuming loyalty. They were devoted to their kind from birth and it was that devotion that fueled much of the aggression of their warfare.

There had been only one time before when Pyra and the other warriors had been forced to fight against one of their own. It was a painful memory, one that he didn't allow himself to dwell on if he didn't have to. Ullie's betrayal of the rest of the Denynso clan had been gut-wrenching for all of them. It had been his cooperation with a human flight attendant set on seeking revenge that had made it possible for the Klimnu to infiltrate the underground realm beneath the Denynso compound that had once been the home to the Irisa. Only Loralia was left by the time that they swarmed, but it was the attacks of those Klimnu that had threatened the life of Eden, Elianna, and Zuri. It was their presence that had taken Jem from them.

Thoughts of Jem immediately reminded Pyra why it had been so easy for them to eliminate Ullie when and how they did. If he hadn't turned his back on his clan and forgotten the loyalty that held them together, the Klimnu would have been kept away from the compound and their suffering could have been avoided. The only comfort that he had was that through that suffering had grown the bonds between the women and the warriors, and Loralia had been saved from a life of solitude and emptiness, longing alone for the family that had been decimated many years before. And Jem came back to them. Miraculously and inexplicably, the beloved warrior who had become a symbol of everything that they fought for and had touched each of them in a deep way, had come back. Seeming to rise from the dead, Jem had made them aware of the tremendous expanse of the world beyond Uoria and how much they were truly fighting to protect.

They had approached Jonah and Rain's vehicle and passed it, telling Pyra that they were getting close to the compound. Suddenly he heard drums in the distance. They were faint at first, thudding low in the back of his mind almost as though he were hearing his own heartbeat outside of his body, but grew louder as they continued on. He paused, looking around at the rest of the group to see if they were hearing it as well. Eden was staring at the horizon ahead of them, her eyes narrowed. Beside her, Azra was looking around, his hand hovering over the weapon across his chest. Murmurs were rippling through the group and Pyra took a few steps out in front of them, holding up his hand to quiet them. As they hushed, the sound of the drums became deeper and more insistent.

"What is that?" he muttered.

Azra stepped up beside him.

"Elise hears the drums," he said. "She says it means that the hybrids are coming."

Maxim looked beside him to make sure that Zyyr was really ready to handle this. The warrior stood strong, his eyes focused steadfastly in front of him with an expression of determination in his deep orange eyes. The leg that had been injured was wrapped tightly in bandages, but he didn't seem to be favoring it. The injury had either healed successfully or he was putting the pain out of his thoughts and refusing to allow it to control him. Either way, he looked ready to leave the compound and venture out toward the incessant sound of the drums.

The rhythm of the drums had become a consistent source of torment. Even when the hybrids didn't appear, the drums were a reminder that they were there, just waiting. Now Maxim felt that this time, the soldiers were coming. They weren't just calling to them, taunting them from the outer, unseen edges of the planet. The sound of the drumming was getting louder with each moment, each pound resonating deeper within him. Now that Elise had told him that Pyra and the rest had finally arrived on Penthos and were starting toward them, Maxim felt empowered and even more prepared to face the army. He knew that they were calling him out, wanting him specifically, and he was ready to take them on whether there were people behind him or not, but the knowledge that they had come for him and were ready to face this with him gave him strength.

"Are you ready?" he asked.

"Yes," Zyyr responded.

"Yes," Lynx said from his other side.

"I am," Avery said from behind him.

It was the sound of the human man's voice that meant the most. The other two men had been alongside him for the entire journey. He knew that each of them had their own powerful motivations and the intrinsic drive to fight that came from their Denynso birth as much as they had the desire to support and protect him. Avery, though, was different. He was giving of himself openly and freely, even more committed now that he had heard the full story of what was happening. It was true selflessness, a trait that reminded Maxim strongly of his father.

The two women had remained behind in the compound,

preparing the buildings for those who were joining them. Though he wanted to think that just meant making sure that there were enough places for them to sleep and preparing what food they had left to strengthen them, Maxim knew that that wasn't all that Lila and Elise were doing while the men were gone. He knew that they were also tearing blankets to prepare bandages and laying out the remaining healing supplies, readying the buildings to act as makeshift clinics for those that may be injured during the battle to come. Though the battles that they had had with the hybrid army thus far had been only brief, Maxim knew that by now they had heard of the arrival of those from Earth and that likely that would fuel them into more intense fighting. Rather than making him afraid, this made him even more resolute and he took the first steps out of the compound with the other three men close around him.

The sun was beating down on them as they walked across the sand, the sound of the drums marking each step. It seemed that the sound surrounded them and Maxim didn't know which direction to turn, so he kept his focus ahead and walked forward. They had been walking in silence for some time when the sound of the drums seemed to shift, morphing until it was coming from one side. Maxim turned his attention and saw the silhouette of the soldiers along the horizon. It was like the first time that they had seen them through the windows of the ship, but this time they were close enough that he could see the variation in their coloring and the hazy indications of their facial features. He didn't hesitate another moment. Pulling the sword from the sheath at his hip, he let out a yell and started running toward the soldiers.

Avery, Lynx, and Zyyr ran after him, and in an instant, they were locked in a clash with the hybrids. His field of vision closed in so that all he could see was the man in front of him. The creature's eyes were cold and grey, the color of the stones that lined the bottom of the river back home in the kingdom. Maxim swung his sword up over his head and down toward the creature, who lifted his own blade in response, catching the blow and forcing him back. Beside him, Maxim could see Avery caught in hand-to-hand combat with another of the hybrids. On the other side, Zyyr used a smaller blade to slash at another soldier's chest.

The violence burned around him, filling the air with the sound of grunting, blades clashing, and cries of pain. Maxim could feel the sweat pouring down his face and the dirt kicked up by their feet sticking to his skin as he fought. He suddenly became aware of a louder sound. It filled his ears much like the drums, but it was a deeper, richer, and more continuous sound, familiar in the way that he knew he had heard it before. It reverberated through his thoughts and when he looked up toward the faces of the hybrid soldiers he saw that they were listening to it as well. Seeing their reactions caused the sound to crystallize in his mind, becoming the image of a memory and he knew what he was hearing.

Maxim ran backward a few steps to create more space between him and the hybrid, and turned toward the sound of the Denynso war cry. It was growing around him and the force of it seemed to be pushing the soldiers back away from them, demanding their attention and pausing their violent attack. Just as the hybrids had, the group appeared on the horizon as dark silhouettes, hazy in the concentrated sunlight that was seeming to deepen around them in preparation for evening to fall. They approached first in a cluster, then spread out into a row that showed their true numbers. Maxim felt eyes on his back and turned to look behind him.

As if they had been watching and noticed the approach of the much larger group from the vehicle and the shuttle, another swarm of hybrid soldiers started toward them.

Turning back to look at the group that had arrived from Earth, Maxim heard their yells get louder and they started toward the battle already going on. He lifted his sword high above his head and let out his own yell, reaching out to them with his voice. The men around him followed suit and the sky seemed to explode with the power of their shouts. He ran further from the battle so that he could watch the group approach and guide them toward the clash. A figure ran ahead of the rest of the group, quickly leaving them behind.

At first Maxim thought that it was Pyra leading the pack, but quickly realized that the figure was not large enough to be the tremendous Denynso warrior. Not tall enough nor broad enough to be one of that kind, and with a blazing speed that instantly set him apart from the rest, Maxim suddenly realized that this could only be one of his kind, a Mikana. But the ship had not returned from Uoria. Kyven was still wounded, so it could not be his brother rushing toward him across the desert that was quickly becoming blanketed in shadowy purple darkness. There had been no other Mikana that had traveled to Earth with Pyra and his crew, or that had been onboard the ship that had been detoured to Penthos or could have traveled in Jonah and Rain's vehicle.

He took a step toward the advancing figure and saw his hand shoot up above his head, thrusting a sword into the sky. The world around Maxim faded and he saw only the figure. He saw only the man running through the coming night as if running through the veil of years.

He saw only his father.

10

Severine tightened the cloth strips around Rilcx's chest, positioning the baby high on his body so that his tiny head rested on the man's shoulder. She immediately felt the relief of not having the pressure of the ties around her own ribs and stretched to either side to loosen up her movements. She didn't know how long they had been weaving their way through the bunkers. It had been quite some time since they had walked away from the body and the image of it was still lingering in her mind. There were plenty of times when she had seen the products of death, but this was the first time that she had seen bones in that way. Hybrids that died during training or the brief battles that they had engaged in on other planets as part of their preparation, or even those who had been lost as a result of the breeding itself, were quickly and unceremoniously removed or simply left where they fell, abandoned when Ryan took the rest of them back to the breeding facility or these bunkers. There was never an opportunity to see what happened in the days, weeks, months, or even years after the life drained from those bodies and they were left as nothing more than empty shells.

She wasn't sure how she should feel about it. There was an emotion inside of her that seemed blocked by a wall created by Ryan's brutal training. It was the same wall that had enabled her to kill indiscriminately and to allow the children that she raised to be taken away and submitted to the same training that she had been throughout her life. Fractures had appeared in that wall a few times in the last several years, but she had avoided thinking about it until the weeks leading up to the arrival of the group in the laboratory. They knew that Ryan had had his Valdicians capture a man named Creia and hold him captive on Uoria, but only Severine had felt the shift that came with that announcement. When Ryan told them that this was the King of the Denynso, she knew that they were on a new path now. No longer training. No longer preparing. No longer thinking in abstracts about the possibility that they would one day face down the enemies that they had been bred and born to destroy. There was no context to it, no explanation of why he hated them so intensely or what he hoped to achieve by eliminating them. Now, though, they were on an irreversible course that had them rushing toward what she knew could prove to be a catastrophe.

Then they were there. It was real. They were standing in the corridor of the laboratory in the dim lighting of the night, staring across just a few feet of space at a group of people who looked different from themselves but only slightly. Rather than seeming like strange, monstrous creatures, they seemed more like shattered versions of themselves. On each of the faces of the people who they encountered in that battle, she saw the features that pieced the hybrids together. Familiar eyes stared back at her. Lips that had spoken to her since birth held sneers and spat vicious, hate-filled words. She had seen the hair, the skin, the bodies that were in front of her, scattered among the creatures that Ryan had created.

Then Severine saw the human woman with a baby strapped to her chest, fighting alongside the rest without even a moment of hesitation. Something within her broke in that moment. She continued to fight, doing what she had been taught to do, but she no longer cared what happened to her. She knew that if she died, it would be nothing more than deliverance. In her heart, though, Severine knew that she was going to make the last breaths that she had matter more than any other moment that she had ever breathed. She reached out to that human woman and begged her to save the others, hoping that she would get enough meaning from the meager words that she was able to say to make the difference that she had never been able to make herself.

The Others. Severine felt a smile come to her lips at the sound of the words running through her thoughts. They were so much more now than she ever would have thought that they could be. Simple but impactful, they were the identity that she had never thought that she would have. They reassured her that no matter had happened in her past, she had a future. Soon she would make sure that the skeleton that they found didn't continue on with no name and no identity.

Able to move more freely now that she was taking a break from carrying the baby, Severine strode ahead of Rilex. The tunnels still looked abandoned and she began to wonder how long the network had been there before Ryan found it. She had always assumed that Ryan had designed and created them, because in her existence he was responsible for everything. When Rilex pointed out that that body had been lying in the chamber for far longer than Ryan had been alive, it occurred to her that he hadn't made these bunkers, but simply utilized them for his own purposes. The longer that she thought of that, the more she realized that that was all that he did. He took what was already there and manipulated it, adapting and molding it until it served his purposes. Somehow that thought took away some of the power and intimidation that had always hung around Ryan.

She felt like they had been walking through the same stretches of tunnels, coiling around their own steps as they tried to navigate the complex bunkers. Finally, she turned a corner and walked out into a section that she knew that they hadn't been in that day. It didn't look familiar and she wondered if this was a place that she had been when she was first permitted down into these bunkers before Ryan cut them off. This corridor was much wider than the others and the light from the torch that she had taken from Rilex when he took over carrying the baby illuminated what looked like deep gashes along the walls. Like the chamber where they had found the body, this corridor didn't have the finish as other sections. The floor and the walls were solidly packed dirt rather than stone, and she only noticed a few primitive torch holders positioned every few yards rather than the more intricate lighting systems from the newer sections of the bunker.

Severine instinctively slowed as she made her way down this corridor. In the darkness in the distance she thought that she heard deep, rumbling breaths. She paused and glanced over her shoulder at Rilex, who stepped up behind her.

"What?" he whispered.

"Do you hear that?"

As soon as she asked the question, she heard heavy,

thudding footsteps and felt the ground shiver beneath her feet. Her heart started pounding in her chest as she realized that they weren't alone in the corridor.

"Is it them?" Rilex asked.

Severine shook her head.

"I don't think so," she said. "That doesn't sound like multiple people."

"Then what is it?"

Bracing herself, Severine took a few steps forward. The footsteps had paused, but she could still hear the breathing. There was a loud grunt like an animal snorting and she stumbled back.

"I think it's the Meldor," she said, her voice catching fearfully in her throat.

"What is that?" Rilex asked.

"Ryan told us once that there was an animal under the ground here. I've never seen it and he never described it."

"What does it do?" Rilex asked. "Why is it here?"

Severine shook her head.

"I don't know," she said. "He never explained. But if it was what created these claw marks in the walls, it is a very dangerous creature."

There was another loud snort and Rilex reached forward to wrap his hand around her wrist.

"What do we do?" he asked. "Where do we go? Do we turn back?"

"If we turn back, we'll have to find our way again and we may just end up back where we started, or lost in the tunnels. Forward is the only way that we're going to make it out. We have to go past it."

"How?" he asked.

"We just..." she hesitated, not really sure how to answer the question, "go."

Thankful that the baby was better protected cradled against Rilex's chest than he would have been with her, Severine lifted the torch up higher and started down the corridor toward the sound of the breathing. In an instant, she saw a dark form rush across the corridor in front of them. It disappeared into a chamber and Severine felt the urge to follow it. She knew that it was dangerous, but it seemed like another link to Ryan, another piece of the connection of pure manipulation and control that she was determined to end. She had only taken a few steps, however, when she felt Rilex pull her back.

"No," he said. "I'm going first. Take the baby."

He took the torch from her hand and rested it into one of the holders in the wall, then released the baby from his chest so that he could hand him to her. Severine took him almost reluctantly. She wanted to protect the tiny child and could feel her affection for him deepening with each passing moment that she cared for him, but she also wanted to do this, to face these challenges, on her own rather than letting Rilex do it for her. She knew that he loved her and wanted to protect her, but she also knew that she was never going to feel as though she had truly escaped Ryan until she was able to make decisions and do things for herself. If Rilex loving her meant that he could put himself in danger to protect her, then her loving him meant the same. The baby in her arms, however, stopped her from simply following him down the corridor and into the chamber with the creature.

Rilex had been gone only a matter of seconds when she heard a growl and a cry of pain.

"Rilex!" she screamed.

There was another cry and Severine knew that she couldn't wait any longer. She pressed a kiss to the baby's head and settled him onto the ground, wrapping the cloth that they had used as a carrier around him to keep him warm. Grabbing the torch, she ran toward the sound of the Rilex's voice. He was coming through the entrance to the chamber when she arrived. She could see blood on his face and his shirt torn open, a long cut over his collarbone beginning to seep more blood along his chest.

"What happened?" she demanded.

There was another growl from behind him and Severine instinctively thrust the torch forward to fill as much of the space behind Rilex as she could with the illumination of the flames. As soon as she did, there was a whimpering grunt and she heard the same footsteps retreating from them.

"Where's the baby?" Rilex asked, his voice tense with the pain he was obviously feeling.

"I put him down," Severine said, taking him by his wrist and pulling him toward her. "Are you alright?"

"I think so," Rilex said. "I kept moving, so I don't think that whatever it is in there got me very deeply. The cuts are long, but I don't think that they are serious."

Severine's hand lowered slightly as she pushed aside the tatters of his shirt to look at the cut and almost immediately she heard the stomach-churning sound of the creature advancing again. She pushed Rilex back out of the way and held the torch forward, wanting to see whatever this creature was that had attacked Rilex. Just as it had before, the creature groaned and retreated from the light. Behind her the baby started to cry and she touched Rilex's shoulder.

"Go to him," she said. "Make sure that he's alright."

"What are you going to do?"

"I'm going to find out what this thing is."

"No," Rilex insisted, but she shook her head at him and

pulled away from his attempt to grab onto her. "You can't go in there."

"Yes, I can," she said. "Don't forget. I've been down here before. I know this planet, these hybrids, and Ryan in a way that you never will. If either of us should be in there with this creature, it's me."

She could see Rilex's face change as he relented. It wasn't sadness or anger, but a different emotion, one that seemed to tell her that he knew that as much as he wanted to wrap himself around her and guard her from anything else that might hurt her, that just wasn't possible. There was nothing that he could do to take away the memories that she had or to prevent anything from ever happening to her again. All that he could do was walk beside her through this and hope that together they could keep each other safe.

He nodded and took a step out of her way, starting down the corridor toward where the baby lay. Without the torch, he was walking in darkness, and she turned to give him enough illumination to get to the baby where he lay. The moment that the light left the chamber, she felt a rush of hot breath on her and felt the ground tremble as the creature approached her.

"The light!" Rilex shouted at her. "Get out of the way and shine the light on it!"

Severine ducked out of the way just as a heavily furred mass hit her legs and she felt a large paw swipe through the air toward her head. She swept the torch toward it and caught sight of a massive dark brown creature quickly pulling away from the light. She stepped toward it, pushing the torch closer so that more light touched it and heard it whimper again as it tried to press itself as far against the wall as it could. She saw it turn its head away from her, its dark eyes closing tightly as it continued to groan and whimper. Its body started to shake and soon its legs folded and it lowered to the ground.

"It won't get near the light," Severine confirmed to Rilex. "It's cowering from me."

She glanced over her shoulder and saw the corridor filled with a pale light. Backing up carefully to ensure that she didn't take the illumination from the torch out of the room, she looked into the tunnel and saw a small cluster of stars swirling over Rilex's head and shimmering down onto the baby where he lay in Rilex's arms. She felt a smile touch her lips. It wasn't the first time that she had seen Rilex's stars, but they were no less astonishing and beautiful.

"Can you bring them in here?" she asked.

Rilex held the baby in one arm and reached up toward the stars. They seemed to respond to him and he started to guide them toward the chamber. When he got to the entrance, he swept his hand forward, scattering the tiny balls of light across the ceiling so that they spread out and filled the space with their glow. Severine brought the torch back out into the corridor and settled it into the nearest holder so that there would be light when they left the chamber and then returned to look at the creature. It was curled against the wall, its head tucked as far away from the light of the stars as it could get it.

"What's wrong with it?" Rilex asked. "Why does the light do that to it?"

Severine took a step closer to it.

"It might be the species," she said. "I don't know anything about it."

"I don't either," Rilex agreed. "I've never even heard of the Meldor. Is it just this one creature, or are there many?"

Severine shook her head.

"I don't know."

She walked closer to it and out of the corner of her eye she could see Rilex tighten nervously.

"What are you doing?" he asked.

"I want to get a better look at it," Severine said. "It doesn't make sense that something this big would stay underground all the time," she said. "There aren't any other animals down here naturally, as far as I know."

"So?" Rilex asked.

"So, what would it eat?" she asked. "If it is this resistant to light, it wouldn't be able to go on the surface ever. Even the starlight incapacitated it. But something of this size would need food consistently to keep it alive. It just doesn't make sense that there would be an animal that would be born to live underground when there is no natural food source to sustain it."

"I don't think I understand," Rilex said. "There has to be a reason that it's here and it's obvious that the light is hurting it."

Severine looked at him sharply.

"You're right," she said. "It isn't just bothered. It's in pain. Something is hurting it, even though it's eyes are closed. It can't see the light, but it is still afraid and in pain."

She approached the Meldor and gingerly reached out to touch it. The animal bristled at her touch and Severine pulled her hand away defensively. When she realized that it wasn't moving toward her, she reached forward again and rested her hand on its thick fur. The animal was tremendous and she could feel strong muscles beneath its fur. It would definitely need to eat far more than she could imagine would wander down here on its own. Something was bringing it food, which meant that maybe something was keeping it down here. She stepped up until she was just inches from it and continued to run her hand along it.

Though the creature was still shaking and groaning in pain, she felt it seem to relax slightly as she petted it. Finally, she felt confident to reach toward the animal's huge head. Its face was still turned away from her and it had made no move to claw or bite her, so she let her hand run up between its shoulder blades. When it reached the Meldor's neck, her fingertips hit something hard.

Severine felt it further and found that it seemed to stretch around the creature's neck. She glanced over at Rilex.

"There's something here," she said.

She put both hands into the creature's thick hair, pushing through mats and clusters of dirt to get to the hard object that she had felt. Looking down at it, she felt her stomach turn and tears come to her eyes.

"Get rid of the stars," she said.

"What?" Rilex asked.

"Get rid of the stars," she demanded more insistently. "All of them. Make it dark in here."

"Are you sure?" he asked.

"Yes," Severine responded. "Do it now. But keep them close and ready to put up again."

As Rilex reached up toward the balls of light floating close to the ceiling, Severine reached into the pouch at her hip and pulled out a knife. She brought the tip of the blade to the thick collar and tucked her fingers as far under it as she could, feeling sharp metal teeth on the underside. As soon as the stars were gone, the teeth retracted, but only partially. She realized that the torch in the corridor was still putting a small amount of light into the chamber.

"Go take the torch and bring it down the tunnel until you can't see the door anymore," she instructed. "Now."

Severine was relieved when Rilex did as she asked

without hesitation and she tightened her grip in the collar in preparation. As the light from the torch faded around her, the animal's shaking stopped and she could hear the rumble of its growling start again. She fought the nervousness that was encouraging her to release the collar and leave the room. Instead, she held on tighter and waited until the light was gone completely. The instant the light disappeared, Severine felt the metal teeth retract the rest of the way into the collar and the Meldor start to rise to its feet. Its head reared back, but she grasped the collar and started to saw at it with her knife. The creature climbed to its feet and Severine stood on her toes to keep cutting at the thick collar. It let out a roar and shook, nearly sending her onto the ground. She swung herself up onto its back, holding tight with her thighs to keep herself steady. She was nearly through the collar. She couldn't stop. The animal thrashed and Severine cried out as she felt her body hit the wall that the Meldor had been curled against, but she held on.

Finally, she felt the blade go the rest of the way through the collar and it fell away from the creature's neck.

"Rilex!" she screamed, reaching down to grasp the Meldor's thick fur to keep her in place on its back. "Come back! Bring the torch."

Rilex ran into the room and held the torch violently toward the creature. He shook it at the animal, taking an intimidating step forward. Severine held her hand up to stop him, shaking her head.

"No," she said. "Don't. Just wait."

Still holding onto its fur, Severine reached forward and gently stroked the Meldor, trying to ignore the feeling of fresh blood on her fingertips from where the collar had been positioned. The creature continued to growl and thrash for a few moments, but finally she started to feel it calming down beneath her.

"That's right," she murmured. "It's alright. You're safe now. The light won't hurt you."

The Meldor settled and she heard it make a sound close to a sigh of relief.

"What happened?" Rilex asked.

Severine slid down off of the creature's back.

"Make the stars again and put the torch back," she said. Rilex complied and when he came back, she held up the cut collar. "It wasn't the light that was bothering it. It was this."

"What is it?" Rilex asked, coming toward her.

"It's a collar," she said. "I think it has a chip in it that responds to light. There are metal teeth that retracted when the light went away. It's been trained to be afraid of the light because of the pain that this causes it. It doesn't live down here naturally. It was put down here."

"By Ryan?" Rilex asked.

"I think so. It's part of his war tactics."

"But why?" Rilex asked. "Why would he take a creature this big and put it where no one goes, then make it so that it would never go near light?"

"Think about it," Severine said. "You saw how vicious this thing can be. Ryan planned for virtually everything, but even he knew that there was always the possibility that things would work out differently than he intended. There was a chance that he wouldn't get the people here that he wants destroyed, that it might take longer than expected, or that he was going to be able to get to them without bringing them here. And if that happened, there would be no reason for him to maintain the army that he trained specifically for this mission."

"I thought that he was intending on weaponizing the army," Rilex said.

"Do you honestly believe that we are the only ones?" Severine asked. She could see Rilex's face fall and she felt the tremble inside her as her mind was flooded with thoughts that she had been fighting not to let through. "There would have been questions if Ryan had bodies to handle on Earth, so he took care of that. The Meldor didn't need to find its own food down here because Ryan made sure that the Valdicians brought it plenty. But that wasn't its only purpose. It's here as a backup plan."

"In case Ryan didn't need any of this army any longer," Rilex said. "He could just remove the lights and release the Meldor on them."

Severine nodded.

"We can't leave it here," she said. "It deserves to be free, too."

11

Athan found himself in the oldest section of the tunnels without fully realizing where he was running. This was the section of the lair of the Order that was rarely used, but that contained some of the most precious, and most fearsome, of possessions that the organization had been holding and protecting throughout time. He avoided this area as much as he could and now he felt even more uncomfortable there. The tense energy that had filled the tunnels when he first got down into them was thicker in this area and Athan felt like he was struggling to draw the air into his lungs enough to keep him breathing steadily. At least here he couldn't hear the whispers of the other Order members seeking him out. He still needed to find Ellora, but being in this area meant that he could escape far more easily.

He was weaving through the back tunnels, feeling his way along the darkness with his fingertips along the walls, when he heard whispers starting again. His body tensed and Athan pressed himself against the wall to protect his back. There were no lights in this area. It was that way by design with the intention that anyone who came to this area would be forced to bring along their own source of light. It was meant to create a heavier, more foreboding feeling in this area that would stand in stark contrast to the newer, more welcoming areas filled with colored light that ushered them through. The effect was boldly, intensely evident now. In the other times when he had been in this area, Athan had gone there with purpose and direction. He had been carrying light with him and was confident in what lay ahead. As he stood there in the darkness, however, he could imagine the thoughts and feelings suffered by those who were brought down to these chambers. The darkness was oppressive and even the light of a torch or a lantern would only penetrate it a few feet ahead. That made it so that all that lay ahead of someone forced down into this area of the tunnels would be the unknown, increasing the fear that they would likely already be feeling. For those who were not being brought to one of the fearsome prison cells at the end of the corridor, but rather were being escorted through this area for some other reason, the purposeful darkness would prevent them from being able to see any more of this space than their escort deemed necessary. It was a primitive, and yet highly effective, layer of secrecy and protection that the Order used to keep all that they did concealed in mystery.

Athan didn't know which direction to move. He could either go toward the sound of the voices deeper in the tunnels or he could go back the way that he had come and risk encountering the rest of the Order again. He was starting back toward the main section of the tunnels when he heard the voices in the darkness get louder. Though he couldn't understand the words through the muffling of the distance, the tone of each voice sounded familiar enough that he paused. The voices grew closer and he heard a voice that took the breath out of his lungs.

"I don't understand why you can't tell me more."

Ellora.

He didn't know who she was talking to, but Athan started in the direction of her voice as fast as he could move confidently through the darkness. He turned a corner and saw a flicker of light cross the corridor in front of him. There were two dark figures in the illumination and he let out a sigh of relief. Though they were moving quickly, the smaller form that he assumed was Ellora didn't seem to be resisting. She was going along with the other one willingly, telling Athan that she hadn't been captured. Though the very fact that she was still in the tunnels kept her in danger, it was comforting to know that she wasn't alone. Someone was with her, which gave her a better chance of getting out of the lair alive.

Athan ran toward the light and turned the corner sharply. He heard Ellora gasp and felt a hard blow in his stomach. Grunting, he bent over the pain in his stomach and leaned against the wall beside him. He felt the warmth of the light from a torch touch his face and he looked up into it.

"Athan!" Ellora gasped.

"You know him?" a man's voice demanded.

Athan looked beyond the glow of the flame form the torch and saw an unfamiliar face in the shadows. He wasn't anybody that he knew and there was something about him that was very different than the rest of the Mikana in the Order. His age was impossible to determine. While he looked young, there was an ancientness in his eyes that seemed to carry the weight of endless years in them.

"Yes," Ellora said. "This is Athan. Don't you know him? He was Aegeus's best friend."

Athan felt his spine straighten defensively. The mention of Aegeus was uncomfortable in a way he couldn't quite define.

"I'm sorry," the man said. "Are you alright?"

"I don't know him," Athan said, choosing not to justify the apology as he straightened.

"This is Mhavrych," Ellora said. "He said that he knew Aegeus."

Athan saw her take a step away from the man, looking at him suspiciously as if she was concerned now that he had lied to her.

"I did know him," the man said. "But very few know me."

Suddenly what Ellora had said was the man's name sunk into Athan's mind. He looked at the man, scrutinizing him, trying to remember exactly when he had heard that before.

"Mhavrych," he said.

"Yes," the man said. "That is the name that I was given when I was younger."

"You were on Penthos," Athan said as realization struck him. "You were there the night that Kyven and Emerie were trapped in the quarry. You saved Nylek."

"Yes," Mhavrych said.

"You left before anyone was able to thank you," Athan said. "You didn't even stay to make sure that they were going to be found."

"I didn't need to be thanked," Mhavrych said. "That wasn't why I did it. And just because you couldn't see me doesn't mean that I wasn't still there to make sure that they were alright."

"But you..." Athan started, but then hesitated. He didn't

want to offend the man, but he needed to understand. "You're one of the…"

"Hybrids?" Mhavrych asked. "I know."

"I don't understand," Athan said.

"You don't have to," Mhavrych said. "Not now. What matters now is that we get out of these tunnels and back where the Order can't access us. We need to get back to Penthos as quickly as possible."

"How did you get here?" Athan asked. "The only ship that has traveled here since we were on Penthos is the one that we were on."

"I have traveled back and forth far more than just then," Mhavrych said.

"What are you doing down here?" Athan asked.

The man looked frustrated, on the brink of anger, but Athan didn't care. He said that he knew Aegeus, but that didn't make any sense. Why would a man who knew Aegeus not know Athan? Why would Aegeus have anything to do with a hybrid? And why would one of the hybrids not only rescue members of their group, but also be connected to the Order in such a way that he knew how to get into the tunnels, and about this specific area of the lair? He was suspicious and defensive, and felt like he needed to protect Ellora, himself, and everyone else.

"It needs protecting," Mhavrych said solemnly.

The words were simple and straightforward, but they held tremendous meaning. Athan felt a shock go through his heart and he took an involuntary step back. His hands were shaking and everything around came into sharp, crisp focus.

"Do you have it?" he asked.

Ellora was looking back and forth between them, her expression one of confusion, but there wasn't time to explain. Mhavrych held up a worn, dirt-streaked sack briefly and then tucked it back to his side.

"What is it?" Ellora asked. "What are you protecting?"

Athan ignored her question. Now wasn't the time. At some point, she would need to know everything, but for now they needed to put all of their focus on finding their way out of the tunnels and back to Creia. He hoped that when the time came for her to understand what was in that bag and its significance, that her husband would be the one who would explain it all to her.

"What do you know about these tunnels?" he asked Mhavrych.

He still didn't understand who this man was or what he had to do with all of this, but he had to trust him. There was no other choice but to put his faith in him and hope that he wasn't making the wrong decision.

"Everything," the man said.

"What is the fastest way to get out of here?" Athan asked. "The Order isn't just looking for Ellora, they're looking for me, too."

"We'll have to go through the cells," Mhavrych said. "There's still a possibility that we'll run into one of them, but it's less likely, and even if we do, we'll have a better chance of getting through only one or two than we would a larger group."

Athan nodded despite the hesitation in his chest. The cells were nothing that he wanted to experience. When he was younger, they were rarely used, only employed in the most extenuating of circumstances, but it hadn't remained that way. The years brought tremendous change to the Order and how it operated, change that was the cause of Aegeus's resistance and rebellion, the motivation behind the plan that Athan knew he was making, but never knew the details. In more recent times the cells had been used far more frequently, and once people were damned to time in those cells, they were rarely, if ever, seen again. He didn't know what they might find within the crumbling walls, but if that was the only option, they could have no hesitation.

Mhavrych lifted his torch above his head and looked to either side as if to confirm that they were still alone. He then gestured in the direction that they had been heading when he encountered them.

"That way," he said. "Listen carefully. Follow my instructions as I say them. Don't hesitate."

Athan stepped ahead of Ellora, not wanting her to go first down the corridor and watched over his shoulder as Mhavrych took the place at the end of the line. They remained close together as they walked quickly further into the darkness, only the light of the torch making a small pool of illumination at his feet guiding his way. He listened carefully for Mhavrych to give instructions and followed them immediately as he did. They moved through sections of the lair that Athan had visited before and then he found himself turning into a corridor that even he hadn't seen. The feeling was unnerving, but he kept listening to Mhavrych and letting his words guide them through a series of quick turns that had them coiling in on themselves and then back out to make a larger circle before leading into a corridor so narrow that Athan could touch the walls on either side of him simply by leaning slightly in either direction. The light from the torch touched narrow doors only as high as his waist on one side, and above his head on the other, slightly offset rather than being regularly stacked with the lower doors.

"They are meant to torment the prisoners further," Mhavrych explained without Athan having to ask. "Some are kept in the cells beneath while others are kept in the upper cells on the other side. They know that they are there, yet they aren't able to see each other. Guards prevent them from communicating."

Athan felt a chill roll down his spine. This wasn't the way of the Order. This wasn't what they were intended to do or how they were meant to care for the precious ward placed in their protection. This was purely the product of the corruption that had grown within the Order like thick, choking vines that could infiltrate and break through even the strongest buildings over time. He tried to ignore the thick, musty smell in this area that seemed to grow stronger the further they walked through it. He kept his eyes focused on the path ahead rather than allowing himself to look through the miniscule barred windows at the tops of the doors. He didn't want to see what was still inside any of them.

At last they reached a dead-end of the corridor and Athan stopped. Mhavrych walked up behind him and looked up. Athan followed his gaze and saw a small hatch in the ceiling above. It appeared to be made of slats of wood held together by metal straps. A metal ring in the center told Athan that this door was meant to be pulled down into the tunnel much like the ramp that led down from the wall above.

"How do we get up there?" Athan asked.

"We climb," Mhavrych said.

Athan's heart sunk as the other man extinguished the torch and sent them into thick blackness. He heard the sound of Mhavrych searching through the pouch that he had tied to his belt. A moment later there was a milky glow. The glow grew and when his eyes grew accustomed to it, Athan could see that Mhavrych was holding a ball of light in his hand. Though he hadn't seen it, it occurred to him that this was not the first time that he had conjured that type of light in an emergency situation.

"That's the light that you used to save Kyven," he said.

Mhavrych nodded.

"Does he still have it?" he asked.

"He never showed it to me," Athan said, "but I'm guessing that he kept it."

"Good," Mhavrych said.

With no further explanation, he planted one foot into the wall on one side of the corner, and then jumped up slightly so that his foot planted into the other. He tossed the ball down to Athan and used his hands to help him scale the walls until he was close enough to the ceiling to grasp the ring in the door. Athan saw him pull the door down and disappear up through the gap in the ceiling. He was gone for several seconds and then Mhavrych's face appeared in the opening.

"Help Ellora up," he said.

Athan rested the ball of light at his feet and helped Ellora up toward Mhavrych's waiting hand. A few moments later she was through the gap and it was only him left.

"I'm going to toss the light up to you," he called up.

The darkness that fell when the ball left his hand was disconcerting, but Athan mimicked the movements that he had seen Mhavrych use and was soon close enough to the ceiling that he could see the glow of the ball through the gap. He could feel the cool air from outside and filled his lungs eagerly with the freshness. Grasping the sides of the gap, he pulled himself through and rolled away. There was a low thud as Mhavrych pulled the hatch back into place, but Athan didn't move. He lay on his back, his eyes closed as he willed his breath to normalize. When he felt in control again, he opened his eyes and saw that they weren't out in the open as he would have expected them to be. Instead, they seemed to be surrounded by the low overhanging branches of a tremendous tree that had bent down to create a clearing beneath. This created the ideal concealment of the entrance to the lair, but Athan wanted to get out of it. After even the brief time in the tunnels, he didn't want to feel closed in any longer.

Athan climbed to his feet and they started out from under the tree. They appeared to be deep in the forest behind the kingdom, further out than he had ventured, and he immediately increased his pace. He wanted to get to the kingdom as quickly as possible, knowing that he would feel safer once they were back within the walls of the kingdom with Creia and the rest of the crew.

12

Rain piloted the vehicle that Athan had given them and that they had left in the orchard through the gates to the human settlement and pulled it to a stop beside the wall. She had been relieved when she found that the vehicles were waiting for them upon arrival from Penthos, knowing that they were going to be vital not just for gathering everyone and everything that they would need from Uoria, but also once they returned to the desolate planet. Having these vehicles at their disposal meant that they could move much more quickly and easily, enabling them to fight more efficiently and get people and supplies where they needed to be without having to rely on walking.

She climbed out of the vehicle and looked around at the settlement that she hadn't seen since she and Jonah returned for their own vehicle. It had been less than a month, but it felt like so much longer. In all of the chaos that she had been experiencing, the settlement seemed quiet and calm. She could still see the remnants of the horrific battle with the Covra, including the huge wall that had been instrumental in their final battle once the Denynso came. It was strange to see it standing there. She knew that it was like everything else that had been created by Loralia – a reflection. It was only there because the lovely, but unusual woman had used her compact to reflect it and it could only linger because of the belief of those who saw it. If they questioned it or didn't believe that it was there, it would disappear. Despite knowing this, Rain could see that the wall was still there, solid and strong in the middle of the road. She knew that it was those pinnacle moments as they stood behind the wall and engaged in their final clash with the disturbing creatures that had implanted the humans with their eggs, knowing that the birth of the next generation would destroy them. There was utter disregard for their lives, but there was nothing that they could do. The arrival of the Denynso and then the human scientists had been the only thing that saved them. If they had arrived only shortly after they did, the entire settlement would have been lost forever.

That thought made her think of Lynx. It wasn't just the lives of those who were being used as incubators that would have been lost had the warriors not arrived when they did. In the hundred years that she had been lying in the compound, locked in place by the toxins of the Covra, the planet had changed, the Denynso compound had shifted, and Lynx had been born. Though she had already lived for many decades by the time that he lived, they were connected from his first moment. It would take until he was an adult and stormed the human settlement with no idea what he was going to find to discover it, but from the minute that he was born, his heart was looking for her. She was his intended mate, the only woman who he would ever love and the person who would help him to fulfill his potential. He knew as soon as he found her and even though it was days upon days before he would even see her eyes or hear her voice, he cared for her and protected her, staying by her side until they finally discovered how they could release them from their lock and bring them back, saving most of them before the birth of the Covra young could destroy them.

If he hadn't, all of the love that they had shared would have been lost.

The sound of children laughing in the distance brought Rain out of her thoughts and she felt herself smile. These were the children born in the fifteen years that passed between the Nyx 23 crew crashing on the surface of Uoria and the Covra locking them, children who, like she was, were more than one hundred years older than the youth on their faces told, and would likely never understand how truly extraordinary they really were. It had been a blessing that none of the children had been lost when the new generation of Covra began to hatch, though Rain knew in her heart that is was likely only because the Covra didn't feel that it was worthwhile to put their eggs inside such small hosts, not thinking that their bodies would provide enough sustenance for their young at birth. Whatever the reason, they were all still alive. They had made it through the horrible ordeal and were back beneath the starlight, laughing as they played, seemingly carefree and without any lingering impact. They were blissfully resilient, and for that, Rain was grateful. She knew that many of the families had already decided that they were not going to leave their settlement on Uoria. Though they now had the means that they didn't in the aftermath of the crash, they had lost their drive to return to Earth. That planet was a memory now and after the long years that they had spent on Uoria, the settlement that they had built together had become their home.

This was where they learned more about their strength and capabilities than they had ever known. This was where they had overcome the despair and helplessness and took the remnants of their ship to create their new village. This was where many of them had found each other and fallen in love. This was where their children were born. Rain wondered how many of those people hadn't told their children about their true origin. If they didn't intend on leaving Uoria for Earth, there may be no reason to share with them the pain and darkness of the past and instead simply let them live their lives in peace and comfort.

Rain knew that much of that rested on the battle that awaited them on Penthos. If Ryan had his way, Uoria would soon be under his control and there would no longer be a way to protect those children or to keep them from knowing what really existed beyond Uoria. She couldn't let that happen. She hadn't been given a choice. When the ship crashed, she was stuck in place with the rest of the survivors. There was nothing that she could do but take one step after the next and try to piece together the life that eventually formed in the settlement. These children would have a choice. She could help to ensure that no matter what their parents chose, when they were adults, they would have the freedom to go where they wanted to go and live the way that they wanted to live.

Gathering the empty bags that she had brought with her, Rain started toward the center of the village. Evening had fallen quickly and the brighter the stars grew above her, the quieter the laughter of the children became as they ventured into their homes for the night. She was nearly to her former home when she saw two people step out onto the street ahead of her.

"Brandon!" she called. "Emmaline!"

The two turned toward her voice and were soon running to her.

"Rain!" Brandon exclaimed as he came close to her. "What's going on? Where's Jonah?"

"I can't explain everything right now," Rain said, "but I need your help. I need everyone who might be willing."

"Does this have to do with why Creia and others from the compound are in the Mikana kingdom now?" Emmaline asked.

"Yes," Rain said. "They're preparing for the same thing. What we've been waiting for, for more than one hundred years. It's time that we go back to Penthos and finish the fight that we started so long ago."

Brandon and Emmaline exchanged glances, but she could see the look of steadfast determination already forming in their eyes and knew that they would be there with her when she left the settlement to return to the Mikana kingdom. She told them to gather whoever else they thought would help and to collect any supplies that they could get their hands on, then Rain continued on toward her house. She knew that she only had a few minutes, but she longed to see her bedroom one more time. She didn't know when she would have the opportunity to see it again, or if she ever would, and wanted to have a few final moments in it to both collect the things still there that might be helpful, and to say goodbye.

The room felt somehow even more still and quiet than the rest of the settlement when she stepped inside. On Earth, it would have been unheard of to simply walk away from a house and have it remain untouched, but here in the settlement there was no other expectation. The rest of the group already had their own homes, each customized to their own needs and desires, and filled with the possessions that they were able to salvage from the crash, as well as what they had found, made, and repurposed from Uoria. There would be no reason for anyone to take over her house. Not yet. Perhaps when the children got older and were ready to separate from their parents, but for now it was sitting just as it had been the day that she last walked away from it.

Rain let her eyes scan around the room, saving the bed for last. That was where Lynx had first seen her, and where she had been when she first became aware of his presence in her life. It looked so benign now, its white covers pristine and crisp as if just waiting for her to climb inside and go to sleep. In her mind, though, that bed would always be a bitter reminder of the time that she spent locked away from reality, lying in place helplessly as the Covra eggs developed inside her. But that was also the first place where she had heard Lynx's voice, coming to her through the emptiness. It had been the first place that she had felt the warmth of Lynx's body and knew the depth of his heart.

She walked around the room and let her fingertips touch each of the possessions there. They all meant so much more to her now than they did. Even when she first settled into this home and filled it with these little mementos of the life that she had had before the ill-fated journey aboard the StarCity, they hadn't carried the same incredible weight that they did now. Though Rain had been one of the first of the group to accept what was happening and encourage them to try to create a new home, part of her heart had always held onto the hope and belief that they wouldn't actually live out the rest of their lives on this unknown planet. She didn't talk about it, but that piece of her refused to admit that they didn't have the ability to get back to Earth, or that this was the life that she was going to have, that one day it would be her body that they were submitting to the strange ground so far from everything that she had ever known and loved. It wasn't fear or hopelessness. Instead, it was stubbornness, and through that stubbornness came the creation of the vehicle that she built with Jonah, and the strength to follow Lynx when they left the settlement.

The feeling of these items had changed. Now they were a link to the past rather than a hope for the future. These pieces were who she once was and reminders of not just the potential that was taken from her during that crash, but the life that was snatched from members of her crew at the crash and in the days and weeks following. In those fifteen years before the final invasion of the Covra, they had added many bodies to the cemetery. These were people who would truly never have the chance to see home again and whose family would never have the opportunity to grieve for them properly. This was final and concrete. Rain knew that she couldn't allow them to be forgotten or dishonored. No matter what happened to the crew and where the remaining survivors decided to live out their lives, the people who had already been lost deserved justice, and it was up to her to make sure that they got it.

Hastily grabbing everything that she needed from the room, Rain ran back out into the settlement and the rapidly growing group of survivors who had taken up their own bags and weapons, and were ready to follow her.

13

———

Kyven cupped Emerie's face with both hands and drew her closer to him for a deep kiss. It felt like it had been months since he had been able to feel her skin and taste her lips like this, though he knew that it hadn't been nearly that long. The time that he was trapped in the clinic on the ship and then in the infirmary had been brutal, with each hour like days stretching between them. Now he was finally able to walk around outside of the infirmary and they had stolen some time to themselves among the protective trees of the fruit orchard. He couldn't wait another moment to touch her, to hold her, to kiss her lips and reconnect them.

Emerie seemed to melt beneath the familiar feeling of his mouth on hers and the taste of his tongue as it slipped past her lips. He allowed it to massage hers and explore her eagerly. When he ended their kiss, Kyven reached up into the branches of the tree that they were sitting beneath and pulled down a cluster of the sweet fruit. He pulled one from the cluster and held it to her lips.

Emerie closed her lips around the fruit and bit down into it, a gentle moan escaping her lips as the tart-sweet juice washed across her tongue. Some of the richly dark liquid slipped over her bottom lip and Kyven dipped his head forward to catch the drips with his tongue. Emerie took the small fruit from his fingers and brought it to his mouth so that he could take the rest of it in. Emerie took another of the fruits from his hand and crushed it in between her fingers. She trailed the juice down the center of his chest, still exposed after leaving the infirmary without bothering to put a shirt on, and glazed it across one of his nipples.

He let out a long, growling breath as she whisked the cool juice away from his skin with the tip of her tongue. As she swirled her tongue against his chest, seeming to indulge as much in the taste and feeling of his skin as she was the juice itself, Kyven brought his hands to her shirt so that he could gather it at her waist and pull it off over her head as soon as she drew back from him, revealing her breasts to him. He moaned at the sight of the lush curves and dipped his thumb into the juice on her hand so that he could paint one taut pink nipple. Forgoing the delicate tracing of her nipple, he leaned forward and closed his mouth over her breast, his tongue flicking across her skin as he licked away the juice.

Emerie bit down into her bottom lip and she arched her back to press her breast deeper into his mouth. Kyven's hands smoothed down over her hips to grip them tightly, pulling her closer to him so that he could glide his mouth along her skin to the other breast and repeat his lavish attention there. He felt her hands move to the front of his pants and she worked the narrow ties free. She pushed the sides of the fabric open and his already surging erection sprung free. Her hand wrapped around his shaft eagerly and she let out a sigh of happiness. Her other hand flattened in the center of his chest and she guided him to lie back on the cool grass so that she could straighten his legs. Moving down, she tugged his pants off. Kyven relaxed back and let his eyes close as she used her fingers to trace more lazy patterns along the skin of his chest with juice.

Emerie followed the patterns with her tongue as she made her way from his chest down his belly. There was nothing rushed or frantic in her movements. Just as he had craved her and ached just to be close to her, Emerie seemed to be luxuriating in her ability to touch Kyven, and enjoying every moment of their skin connecting. He lifted his hips up toward her, but she seemed to purposely avoid touching his cock. Instead, she tilted her head to create a trail of kisses down the deep muscular V at the front of his hips. Her mouth glided along one inner thigh and Kyven felt his skin trembling in response to the touch. She continued the delightful torment up the other thigh and along the juncture of his leg and hip until she reached his belly again.

Kyven's breath had become rough and ragged and his hands were gripping at the grass beside him. Emerie adjusted her body so that she straddled his legs and leaned forward. Her breasts grazed across his erection, tempting it to rise up toward her. As she continued to stroke along his cock with her warm, soft breasts, she licked from his belly up to his chest, and then flicked her tongue across his nipple again. Lifting up to this position had caused Kyven's erection to slide across her stomach and he could feel it gliding easily with the warm drops of fluid that were slipping out and onto her skin. Emerie slid against him again and he reached up to tuck his hand at the back of her head, guiding her back down his body.

Emerie rose up on her knees to slip out of her skirt before she leaned back down and took Kyven's erection into her mouth. A loud groan tore from his chest as he felt a deep need within him fulfilled by the warm, soft embrace of her lips and tongue. She glided her mouth down until she fully enveloped him and the tip dipped down into her throat.

Kyven clutched at her hair and used it to gently guide her into a smooth, fast rhythm. The sensation that she created was nearly overwhelming and he lifted his hips to thrust into her mouth. Soon he knew that he wasn't going to be able to hold off much longer. He grasped her by her arms and pulled her up his body, positioning her thighs on either side of him. He reached down with one hand and held his shaft so that he could position his tip at her opening. Emerie released her thighs and settled down onto his hips, taking him fully inside her in one slow glide.

Kyven watched her back arch and heard Emerie let out a moan of pleasure. When she finally held him completely, he grabbed her hips and led her to roll them so that they stay connected even while he massaged her walls and nurtured her to a shattering climax. She screamed out as her body drew him deeper and within seconds he felt the rush of dizzying sensation surge through him and his cock throbbed inside her. Kyven thrust up into her until his climax eased, and Emerie finally fell forward, her sweaty body trembling against his.

Their breath slowed and her shaking quieted as he cradled her against his chest, but Kyven stayed inside her, the feeling of her body holding him and them being melded into one was comforting and intimate. He ran his hands down her back and tenderly kissed her shoulder, closing his eyes so that he could lose himself in the feeling, smell, taste, and sound of her.

"Thank you," Emerie whispered, the word sounding almost like an exhalation of breath.

Kyven laughed softly.

"For what?" he asked.

She lifted her head and looked into his eyes.

"For coming back to me."

"Did I ever leave?" he asked.

"You almost did," she said. "That beast could have killed you with little more than one more swipe. A single bite. Slashing just a little to either side."

Her breath caught in her throat and she looked down, shaking her head slowly as if to will away the tears that Kyven could hear forming in her voice. He sat up, gathering her into his lap and rested his hands on either side of her face so that he could look at her, wanting her to see the sincerity and life in his eyes.

"I am right here, Emerie," he said. "I never went anywhere, and I'm not going to. I was injured, yes. The Meldor was horrible, I'm not going to pretend that it wasn't. But I survived. I'm alright now. I've healed and I will continue to heal until it will be like nothing happened. If anything, this will only make me stronger." She tried to glance down again and he kept his hands steady to prevent her from looking away. "I love you," he said. "With everything in me, I love you."

"I love you, too," Emerie said.

Relief came over her face and Emerie kissed him softly.

"You know that this will all be over soon," he said, hoping that she would believe him, even if he wasn't completely sure of this himself. "This will all be over and we'll have a life waiting for us."

Emerie nodded.

"I know," she said quietly.

"And when that happens, we'll decide together what we're going to do."

"What do you mean?" she asked, sounding concerned.

"This isn't your world, Emerie," he said. "You are here by chance and by force. You never meant to not return to Earth and live out your life there after your mission, and I wouldn't blame you if you wanted to leave Uoria and not have to see it again. I can imagine that you want to get back to Earth."

Emerie shook her head.

"I don't know that for sure," she said.

"You don't?" Kyven asked. "You don't want to go back to Earth?"

"No," Emerie said. "I mean...yes, I have thought about going back at some point to see it again, but I can't tell you for sure that that is where I want to stay. They still don't know what happened to us and I can honestly say that I have no idea how they would respond to finding out that we are still alive. If it was me, I'm not sure what I would do or think. Going back to Earth would give me some closure. I'd like to see that everything has moved on alright without me. I'd like to pay my respects to my family and see that someone else is living in my home. I feel like I need that in order to be able to really say goodbye to the life that I had before I boarded the StarCity. But I don't know what's going to come after that. I don't really want to think about it."

"Then we don't have to," Kyven said, wrapping his arms tightly around her waist and cuddling her close. "We don't have to think about any of it. All that matters is that we're together. Just know that I want you to be happy."

"I know," Emerie said. "And when the time comes, we'll think about it. We'll know what's right for us when we find it. For now, we get through this. All we can think about it getting through it, then we can figure out what is beyond it."

UNTITLED

To be continued...

AZRA & ELISE'S STORY

1

———

The world fell strangely silent around him as Azra ran across the deep desert sand toward the clash that he saw ahead. He felt the battle yell coming from his throat, but he couldn't hear it. It was as if there was so much happening around him that his senses had shut down to prevent his mind from becoming overwhelmed. The lack of sound allowed him to focus intently on the people around him and the weight of the weapon that he had taken into his hand. As soon as his feet brought him into the center of the battle, though, all of the sound rushed back. Azra could suddenly hear the roar of voices, punctuated by the metallic sound of blades hitting. Pyra's voice rose above all the others, and Azra felt galvanized.

Ahead of him he could see a hooded man that appeared nearly as tall as the Denynso warriors but more slender. The man had one hand outstretched in front of him and George was lying on the sand, struggling against an unseen force that appeared to be holding him down in the burning grains. The human scientist clawed at his neck and chest, his heels digging down into the ground beneath him as if he was trying to pull hands away. Azra knew that meant that this particular hybrid had Valdician blood. He ran forward and dug his blade into the back of the man's shoulder. He didn't intend to kill him, but rather force him to lose the concentration that was necessary for him to maintain his hold on George.

The hybrid reared back with the pain of the stab and almost instantly George scrambled to his feet. Azra lifted his blade above his head and brought it down again, slashing at the hood so that it fell away from the creature's head. He wanted to see its face. He needed to break through the ambiguity, to see this being for itself rather than allowing it to remain an abstract thought in his mind. Abstracts enabled him to fight indiscriminately, to simply put the inborn compulsion for war in control and lash out at whatever was near him without thought. That was no longer an option. Surrounded by more species than he had ever known existed, Azra knew that the battle lines were no longer like they used to be. Before the Denynso warriors left the compound, things had been straightforward and easy to understand. There had been the Denynso and everyone else. There was a vague understanding that there were species in other places throughout the galaxy, and even the entirety of the Universe, that respected the Denynso and considered themselves neutral with them, never interested in fighting and always happy for the warriors to handle the enemies that they did have if they happened to venture on to Uoria. For the most part, however, there was only the warriors and the enemies that came onto the planet in an effort to destroy his kind or to take over his planet.

During those days, when they stood on a battlefield, it was easy to recognize who was the enemy. This was no longer the case. Now he could look to either side and see people of all kinds embroiled in the battle that raged hotter with every passing second. Though most of the hybrid army soldiers wore hooded cloaks, it wasn't enough to delineate clearly which people were fighting for the same convictions and which were pushing back against them. He couldn't help but remember what the hybrid that Rilex had left with, the one that the women now called Severine, had told them about the hybrids. Not all of them had the violent compulsions within them or had any belief in what Ryan wanted them to do. They were slaves forced to follow through with the scientist's grisly ideals, and that made the delicate delineation between those who were on his side and those who he was meant to be fighting against much more difficult to discern. He had to pay close attention to each person, hoping that this time, this fight, would be different. This time maybe he would have the chance to change the outcome.

Ahead of him Azra saw one of the hooded figures run past with incredible speed that reminded him of Ero. He knew this meant that that hybrid was part Mikana, like the Denynso warrior that descended from a Denynso and Mikana pairing many generations before. Soon he was aware of others, of the people in both his group and the hybrid army moving at the same blazing speed while others moved people and objects around them without ever placing their hands on them, and still others grabbed those around them with massive hands and tossed them with overpowering strength. It was as if his mind had isolated each of the different species and separated them, allowing the most prevalent abilities in each of the people, both hybrid and not, to show through the strongest. Suddenly they seemed at once indescribably different and yet more alike than ever before.

As the battle raged on around him, Azra became aware of a gnawing feeling in his stomach. No matter what he did or how hard he tried to push the thoughts away, he couldn't get the image of Elise out of his mind. He was deeply concerned about her, even more so now that they had actually arrived on Penthos and were facing the battle that had been building up in their minds for so long. He was conflicted by her not being there with him. He was thankful that she wasn't on the battlefield in danger and witnessing the carnage that was quickly escalating around him, but not being able to see her made him wonder where she was and if she was safe. His eyes fell on Lynx and he ran toward his brother, ducking out of the way of a blow from a hybrid soldier wearing tattered and bloody robes.

"Lynx!" he shouted. "Where is Elise?"

Lynx turned toward him.

"She stayed behind," Lynx said. "She's safe. She and Lila are preparing the compound for everyone to come back."

Azra nodded. Reassured by knowing that his mate was safe and secure, he turned back to the battle and began to slash his way through the wall of soldiers approaching him. Out of the corner of his eye he saw a warrior double over as a blade went into his belly. He started toward him, immediately realizing that it was Ero. The young warrior lay on the ground, curled over onto his hip as he dug his fingers into the ground as if trying to pull himself away from the hooded creature that was lifting his weapon again. He dropped to his knees beside Ero and blocked him with his body as he forced his own blade forward into the man's gut, reciprocating the injury that he had caused Ero. As the soldier stumbled back, he grasped Ero's shirt and started to drag him back toward Pyra and Gyyx several feet away. He shouted their names and they rushed toward him. Pyra leaned down and scooped Ero up off of the ground as Azra continued to support his legs.

They rushed out of the center of the fray toward an empty expanse of the desert sand.

2

Elise shook out the thin blanket in her hands and folded it over, then unfolded it and shook it again. The snap through the air was somehow comforting, as if it was reassuring her that each time that she did it she would remove any dirt that might be clinging to the fabric and would soften the fibers. She wanted it to be the best it could be when the men got there, just in case this was the blanket that Azra was going to use.

"Can you hand me another of the blankets?"

Elise turned toward Lila's soft voice and saw the woman holding out one slim hand toward her. She noticed that there was a small stack of neatly folded blankets on the table in front of her. Elise nodded, wondering how long she had been standing there with this one blanket in her hands. She lowered it to the table in front of her and handed another to Lila. The other woman swiftly shook it out and folded it before adding it to her stack. Elise could smell the warmth coming from the fabric that came from drying them out in the intense sunlight of the planet after washing them from the one small pump that they had found behind another of the buildings in the compound. That discovery had been a tremendous comfort and reassurance to them. The water that they had brought with them was starting to dwindle and now that the ship had left Penthos they didn't have access to the water caches any longer. Though she knew that the rest of the group had arrived in another ship equipped with a water cache, Elise couldn't be sure that it was properly stocked before they left or that there would be enough to sustain all of them for as long as they were on the planet. Finding the pump, though old, outdated, and working only at a small trickle, ensured that they would have access to other water.

"Are you thinking about Azra?" Lila asked.

Elise felt slightly embarrassed to be caught completely lost in her thoughts about her mate. At that moment, she was supposed to be preparing for the group to get back from the battle, transforming the small, empty building close to their main shelter into a hospital. Though she hoped that it wasn't going to need to be used, it was critical that they had it ready before the men arrived so that if any of them did need care, they would be able to get the treatment and healing necessary as fast as possible. She should be able to focus on that rather than allowing her mind to drift to Azra and how much she had missed him since she had said goodbye to him. If she had known this was going to happen, that in such a short time she would be struggling to keep her emotions under control as she waited to know if Azra got through a battle on a distant and desolate planet, things might have been different.

She nodded and walked out of the building, suddenly needing air. The smell of food cooking in the fire that they had built filled her lungs and she concentrated on that rather than the tears that were threatening her eyes. She stepped up to the cooking pit and stirred the thick stew simmering in a large pot they had found already in place on the pit. It wasn't too long ago that Elise assumed that it had been more than a century since anyone had stepped foot on Penthos, but now she knew that that wasn't the case. She could only hope that this compound was as safe and secure as Maxim seemed to believe that it was. While it looked as though it had been some time since it had been used, there were small details that they had discovered, like the pot in the fire, that made her worry that this section of the planet had been used in more recent memory, and that those who had utilized it might return for it before they left.

"It's alright to be thinking about him," Lila said as she came up behind her and checked on the loaves of bread that they had rising in the heat that was still high even though the sun was dipping low in the sky.

The evening was rushing in and she could see Lila's shadow stretch across the courtyard in front of the building, in the light from the torches that they had positioned around the edge of the compound. Though she didn't like the idea of announcing their presence to the hybrid army, they knew that they needed to be as evident as possible to the men when they were on their way back. With the exception of Maxim, Zyyr, Lynx, and Avery, they didn't know how to get to them, and if they were separated they needed to have a clear path to the safety that waited them here.

"There's too many other things that I need to be doing right now," Elise said. "There's a huge group that will be here soon, and there are only two of us to get this place ready for them. They will need something to eat and water, and they might…"

Her voice trailed off and she turned back to the food.

"There will be injuries," Lila said. "You need to understand that."

The words were stark and the woman's voice held more strength and insistence than Elise had ever heard in it. She turned toward Lila, put off by the seeming lack of care and concern in what she had said. She didn't know how to respond, and suddenly she felt even more alone. Dropping the spoon that she had been using to stir the stew onto a stone platter beside the pot, Elise turned and rushed back into the building that they were outfitting as a makeshift hospital.

Her hands shook as she took up a sheet and spread it over one of the tables to create a bed. She was repeating the process on the other bed when Lila stepped into the room. Elise grabbed a threadbare sheet and started ripping it into long strips, the force that it took and the sound of the fabric tearing was a release for the frustration and fear that she was feeling.

"I'm sorry," Lila said as she took a step toward Elise. "I didn't mean that to hurt you."

Elise tossed the bandages to the table and looked up to stare at the other woman incredulously.

"You didn't mean it to hurt me?" she asked. "So, your idea of comforting me is to point out that they are going to be horribly wounded, and I just need to get my mind around that?"

"That's not what I meant by it," Lila said. "It's not that I want you to think that there are terrible things happening or that they are all going to come back hurt."

"Then what?" Elise asked. "What could you have possibly thought that I was going to think when you said that?"

"You are from Earth," Lila said. "From what the Nyx 23

crew and the human mates of the Denynso warriors have told me, there hasn't been a large-scale war on Earth in a long time. Certainly not during your life. The only warfare that humans have seen has been on other planets or in very small, isolated battles. Even those are technological wars. They are distant, impersonal. War is different on Uoria. Our kind, even those who have never seen battle ourselves, live with the scars passed down through generations that have known what it is to look into the eyes of the person in front of them on the battlefield and watch the life drain away from them as they feel their last breath on their skin. You can't understand what is happening out there because it hasn't been something that has been a part of your existence. I know that in your heart you don't want to think about the fact that they are fighting as ferociously as they are, but you need to remember what you've already seen. You need to remember what Kyven and Emerie went through. What happened to Nylek. What happened to Zyyr. That has to be what is in your mind when you think about what they are going through and what will have happened when they get back here. That is the only way that you are going to be able to be prepared. If you think that everything is going to be fine and that there is nothing for you to worry about, it will be much harder for you to face the real aftermath of a battle. That can cost lives."

Elise drew in a shuddering breath. She knew that Lila was right. She couldn't let herself remain buried in the denial that she had surrounded herself with like a protective casing. It felt comforting in a shallow way, but it also kept her from processing the reality that she needed to accept before she would be able to be any benefit to Azra or to anyone else.

"I don't know what I'm supposed to do," she admitted. "I'm a flight attendant."

Lila shook her head.

"You are the mate of a Denynso warrior. You have been since birth. That makes you so much more than anything that you have ever thought of yourself. None of us really know what to expect here. All we can do is prepare ourselves in the best way that we can, and hope that it is enough."

"And if it isn't?"

"Then we figure out what else we need to do, and we do it. Life is different now, Elise. You don't have someone planning and scheduling your every moment for you anymore. You aren't living for other people or to fill some expectation. You are just...living."

"I don't know if I know how to do that," Elise said.

"You do," Lila told her. "You just have to find it."

Elise concentrated for a few moments on tearing another sheet into long bandages and then looked back up at Lila.

"You know, the most impulsive thing that I ever did was fall in love with Azra."

"What do you mean?" Lila asked.

Elise looked toward the door that was still standing open, staring out into the dancing firelight around the courtyard. She thought of all of the times that she had stood inside the ship staring out of the windows, wondering what else was out there beyond the repeated, back and forth trips that she took as she traveled for work. Never could she have imagined that it would have been like this.

"My life was set. It was a routine. I knew what I was going to do, when I was going to do it. I had plans months and even years in advance. Then I was assigned to a trip picking up passengers from Uoria and bringing them to Earth. It seemed so exotic and exciting. I was used to the usual leisure destinations and the long cruises, and I had never been to somewhere as far or as unique as Uoria. Especially with what happened to the last attendant who interacted with the warriors."

Elise could see the look of confusion on Lila's face and had to remind herself that this woman was not human. She wasn't from Earth and didn't have the same experiences or thoughts that she did. It was a strange realization and one that she knew would take time to process. Though there were things about Lila and the other Mikana that clearly differentiated them from humans, Elise found herself less and less cognizant of them the longer that she spent with them. Being near other species was something that she was accustomed to after the years she spent traveling on the ships, but there had always been distinct separations between them. She considered each of them different and often found herself interacting with them in the way that she thought that she was supposed to based on what she had been taught about each in her training and what she thought that she knew about them. In her brief time with this group, though, she had realized just how ridiculous that was and how skewed she had allowed her perceptions, and the behaviors that they dictated, to become.

"There was another flight attendant, not too long ago, who went to Uoria. She was on the shuttle that brought a couple of the women from the University program to the Denynso."

"What happened to her?" Lila asked.

Elise shrugged.

"No one really knows," she said. "She volunteered to be a part of all of those trips and seemed to really enjoy them, though every time that she came back, she seemed different for a few days."

"What do you mean different?"

"It's hard to explain," Elise said. "She was just different. Distant. Not quite angry, but something close to that. It would linger for a few days after she returned, and then she would go back to normal. Then one time, we just didn't see her again."

She could see the look of shock on Lila's face.

"She didn't come back from Uoria?"

"Oh, she came back," Elise said. "But not to work. No one is completely sure what actually happened, but she was sent back locked in a pod and disappeared. The official word of the company was that she had been relieved of her responsibility after an issue during that last trip, but we knew that there was much more to it than that. The University was extremely touchy about the program with the Denynso. If she did something to offend them, there could be very serious trouble for her. It was well-known that there were government agencies involved in the exchange program and that there have been conflicts with Earth before. The last thing that either group would want is for a human woman to show up and cause an issue with the warriors."

"So, what do you think happened to her?" Lila asked.

"I'm not sure, but I know it's more than just her leaving her position and going off to do something else. If that was the case, we would have heard about it. Someone would have seen her or at least talked to her. You don't just disappear when your job ends. If I had to guess, I would say that the Denynso got in touch with the University to tell them what she had done and when she arrived back on Earth they handed her over to the government agency overseeing the cooperation between the two planets."

"What would that mean?" Lila asked.

"That would depend on what really happened," Elise said. "If it was something serious enough, she could have been sent to a prison facility on Earth or even one of the intergalactic prison colonies."

"Prison colonies?" Lila asked. "Isn't that what was here? I thought that that is what caused the problems with the human crew."

"The colony on Penthos was illegal," Elise explained. "At the time, the cooperation agreements were very new and some of them were still being designed. The idea of punishment for criminal behavior and the expected treatment of species on planets that were overtaken by others was hotly debated. It was one of the most pressing issues of the agreements and part of what had taken so long to get all of them formally settled. Most people believe that is part of why Nyx 23 was kept a clandestine mission. They didn't have the intention of revealing any of their work until they had found the evidence their intelligence told them that they would, and were able to put the steps into place to begin resolution. Unfortunately, that's not how it happened. Instead, everyone found out about it because they went missing."

Elise felt a chill go through her. Her entire life she had heard about Nyx 23 and the tragedy of their loss. Coming up with reasons that they had disappeared and stories of what had happened to them was a popular pastime for many people, and there had been countless books and raving demonstrations based on the conspiracies that grew out of these discussions. She remembered sitting at the top of the stairs when she was a child, peering down through the spindles at the party her parents were hosting. She was supposed to have been asleep hours before, but Elise couldn't sleep when she knew that there were adults filling the home and talking about the wondrous and interesting things that she never got to hear about. Though much of the conversation had been dull at first, soon the direction of the conversation shifted to Nyx 23. It was a favorite topic of her father, though she never understood why. He had his own strong opinions about it, including a harsh condemnation of mission control for not reporting them missing sooner or being more upfront about the mission itself.

Elise had heard all of these thoughts before, but that night there was something new. A man who she had never seen stepped into the conversation and presented the idea that the team didn't die on Penthus or go off track and disappear into deep space where their ship would be destroyed by the environmental forces. That had stopped the conversation, creating a tense, uncomfortable silence that settled over the room.

"What if they lived?"

It was a question that had seemed so mundane, and yet so impactful. Every other conspiracy theory that she had heard up until that point, even in just the small snippets that she had been able to glean from listening in on conversations, were dramatic and complicated, sounding outlandish even to a child. There were people who believed that the crew had, in fact, returned to Earth and been integrated into other scientific programs to watch how the story of their mission spread as a means of researching meme theory and use it as an instrument of population control. There were others who felt that the crew themselves had been a different species who had come to Earth generations before and hadn't been able to leave because of travel restrictions, so they came up with the idea of the mission to allow them to leave and return to their home planet without detection. Still more tried to convince anyone who would listen that the mission had never happened at all, and that the entire story was a complex and intricate cover for another tactical move, using the images of people who had died in other missions or who had been sent to prison colonies to serve life for crimes that the government didn't want to admit.

That one question, though, was different. It was simple and straightforward. That made it at once more plausible and more unbelievable. Elise remembered that the adults at the party had quickly shut down that train of thought, dismissing it as quickly and easily as they had accepted more ridiculous concepts, and soon after that the guests had left and Elise had snuck back to bed before she was caught. She had thought about that question for many months, waiting for the next party that may give her the opportunity to hear more from that unknown man. But it never came. She never saw that man again or heard mention of his theory. Soon, the thought seemed to leave her mind and she didn't contemplate it again. Not until now.

"Did you know?" Elise asked.

Lila looked at her strangely.

"Know what?" she asked.

"About the Nyx 23 crew," Elise said. "Did you know who they really were?"

Lila shook her head.

"You have to remember that the humans had been locked in place by the Covra for more than one hundred years when the Denynso found them and released them. The Mikana hadn't had any interaction with them since before they were locked and had long been distanced from the Denynso. By the time that the warriors came to our kingdom to ask for help, no one was still alive who had engaged with them. Some of the elders remember their parents and grandparents talking about them, and even going out to look for the settlement after their interaction stopped, but they never found them."

"But wouldn't they have told your kind? Wouldn't they have talked about where they came from and what had happened to them? Maybe the Mikana would have been able to help them and get them back to Earth."

Lila shook her head again.

"No," she said. "The Mikana and the humans didn't connect until well after their arrival on Uoria. By then, I suppose the group had settled into place and felt that they had their home."

"Or they didn't trust you," Elise said.

"Why would you say that?"

"They didn't know that Uoria even existed," Elise said. "They didn't know anything about your kind, even less than they knew about the Valdicians. How would they know that they could trust you, or that you weren't a part of the group that caused them to crash?"

"We helped them," Lila said. "The Mikana living in the kingdom at the time taught them about Uoria and how to find food, build their settlement better, everything. How could they think that they were cooperating with a species trying to hurt them?"

Elise shrugged.

"I've never been through what they have, so I can't guess what they were thinking or going through."

They women fell silent and Elise walked back out of the building to check on the food. The bread was ready to bake and she tucked it into the dugout oven near the blazing fire. Her ears strained for the sound of the men approaching, or even the drums, anything that would tell her that something was happening beyond the wall of the compound.

"Did knowing about the other flight attendant make you worry when you met the Denynso?"

Elise glanced over her shoulder and saw Lila standing beside the pot, distributing the finished stew into a large tureen so that she could start another batch. There was a level of forced levity in her voice as if she were trying to make the question that she asked less serious.

"I guess a little," Elise said. "But at the same time, I knew that it was her that did something wrong that caused whatever happened to her, not them. All I knew about the Denynso was that they are fierce, violent warriors. There were rumors that these men are insatiable, and that some of them are so powerful and even ruthless toward women that they avoid them all together until they have a partner. That was intimidating."

"I suppose you didn't know about their mating tradition?" Lila asked.

It was said playfully, a gentle tease from another woman who was in the same position that she had been, falling in love with a man outside of her species who was known not just for their fierce fighting, but also for their intense devotion to their mates.

"I didn't," Elise said with a laugh. "But there was something about Azra. As soon as I saw him, something inside me changed. It was like I somehow knew that there was something special about us."

"I know exactly what you mean."

Elise started toward the pump to gather more water for the next batch of stew and Lila felt into step beside her with another large pitcher in her hand.

"It all happened so quickly. I couldn't believe how strong

my feelings for him were or how much I was longing for him. Finding him in that ship and bonding with him was so impulsive, so unlike anything that I had ever done. I knew that it wasn't a smart choice. We only had the short time from when we left Uoria until we arrived on Earth. I had to continue on with my work and had only a brief time to spend with him. I was worried that that meant that I was going to lose him so soon after I found him, but he reassured me that that wasn't going to happen."

"Of course not," Lila said. "He is totally devoted to you. As a Denynso, he's been waiting for you his entire life and will love you with unimaginable depth and passion every day of your life, whether you are standing right beside him or are a galaxy away."

Elise filled the containers that they carried and they started back toward the fire. There was an ache forming in the base of her throat as she poured water into the now-empty pot and heard the hiss as it reacted to the heat from the fire beneath. She felt her shoulders drop as a long sigh escaped from her lungs.

"It seems so unfair," she said. "I have spent every day that we've been apart thinking about when we would finally be able to be together. I have wanted so much to be able to take care of him the way that his mate should. To cook for him. Make sure his home is clean and ready for him when he gets home. I thought that it would be months until I was able to even begin doing those things for him. Now here I am, taking care of him the way that I'd been dreaming, but these are the circumstances that brought me here."

3
____

The sound of the drums had begun again. It was pounding in Azra's ears, mimicking his pulse until he felt like they had replaced his heart itself and was now trembling through his body. He knew that meant that they were coming. More of the hybrid army was coming their way, fresh and unburdened by the tiredness of already having fought. He looked back over his shoulder at Ero and saw that Ciyrs was kneeling beside him, trying to perform a healing as quickly as he could. The procedure made both men more vulnerable and the healer needed to get through it as fast as possible so that he could return to fighting and Ero would be safer.

Around him Azra could feel the energy of the battle shifting. The group led by Pyra and Maxim had been strong and dominant when they first began to fight, but now that was waning. The men were growing tired and injuries had pushed some of them back. Though they were still fighting with everything in them, some struggling through the blood in their eyes and obvious wounds, the new wave of hybrid soldiers was beginning to arrive, and Azra could see a look of worry beginning to form in the eyes of the those who hadn't before faced such a fierce battle.

War had never been like this. There had never been a battle that Azra hadn't felt completely confident in facing. Even when they had stormed the laboratory and the first time that they had encountered the hybrids in the corridor, he hadn't allowed himself even a moment of entertaining the thought that they could be defeated. They might not know exactly what they were facing. He might be concerned about his own ability to face down the creatures and come out victorious. But there was never a moment that he felt that defeat may be imminent. Now he was starting to wonder if this was that moment. If this could be the time that the Denynso were unable to overcome a challenge that was set before them and would have no other choice but to let Ryan's cruel and disturbing plans come to fruition.

Azra tilted his head to the sky and let out the loudest battle yell that his lungs could create. The feeling of the cry pulsing through him and pouring out of his throat revived him and washed his mind clean of the negative thoughts. He felt new energy rush to the tips of his fingers and through his legs, taking the stiffness and soreness that had formed in his muscles away.

Having to trust that Ciyrs would be able to handle Ero on his own, Azra surged back into the battle, fighting with even greater ferocity as the first fresh soldiers came down on him. He wanted them to see him, to look into his eyes and see that he wasn't going to back down. There was no fear. There was no hesitation. If he died, he would die with Elise in his mind, the power of the Denynso in his heart, and a battle cry on his lips.

The night around him had become so deep and the light from the torches and lanterns around the battlefield so scarce that Azra was able to see the sparks that leapt from blades crashing against each other. They jumped through the sky like tiny shooting stars and suddenly Azra's mind rushed to Rilex. He still hadn't seen him and he was worried that he had encountered danger when he left the ship and journeyed across the planet in pursuit of the hybrid woman. Even if Rilex was able to escape whatever it was that he had faced, the darkness might make it nearly impossible for him to find his way back, making him even more vulnerable to the dangers that awaited all of them.

Suddenly Azra heard a gasping scream ripple through everyone on the battlefield as if they were all reacting in turn to something. He turned away from the man who know lay at his feet and saw a bright light moving toward him through the purplish blackness beyond the clash. The light was moving, shifting as it approached like it was being carried by something, but it was higher in the sky than even a Denynso warrior could have held it. The fighting around him slowed as everyone turned their attention toward the approaching light and the silhouette that was becoming more evident against the sky.

The shape became more defined quickly and soon Azra realized that it was a huge animal unlike anything that he had ever seen. Walking on four massive legs with thick fur that nearly brushed the sand from where it hung from its belly and chest, the creature had a head so large that the eyes it contained appeared larger than Azra's hand. His eyes traveled up to its back where he saw the hybrid woman he had heard Eden call Severine sitting astride it. She seemed to be gripping its fur in one hand to keep herself securely in place while holding a large torch above her head with the other, but the creature wasn't resisting the pressure. Instead, it appeared to be walking along willingly, its pace steady as it approached. Azra took a step forward and noticed that there was another figure walking in the deeper shadow cast by the creature. After a moment, he realized that it was Rilex.

The man had a bandage wrapped around his body, but he didn't appear afraid or as though he were being forced to walk along, and Azra felt a boost of hope within him. As the animal approached, he noticed the hybrid soldiers around him becoming anxious. They stepped away from the people they were fighting and started to back away. Azra could see the look of fear on their faces and their weapons drop to their sides as they took their focus away from their assaults and turned it instead toward the oncoming creature. He got the immediate impression that they knew what this animal was and why it was there.

As the hybrid soldiers backed away, seeming to come together in the center of the battlefield, Azra noticed that they were leaving the wounded behind. Without another thought, he rushed forward toward the closest prone figure and scooped it into his arms, turning to bring it back to where Ero lay. The young warrior's eyes were closed and his breathing was deep, telling Azra that Ciyrs had had to perform a complete healing on him. While this was the only way that the healer would be able to save Ero's life, it also took away his strength and energy as his body accepted the healing and then rebuilt itself. This meant that the healing would ensure that Ero would survive to the compound, but it left him incapacitated.

Azra lay the wounded man on the ground and noticed that it was a hybrid. For a moment, he was startled and felt unnerved, but then he realized that this man wasn't wearing a hood and was one of the men that they had rescued from the breeding facility in the laboratory building on Earth.

The man looked up at him and Azra was surprised to see a slight smile on his lips.

"You're going to be alright," Azra said to him. "Ciyrs will help you."

"I know," the hybrid man said, his voice breathy with the pain that he was feeling. "Even if he didn't, I'll be alright."

"What do you mean?" Azra asked.

"I fought," he said. "I looked them in the eye and I fought. It felt wonderful. I can be done now."

His eyes started to flutter closed and Azra tucked his hand beneath the soldier's head to lift it up, trying to wake him.

"No," Azra said. "You're not done. You're far from it. Wake up."

Ciyrs grabbed Azra by his arm and pulled him back.

"I've got him," the healer said. "I'll take care of him. You go help the rest."

Azra climbed to his feet and rushed back to the battlefield. The huge animal was standing at the edge now, baring his ferocious teeth as he strained toward the hybrids. Rilex stood in front of it, pushing against it as Severine tugged on its fur, talking to it and trying to calm it. The hybrid soldiers backed away from it, scrambling over each other as they tried to gather in the center and then move away from the battlefield. Out of the corner of the eye, Azra saw the flicker of another warrior rushing past him. He turned to look at him and watched him disappear behind a tight clutch of hybrid soldiers. Azra felt like something had hit him in the center of the chest, taking the breath out of him. It had been a glimpse into the past: the image of Jem fighting alongside him. Reinforced by the image, he ran past them toward the creature. When he was within a few feet, he shouted toward Rilex.

"We need help," he yelled. "The injured need to get to the compound."

Rilex looked up at Severine, who nodded. She used the fur in her hand to guide the animal forward at a slightly faster pace.

"Gather them up," she called down. "Get them onto the Meldor's back. I'll be able to get them there faster than carrying them."

Azra nodded and ran back toward Ciyrs and the injured men. Together the warriors lifted the injured men up and draped them over the animal's back. Azra climbed up with them so that he could help to hold the unconscious men in place. Before he had the chance to really prepare himself, Rilex jumped up with him and Severine urged the animal ahead. In an instant, they were running away from the sounds of the battlefield and into the deeper darkness of the planet, heading toward the compound that had been their goal when they arrived on Penthos.

4

———————

Elise could hear heavy thudding sounds outside and for a moment thought that they were the drums again. The longer that she listened, though, the clearer it became that these were not drums, but something else, something stronger and deeper coming closer with every passing moment. Soon she heard voices along with the sound and she realized that someone was coming toward the compound. Dropping the blankets in her hands, she ran out of the building and toward the entrance to the compound, her heart pounding in her chest.

Lila was close behind her and they ran in silence until they reached the arched entryway.

"Do you see them?" Lila asked.

Elise scanned the darkness outside of the compound, trying to see through it to find any indication of anyone who might be approaching. The heavy sound stopped and an instant later she saw a wall of people coming toward her. She stepped out of the way and they streamed past her, rushing into the protective surroundings of the stone wall. She noticed one of the warriors carrying a man over his shoulder, and then another, and another. She ran toward the first man and gestured for him to follow her.

"Bring them in here," she said, rushing toward the building that she and Lila had prepared.

Elise stepped inside the building and turned to the door. All at once the space around her was filled with sound and tense energy that bordered somewhere between fear and anger. She watched as the men placed the wounded on the tables and then spread blankets on the floor to add more. She scanned the group for familiar faces, but she saw only Zyyr and Lynx. The rest were unknown to her, and she felt off-balance and bombarded. There were more of them than she expected, and though it was reassuring to know that their numbers were high enough that they might have a chance against the army that she had seen swarm the ship, it was also overwhelming.

Ciyrs stepped up beside one of the tables and used a small knife to cut away the bloodstained clothing that the man was wearing. His chest exposed, Elise saw a deep gash across it and felt her stomach turn. Lila's warning to her repeated through her mind. *There are going to be injuries.* Now she fully understood why the Mikana woman would give her this stark warning. Even coming to terms with the idea of the true hand-to-hand combat in her mind hadn't fully prepared her for this. She remembered the injuries that Nylek and Kyven had suffered, but she hadn't expected to see so many people suffering similar wounds after this first battle. It didn't seem that these men were as severely wounded as either of those men who were now on Uoria, but the wounds that she did see were still horrifying and she felt her mind starting to reject everything that was happening around her.

Pushing through the men, Elise ran outside and ducked

behind a nearby house. She pressed her back against the stone wall and drew in a breath, willing her muscles to stop shaking and her mind to stop racing. Everything was pressing down on her. It felt almost as though she were watching it, standing on the other side of a screen just witnessing what was happening and not able to affect it at all. She struggled to bring herself into the reality of the moment, reminding herself that she was there, she was a part of this, and she could interact with it. She could make a difference.

Opening her eyes, Elise forced herself to look down at her hands. They were streaked with blood from pressing through the group on her way out of the building. The longer she looked at them, the less terrifying it seemed. Soon the fear gave way to anger and then determination. It wasn't just blood, it was a strong and vivid reminder of each of the people who had suffered at the hands of the hybrids. That filled her with a drive that she hadn't experienced before, and she pushed away from the building, turning back and rushing toward the makeshift hospital. More of the group were streaming through the compound entrance and she ran toward them.

"What can I do?" she asked.

"Water," a man with large, damaged wings said with a low, gravelly voice. "Bring water."

Elise nodded and ran to get the pitcher filled with water. She carried it back toward the men who were gathered outside and offered it to the winged man. He held it to his lips and drank it down eagerly before passing it to another man standing close behind him. Elise realized that none of these men were showing signs of injury and felt hopeful. The more she saw who had gotten through without damage, the more confident she felt that this was not the end. As the men passed the pitcher of water, she headed back to the fire and grabbed up another pitcher, bringing it to the pump to fill. When she got back, she handed off the pitcher and offered to bring the winged man some of the food that she and Lila had prepared.

For the next several minutes she scurried around the courtyard, refilling the water pitchers, serving food, and helping men distribute fresh clothes that they had brought with them on the ship. She was accepting back the half-filled water pitcher when she looked up and felt the pitcher fall from her fingers. A gasp stuck in her throat and she stumbled back a few steps. Ahead of her a massive beast was coming through the entrance into the compound. Though none of those around her seemed frightened by its presence, Elise felt herself shaking.

"What is that?" she asked one of the few women who had come with the group and who had started helping her with her tasks.

"It's a Meldor," the woman said.

The word sent a shiver through Elise. Hearing it reminded her of what Kyven had gone through under the ground because of that creature. The animal started coming closer and Elise backed up further, not wanting to turn her back on it for fear that it would attack her in the same way.

"You don't have to be afraid," a voice told her.

Elise looked up and saw a woman sitting astride the Meldor.

"Is this thing safe?" she called back.

The woman patted the animal's flank and it stopped walking. She reached behind her back and Elise saw that she was untying the fabric from the front of her body. That was the first time that she noticed that the woman was holding a baby. The woman leaned down and carefully handed the baby to a man who stood close beside the animal. Once the baby was safe, the woman swung her legs over to the side and carefully climbed down until she could jump to the sand in front of Elise.

"This is a Meldor," the woman said. "I can assure you that it is perfectly safe."

"And who are you?" Elise asked.

The question came out sounding more aggressive and accusatory than she had intended, but she felt intensely protective of the compound and everyone in it, and this woman and the creature that she rode felt like a threat.

"My name is Severine," the woman said. "This is my mate, Rilex." She gestured toward the man now cradling the baby. "I have the trust of those who were on Earth. You can trust me. And you can trust the Meldor. It is just an animal. All it needs is to be taken care of, just like the men. Food, water, and rest. That's all."

Elise looked at the animal again and saw it turn its head toward her. Huge dark eyes stared at her and she saw no viciousness in them. Instead, they seemed deep and soulful, with a hint that seemed like a slight veil of fear over them, as if it, too, had experienced something harsh and painful. She turned back to Severine and nodded.

"Alright," she said, gesturing to the cluster of buildings on the other side of the compound. "We aren't using those buildings. They might have some things left in them, but they should be mostly empty. There is one that has double doors nearly the size of one wall, like it might have once been a barn or a stable. If it fits inside, it will be safe there. Bring it there and I'll bring some water."

"Thank you," Severine said.

A few minutes later, Elise was walking away from the building that now housed the Meldor. Though there were still people rushing around, the compound felt calmer and more under control than it had when the group had first arrived. Feeling as though everything had settled down, she took up one of the lanterns from the ground and started through the clearing toward the far side of the compound. She knew that many of the people who had arrived would settle into the buildings closest to the main headquarters that they had established, which left much of the back portion of the compound empty and quiet.

The lantern created a pool of yellow light in front of her and she followed it into the peaceful stillness of the shadows. Elise chose a spot beside one of the buildings and eased herself onto the ground. Her body relaxed as she settled down, tension from her muscles sliding out and her joints loosening. She sighed and leaned her head back against the wall, closing her eyes to rest for a moment. She had been sitting there for only a few moments when she heard footsteps coming toward her.

5

Azra felt his heart swell when he saw the figure leaning back against the wall and recognized that it was Elise. It felt like it had been so long since he had seen her, and just getting a glimpse of her felt like a rush of cool air into his lungs. He took a few steps toward her, then paused, not wanting to startle her in the quiet privacy that she had found.

"Elise?" he said loudly enough that she would hear him, but softly enough that it wouldn't frighten her.

Despite his efforts, Elise's head snapped up off of the wall and she looked over at him sharply. He took another step forward, holding his own torch so that she could see his face. Even at the distance, he could see her eyes light up and in an instant, she was on her feet and running toward him. No longer caring about the illumination that the torch provided, he dropped it to the ground. It hissed loudly as it hit and the sand extinguished the flame, but he didn't have a chance to see it. He was running toward Elise as fast as he could, holding his arms open toward her so that he wouldn't have to wait a second longer than he had to to hold her.

Elise came to within a couple of feet of Azra and leapt forward. Azra caught her in his arms and pulled her up against his chest so that he could tuck his head into the curve of her neck and breath in her scent. She felt warm and soft in his arms and he wished that he could stand there holding her forever. Her arms wrapped around his neck, holding him tightly as she kissed his neck and encircled his waist with her legs.

"I've missed you so much," she murmured in between kisses. "I was so scared that I was never going to see you again."

Azra made soothing sounds to quiet her and cuddled her a little closer, trying to comfort her.

"I've missed you, too," he said. "But you never have to worry about me. I will go through anything to be with you. There's nothing that I wouldn't do to make sure that I was with you again."

Elise pulled her head back and looked into his eyes, leaning forward to touch their foreheads together.

"I know you would," she said. "I would, too."

"You did," Azra said.

Elise pulled back to look at him again.

"What do you mean? I didn't do anything."

Azra gave her another little squeeze and then lowered her gently to her feet.

"Of course, you did," he said. "You're still here, aren't you? You didn't have to be. You could have gone back with the rest of them to Uoria. You could have gone to Creia and had him contact Earth for a shuttle that would bring you back, and you never would have had to see any of us again, but you didn't."

"I couldn't have done that."

"Yes, you could. You could have decided that you weren't

going to deal with all of this, and that you would rather just put it behind you. That would be so easy for you. But you didn't. You decided to stay here and wait for me. You've helped more than you will ever understand, and I am so proud of you. You are so strong."

He stroked her cheek with the back of his hand, gazing at her tenderly. She was even more beautiful than the first time that he saw her. Even with the exhaustion evident on her face, there was a radiance in her eyes that made him feel as though he were seeing the real her that he hadn't encountered when they were on the ship. There was an authenticity, a depth about her now that seemed like she had just discovered a level of herself that even she had never known and was now prepared to share it with him.

"I would do it all again," she said. "I would do anything to protect you."

It sounded strange coming out of her mouth, but as he thought about it, Azra realized that it was absolutely true. Though he was accustomed to being the one in the position of protecting others and would have thought that it would always be him who would be protecting Elise, he knew that what she had done for him, for all of them, had been invaluable. Without her, they wouldn't have been able to use the ship properly or know how to access all of the supplies within it. Without her, they wouldn't have been able to communicate between Penthos and Earth, or between the groups after they arrived. Without her, the compound wouldn't have been prepared for their return, and they wouldn't have been able to get the wounded the care that they needed, or the rest, the food and water they had been lacking in the battle. In her own way, she had protected him and all of them.

"I love you," he said. "I love you, Elise. I don't know if I've ever said that to you, but if you'll let me, I'll say it to you a million more times, and then when I am finished, I will start again. I never want you to go a day without hearing me tell you that I love you."

Even in the dim lighting of the lantern in the desert sand, Azra could see the joyful sparkle of Elise's eyes. She reached up and flattened her hand into the center of his chest, pausing as if she just wanted to feel the rhythm of his heart beating against her palm.

"I love you, too, Azra," she said. "I have been longing to hear those words. Thinking about them is what has kept me going. I don't care how many times you say them to me, it will never be enough, and no matter how many times you say them to me, I will say them back to you. I can never tell you enough times how deeply I love you, how tightly I hold you in my heart, or how intensely I have longed for you since we've been apart. I'm sorry for every moment that I have missed with you."

Azra shook his head at her. He cupped her face with both hands, supporting it so that she wouldn't look away and she would continue to look into his eyes. He wanted her to see the rich orange coloration that had formed when they had completed their bond. It was a visual reminder, a tangible change that proved his devotion to her and ensured that anyone who looked at him would know that he had a mate. This along with a searing heat that would emanate from his skin if another woman not in his close personal circle approached him ensured no other woman attempted to get close to him, keeping him set apart fully and completely for Elise.

"You had no way of knowing what was going to happen," Azra told her, trying to reassure her that it wasn't her fault. "You made the decision that was right for you. You thought that finishing your contract would only keep you away for a short time and that we would be able to choose what we did from there. You couldn't have known that this was going to be how it turned out."

"But it wasn't the decision that was right for me," Elise said. "The right decision would have been to stay with you."

"You can't think that," Azra said. "Your career is important to you. It's something that you worked hard to accomplish, and you wanted to fulfill the commitment that you made. That's honorable. What matters is not the minutes that we've lost, but the ones that we still have."

"Every one of those moments is precious," Elise said. "All of them. I can't bear the thought of losing any more time with you. I can't stand the idea that we will ever be apart again."

"Then don't think about it," Azra said. "Just don't think about it anymore. You don't have to miss me. You don't have to worry about me. I'm right here. I'm right here with you. You can see me here in front of you. You can hear my voice." Azra's belly was starting to tremble and he took a step closer to her to close the small space between them. He dipped his head down and ran his lips along the side of her neck. "You can smell my skin. You can feel my lips on yours."

Elise let out a slightly shivering sigh.

"Azra," she breathed.

Azra touched a hand to the front of her hips and guided her back toward the building where she had been sitting when he approached. He pressed her back gently so that she stood against the wall and reached down to grasp her wrists and sweep them up over her head. Pinning both hands in place with one of his, he paused and stared into Elise's eyes.

"Every moment that we have together is precious," he

said, repeating the sentiment that she had shared with him. "I don't want to waste any of them. I want to spend every moment that I am close to you treasuring you." He kissed the soft dip in between her collar bones. "Cherishing you." He ran his lips up the front of Elise's throat and brought them right above hers so that he could feel them as he spoke. "Worshipping you."

Their mouths met and Azra felt Elise melt beneath the impact of their kiss. He could taste the heat and sweetness of her and longed for more. His tongue tempted her lips, coaxing them to open for him so that it could glide in and taste her more fully.

6

———

Azra's eyes burned into Elise's as he stared deeply at her, the intensity of his gaze seeming to hold her in place as she looked back at him. He could see the intensity of the desire in her eyes, and knew that she was feeling the same craving to revisit their bond that he was. They had both been through so much in their time apart, and now they needed to find their reassurance and grounding in each other's arms.

Still gently pushing against her wrists to hold Elise against the stone wall of the house, Azra lowered himself to his knees to close the height difference between them. This put him at a much better vantage point and he dipped his head to touch his mouth to the dip between her breasts. He nuzzled the fabric of her dress away with the sides of his face, exposing a little more of her skin, and pressed another kiss to the warm valley. Whether from the exertion of all of her efforts to help them after the battle, excitement at being reunited with Azra, desire for him, or a combination of all of them, sweat was beading on her soft skin and Azra let the tip of his tongue slip past his lips to gather some of the salty drops into his mouth.

Elise's breath caught in her throat and he felt her writhing slightly as he licked from the center of her breasts up her chest. He sighed in response to the sound and continued along her neck so that he completed his journey with his face poised just inches from hers. His breathing was becoming deeper and more labored, but Azra kept his movements slow and controlled. Just as they had said, the moments that they were sharing were precious and he didn't want to move through even a single one of them too quickly and miss the delicious pleasure waiting in each. He nudged her nose with his and she complied with his unspoken request, offering her mouth to him.

Wanting to fill his mouth with the taste of her and breathe into her, but needing to maintain his control so that he could properly express to her everything that he had been thinking and feeling, Azra allowed himself to only glide the tip of his tongue against her lips. When she whimpered and parted her lips he couldn't resist delving just a bit further, dipping his tongue into her mouth to lightly stroke the soft warmth waiting there. It was a tender, subtle promise of what else awaited him, and he felt his mind, heart, and body longing for more.

Azra released her wrists and felt Elise's arms lower down to rest on his shoulders. He touched a kiss to each cheek, then her forehead, and the tip of her nose. Elise sighed and let her eyes flutter closed, a gentle smile coming to her lips.

"We have all the time that we want," Azra whispered to her. "We are all alone."

"No, we aren't," she whispered back. "They are all on the other side of the compound."

Azra shook his head.

"No," he said, kissing her cheeks again. "We are alone. It's only us. There's nothing else. All you need to do is let go."

Azra felt Elise surrender herself to him and Azra swept her into his arms. He carried her back behind the building, finding even more privacy for them. He lowered her to the sand again and knelt down to remove her shoes. The sun going down had allowed the sand to cool enough that she could stand in it comfortably and he ran his hands from her ankles up her legs indulgently, touching her skin as he moved her dress up. He moved painstakingly slowly, gradually revealing her body and discovering that she wore nothing beneath the long skirt. Finally, he slipped it up over her head and spread it out on the ground to create a bed for them. Azra groaned deep in his throat when he saw the full beauty of her body revealed to him, and in smooth, fast movements he peeled away his clothes and dropped them to the ground.

For a moment, he considered lifting her up again so that he could lay her down, but then he changed his mind. He needed more than that. Instead, Azra moved her dress closer to the wall of the house and sat down, leaning against the building with his back. He used one finger to beckon her toward him and she complied, lowering herself down to her knees and crawling toward him. Azra reached forward with one hand and took her thigh, guiding it over his lap so that she straddled him. He stopped her before she settled fully onto him, allowing her to hover over his hips as she brought her hands up to rest on the back of his neck.

The sun was beginning to rise, gradually cutting through the thick purple and dark blue of the night with streaks of orange and pink at the horizon. The last time Azra saw the sunrise, he didn't know how long it would be before he was able to hold Elise in his arms again, and now she gazed down at him, her eyes drinking him in as he held her hips firmly and slowly, carefully led her down to nestle on his lap.

The tip of his erection touched her core and Azra could feel that her body was hot and ready for him. Her sweet wetness slickened his swollen head as if in invitation, and he tightened his hips slightly so that she could welcome him in. Elise cried out as Azra filled her, tossing her head back and squeezing his thighs with hers. This offered greater access to her tender throat and he took the opportunity to touch her skin with his open mouth. He followed the flow of her breath as he ran his tongue down her throat and then along her breasts. His teeth playfully caught one nipple and Elise gasped, lifting her head to stare down at him again. Azra lifted his hips again to push deeper inside her and she responded by parting her thighs. The movement caused her body to lower even further into his lap and her walls to open more, allowing her to accept him fully.

Almost instantly Azra knew that he couldn't keep moving so slowly. He needed to show her the passion that was flowing through him and find solace in the blissful release of the emotions and energy that had built up within him during the battle. He wrapped one around her hips and cupped the other hand around her face, tilting it forward to rest against his. Their movements grew faster and soon Azra felt the incredible sensations build to a dizzying peak and then his cock pulsed as he began to spill into her. Elise moaned and he felt her walls clutch tightly around his erection, milking him with her spasms and drawing him deeper into her body.

When their panting finally slowed and he felt like he could move again, Azra gently lifted Elise off of his lap and laid her down on the dress before settling down beside her. Elise nestled against him and he cuddled closer, relishing the feeling of her sweat-dampened skin and the salty, musky smell of her body.

"I love you," he said into her hair, not wanting to wait to begin to fulfill his promise to her.

"I love you, too," she said. "More than I can ever tell you."

7
___

zra knew that he hadn't slept long, but his mind wouldn't allow him to lay in bed any longer. He could hear the people already moving throughout the compound, preparing for the day that lay ahead of them. By the time that he and Elise had returned to the main part of the compound and she brought him to the bed that she had been sleeping in since the ship left Penthos, the sun was nearly fully in place, and now it had started its gradual glide across the sky. Even though he knew it was morning, the planet still looked dark and forbidding, and he found himself tempted to light a lantern to bring with him, if only to burn away the oppressive energy from around him.

Elise was still sleeping peacefully when he slipped out of the bed and walked into the main room of the building. Zyyr was there and he greeted the other warrior happily, glad to see one of the men who had been trapped here on Penthos when he was on Earth.

"There is water to bathe and fresh clothes in the next

room," Zyyr told him. "The women have food waiting outside, too."

It all sounded wonderful, but Azra couldn't concentrate on those simple pleasures yet.

"How are the wounded?" he asked. "Ero? George?"

Zyyr nodded.

"They're doing fine," he said. "George didn't even need healing. Jacob dressed his wounds and he's out with the rest now. Ero is still sleeping. He had to undergo another healing and Ciyrs says that he needs to stay in the clinic building for at least the rest of the day."

"Does he think that he's going to be alright?" Azra asked.

Zyyr nodded again, as if the gesture was going to give him more than any words that he would be able to say.

"He's optimistic. Ero just needs more rest."

"Has there been more contact with those on Uoria?"

"Lynx reached out to Rain this morning. It shouldn't be much longer before they arrive."

It was Azra's turn to nod. It was reassuring to know that the rest of them would be there soon, reinforcing their numbers and boosting their morale to carry them through.

"What do we do now?" he asked.

"Take a bath," Zyyr said. "Change your clothes. Get something to eat. After that, we wait. That's all we can do."

Azra waited until Zyyr walked out of the building to go into the other room. He found a large basin and several pitchers of water, along with a stack of fresh clothing. He was thankful for the supplies that had already been packed in the ship for the human crew as well as those brought along by those in the ship from Earth as he bathed and stepped into a clean set of clothes. When he finished, he walked out of the building and into the busyness of the courtyard. All around him people were scurrying between the buildings, getting food from the same fire pit as the night before, and gathering in small groups for a few moments before splintering off and going their separate ways. It wasn't until then that Azra had really noticed how many people were in the compound. It seemed like far more than he would have guessed, and he knew that there were more still waiting in the ship.

Across the courtyard he saw Jem and Azra smiled. Though he had known since they were on Earth that he had returned, seeing him in battle had been different. Azra strode toward him, but before he could reach him, he heard Lynx's voice.

"Jem!" he shouted.

Azra saw the warrior run toward Jem and gather him into his arms in a tight embrace. Lynx grabbed onto Jem's upper arms and pushed him back, laughing as he looked into his face and then pulled him back in for another hug.

"I can't believe this!" he said. "They told me that you were back, but I couldn't believe it. How can this be true?"

Azra stepped up beside them.

"It's a miracle," he said, patting Jem on the back.

Jem grinned, looking between the men.

"I'm not the miracle," he said. "You are. This is. I thought that you would have put me behind you by now."

"Never," Lynx said. "What happened to you? How did you get back with them?"

Before he could answer, Angela came up beside Jem and wrapped her arm around his waist. Jem leaned down to kiss her, and then turned back to Lynx.

"Lynx, this is Angela, my mate."

Lynx smiled broadly, but Azra could see the flicker of sadness in his eyes. He knew that the other warrior was thinking about Rain and hoping that she would get back to

Penthos soon. Seeing them made Azra's heart clench. He thought to the night before, holding Elise in his arms and listening to the slow rhythm of her breathing as she fell asleep. That had been an incredible, blissful indulgence despite being such a simple pleasure. He knew that it had been completely true when they said that they couldn't stand being apart again. It wasn't enough for him just to know that they were together now. He needed to know that they were going to be together permanently, and though completing their bond had fulfilled that for him, he wanted to give it to her as well.

"Jem," he said, interrupting Jem explaining to Lynx how he and Angela had met. "I'm sorry to interrupt, but I need your help. Yours, too, Angela. If you're willing."

The couple exchanged glances and then nodded at him.

"Of course," Angela said. "What can we do for you?"

Azra gave a sigh to steel himself, and started talking, explaining the idea that was forming in his mind. He didn't know if it was going to be good enough. He didn't know if it was going to work out the way that he wanted it to and tell her what he wanted it to tell, but it was all he had. He had to try.

When he was finished explaining it to this group, they split off, rushing to other parts of the compound to find other members of the group whose help he needed to carry through with his plan. He knew that they didn't have much time. It wouldn't be long before Elise woke up and he would need to avoid her until everything was in place. That would be too hard if he needed to wait long, so he needed to get everything ready as quickly as possible.

The first person he sought out was Loralia. He knew that of everyone who he would ask to help him, it was her who might struggle the most, but what she had to offer was important and he hoped that he could convince her to be a part of it. He found her in the clinic with Azrael, checking on a wound in her father's arm. Reassured that he was well and would soon be able to leave the clinic, Azra asked Loralia if she would step outside to talk to him. She agreed, but they were stepping out of the door when Azra turned back around to look at the battle-worn winged man.

"Azrael," he said. "If you are willing, I would greatly appreciate your help as well."

Azrael nodded.

"What can I do for you?"

8

———

Elise sliced the final loaf of bread and piled it onto a platter with the rest of the pieces. It was the middle of the afternoon and she was still working toward making sure that everyone was fed. There were too many of them to eat all at once when there only a few of them preparing food, but she hoped that if they were going to spend much longer on Penthos that they would be able to find a more efficient process. She was happy to help in whatever way she could, including preparing these meals with Lila as well as Eden, Zuri, and Zsilvia, some of the other women she had met that morning, but she would prefer if they were all able to eat at the same time. Somehow, she felt like it would make them stronger, tightening their connection and helping to create a more unified feeling among a group so splintered and varied.

Not for the first time that day she paused and listened as intently as she could. She was waiting to hear the drums, to know that the hybrid army was on its way and that soon the group would have to mobilize and leave the compound again. The thought was terrifying. She hadn't seen Azra at all that day and she couldn't bear the thought of him having to go into battle without having a chance to hold him again. Waking up without him beside her had been upsetting. The emptiness in the place where he had been lying felt hollow and she had instantly felt her stomach drop. As she walked around the compound, however, she had been reassured by everyone she asked that Azra was fine, that he was just getting himself ready for what was to come and talking through what had already happened with the warriors who had been here on Penthos while he was on Earth.

She had wanted to believe them and to go along with it, not allowing it to upset or discourage her. This was the life that she would be leading. If there was a battle to be fought, that would be his priority, and rightfully so. If that meant that he would barely sleep or that she would have to sacrifice seeing his face first thing in the morning, it was something she would have to be willing to do. At the same time, she felt the longing for him again and worried that they would forever be defined by the ways of a culture that she didn't understand, and may never understand. She could only hope deep within her soul that she would be able to learn like the other women had. They all seemed so comfortable, so at ease among the other species and with their mates. None seemed as out of place as she felt, with the exception of Angela who had been introduced to her as the mate of Jem. That woman clung to her Denynso warrior and seemed somewhat timid about what was happening around her. Elise didn't know how long she and Jem had been bonded, but it gave her some reassurance that she was not the only one who felt an overpowering love for a man she was still struggling to understand.

Suddenly she saw Azra approaching and Elise felt her heart soar. A smile broke across her lips and all of the fear that she had been feeling dissipated. Coming around the heavy pot that still hung above the fire, she walked toward him, her arms extended to embrace him. Azra held her for only a moment before stepping back and giving her a hard, insistent kiss as if confirming something to himself. He took both of her hands in his and stared into her face.

"Can you come with me for a minute?" he asked.

"Of course," Elise said. "Is everything alright?"

"Yes," Azra said. "At least...I hope it is."

Elise looked up at him quizzically.

"What do you mean?" she asked.

"Just come with me," he said.

He continued to hold both of her hands as he backed up a few steps, and then turned so that he walked along beside her. He led her across the courtyard and toward the buildings that had been quiet and still the night before. At first, she thought that he might be trying to steal a few more moments alone with her, and then she noticed a figure standing at the first building.

"What are we doing?" she asked.

"Just trust me," he said.

They approached the building and she realized that the figure was Angela, the woman she had just been thinking about. Azra brought her up to Angela.

"Elise," he said. "This is Angela."

"I know," Elise said, but Angela was already starting to speak.

"I'm from Earth," she said. "Like you. Only I left several years ago. I was part of an archeological team assigned to uncovering more about an ancient culture, and I accidentally used a portal that no one knew was there to bring me into a different stream. I was in another place and time for years with only my friend Jacob. Then I met Jem. We remained together on his own planet for some time before he decided that he wanted to return to Uoria and his people."

Elise felt a wave of confusion flow over her.

"His planet?" she asked. "I thought Jem was Denynso."

"I am," Jem said as he stepped around the corner of the building to join his mate in front of Elise. "I was born into the Denynso clan as a warrior. During a battle against the Klimnu, I was faced with a dangerous situation in which the only other option that I had was to sacrifice my life to eliminate the enemy and protect my kind and my home. I jumped literally into the unknown, but I didn't die. Instead, I went through another portal and ended up on a distant planet. I had no way of knowing where I was or how to get back to Uoria, so I had to settle there. In the time that I spent there, I never encountered another occupant. Then I met two people, Galadriel and Vyker, and they eventually led me to Angela. We came back here to reunite with my kind."

Elise nodded, feeling as though she were being to understand more. Azra took her hand again.

"Thank you, Jem, Angela," he said and started guiding her to the next house.

Here stood the man who had been introduced to her as Rilex. He waved at her as she approached.

"This is Rilex," Azra said.

She didn't speak this time, but gave a single nod and continued to look at the man.

"I am from a very different time and place. I come from

the same place as the man Vyker who Jem just told you about. We are an ancient race, one that you may never even have heard about. We are responsible for the care and protection of the stars. I went to Earth much as Jem and Angela traveled: accidentally through a portal. I was searching for something for my dearest friend, Vyker's father, and I ended up on Earth many, many years ahead of my own time. I was alone there, unable to get back home, and all I could do was research and hope that someday I would be able to accomplish the goal that I had set for myself so long before. Then I met Galadriel. I could have returned to my time permanently, but I knew that I still had work to do. I went back to Earth and continued my research. That's when Jem and Angela arrived and we joined the group in the laboratory. There I met Severine."

Just as Jem had, Severine stepped out from around the side of the building and joined Rilex. He looped his arm around her affectionately and pulled her close to touch a kiss to the side of her head. As he had before, Azra introduced her to the woman.

"I was born on Earth, but I come from many other places. I am a hybrid, designed and created by Ryan to help him fulfill his goal of creating weaponized beings and the ultimate army against the Denynso and the Mikana. I am a combination of several species, but all I know is the breeding facilities where I grew up, and this planet. I was trained for war here after years of service in the nursery caring for and raising the babies who would one day become soldiers in Ryan's experimental army. I was born for a specific, horrible purpose, but I knew that there was more for me. I asked Eden for help and with the help of her mate Pyra and more from her crew, they were able to save the breeding women, as well as me and some of the other hybrids from the program. That was when I met Rilex and soon after he gave me the name Severine. I hadn't had one before. Now I represent The Others. We are at once nothing and everything, abominations," she took a long breath, "and miracles. We have adopted the newborn son of one of the human women who was liberated from the program and intend to raise him together understanding everything that went into creating him, but also everything that he has the potential to be. Beneath the ground here on Penthos we encountered the Meldor. It was being held under torture and trained to kill. We've freed him as I was freed and will bring him with us as we continue to fight."

Azra thanked them and guided Elise on again.

They reached a third house and she saw a Denynso warrior standing beside a beautiful woman with flowing silver hair.

"Bannack," Azra said, gesturing toward the warrior.

"I'm a Denynso warrior," Bannack said. "I was born on the compound as nearly all Denynso have been for generations. I had fought many battles by the time that I found Loralia living below the ground, but the one that I had to fight against myself simply to accept the love that she was offering me was likely the hardest thing that I have ever done. It was also the most wonderful."

"Loralia," Azra said.

"I, too, and a combination," the woman said, "but not like Severine. I wasn't created in a laboratory and was never intended to be a source of pain for anyone. In fact, I didn't know that I was anything more than Irisa until very recently. I grew up beneath the ground in the Irisa realm that mirrored the beloved ground above. I've been alone most of my life. My entire family was killed by a vicious plague that burned through when I was younger. I was the only survivor and remained by myself until the Klimnu invaded my realm and began to attack the Denynso above. Soon there was a battle and the Denynso were victorious. I knew that I couldn't remain hidden there on my own for the rest of my life. That was when I fell in love with Bannack. It took quite some time after that for me to embrace what had saved me from the ravages of that sickness and what set me apart from the other Irisa who I had known my entire life. Then I met my father."

The winged man who Elise had spoken to the night before stepped around the building and stood next to Loralia.

"Azrael," Azra said.

"I am Eteri," the man said. "I fell in love with an Irisa woman when I was very young, but there was turmoil on Uoria then. Our planet was being ravaged and the Irisa were not safe. They were already suffering early signs of the plague that would destroy them and they knew that they needed some way to protect themselves. They moved beneath the ground into a realm that would guard them. The woman I loved had to go to protect herself, but also to protect the baby that she carried. We both hoped that soon we would be reunited, but I never saw her again. I lived for many years giving myself into battle so that I didn't have to accept the pain. It was only recently that I learned my child had survived, and then I had the honor to meet her."

Elise felt emotion tightening in her chest, but the confusion was still there. She turned to Azra, expecting him to lead her further, but he didn't.

"I don't understand," she said. "What is this?"

Azra looked around him at the people who had introduced themselves to Elise and told them about their lives.

Then he looked back at her. The orange of his eyes seemed deeper and more intense, and she felt her heart flutter.

"I know how important your career was to you," he said. "It was a way for you to see the galaxy and experience new things and new people. It helped you to learn and kept you from feeling trapped. Now you have seen so much more of the galaxy than you ever would have through those leisure cruises. You have met species that you never would have encountered, and heard stories unlike anything any passenger could tell you. I can't tell you that you have seen everything or that there isn't more for you to experience, but I can promise you that, if you will allow me to, I will be there alongside you when you do." Feeling breathless, Elise watched as Azra lowered himself to his knees in the sand in front of her. He took both of her hands in his again and kissed them both in turn. "I have given you a glimpse into the galaxy, now I'm asking you to give me an adventure far greater than anything that I have ever imagined. Will you marry me?"

Elise gasped and immediately felt tears streaming down her cheeks. She laughed through them and nodded, again not feeling as though she could come up with the words that she wanted to say to him.

"Yes," she finally managed. "Yes. Of course, I will marry you."

Azra jumped to his feet and swept her into his arms, capturing her mouth in a powerful kiss. She clung to him, feeling her body shaking against his. She could never have dreamed this. It was all too incredible, too truly breath-taking for her to accept as real. As if hearing her thoughts, her mate kissed her again, reassuring her that he was completely real and that this truly was happening.

"I'd like to wait to have the ceremony," he said. "Just

until everyone who is still on Uoria can get here. That way we can all be together."

Elise buried her fingers into her future husband's thick white hair and smiled at him.

"Of course," she said. "Anything as long as I get to be your mate and your wife."

"My everything," Azra said. "Always."

UNTITLED

To Be Continued in Series V...